POKÉMON™
ADVENTURES
FIRERED & LEAFGREEN

Pokémon ADVENTURES
FireRed & LeafGreen
Volume 25
Perfect Square Edition

Story by HIDENORI KUSAKA
Art by SATOSHI YAMAMOTO

English Adaptation/Bryant Turnage
Translation/Tetsuichiro Miyaki
Touch-up & Lettering/Annaliese Christman
Design/Shawn Carrico
Editor/Annette Roman

The stories, characters and incidents mentioned
in this publication are entirely fictional.

Printed in the U.S.A.

Published by VIZ Media, LLC
P.O. Box 77010
San Francisco, CA 94107

10 9 8 7 6 5 4 3 2 1
First printing, November 2014

www.perfectsquare.com   www.viz.com

SPECIAL OBJECT

The Pokédex holders and their stories

Kanto region

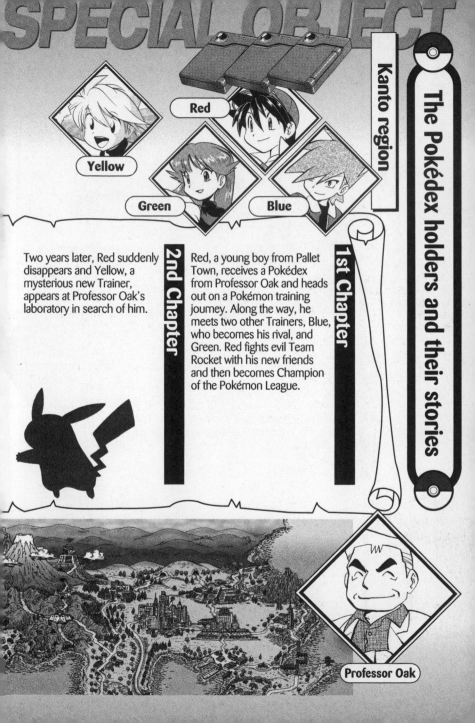

Red
Yellow
Green
Blue

1st Chapter

Red, a young boy from Pallet Town, receives a Pokédex from Professor Oak and heads out on a Pokémon training journey. Along the way, he meets two other Trainers, Blue, who becomes his rival, and Green. Red fights evil Team Rocket with his new friends and then becomes Champion of the Pokémon League.

2nd Chapter

Two years later, Red suddenly disappears and Yellow, a mysterious new Trainer, appears at Professor Oak's laboratory in search of him.

Professor Oak

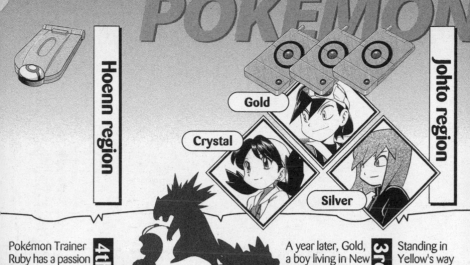

POKEMON

Johto region

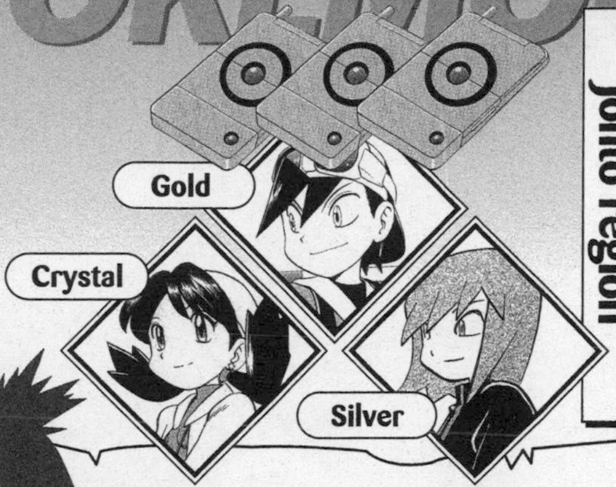
Gold
Silver
Crystal

Hoenn region

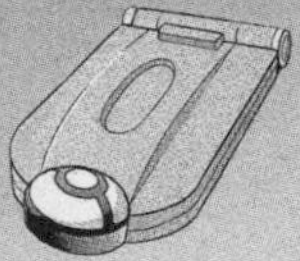

Standing in Yellow's way is the Kanto Elite Four, led by Lance. In a major battle at Cerise Island, Yellow manages to stymie the group's evil ambitions.

3rd Chapter

A year later, Gold, a boy living in New Bark Town in a house full of Pokémon, sets out on a journey in pursuit of Silver, a Trainer who stole a Totodile from Professor Elm's laboratory. The two don't get along at first, but eventually they become partners fighting side by side. During their journey, they meet Crystal, the trainer who Professor Elm entrusts with the completion of his Pokédex. Together, the trio succeed to shatter the evil scheme of the Mask of Ice, a villain who leads what remains of Team Rocket.

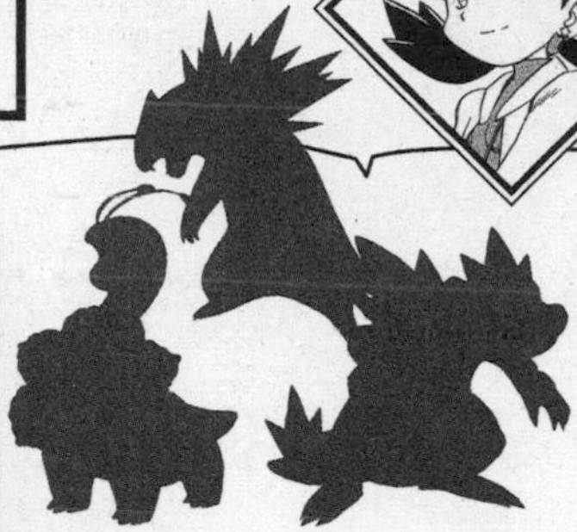

4th Chapter

Pokémon Trainer Ruby has a passion for Pokémon Contests. He runs away from home right after his family moves to Littleroot Town. He meets a wild girl named Sapphire and they pledge to compete with each other in an 80-day challenge to...

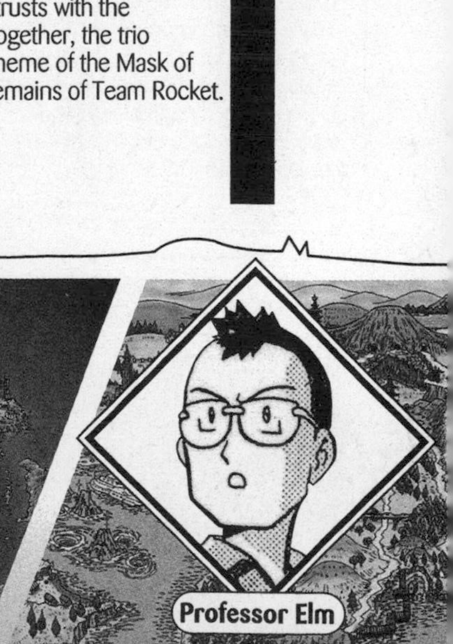
Professor Elm

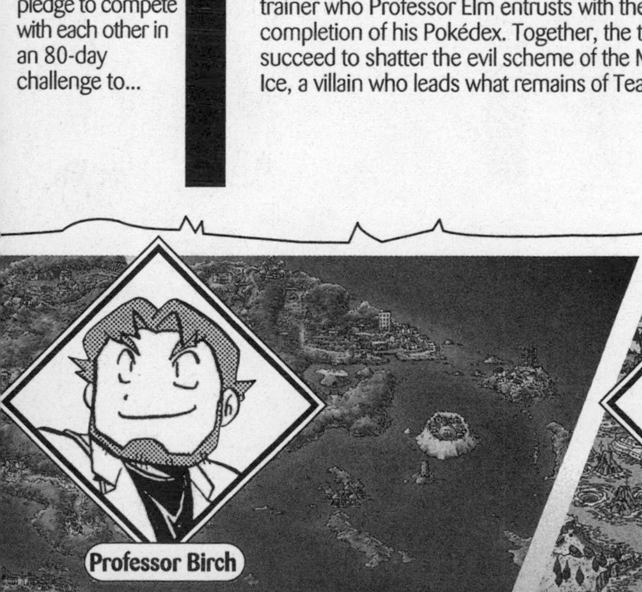
Professor Birch

SPECIAL OBJECT

Kanto region

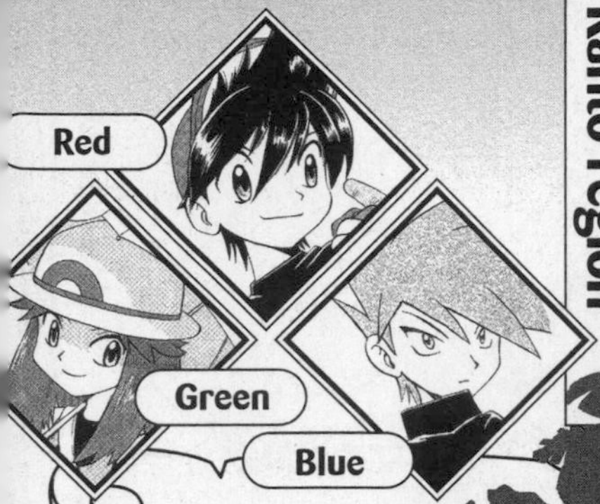

Red
Green
Blue

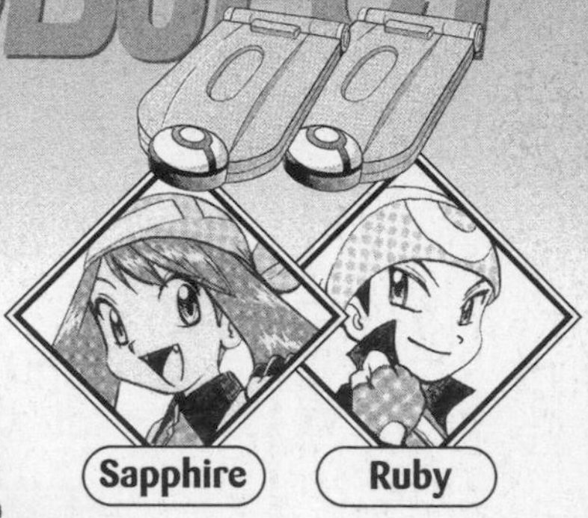

Sapphire
Ruby

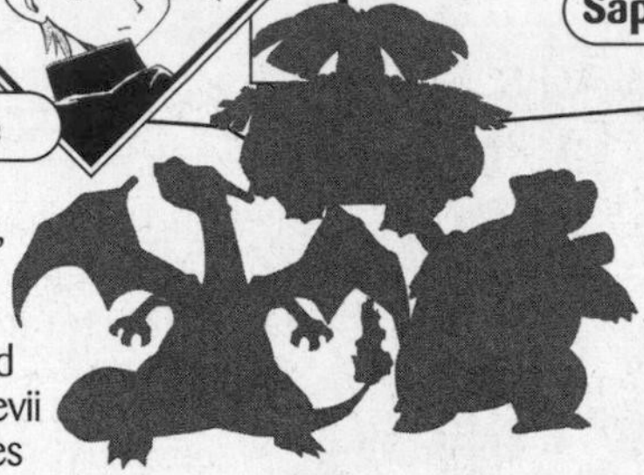

5th Chapter

Six months later, Red is badly defeated by a Pokémon named Deoxys at the Sevii Islands. Red loses faith in himself, but after much soul-searching he decides to face Deoxys again. Together, Mewtwo and Red launch an attack on the Trainer Tower, which is rife with traps. Giovanni, the leader of Team Rocket, keeps Red and the others occupied inside the tower while he follows up on a lead from Deoxys that directs him to find what he has long been searching for in Viridian City...

...win every Pokémon Contest and every Pokémon Gym Battle, respectively. Meanwhile, in the Hoenn region, Team Aqua and Team Magma set their evil plot in motion. As a result, Legendary Pokémon Groudon and Kyogre are awakened and inflict catastrophic climate changes on Hoenn. In the end, thanks to Ruby and Sapphire's heroic efforts, the two legendary Pokémon go back into hibernation.

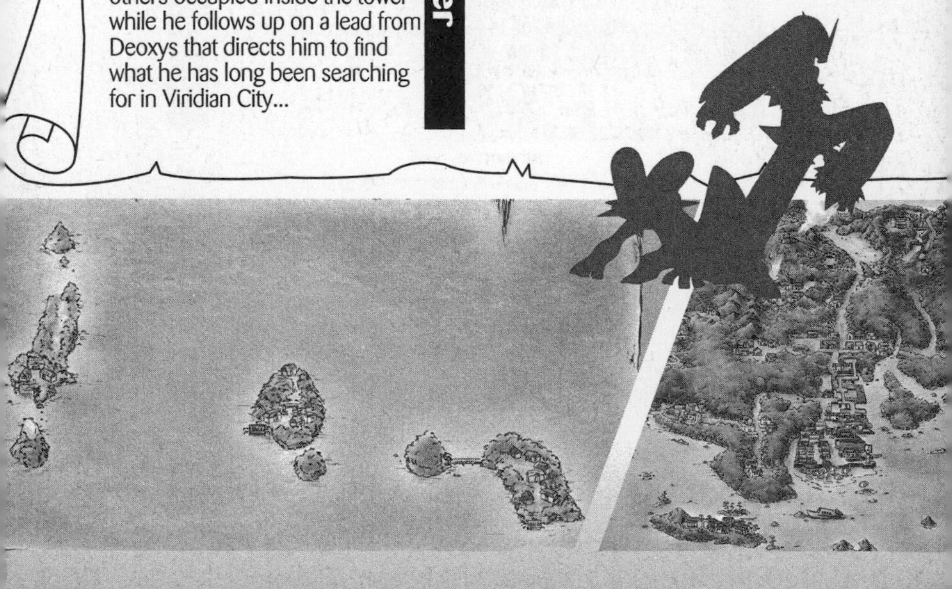

POKÉMON™
ADVENTURES
FIRERED & LEAFGREEN

25
VOLUME TWENTY-FIVE

CONTENTS

● **Adventure 288** ●
Give It Your Best, Blastoise

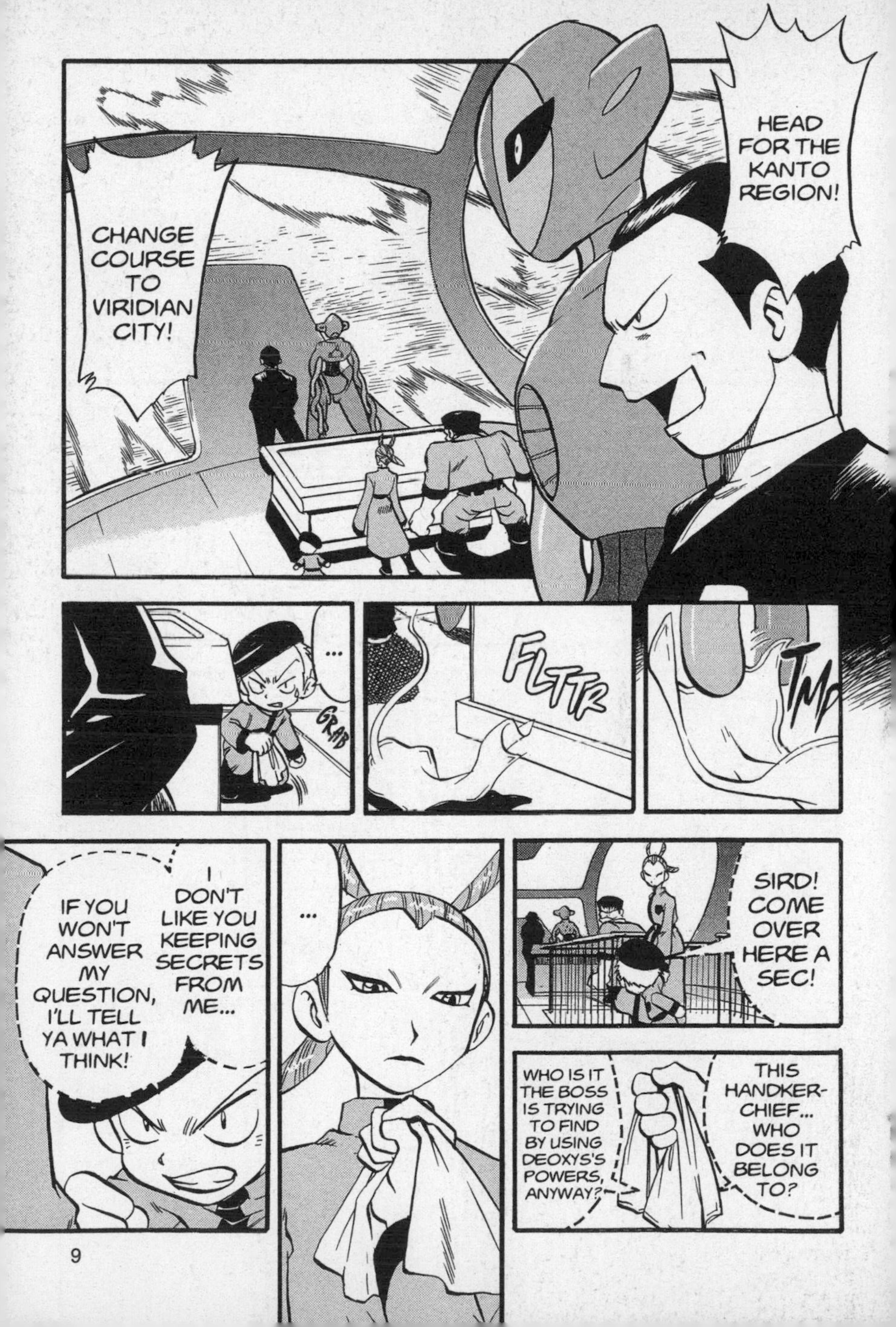
HEAD FOR THE KANTO REGION!
CHANGE COURSE TO VIRIDIAN CITY!
TMP
FLTTR
...
GRAB
SIRD! COME OVER HERE A SEC!
THIS HANDKER-CHIEF... WHO DOES IT BELONG TO?
WHO IS IT THE BOSS IS TRYING TO FIND BY USING DEOXYS'S POWERS, ANYWAY?
...
I DON'T LIKE YOU KEEPING SECRETS FROM ME...
IF YOU WON'T ANSWER MY QUESTION, I'LL TELL YA WHAT I THINK!

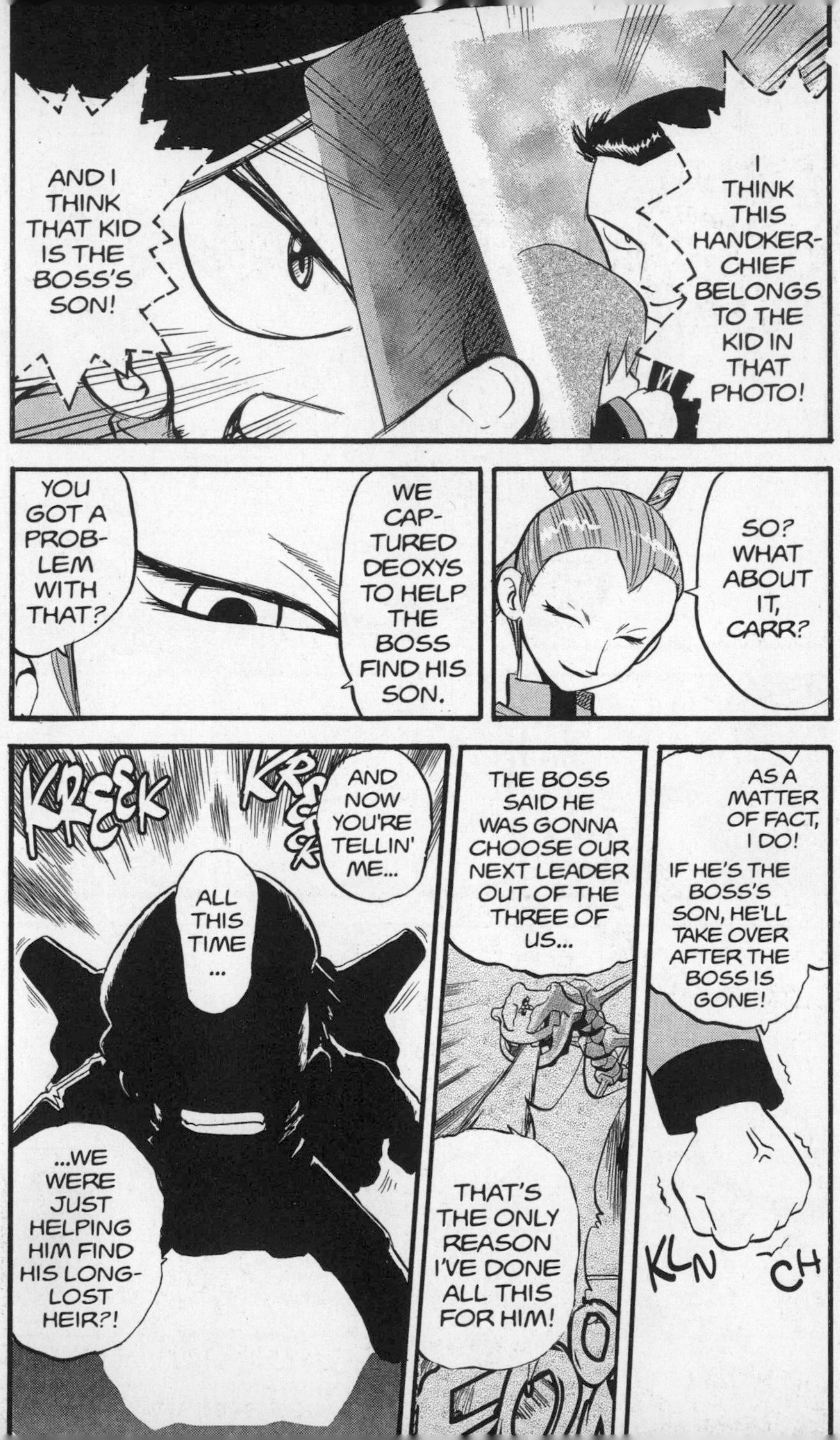
I THINK THIS HANDKER-CHIEF BELONGS TO THE KID IN THAT PHOTO!
AND I THINK THAT KID IS THE BOSS'S SON!
SO? WHAT ABOUT IT, CARR?
WE CAP-TURED DEOXYS TO HELP THE BOSS FIND HIS SON.
YOU GOT A PROB-LEM WITH THAT?
AS A MATTER OF FACT, I DO!
IF HE'S THE BOSS'S SON, HE'LL TAKE OVER AFTER THE BOSS IS GONE!
KLNCH
THE BOSS SAID HE WAS GONNA CHOOSE OUR NEXT LEADER OUT OF THE THREE OF US...
THAT'S THE ONLY REASON I'VE DONE ALL THIS FOR HIM!
KREEK
AND NOW YOU'RE TELLIN' ME...
ALL THIS TIME...
...WE WERE JUST HELPING HIM FIND HIS LONG-LOST HEIR?!

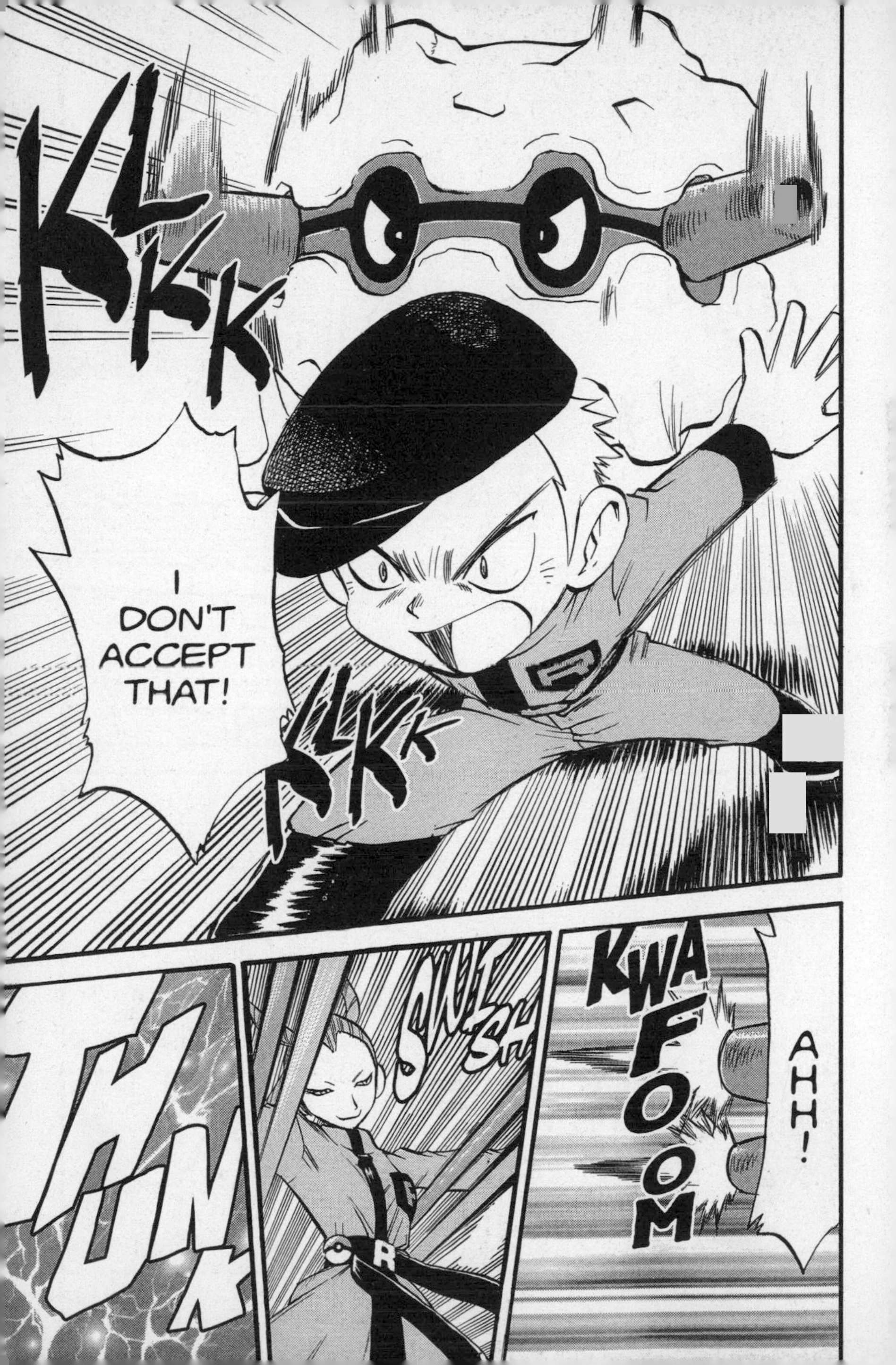
I DON'T ACCEPT THAT!
AHH!
KWAFOOOM
THUNK

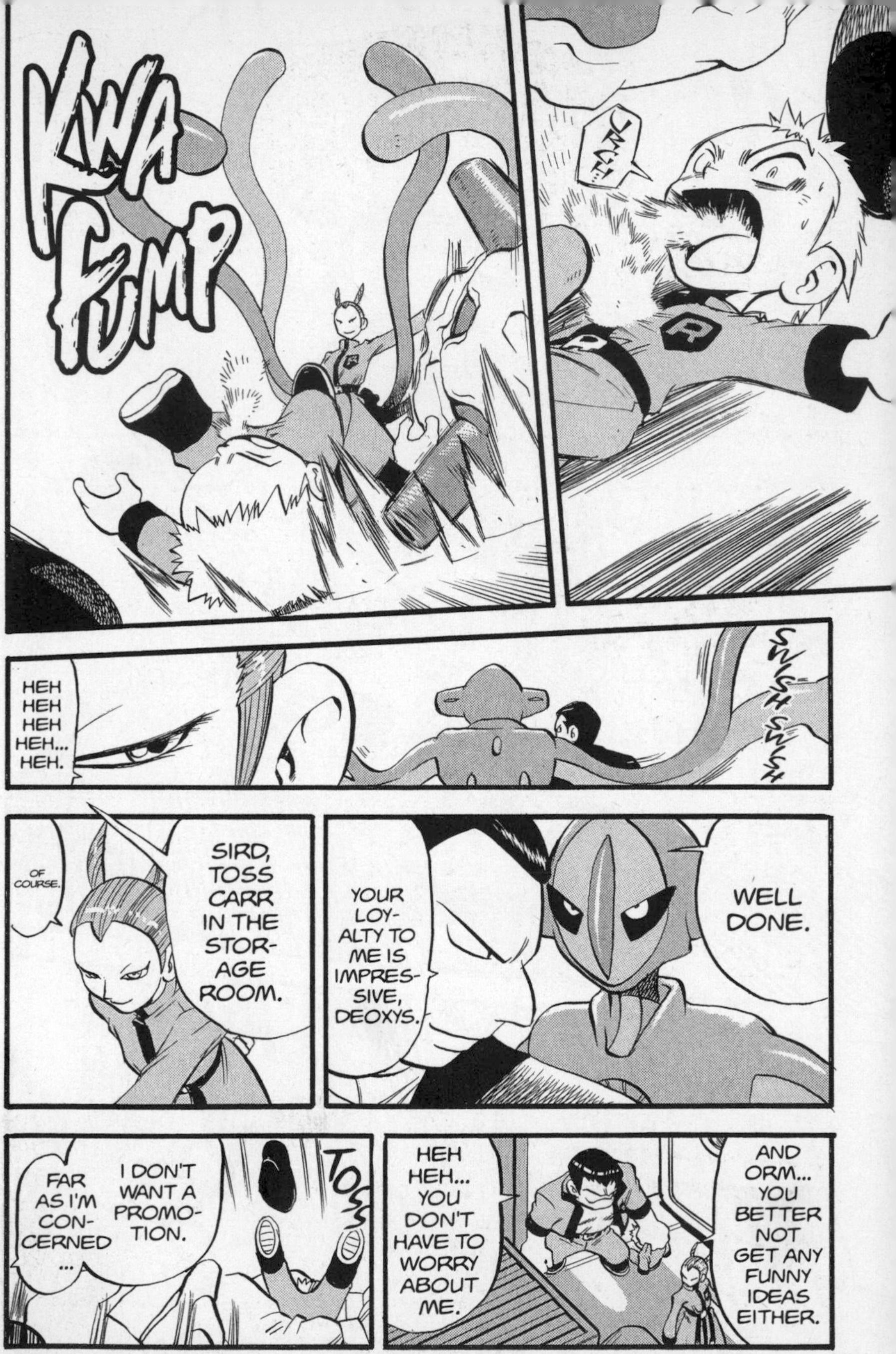
URGH...
KWA
FUMP
SWISH SWISH
HEH HEH HEH HEH... HEH.
WELL DONE.
YOUR LOY-ALTY TO ME IS IMPRES-SIVE, DEOXYS.
SIRD, TOSS CARR IN THE STOR-AGE ROOM.
OF COURSE.
AND ORM... YOU BETTER NOT GET ANY FUNNY IDEAS EITHER.
HEH HEH... YOU DON'T HAVE TO WORRY ABOUT ME.
TOSS
I DON'T WANT A PROMO-TION.
FAR AS I'M CON-CERNED ...

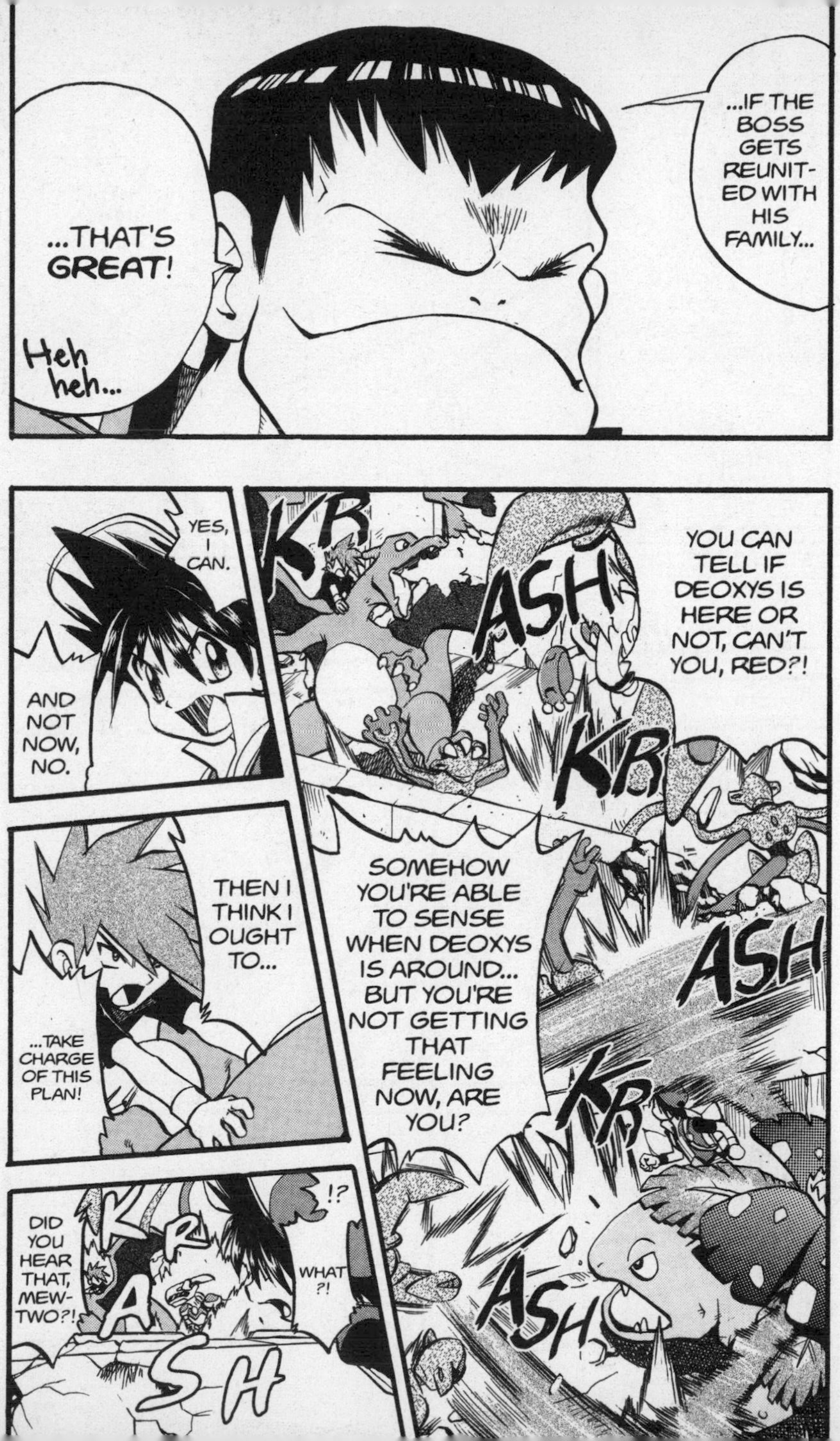
...IF THE BOSS GETS REUNIT-ED WITH HIS FAMILY...
...THAT'S GREAT!
Heh heh...
KRASH
YOU CAN TELL IF DEOXYS IS HERE OR NOT, CAN'T YOU, RED?!
KRASH
SOMEHOW YOU'RE ABLE TO SENSE WHEN DEOXYS IS AROUND... BUT YOU'RE NOT GETTING THAT FEELING NOW, ARE YOU?
KRASH
YES, I CAN.
AND NOT NOW, NO.
THEN I THINK I OUGHT TO...
...TAKE CHARGE OF THIS PLAN!
!?
WHAT?!
DID YOU HEAR THAT, MEW-TWO?!
KRASH

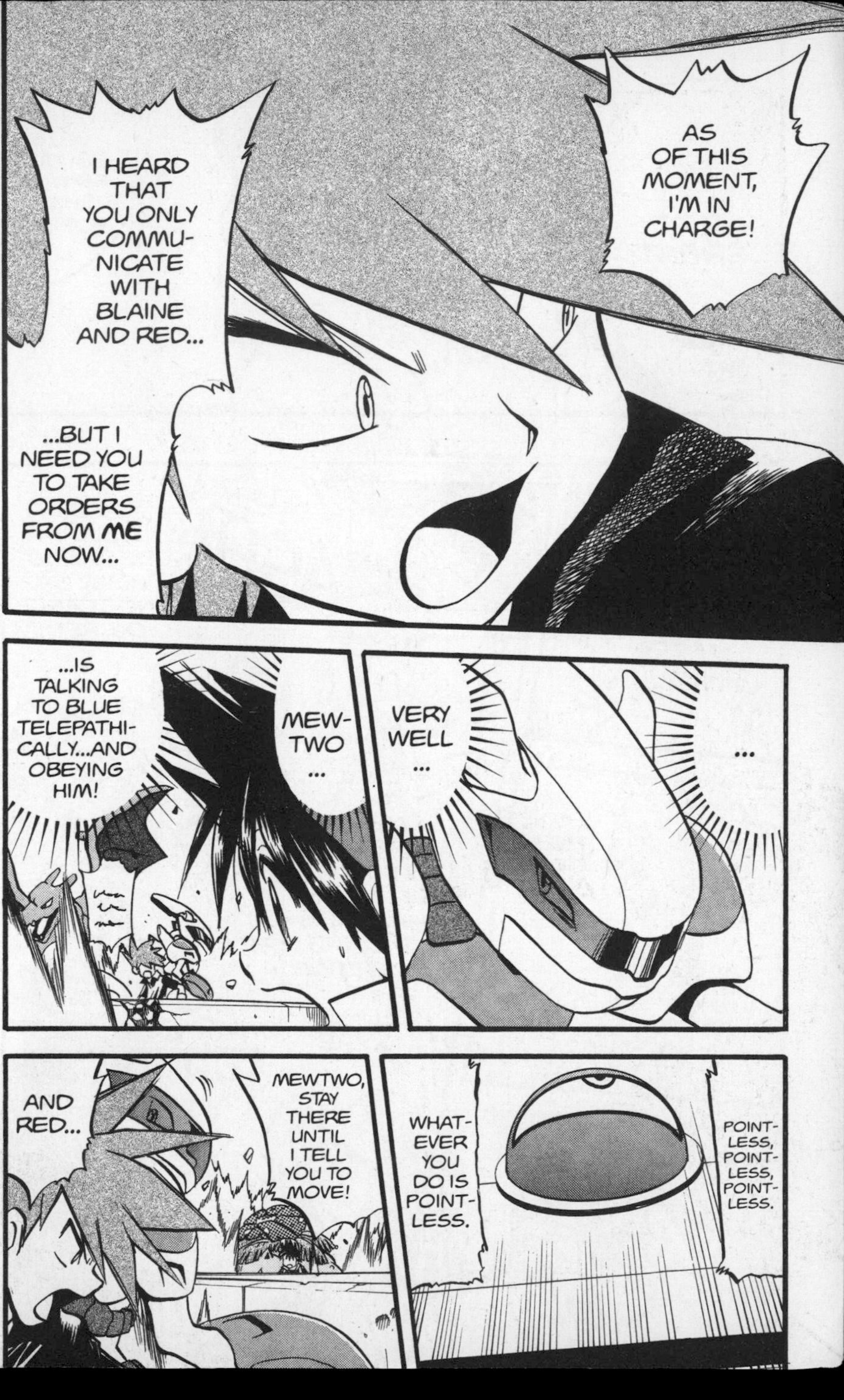
I HEARD THAT YOU ONLY COMMUNICATE WITH BLAINE AND RED...
...BUT I NEED YOU TO TAKE ORDERS FROM **ME** NOW...
AS OF THIS MOMENT, I'M IN CHARGE!
...
VERY WELL ...
MEW-TWO ...
...IS TALKING TO BLUE TELEPATHICALLY...AND OBEYING HIM!
POINTLESS, POINTLESS, POINTLESS.
WHATEVER YOU DO IS POINTLESS.
MEWTWO, STAY THERE UNTIL I TELL YOU TO MOVE!
AND RED...

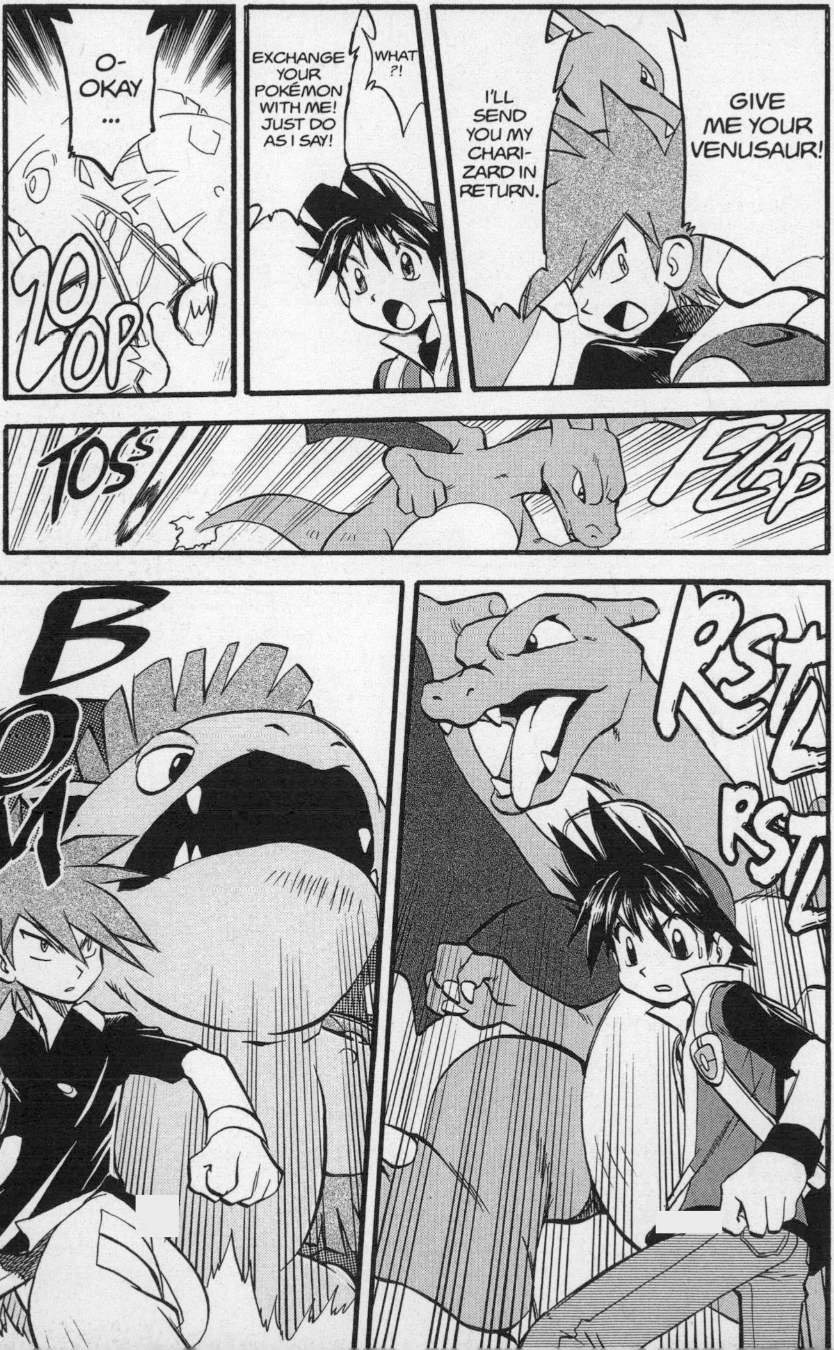
GIVE ME YOUR VENUSAUR!
I'LL SEND YOU MY CHARI-ZARD IN RETURN.
WHAT ?!
EXCHANGE YOUR POKéMON WITH ME! JUST DO AS I SAY!
O-OKAY ...
ZOOP
FLAP
TOSS
RSTL
RSTL
BOOM

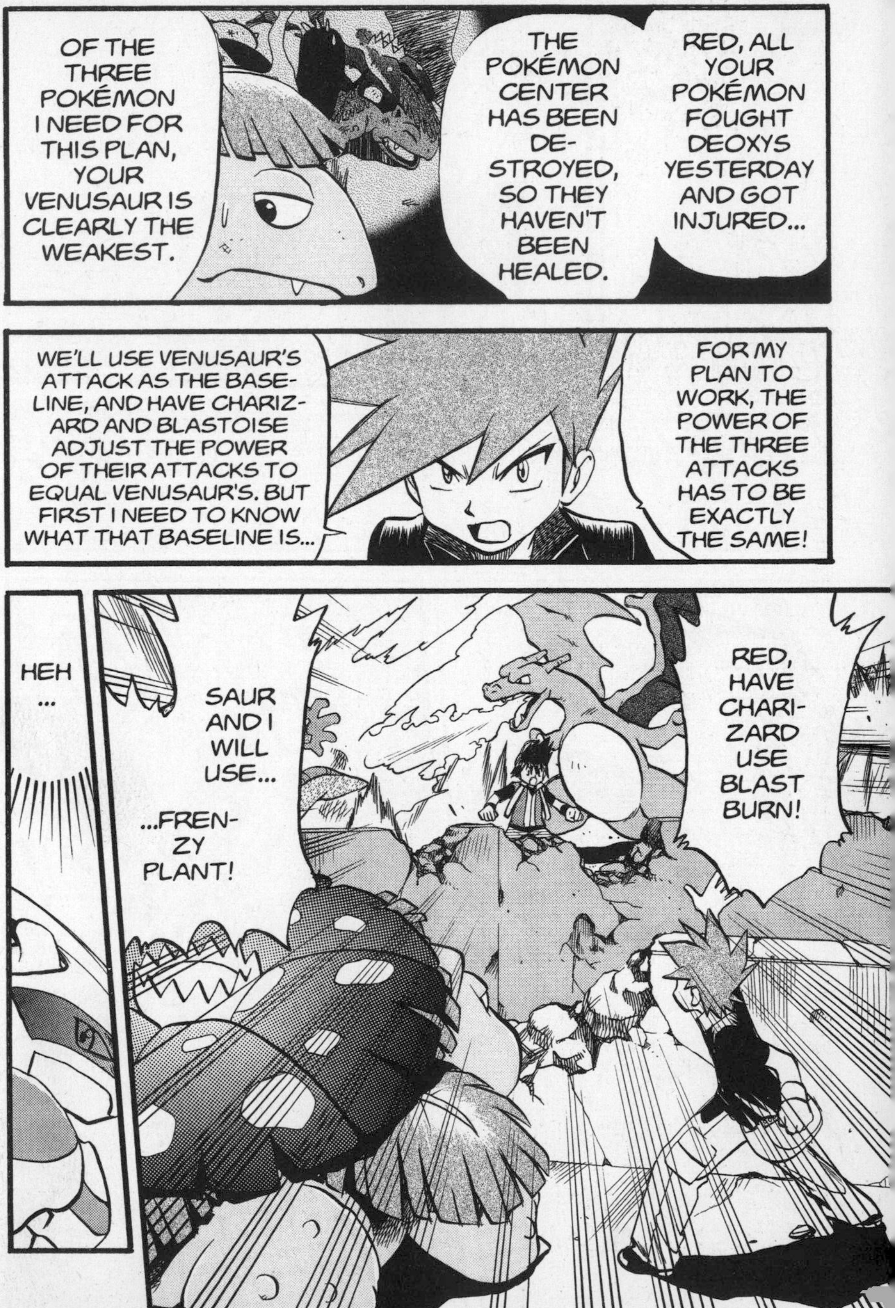
RED, ALL YOUR POKÉMON FOUGHT DEOXYS YESTERDAY AND GOT INJURED...
THE POKÉMON CENTER HAS BEEN DE-STROYED, SO THEY HAVEN'T BEEN HEALED.
OF THE THREE POKÉMON I NEED FOR THIS PLAN, YOUR VENUSAUR IS CLEARLY THE WEAKEST.
FOR MY PLAN TO WORK, THE POWER OF THE THREE ATTACKS HAS TO BE EXACTLY THE SAME!
WE'LL USE VENUSAUR'S ATTACK AS THE BASE-LINE, AND HAVE CHARIZ-ARD AND BLASTOISE ADJUST THE POWER OF THEIR ATTACKS TO EQUAL VENUSAUR'S. BUT FIRST I NEED TO KNOW WHAT THAT BASELINE IS...
RED, HAVE CHARI-ZARD USE BLAST BURN!
SAUR AND I WILL USE...
...FREN-ZY PLANT!
HEH ...

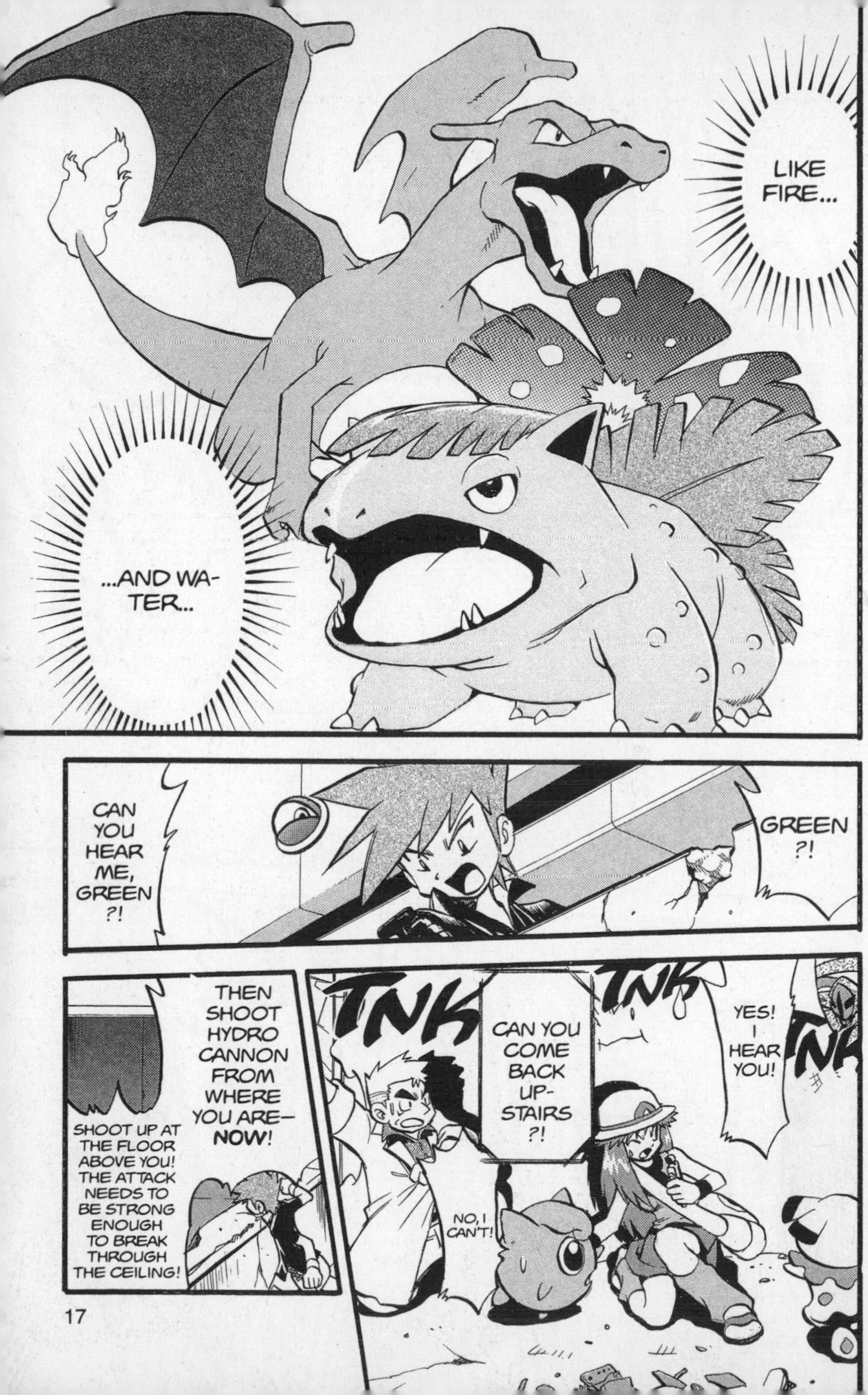
LIKE FIRE...
...AND WATER...
GREEN ?!
CAN YOU HEAR ME, GREEN ?!
TNK
TNK
TNK
YES! I HEAR YOU!
CAN YOU COME BACK UPSTAIRS ?!
NO, I CAN'T!
THEN SHOOT HYDRO CANNON FROM WHERE YOU ARE—**NOW**!
SHOOT UP AT THE FLOOR ABOVE YOU! THE ATTACK NEEDS TO BE STRONG ENOUGH TO BREAK THROUGH THE CEILING!

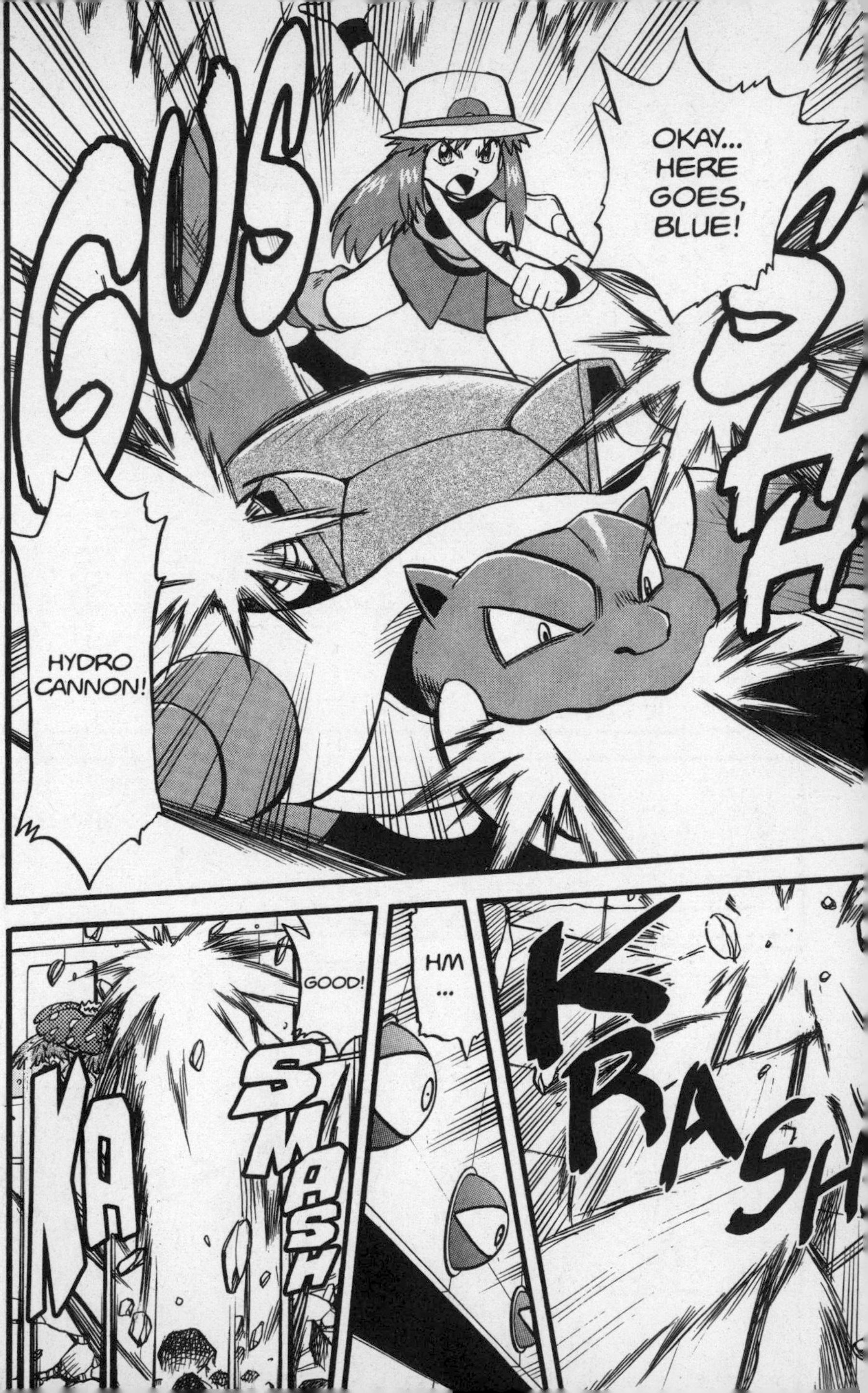
OKAY... HERE GOES, BLUE!
HYDRO CANNON!
KRASH
HM ...
GOOD!
SMASH

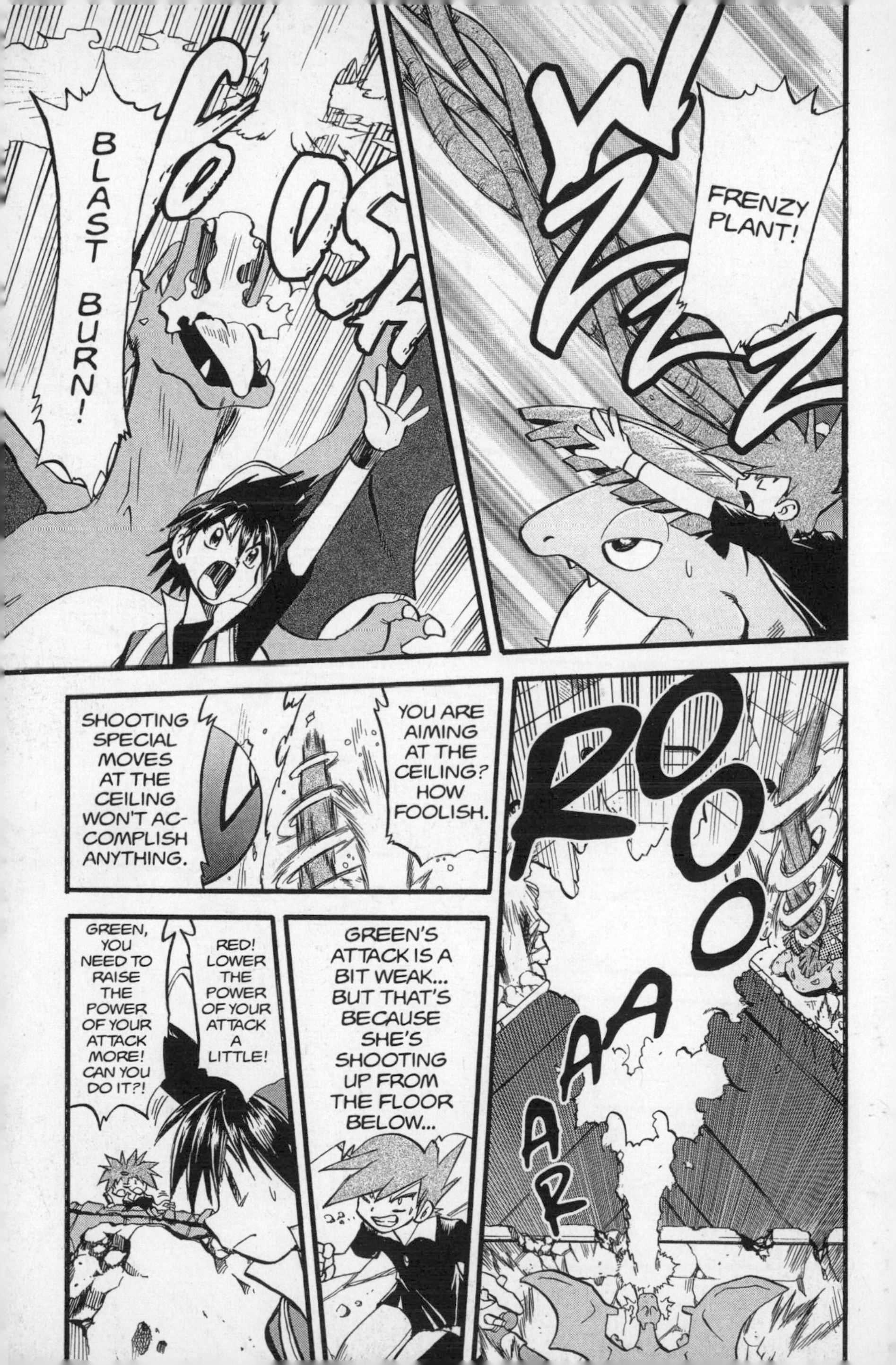

FRENZY PLANT!
BLAST BURN!
ROOOOAAAR
YOU ARE AIMING AT THE CEILING? HOW FOOLISH.
SHOOTING SPECIAL MOVES AT THE CEILING WON'T AC-COMPLISH ANYTHING.
GREEN'S ATTACK IS A BIT WEAK... BUT THAT'S BECAUSE SHE'S SHOOTING UP FROM THE FLOOR BELOW...
RED! LOWER THE POWER OF YOUR ATTACK A LITTLE!
GREEN, YOU NEED TO RAISE THE POWER OF YOUR ATTACK MORE! CAN YOU DO IT?!

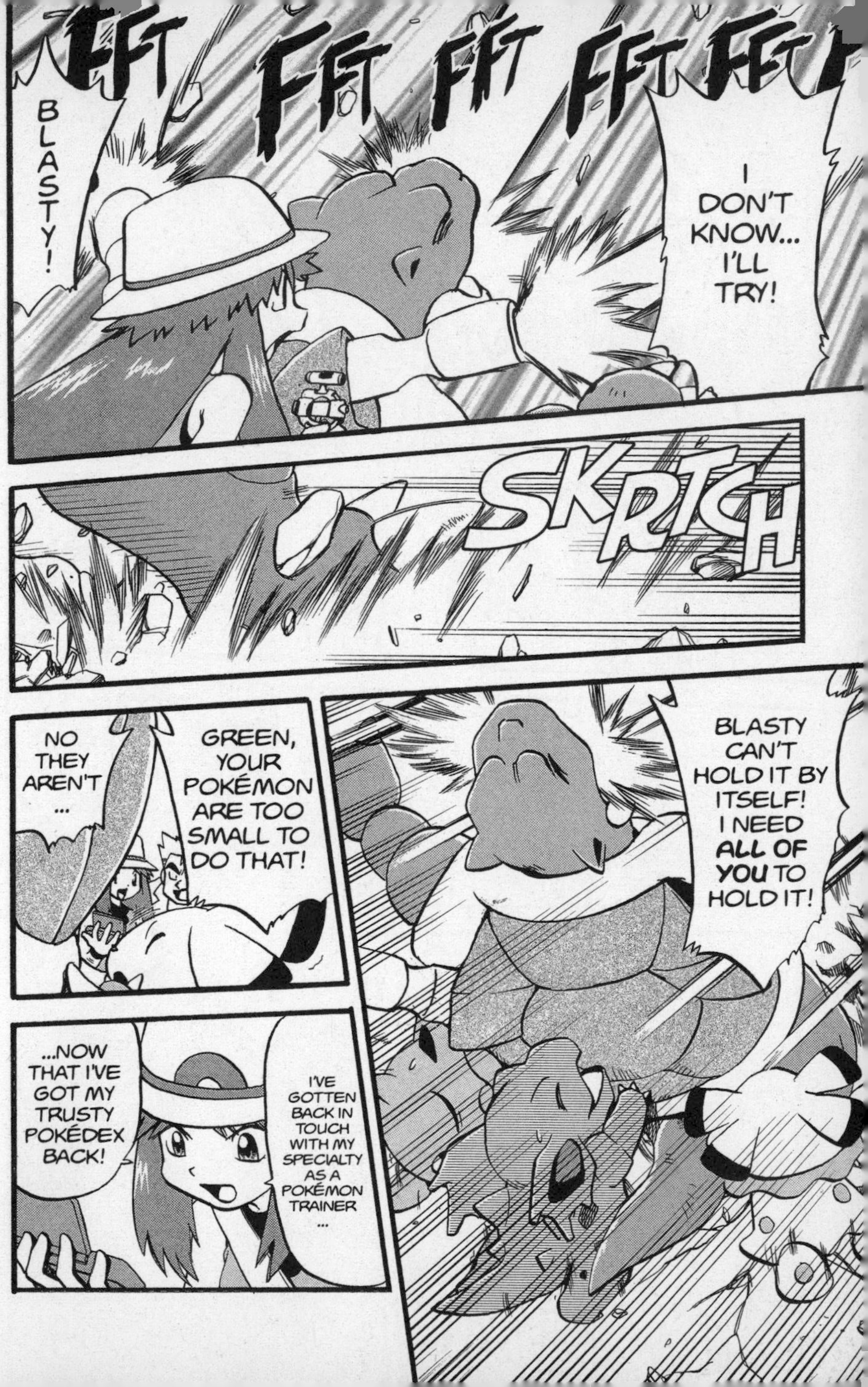
FFT
FFT
FFT
FFT
FFT
I DON'T KNOW... I'LL TRY!
BLASTY!
SKRTCH
BLASTY CAN'T HOLD IT BY ITSELF! I NEED **ALL OF YOU** TO HOLD IT!
GREEN, YOUR POKÉMON ARE TOO SMALL TO DO THAT!
NO THEY AREN'T ...
I'VE GOTTEN BACK IN TOUCH WITH MY SPECIALTY AS A POKÉMON TRAINER ...
...NOW THAT I'VE GOT MY TRUSTY POKÉDEX BACK!

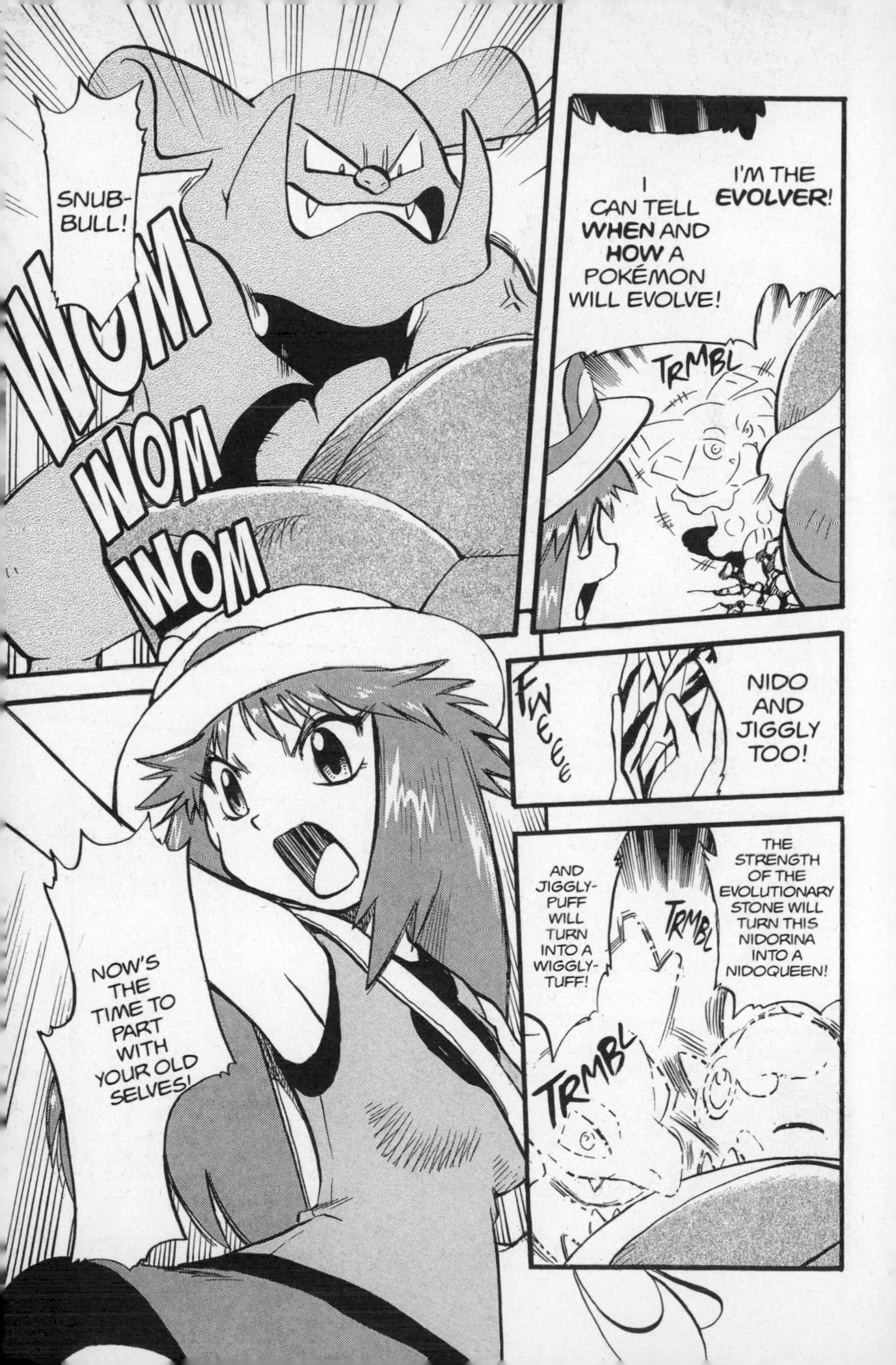
I'M THE EVOLVER!
I CAN TELL WHEN AND HOW A POKÉMON WILL EVOLVE!
TRMBL
SNUB-BULL!
WOM
WOM
WOM
FWEEEE
NIDO AND JIGGLY TOO!
THE STRENGTH OF THE EVOLUTIONARY STONE WILL TURN THIS NIDORINA INTO A NIDOQUEEN!
AND JIGGLY-PUFF WILL TURN INTO A WIGGLY-TUFF!
TRMBL
TRMBL
NOW'S THE TIME TO PART WITH YOUR OLD SELVES!

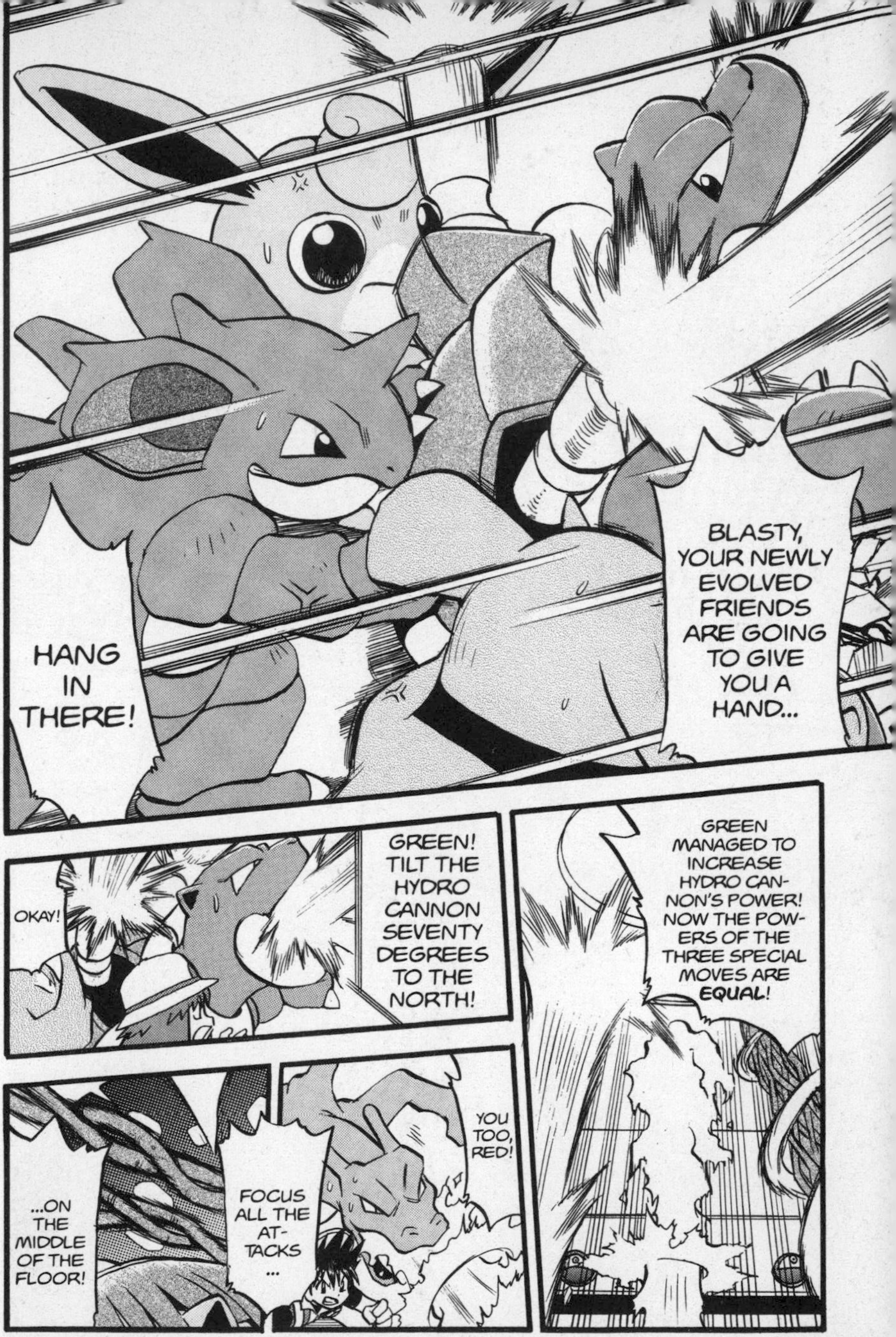
BLASTY, YOUR NEWLY EVOLVED FRIENDS ARE GOING TO GIVE YOU A HAND...
HANG IN THERE!
GREEN MANAGED TO INCREASE HYDRO CANNON'S POWER! NOW THE POWERS OF THE THREE SPECIAL MOVES ARE **EQUAL**!
GREEN! TILT THE HYDRO CANNON SEVENTY DEGREES TO THE NORTH!
OKAY!
YOU TOO, RED!
FOCUS ALL THE ATTACKS...
...ON THE MIDDLE OF THE FLOOR!

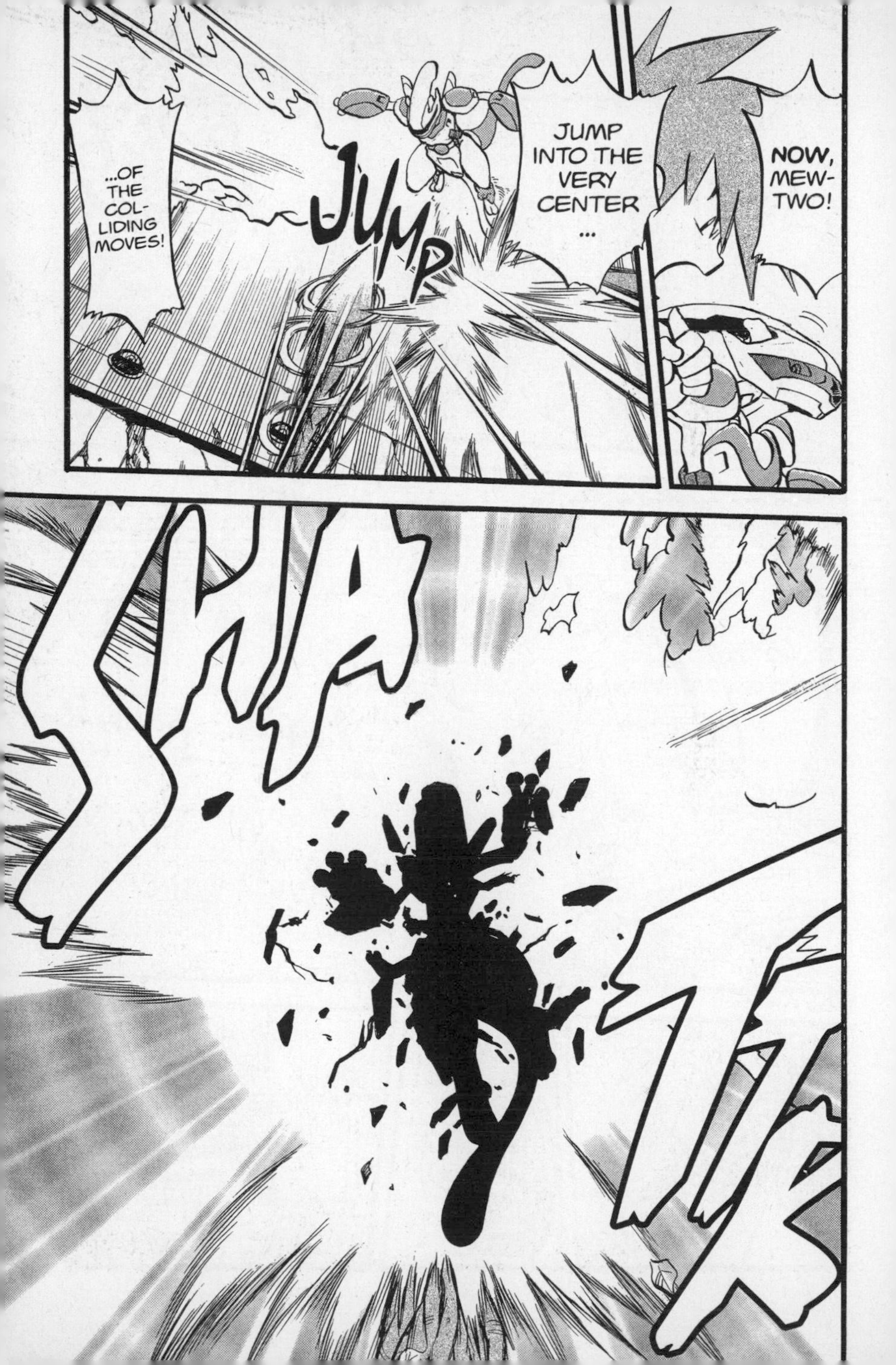
NOW, MEW-TWO!
JUMP INTO THE VERY CENTER ...
JUMP
...OF THE COL-LIDING MOVES!

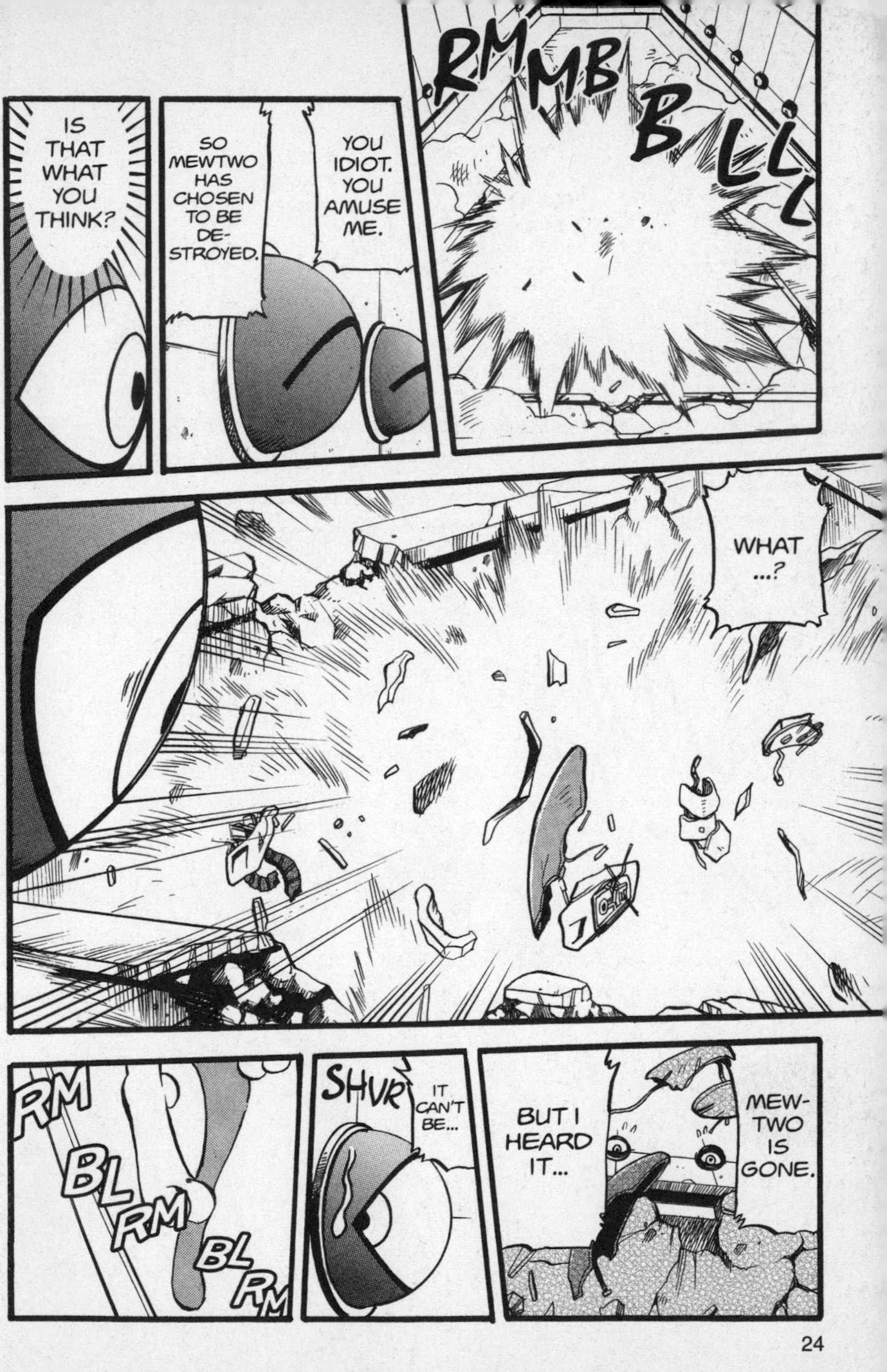
RMMB
BLLL
YOU IDIOT. YOU AMUSE ME.
SO MEWTWO HAS CHOSEN TO BE DE-STROYED.
IS THAT WHAT YOU THINK?
WHAT ...?
MEW-TWO IS GONE.
BUT I HEARD IT...
SHVR
IT CAN'T BE...
RM
BLRM
BLRM

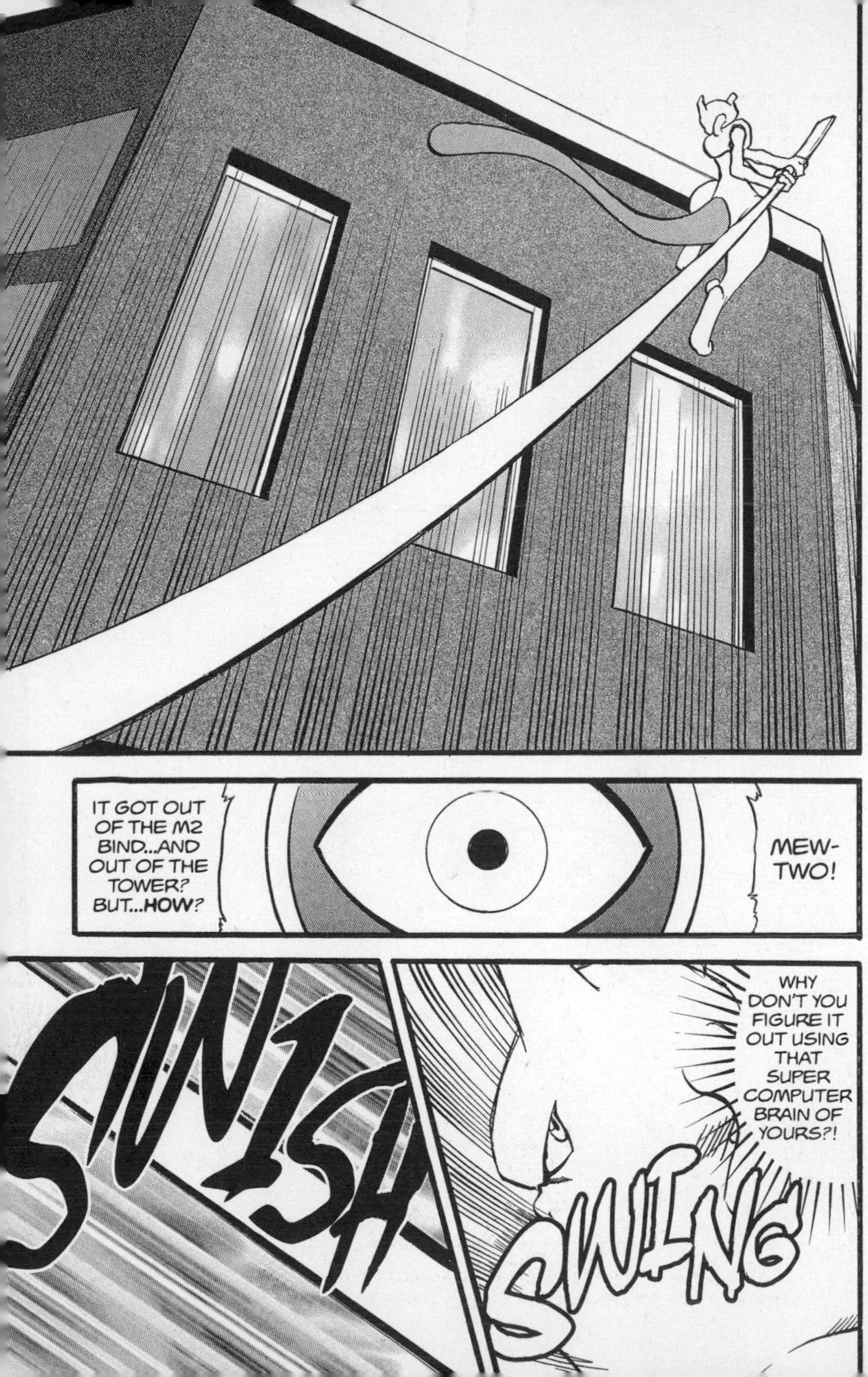
MEW-TWO!
IT GOT OUT OF THE M2 BIND...AND OUT OF THE TOWER? BUT...HOW?
WHY DON'T YOU FIGURE IT OUT USING THAT SUPER COMPUTER BRAIN OF YOURS?!
SWING
SWISH

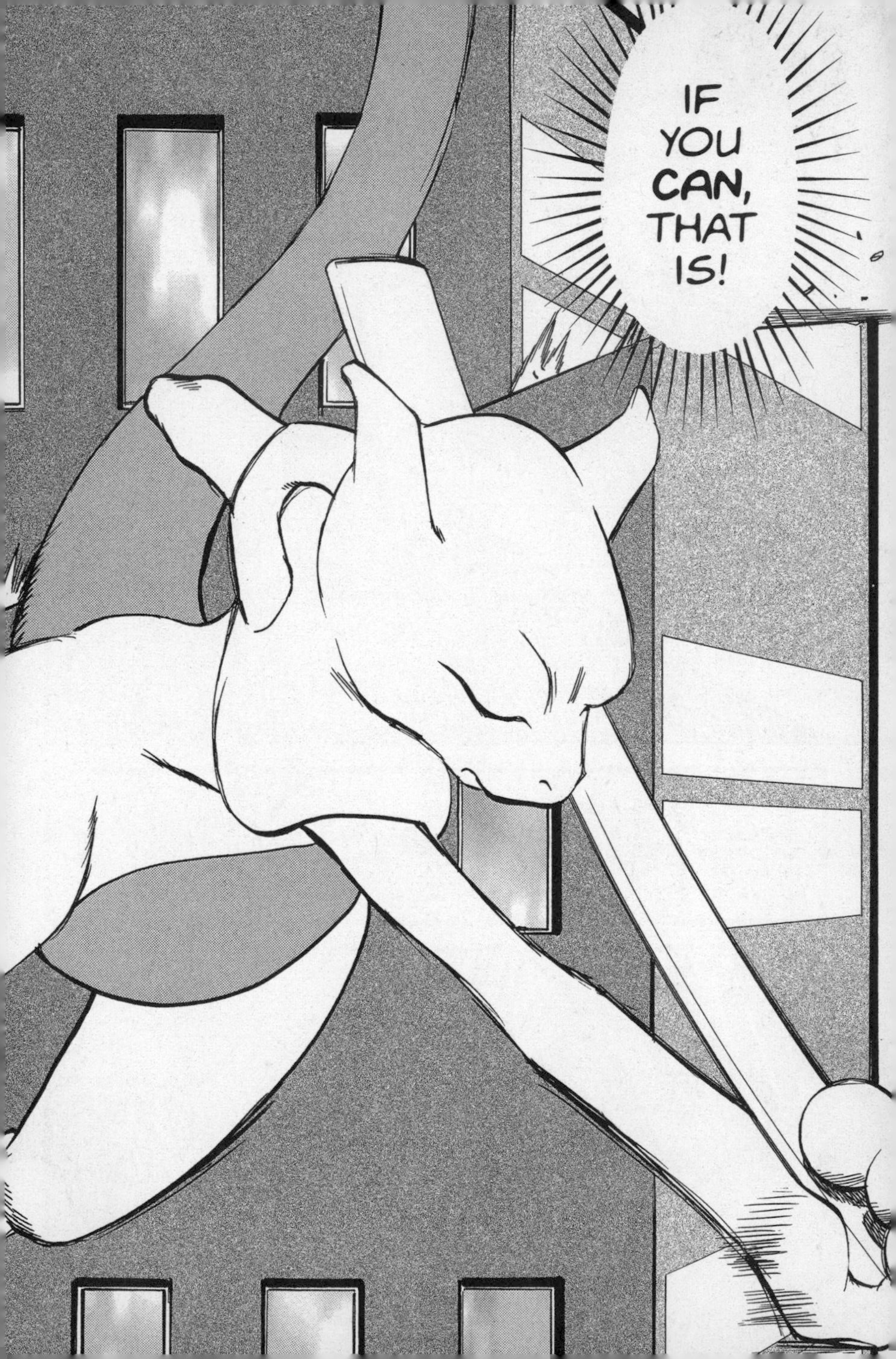
IF YOU CAN, THAT IS!

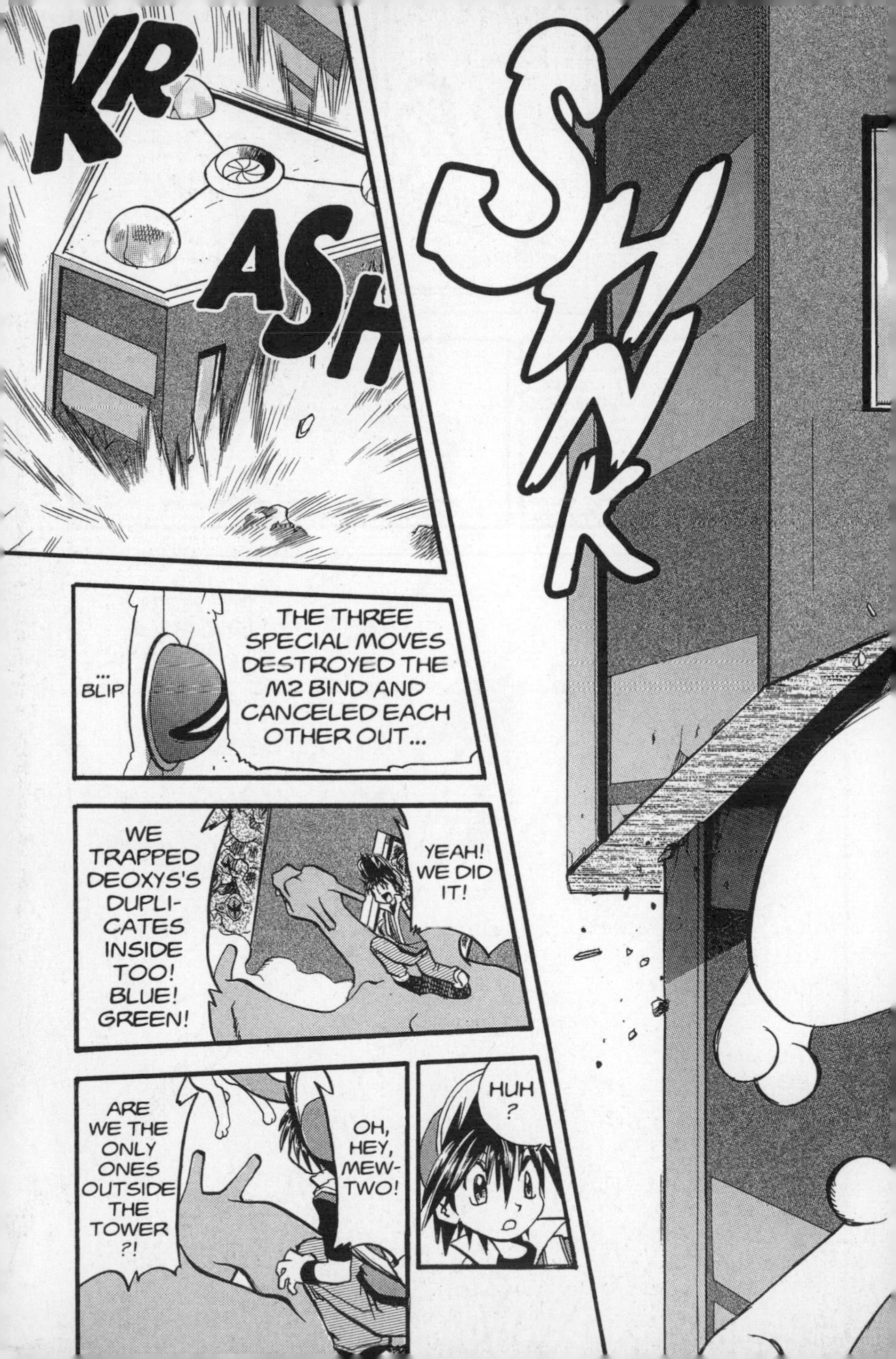
SHINK
KRASH
THE THREE SPECIAL MOVES DESTROYED THE M2 BIND AND CANCELED EACH OTHER OUT...
... BLIP
YEAH! WE DID IT!
WE TRAPPED DEOXYS'S DUPLICATES INSIDE TOO! BLUE! GREEN!
HUH?
OH, HEY, MEW-TWO!
ARE WE THE ONLY ONES OUTSIDE THE TOWER?!

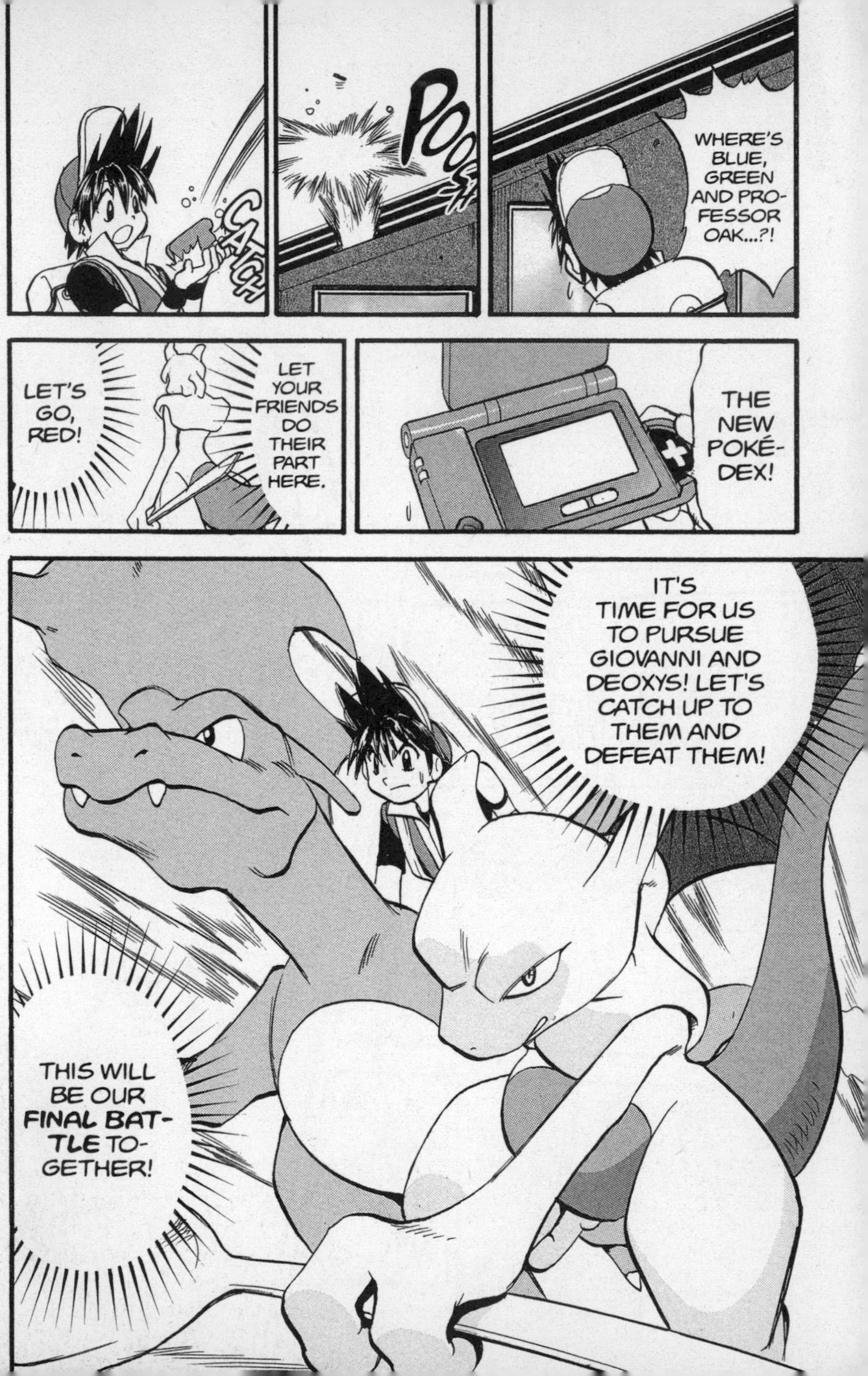
WHERE'S BLUE, GREEN AND PRO-FESSOR OAK...?!
POOF
CATCH
THE NEW POKÉ-DEX!
LET YOUR FRIENDS DO THEIR PART HERE.
LET'S GO, RED!
IT'S TIME FOR US TO PURSUE GIOVANNI AND DEOXYS! LET'S CATCH UP TO THEM AND DEFEAT THEM!
THIS WILL BE OUR **FINAL BAT-TLE** TO-GETHER!

PROFESSOR OAK

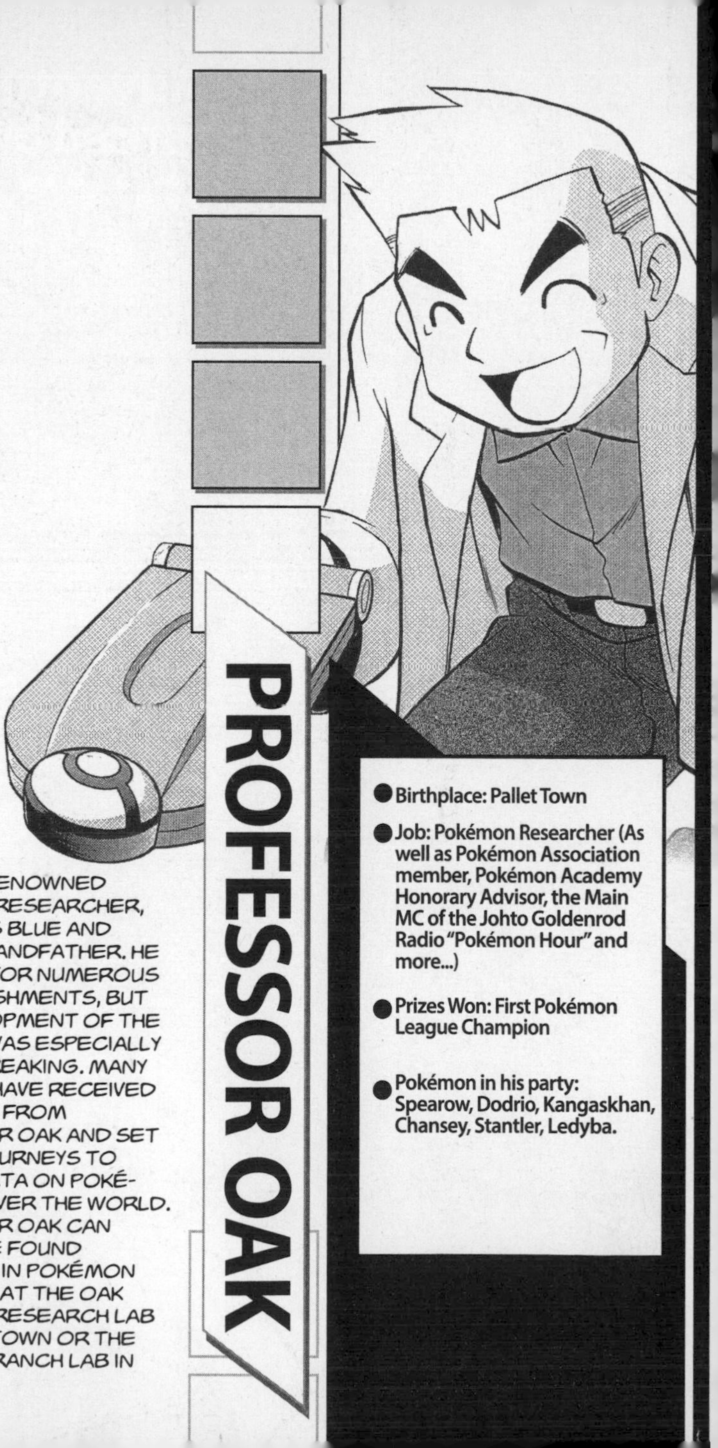

- Birthplace: Pallet Town
- Job: Pokémon Researcher (As well as Pokémon Association member, Pokémon Academy Honorary Advisor, the Main MC of the Johto Goldenrod Radio "Pokémon Hour" and more...)
- Prizes Won: First Pokémon League Champion
- Pokémon in his party: Spearow, Dodrio, Kangaskhan, Chansey, Stantler, Ledyba.

A WORLD RENOWNED POKÉMON RESEARCHER, AS WELL AS BLUE AND DAISY'S GRANDFATHER. HE IS KNOWN FOR NUMEROUS ACCOMPLISHMENTS, BUT HIS DEVELOPMENT OF THE POKÉDEX WAS ESPECIALLY GROUNDBREAKING. MANY CHILDREN HAVE RECEIVED A POKÉDEX FROM PROFESSOR OAK AND SET OUT ON JOURNEYS TO GATHER DATA ON POKÉMON ALL OVER THE WORLD. PROFESSOR OAK CAN USUALLY BE FOUND IMMERSED IN POKÉMON RESEARCH AT THE OAK POKÉMON RESEARCH LAB IN PALLET TOWN OR THE SECOND BRANCH LAB IN JOHTO.

•Adventure 289•
Surprised by Sneasel

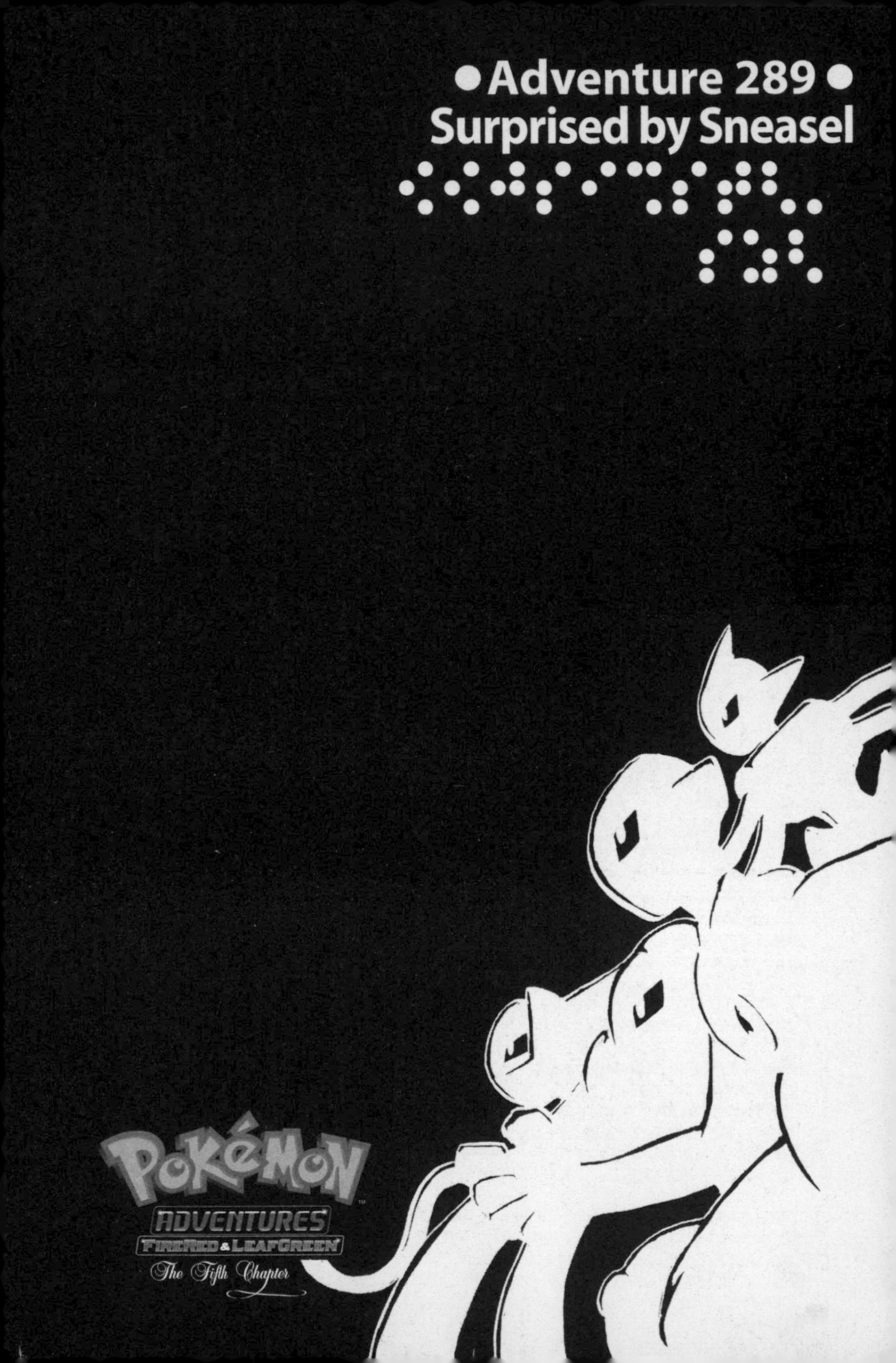

POKÉMON
ADVENTURES
FIRERED & LEAFGREEN
The Fifth Chapter

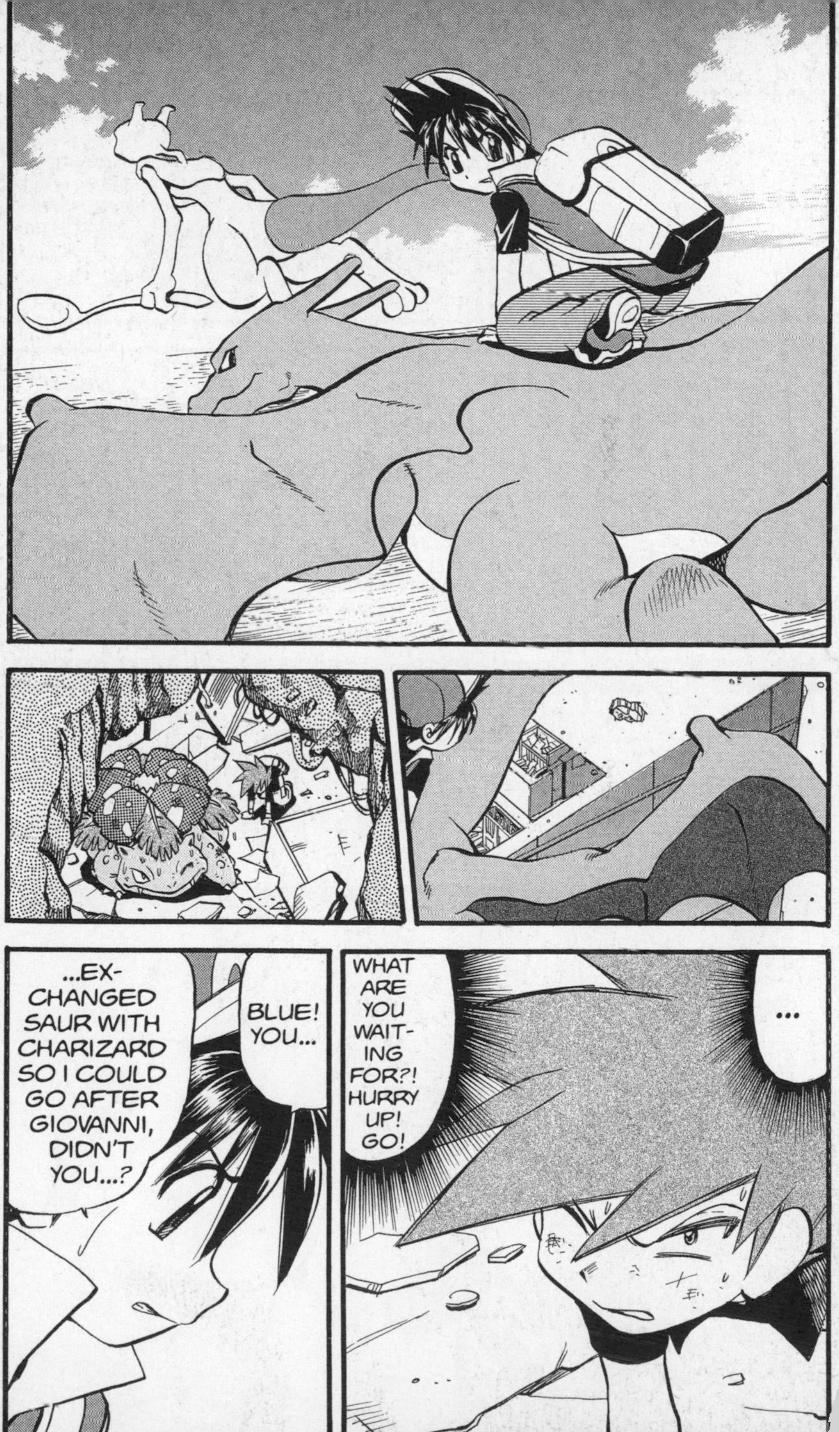
...
WHAT ARE YOU WAIT-ING FOR?! HURRY UP! GO!
BLUE! YOU...
...EX-CHANGED SAUR WITH CHARIZARD SO I COULD GO AFTER GIOVANNI, DIDN'T YOU...?

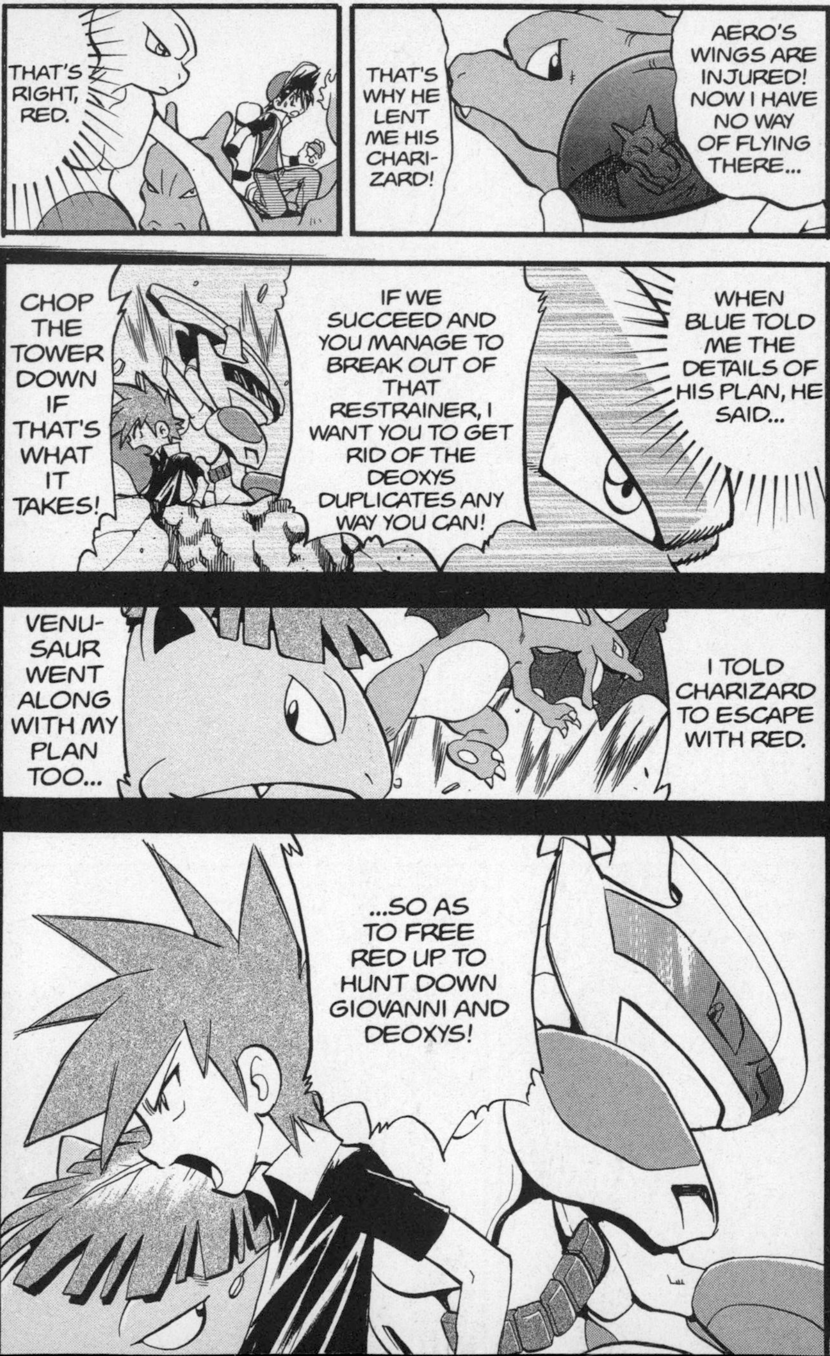
AERO'S WINGS ARE INJURED! NOW I HAVE NO WAY OF FLYING THERE...
THAT'S WHY HE LENT ME HIS CHARI-ZARD!
THAT'S RIGHT, RED.
WHEN BLUE TOLD ME THE DETAILS OF HIS PLAN, HE SAID...
IF WE SUCCEED AND YOU MANAGE TO BREAK OUT OF THAT RESTRAINER, I WANT YOU TO GET RID OF THE DEOXYS DUPLICATES ANY WAY YOU CAN!
CHOP THE TOWER DOWN IF THAT'S WHAT IT TAKES!
I TOLD CHARIZARD TO ESCAPE WITH RED.
VENU-SAUR WENT ALONG WITH MY PLAN TOO...
...SO AS TO FREE RED UP TO HUNT DOWN GIOVANNI AND DEOXYS!

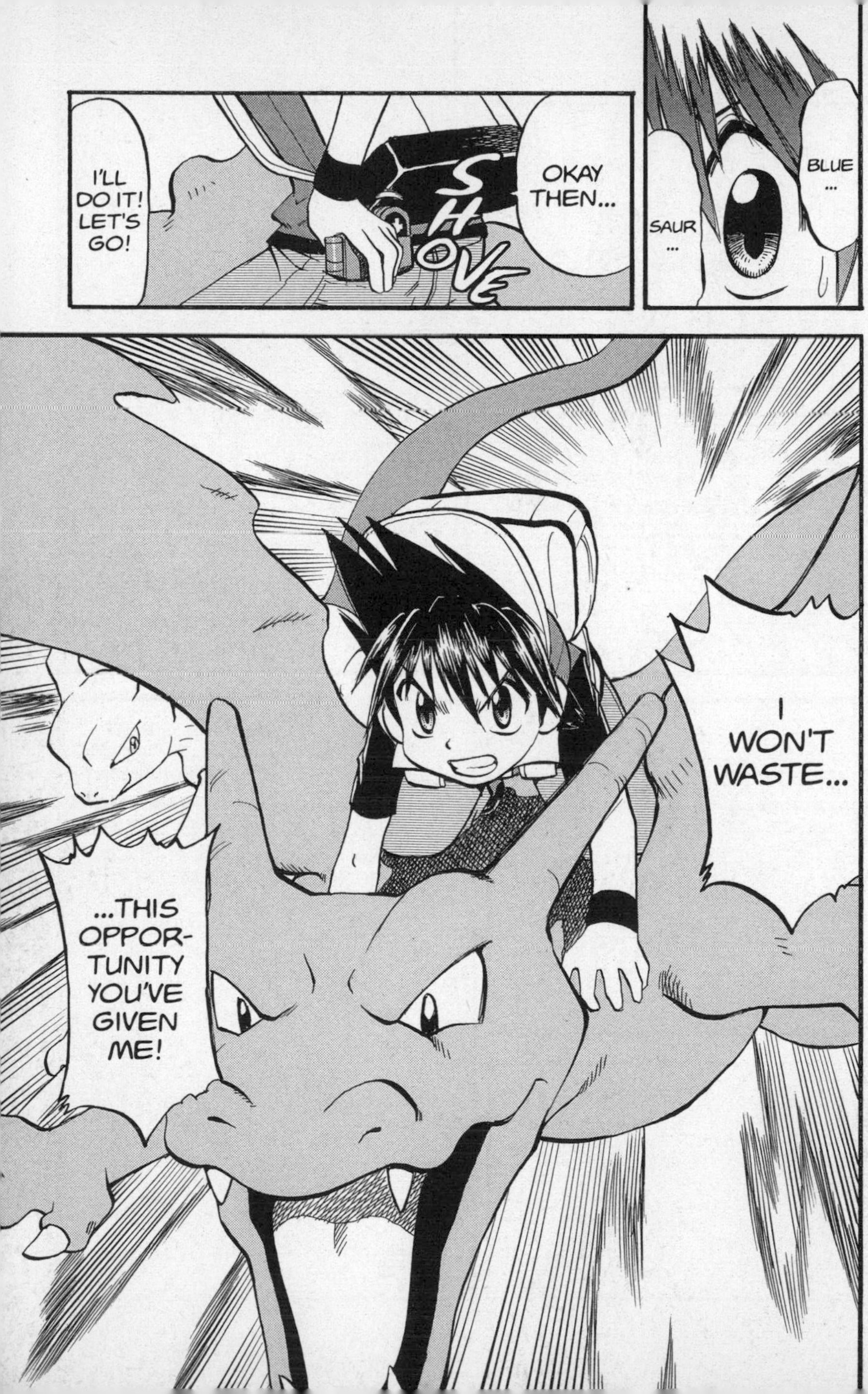

BLUE...
SAUR...
OKAY THEN...
SHOVE
I'LL DO IT! LET'S GO!
I WON'T WASTE...
...THIS OPPOR-TUNITY YOU'VE GIVEN ME!

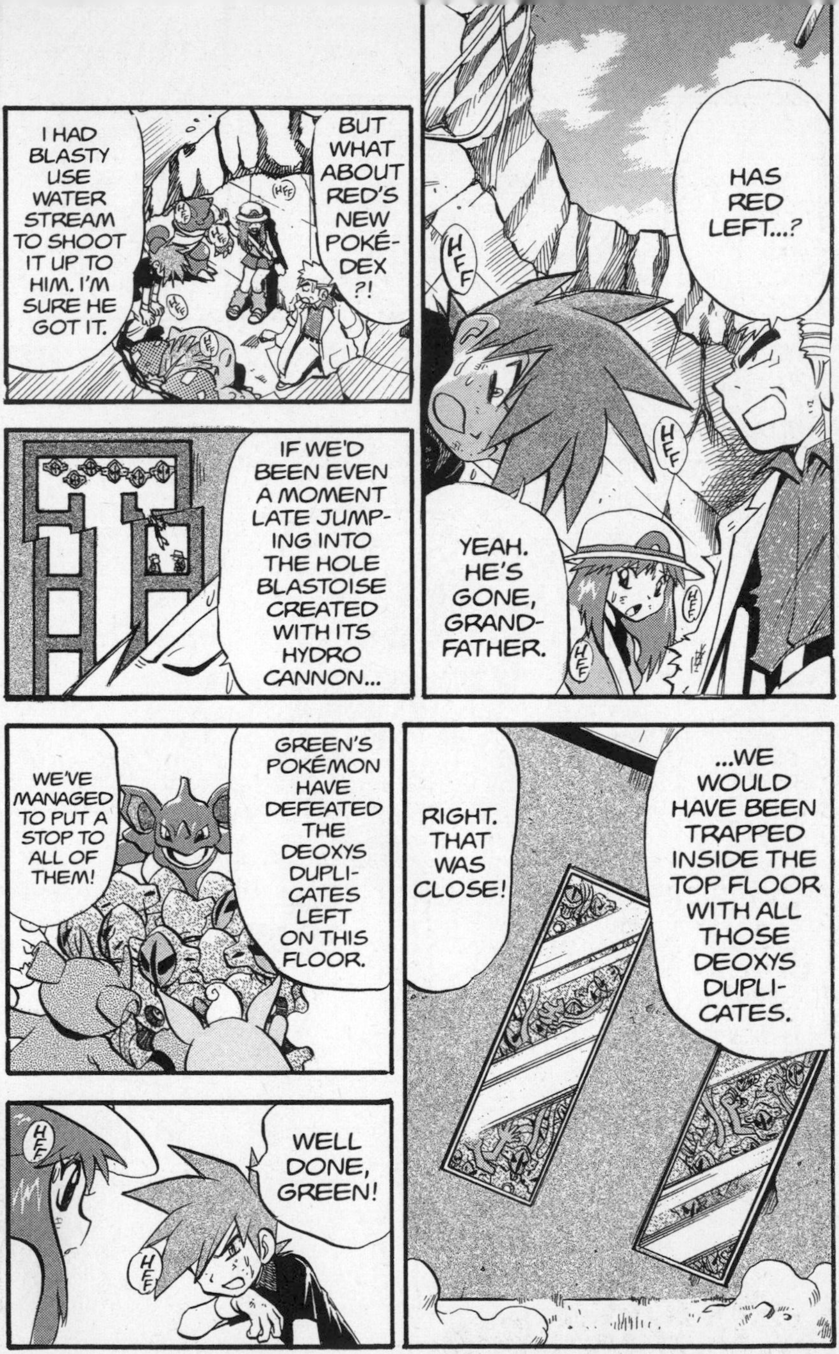

HAS RED LEFT...?
YEAH. HE'S GONE, GRANDFATHER.
BUT WHAT ABOUT RED'S NEW POKÉDEX ?!
I HAD BLASTY USE WATER STREAM TO SHOOT IT UP TO HIM. I'M SURE HE GOT IT.
IF WE'D BEEN EVEN A MOMENT LATE JUMPING INTO THE HOLE BLASTOISE CREATED WITH ITS HYDRO CANNON...
...WE WOULD HAVE BEEN TRAPPED INSIDE THE TOP FLOOR WITH ALL THOSE DEOXYS DUPLICATES.
RIGHT. THAT WAS CLOSE!
GREEN'S POKÉMON HAVE DEFEATED THE DEOXYS DUPLICATES LEFT ON THIS FLOOR.
WE'VE MANAGED TO PUT A STOP TO ALL OF THEM!
WELL DONE, GREEN!

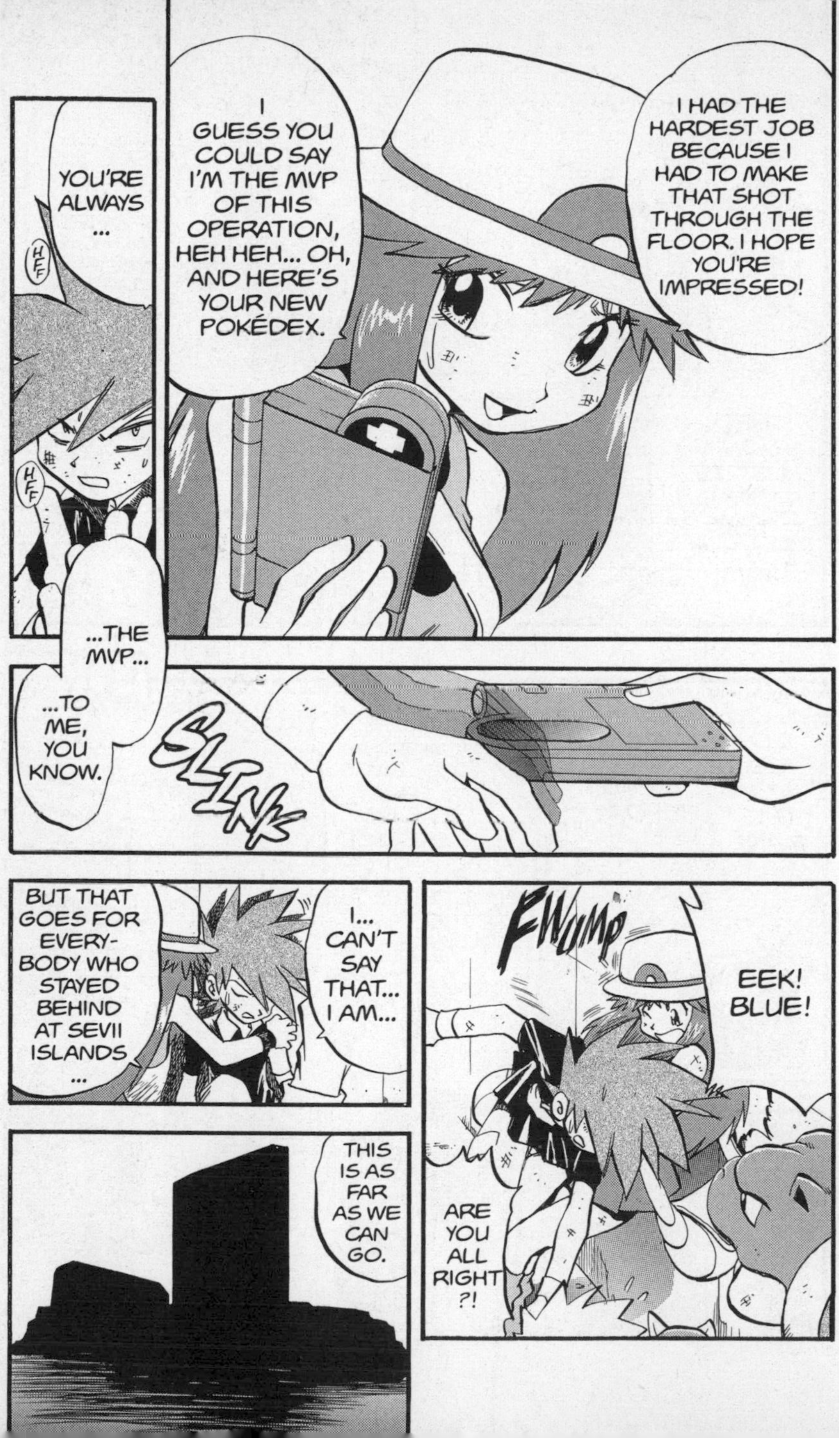
I HAD THE HARDEST JOB BECAUSE I HAD TO MAKE THAT SHOT THROUGH THE FLOOR. I HOPE YOU'RE IMPRESSED!
I GUESS YOU COULD SAY I'M THE MVP OF THIS OPERATION, HEH HEH... OH, AND HERE'S YOUR NEW POKÉDEX.
YOU'RE ALWAYS ...
HFF
HFF
...THE MVP...
...TO ME, YOU KNOW.
SLINK
FWUMP
EEK! BLUE!
ARE YOU ALL RIGHT ?!
I... CAN'T SAY THAT... I AM...
BUT THAT GOES FOR EVERY-BODY WHO STAYED BEHIND AT SEVII ISLANDS ...
THIS IS AS FAR AS WE CAN GO.

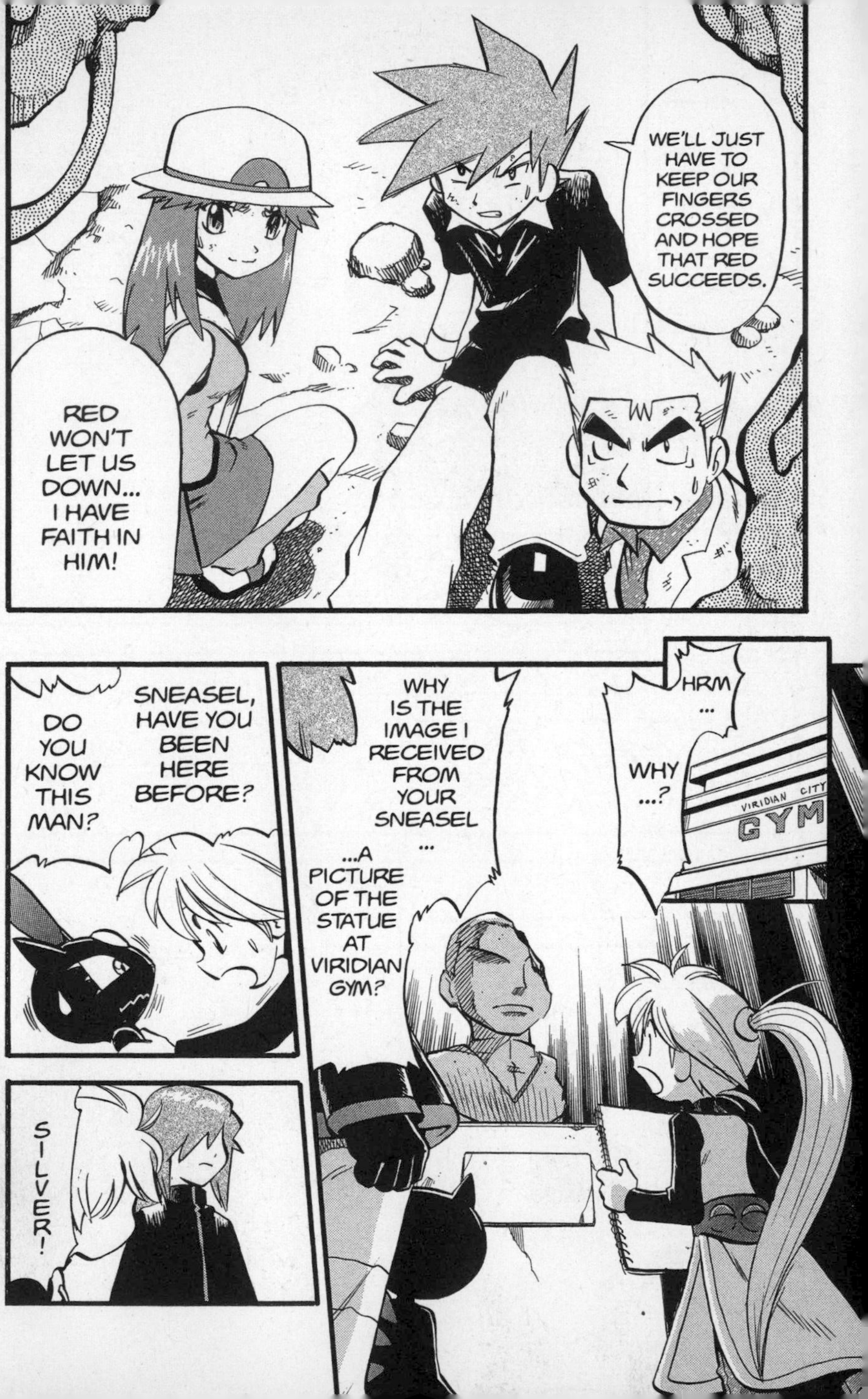
WE'LL JUST HAVE TO KEEP OUR FINGERS CROSSED AND HOPE THAT RED SUCCEEDS.
RED WON'T LET US DOWN... I HAVE FAITH IN HIM!
HRM ...
WHY ...?
VIRIDIAN CITY GYM
WHY IS THE IMAGE I RECEIVED FROM YOUR SNEASEL ...
...A PICTURE OF THE STATUE AT VIRIDIAN GYM?
SNEASEL, HAVE YOU BEEN HERE BEFORE?
DO YOU KNOW THIS MAN?
SILVER!

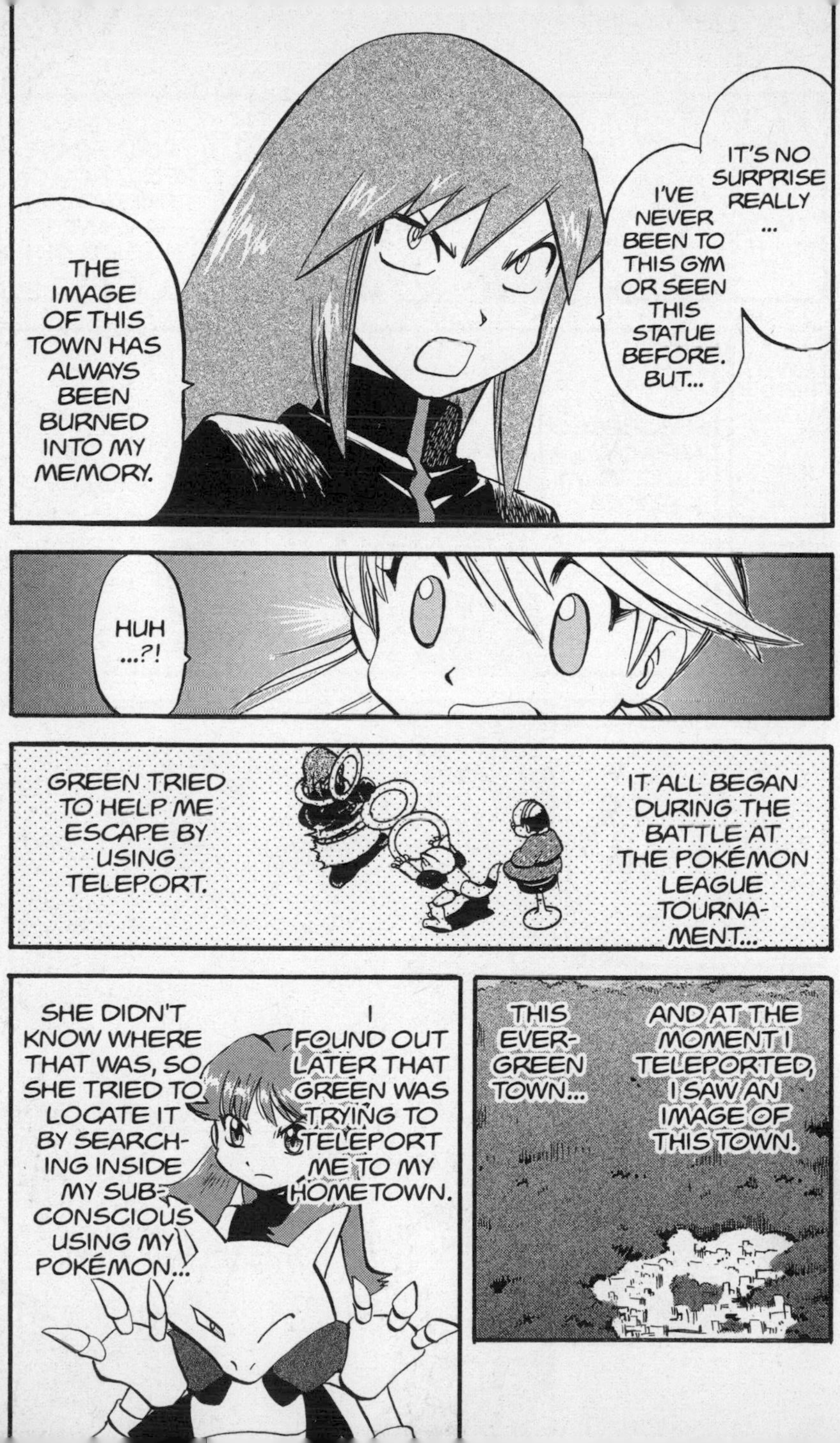
IT'S NO SURPRISE REALLY...
I'VE NEVER BEEN TO THIS GYM OR SEEN THIS STATUE BEFORE. BUT...
THE IMAGE OF THIS TOWN HAS ALWAYS BEEN BURNED INTO MY MEMORY.
HUH ...?!
IT ALL BEGAN DURING THE BATTLE AT THE POKÉMON LEAGUE TOURNA-MENT...
GREEN TRIED TO HELP ME ESCAPE BY USING TELEPORT.
AND AT THE MOMENT I TELEPORTED, I SAW AN IMAGE OF THIS TOWN.
THIS EVER-GREEN TOWN...
I FOUND OUT LATER THAT GREEN WAS TRYING TO TELEPORT ME TO MY HOMETOWN.
SHE DIDN'T KNOW WHERE THAT WAS, SO SHE TRIED TO LOCATE IT BY SEARCH-ING INSIDE MY SUB-CONSCIOUS USING MY POKÉMON...

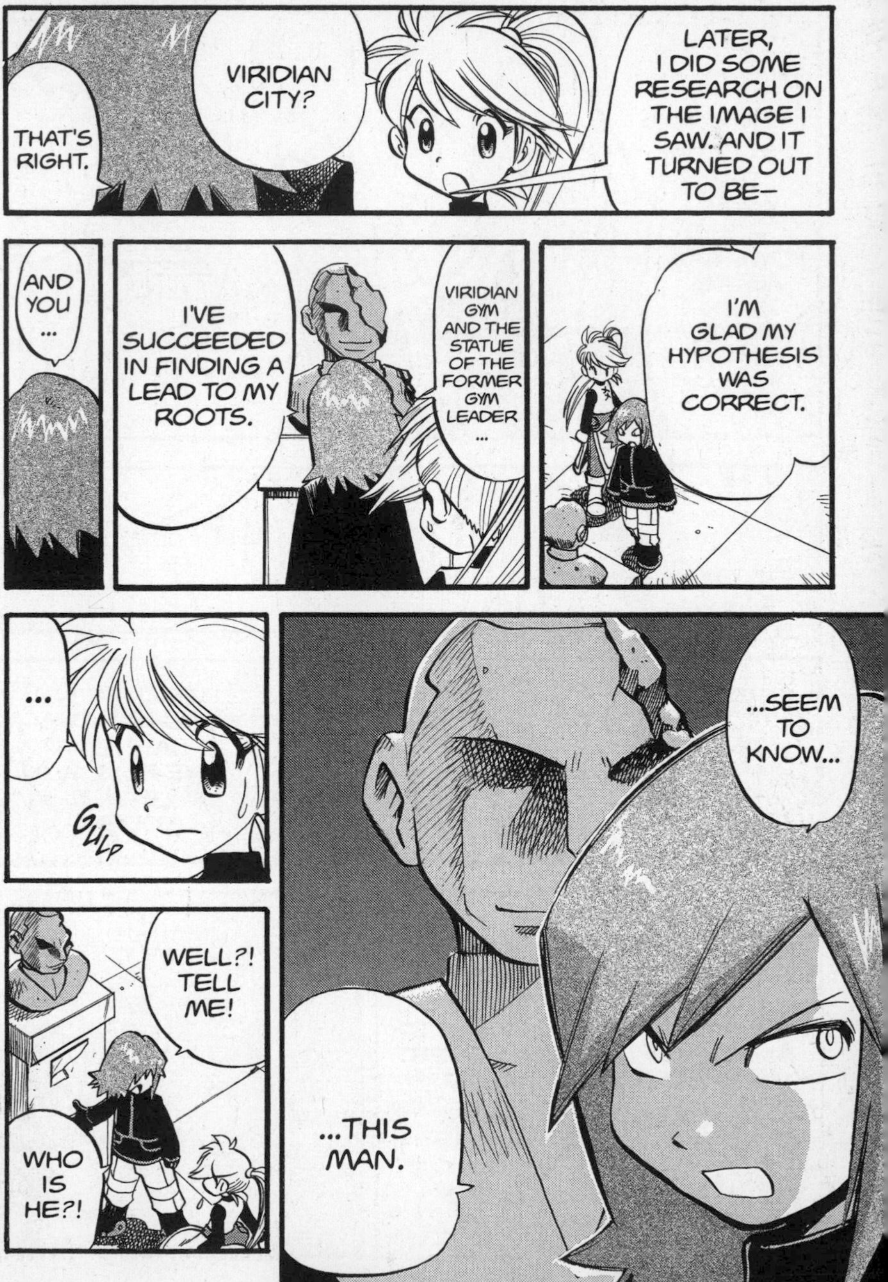
LATER, I DID SOME RESEARCH ON THE IMAGE I SAW. AND IT TURNED OUT TO BE—
VIRIDIAN CITY?
THAT'S RIGHT.
I'M GLAD MY HYPOTHESIS WAS CORRECT.
VIRIDIAN GYM AND THE STATUE OF THE FORMER GYM LEADER ...
I'VE SUCCEEDED IN FINDING A LEAD TO MY ROOTS.
AND YOU ...
...SEEM TO KNOW...
...THIS MAN.
...
GULP
WELL?! TELL ME!
WHO IS HE?!

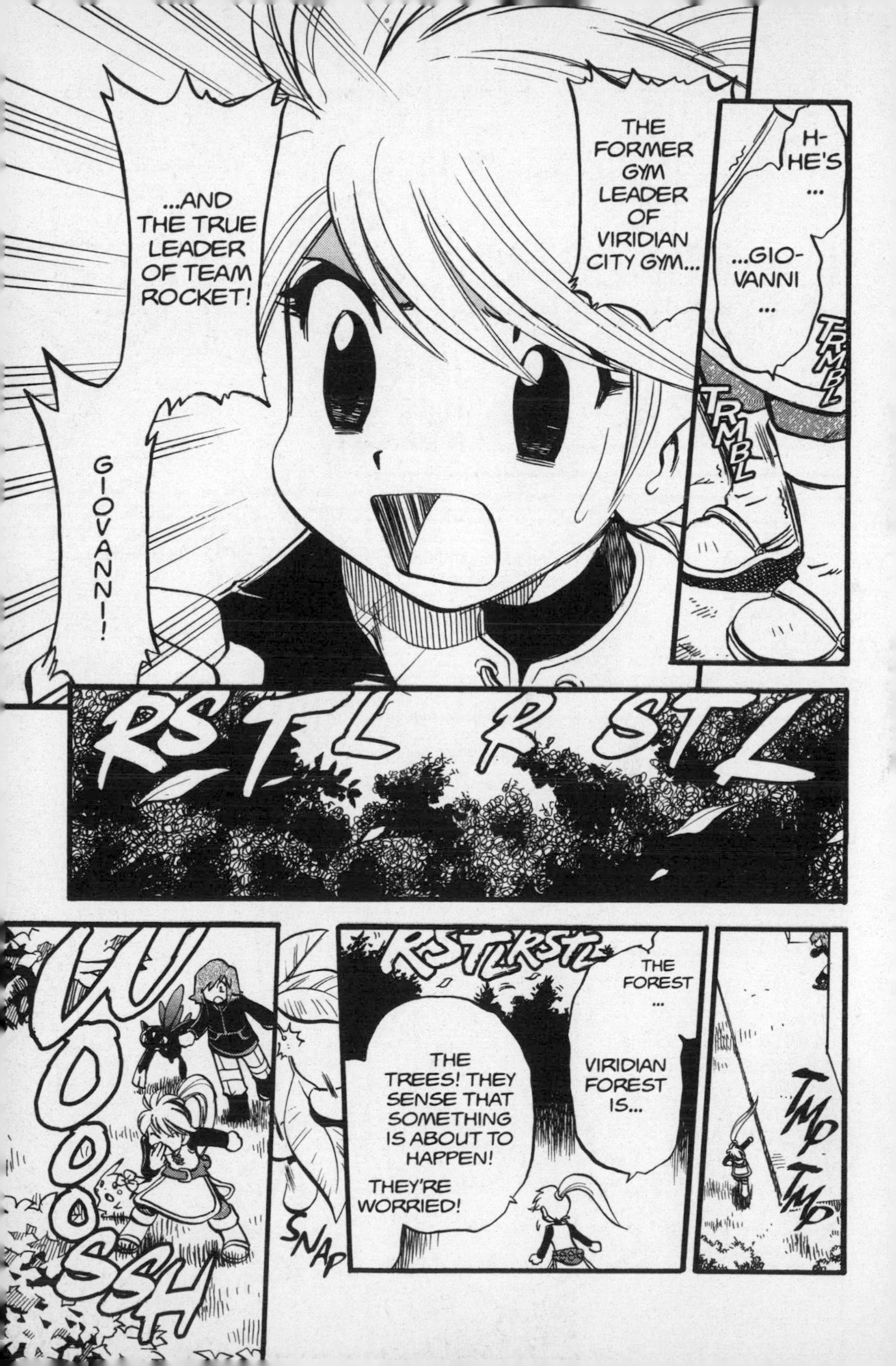
H-HE'S...
...GIO-VANNI...
TRMBL
TRMBL
THE FORMER GYM LEADER OF VIRIDIAN CITY GYM...
...AND THE TRUE LEADER OF TEAM ROCKET!
GIOVANNI!
RSTL RSTL
TMP TMP
RSTLRSTL
THE FOREST...
VIRIDIAN FOREST IS...
THE TREES! THEY SENSE THAT SOMETHING IS ABOUT TO HAPPEN!
THEY'RE WORRIED!
SNAP
WOOOOSSH

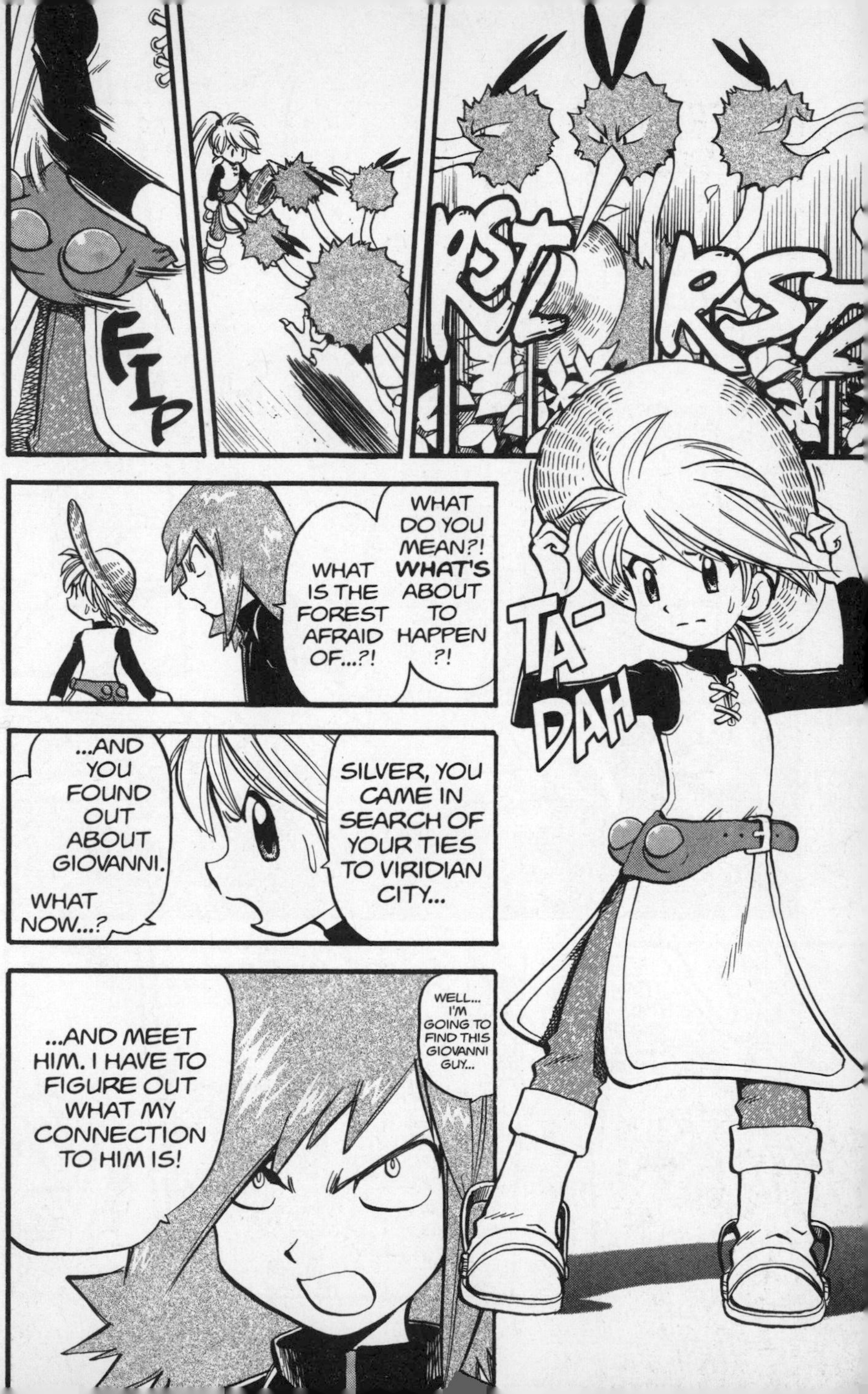
RSZ
RSZ
FIP
TA-DAH
WHAT DO YOU MEAN?! WHAT'S ABOUT TO HAPPEN?!
WHAT IS THE FOREST AFRAID OF...?!
SILVER, YOU CAME IN SEARCH OF YOUR TIES TO VIRIDIAN CITY...
...AND YOU FOUND OUT ABOUT GIOVANNI.
WHAT NOW...?
WELL... I'M GOING TO FIND THIS GIOVANNI GUY...
...AND MEET HIM. I HAVE TO FIGURE OUT WHAT MY CONNECTION TO HIM IS!

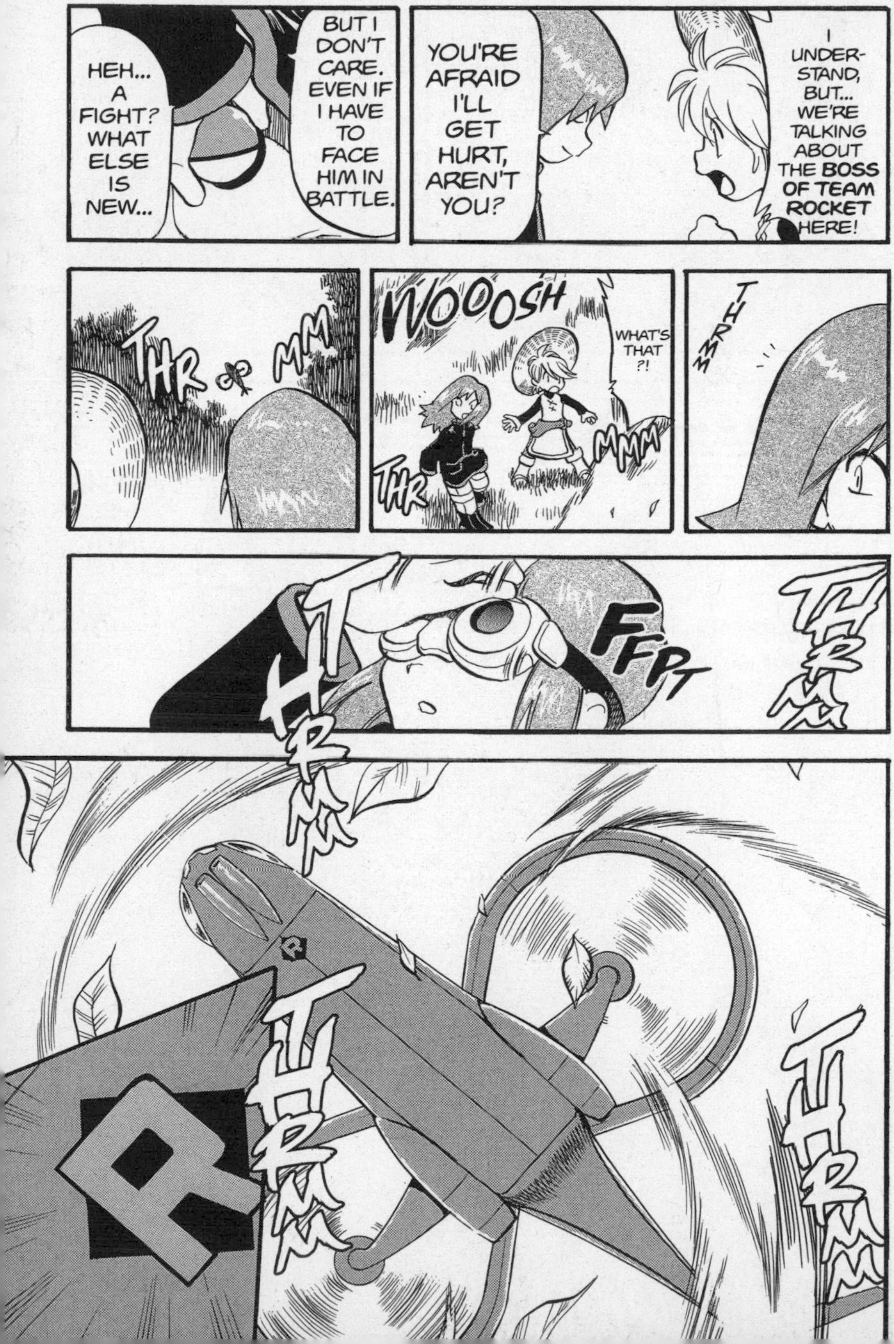
I UNDERSTAND, BUT... WE'RE TALKING ABOUT THE BOSS OF TEAM ROCKET HERE!
YOU'RE AFRAID I'LL GET HURT, AREN'T YOU?
BUT I DON'T CARE. EVEN IF I HAVE TO FACE HIM IN BATTLE.
HEH... A FIGHT? WHAT ELSE IS NEW...
THRMM
WOOOSH
WHAT'S THAT?!
THR MMM
THR MM
THRM
FFPT
THRM
THRMM
THRM
THRM

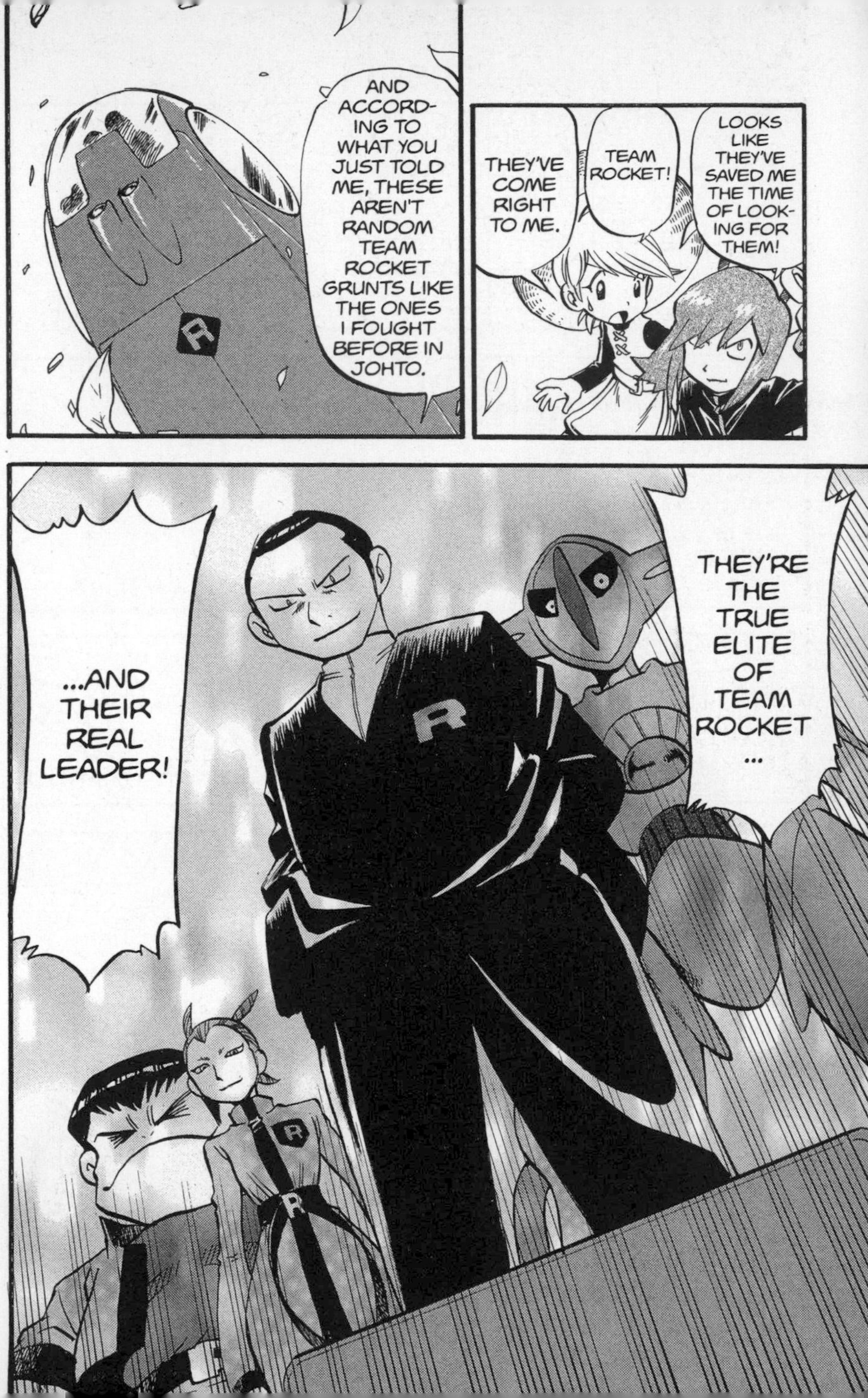
LOOKS LIKE THEY'VE SAVED ME THE TIME OF LOOK-ING FOR THEM!
TEAM ROCKET!
THEY'VE COME RIGHT TO ME.
AND ACCORD-ING TO WHAT YOU JUST TOLD ME, THESE AREN'T RANDOM TEAM ROCKET GRUNTS LIKE THE ONES I FOUGHT BEFORE IN JOHTO.
THEY'RE THE TRUE ELITE OF TEAM ROCKET ...
...AND THEIR REAL LEADER!

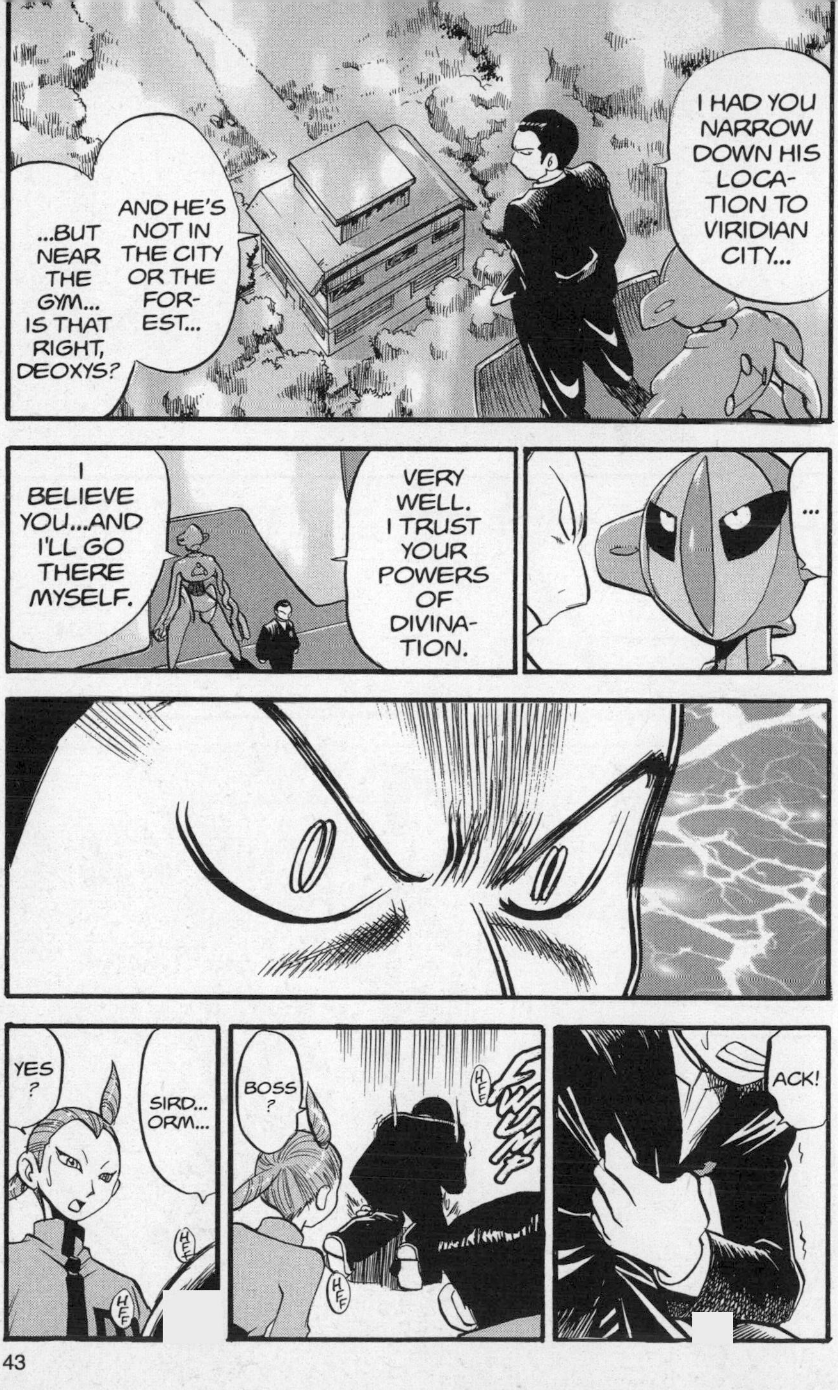
I HAD YOU NARROW DOWN HIS LOCATION TO VIRIDIAN CITY...
AND HE'S NOT IN THE CITY OR THE FOREST...
...BUT NEAR THE GYM... IS THAT RIGHT, DEOXYS?
...
VERY WELL. I TRUST YOUR POWERS OF DIVINATION.
I BELIEVE YOU...AND I'LL GO THERE MYSELF.
ACK!
BOSS?
HFF
WUMP
HFF
YES?
SIRD... ORM...
HFF
HFF

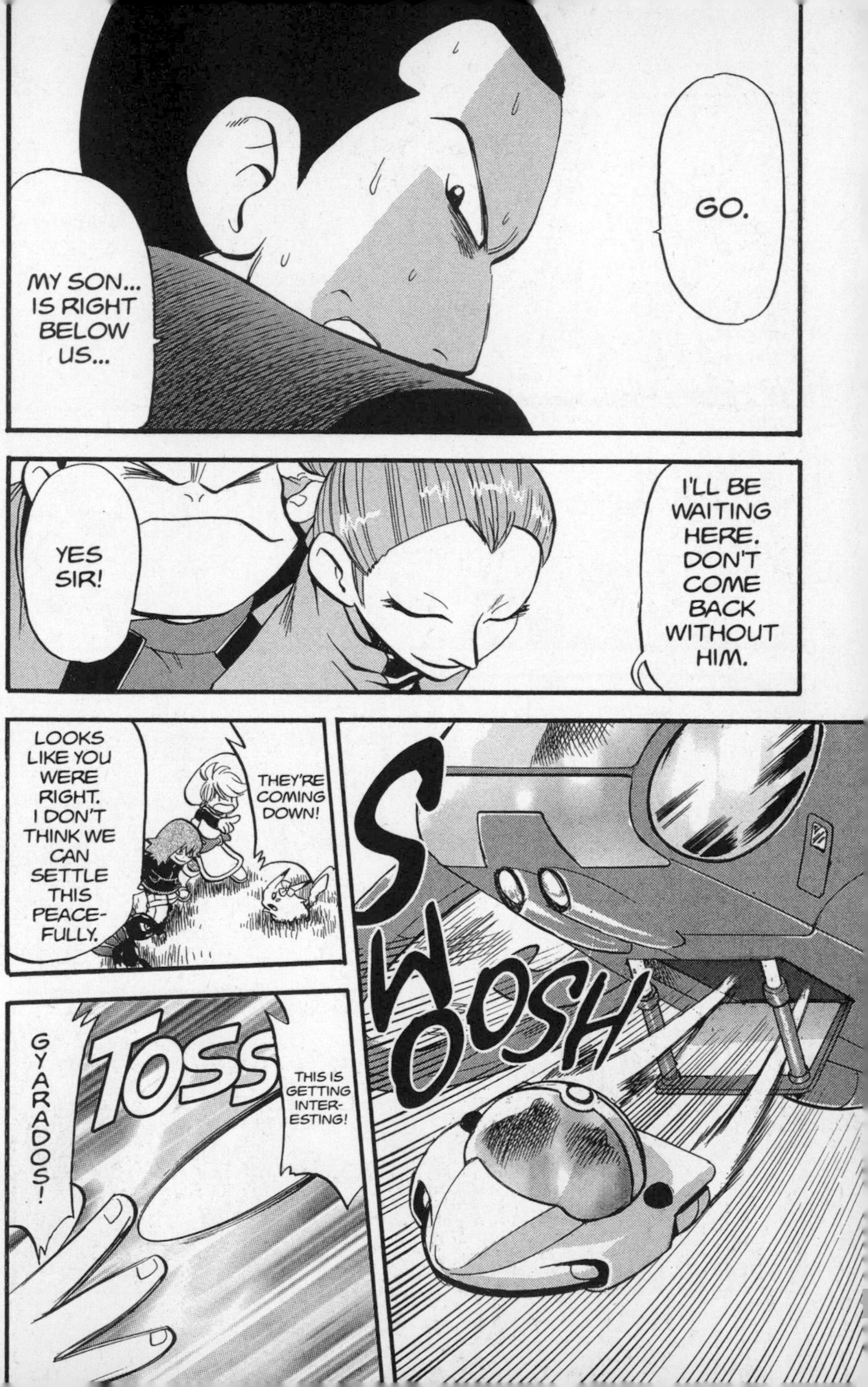
GO.
MY SON... IS RIGHT BELOW US...
I'LL BE WAITING HERE. DON'T COME BACK WITHOUT HIM.
YES SIR!
SWOOSH
THEY'RE COMING DOWN!
LOOKS LIKE YOU WERE RIGHT. I DON'T THINK WE CAN SETTLE THIS PEACE-FULLY.
THIS IS GETTING INTER-ESTING!
TOSS
GYARADOS!

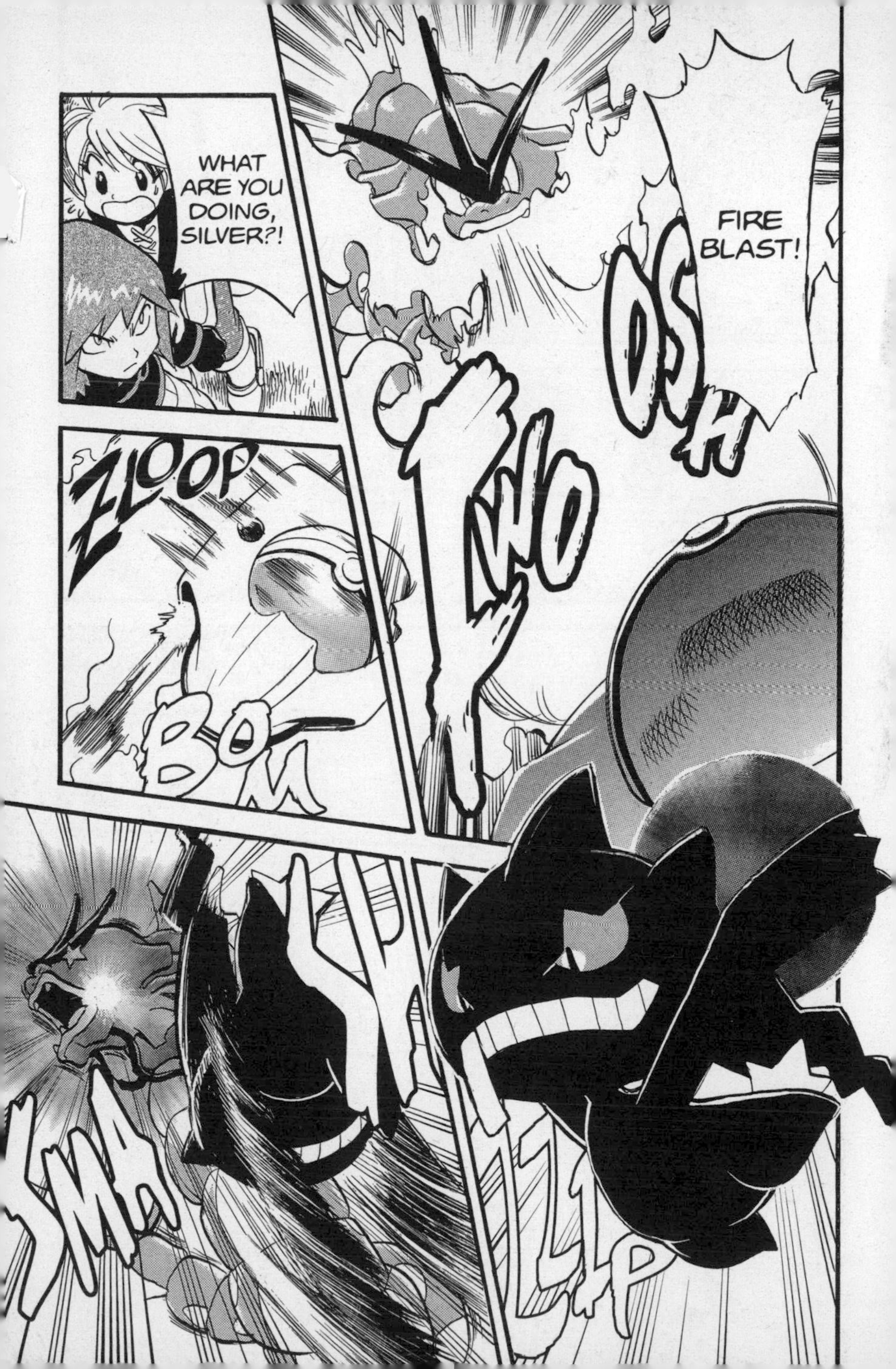
FIRE BLAST!
WHAT ARE YOU DOING, SILVER?!
ZLOOP
BOM

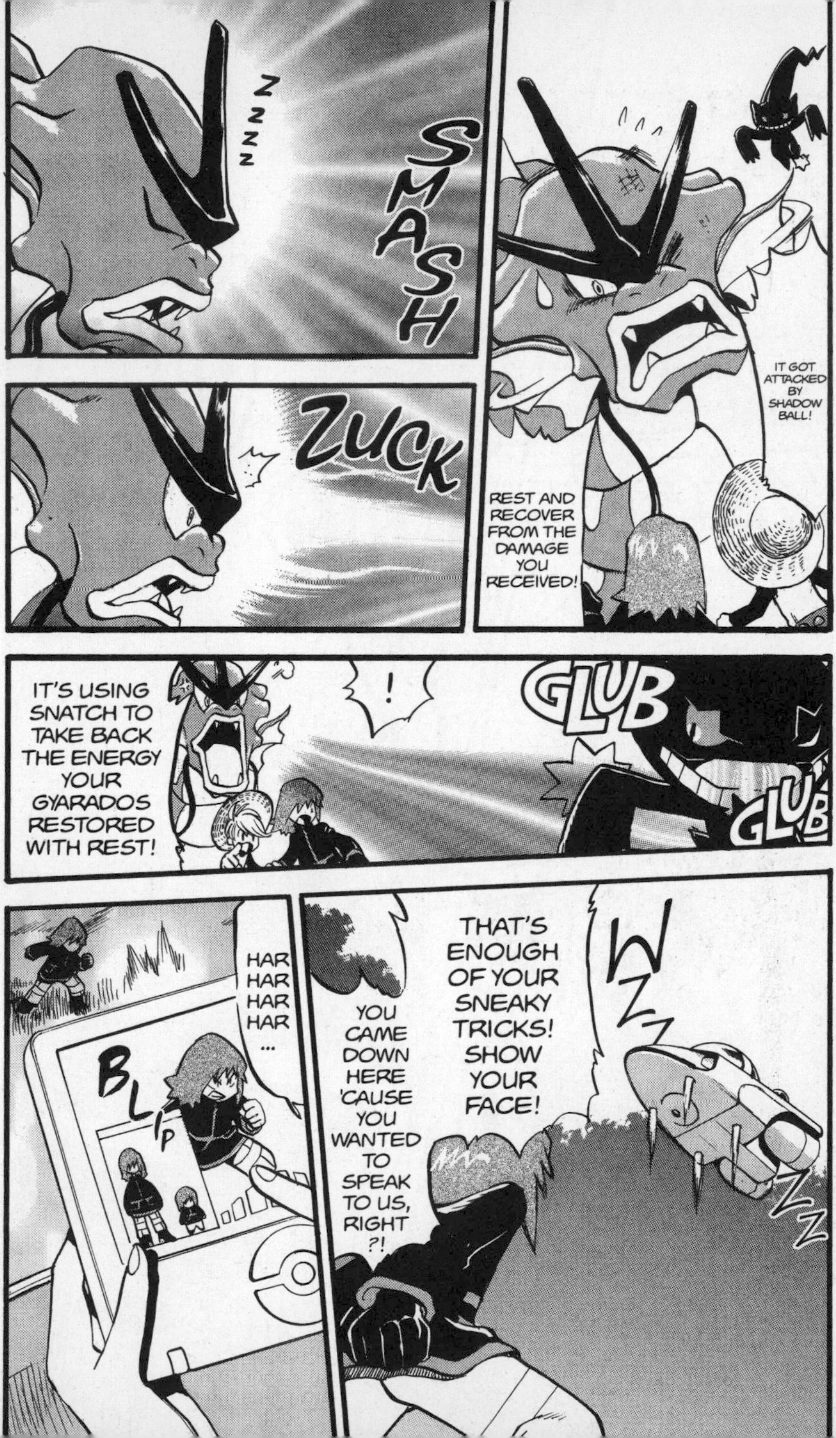
IT GOT ATTACKED BY SHADOW BALL!
REST AND RECOVER FROM THE DAMAGE YOU RECEIVED!
ZZZZ
SMASH
ZUCK
GLUB
GLUB
!
IT'S USING SNATCH TO TAKE BACK THE ENERGY YOUR GYARADOS RESTORED WITH REST!
THAT'S ENOUGH OF YOUR SNEAKY TRICKS! SHOW YOUR FACE!
YOU CAME DOWN HERE 'CAUSE YOU WANTED TO SPEAK TO US, RIGHT?!
HAR HAR HAR HAR ...
BLIP

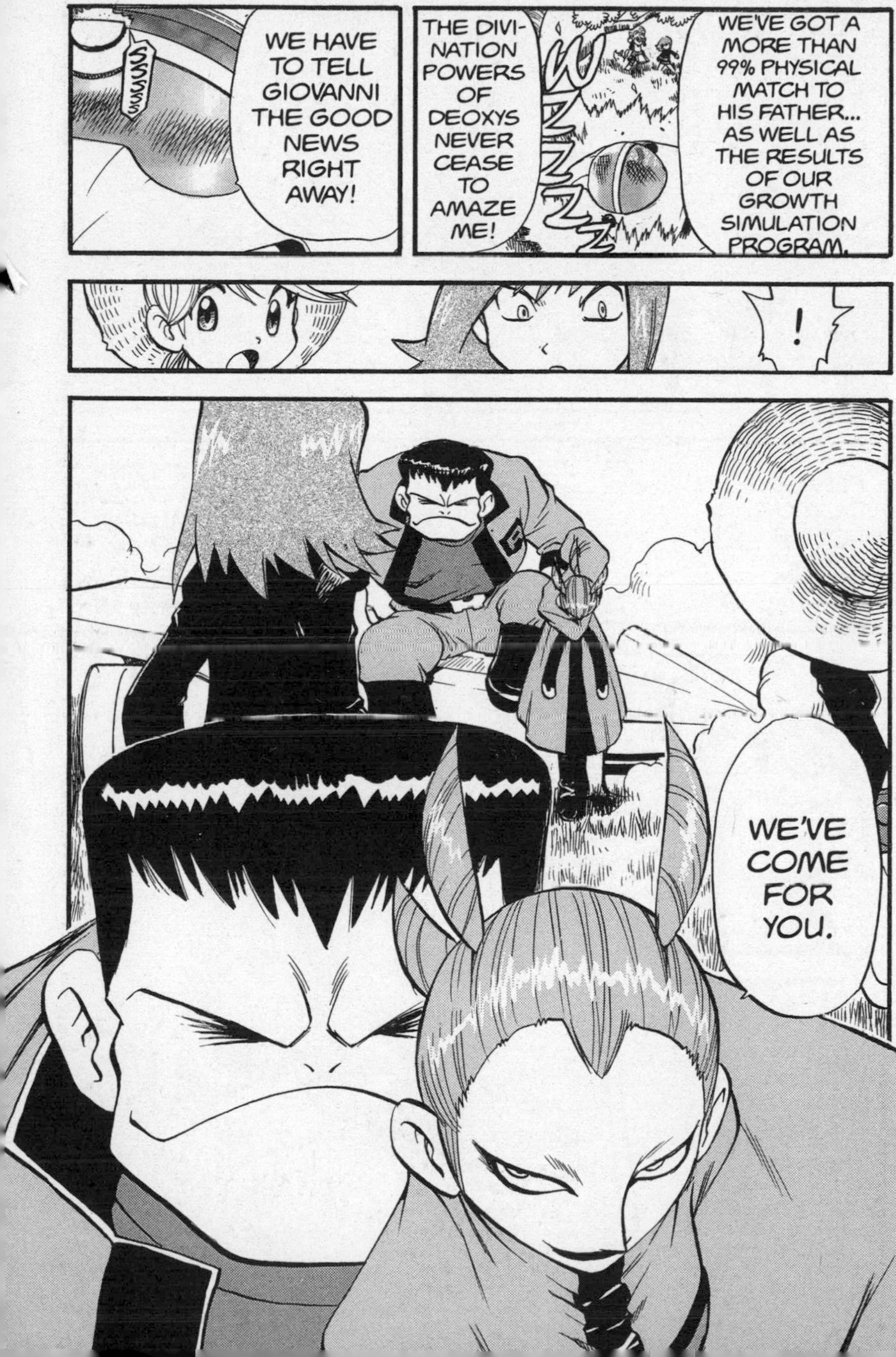
WE'VE GOT A MORE THAN 99% PHYSICAL MATCH TO HIS FATHER... AS WELL AS THE RESULTS OF OUR GROWTH SIMULATION PROGRAM.
THE DIVINATION POWERS OF DEOXYS NEVER CEASE TO AMAZE ME!
WE HAVE TO TELL GIOVANNI THE GOOD NEWS RIGHT AWAY!
!
WE'VE COME FOR YOU.

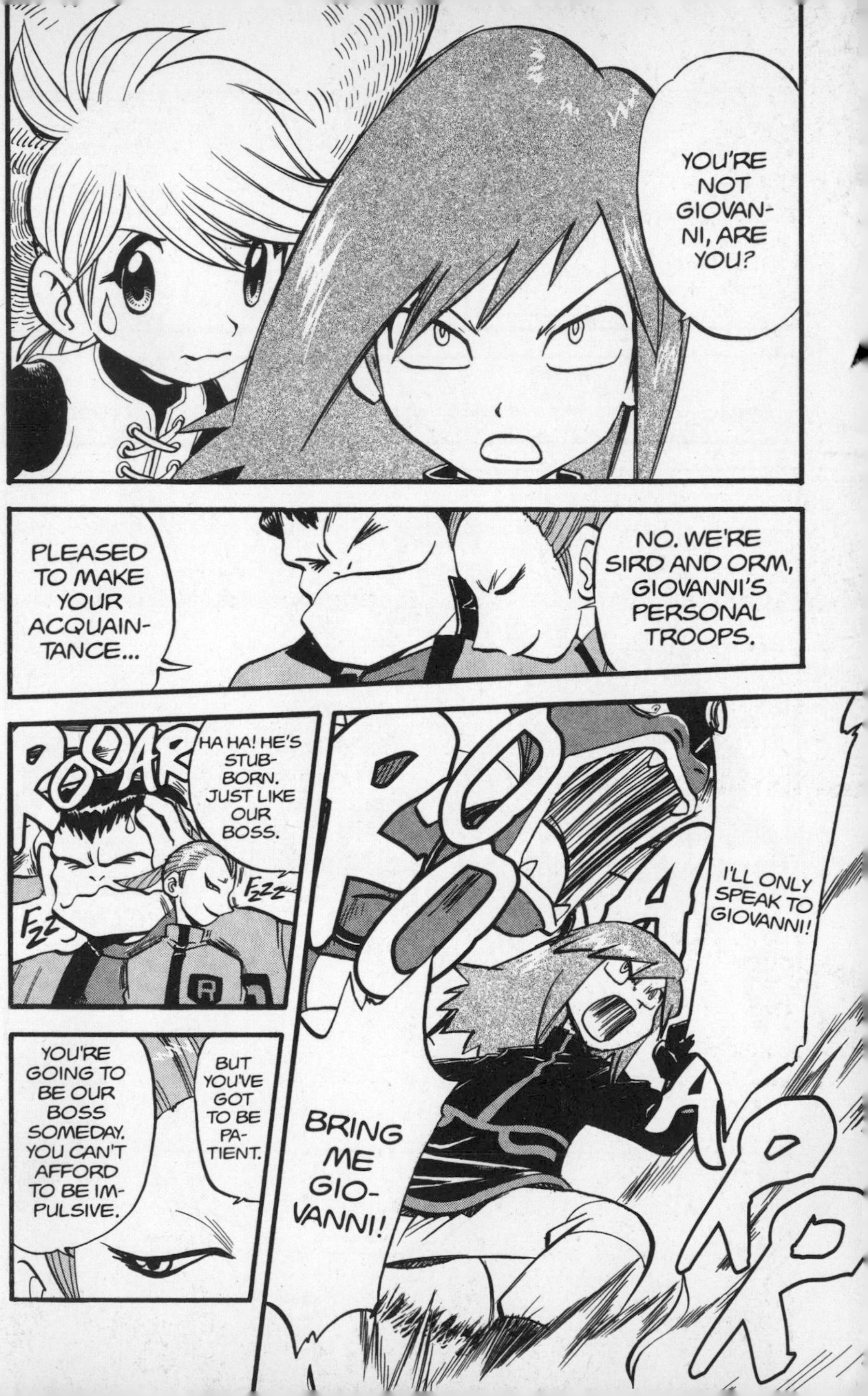
YOU'RE NOT GIOVANNI, ARE YOU?
NO. WE'RE SIRD AND ORM, GIOVANNI'S PERSONAL TROOPS.
PLEASED TO MAKE YOUR ACQUAINTANCE...
I'LL ONLY SPEAK TO GIOVANNI!
BRING ME GIOVANNI!
HA HA! HE'S STUBBORN. JUST LIKE OUR BOSS.
FZZZ
FZZZ
BUT YOU'VE GOT TO BE PATIENT.
YOU'RE GOING TO BE OUR BOSS SOMEDAY. YOU CAN'T AFFORD TO BE IMPULSIVE.

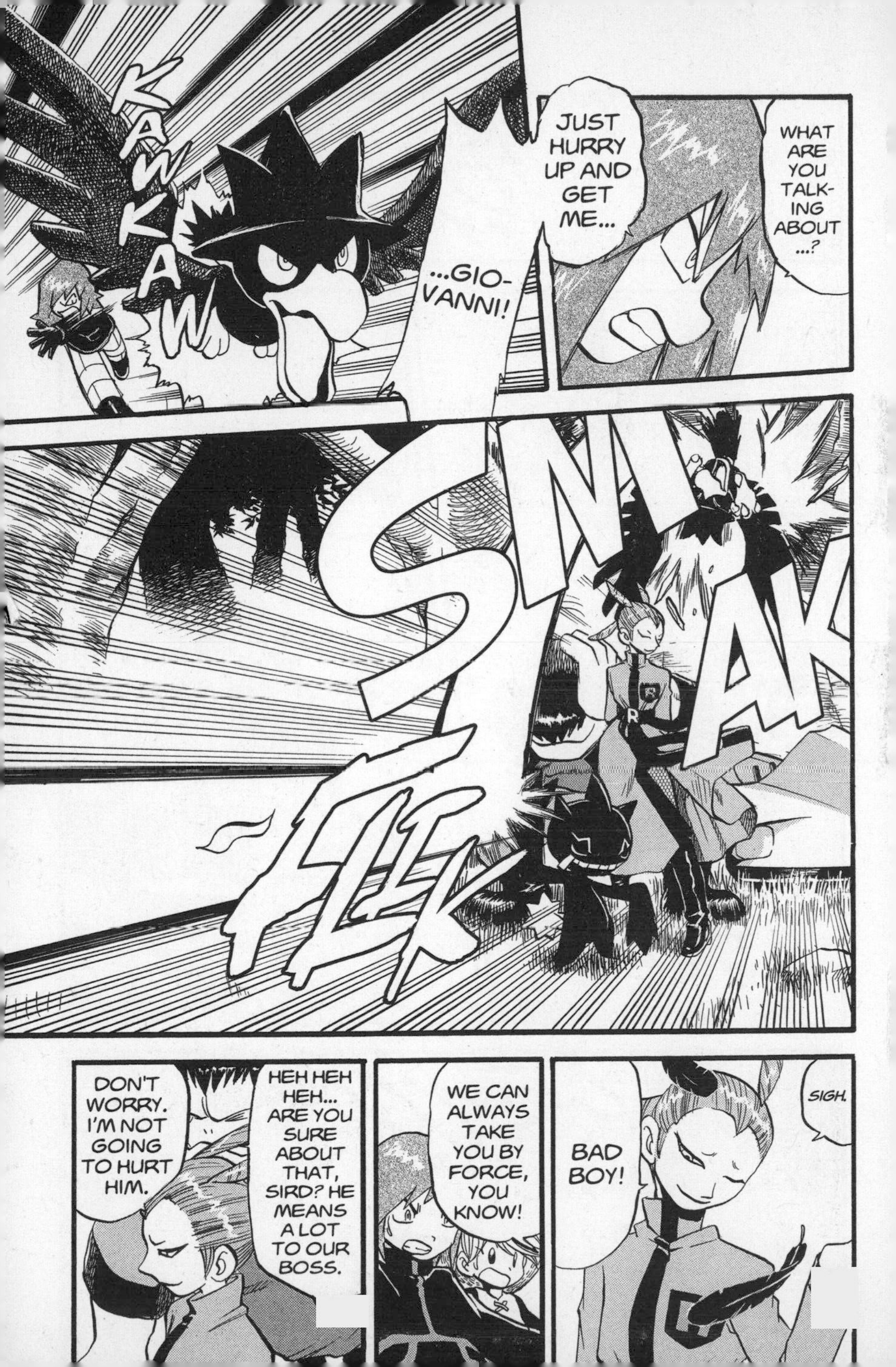
WHAT ARE YOU TALKING ABOUT...?
JUST HURRY UP AND GET ME...
...GIO-VANNI!
KAW KAW
SMAK
FLIK
SIGH.
BAD BOY!
WE CAN ALWAYS TAKE YOU BY FORCE, YOU KNOW!
HEH HEH HEH... ARE YOU SURE ABOUT THAT, SIRD? HE MEANS A LOT TO OUR BOSS.
DON'T WORRY. I'M NOT GOING TO HURT HIM.

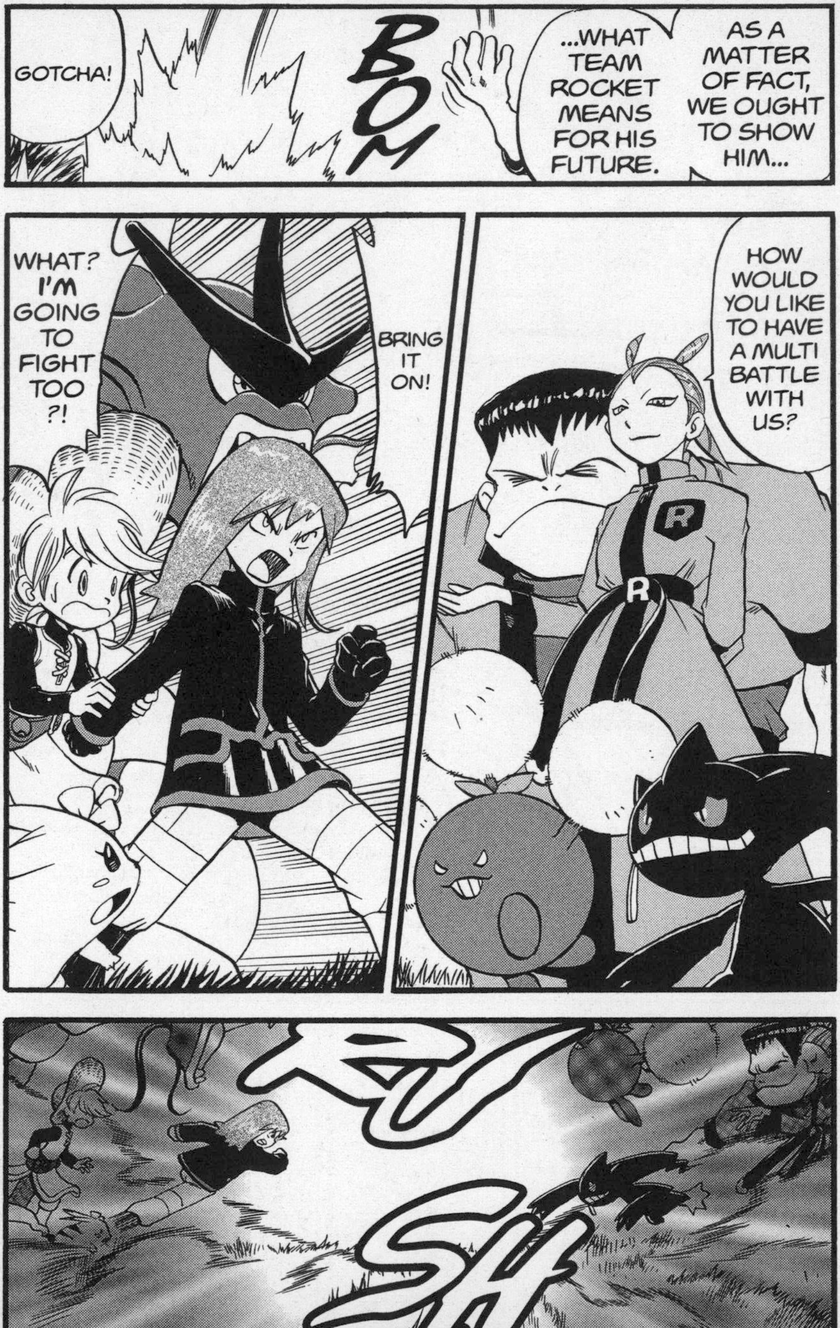
AS A MATTER OF FACT, WE OUGHT TO SHOW HIM...
...WHAT TEAM ROCKET MEANS FOR HIS FUTURE.
BOOM
GOTCHA!
HOW WOULD YOU LIKE TO HAVE A MULTI BATTLE WITH US?
BRING IT ON!
WHAT? I'M GOING TO FIGHT TOO ?!
RUSH

LANETTE & BRIGETTE

LANETTE & BRIGETTE

THESE TWO BRILLIANT SIS-
TERS ARE IN CHARGE OF
THE HOENN REGION POKÉ-
MON TRANSPORTER SYS-
TEM. THEY ARE FRIENDS OF
BILL AND CELIO, AND THE
FOUR TECHNOLOGY DEVEL-
OPERS OFTEN
PROBLEM-SOLVE
TOGETHER. BRIGETTE,
THE OLDER SISTER, IS A
LINEAR THINKER, WHILE
LANETTE, THE RESTLESS
YOUNGER SISTER, IS PRONE
TO FLASHES OF INTUITION.
THEY ARE POLAR
OPPOSITES, BUT THEY
COMPLEMENT WHAT THE
OTHER LACKS. DURING THE
SEVII ISLANDS INCIDENT,
THEY AIDED BILL BY
FIGURING OUT HOW A GEO-
GRAPHICAL LOCATION
COULD INFLUENCE A
POKÉMON'S FORM.

- Workplace: Route 114, Hoenn region

- Job: Pokémon Transporter System Developer (Lanette). Pokémon Storage Management (Brigette).

- Hobby: Finding bargains at the Lilycove Department Store (Lanette). Playing roulette at Mauville City (Brigette).

•Adventure 290•
A Well-Journeyed Jumpluff

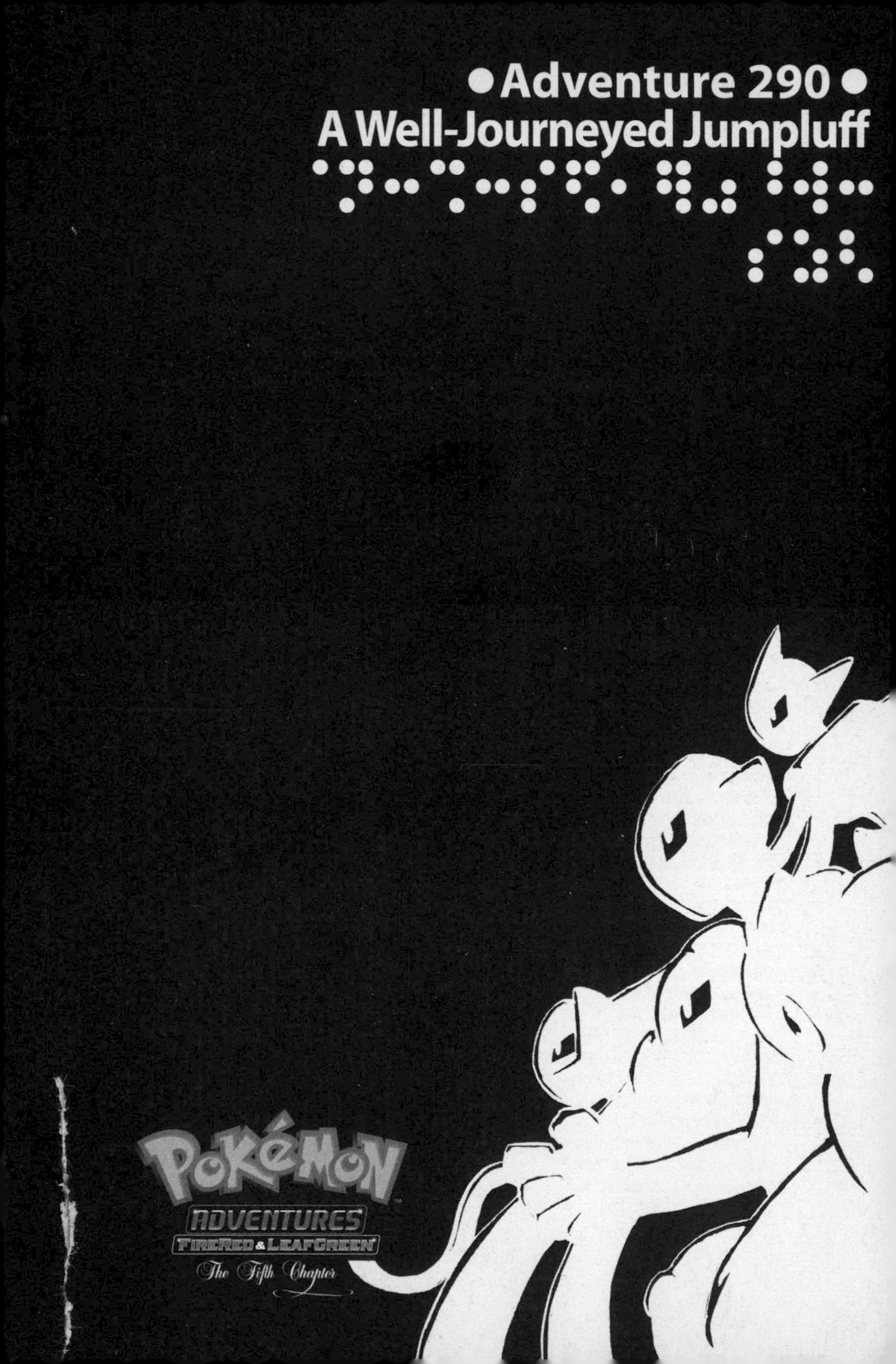

Pokémon Adventures
FireRed & LeafGreen
The Fifth Chapter

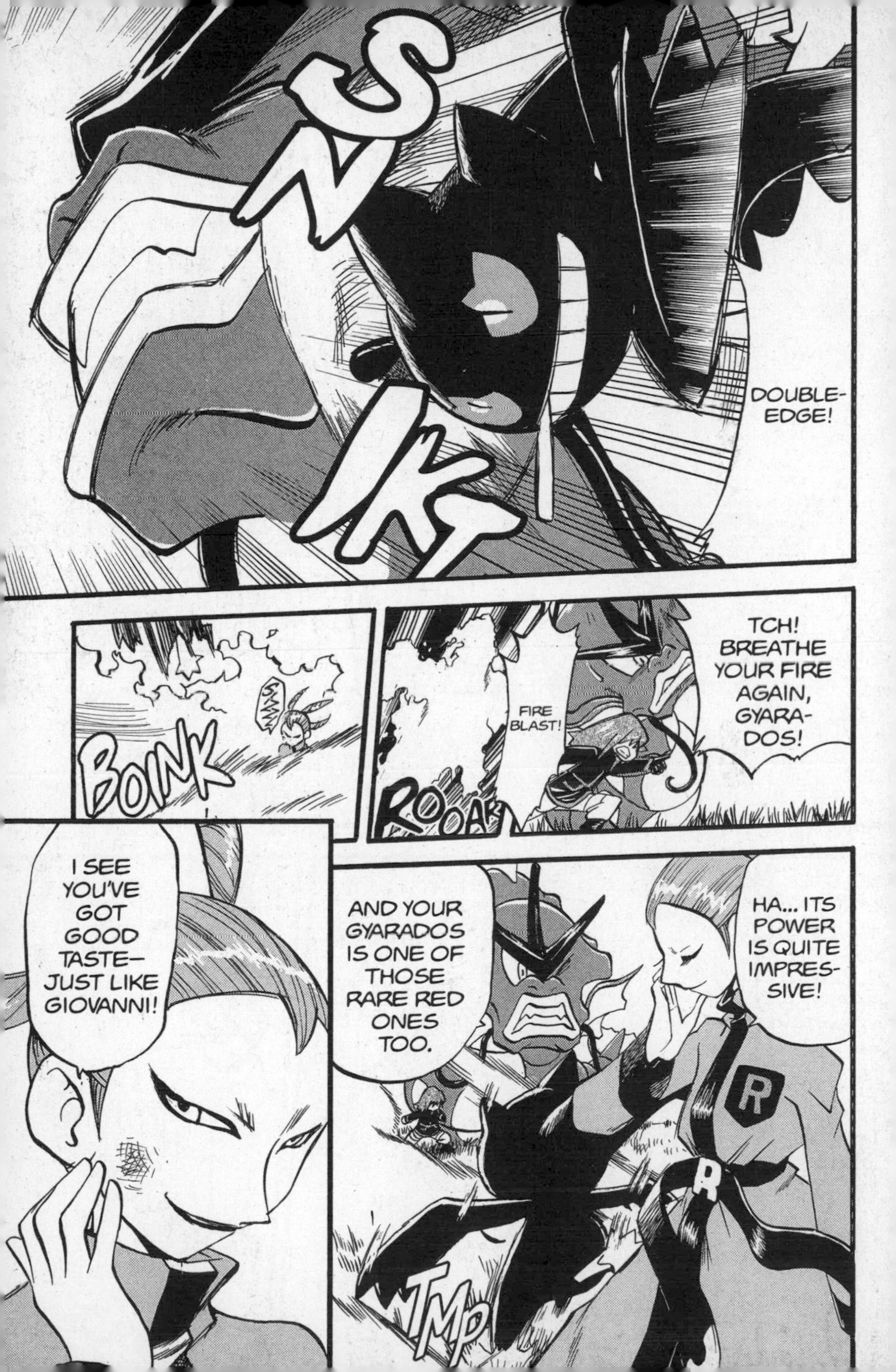
SNIKT
DOUBLE-EDGE!
TCH! BREATHE YOUR FIRE AGAIN, GYARADOS!
FIRE BLAST!
ROOAR
BOINK
HA... ITS POWER IS QUITE IMPRESSIVE!
AND YOUR GYARADOS IS ONE OF THOSE RARE RED ONES TOO.
TMP
I SEE YOU'VE GOT GOOD TASTE—JUST LIKE GIOVANNI!

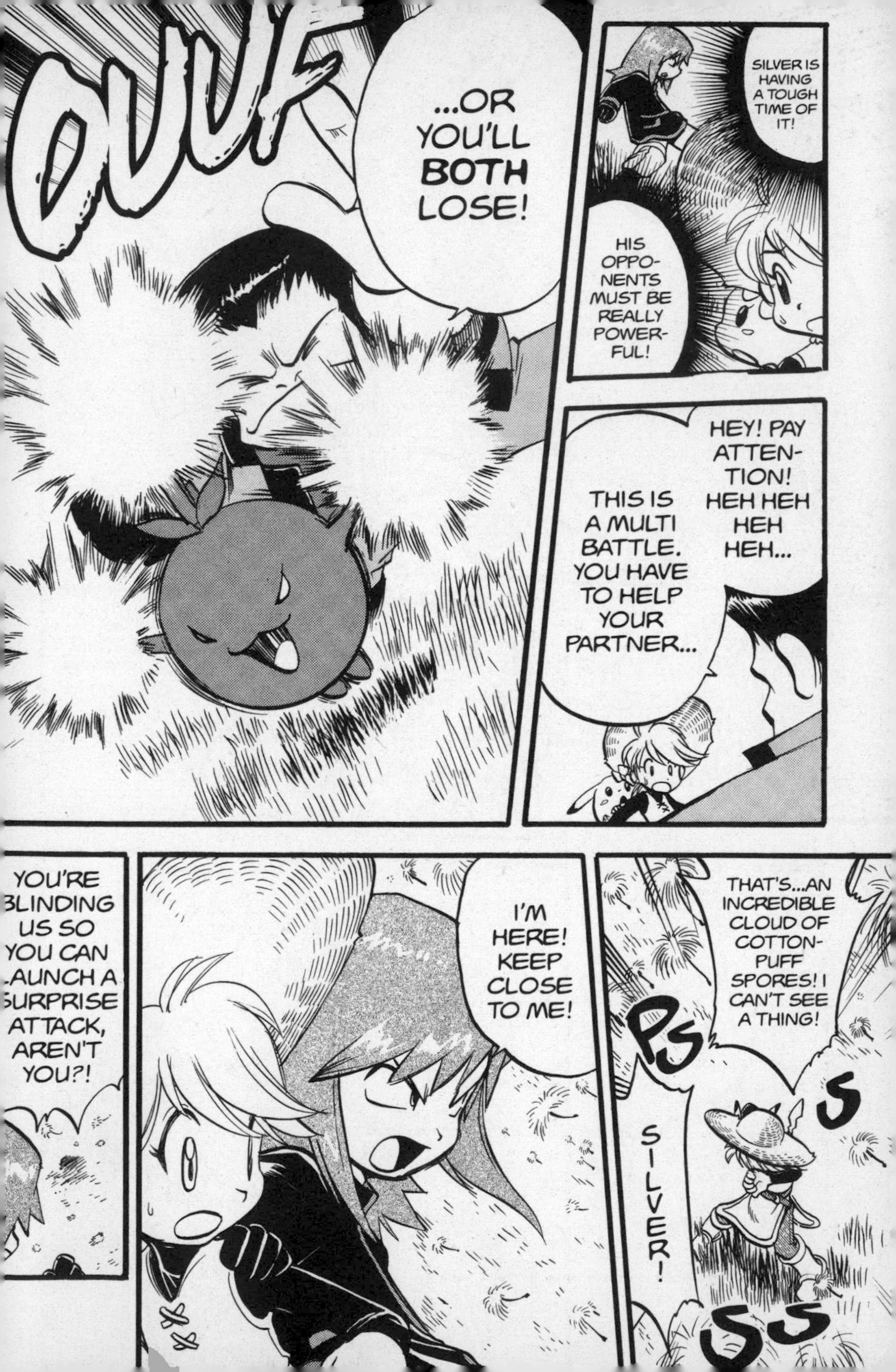
SILVER IS HAVING A TOUGH TIME OF IT!
HIS OPPONENTS MUST BE REALLY POWERFUL!
HEY! PAY ATTENTION! HEH HEH HEH HEH...
THIS IS A MULTI BATTLE. YOU HAVE TO HELP YOUR PARTNER...
OWF
...OR YOU'LL BOTH LOSE!
THAT'S...AN INCREDIBLE CLOUD OF COTTON-PUFF SPORES! I CAN'T SEE A THING!
PS
SILVER!
S
SS
I'M HERE! KEEP CLOSE TO ME!
YOU'RE BLINDING US SO YOU CAN LAUNCH A SURPRISE ATTACK, AREN'T YOU?!

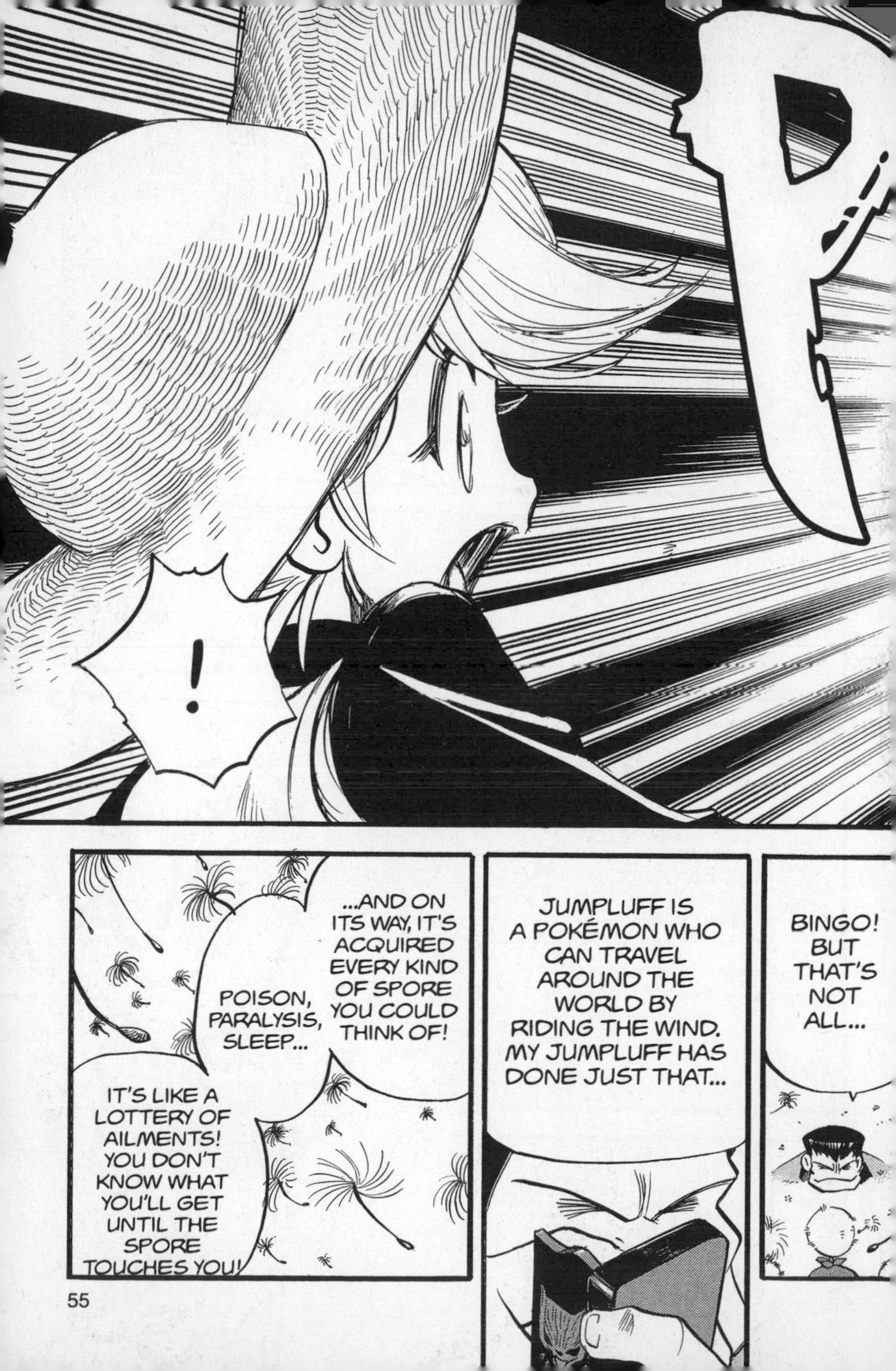
!
BINGO! BUT THAT'S NOT ALL...
JUMPLUFF IS A POKÉMON WHO CAN TRAVEL AROUND THE WORLD BY RIDING THE WIND. MY JUMPLUFF HAS DONE JUST THAT...
...AND ON ITS WAY, IT'S ACQUIRED EVERY KIND OF SPORE YOU COULD THINK OF!
POISON, PARALYSIS, SLEEP...
IT'S LIKE A LOTTERY OF AILMENTS! YOU DON'T KNOW WHAT YOU'LL GET UNTIL THE SPORE TOUCHES YOU!

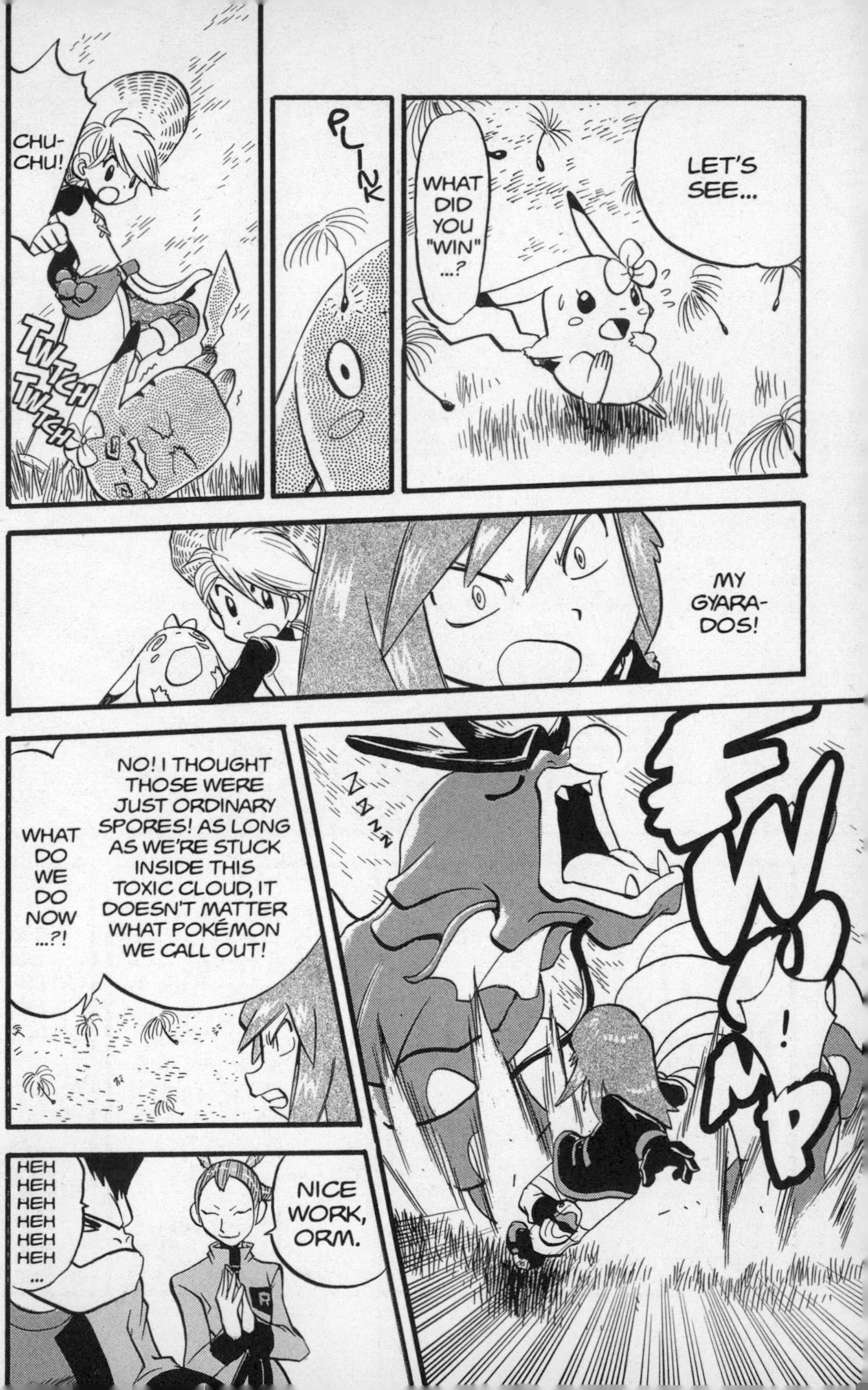
LET'S SEE...
WHAT DID YOU "WIN" ...?
PLINK
CHU-CHU!
TWITCH TWITCH
MY GYARA-DOS!
FWUMP!
NO! I THOUGHT THOSE WERE JUST ORDINARY SPORES! AS LONG AS WE'RE STUCK INSIDE THIS TOXIC CLOUD, IT DOESN'T MATTER WHAT POKéMON WE CALL OUT!
WHAT DO WE DO NOW ...?!
NICE WORK, ORM.
HEH HEH HEH HEH HEH HEH ...

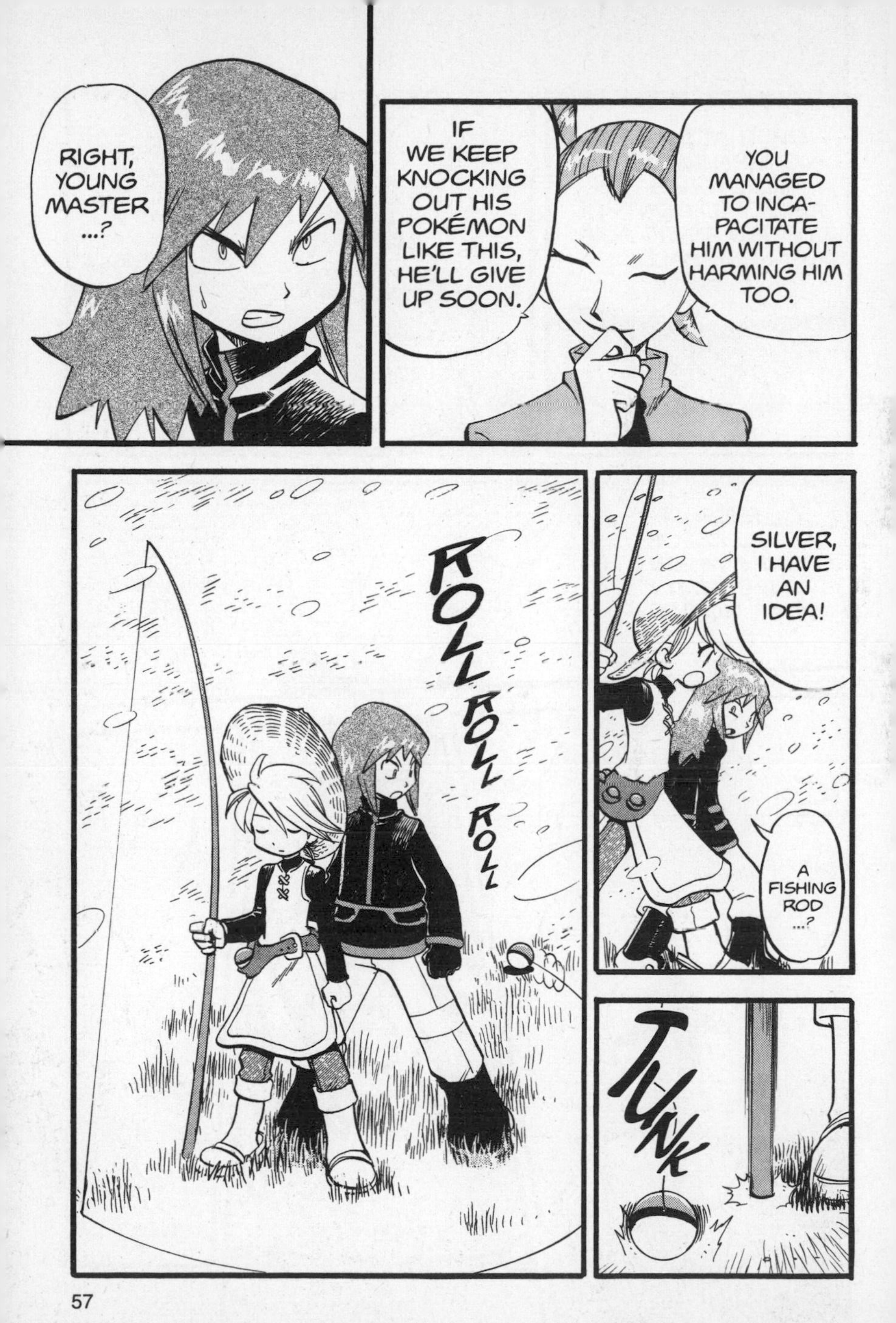
YOU MANAGED TO INCAPACITATE HIM WITHOUT HARMING HIM TOO.
IF WE KEEP KNOCKING OUT HIS POKÉMON LIKE THIS, HE'LL GIVE UP SOON.
RIGHT, YOUNG MASTER ...?
SILVER, I HAVE AN IDEA!
A FISHING ROD ...?
TUNK
ROLL ROLL ROLL ROLL

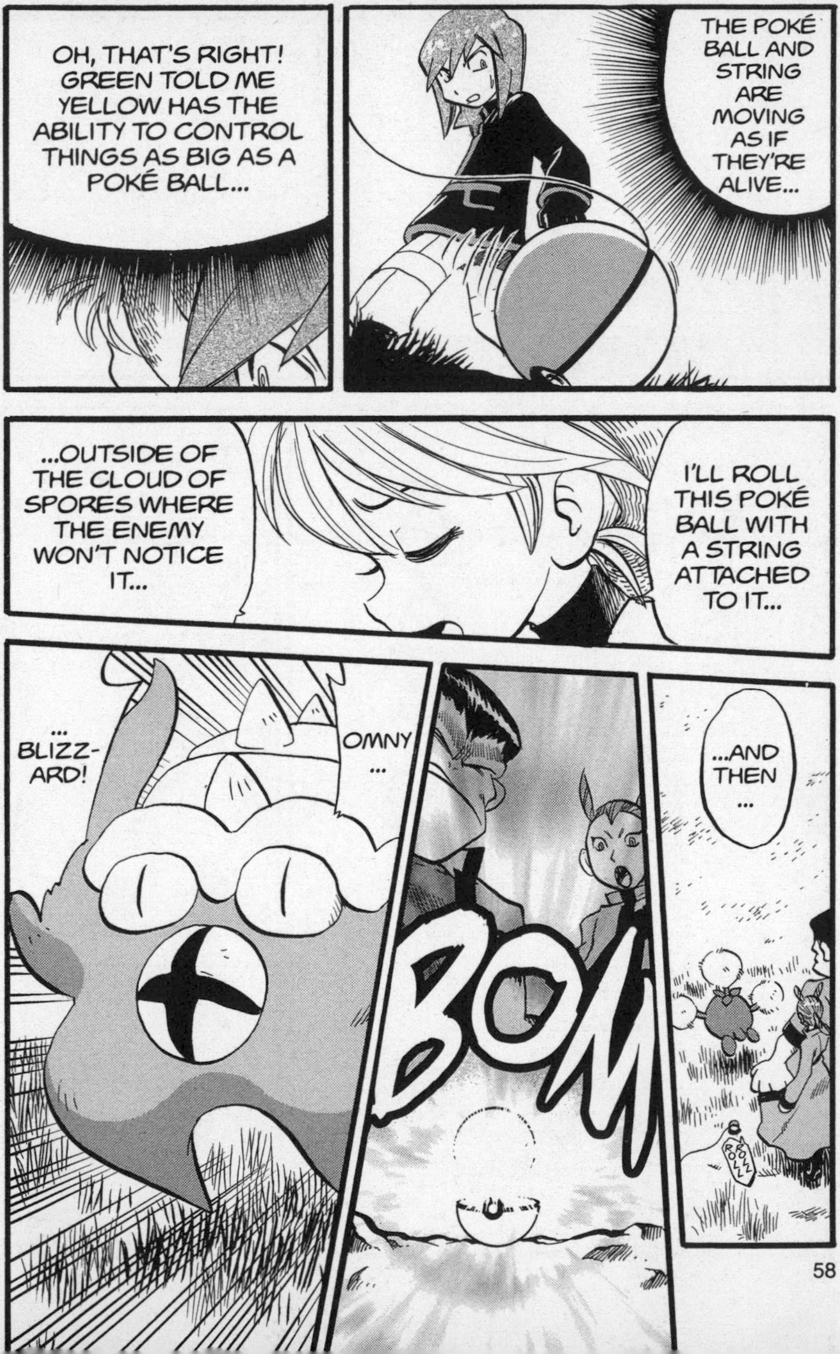
THE POKÉ BALL AND STRING ARE MOVING AS IF THEY'RE ALIVE...
OH, THAT'S RIGHT! GREEN TOLD ME YELLOW HAS THE ABILITY TO CONTROL THINGS AS BIG AS A POKÉ BALL...
I'LL ROLL THIS POKÉ BALL WITH A STRING ATTACHED TO IT...
...OUTSIDE OF THE CLOUD OF SPORES WHERE THE ENEMY WON'T NOTICE IT...
...AND THEN ...
ROLL ROLL
OMNY ...
BOM
... BLIZZ-ARD!

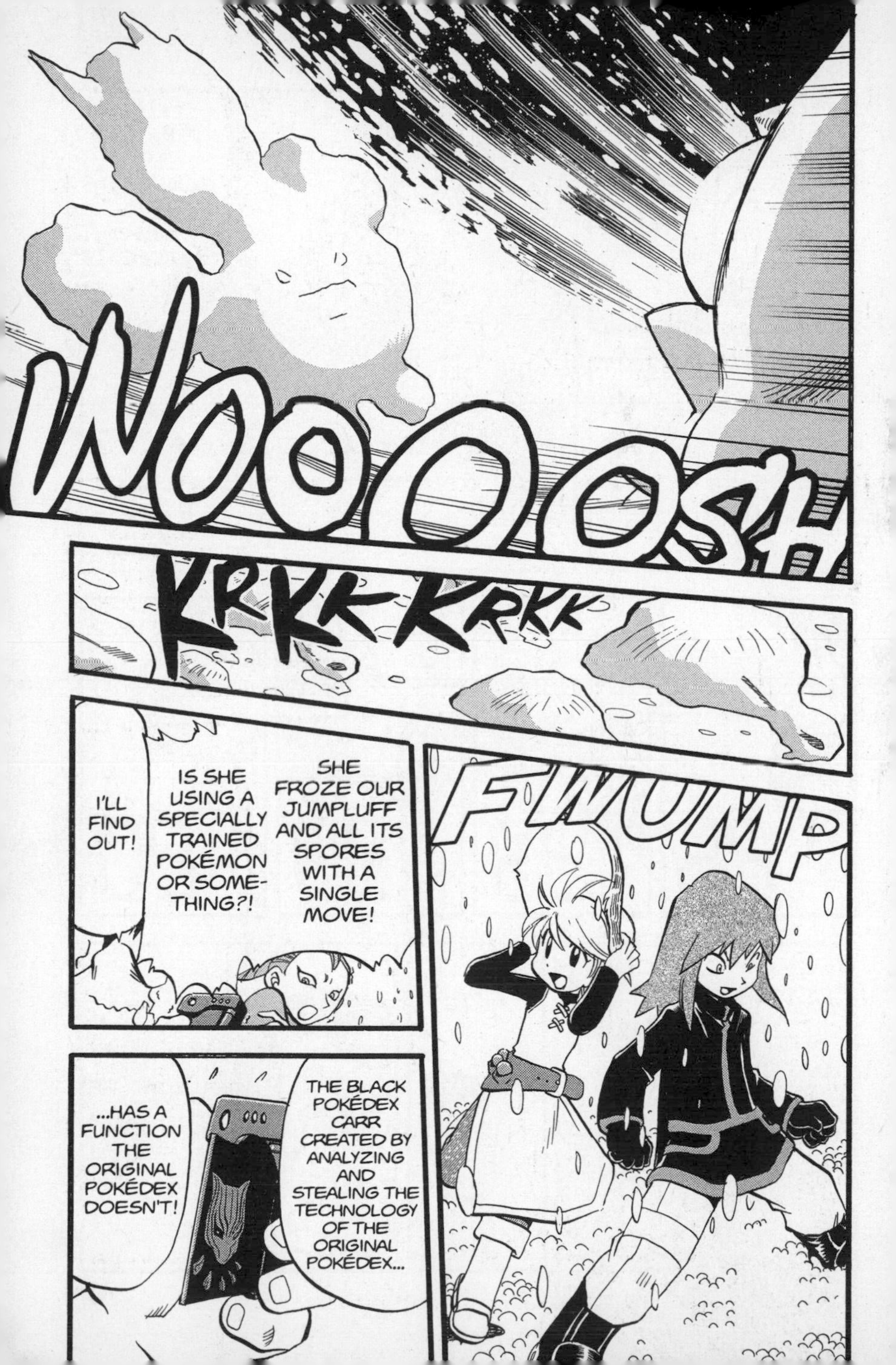
WOOOOSH
KRKK KRKK
FWUMP
SHE FROZE OUR JUMPLUFF AND ALL ITS SPORES WITH A SINGLE MOVE!
IS SHE USING A SPECIALLY TRAINED POKÉMON OR SOME-THING?!
I'LL FIND OUT!
THE BLACK POKÉDEX CARR CREATED BY ANALYZING AND STEALING THE TECHNOLOGY OF THE ORIGINAL POKÉDEX...
...HAS A FUNCTION THE ORIGINAL POKÉDEX DOESN'T!

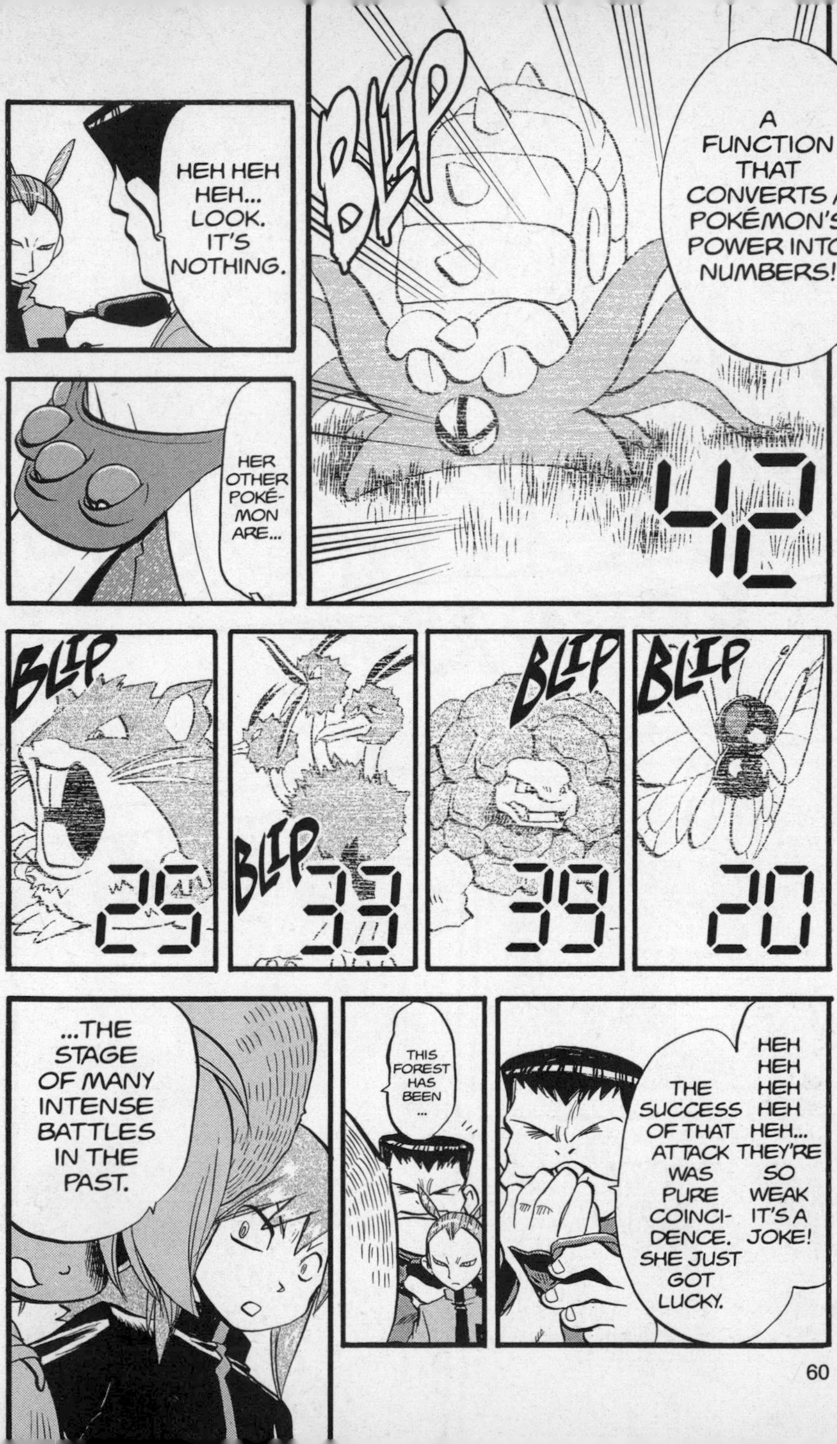

BLIP
A FUNCTION THAT CONVERTS A POKÉMON'S POWER INTO NUMBERS!
42
HEH HEH HEH... LOOK. IT'S NOTHING.
HER OTHER POKÉMON ARE...
BLIP
20
BLIP
39
BLIP
33
BLIP
25
HEH HEH HEH HEH HEH... THEY'RE SO WEAK IT'S A JOKE!
THE SUCCESS OF THAT ATTACK WAS PURE COINCIDENCE. SHE JUST GOT LUCKY.
THIS FOREST HAS BEEN ...
...THE STAGE OF MANY INTENSE BATTLES IN THE PAST.

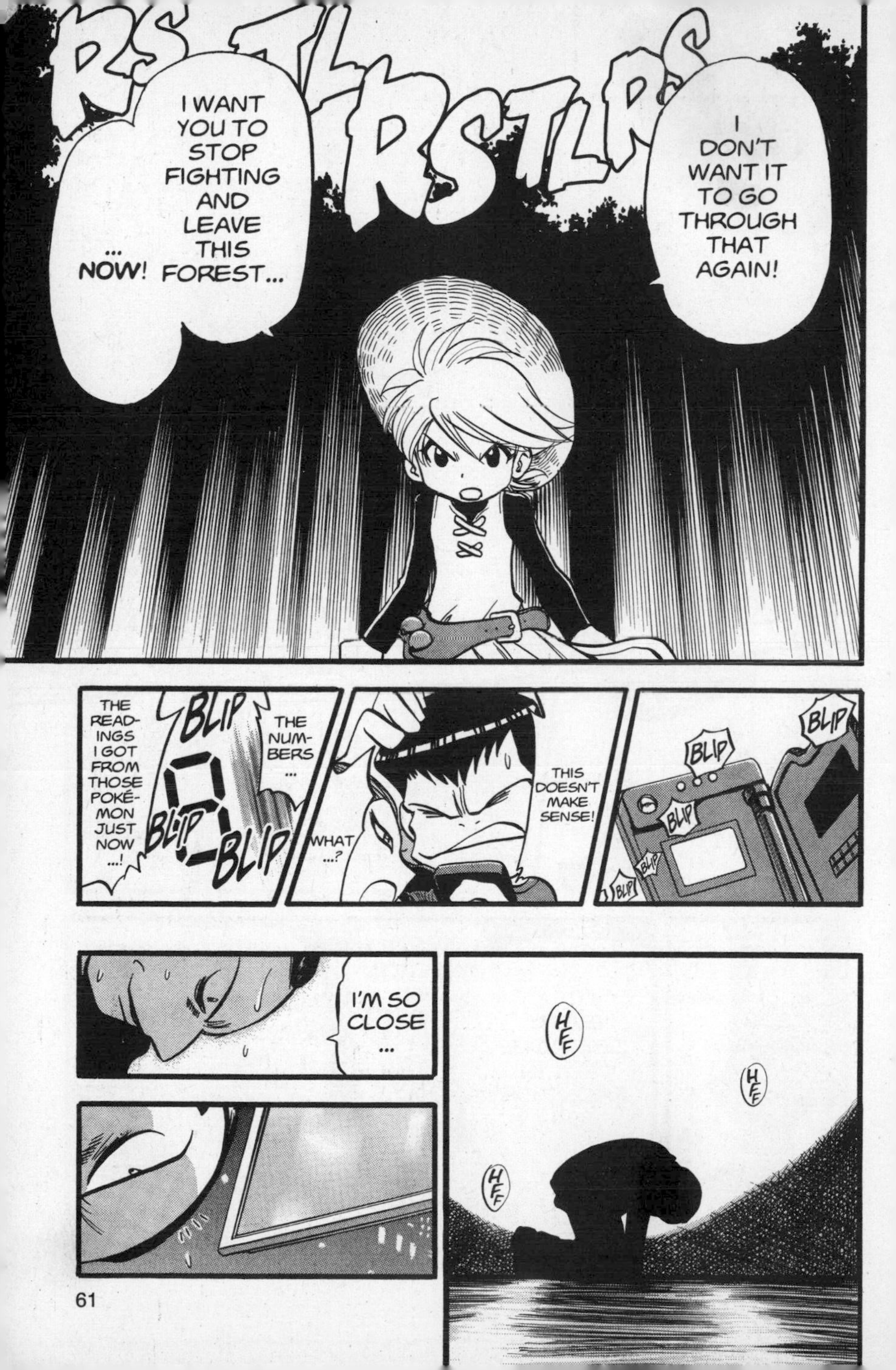
I DON'T WANT IT TO GO THROUGH THAT AGAIN!
I WANT YOU TO STOP FIGHTING AND LEAVE THIS FOREST...
... NOW!
BLIP
BLIP
BLIP
BLIP
BLIP
THIS DOESN'T MAKE SENSE!
WHAT ...?
THE NUMBERS ...
THE READINGS I GOT FROM THOSE POKÉMON JUST NOW ...!
BLIP
BLIP
BLIP
HFF
HFF
HFF
I'M SO CLOSE ...

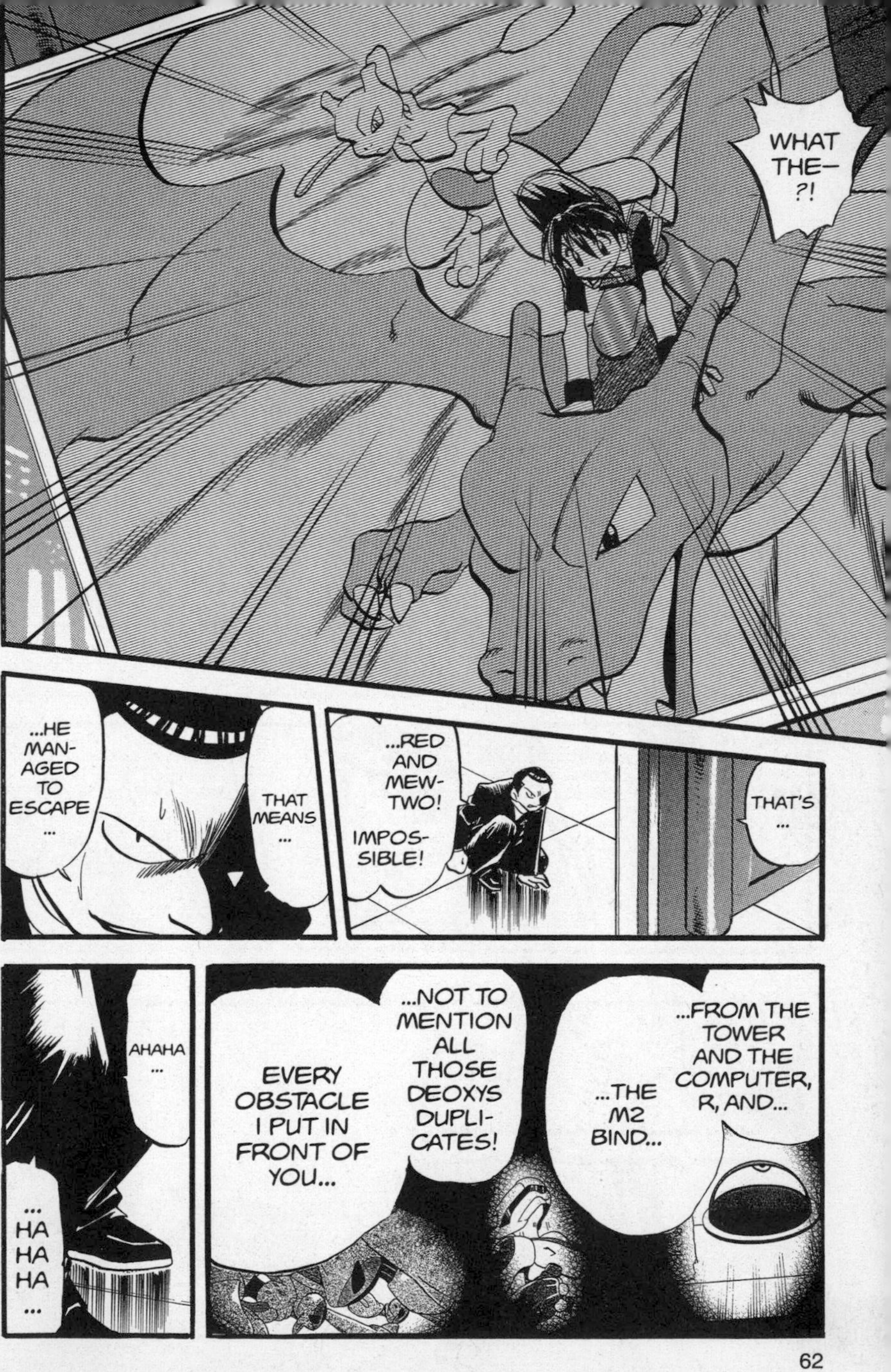
WHAT THE— ?!
THAT'S ...
...RED AND MEW-TWO!
IMPOSSIBLE!
THAT MEANS ...
...HE MANAGED TO ESCAPE ...
...FROM THE TOWER AND THE COMPUTER, R, AND...
...THE M2 BIND...
...NOT TO MENTION ALL THOSE DEOXYS DUPLICATES!
EVERY OBSTACLE I PUT IN FRONT OF YOU...
AHAHA ...
... HA HA HA ...

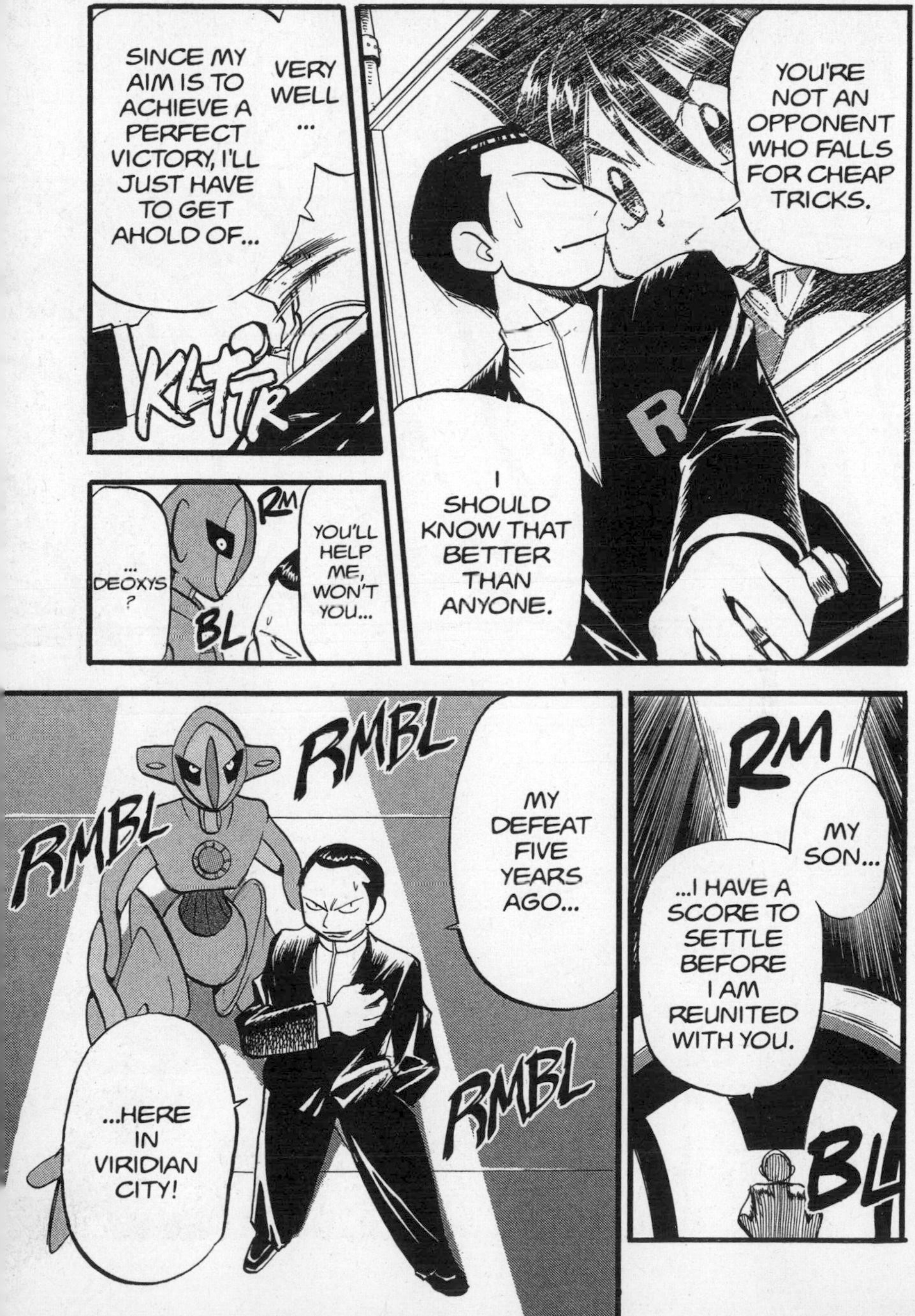
YOU'RE NOT AN OPPONENT WHO FALLS FOR CHEAP TRICKS.
I SHOULD KNOW THAT BETTER THAN ANYONE.
VERY WELL ...
SINCE MY AIM IS TO ACHIEVE A PERFECT VICTORY, I'LL JUST HAVE TO GET AHOLD OF...
KLTTR
RM
YOU'LL HELP ME, WON'T YOU...
... DEOXYS ?
BL
RM
MY SON...
...I HAVE A SCORE TO SETTLE BEFORE I AM REUNITED WITH YOU.
BL
RMBL
MY DEFEAT FIVE YEARS AGO...
RMBL
...HERE IN VIRIDIAN CITY!
RMBL

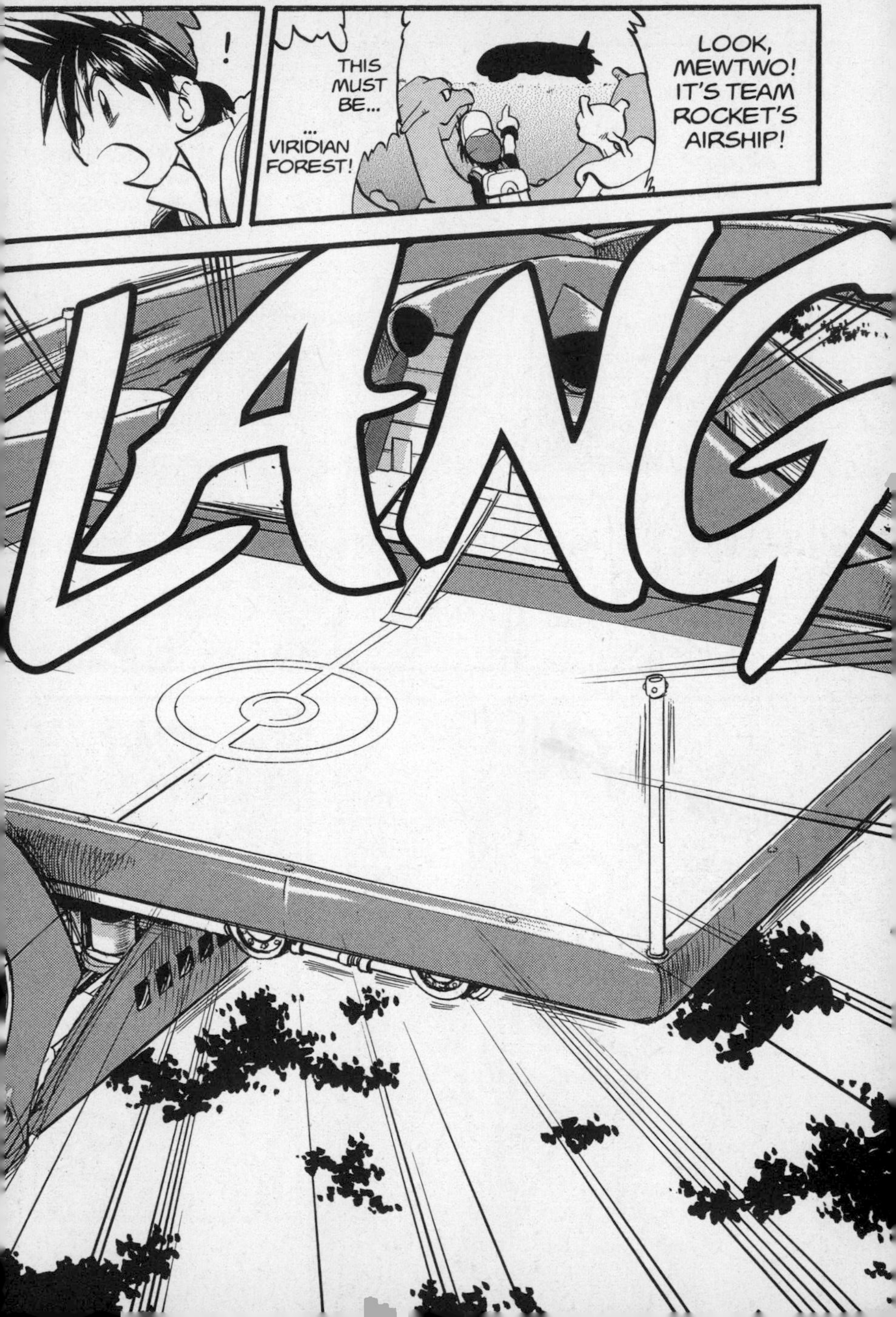
LOOK, MEWTWO! IT'S TEAM ROCKET'S AIRSHIP!
THIS MUST BE...
...VIRIDIAN FOREST!
!
LANG

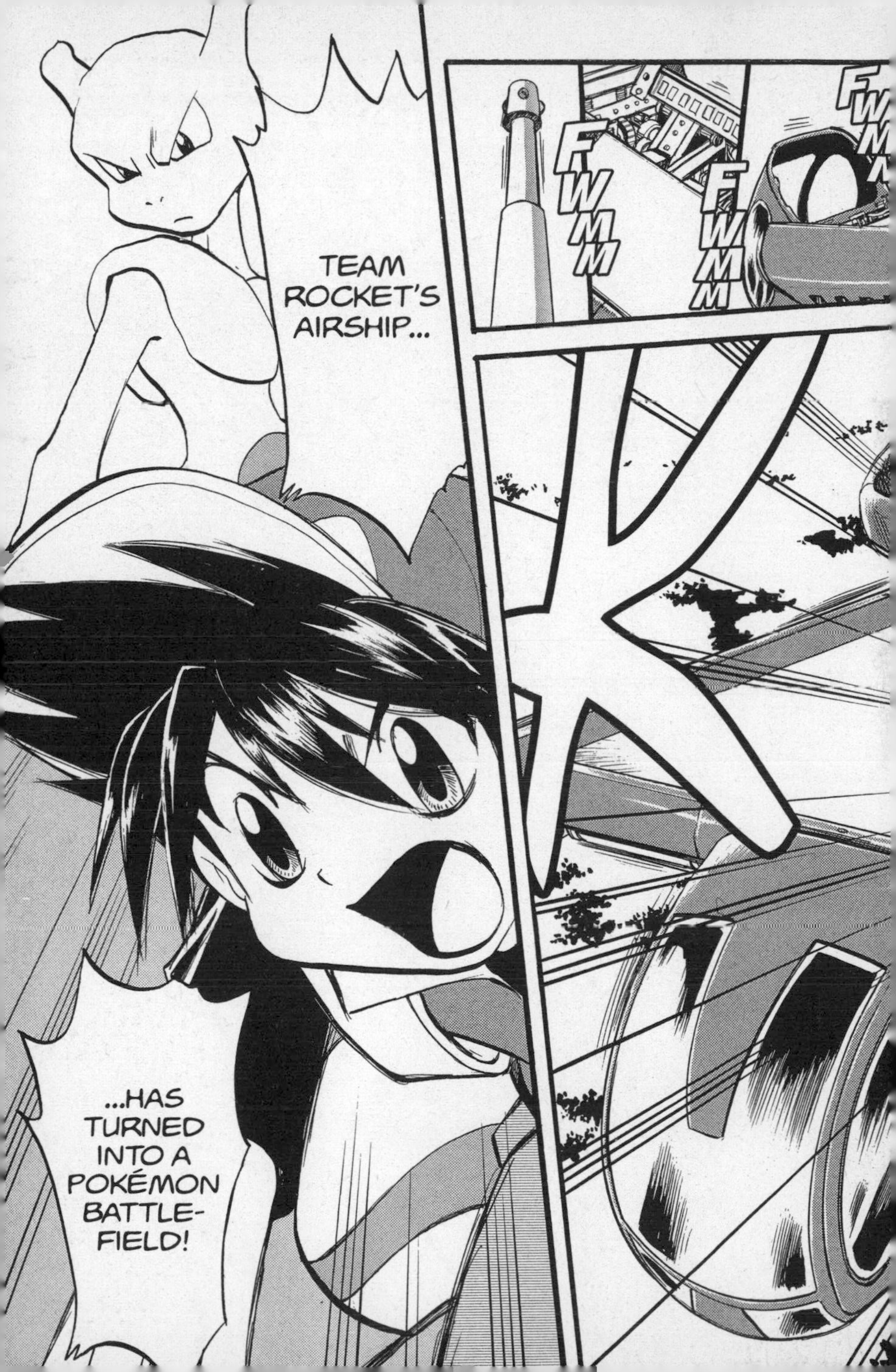
FWMM
FWMM
FWMM
TEAM ROCKET'S AIRSHIP...
...HAS TURNED INTO A POKÉMON BATTLE-FIELD!

• Adventure 291 •
Can Mewtwo Dish It Out with a Spoon?

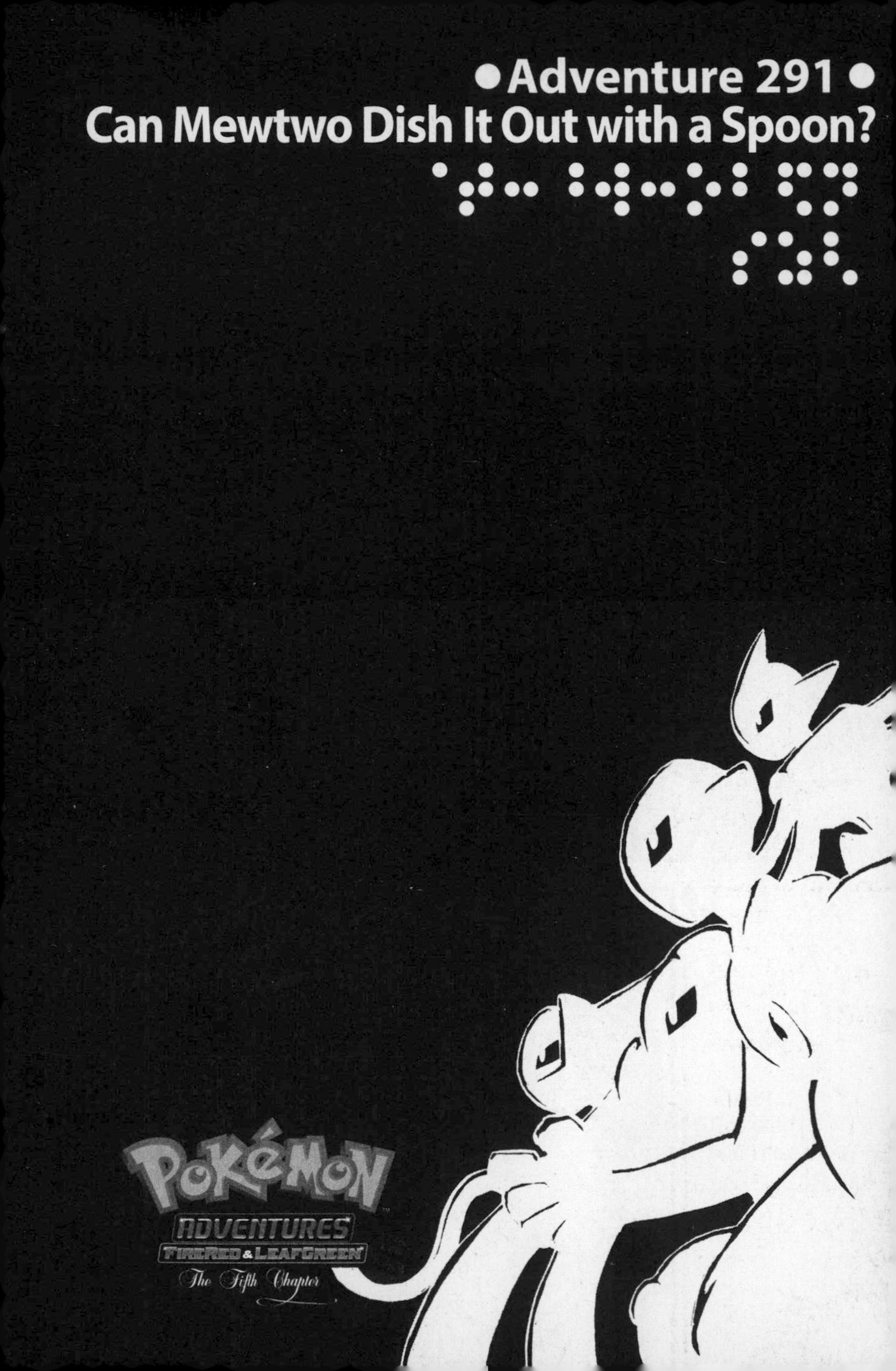

Pokémon Adventures
FireRed & LeafGreen
The Fifth Chapter

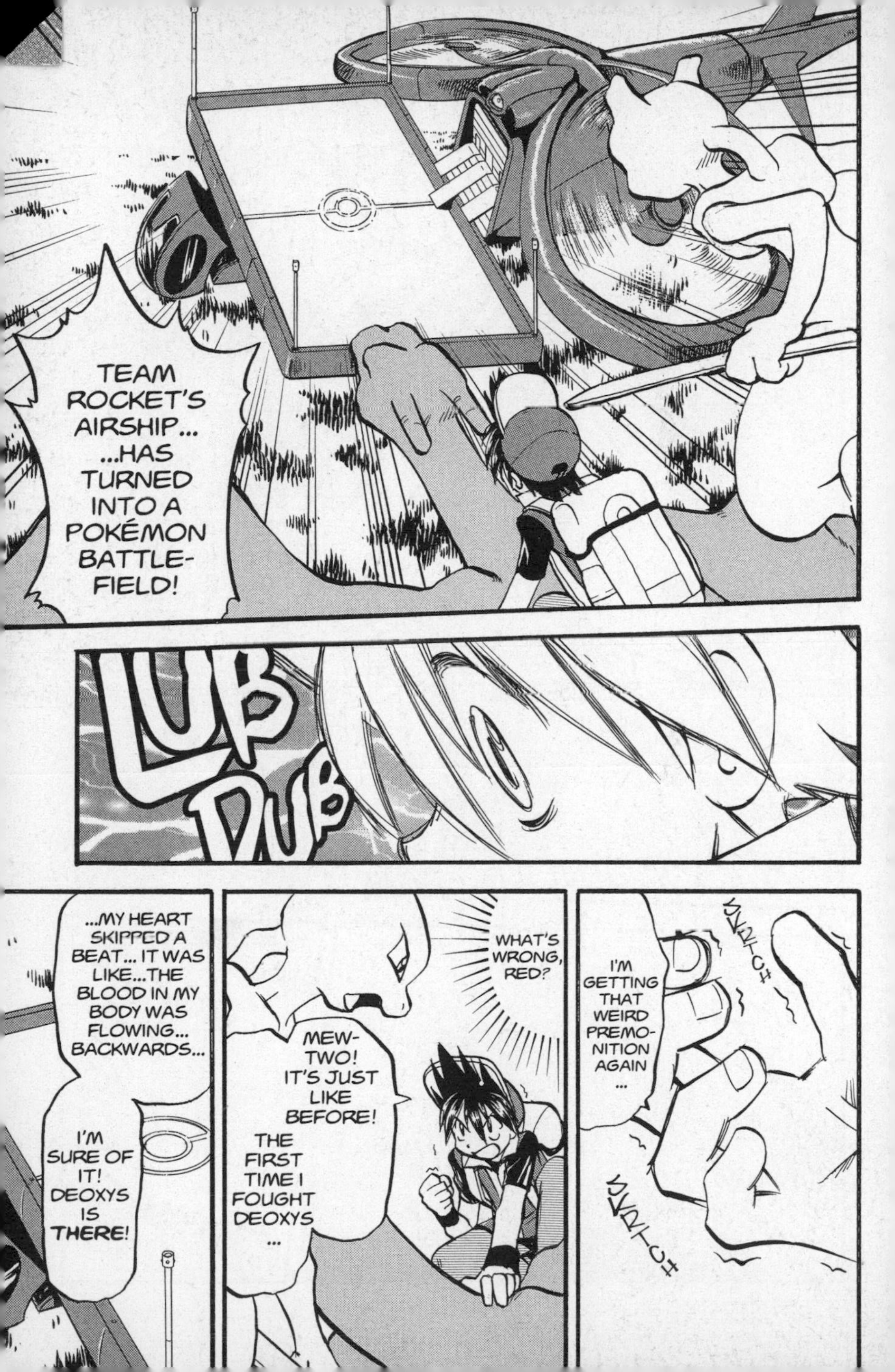
TEAM ROCKET'S AIRSHIP... ...HAS TURNED INTO A POKÉMON BATTLE-FIELD!
LUB
DUB
I'M GETTING THAT WEIRD PREMO-NITION AGAIN ...
SKRITCH
SKRITCH
WHAT'S WRONG, RED?
MEW-TWO! IT'S JUST LIKE BEFORE!
THE FIRST TIME I FOUGHT DEOXYS ...
...MY HEART SKIPPED A BEAT... IT WAS LIKE...THE BLOOD IN MY BODY WAS FLOWING... BACKWARDS...
I'M SURE OF IT! DEOXYS IS **THERE**!

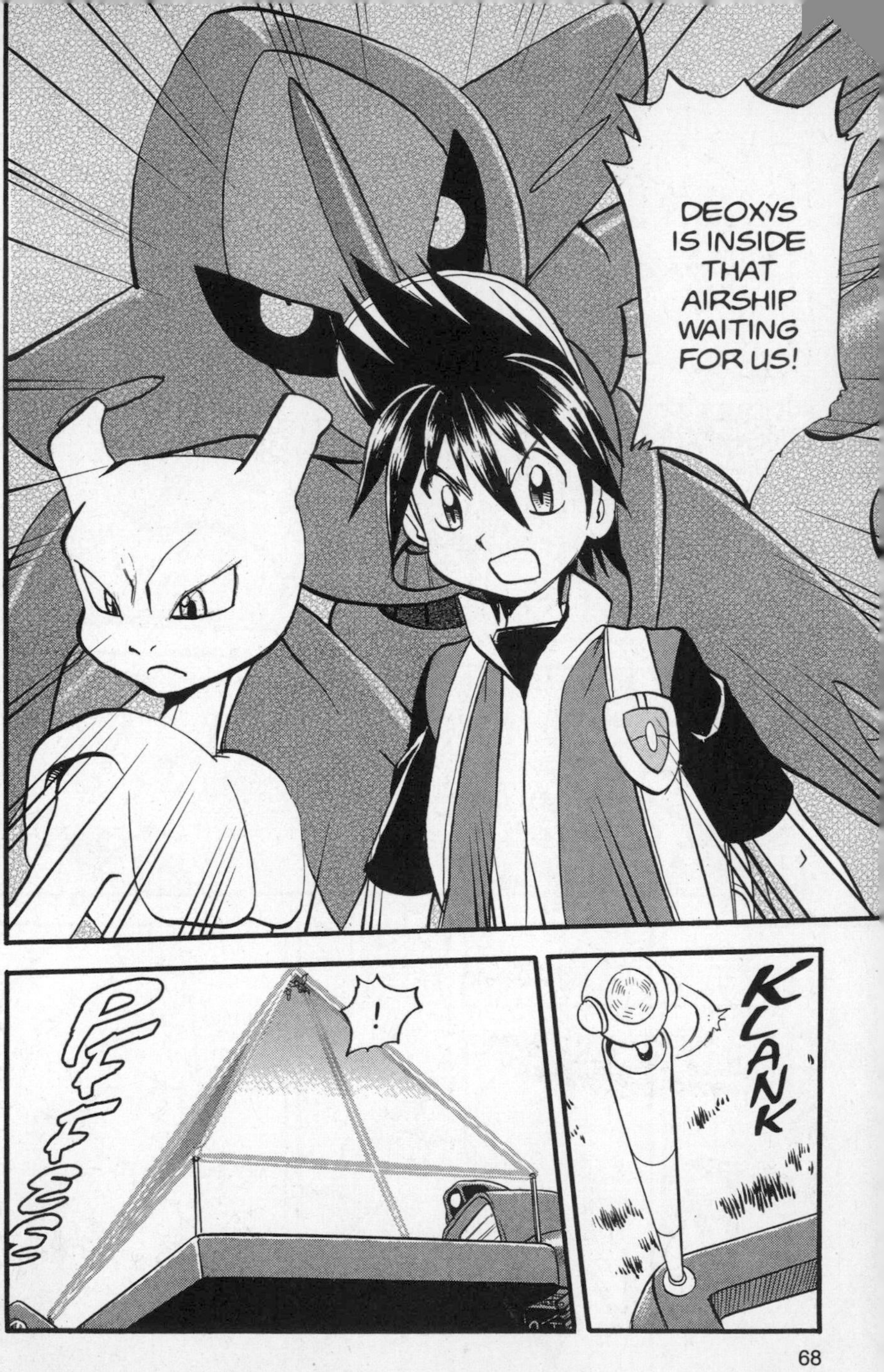
DEOXYS IS INSIDE THAT AIRSHIP WAITING FOR US!
KLANK
!
PFFEE

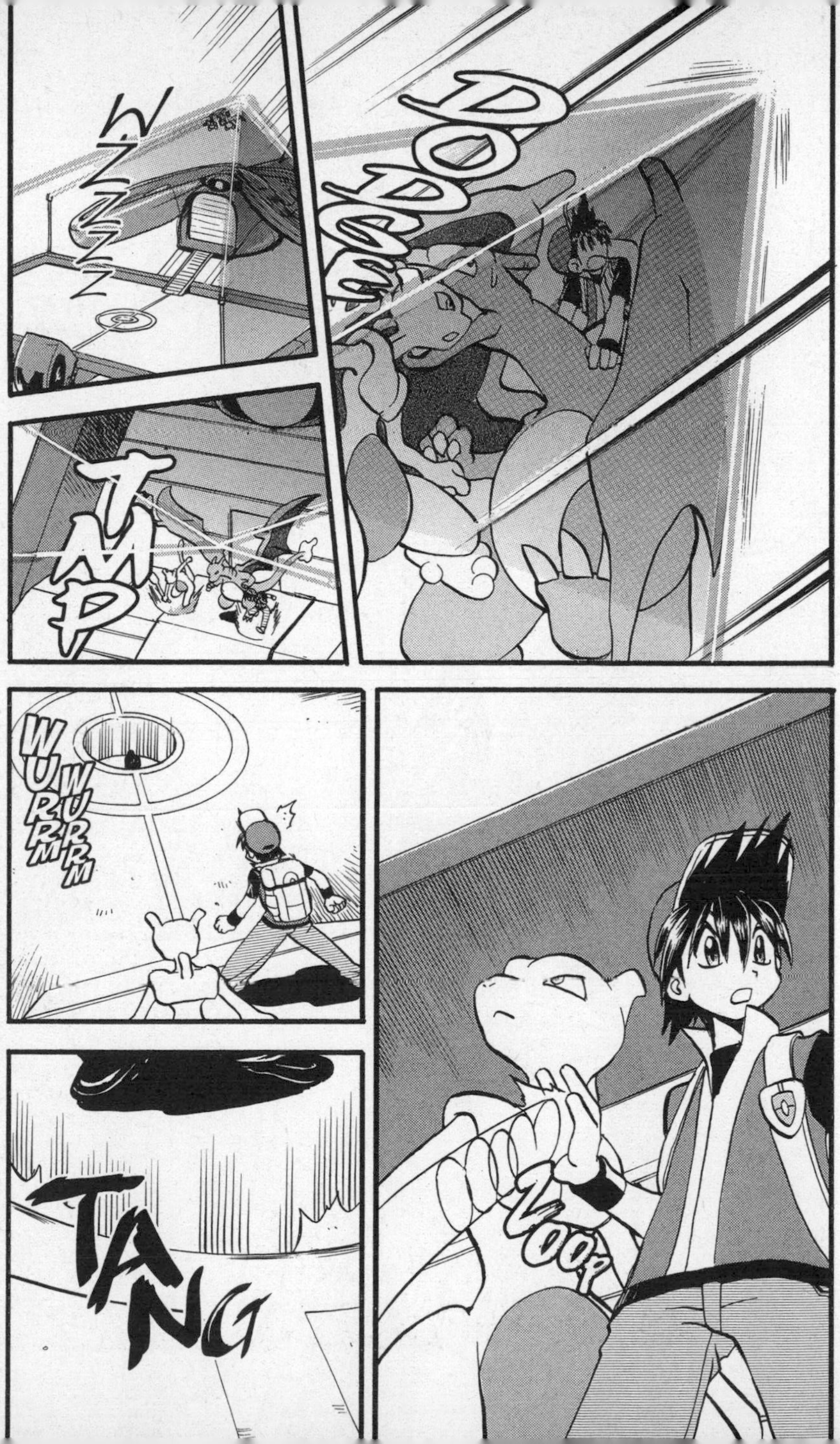
DODGE
WIZZZZ
TMP
ZOOP
WURRM
WURRRM
TANG

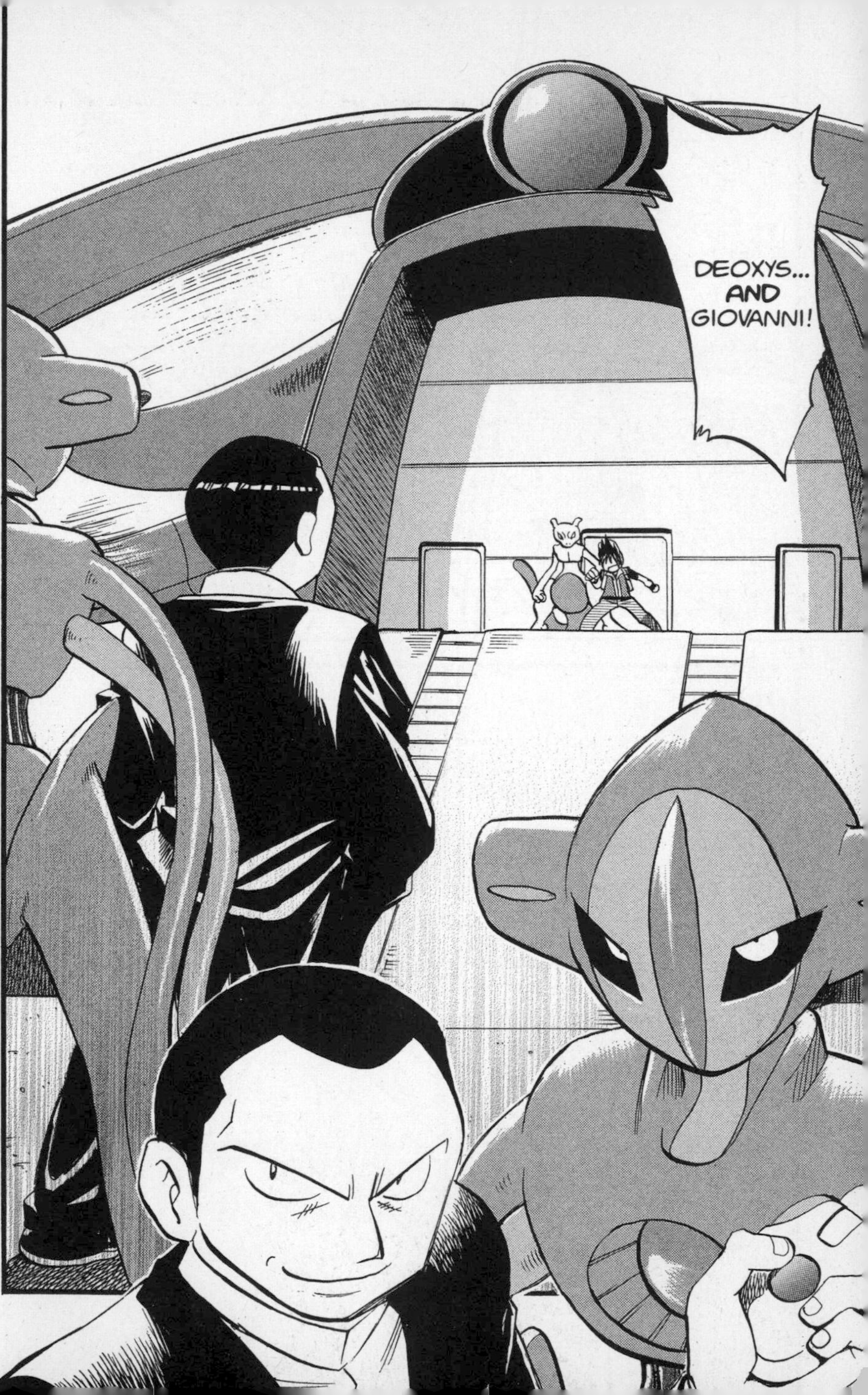
DEOXYS... AND GIOVANNI!

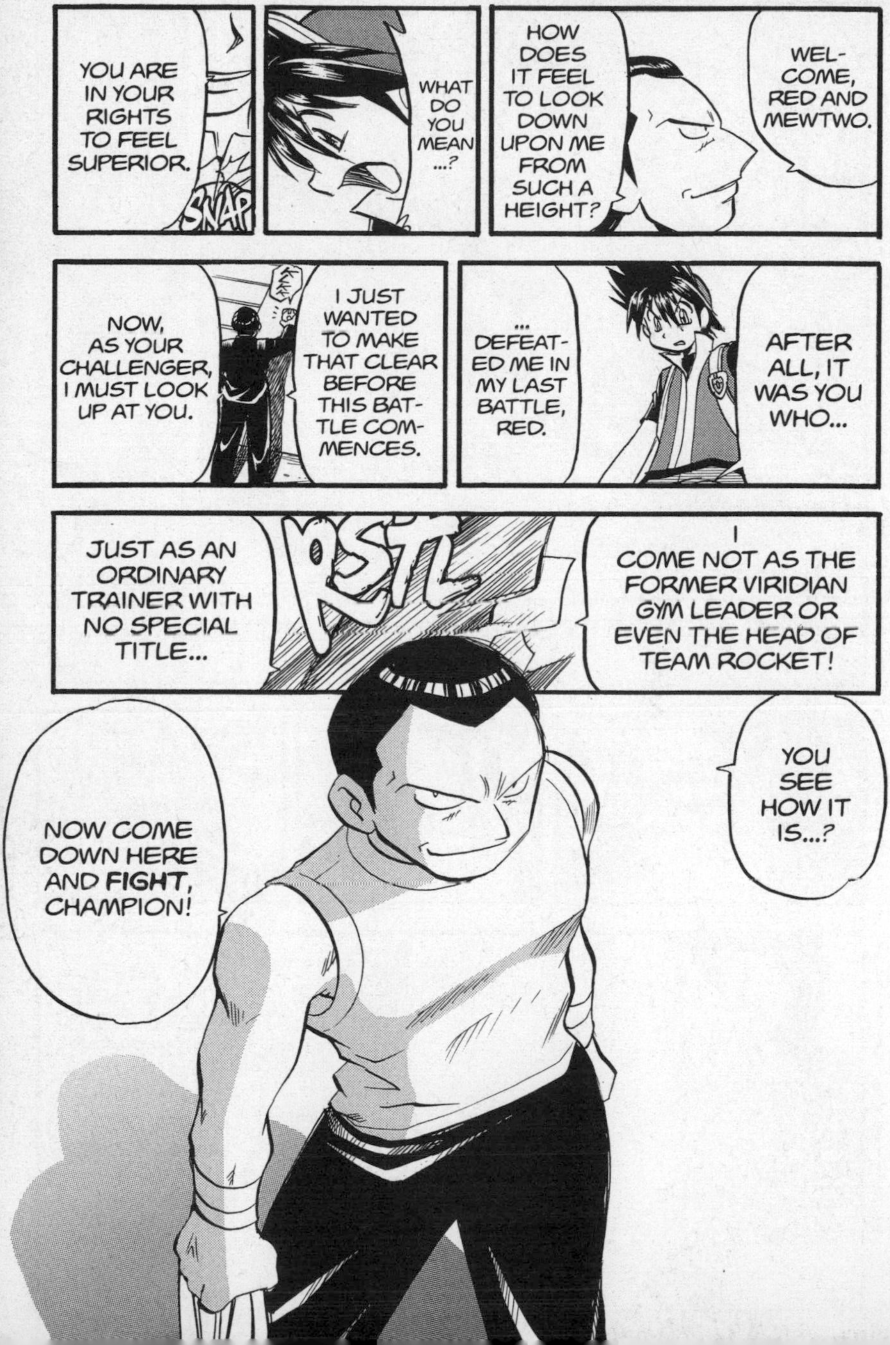
WELCOME, RED AND MEWTWO.
HOW DOES IT FEEL TO LOOK DOWN UPON ME FROM SUCH A HEIGHT?
WHAT DO YOU MEAN ...?
YOU ARE IN YOUR RIGHTS TO FEEL SUPERIOR.
SNAP
AFTER ALL, IT WAS YOU WHO...
... DEFEATED ME IN MY LAST BATTLE, RED.
I JUST WANTED TO MAKE THAT CLEAR BEFORE THIS BATTLE COMMENCES.
NOW, AS YOUR CHALLENGER, I MUST LOOK UP AT YOU.
I COME NOT AS THE FORMER VIRIDIAN GYM LEADER OR EVEN THE HEAD OF TEAM ROCKET!
RSTL
JUST AS AN ORDINARY TRAINER WITH NO SPECIAL TITLE...
YOU SEE HOW IT IS...?
NOW COME DOWN HERE AND **FIGHT**, CHAMPION!

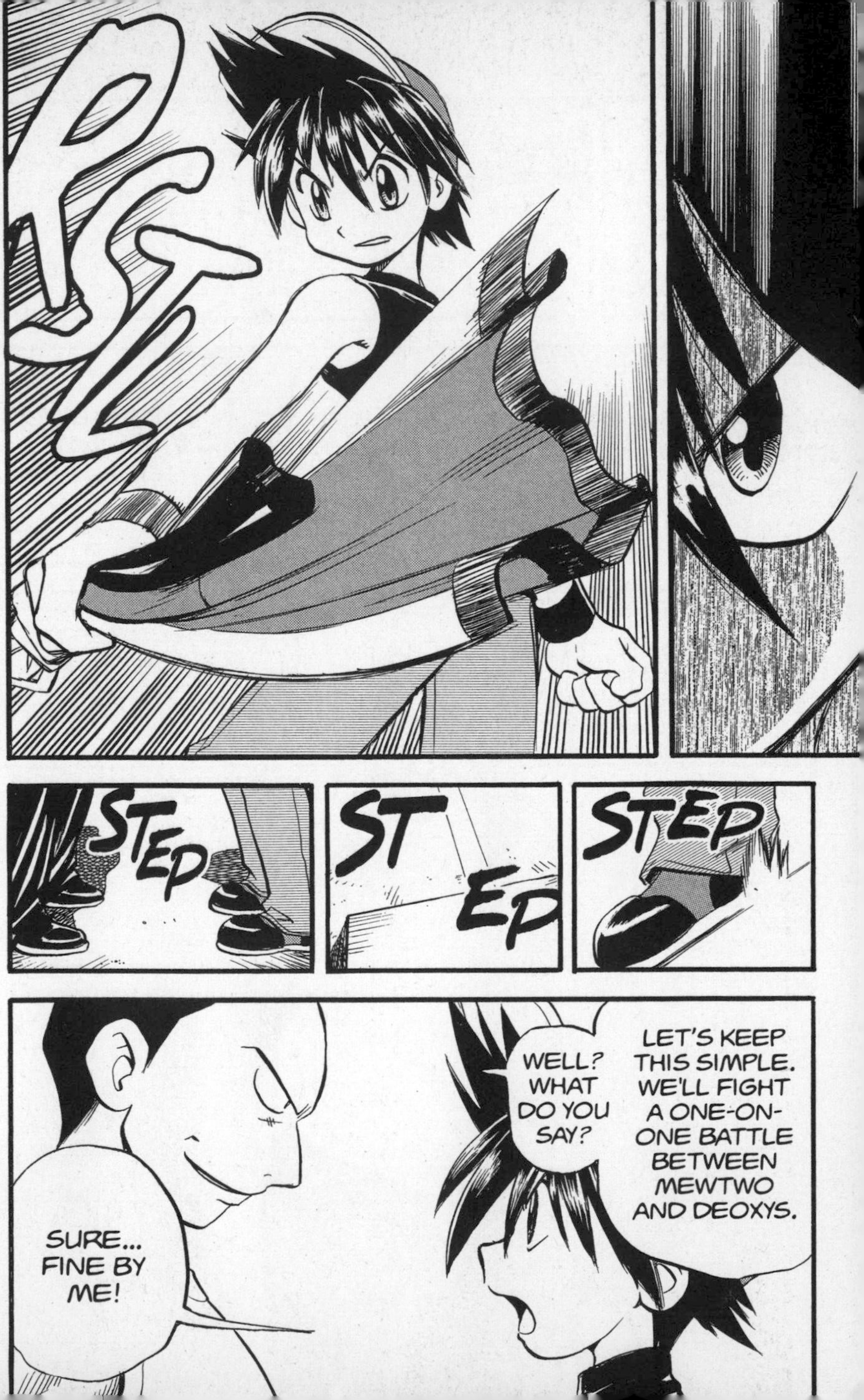
STEP
ST EP
STEP
LET'S KEEP THIS SIMPLE. WE'LL FIGHT A ONE-ON-ONE BATTLE BETWEEN MEWTWO AND DEOXYS.
WELL? WHAT DO YOU SAY?
SURE... FINE BY ME!

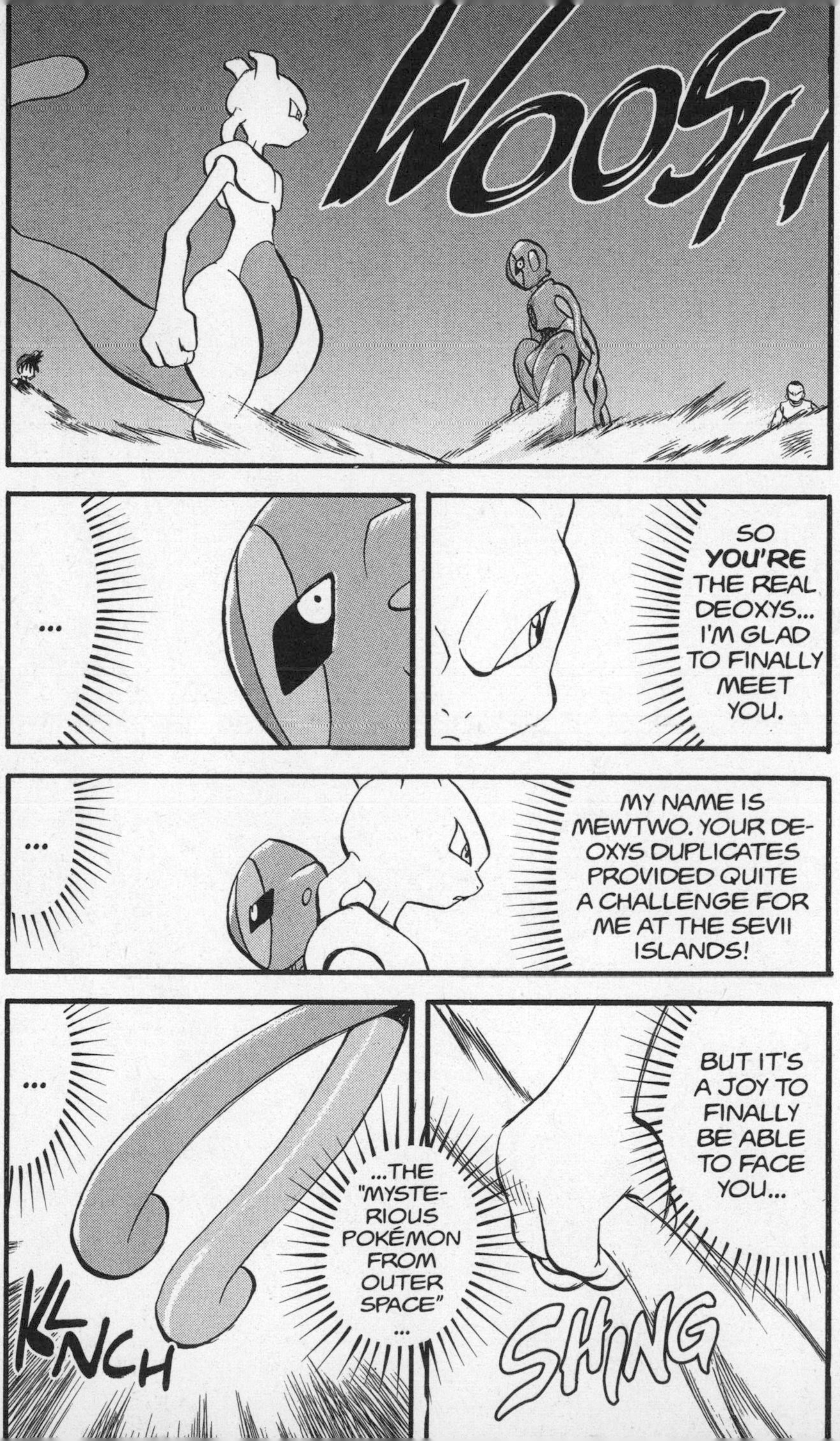
WOOSH
SO YOU'RE THE REAL DEOXYS... I'M GLAD TO FINALLY MEET YOU.
...
MY NAME IS MEWTWO. YOUR DE-OXYS DUPLICATES PROVIDED QUITE A CHALLENGE FOR ME AT THE SEVII ISLANDS!
...
BUT IT'S A JOY TO FINALLY BE ABLE TO FACE YOU...
...THE "MYSTE-RIOUS POKÉMON FROM OUTER SPACE"...
SHING
...
KLNCH

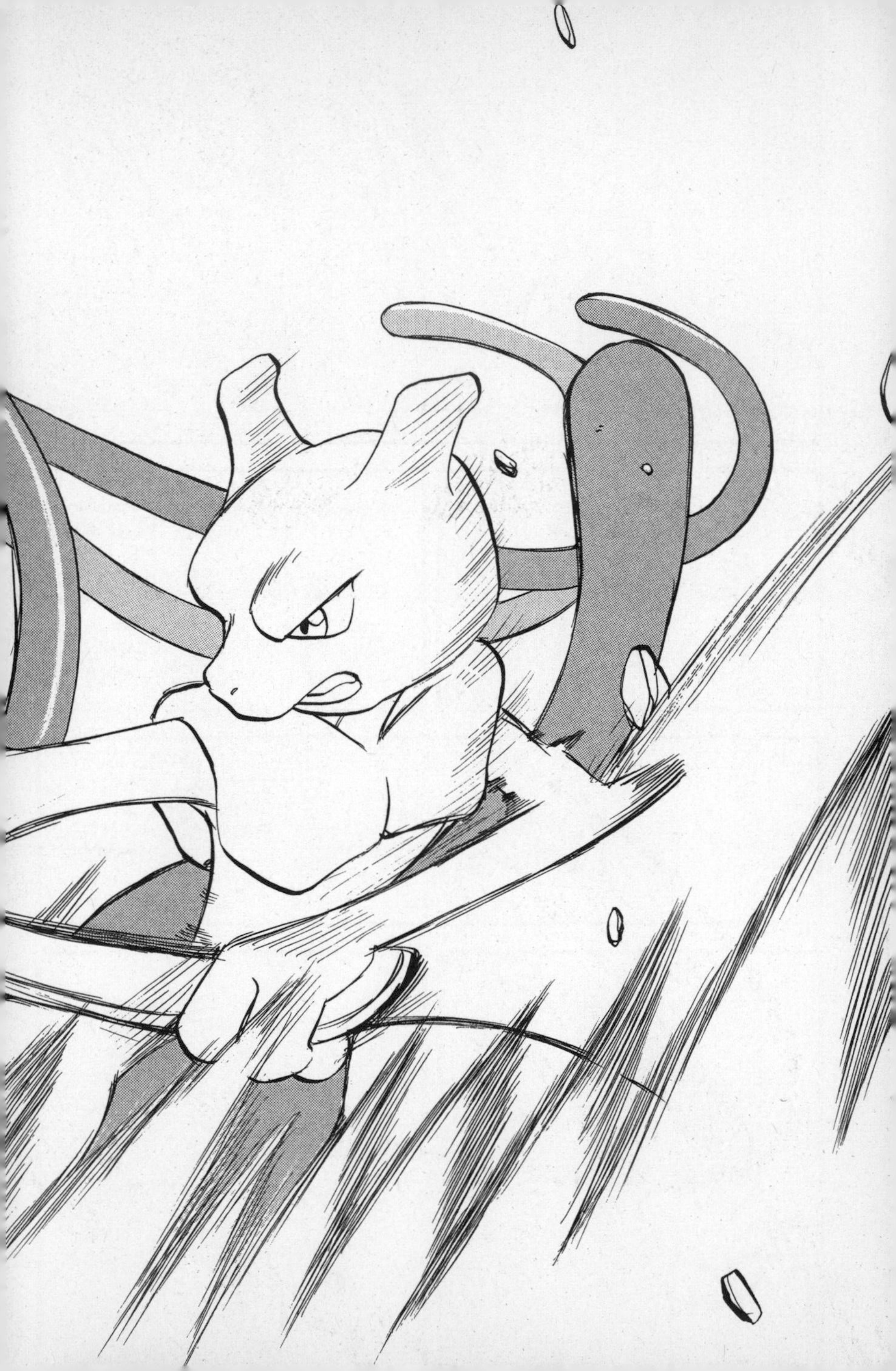

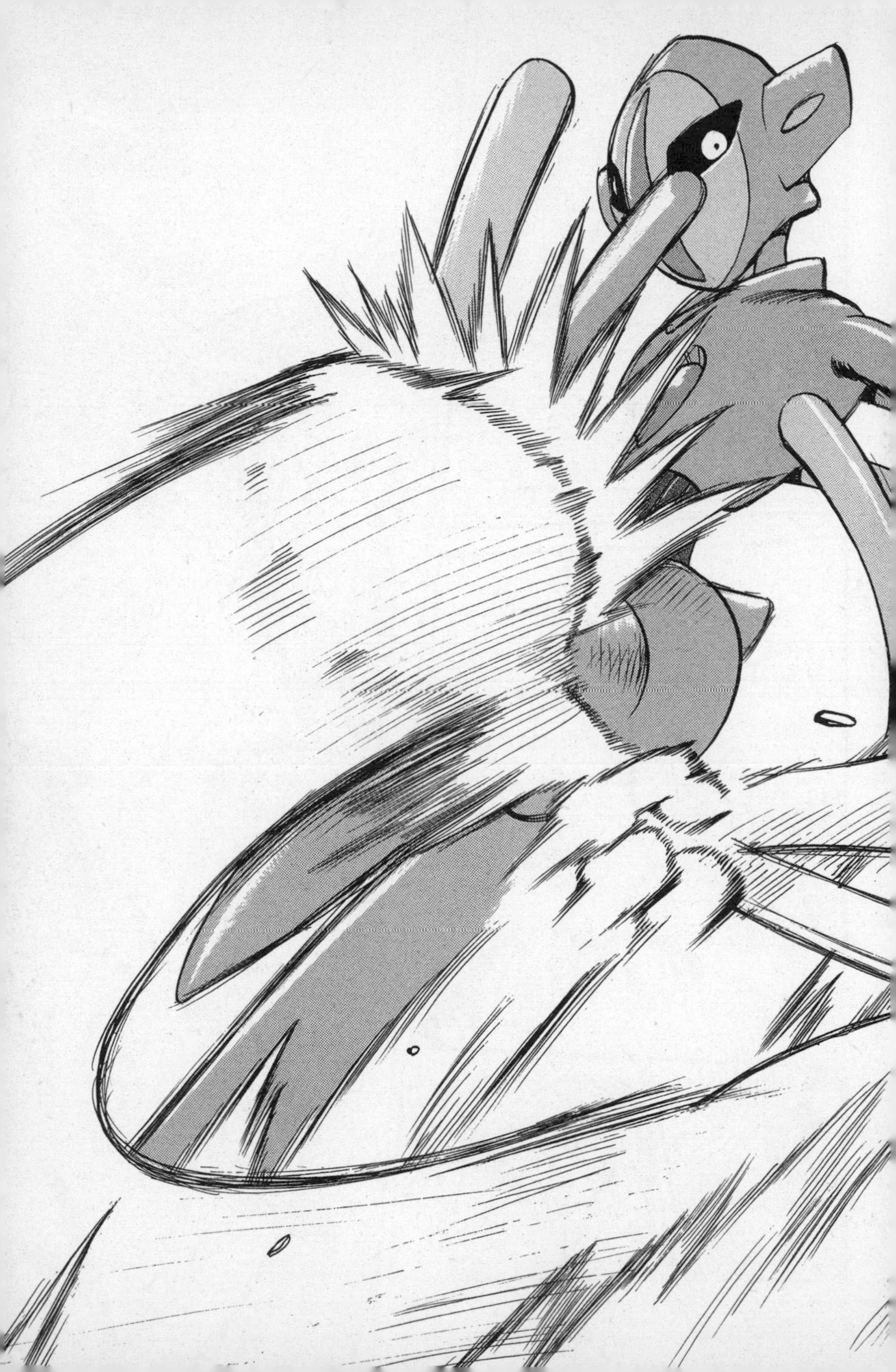

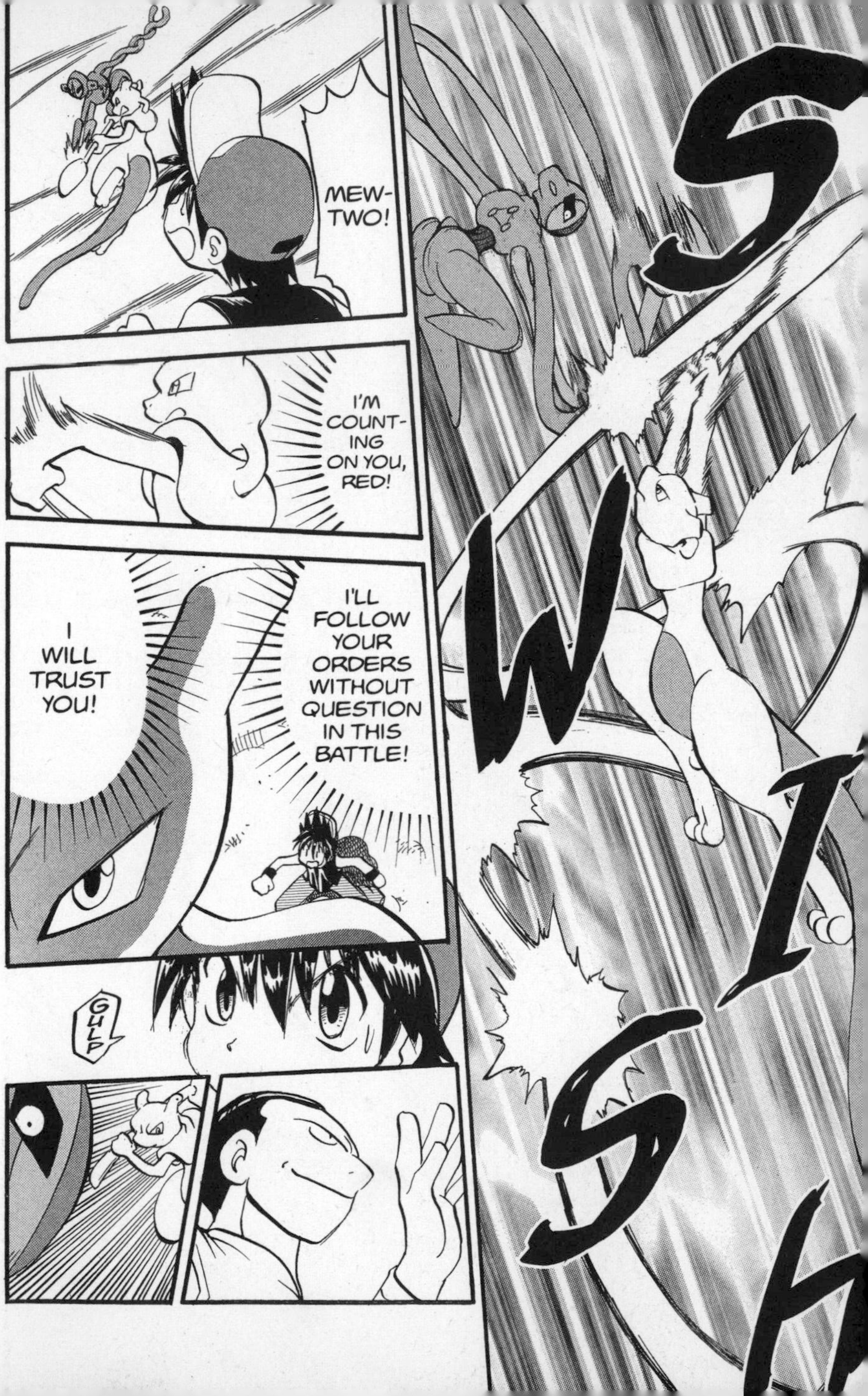
SWISH
MEW-TWO!
I'M COUNTING ON YOU, RED!
I'LL FOLLOW YOUR ORDERS WITHOUT QUESTION IN THIS BATTLE!
I WILL TRUST YOU!
GULP

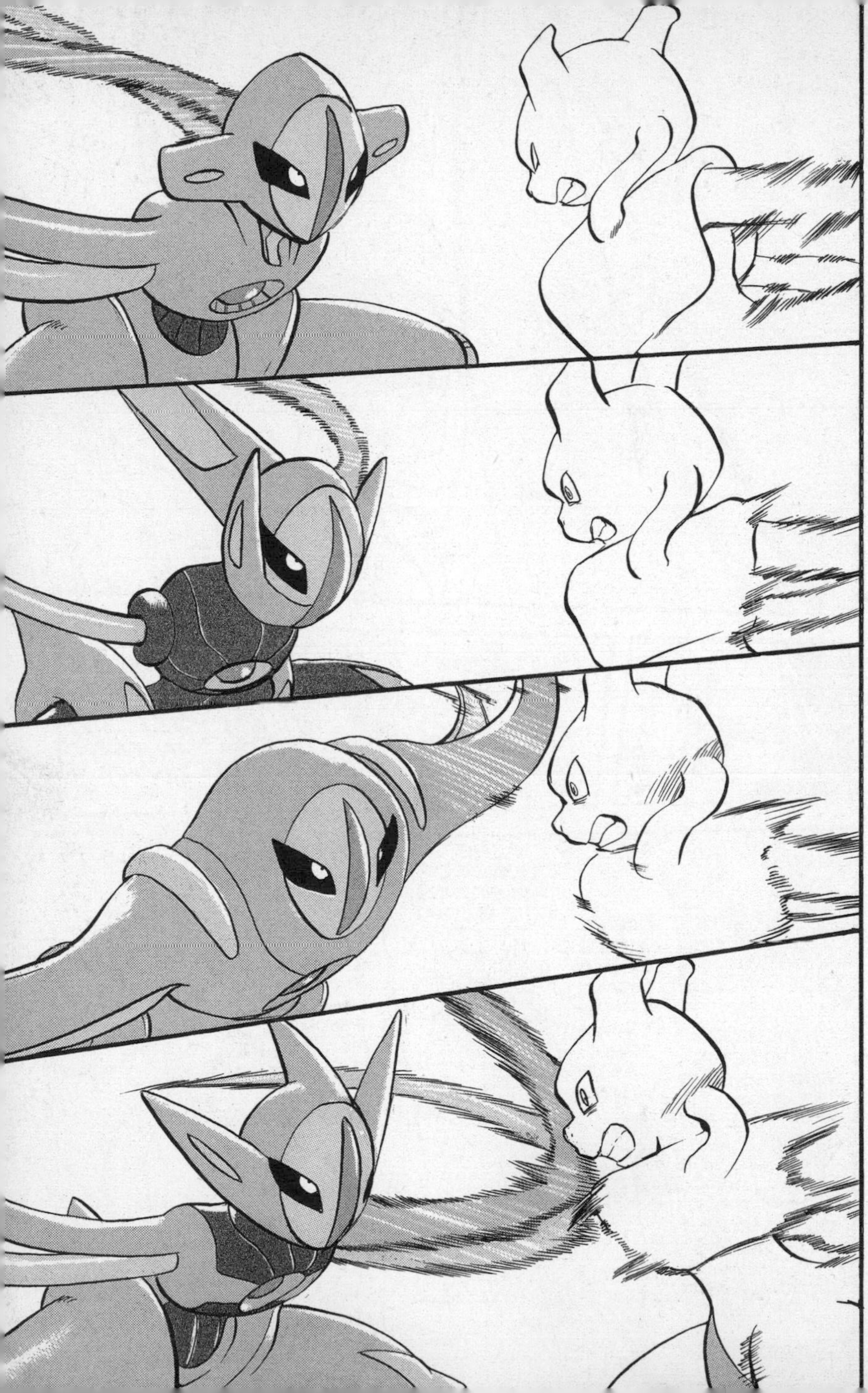

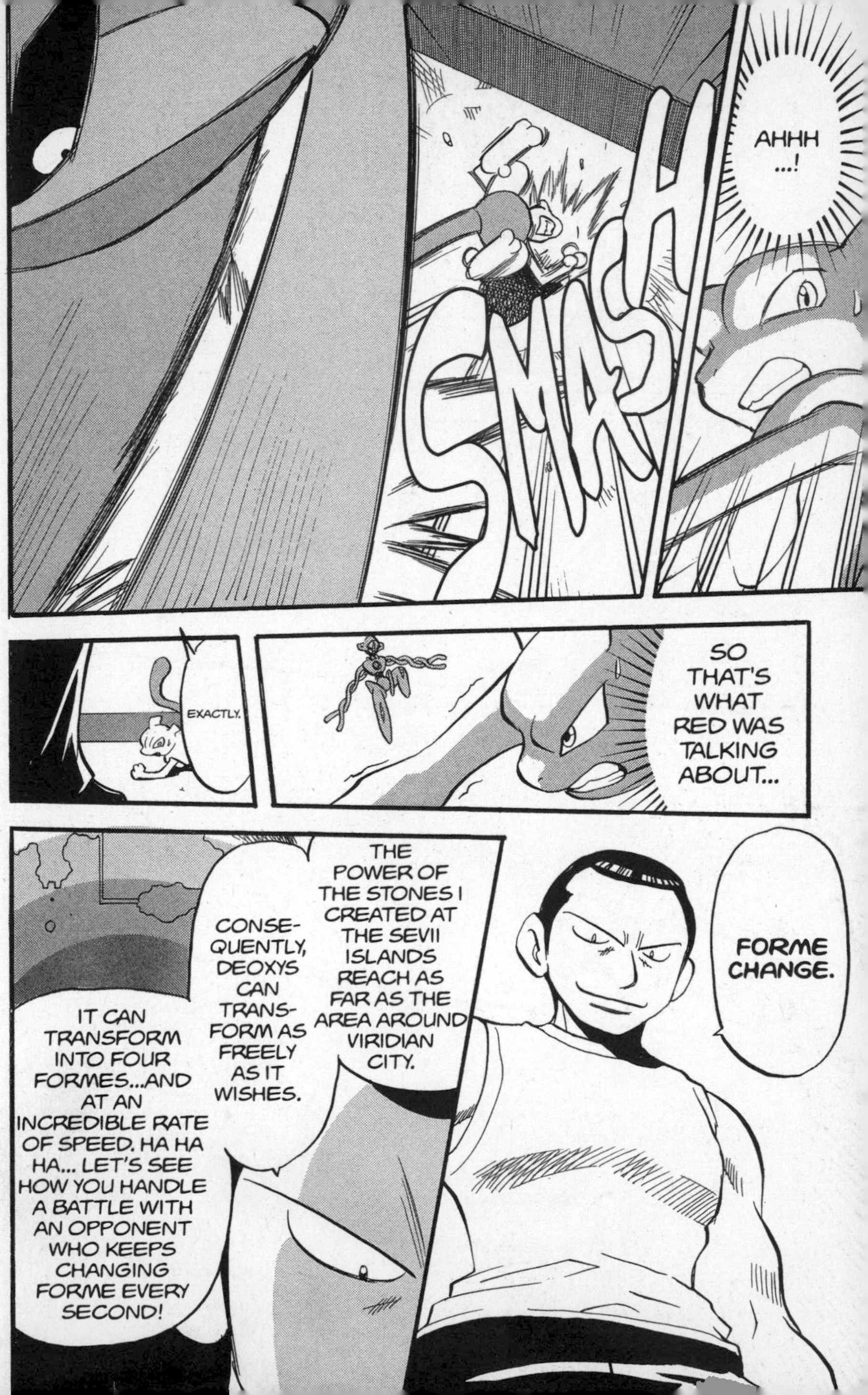
AHHH ...!
SMASH
SO THAT'S WHAT RED WAS TALKING ABOUT...
EXACTLY.
FORME CHANGE.
THE POWER OF THE STONES I CREATED AT THE SEVII ISLANDS REACH AS FAR AS THE AREA AROUND VIRIDIAN CITY.
CONSE-QUENTLY, DEOXYS CAN TRANS-FORM AS FREELY AS IT WISHES.
IT CAN TRANSFORM INTO FOUR FORMES...AND AT AN INCREDIBLE RATE OF SPEED. HA HA HA... LET'S SEE HOW YOU HANDLE A BATTLE WITH AN OPPONENT WHO KEEPS CHANGING FORME EVERY SECOND!

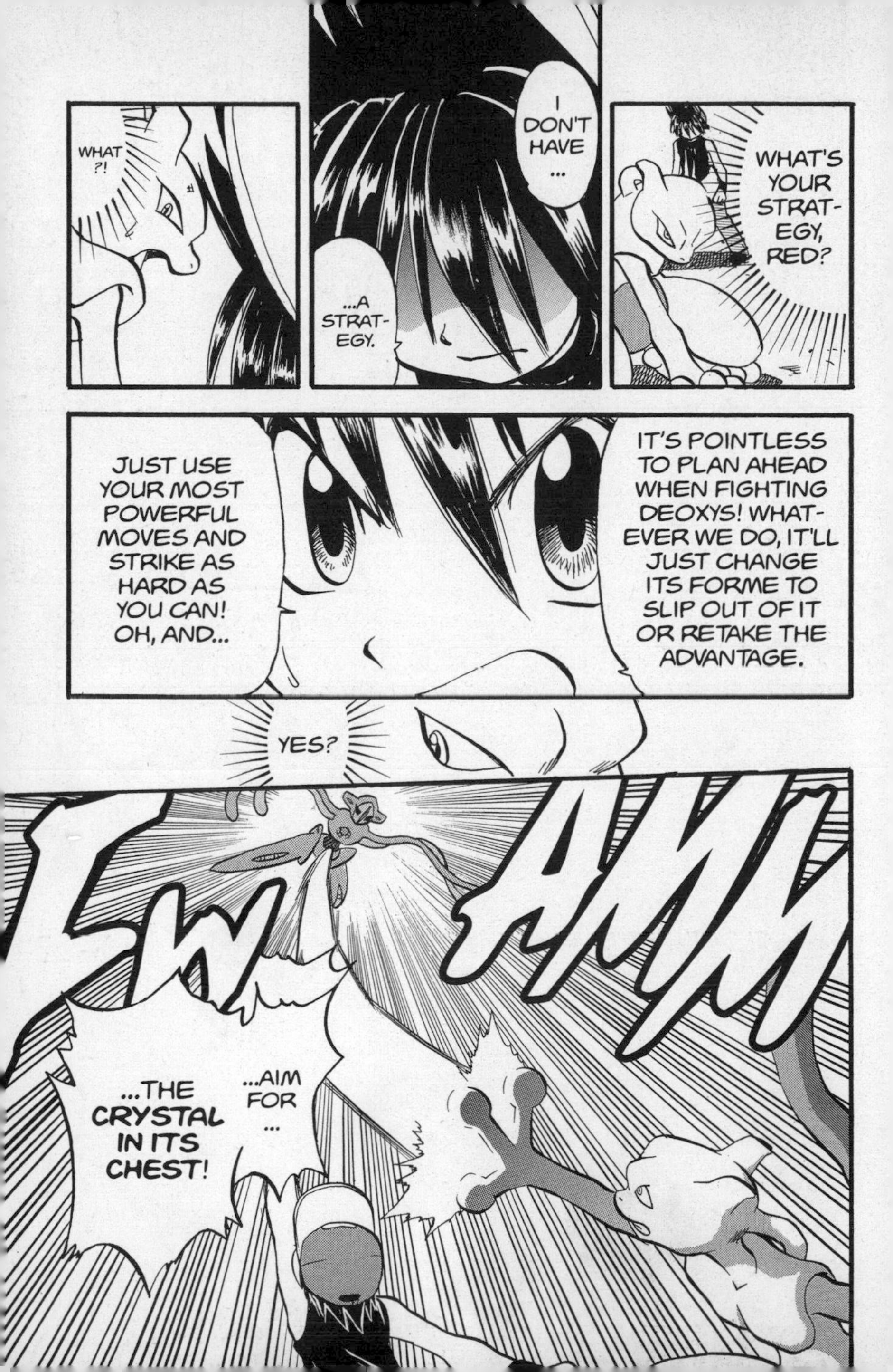
WHAT'S YOUR STRAT-EGY, RED?
I DON'T HAVE...
...A STRAT-EGY.
WHAT?!
IT'S POINTLESS TO PLAN AHEAD WHEN FIGHTING DEOXYS! WHAT-EVER WE DO, IT'LL JUST CHANGE ITS FORME TO SLIP OUT OF IT OR RETAKE THE ADVANTAGE.
JUST USE YOUR MOST POWERFUL MOVES AND STRIKE AS HARD AS YOU CAN! OH, AND...
YES?
...AIM FOR...
...THE CRYSTAL IN ITS CHEST!

• Adventure 292 •
Bested by Banette

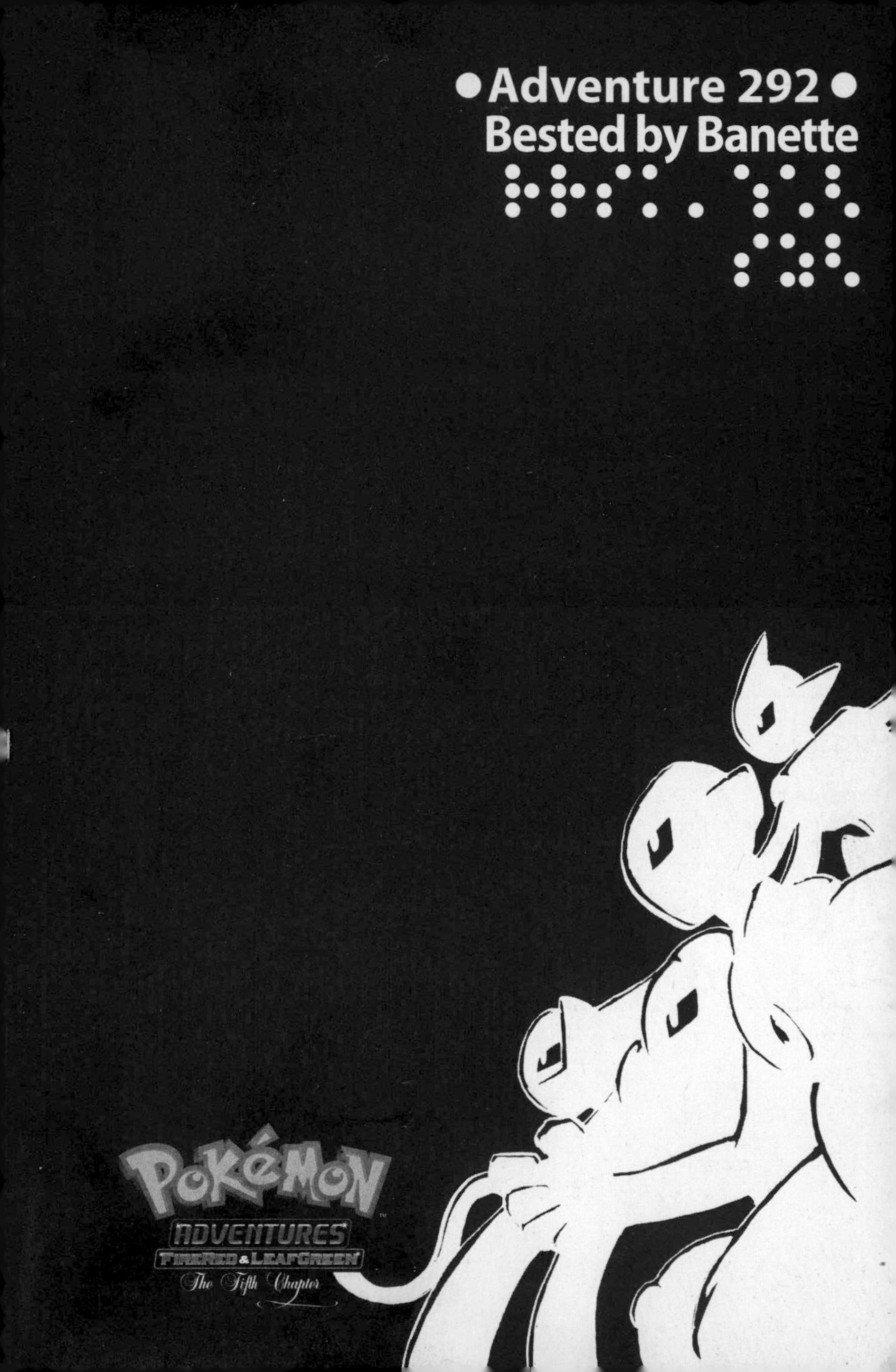

Pokémon Adventures
FireRed & LeafGreen
The Fifth Chapter

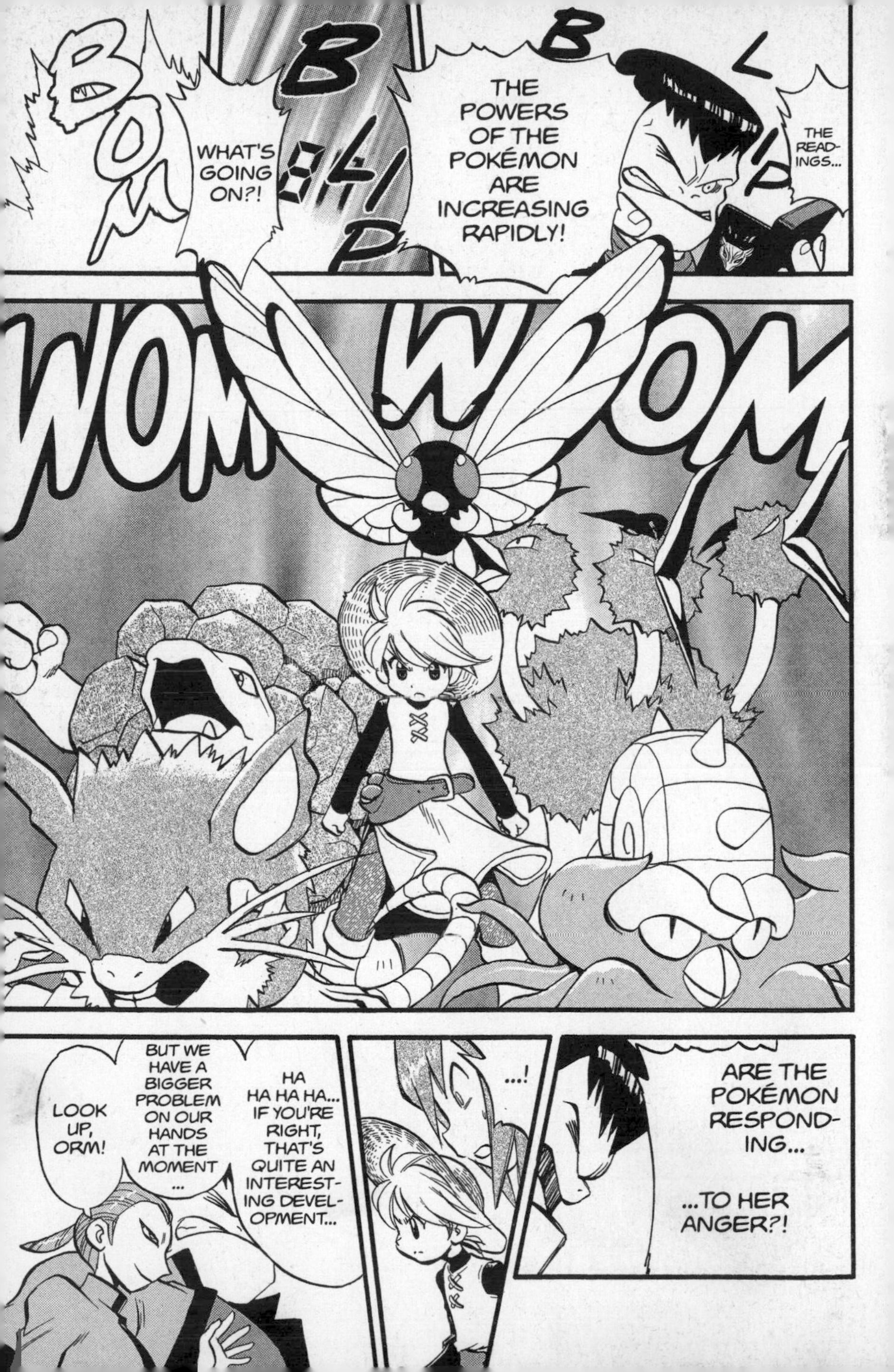
BLIP
THE READINGS...
BLIP
THE POWERS OF THE POKÉMON ARE INCREASING RAPIDLY!
BOOM
WHAT'S GOING ON?!
WOOM WOOM
ARE THE POKÉMON RESPONDING...
...TO HER ANGER?!
...!
HA HA HA HA... IF YOU'RE RIGHT, THAT'S QUITE AN INTERESTING DEVELOPMENT...
BUT WE HAVE A BIGGER PROBLEM ON OUR HANDS AT THE MOMENT...
LOOK UP, ORM!

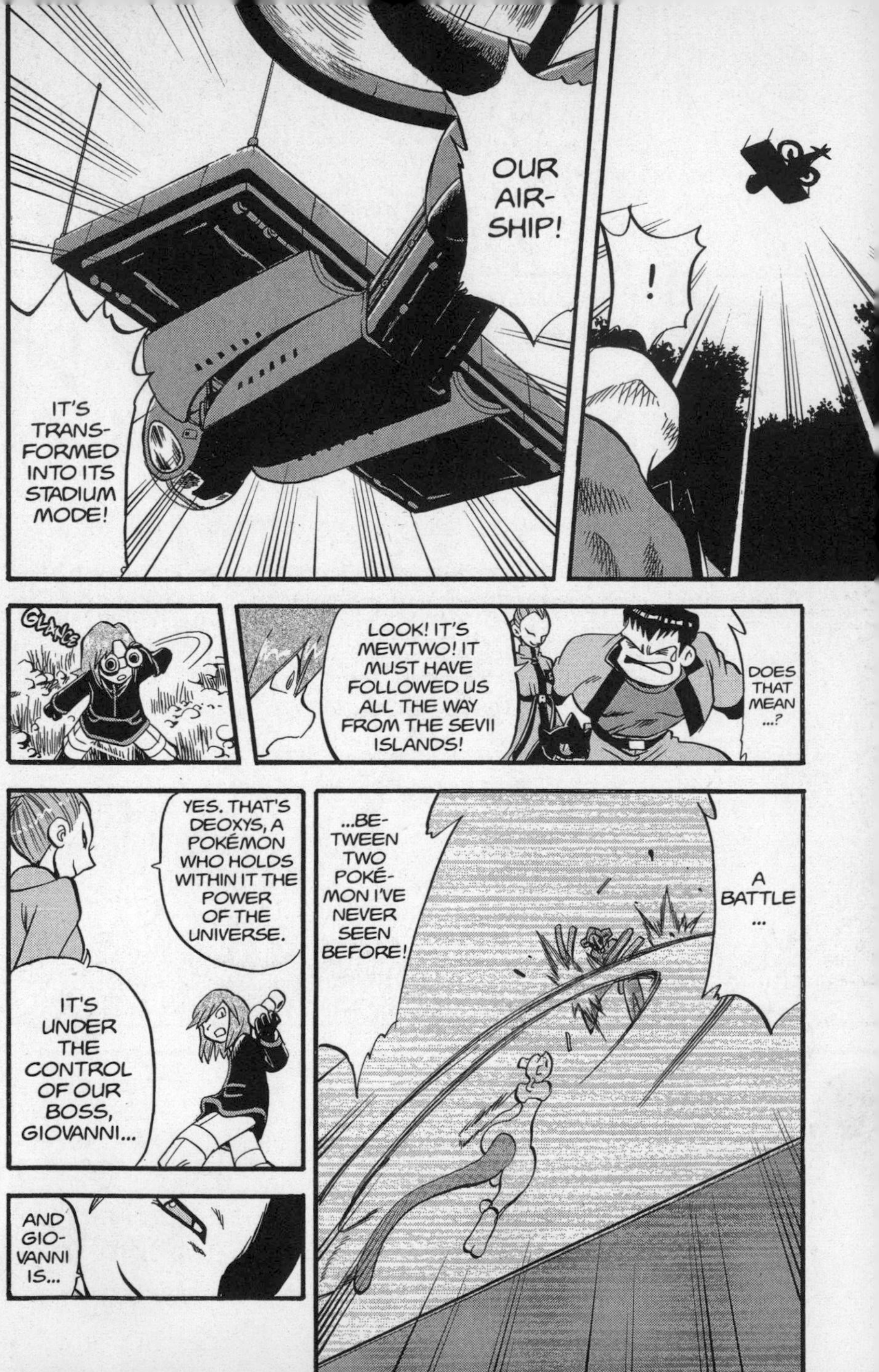
!
OUR AIR-SHIP!
IT'S TRANS-FORMED INTO ITS STADIUM MODE!
DOES THAT MEAN ...?
LOOK! IT'S MEWTWO! IT MUST HAVE FOLLOWED US ALL THE WAY FROM THE SEVII ISLANDS!
GLANCE
A BATTLE ...
...BE-TWEEN TWO POKÉ-MON I'VE NEVER SEEN BEFORE!
YES. THAT'S DEOXYS, A POKÉMON WHO HOLDS WITHIN IT THE POWER OF THE UNIVERSE.
IT'S UNDER THE CONTROL OF OUR BOSS, GIOVANNI...
AND GIO-VANNI IS...

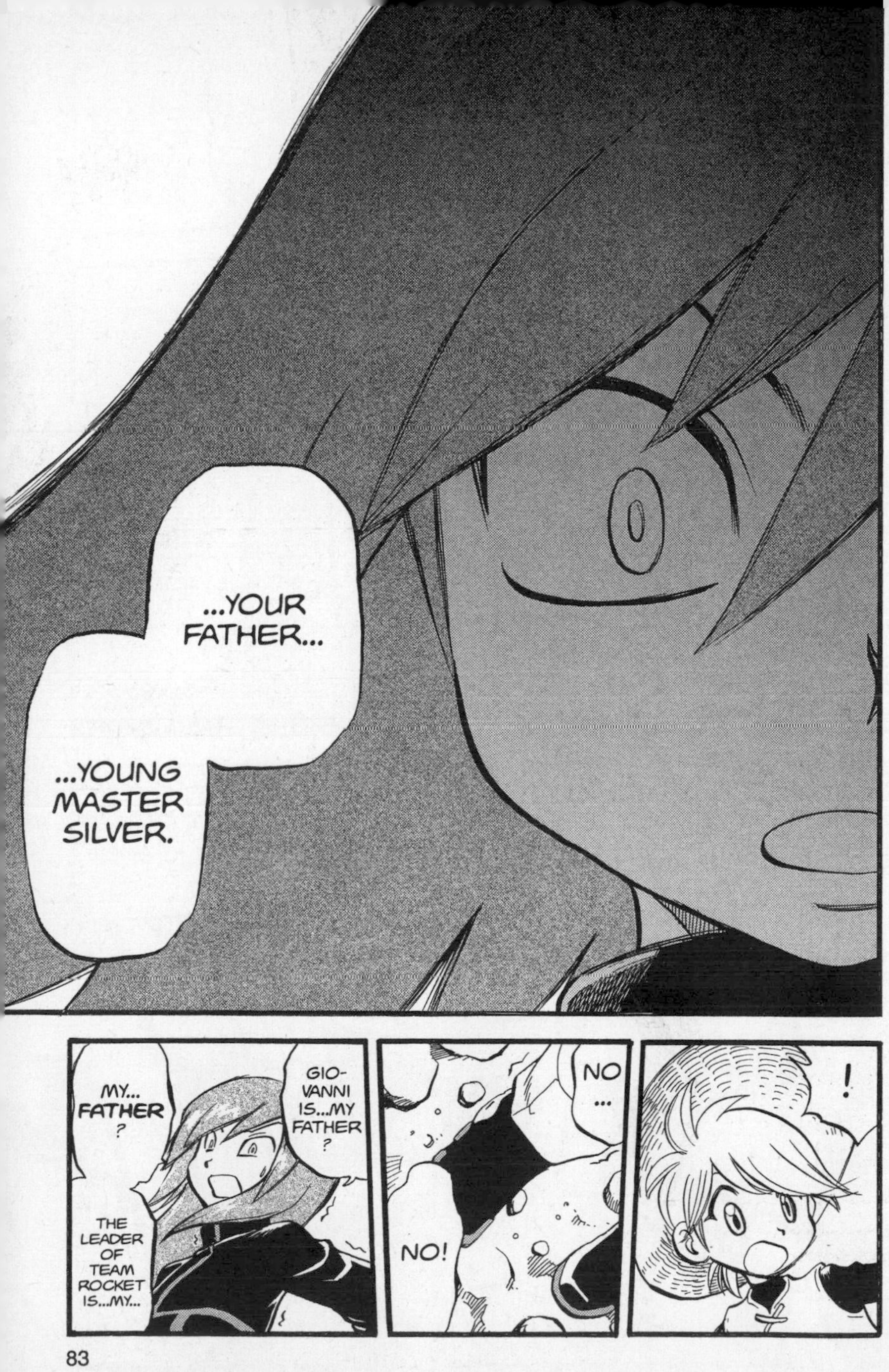
...YOUR FATHER...
...YOUNG MASTER SILVER.
!
NO ...
NO!
GIO-VANNI IS...MY FATHER?
MY... FATHER?
THE LEADER OF TEAM ROCKET IS...MY...

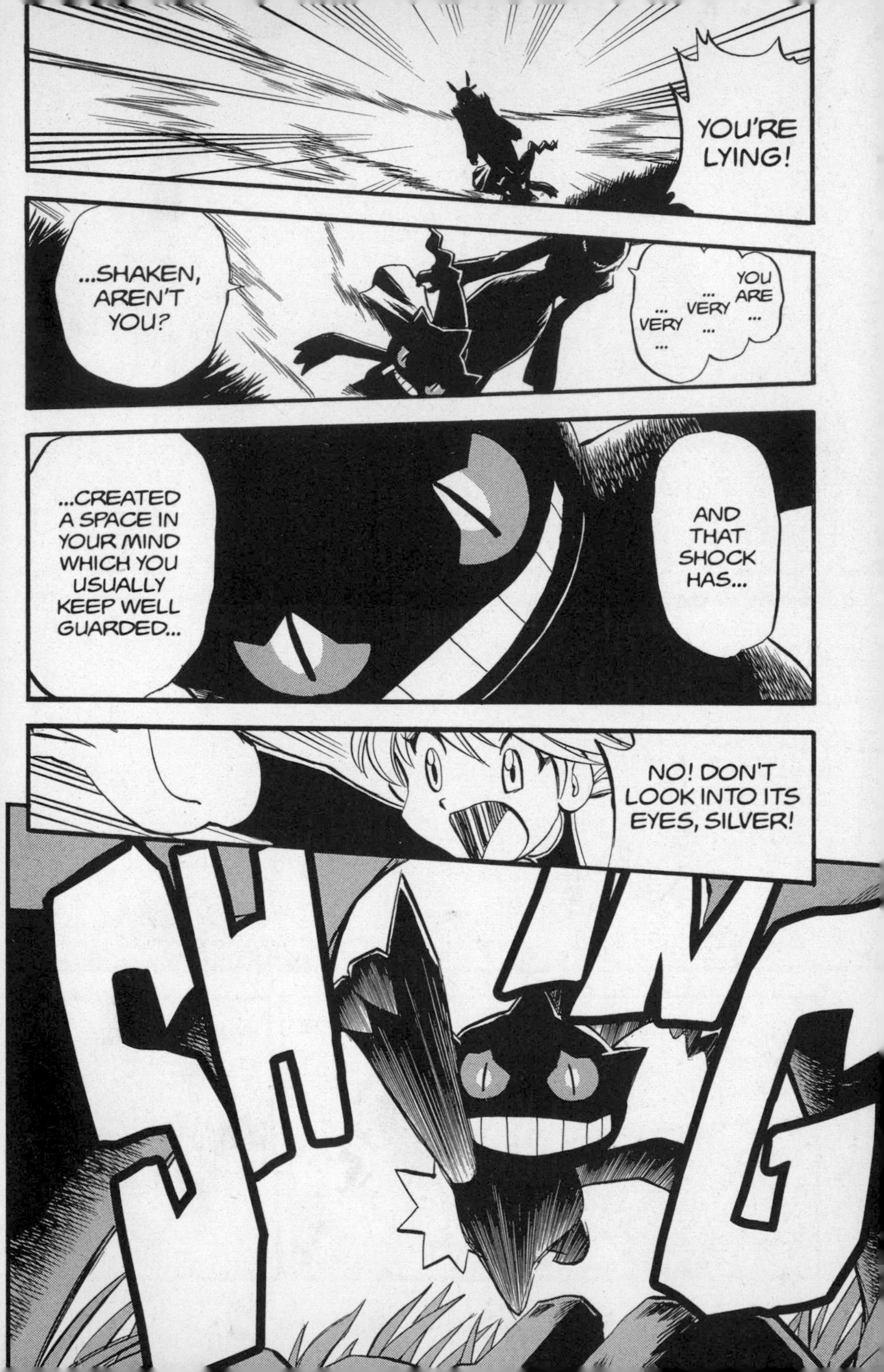
YOU'RE LYING!
YOU ARE ... ... VERY ... ... VERY ...
...SHAKEN, AREN'T YOU?
AND THAT SHOCK HAS...
...CREATED A SPACE IN YOUR MIND WHICH YOU USUALLY KEEP WELL GUARDED...
NO! DON'T LOOK INTO ITS EYES, SILVER!
SHING

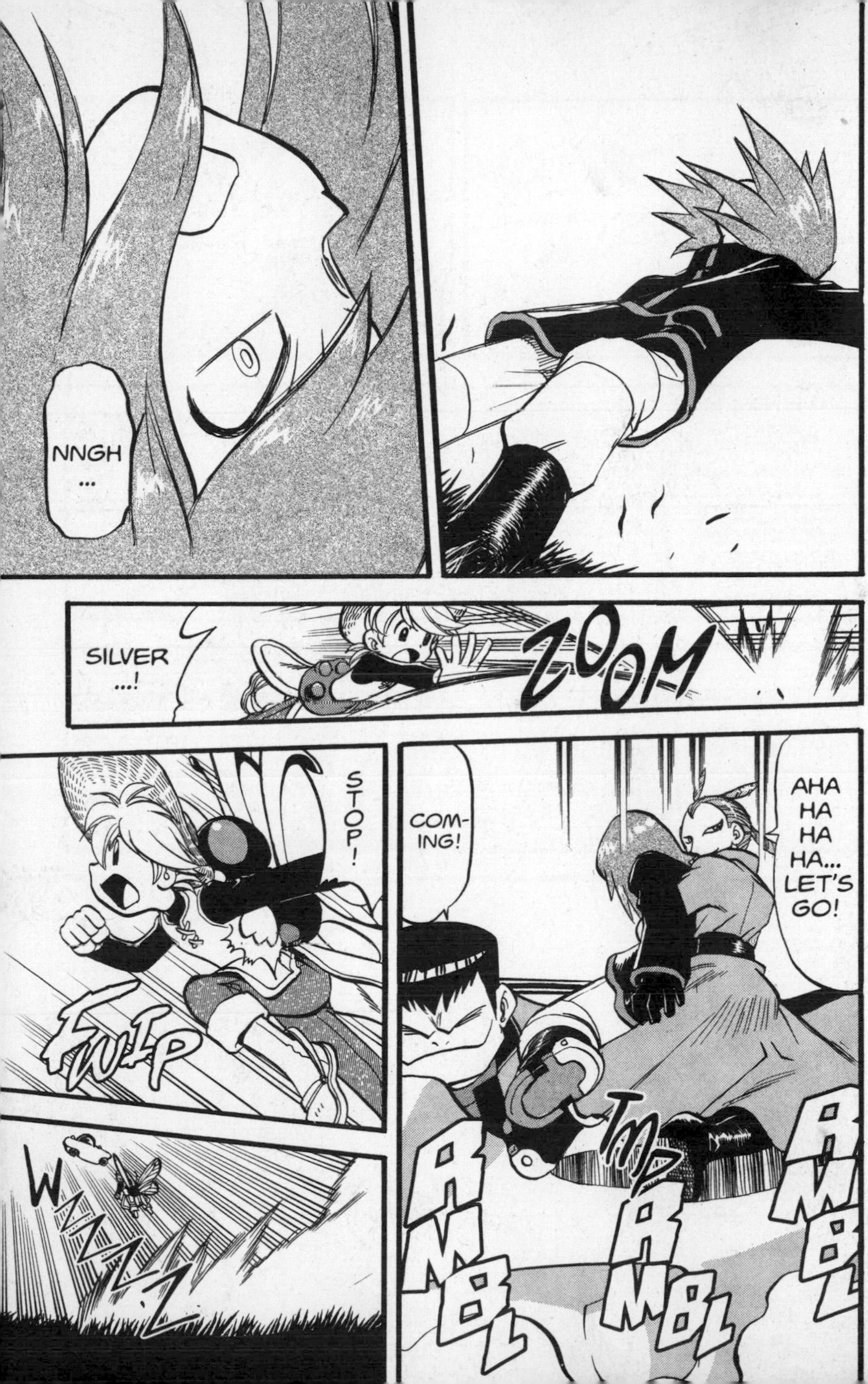
NNGH
...
SILVER
...!
ZOOM
AHA
HA
HA
HA...
LET'S
GO!
COM-
ING!
THMP
RAMBL
RAMBL
RAMBL
STOP!
FWIP

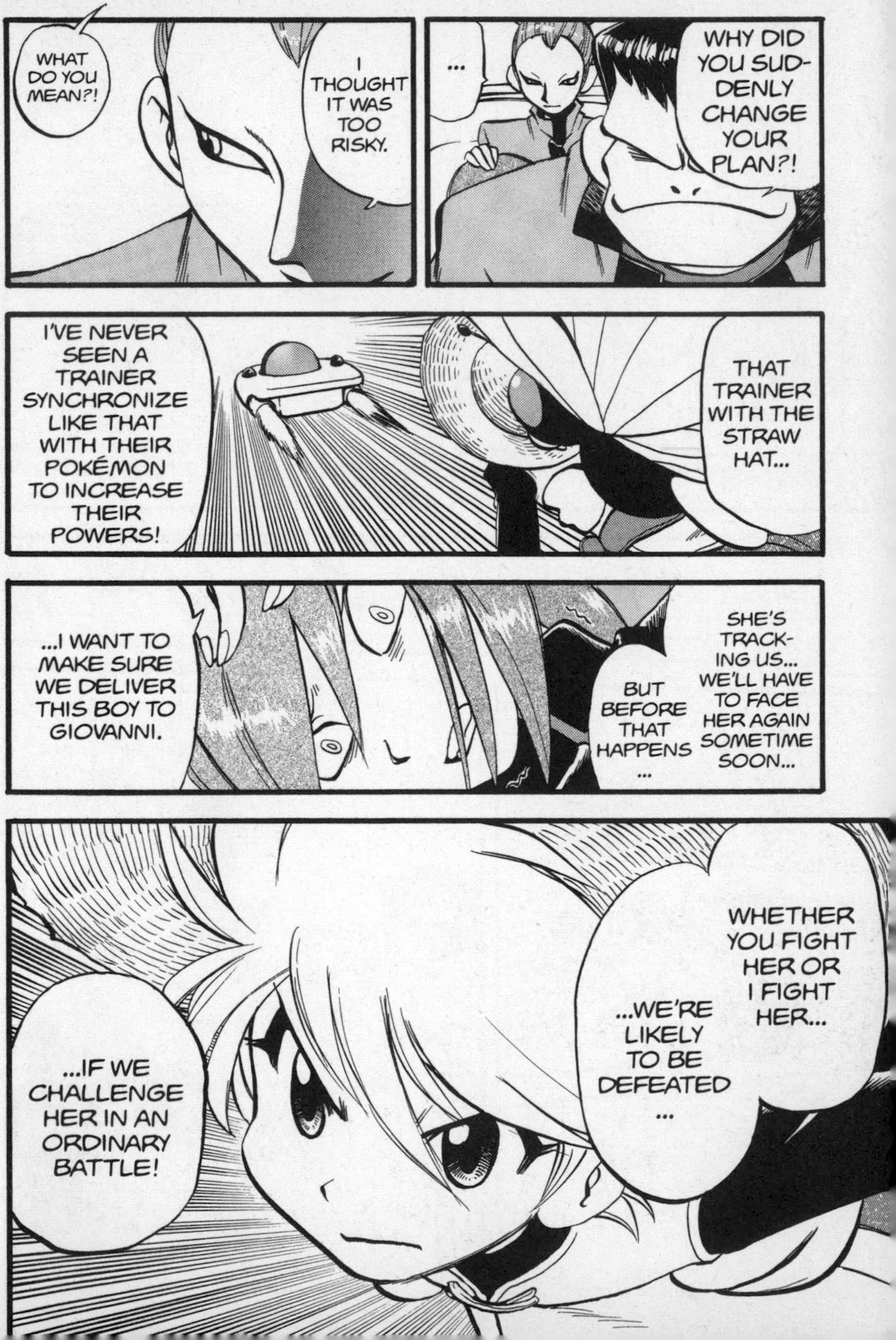
WHY DID YOU SUDDENLY CHANGE YOUR PLAN?!
...
I THOUGHT IT WAS TOO RISKY.
WHAT DO YOU MEAN?!
THAT TRAINER WITH THE STRAW HAT...
I'VE NEVER SEEN A TRAINER SYNCHRONIZE LIKE THAT WITH THEIR POKÉMON TO INCREASE THEIR POWERS!
SHE'S TRACKING US... WE'LL HAVE TO FACE HER AGAIN SOMETIME SOON...
BUT BEFORE THAT HAPPENS...
...I WANT TO MAKE SURE WE DELIVER THIS BOY TO GIOVANNI.
WHETHER YOU FIGHT HER OR I FIGHT HER...
...WE'RE LIKELY TO BE DEFEATED...
...IF WE CHALLENGE HER IN AN ORDINARY BATTLE!

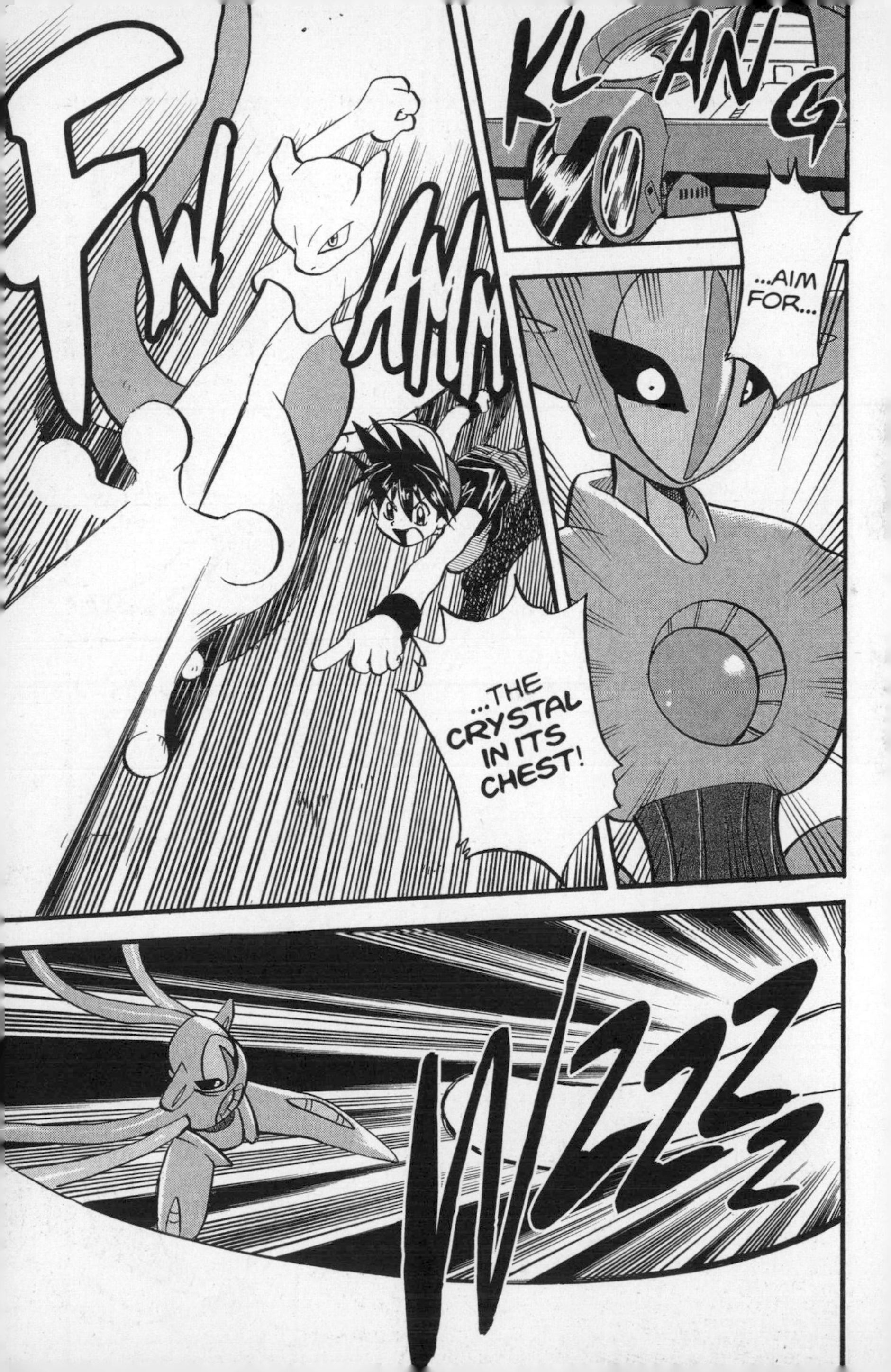
KLANG
...AIM FOR...
...THE CRYSTAL IN ITS CHEST!
FWAMM
WZZZ

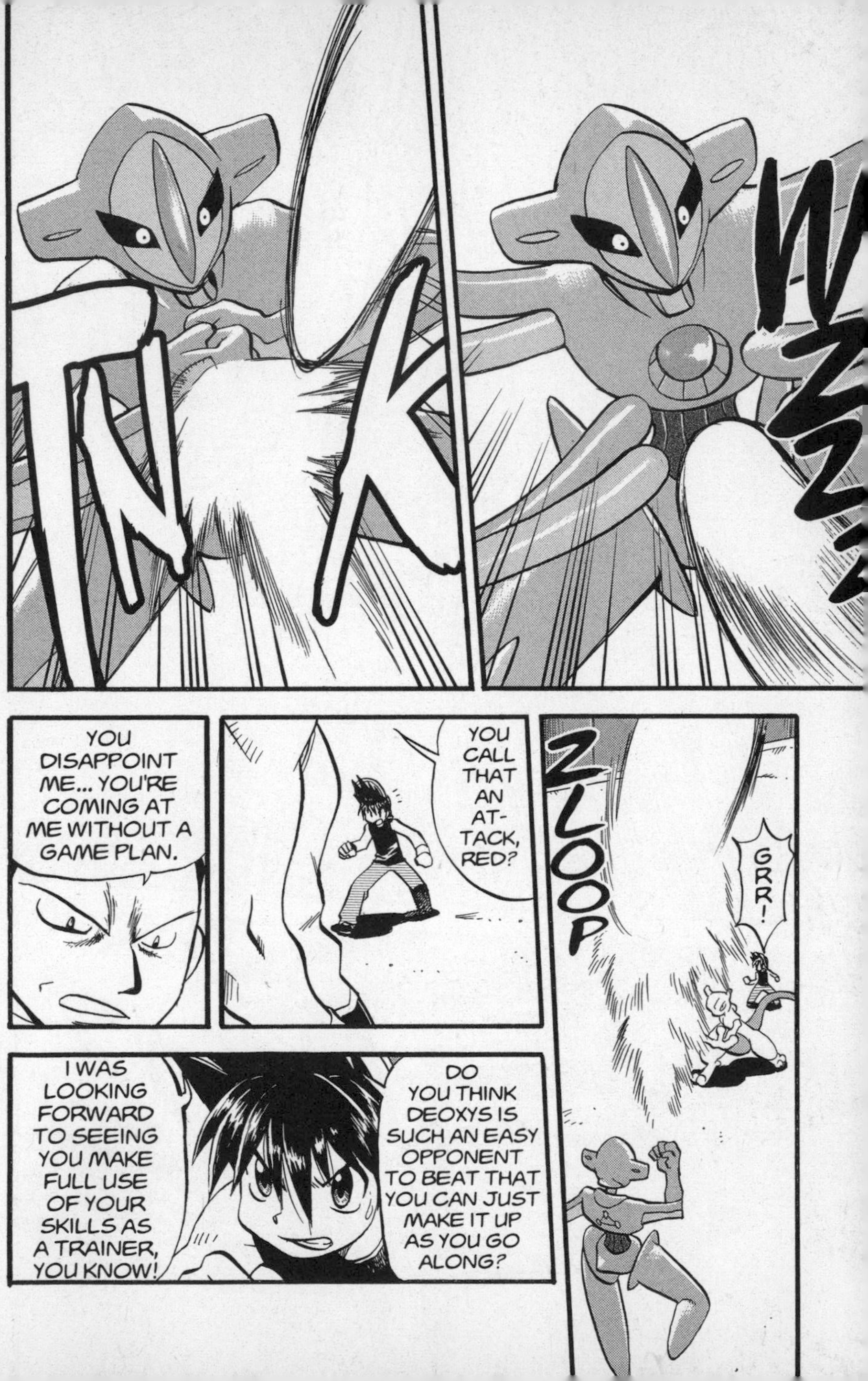
ZLOOP
GRR!
YOU CALL THAT AN AT-TACK, RED?
YOU DISAPPOINT ME... YOU'RE COMING AT ME WITHOUT A GAME PLAN.
DO YOU THINK DEOXYS IS SUCH AN EASY OPPONENT TO BEAT THAT YOU CAN JUST MAKE IT UP AS YOU GO ALONG?
I WAS LOOKING FORWARD TO SEEING YOU MAKE FULL USE OF YOUR SKILLS AS A TRAINER, YOU KNOW!

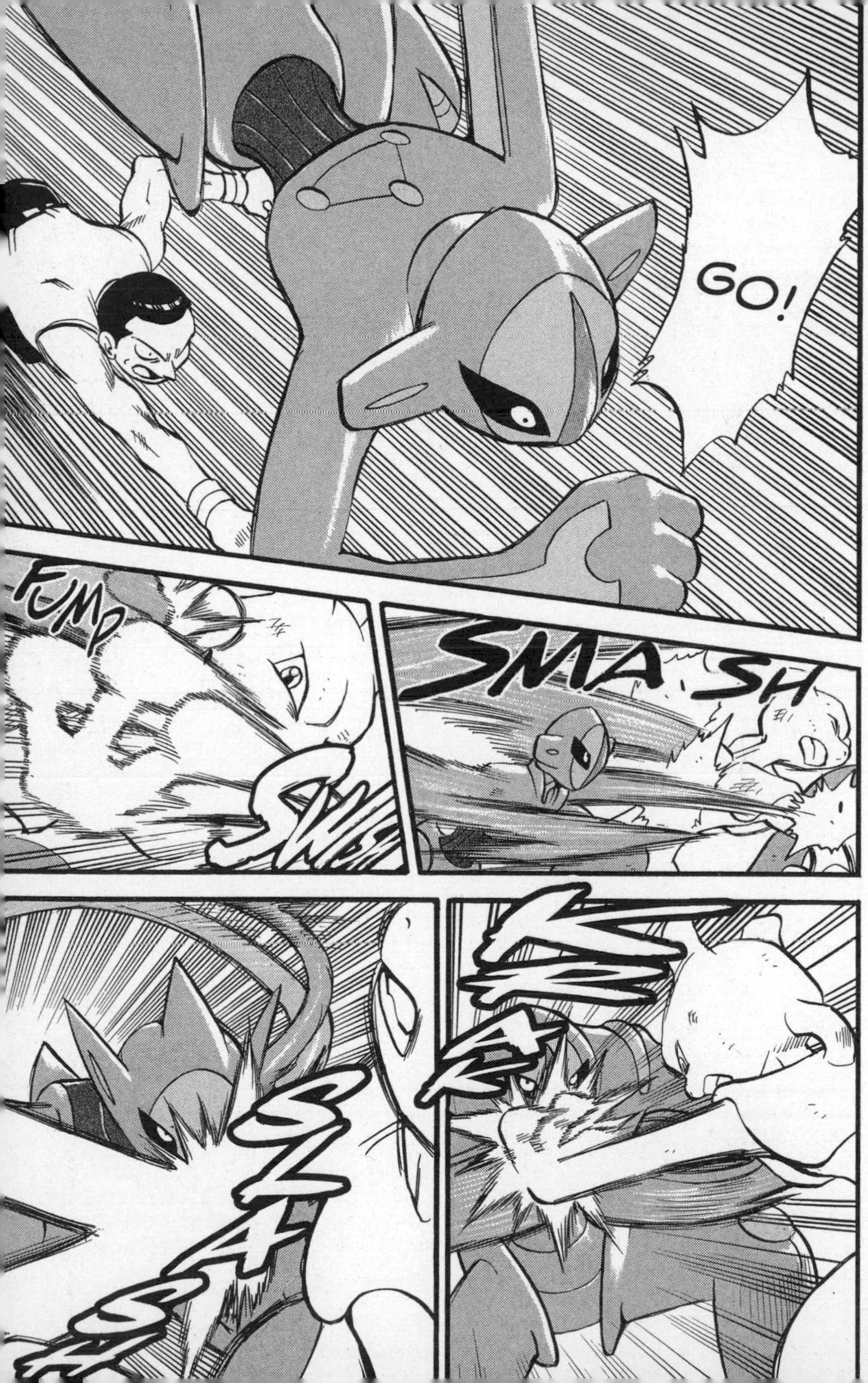
GO!
SMASH
FUMP

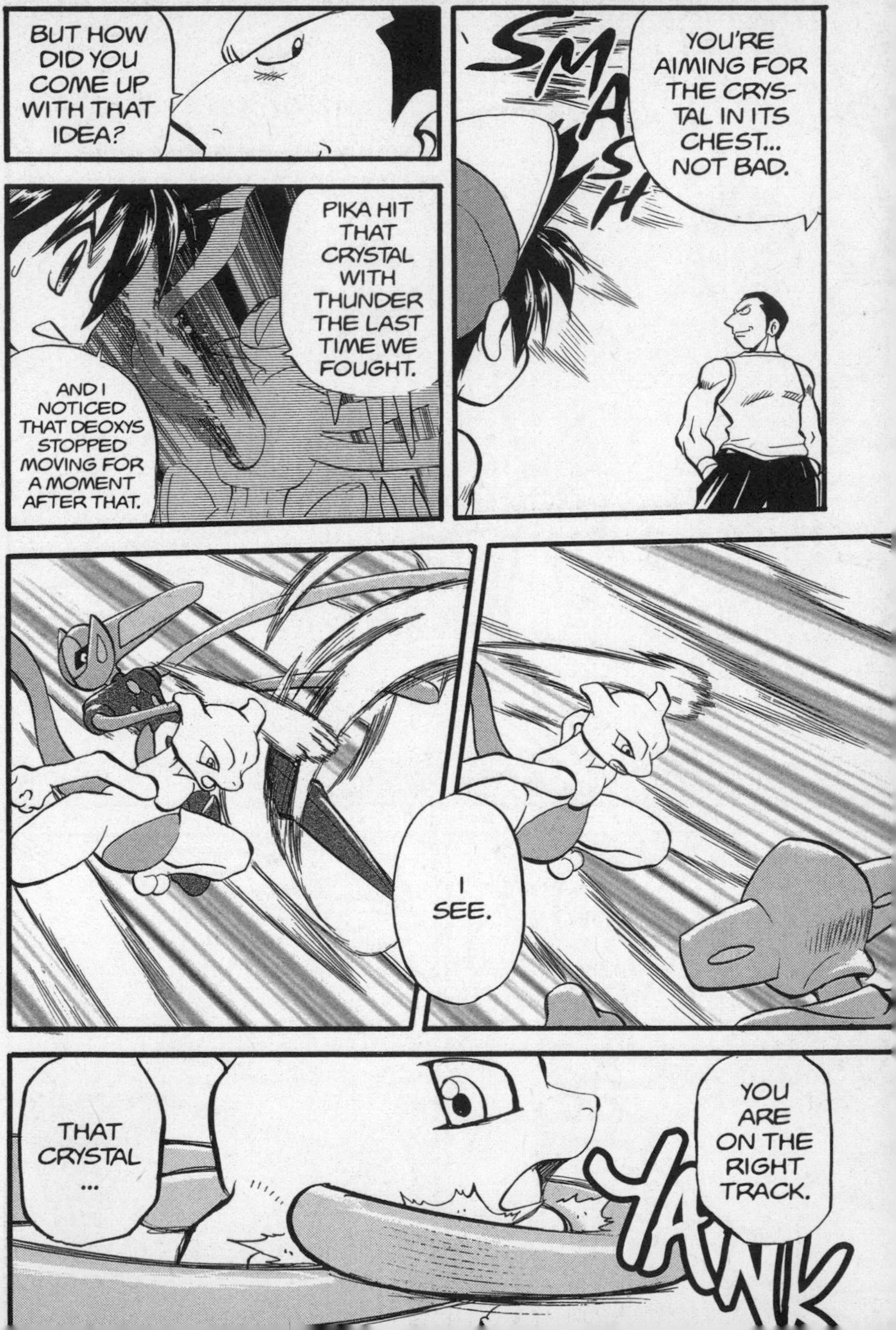
SMASH
YOU'RE AIMING FOR THE CRYS-TAL IN ITS CHEST... NOT BAD.
BUT HOW DID YOU COME UP WITH THAT IDEA?
PIKA HIT THAT CRYSTAL WITH THUNDER THE LAST TIME WE FOUGHT.
AND I NOTICED THAT DEOXYS STOPPED MOVING FOR A MOMENT AFTER THAT.
I SEE.
YOU ARE ON THE RIGHT TRACK.
YANK
THAT CRYSTAL ...

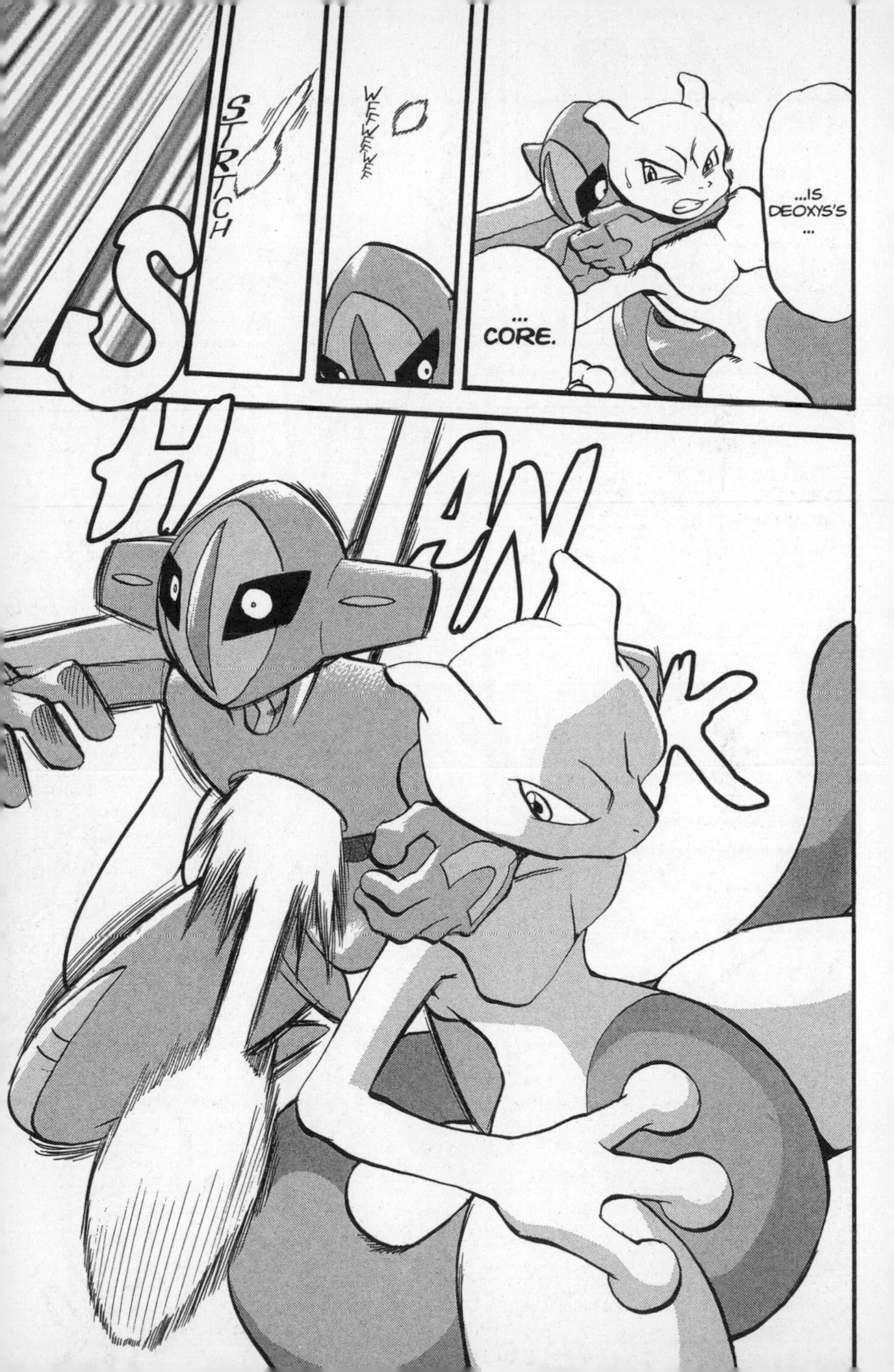
...IS DEOXYS'S ...
... CORE.
WFFWFFWFF
STRTCH
SHWANK

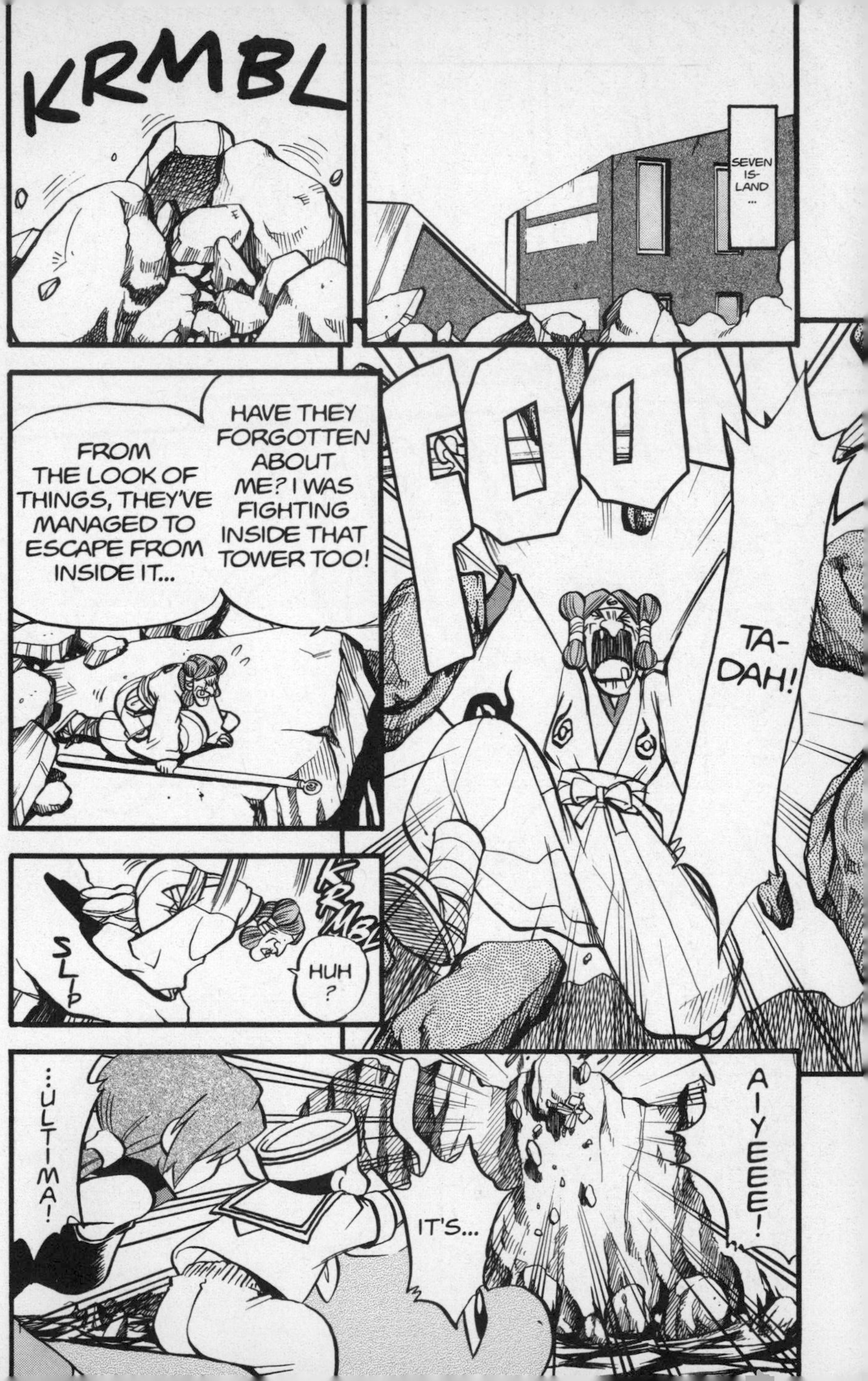
SEVEN ISLAND...
KRMBL
FOO
TA-DAH!
HAVE THEY FORGOTTEN ABOUT ME? I WAS FIGHTING INSIDE THAT TOWER TOO!
FROM THE LOOK OF THINGS, THEY'VE MANAGED TO ESCAPE FROM INSIDE IT...
KRMBL
HUH?
SLIP
AIYEEE!
IT'S...
...ULTIMA!

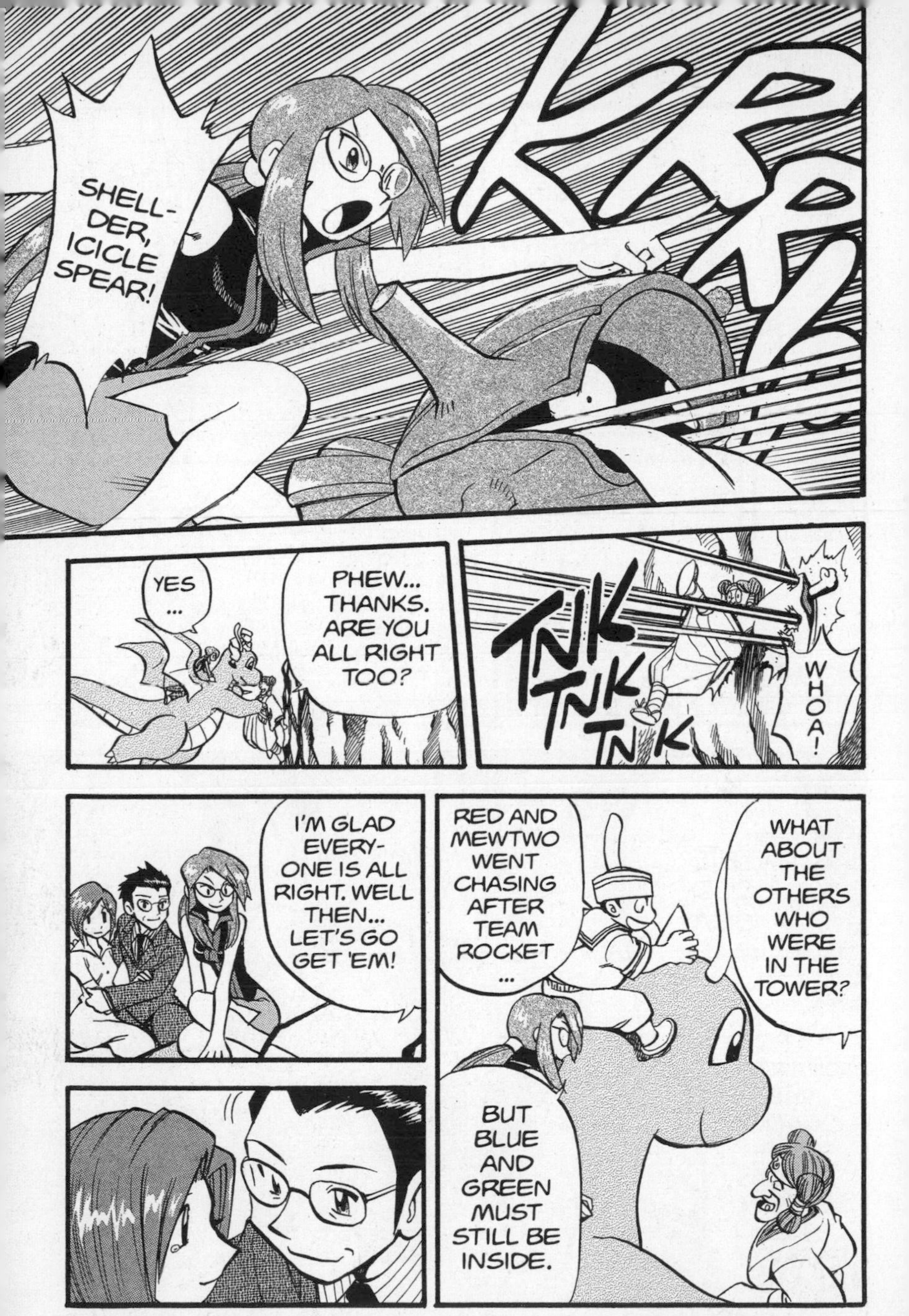
SHELLDER, ICICLE SPEAR!
TNK TNK TNK
WHOA!
PHEW... THANKS. ARE YOU ALL RIGHT TOO?
YES...
WHAT ABOUT THE OTHERS WHO WERE IN THE TOWER?
RED AND MEWTWO WENT CHASING AFTER TEAM ROCKET...
BUT BLUE AND GREEN MUST STILL BE INSIDE.
I'M GLAD EVERYONE IS ALL RIGHT. WELL THEN... LET'S GO GET 'EM!

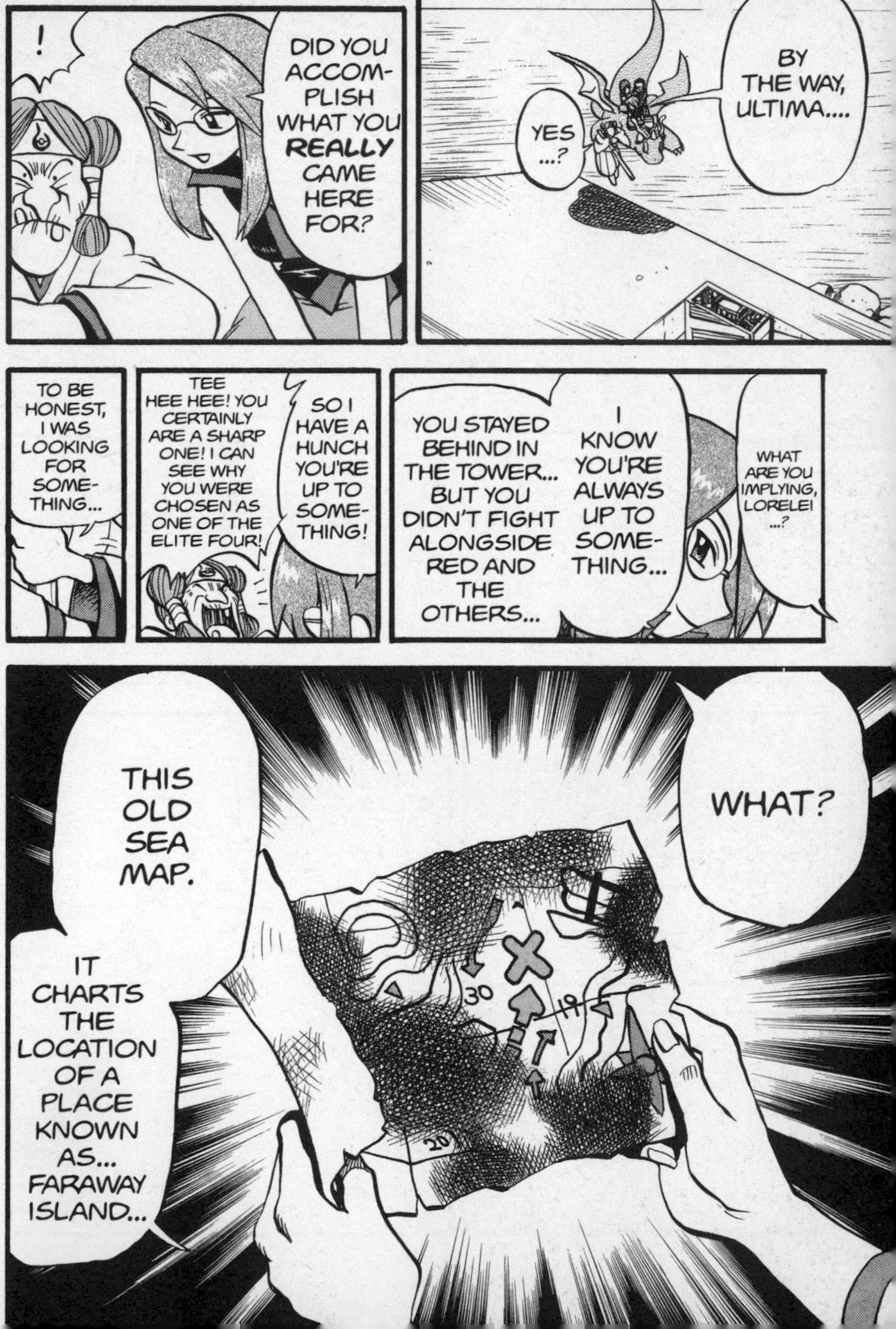
BY THE WAY, ULTIMA....
YES ...?
DID YOU ACCOMPLISH WHAT YOU **REALLY** CAME HERE FOR?
!
WHAT ARE YOU IMPLYING, LORELEI ...?
I KNOW YOU'RE ALWAYS UP TO SOMETHING...
YOU STAYED BEHIND IN THE TOWER... BUT YOU DIDN'T FIGHT ALONGSIDE RED AND THE OTHERS...
SO I HAVE A HUNCH YOU'RE UP TO SOMETHING!
TEE HEE HEE! YOU CERTAINLY ARE A SHARP ONE! I CAN SEE WHY YOU WERE CHOSEN AS ONE OF THE ELITE FOUR!
TO BE HONEST, I WAS LOOKING FOR SOMETHING...
WHAT?
THIS OLD SEA MAP.
IT CHARTS THE LOCATION OF A PLACE KNOWN AS... FARAWAY ISLAND...
30
19
20

●Adventure 293●
Down-for-the-Count Deoxys

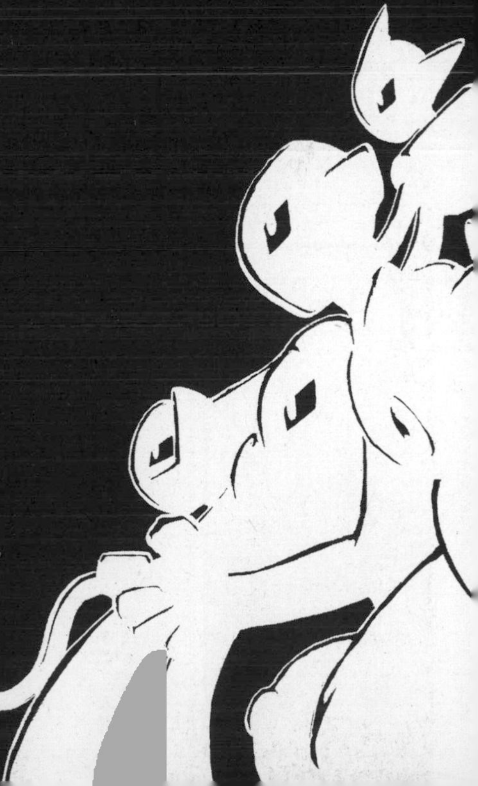

POKÉMON ADVENTURES
FIRERED & LEAFGREEN
The Fifth Chapter

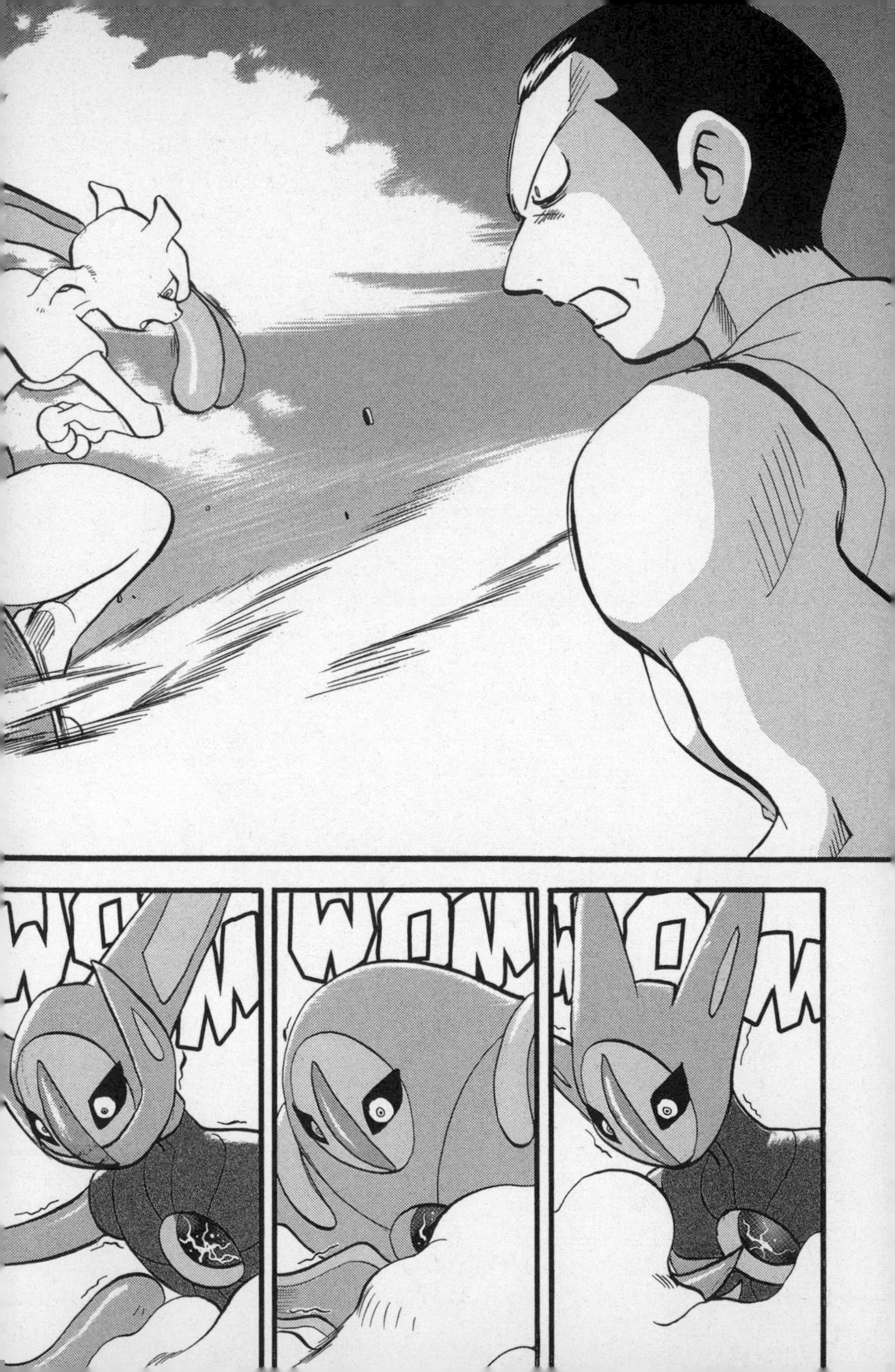
WOM
WOM
WOM

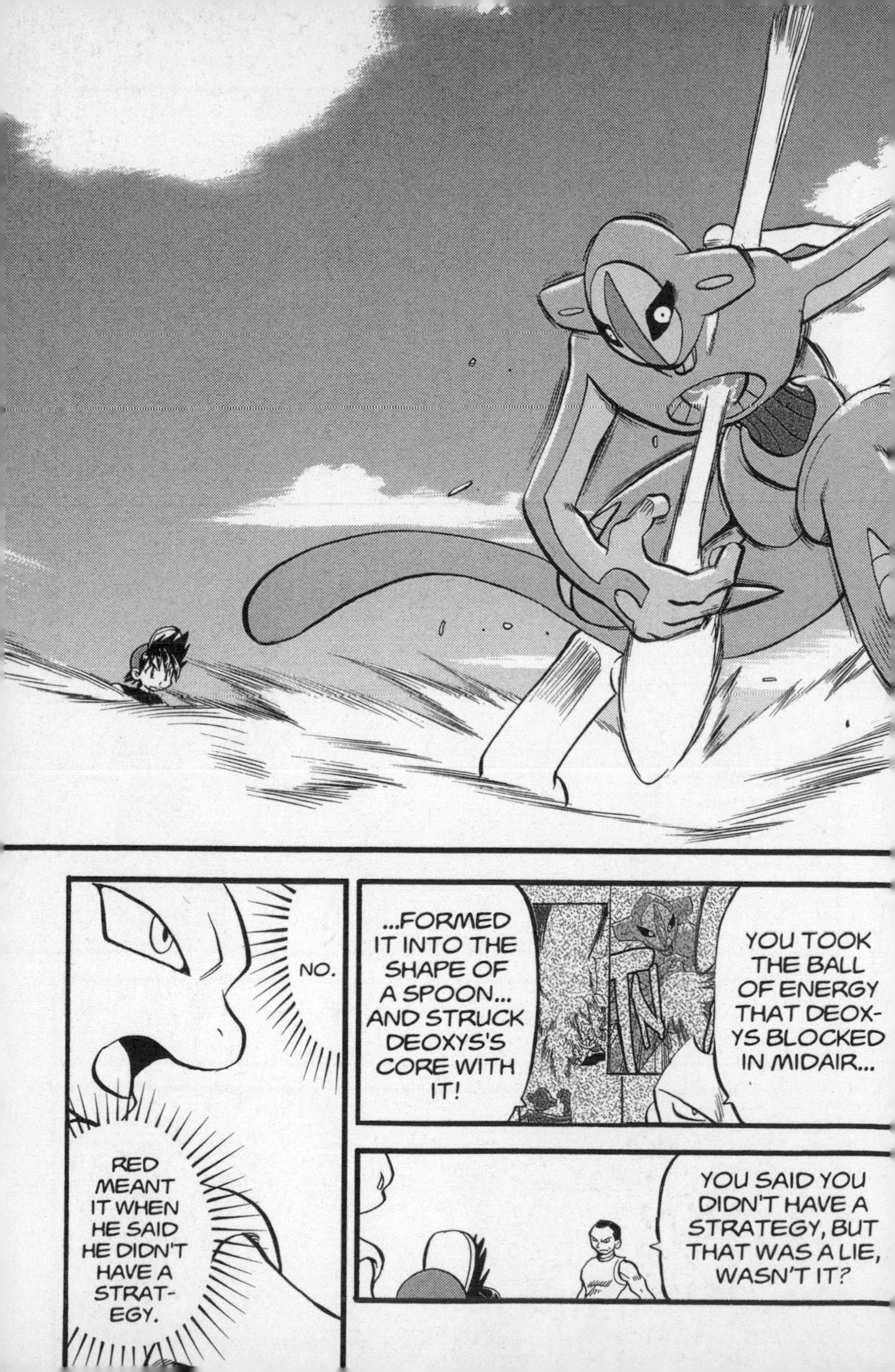
YOU TOOK THE BALL OF ENERGY THAT DEOXYS BLOCKED IN MIDAIR...
...FORMED IT INTO THE SHAPE OF A SPOON... AND STRUCK DEOXYS'S CORE WITH IT!
YOU SAID YOU DIDN'T HAVE A STRATEGY, BUT THAT WAS A LIE, WASN'T IT?
NO.
RED MEANT IT WHEN HE SAID HE DIDN'T HAVE A STRATEGY.

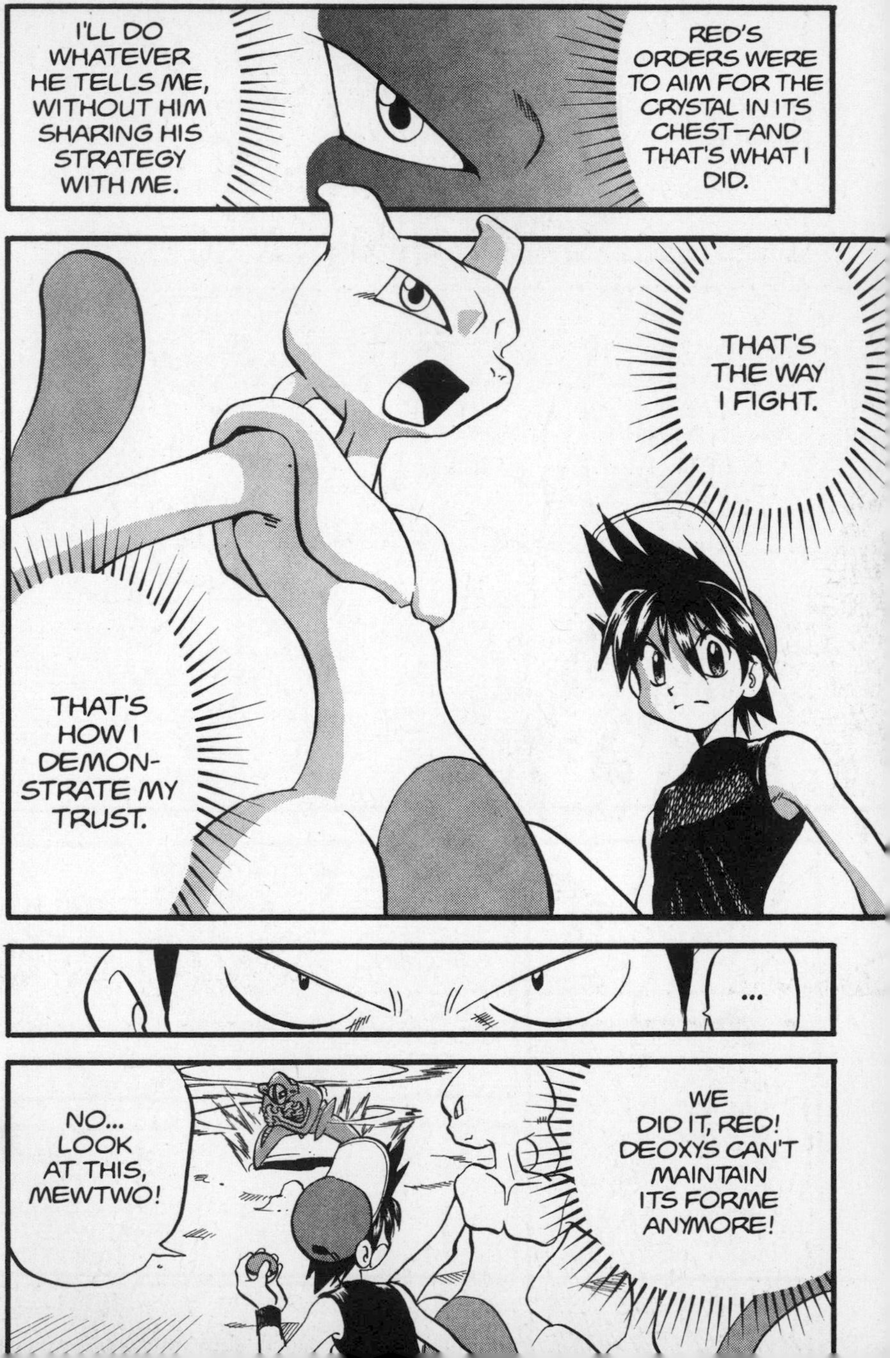
RED'S ORDERS WERE TO AIM FOR THE CRYSTAL IN ITS CHEST—AND THAT'S WHAT I DID.
I'LL DO WHATEVER HE TELLS ME, WITHOUT HIM SHARING HIS STRATEGY WITH ME.
THAT'S THE WAY I FIGHT.
THAT'S HOW I DEMON-STRATE MY TRUST.
...
WE DID IT, RED! DEOXYS CAN'T MAINTAIN ITS FORME ANYMORE!
NO... LOOK AT THIS, MEWTWO!

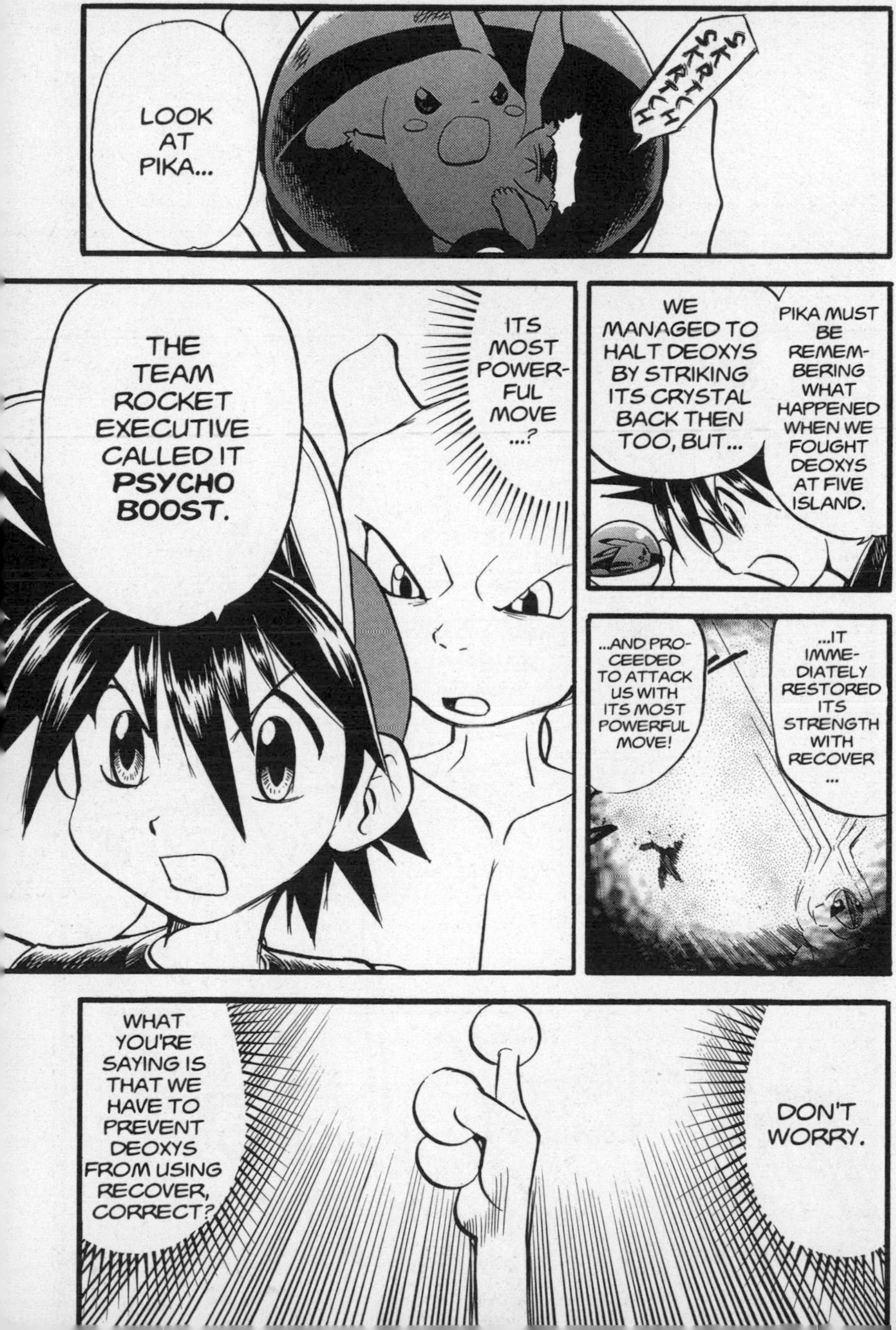
SKRTCH SKRTCH
LOOK AT PIKA...
PIKA MUST BE REMEMBERING WHAT HAPPENED WHEN WE FOUGHT DEOXYS AT FIVE ISLAND.
WE MANAGED TO HALT DEOXYS BY STRIKING ITS CRYSTAL BACK THEN TOO, BUT...
...IT IMMEDIATELY RESTORED ITS STRENGTH WITH RECOVER...
...AND PROCEEDED TO ATTACK US WITH ITS MOST POWERFUL MOVE!
ITS MOST POWERFUL MOVE...?
THE TEAM ROCKET EXECUTIVE CALLED IT **PSYCHO BOOST.**
DON'T WORRY.
WHAT YOU'RE SAYING IS THAT WE HAVE TO PREVENT DEOXYS FROM USING RECOVER, CORRECT?

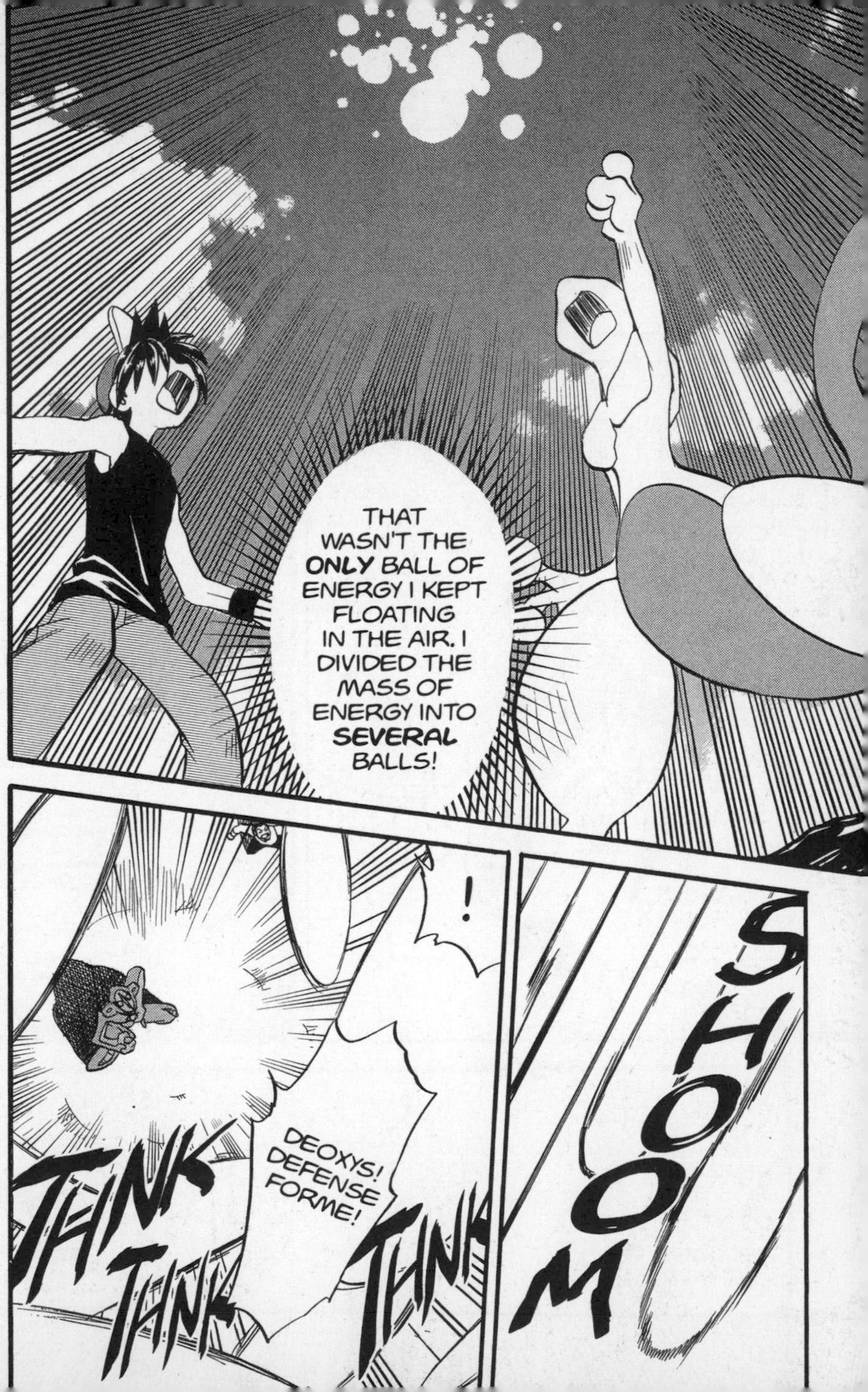
THAT WASN'T THE **ONLY** BALL OF ENERGY I KEPT FLOATING IN THE AIR. I DIVIDED THE MASS OF ENERGY INTO **SEVERAL** BALLS!
SHOOOM
!
DEOXYS! DEFENSE FORME!
THNK
THNK
THNK
THNK

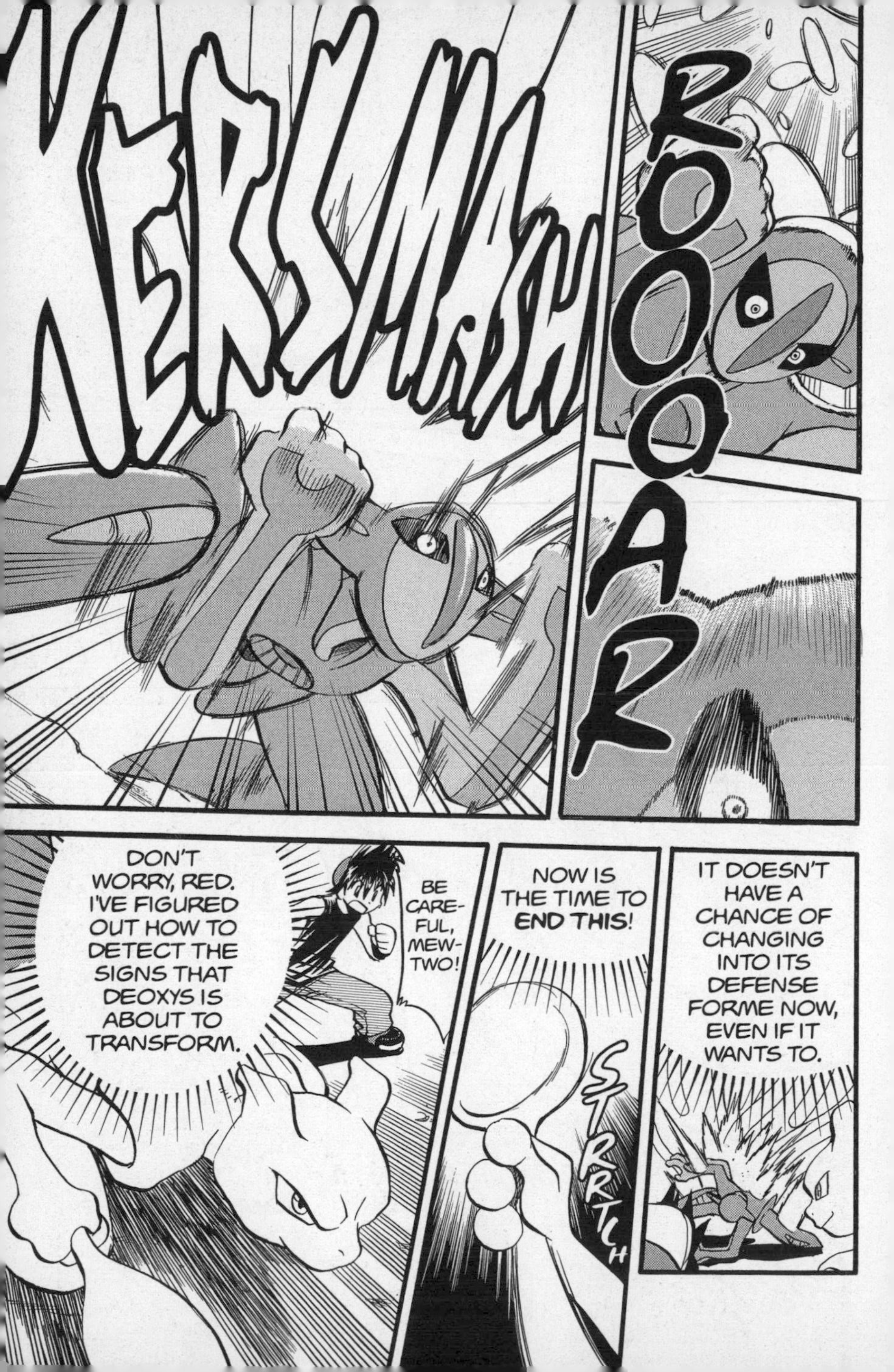

ROOOOAR
KERSMASH
IT DOESN'T HAVE A CHANCE OF CHANGING INTO ITS DEFENSE FORME NOW, EVEN IF IT WANTS TO.
NOW IS THE TIME TO **END THIS!**
STRRRTCH
BE CAREFUL, MEW-TWO!
DON'T WORRY, RED. I'VE FIGURED OUT HOW TO DETECT THE SIGNS THAT DEOXYS IS ABOUT TO TRANSFORM.

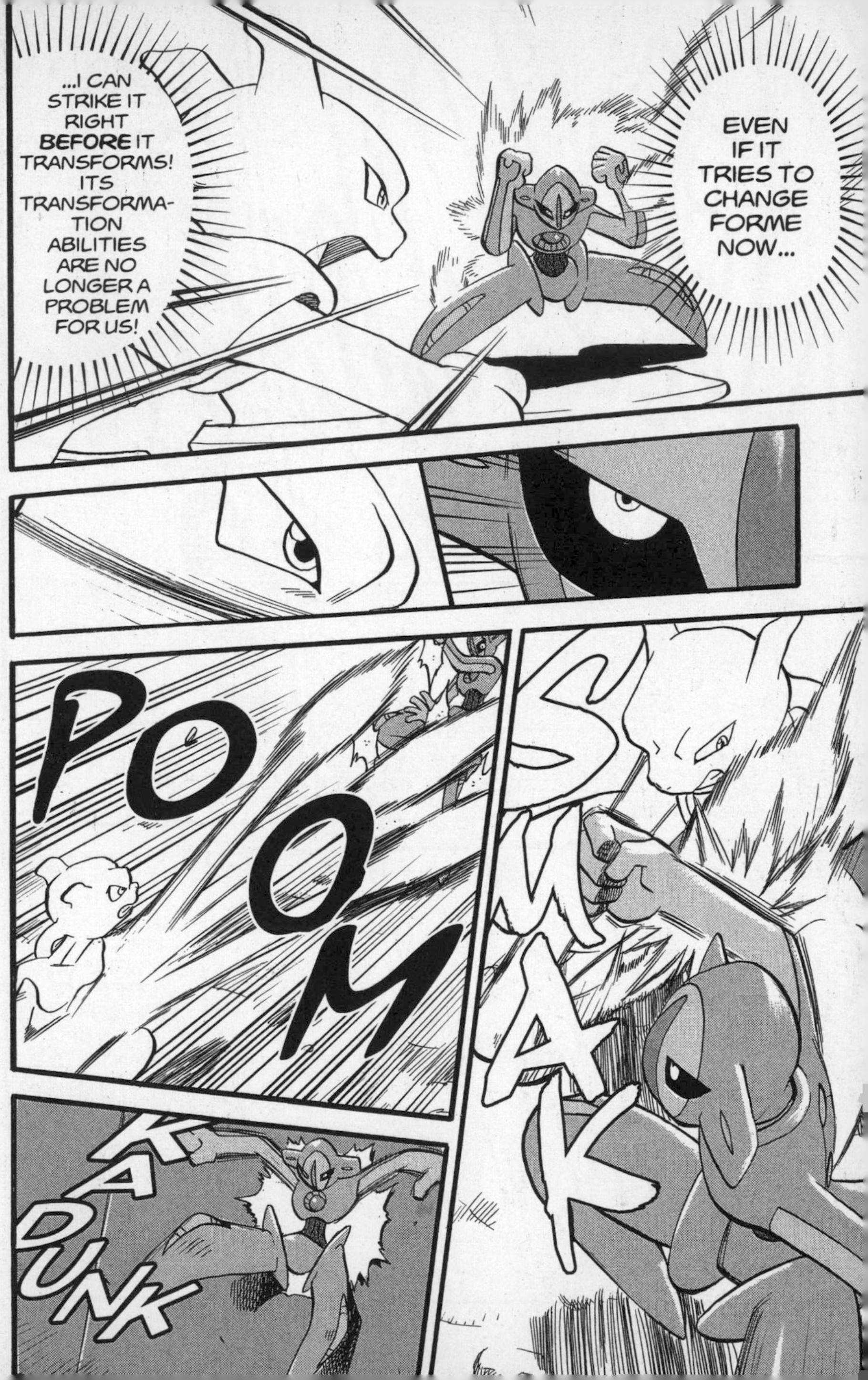
EVEN IF IT TRIES TO CHANGE FORME NOW...
...I CAN STRIKE IT RIGHT **BEFORE** IT TRANSFORMS! ITS TRANSFORMATION ABILITIES ARE NO LONGER A PROBLEM FOR US!
SMAK
POOM
KADUNK

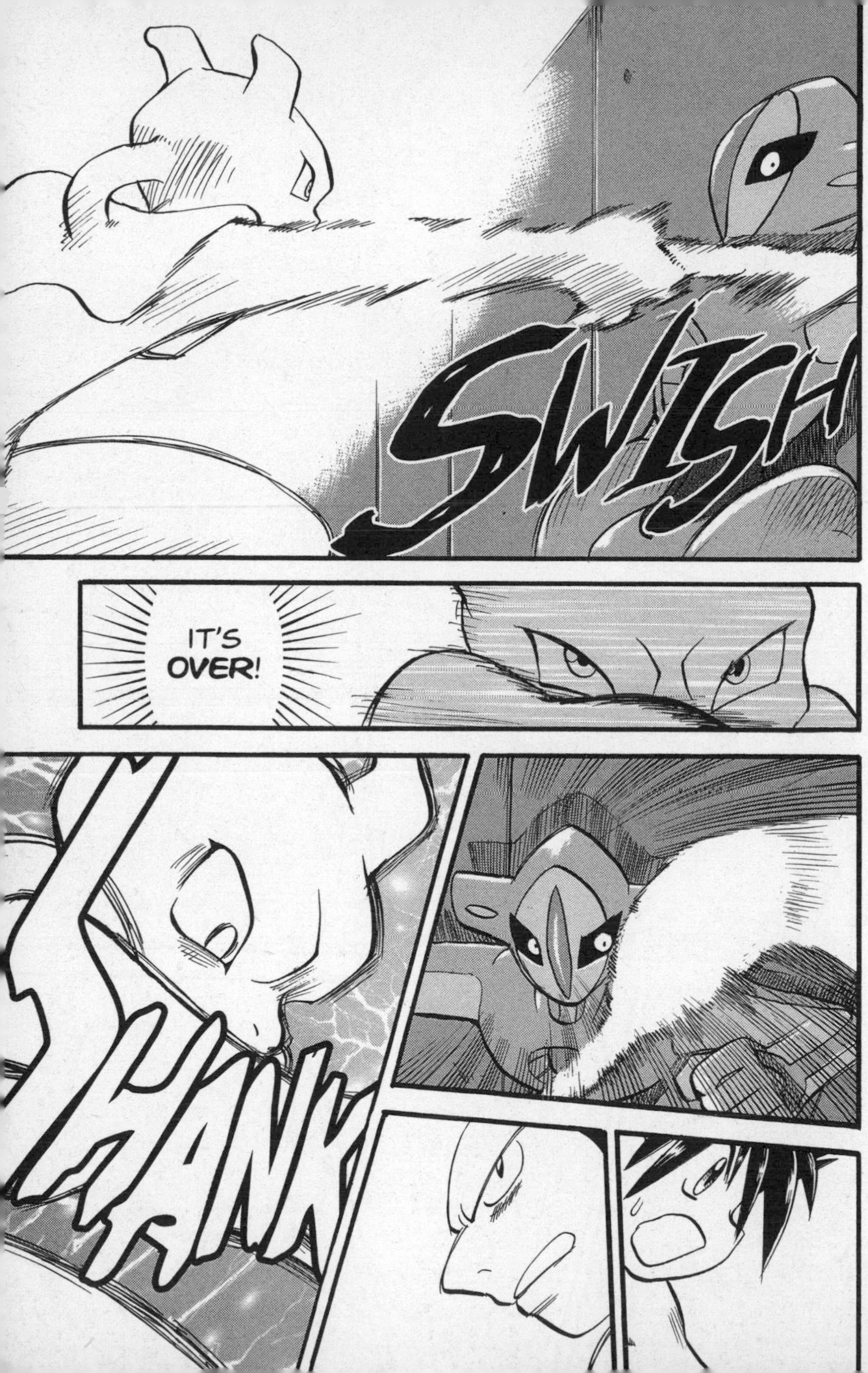
SWISH
IT'S OVER!

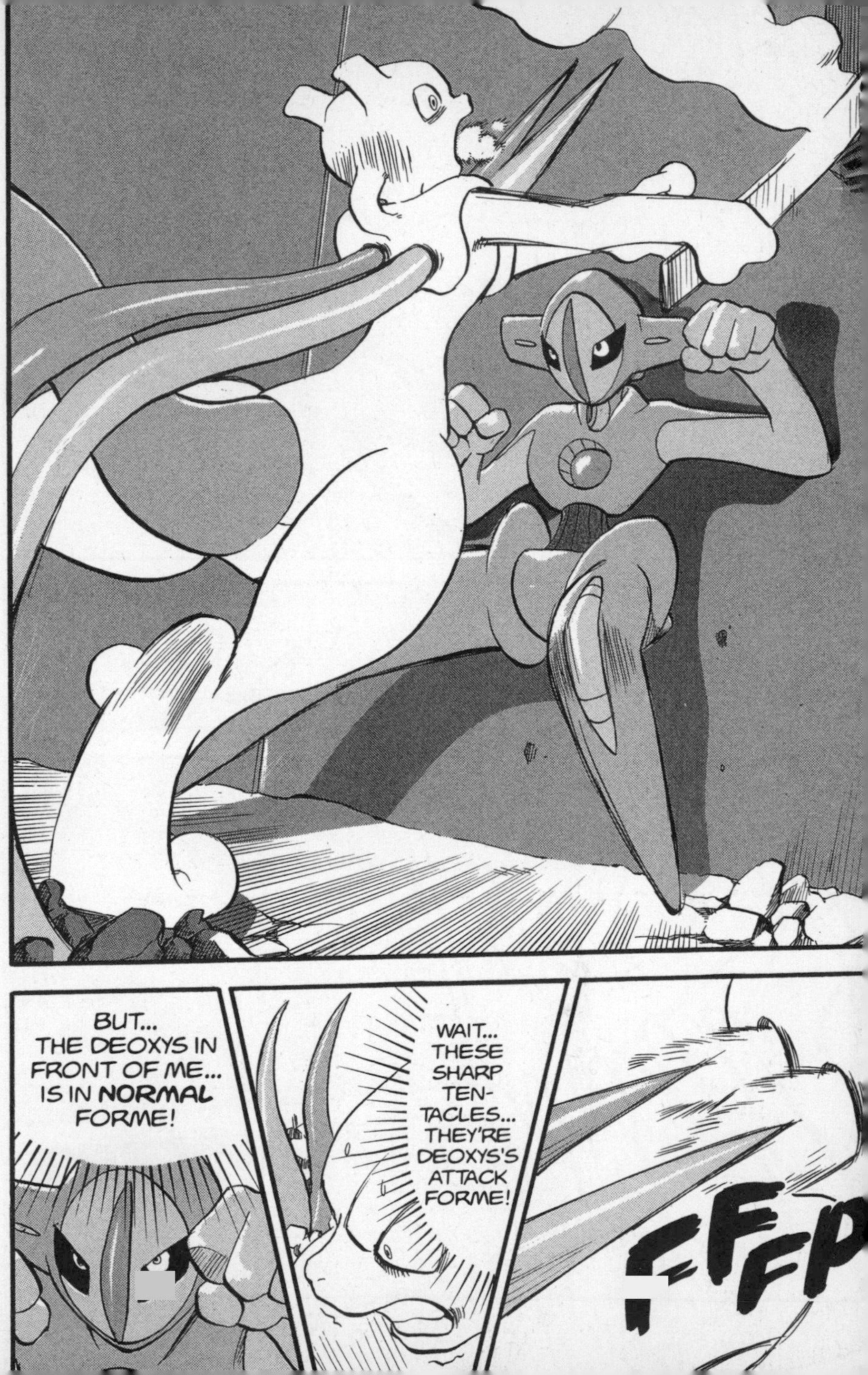
FFFP
WAIT... THESE SHARP TEN-TACLES... THEY'RE DEOXYS'S ATTACK FORME!
BUT... THE DEOXYS IN FRONT OF ME... IS IN **NORMAL** FORME!

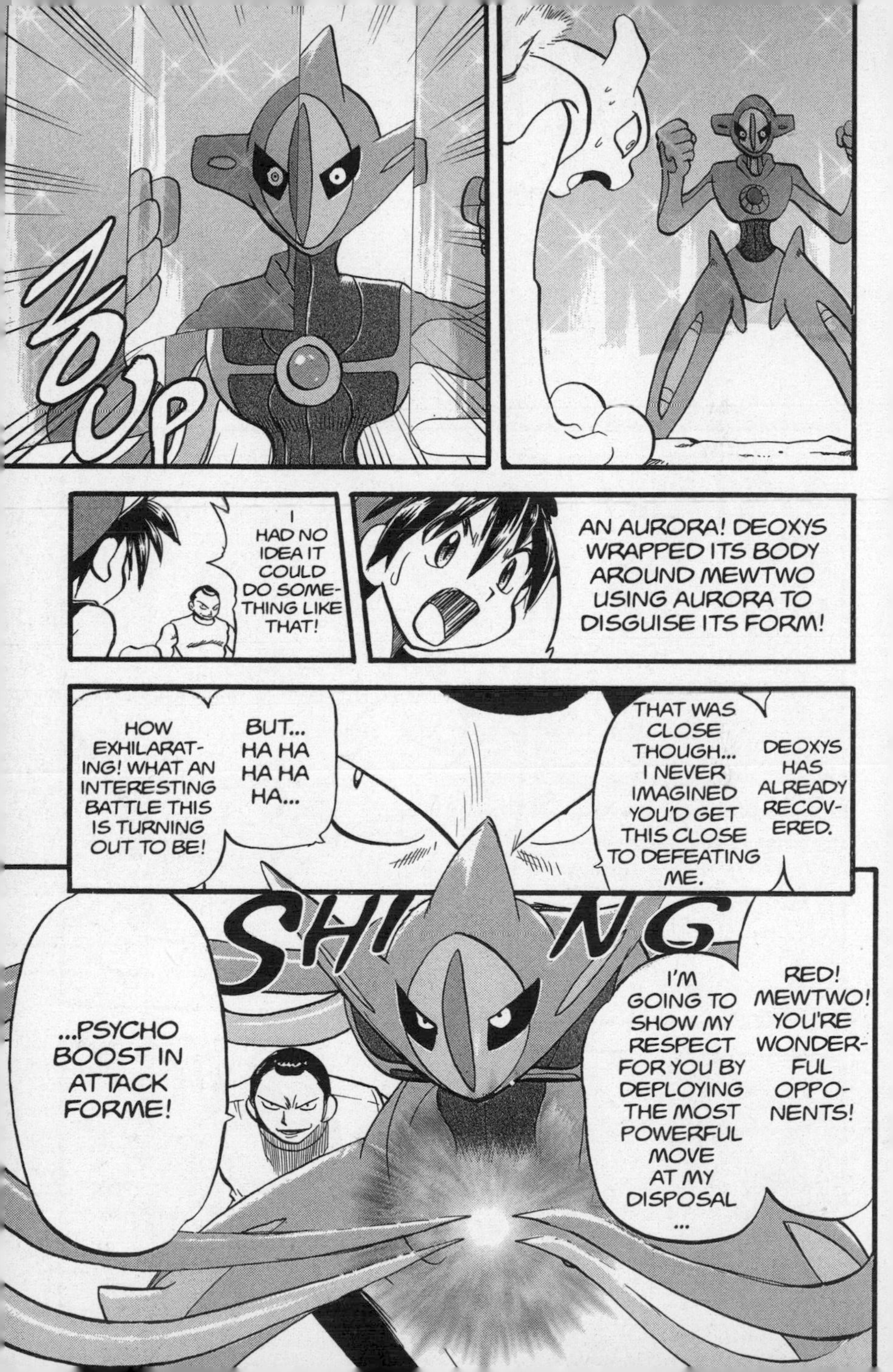
AN AURORA! DEOXYS WRAPPED ITS BODY AROUND MEWTWO USING AURORA TO DISGUISE ITS FORM!
I HAD NO IDEA IT COULD DO SOMETHING LIKE THAT!
DEOXYS HAS ALREADY RECOVERED.
THAT WAS CLOSE THOUGH... I NEVER IMAGINED YOU'D GET THIS CLOSE TO DEFEATING ME.
BUT... HA HA HA HA HA...
HOW EXHILARATING! WHAT AN INTERESTING BATTLE THIS IS TURNING OUT TO BE!
SHING
RED! MEWTWO! YOU'RE WONDERFUL OPPONENTS!
I'M GOING TO SHOW MY RESPECT FOR YOU BY DEPLOYING THE MOST POWERFUL MOVE AT MY DISPOSAL...
...PSYCHO BOOST IN ATTACK FORME!

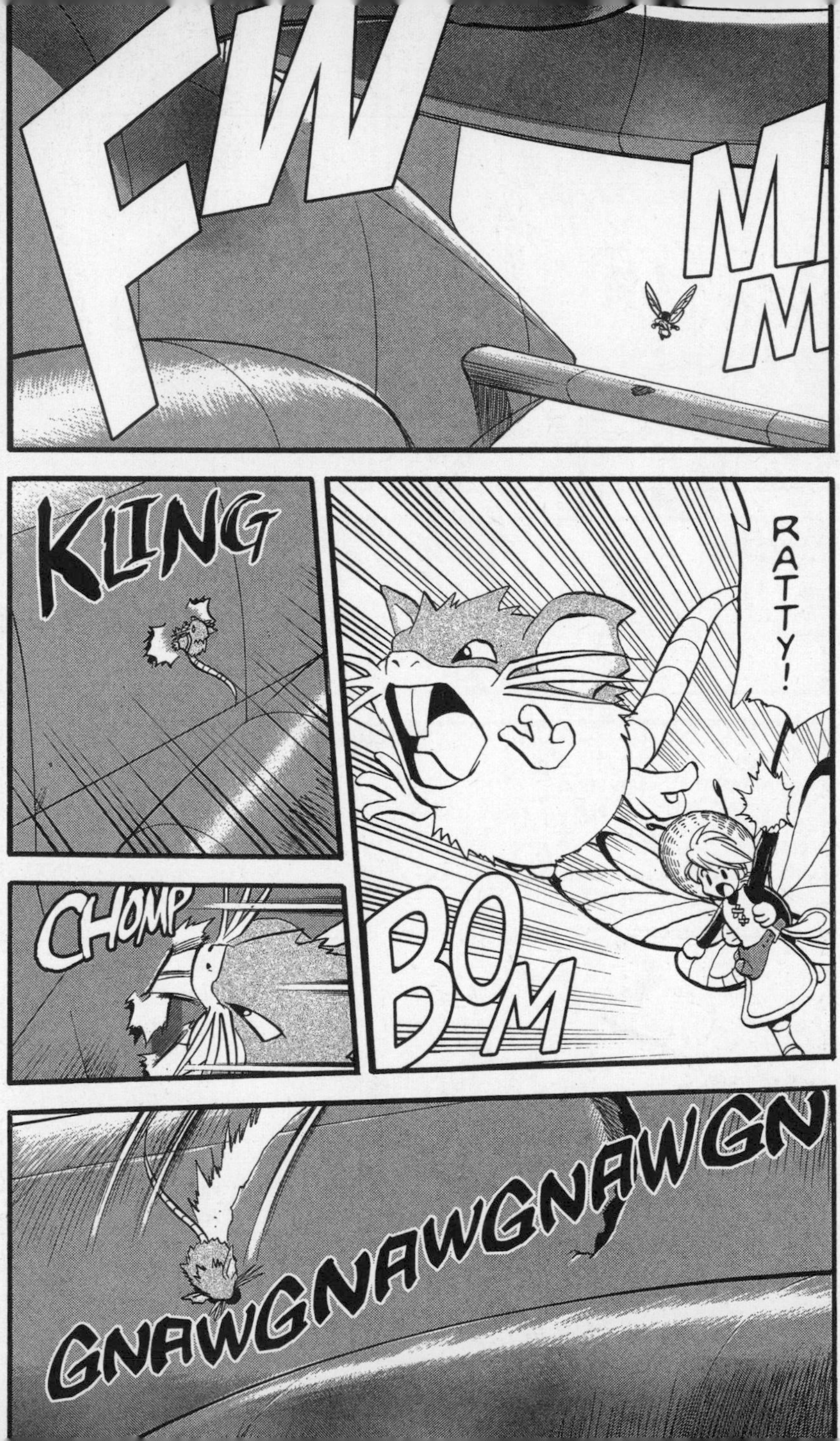
M
M
FW
RATTY!
BOM
KLING
CHOMP
GNAWGNAWGNAWGN

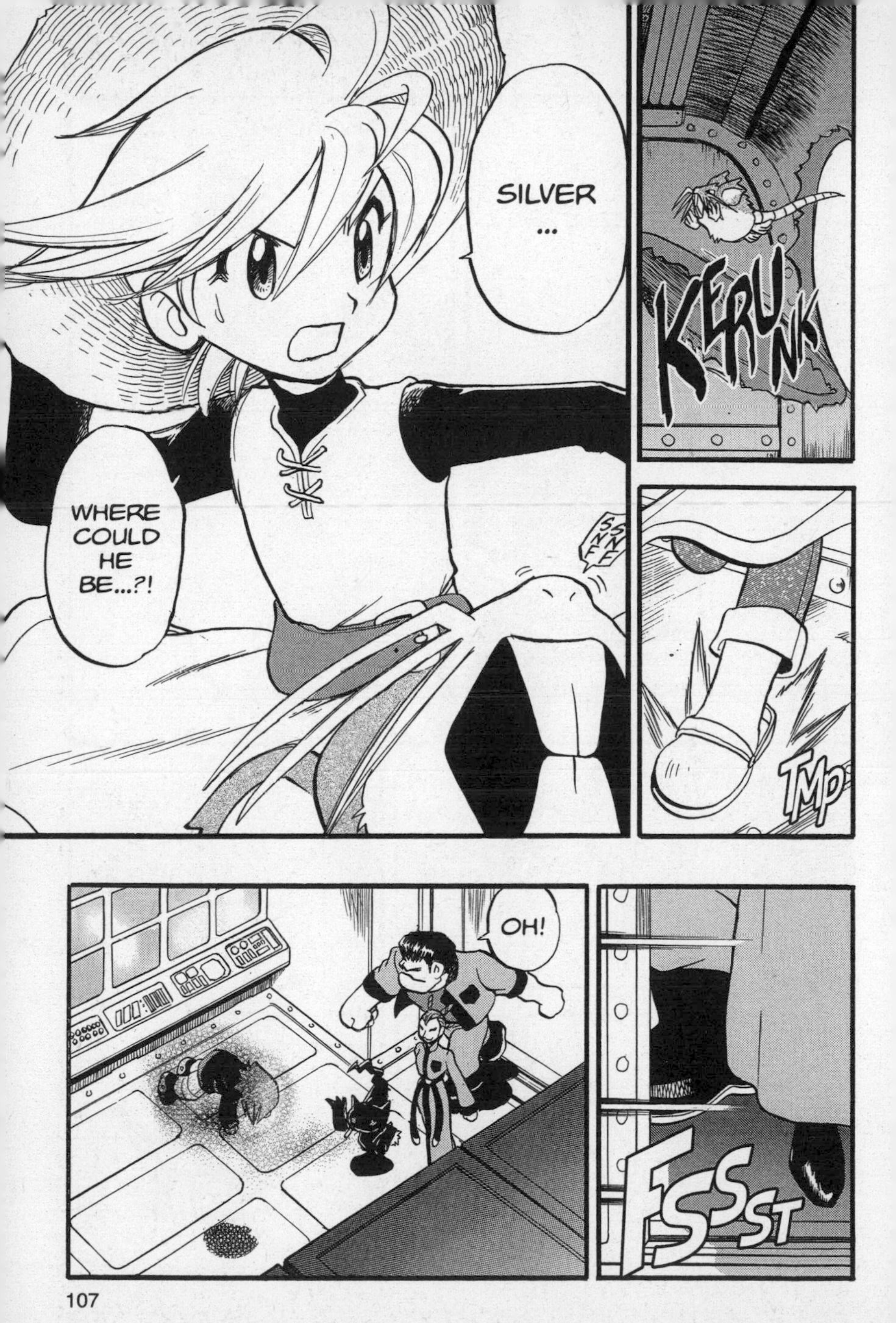
KERUNK
TMP
SILVER ...
SNF SNF
WHERE COULD HE BE...?!
FSSST
OH!

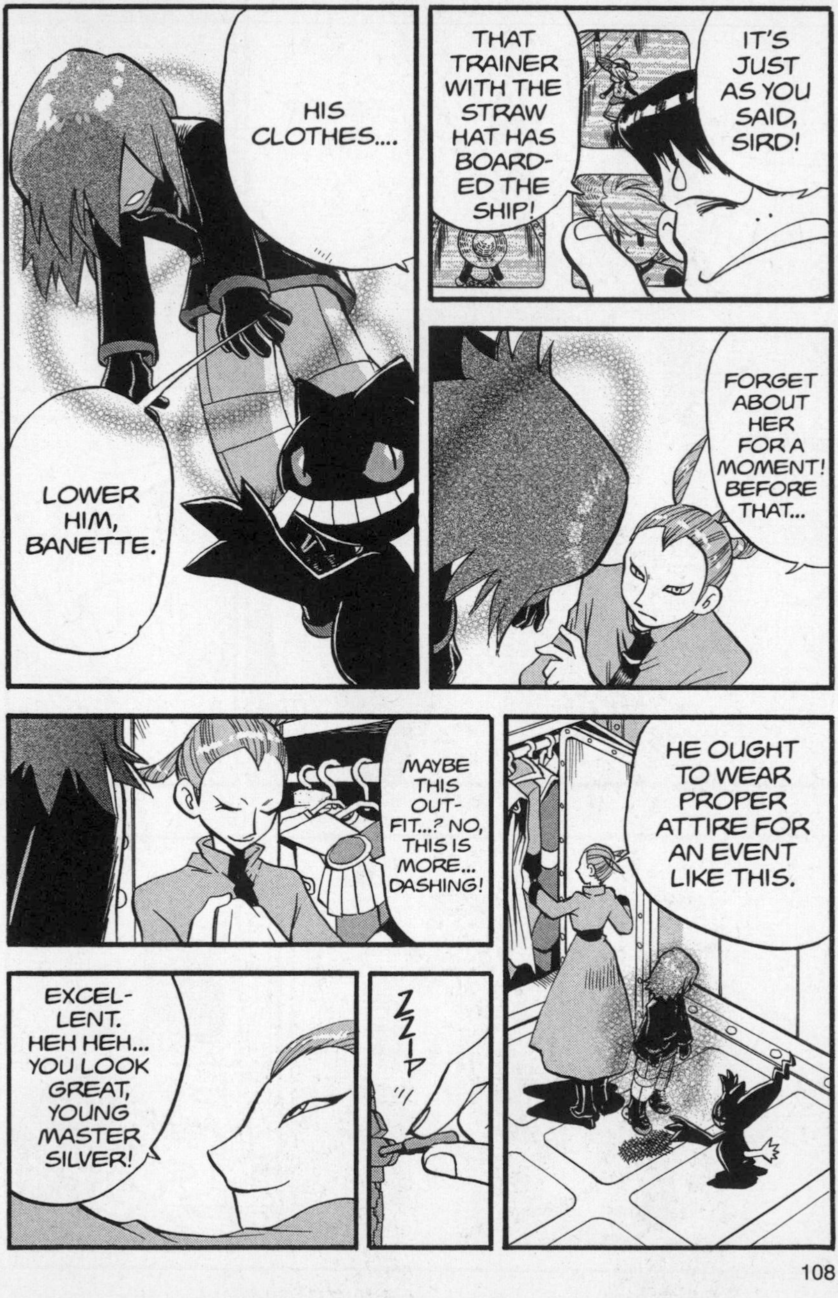
IT'S JUST AS YOU SAID, SIRD!
THAT TRAINER WITH THE STRAW HAT HAS BOARD-ED THE SHIP!
FORGET ABOUT HER FOR A MOMENT! BEFORE THAT...
HIS CLOTHES....
LOWER HIM, BANETTE.
HE OUGHT TO WEAR PROPER ATTIRE FOR AN EVENT LIKE THIS.
MAYBE THIS OUT-FIT...? NO, THIS IS MORE... DASHING!
ZZIP
EXCEL-LENT. HEH HEH... YOU LOOK GREAT, YOUNG MASTER SILVER!

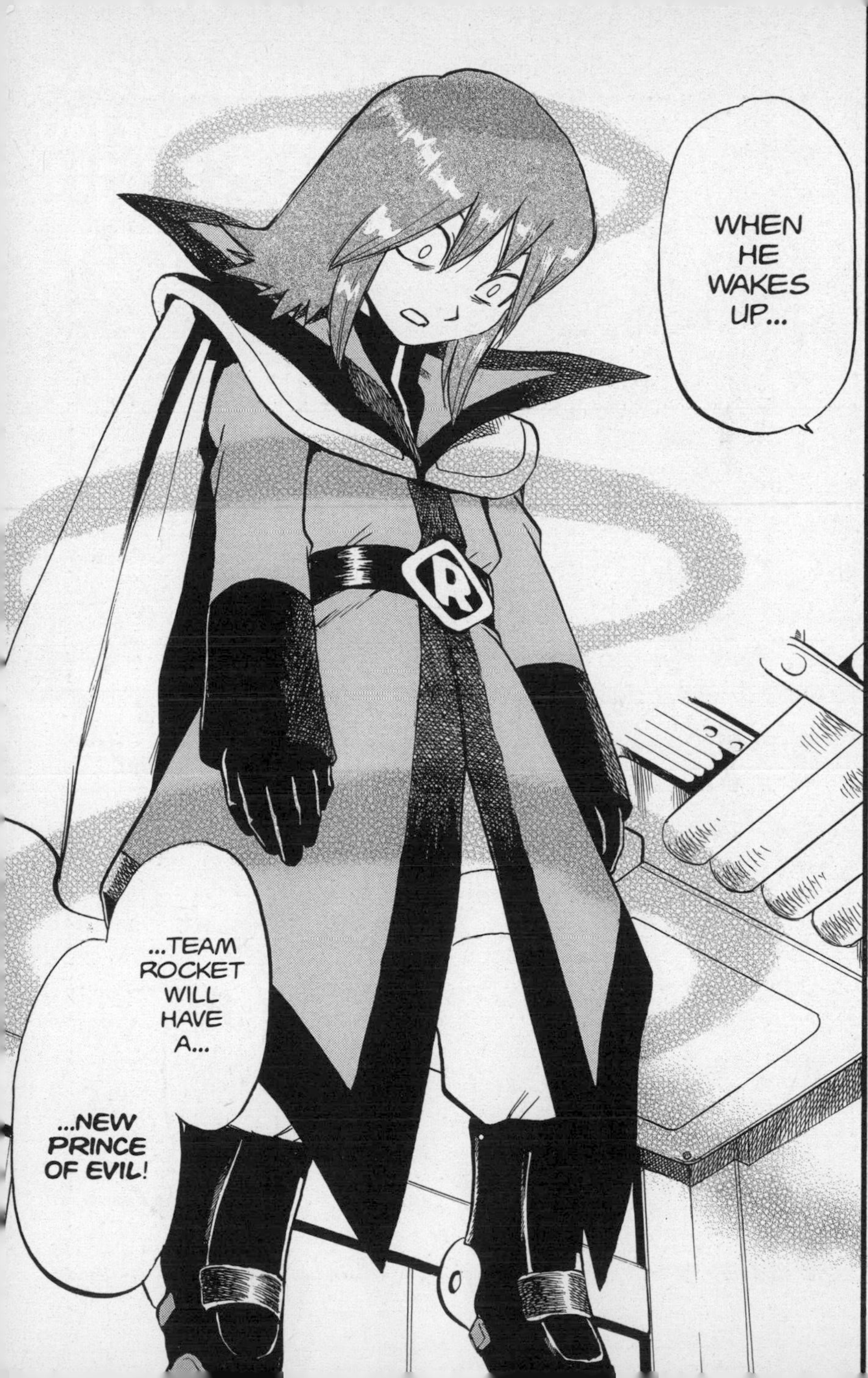
WHEN HE WAKES UP...
...TEAM ROCKET WILL HAVE A...
...NEW PRINCE OF EVIL!

●Adventure 294●
Mewtwo and Mew Too

Pokémon Adventures
FireRed & LeafGreen
The Fifth Chapter

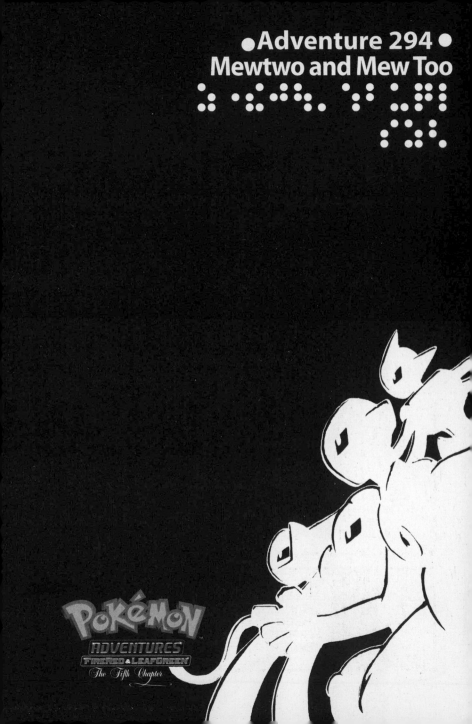

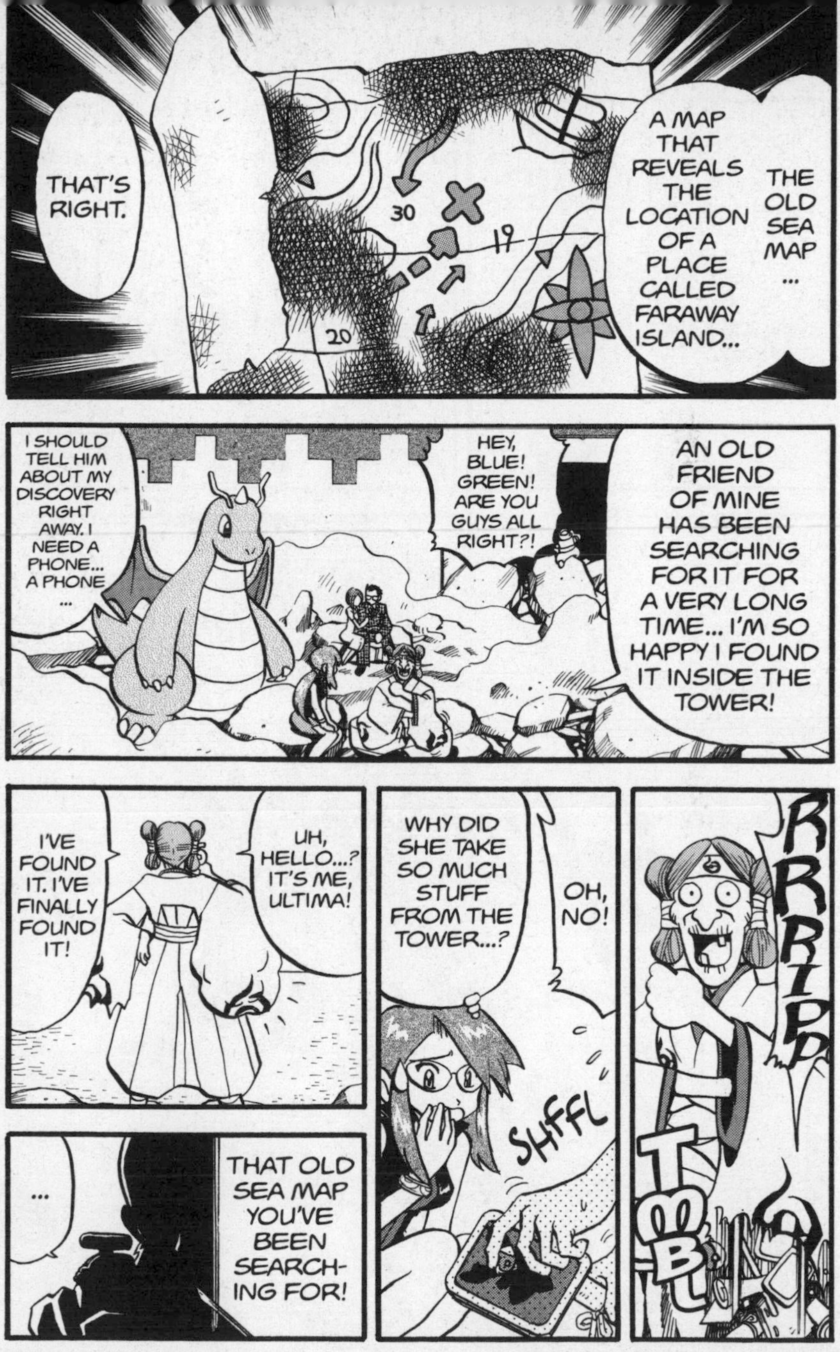

THE OLD SEA MAP ...
A MAP THAT REVEALS THE LOCATION OF A PLACE CALLED FARAWAY ISLAND...
THAT'S RIGHT.
AN OLD FRIEND OF MINE HAS BEEN SEARCHING FOR IT FOR A VERY LONG TIME... I'M SO HAPPY I FOUND IT INSIDE THE TOWER!
HEY, BLUE! GREEN! ARE YOU GUYS ALL RIGHT?!
I SHOULD TELL HIM ABOUT MY DISCOVERY RIGHT AWAY. I NEED A PHONE... A PHONE ...
RRRIPP
TMBL
OH, NO!
WHY DID SHE TAKE SO MUCH STUFF FROM THE TOWER...?
SHFFL
UH, HELLO...? IT'S ME, ULTIMA!
I'VE FOUND IT. I'VE FINALLY FOUND IT!
THAT OLD SEA MAP YOU'VE BEEN SEARCH-ING FOR!
...

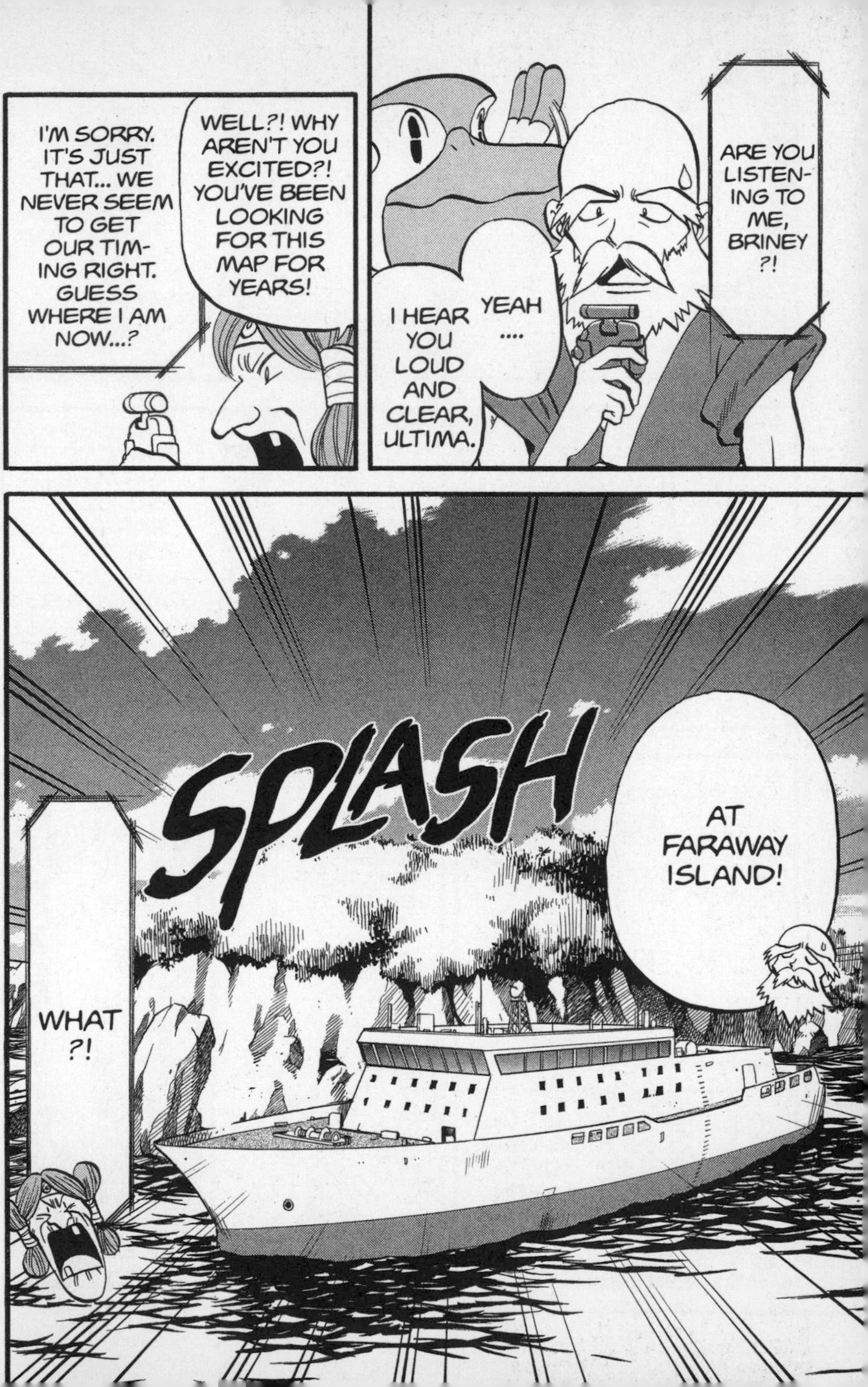
ARE YOU LISTENING TO ME, BRINEY?!
YEAH ....
I HEAR YOU LOUD AND CLEAR, ULTIMA.
WELL?! WHY AREN'T YOU EXCITED?! YOU'VE BEEN LOOKING FOR THIS MAP FOR YEARS!
I'M SORRY. IT'S JUST THAT... WE NEVER SEEM TO GET OUR TIMING RIGHT. GUESS WHERE I AM NOW...?
AT FARAWAY ISLAND!
SPLASH
WHAT?!

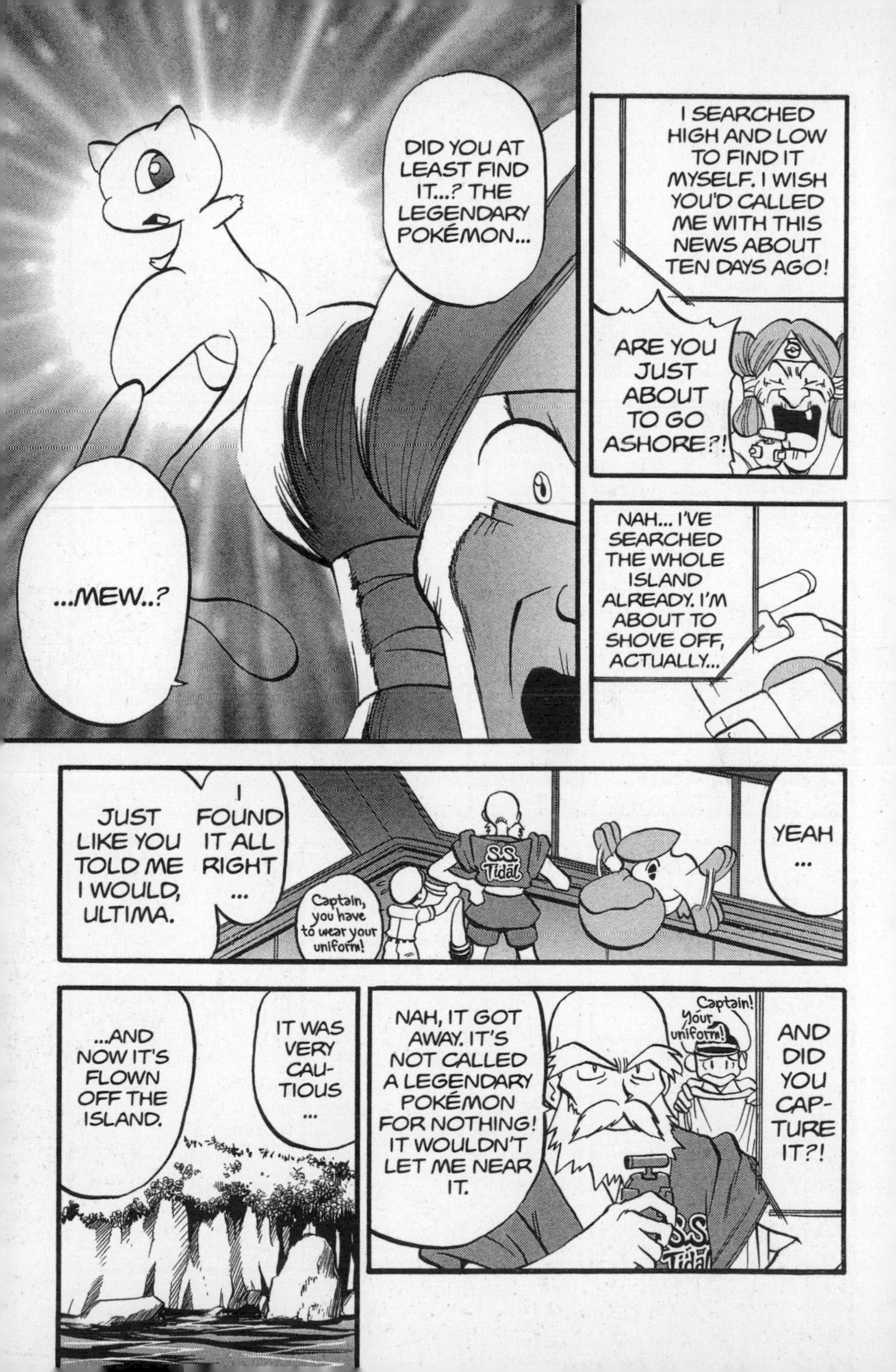
I SEARCHED HIGH AND LOW TO FIND IT MYSELF. I WISH YOU'D CALLED ME WITH THIS NEWS ABOUT TEN DAYS AGO!
ARE YOU JUST ABOUT TO GO ASHORE?!
NAH... I'VE SEARCHED THE WHOLE ISLAND ALREADY. I'M ABOUT TO SHOVE OFF, ACTUALLY...
DID YOU AT LEAST FIND IT...? THE LEGENDARY POKÉMON...
...MEW..?
YEAH ...
Captain, you have to wear your uniform!
I FOUND IT ALL RIGHT ...
JUST LIKE YOU TOLD ME I WOULD, ULTIMA.
AND DID YOU CAP-TURE IT?!
Captain! Your uniform!
NAH, IT GOT AWAY. IT'S NOT CALLED A LEGENDARY POKÉMON FOR NOTHING! IT WOULDN'T LET ME NEAR IT.
IT WAS VERY CAU-TIOUS ...
...AND NOW IT'S FLOWN OFF THE ISLAND.

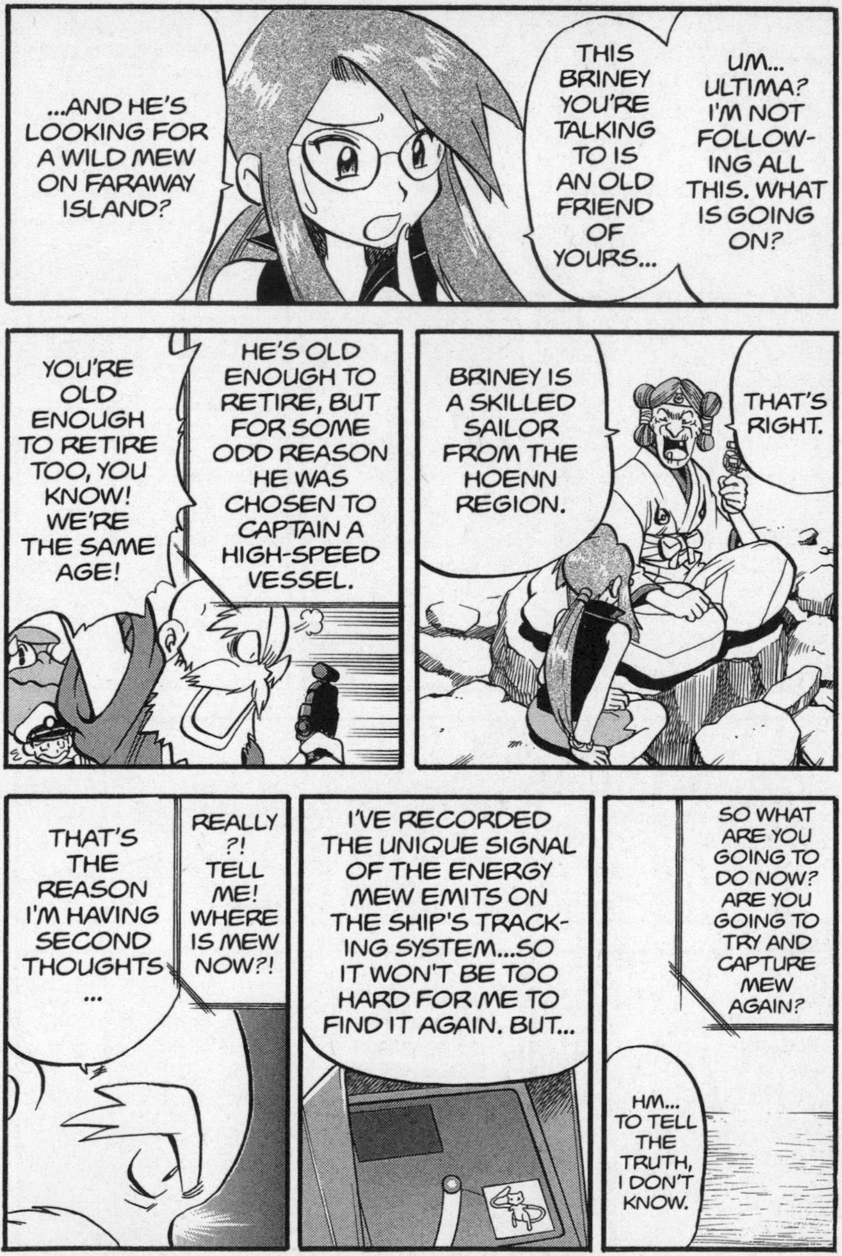
UM... ULTIMA? I'M NOT FOLLOW-ING ALL THIS. WHAT IS GOING ON?
THIS BRINEY YOU'RE TALKING TO IS AN OLD FRIEND OF YOURS...
...AND HE'S LOOKING FOR A WILD MEW ON FARAWAY ISLAND?
THAT'S RIGHT.
BRINEY IS A SKILLED SAILOR FROM THE HOENN REGION.
HE'S OLD ENOUGH TO RETIRE, BUT FOR SOME ODD REASON HE WAS CHOSEN TO CAPTAIN A HIGH-SPEED VESSEL.
YOU'RE OLD ENOUGH TO RETIRE TOO, YOU KNOW! WE'RE THE SAME AGE!
SO WHAT ARE YOU GOING TO DO NOW? ARE YOU GOING TO TRY AND CAPTURE MEW AGAIN?
HM... TO TELL THE TRUTH, I DON'T KNOW.
I'VE RECORDED THE UNIQUE SIGNAL OF THE ENERGY MEW EMITS ON THE SHIP'S TRACK-ING SYSTEM...SO IT WON'T BE TOO HARD FOR ME TO FIND IT AGAIN. BUT...
REALLY?! TELL ME! WHERE IS MEW NOW?!
THAT'S THE REASON I'M HAVING SECOND THOUGHTS...

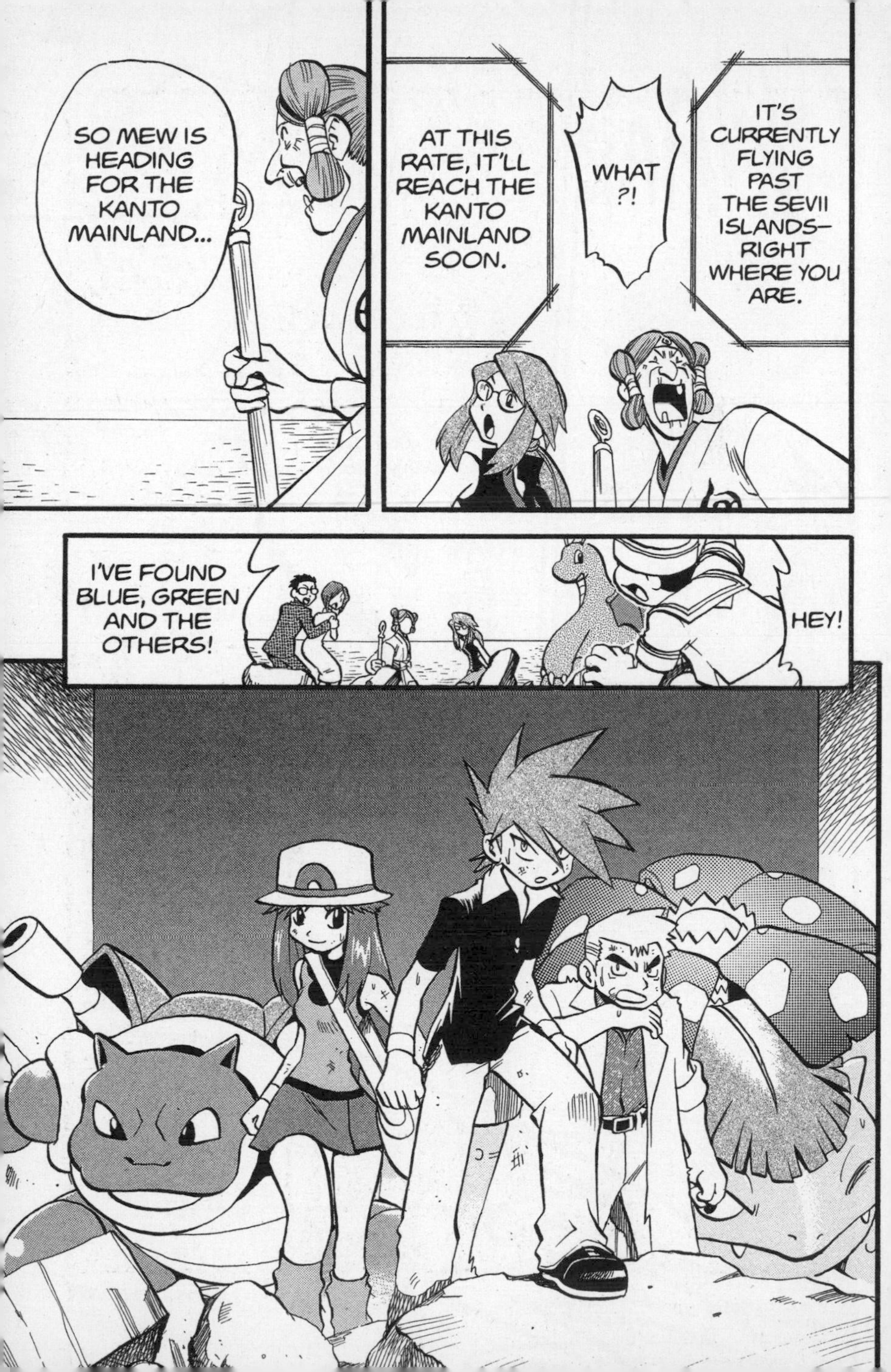
IT'S CURRENTLY FLYING PAST THE SEVII ISLANDS—RIGHT WHERE YOU ARE.
WHAT ?!
AT THIS RATE, IT'LL REACH THE KANTO MAINLAND SOON.
SO MEW IS HEADING FOR THE KANTO MAINLAND...
HEY!
I'VE FOUND BLUE, GREEN AND THE OTHERS!

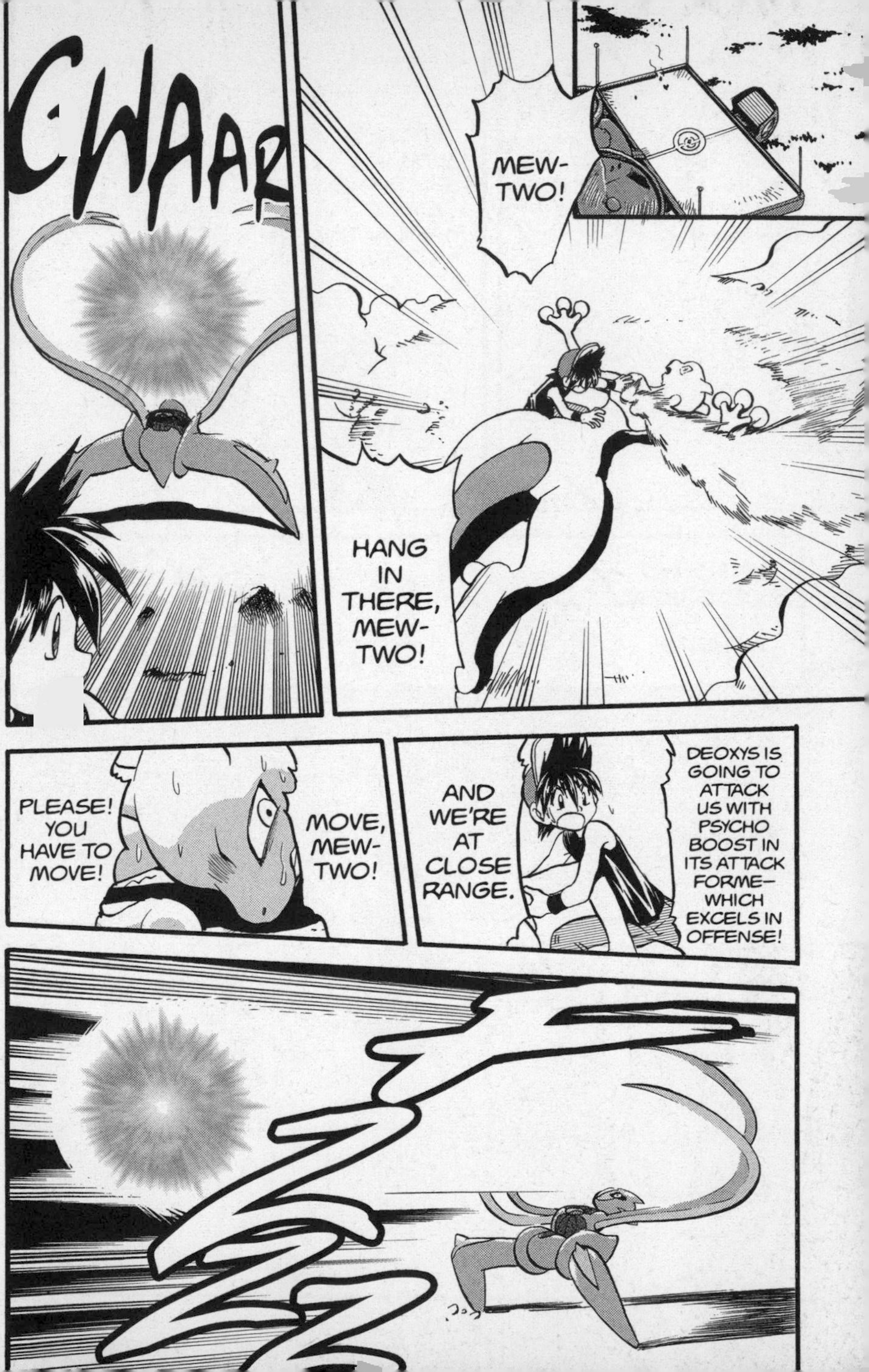
MEW-TWO!
HANG IN THERE, MEW-TWO!
CHAAR
DEOXYS IS GOING TO ATTACK US WITH PSYCHO BOOST IN ITS ATTACK FORME—WHICH EXCELS IN OFFENSE!
AND WE'RE AT CLOSE RANGE.
MOVE, MEW-TWO!
PLEASE! YOU HAVE TO MOVE!

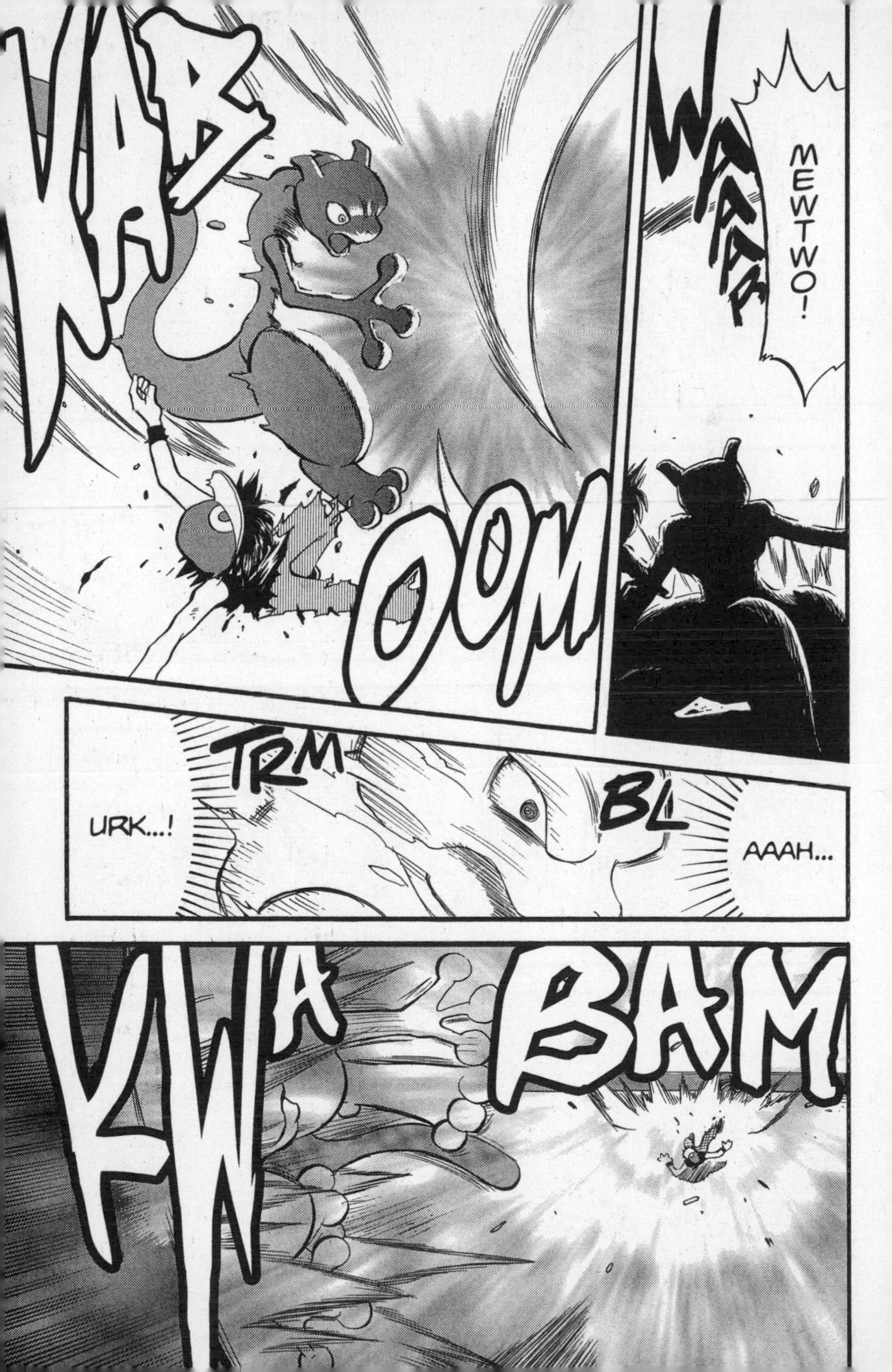
MEWTWO!
KABOOM
AAAH...
BL
TRM
URK...!
KAWA
BAM

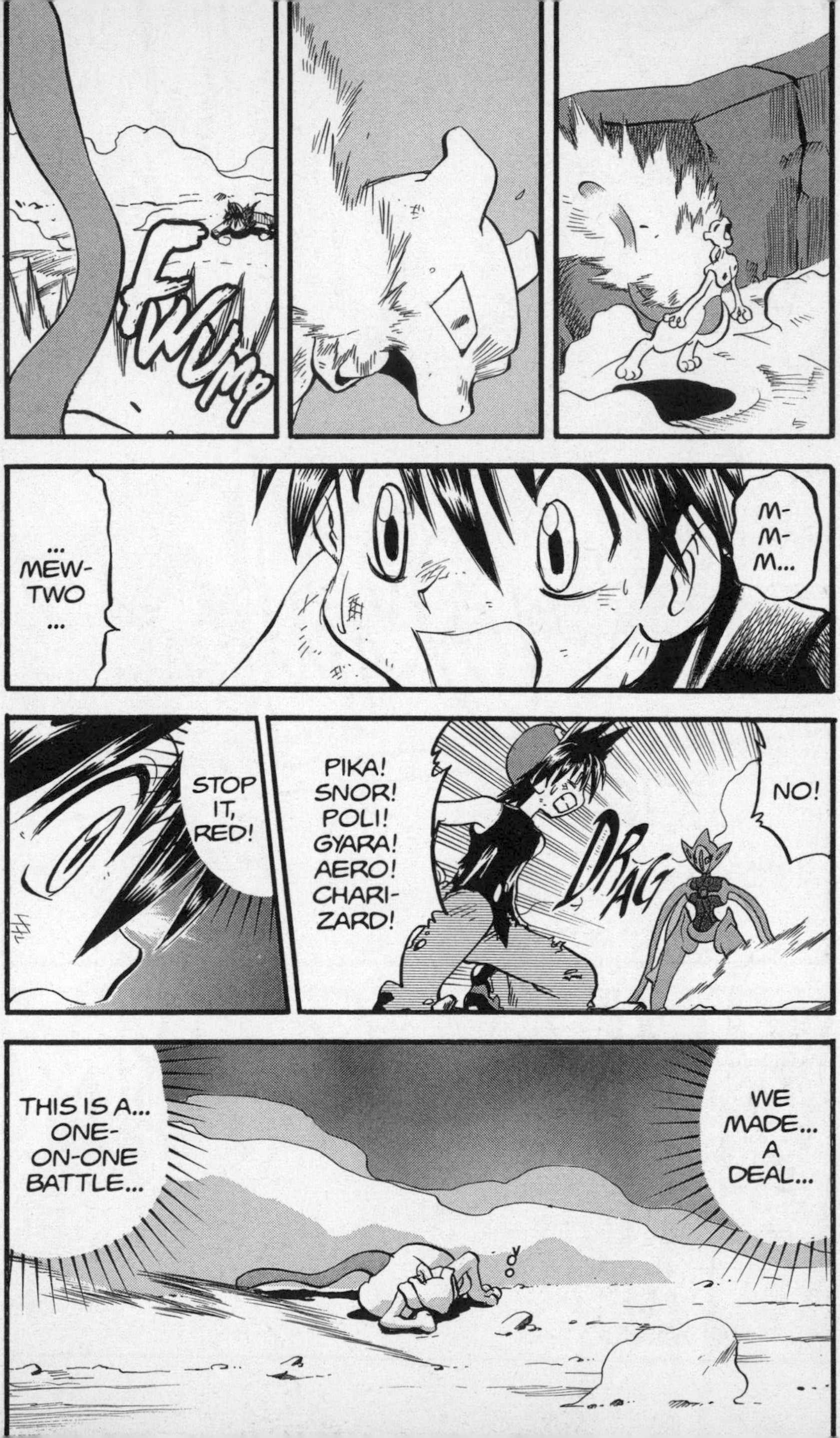
FWUMP
M-M-M...
...MEW-TWO...
NO!
DRAG
PIKA! SNOR! POLI! GYARA! AERO! CHARIZARD!
STOP IT, RED!
WE MADE... A DEAL...
THIS IS A... ONE-ON-ONE BATTLE...

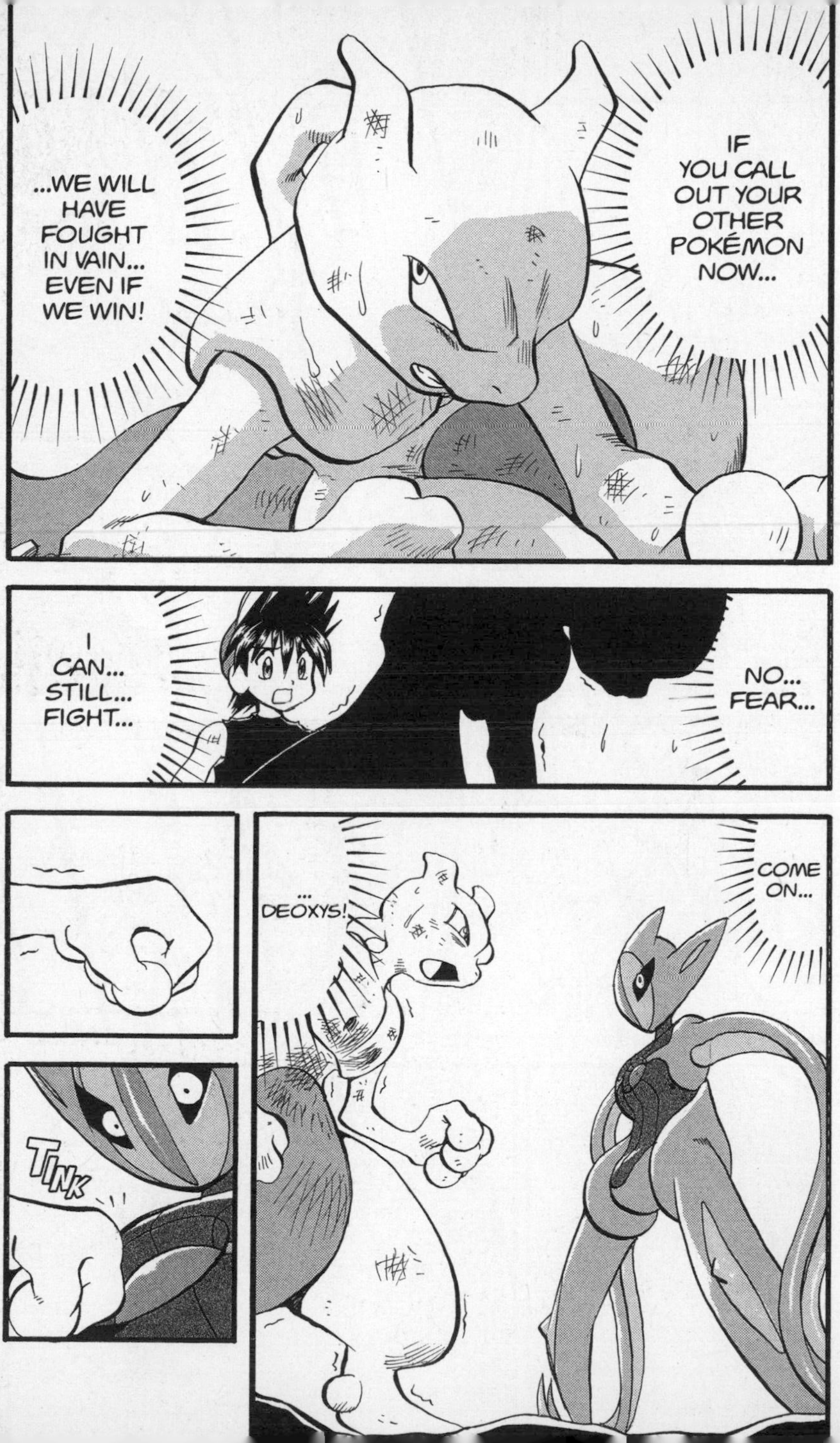
IF YOU CALL OUT YOUR OTHER POKÉMON NOW...
...WE WILL HAVE FOUGHT IN VAIN... EVEN IF WE WIN!
NO... FEAR...
I CAN... STILL... FIGHT...
COME ON...
...DEOXYS!
TINK

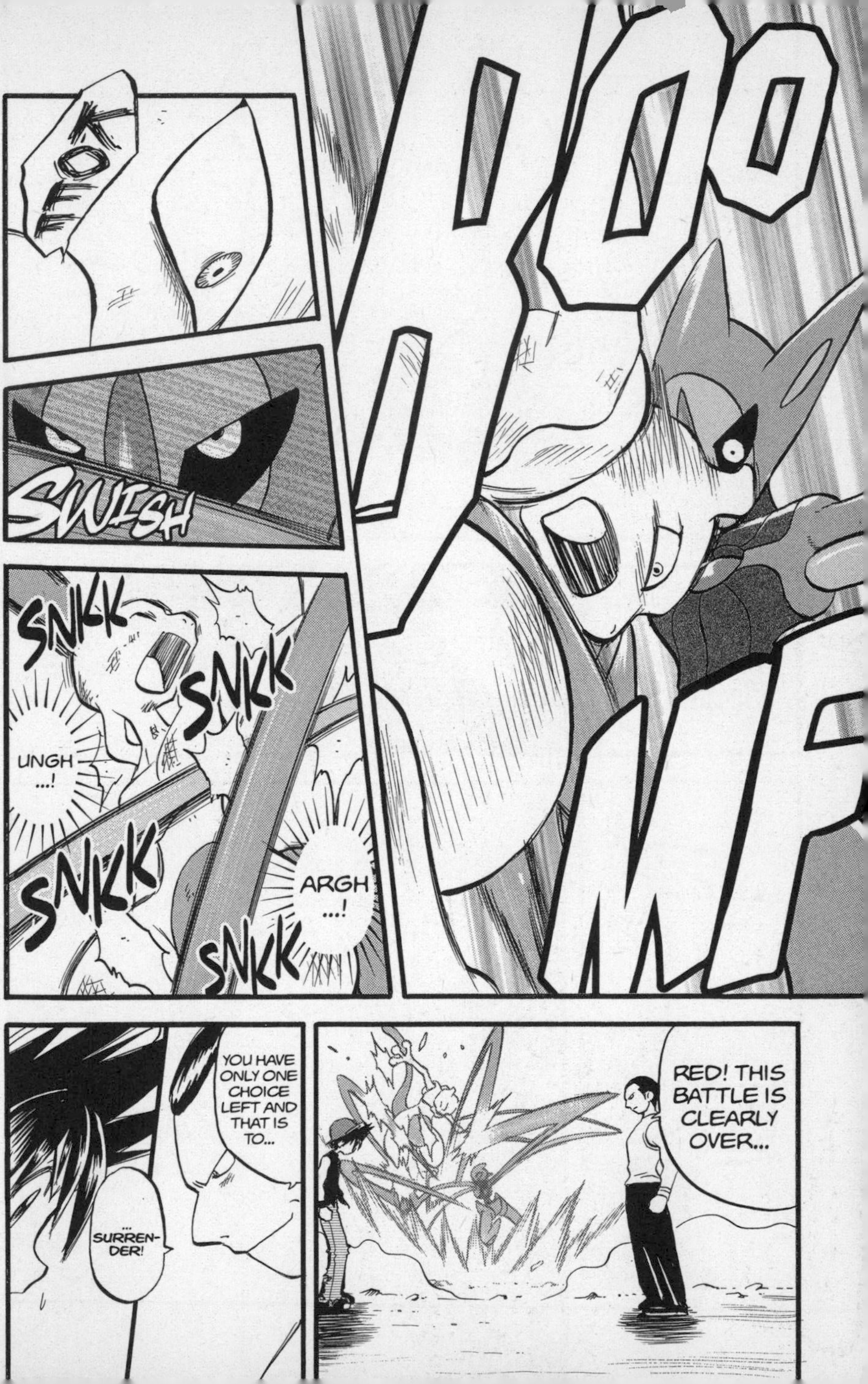
SWISH
SNKK
SNKK
UNGH ...!
ARGH ...!
SNKK
SNKK
RED! THIS BATTLE IS CLEARLY OVER...
YOU HAVE ONLY ONE CHOICE LEFT AND THAT IS TO...
... SURREN-DER!

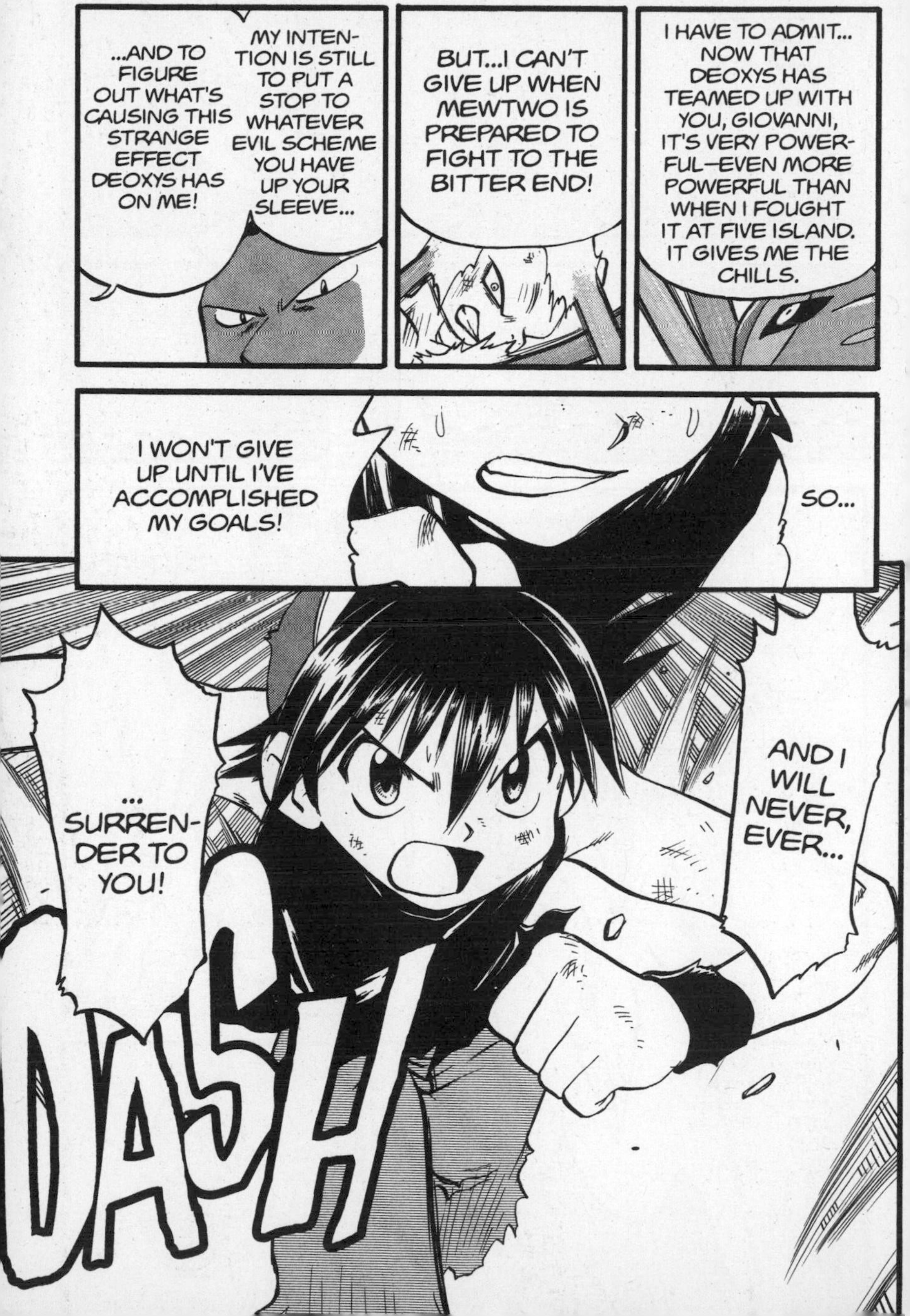
I HAVE TO ADMIT... NOW THAT DEOXYS HAS TEAMED UP WITH YOU, GIOVANNI, IT'S VERY POWERFUL—EVEN MORE POWERFUL THAN WHEN I FOUGHT IT AT FIVE ISLAND. IT GIVES ME THE CHILLS.
BUT...I CAN'T GIVE UP WHEN MEWTWO IS PREPARED TO FIGHT TO THE BITTER END!
MY INTENTION IS STILL TO PUT A STOP TO WHATEVER EVIL SCHEME YOU HAVE UP YOUR SLEEVE...
...AND TO FIGURE OUT WHAT'S CAUSING THIS STRANGE EFFECT DEOXYS HAS ON ME!
SO...
I WON'T GIVE UP UNTIL I'VE ACCOMPLISHED MY GOALS!
AND I WILL NEVER, EVER...
...SURRENDER TO YOU!
DASH

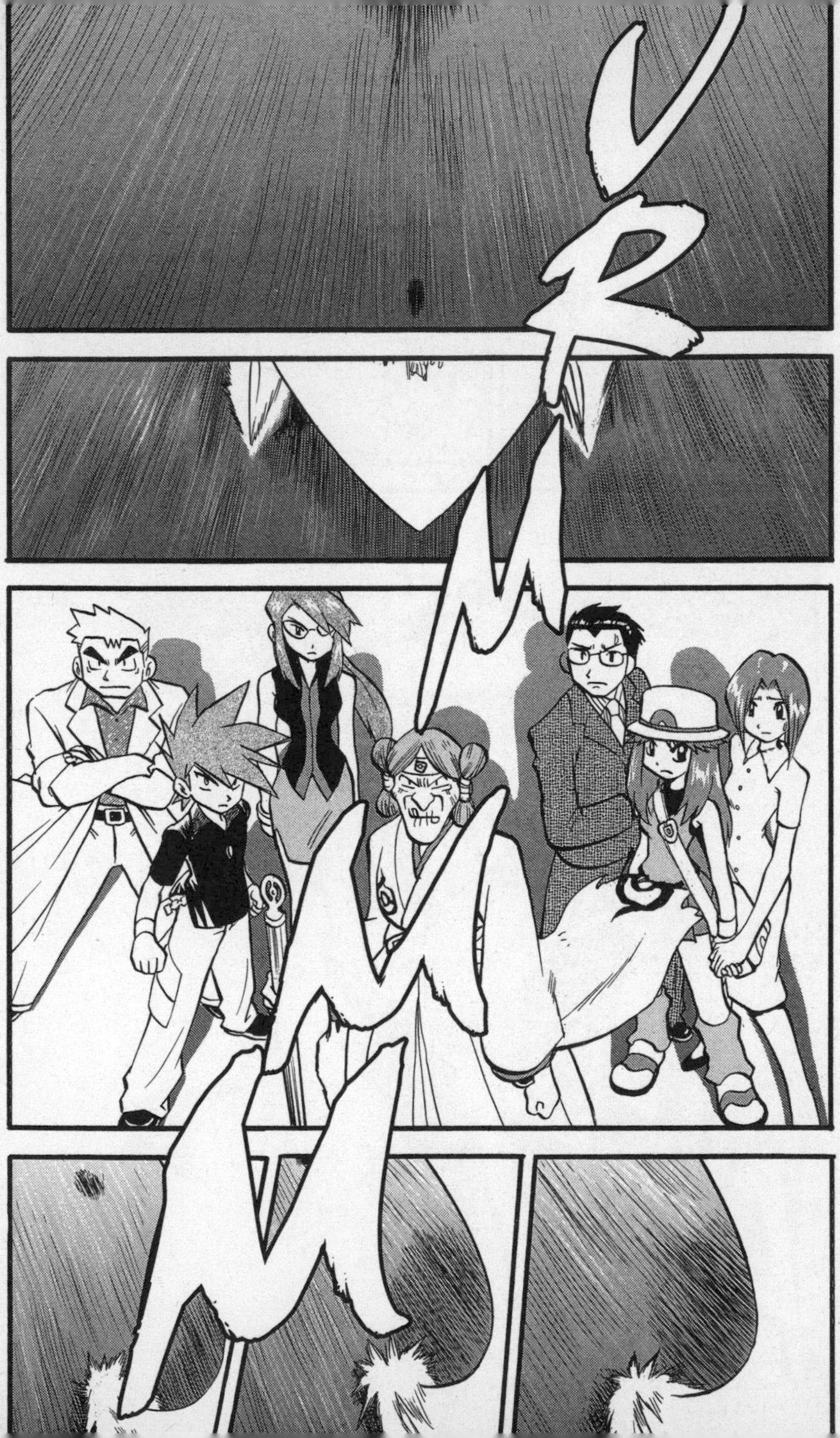
VRMMM

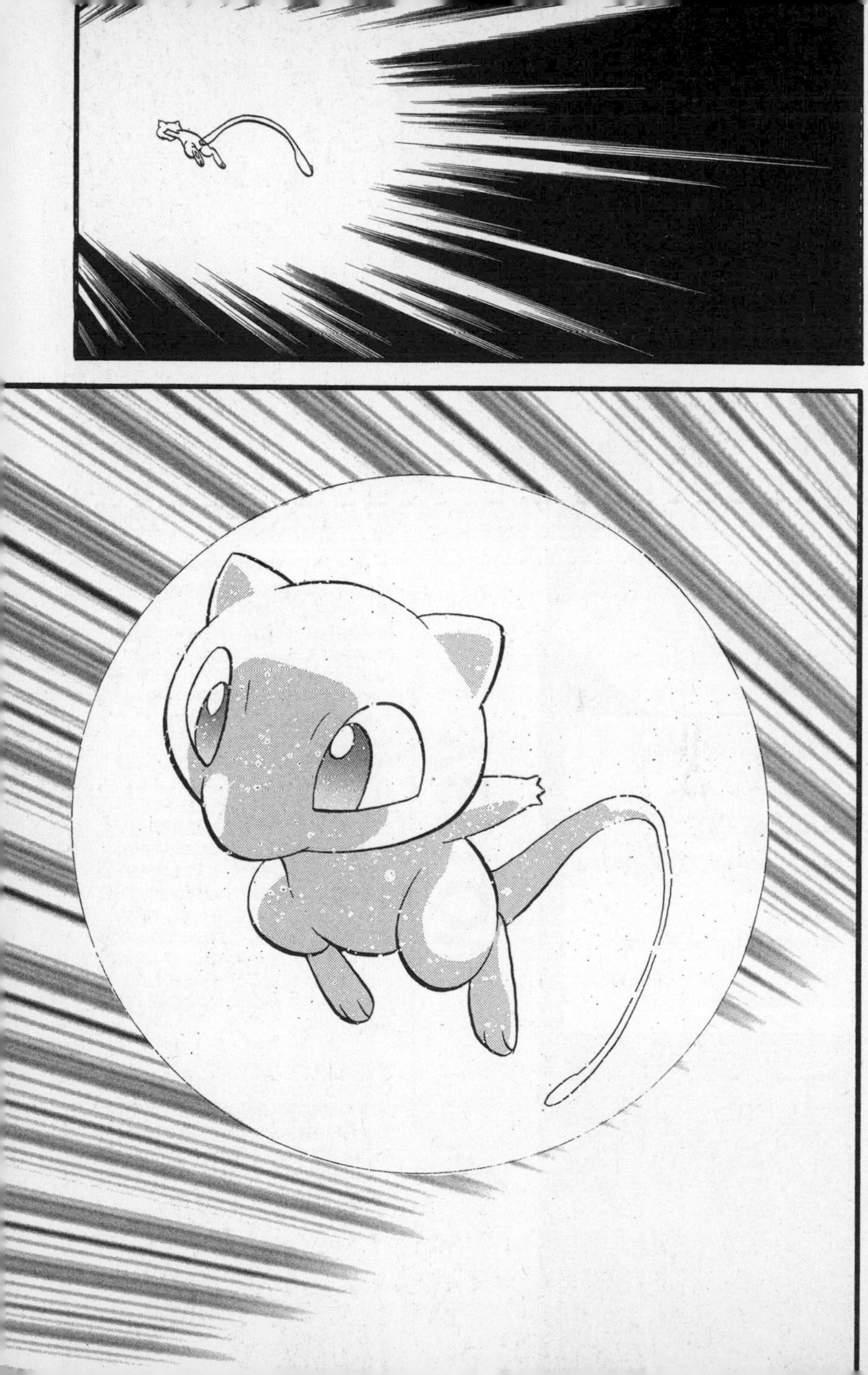

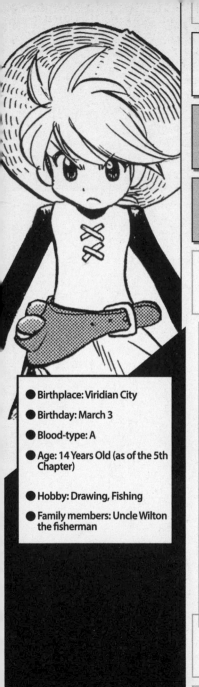

- Birthplace: Viridian City
- Birthday: March 3
- Blood-type: A
- Age: 14 Years Old (as of the 5th Chapter)
- Hobby: Drawing, Fishing
- Family members: Uncle Wilton the fisherman

YELLOW

IT IS SAID THAT EVERY TEN YEARS A GIRL IS BORN WHO IS IMBUED WITH PSYCHIC POWERS FROM THE VIRIDIAN FOREST. YELLOW HAS THE ABILITY TO READ THE MINDS OF POKÉMON AND TO HEAL THEIR WOUNDS. HER FULL NAME IS "AMARILLO DEL BOSQUE VERDE." SHE USED TO LIVE AN ORDINARY LIFE IN VIRIDIAN CITY, BUT HER LIFE CHANGED DRASTICALLY AFTER SHE MET RED. WHEN RED WENT MISSING DURING HIS CHALLENGE AGAINST THE KANTO ELITE FOUR, YELLOW SET OUT WITH RED'S POKÉMON PIKA ON A JOURNEY TO FIND HIM. FOR SOME REASON, SHE CHOSE TO HIDE HER IDENTITY AS A GIRL.

YELLOW IS CURRENTLY TRYING TO RESCUE SILVER, WHO WAS KIDNAPPED BY THE THREE BEASTS OF TEAM ROCKET AND IS NOW ABOARD THEIR AIRSHIP. HOW WILL HER UNIQUE POWERS BE OF USE...?

●Adventure 295●
Double Down Deoxys

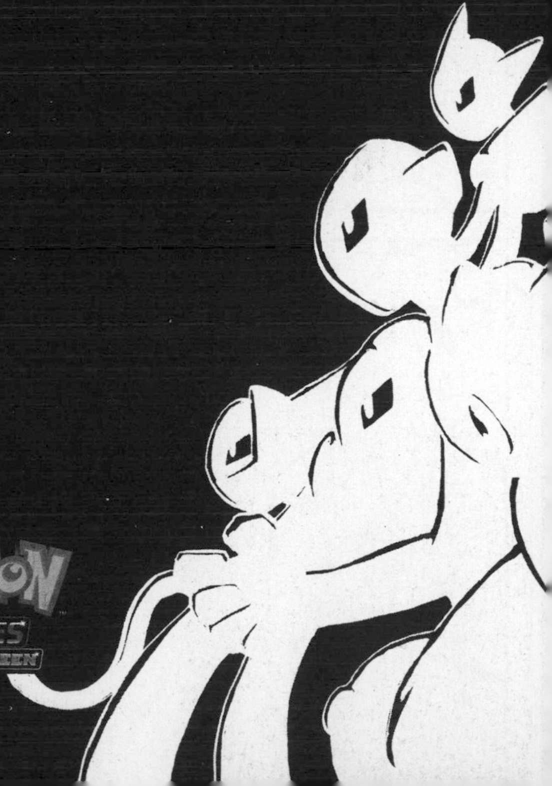

Pokémon Adventures
FireRed & LeafGreen
The Fifth Chapter

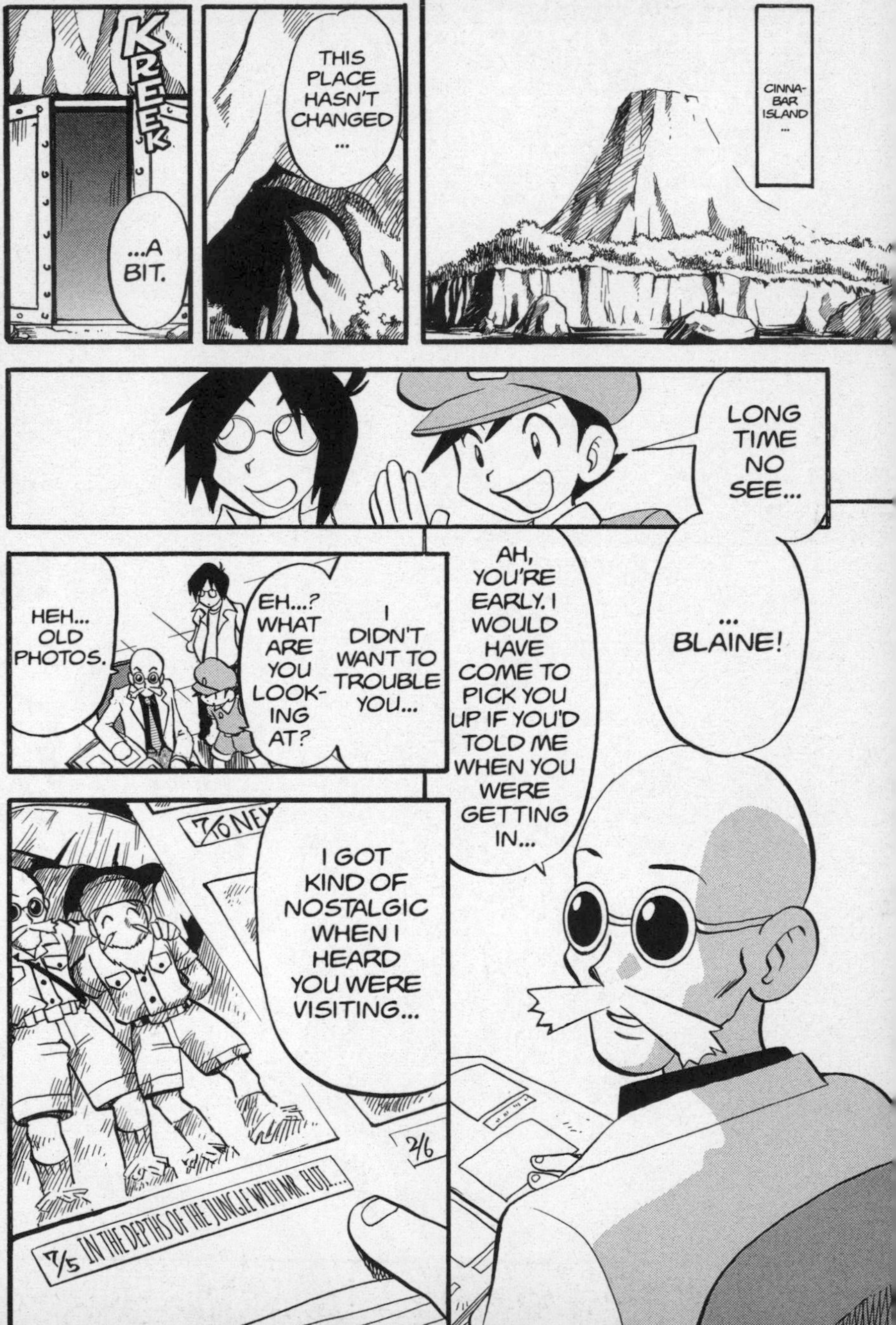
CINNABAR ISLAND ...
THIS PLACE HASN'T CHANGED ...
KREEK
...A BIT.
LONG TIME NO SEE...
... BLAINE!
AH, YOU'RE EARLY. I WOULD HAVE COME TO PICK YOU UP IF YOU'D TOLD ME WHEN YOU WERE GETTING IN...
I DIDN'T WANT TO TROUBLE YOU...
EH...? WHAT ARE YOU LOOKING AT?
HEH... OLD PHOTOS.
I GOT KIND OF NOSTALGIC WHEN I HEARD YOU WERE VISITING...
2/6
7/5 IN THE DEPTHS OF THE JUNGLE WITH MR. FUJI...

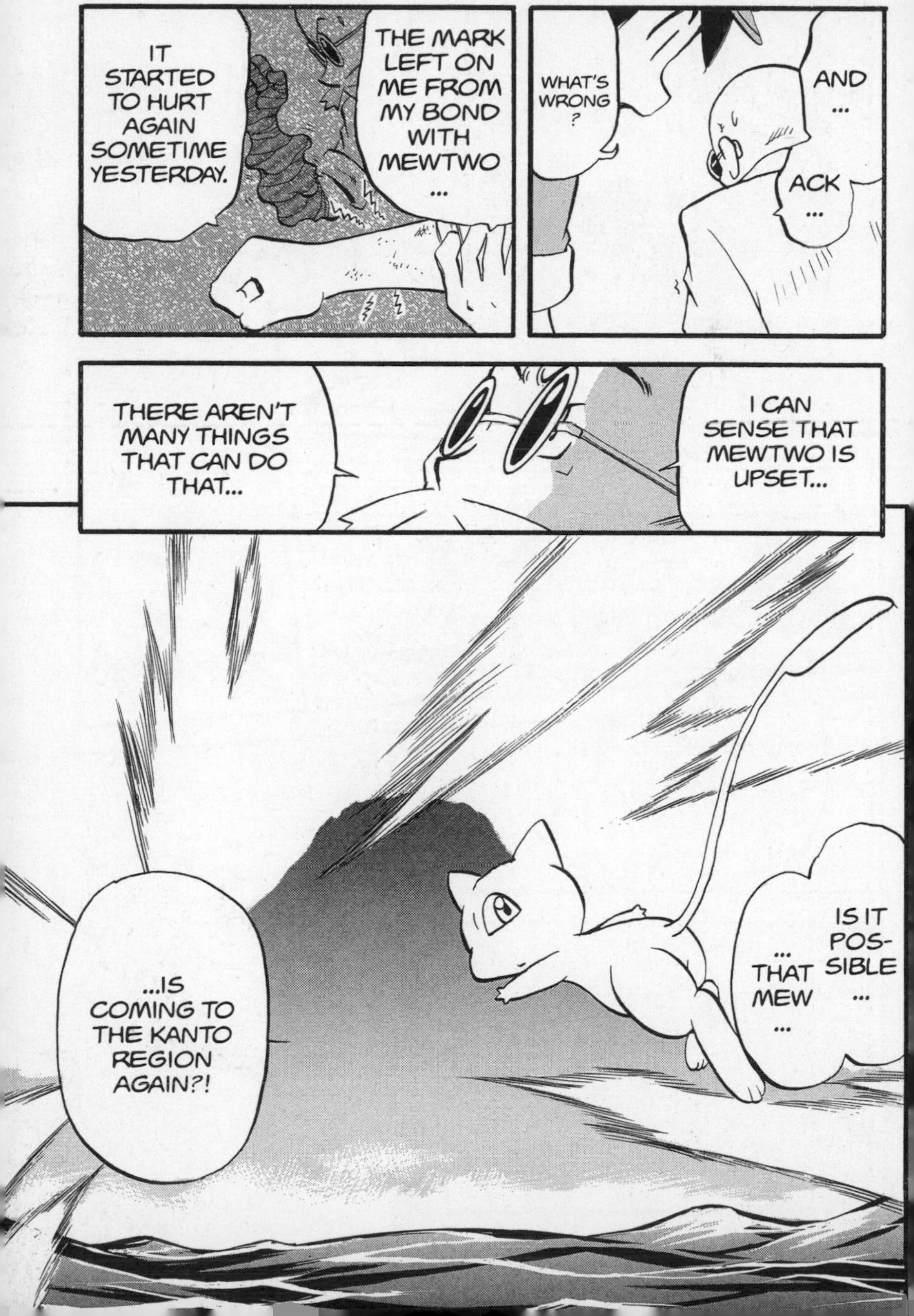
AND ...
WHAT'S WRONG ?
ACK ...
THE MARK LEFT ON ME FROM MY BOND WITH MEWTWO ...
IT STARTED TO HURT AGAIN SOMETIME YESTERDAY.
I CAN SENSE THAT MEWTWO IS UPSET...
THERE AREN'T MANY THINGS THAT CAN DO THAT...
IS IT POS-SIBLE ...
... THAT MEW ...
...IS COMING TO THE KANTO REGION AGAIN?!

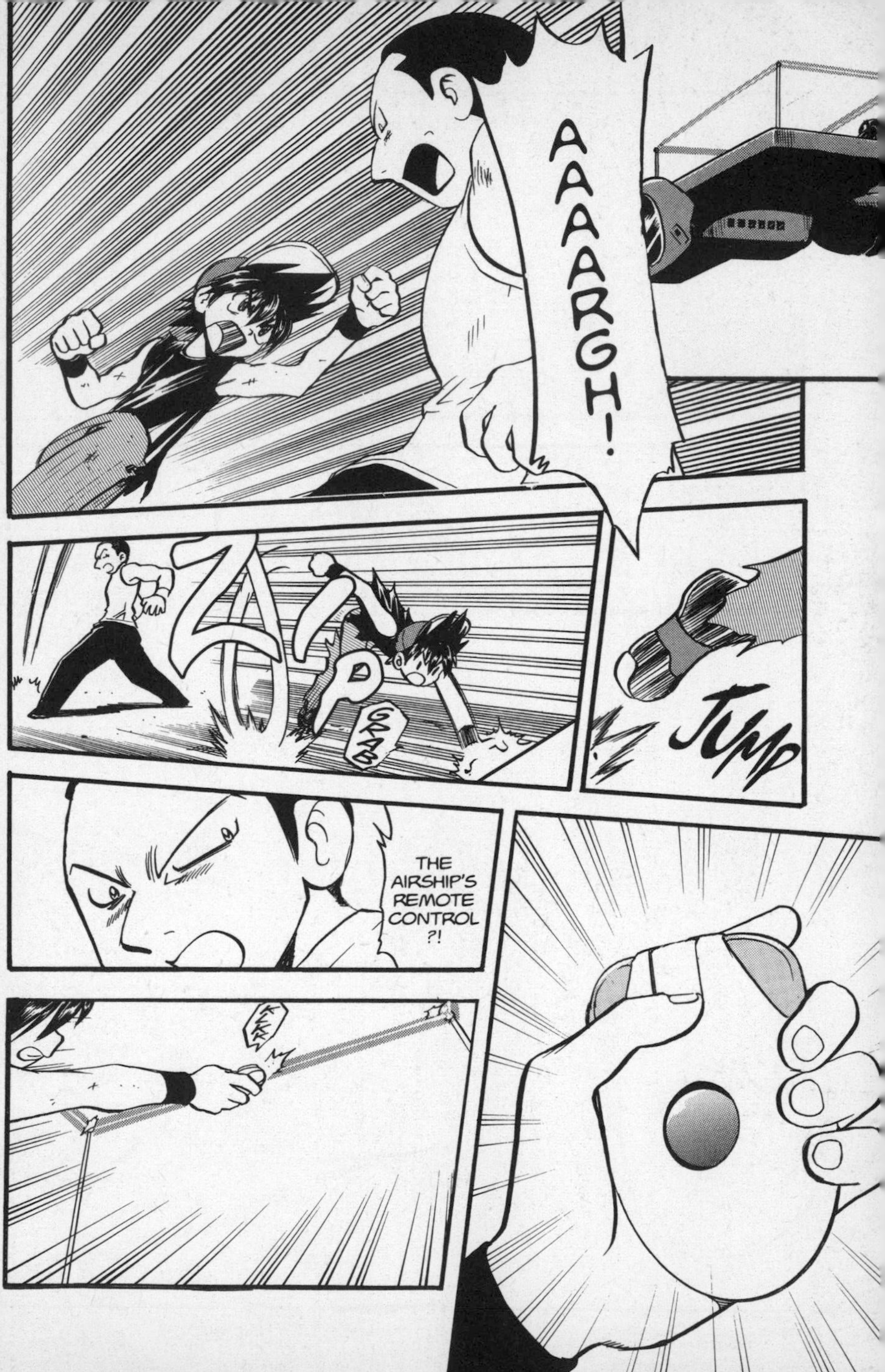
AAAARGH!
JUMP
ZAP
GRAB
THE AIRSHIP'S REMOTE CONTROL ?!

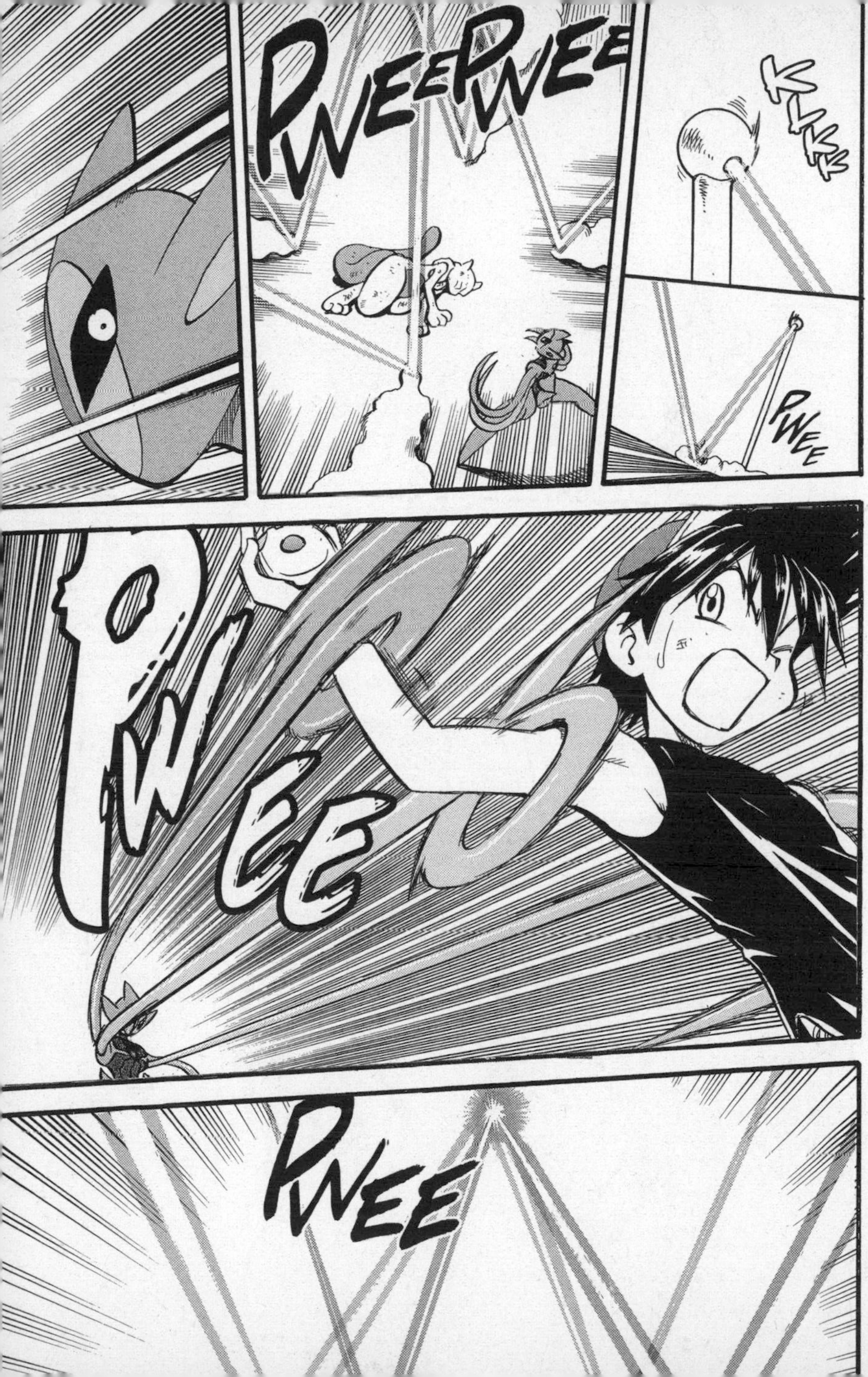
KYKKK
PWEE
PWEEPWEE
PWEE
PWEE

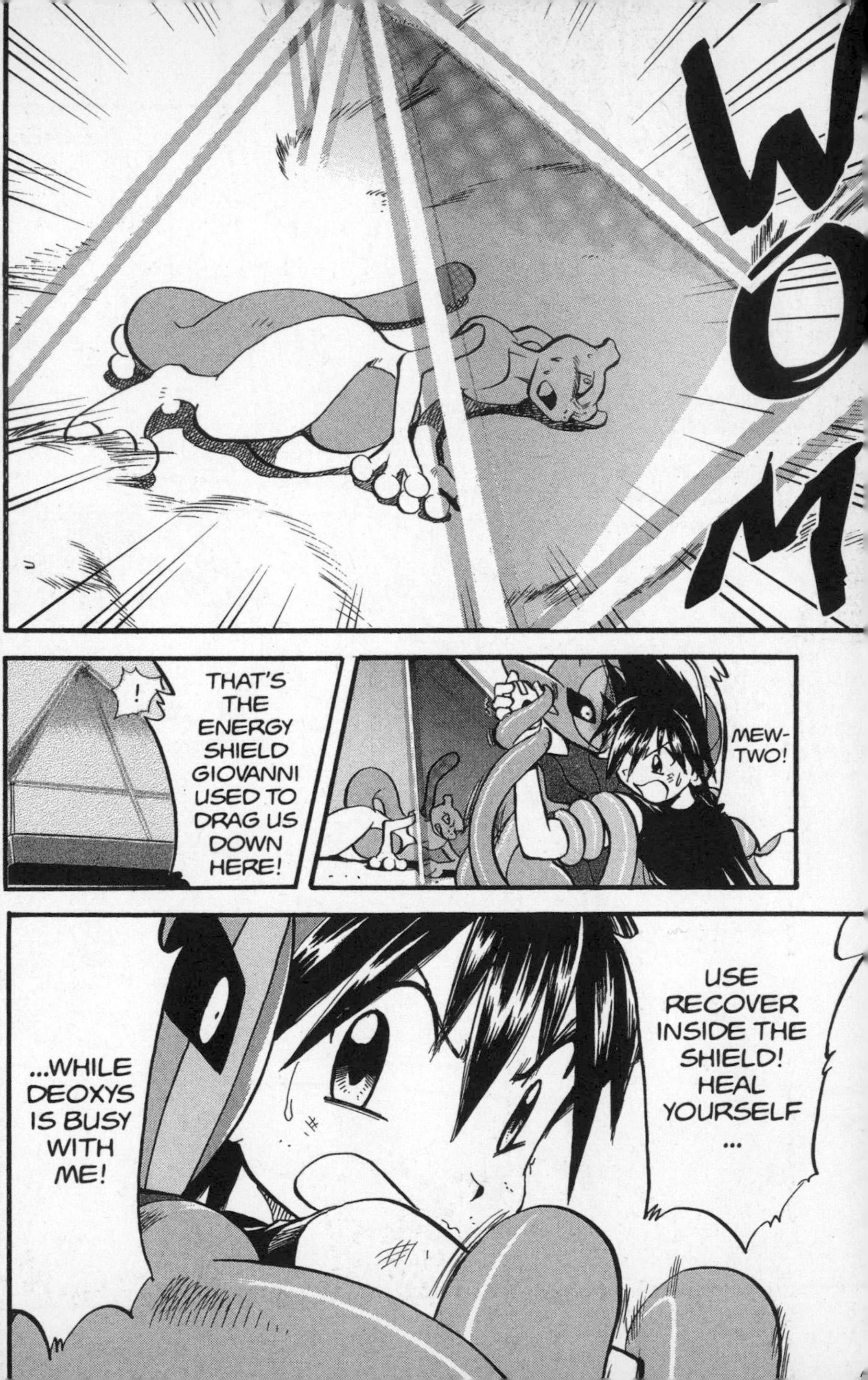
WOOM
MEW-TWO!
!
THAT'S THE ENERGY SHIELD GIOVANNI USED TO DRAG US DOWN HERE!
USE RECOVER INSIDE THE SHIELD! HEAL YOURSELF ...
...WHILE DEOXYS IS BUSY WITH ME!

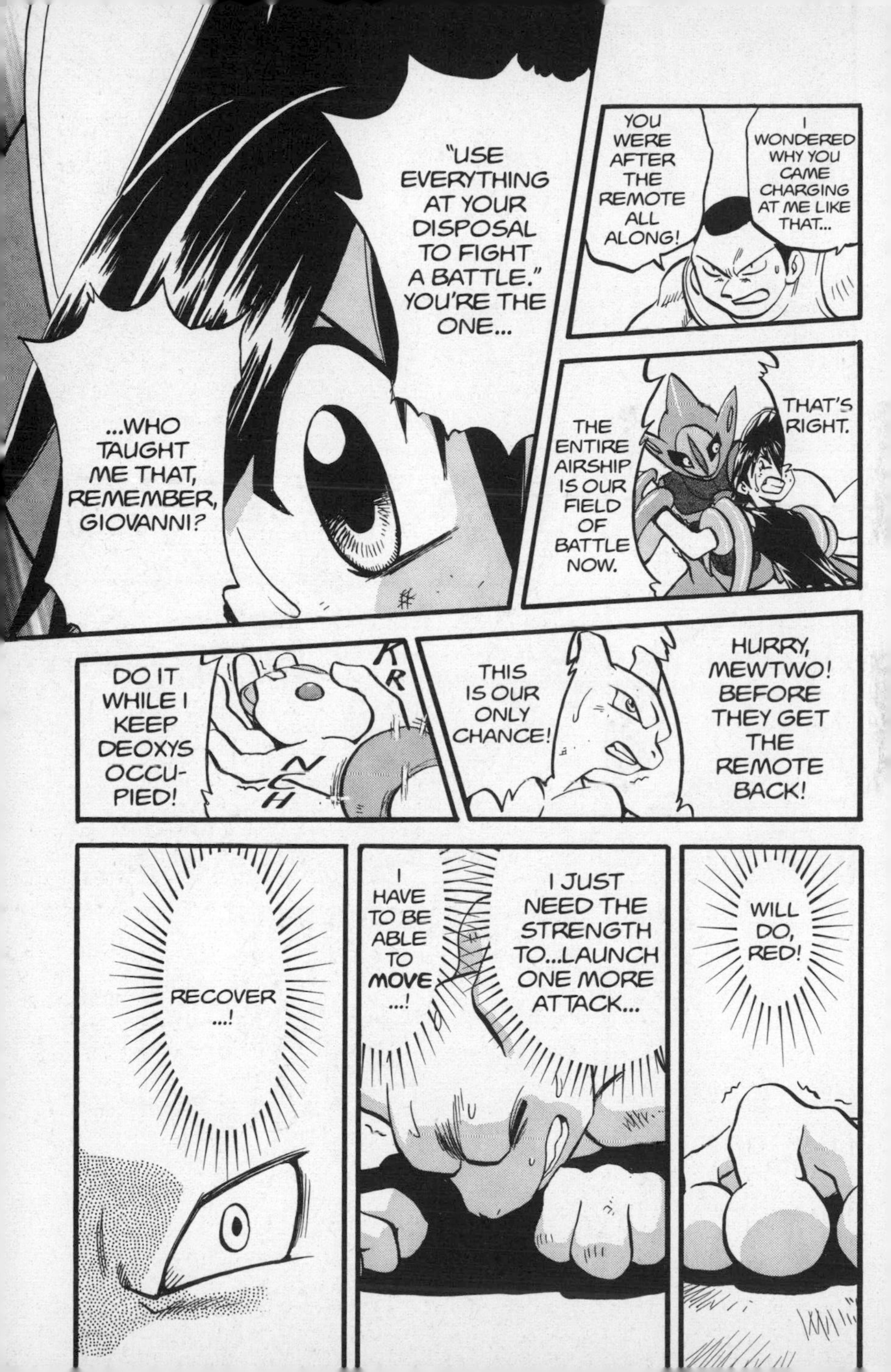
I WONDERED WHY YOU CAME CHARGING AT ME LIKE THAT...
YOU WERE AFTER THE REMOTE ALL ALONG!
THAT'S RIGHT.
THE ENTIRE AIRSHIP IS OUR FIELD OF BATTLE NOW.
"USE EVERYTHING AT YOUR DISPOSAL TO FIGHT A BATTLE." YOU'RE THE ONE...
...WHO TAUGHT ME THAT, REMEMBER, GIOVANNI?
HURRY, MEWTWO! BEFORE THEY GET THE REMOTE BACK!
THIS IS OUR ONLY CHANCE!
KRR
NCH
DO IT WHILE I KEEP DEOXYS OCCUPIED!
WILL DO, RED!
I JUST NEED THE STRENGTH TO...LAUNCH ONE MORE ATTACK...
I HAVE TO BE ABLE TO **MOVE**...!
RECOVER...!

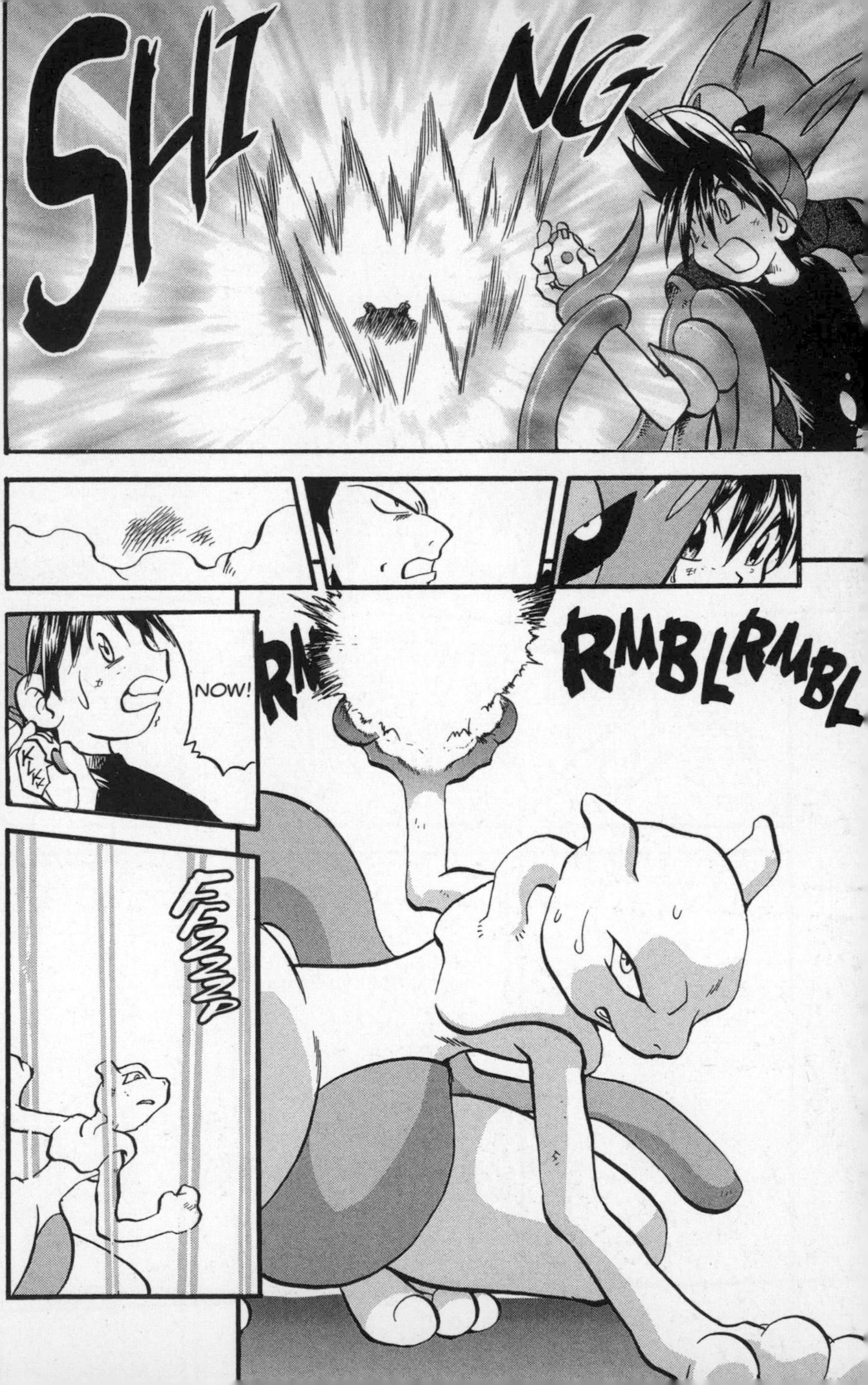
SHI NG
RMBLRMBL
RM
NOW!
FFWWWP

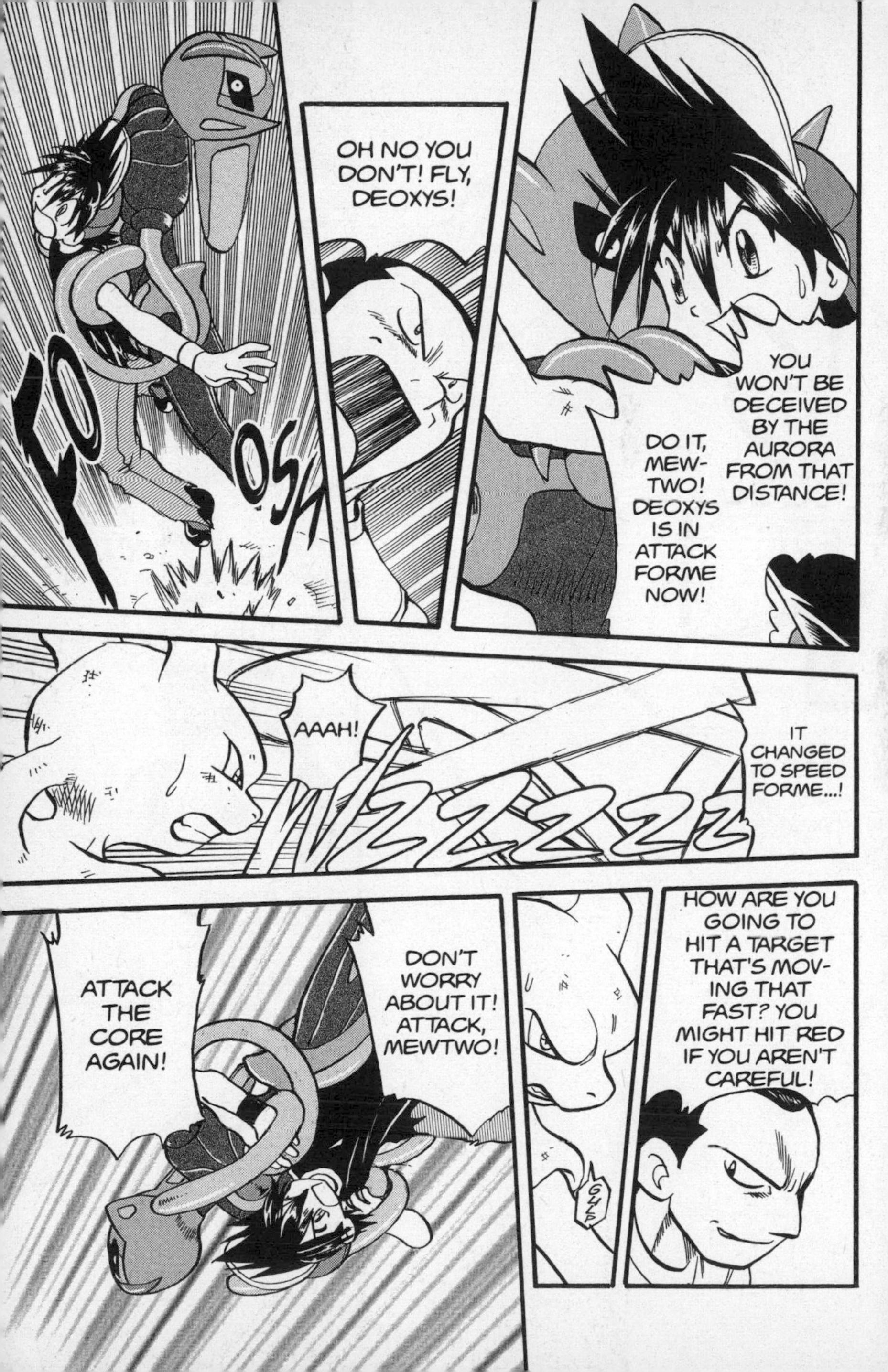
YOU WON'T BE DECEIVED BY THE AURORA FROM THAT DISTANCE!
DO IT, MEW-TWO! DEOXYS IS IN ATTACK FORME NOW!
OH NO YOU DON'T! FLY, DEOXYS!
FOOSH
IT CHANGED TO SPEED FORME...!
AAAH!
HOW ARE YOU GOING TO HIT A TARGET THAT'S MOV-ING THAT FAST? YOU MIGHT HIT RED IF YOU AREN'T CAREFUL!
GULP
DON'T WORRY ABOUT IT! ATTACK, MEWTWO!
ATTACK THE CORE AGAIN!

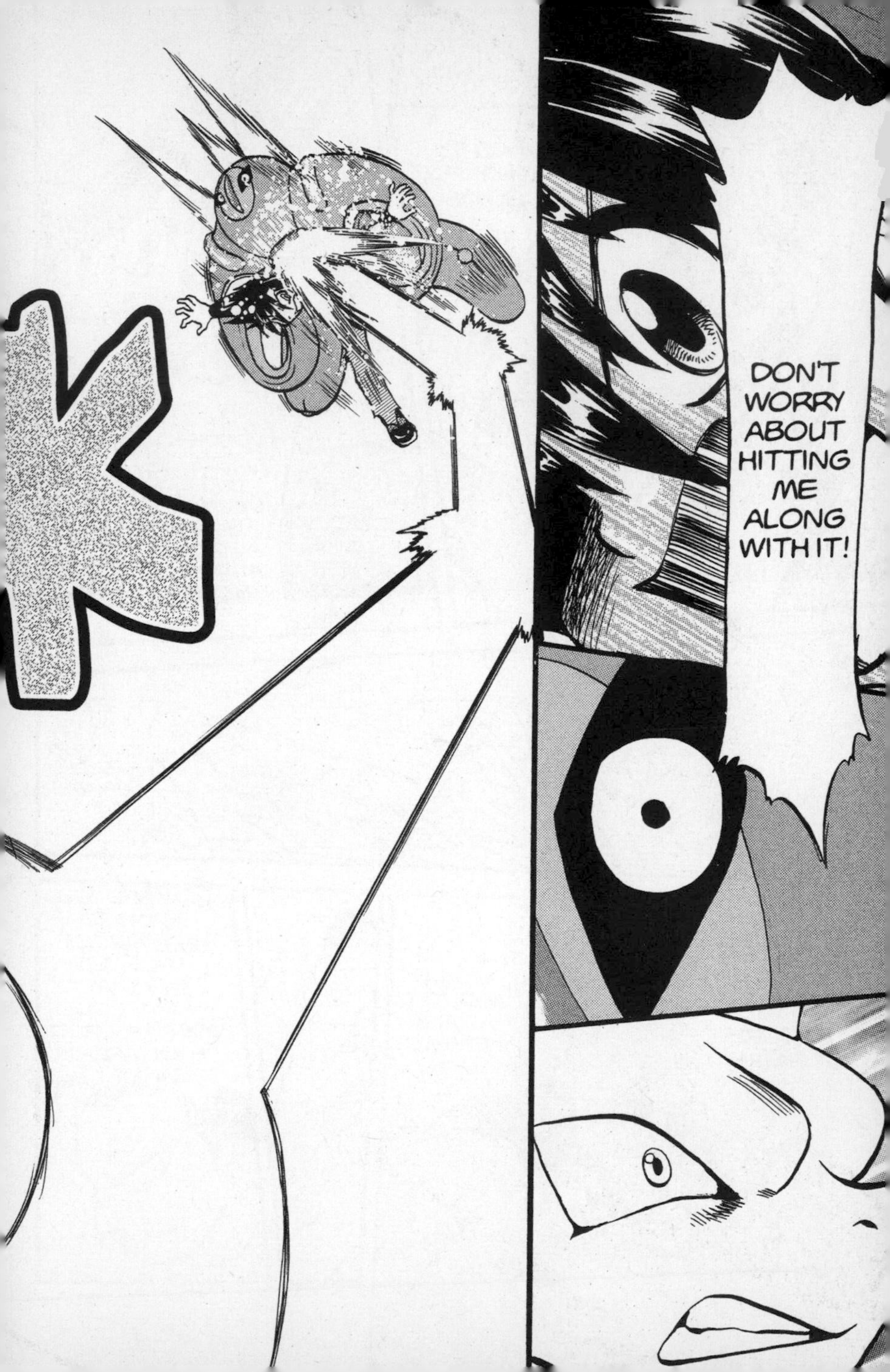
DON'T WORRY ABOUT HITTING ME ALONG WITH IT!

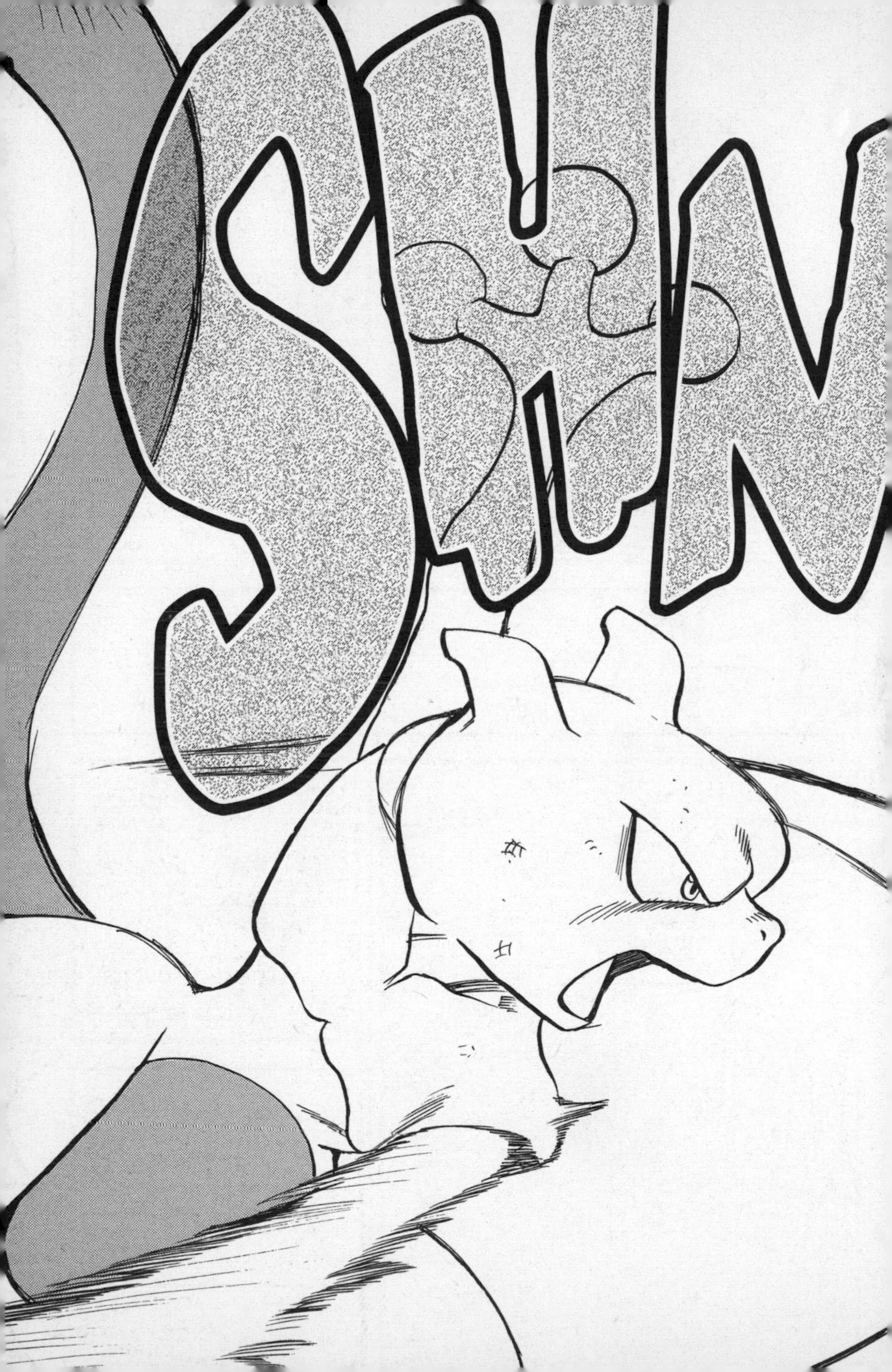
SHIN

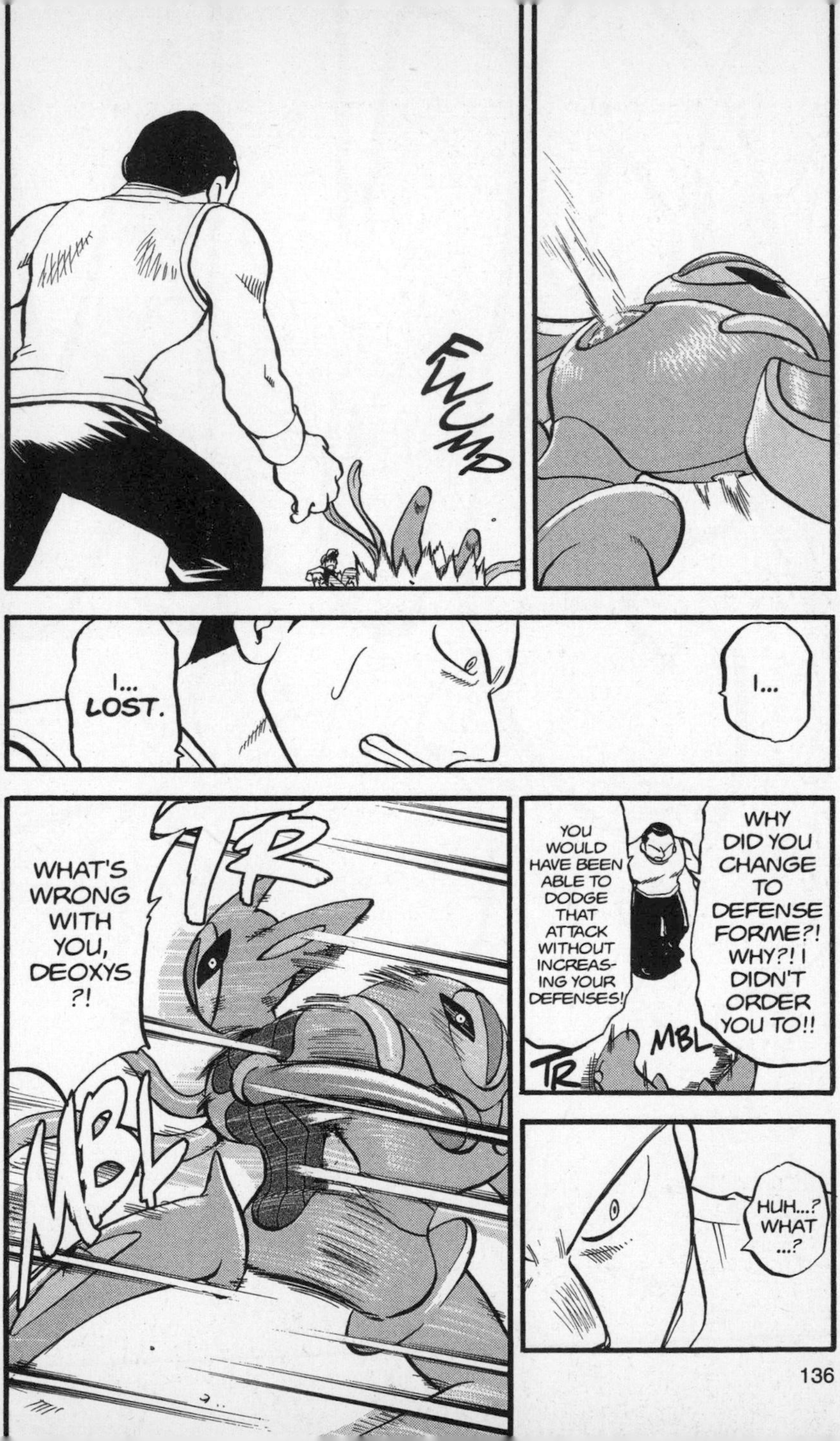
FWUMP
I...
I...
LOST.
WHY DID YOU CHANGE TO DEFENSE FORME?! WHY?! I DIDN'T ORDER YOU TO!!
YOU WOULD HAVE BEEN ABLE TO DODGE THAT ATTACK WITHOUT INCREASING YOUR DEFENSES!
MBL
TR
HUH...? WHAT ...?
TR
WHAT'S WRONG WITH YOU, DEOXYS ?!
MBL

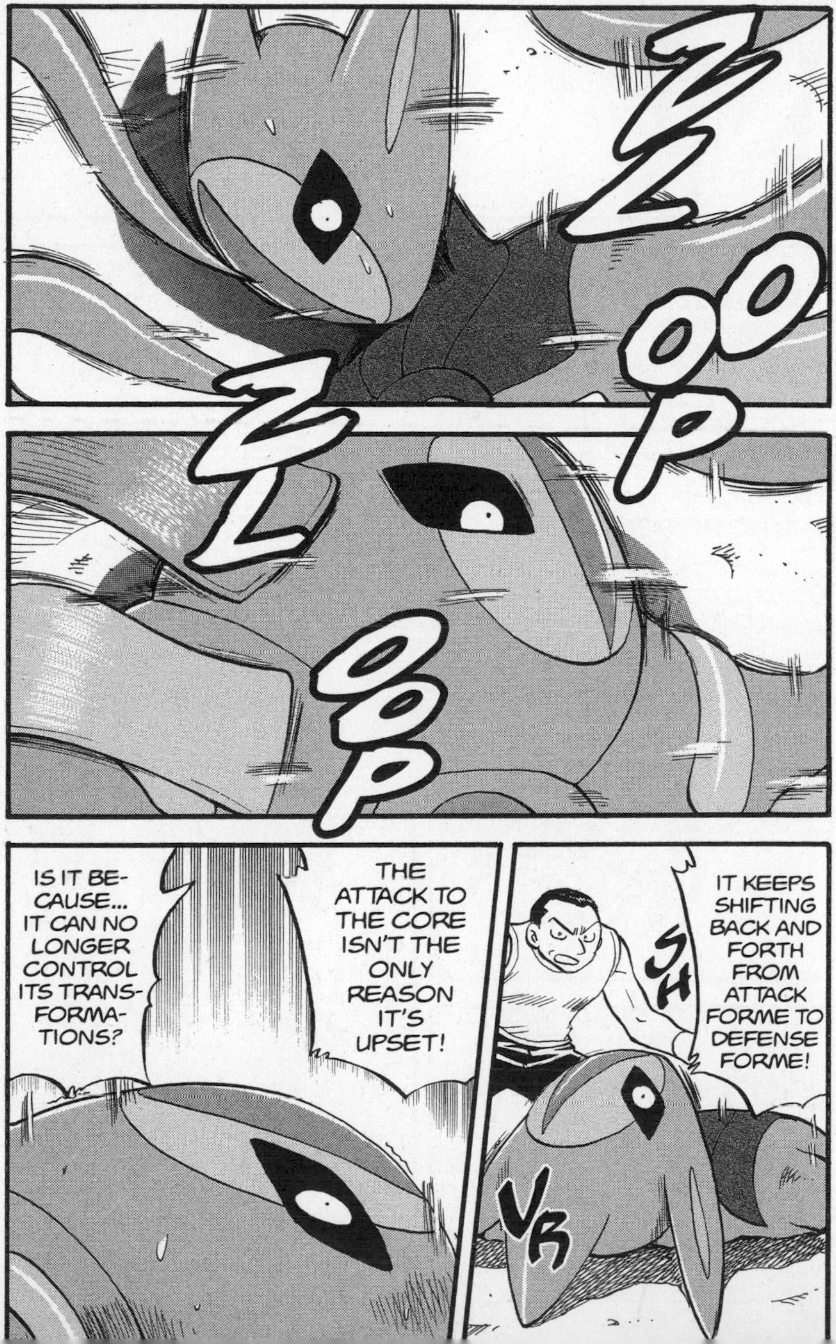
ZOOOP
ZOOOP
IT KEEPS SHIFTING BACK AND FORTH FROM ATTACK FORME TO DEFENSE FORME!
SH
VR
THE ATTACK TO THE CORE ISN'T THE ONLY REASON IT'S UPSET!
IS IT BE-CAUSE... IT CAN NO LONGER CONTROL ITS TRANS-FORMA-TIONS?

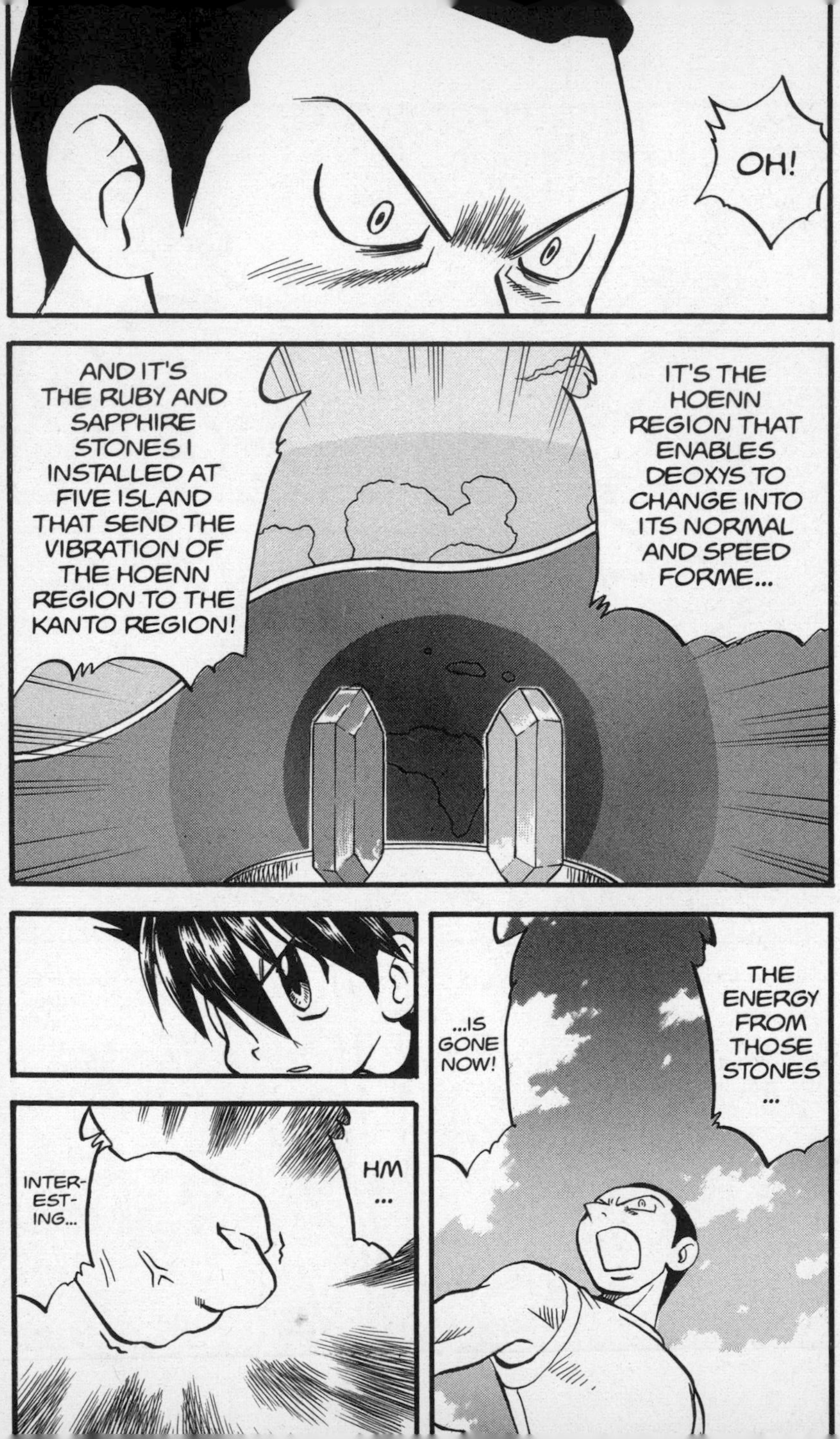
OH!
IT'S THE HOENN REGION THAT ENABLES DEOXYS TO CHANGE INTO ITS NORMAL AND SPEED FORME...
AND IT'S THE RUBY AND SAPPHIRE STONES I INSTALLED AT FIVE ISLAND THAT SEND THE VIBRATION OF THE HOENN REGION TO THE KANTO REGION!
THE ENERGY FROM THOSE STONES ...
...IS GONE NOW!
HM ...
INTER-EST-ING...

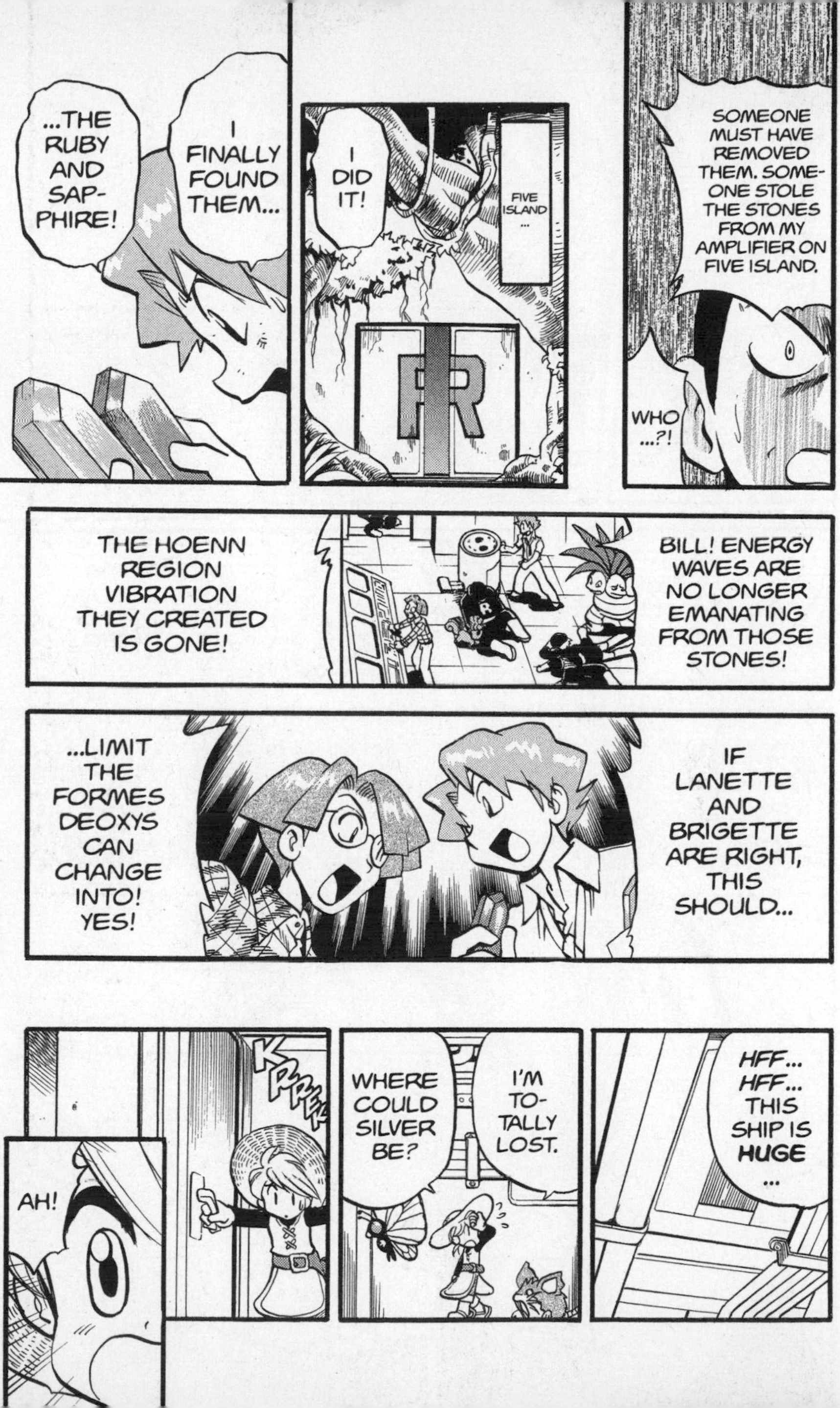
SOMEONE MUST HAVE REMOVED THEM. SOME-ONE STOLE THE STONES FROM MY AMPLIFIER ON FIVE ISLAND.
WHO ...?!
FIVE ISLAND ...
I DID IT!
I FINALLY FOUND THEM...
...THE RUBY AND SAP-PHIRE!
BILL! ENERGY WAVES ARE NO LONGER EMANATING FROM THOSE STONES!
THE HOENN REGION VIBRATION THEY CREATED IS GONE!
IF LANETTE AND BRIGETTE ARE RIGHT, THIS SHOULD...
...LIMIT THE FORMES DEOXYS CAN CHANGE INTO! YES!
HFF... HFF... THIS SHIP IS **HUGE** ...
I'M TO-TALLY LOST.
WHERE COULD SILVER BE?
KPREE
AH!

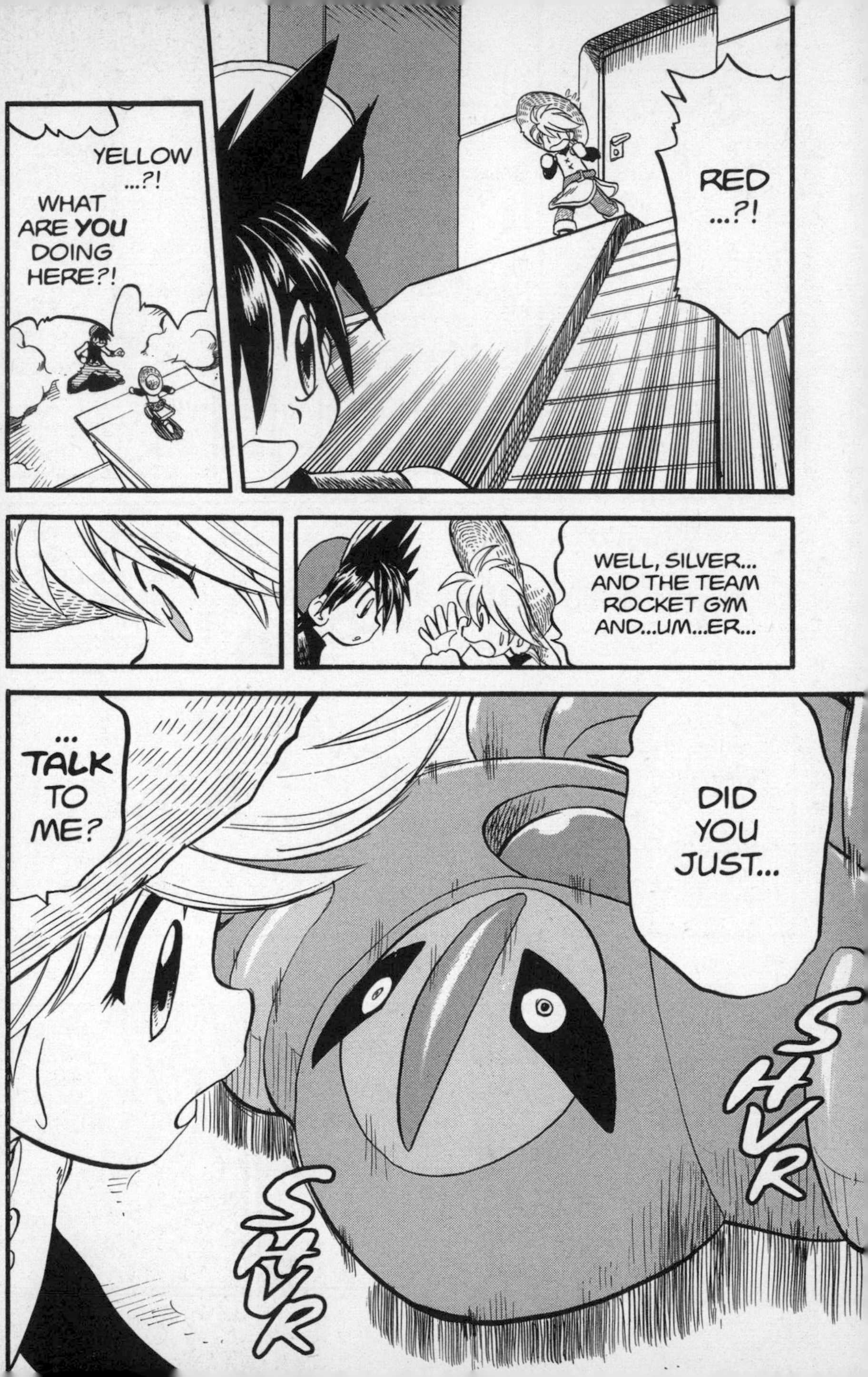
RED ...?!
YELLOW ...?! WHAT ARE YOU DOING HERE?!
WELL, SILVER... AND THE TEAM ROCKET GYM AND...UM...ER...
DID YOU JUST...
... TALK TO ME?
SHVR
SHVR

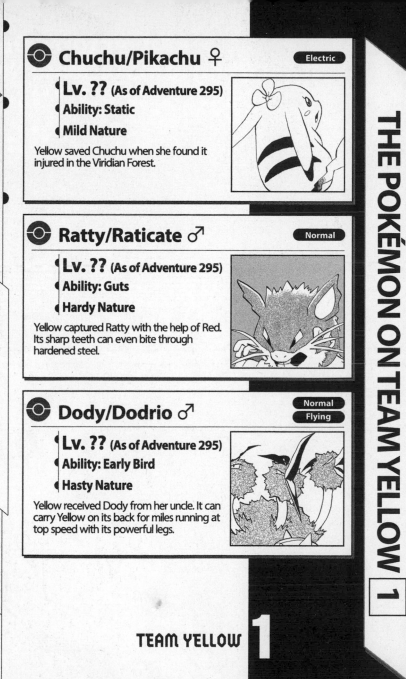

POKÉMON STATS

TEAM YELLOW

Chuchu/Pikachu ♀

Electric

Lv. ?? (As of Adventure 295)

Ability: Static

Mild Nature

Yellow saved Chuchu when she found it injured in the Viridian Forest.

Ratty/Raticate ♂

Normal

Lv. ?? (As of Adventure 295)

Ability: Guts

Hardy Nature

Yellow captured Ratty with the help of Red. Its sharp teeth can even bite through hardened steel.

Dody/Dodrio ♂

Normal
Flying

Lv. ?? (As of Adventure 295)

Ability: Early Bird

Hasty Nature

Yellow received Dody from her uncle. It can carry Yellow on her back for miles running at top speed with its powerful legs.

TEAM YELLOW 1

Adventure 296
It's Starting to Make Sense Now

Pokémon Adventures
FireRed & LeafGreen
The Fifth Chapter

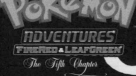

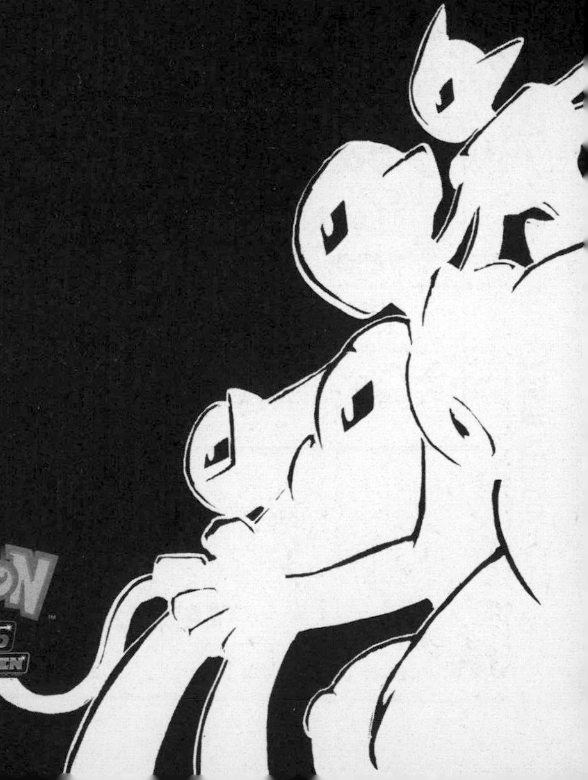

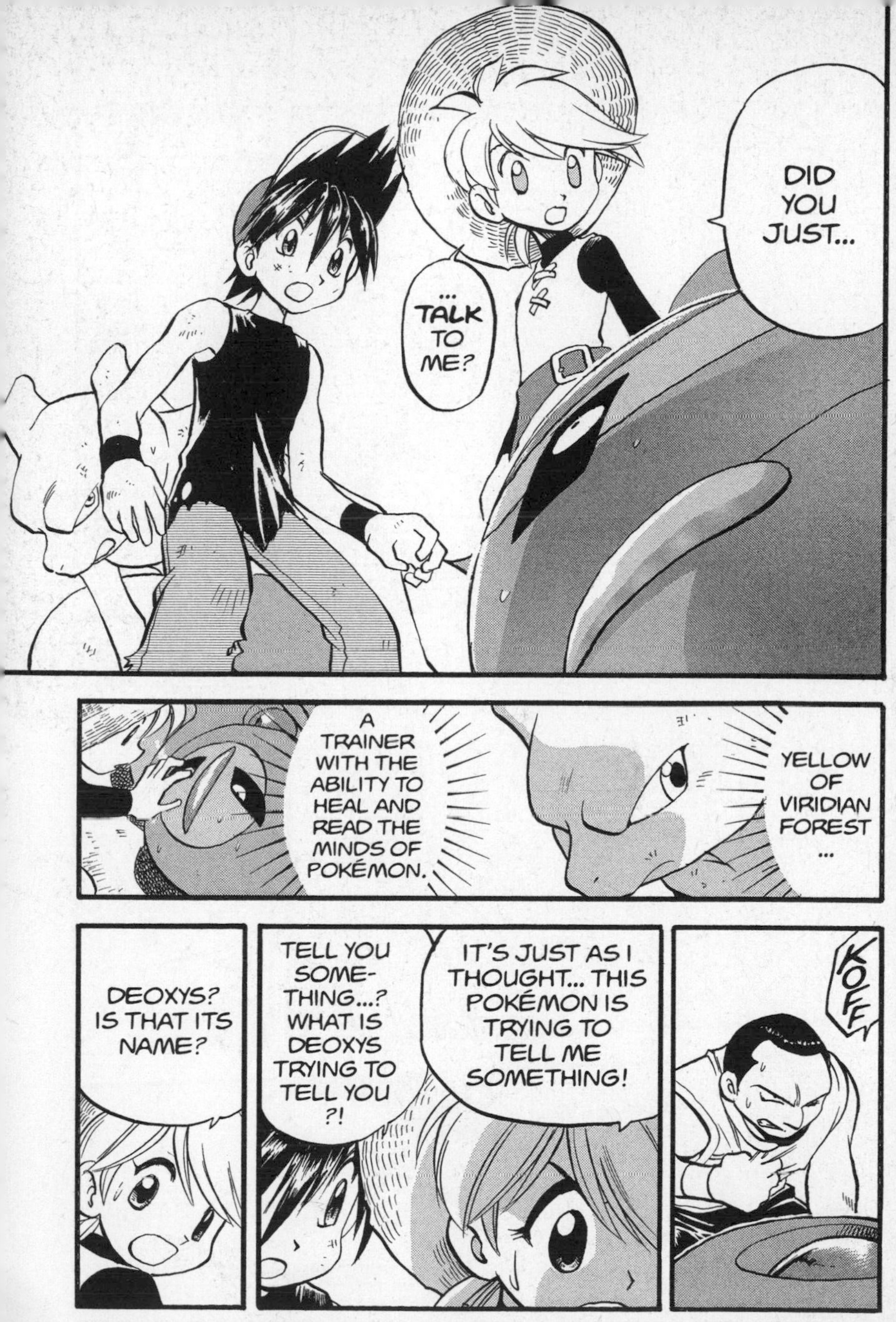
DID YOU JUST...
...TALK TO ME?
YELLOW OF VIRIDIAN FOREST...
A TRAINER WITH THE ABILITY TO HEAL AND READ THE MINDS OF POKÉMON.
KOFF
IT'S JUST AS I THOUGHT... THIS POKÉMON IS TRYING TO TELL ME SOMETHING!
TELL YOU SOMETHING...? WHAT IS DEOXYS TRYING TO TELL YOU?!
DEOXYS? IS THAT ITS NAME?

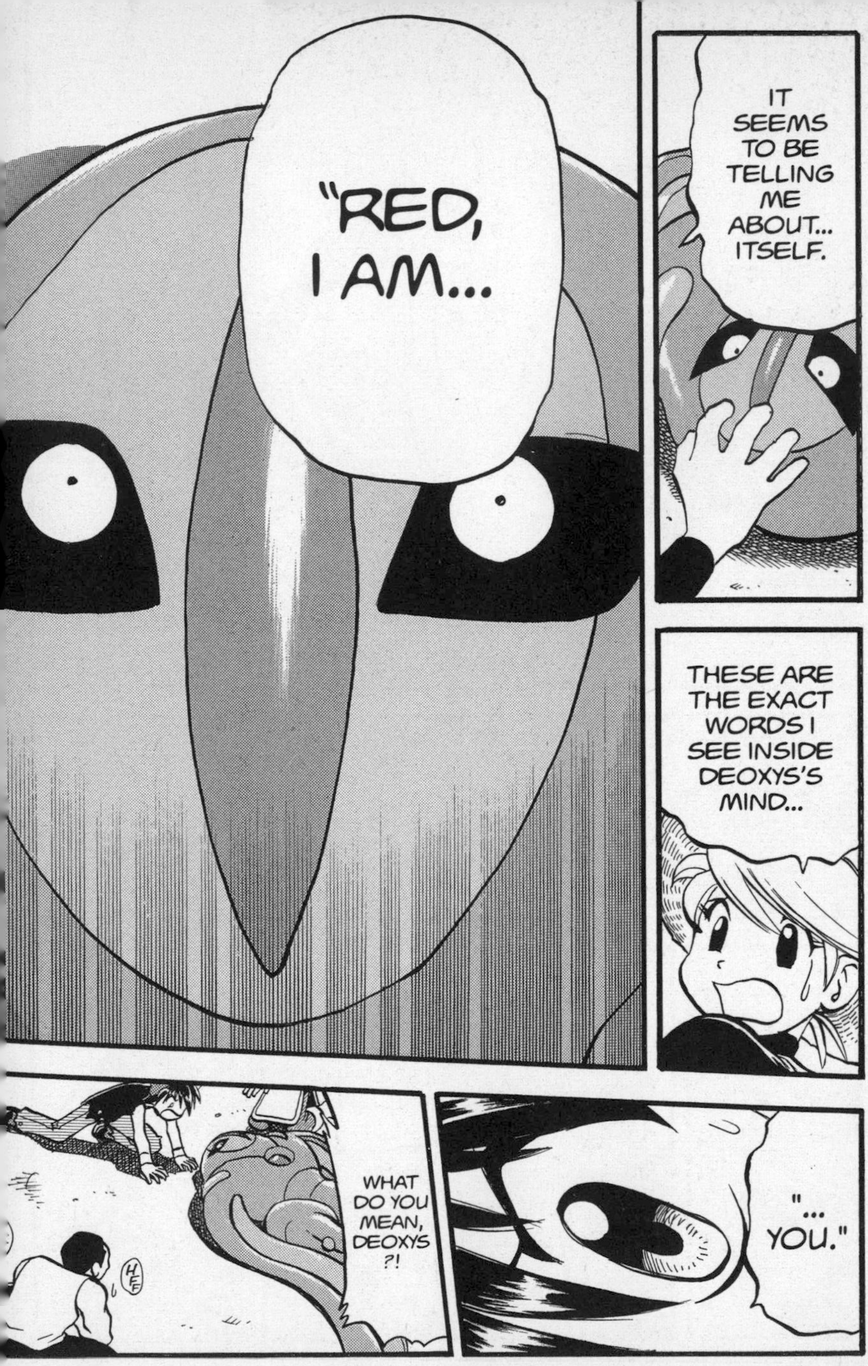
IT SEEMS TO BE TELLING ME ABOUT... ITSELF.
THESE ARE THE EXACT WORDS I SEE INSIDE DEOXYS'S MIND...
"RED, I AM...
"... YOU."
WHAT DO YOU MEAN, DEOXYS?!
HEF

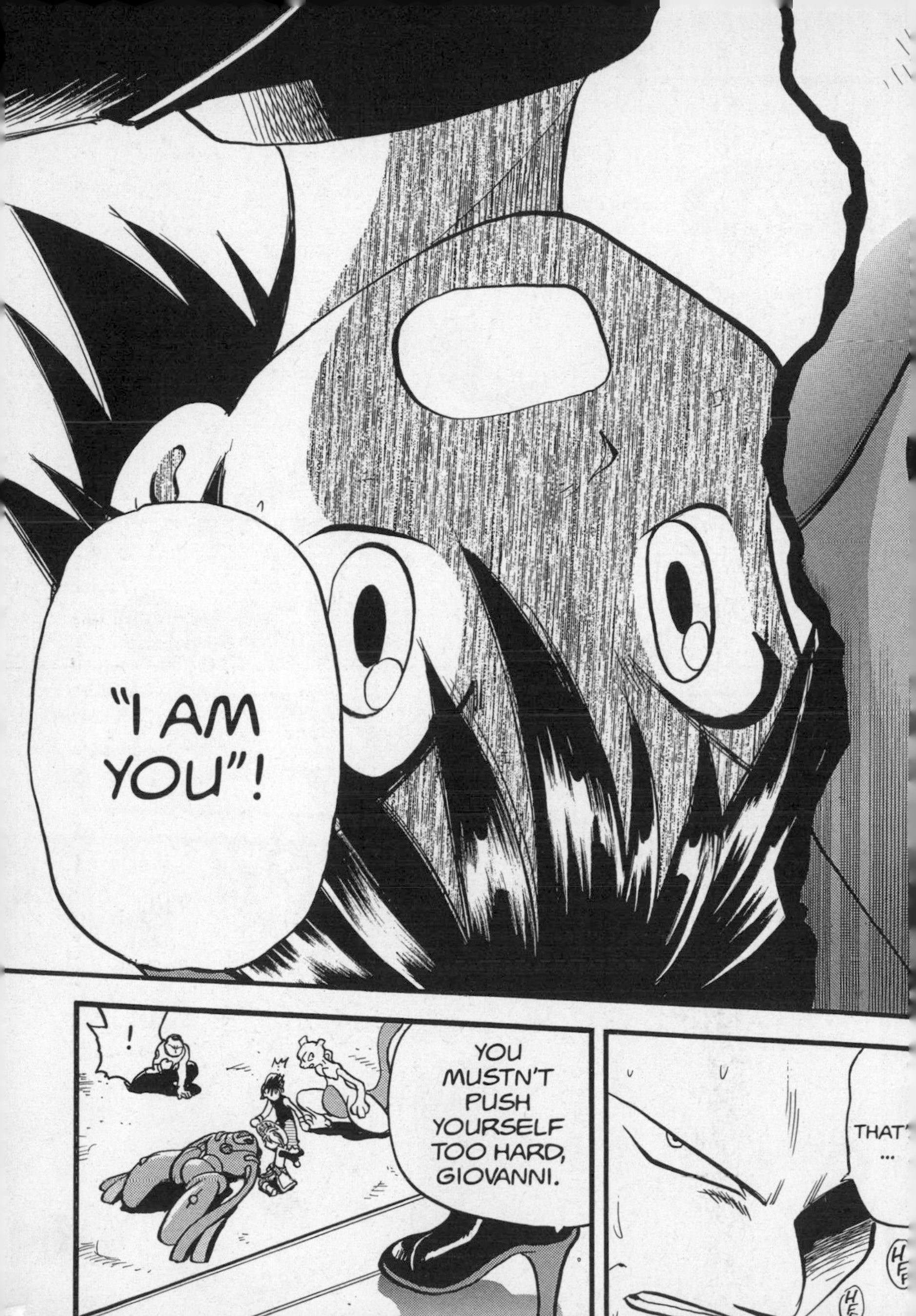
"I AM YOU"!
THAT'...
HFF
HFF
YOU MUSTN'T PUSH YOURSELF TOO HARD, GIOVANNI.
!

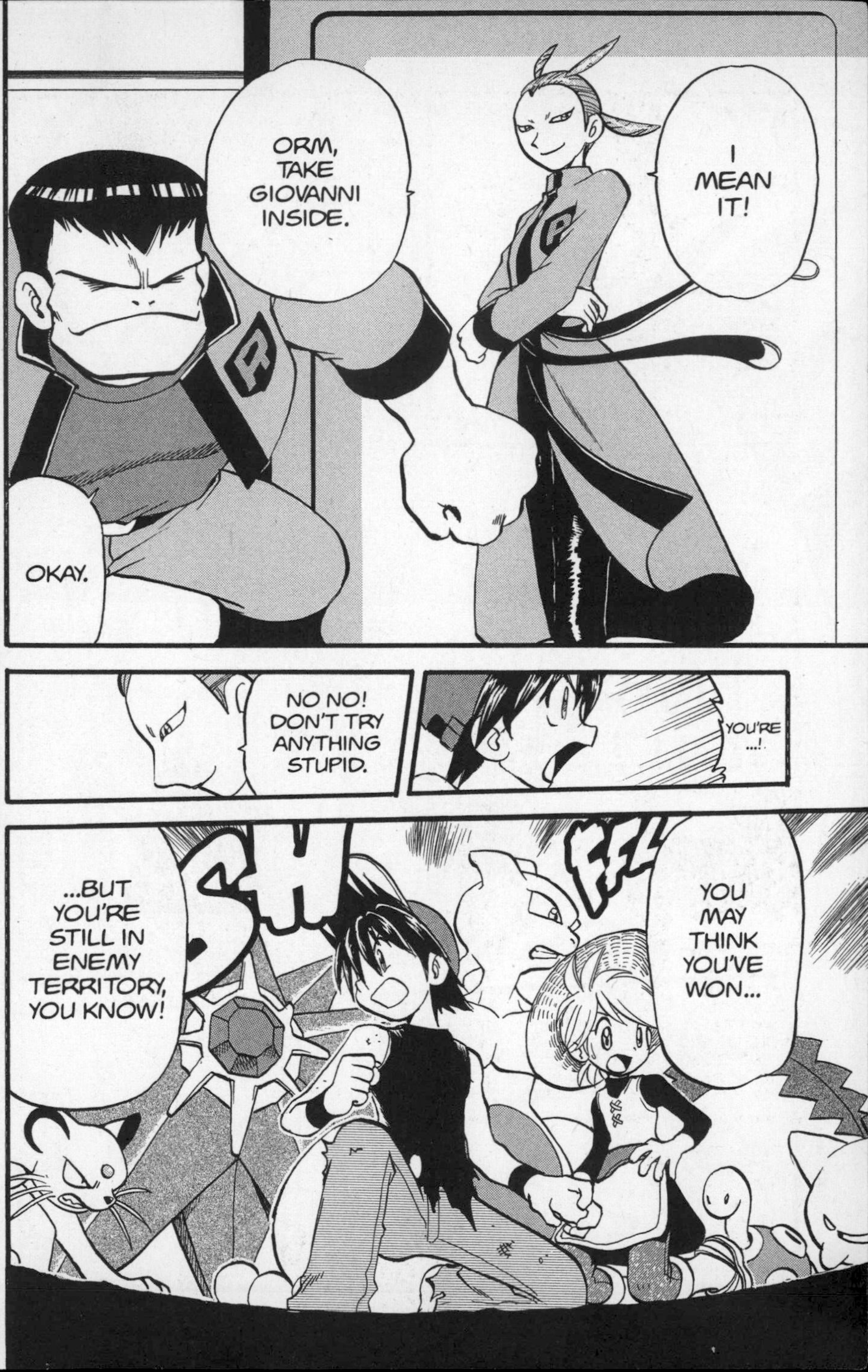
I MEAN IT!
ORM, TAKE GIOVANNI INSIDE.
OKAY.
YOU'RE ...!
NO NO! DON'T TRY ANYTHING STUPID.
YOU MAY THINK YOU'VE WON...
...BUT YOU'RE STILL IN ENEMY TERRITORY, YOU KNOW!

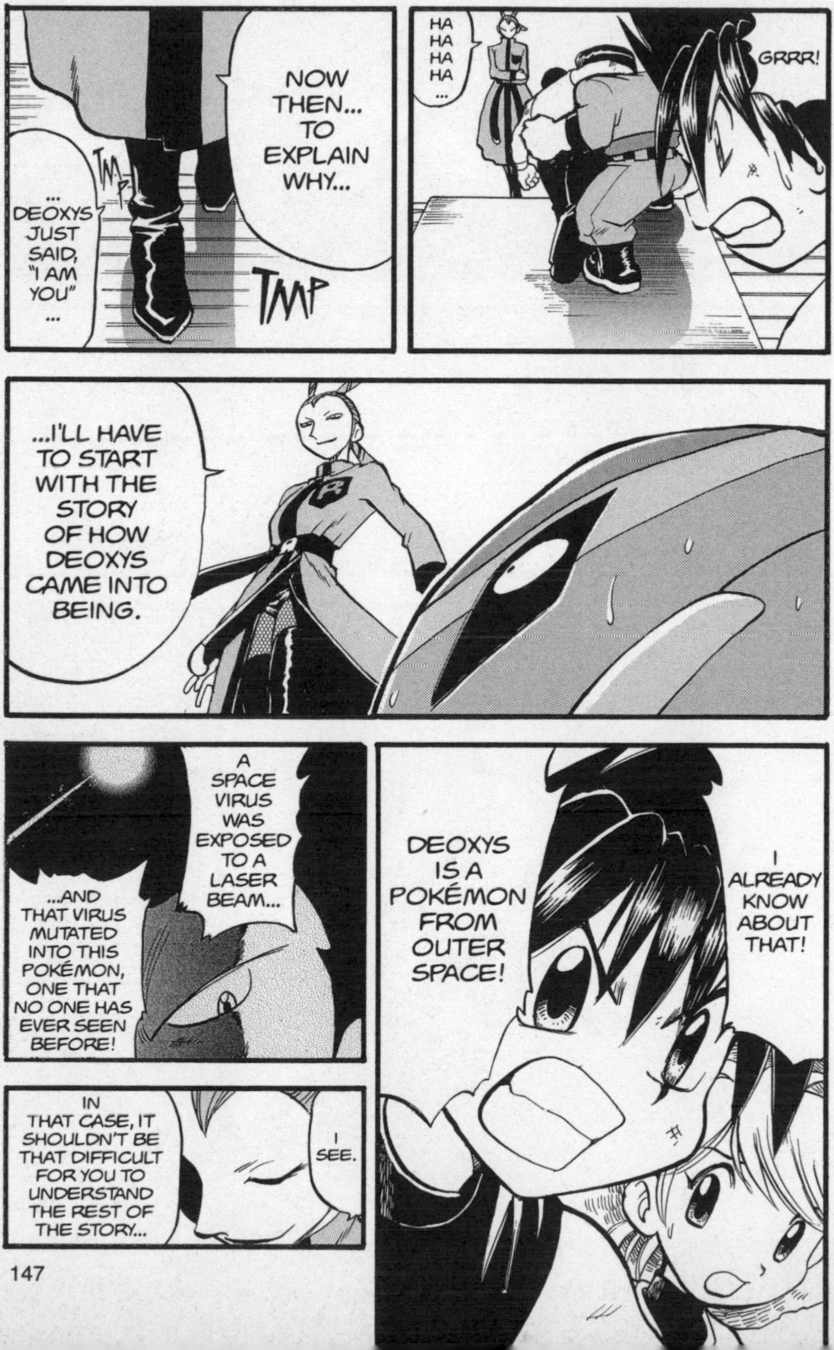
HA HA HA HA ...
GRRR!
NOW THEN... TO EXPLAIN WHY...
... DEOXYS JUST SAID, "I AM YOU" ...
TMP
TMP
...I'LL HAVE TO START WITH THE STORY OF HOW DEOXYS CAME INTO BEING.
DEOXYS IS A POKÉMON FROM OUTER SPACE!
I ALREADY KNOW ABOUT THAT!
A SPACE VIRUS WAS EXPOSED TO A LASER BEAM...
...AND THAT VIRUS MUTATED INTO THIS POKÉMON, ONE THAT NO ONE HAS EVER SEEN BEFORE!
I SEE.
IN THAT CASE, IT SHOULDN'T BE THAT DIFFICULT FOR YOU TO UNDERSTAND THE REST OF THE STORY...

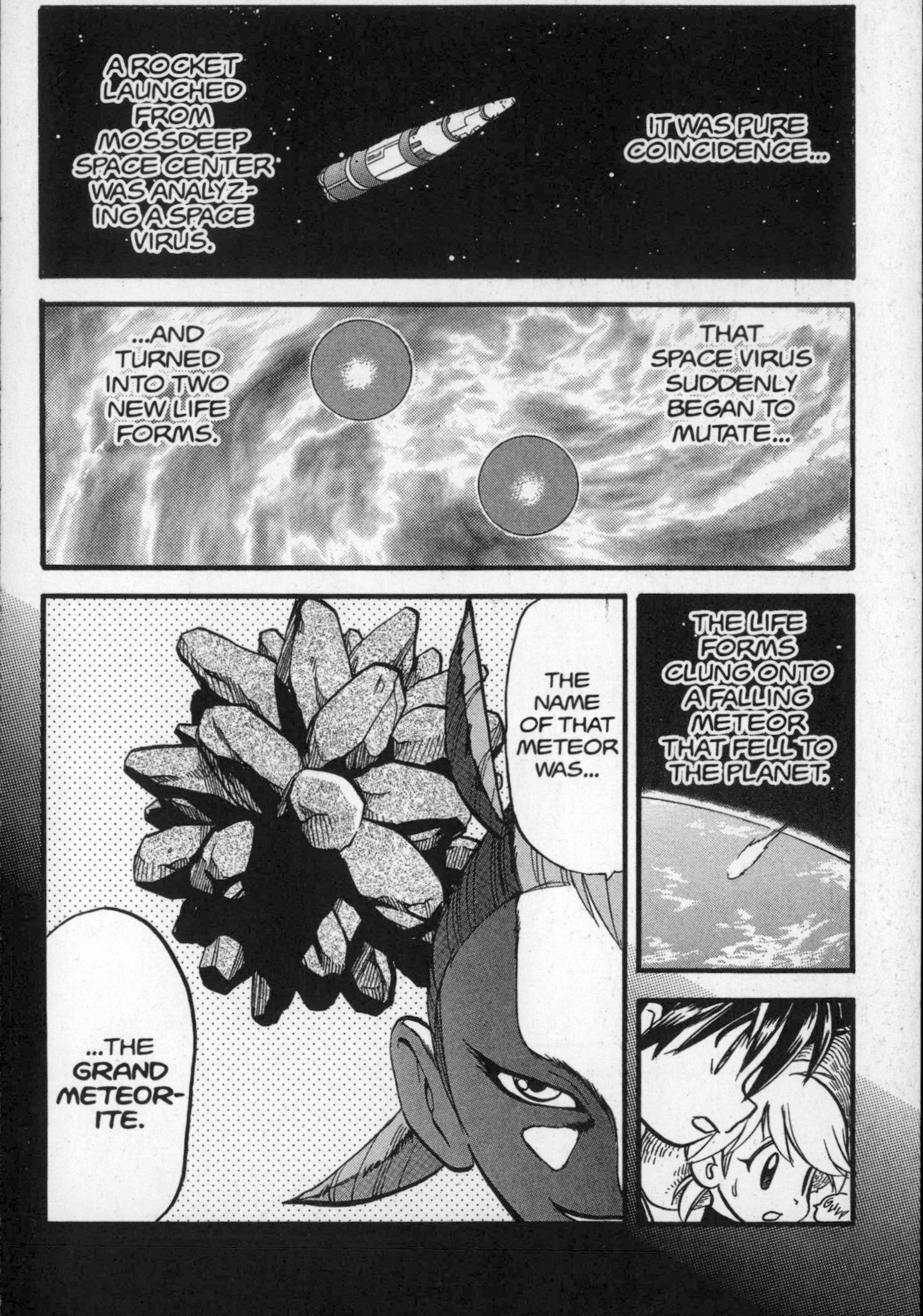
IT WAS PURE COINCIDENCE...
A ROCKET LAUNCHED FROM MOSSDEEP SPACE CENTER WAS ANALYZ-ING A SPACE VIRUS.
THAT SPACE VIRUS SUDDENLY BEGAN TO MUTATE...
...AND TURNED INTO TWO NEW LIFE FORMS.
THE LIFE FORMS CLUNG ONTO A FALLING METEOR THAT FELL TO THE PLANET.
THE NAME OF THAT METEOR WAS...
...THE GRAND METEOR-ITE.

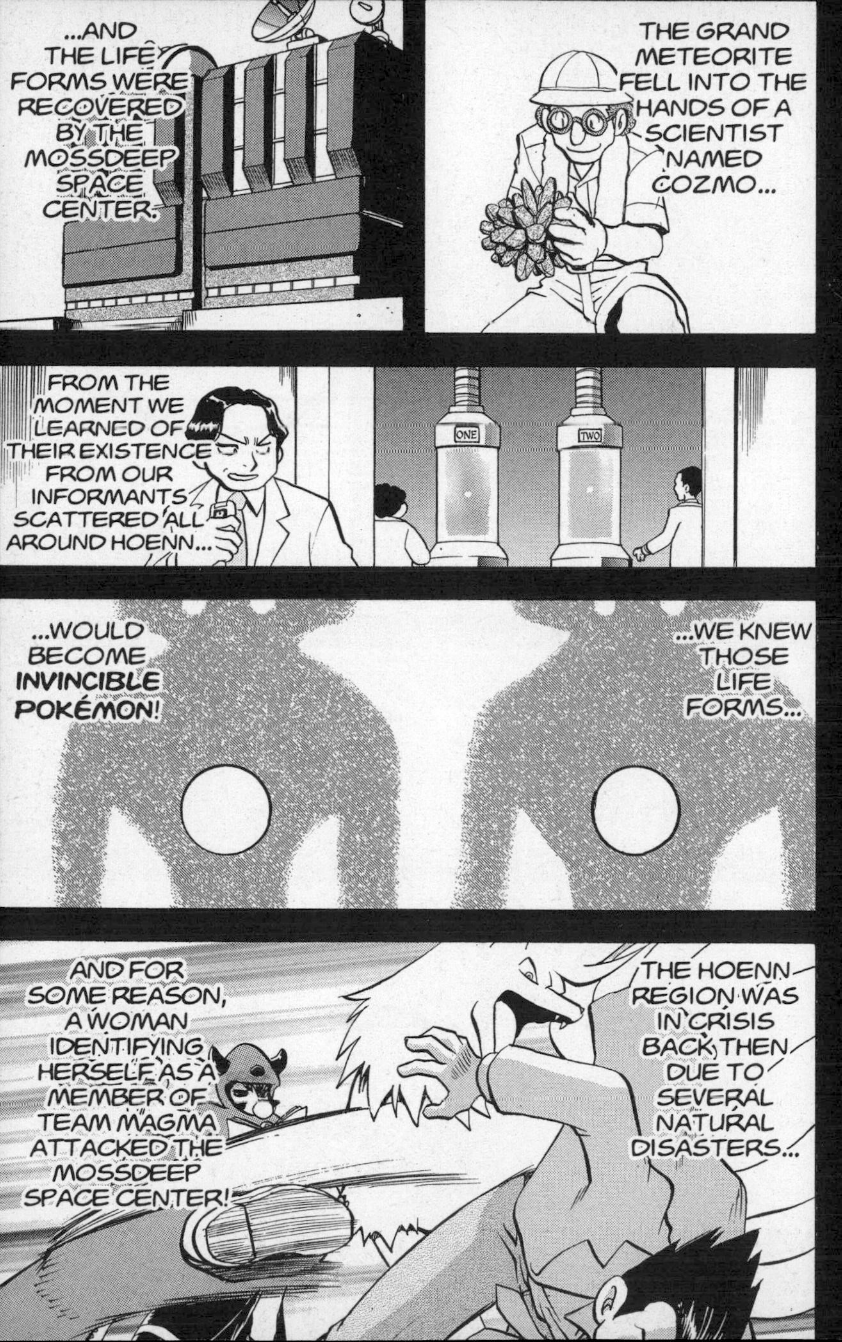
THE GRAND METEORITE FELL INTO THE HANDS OF A SCIENTIST NAMED COZMO...
...AND THE LIFE FORMS WERE RECOVERED BY THE MOSSDEEP SPACE CENTER.
FROM THE MOMENT WE LEARNED OF THEIR EXISTENCE FROM OUR INFORMANTS SCATTERED ALL AROUND HOENN...
ONE
TWO
...WE KNEW THOSE LIFE FORMS...
...WOULD BECOME **INVINCIBLE POKÉMON!**
THE HOENN REGION WAS IN CRISIS BACK THEN DUE TO SEVERAL NATURAL DISASTERS...
AND FOR SOME REASON, A WOMAN IDENTIFYING HERSELF AS A MEMBER OF TEAM MAGMA ATTACKED THE MOSSDEEP SPACE CENTER!

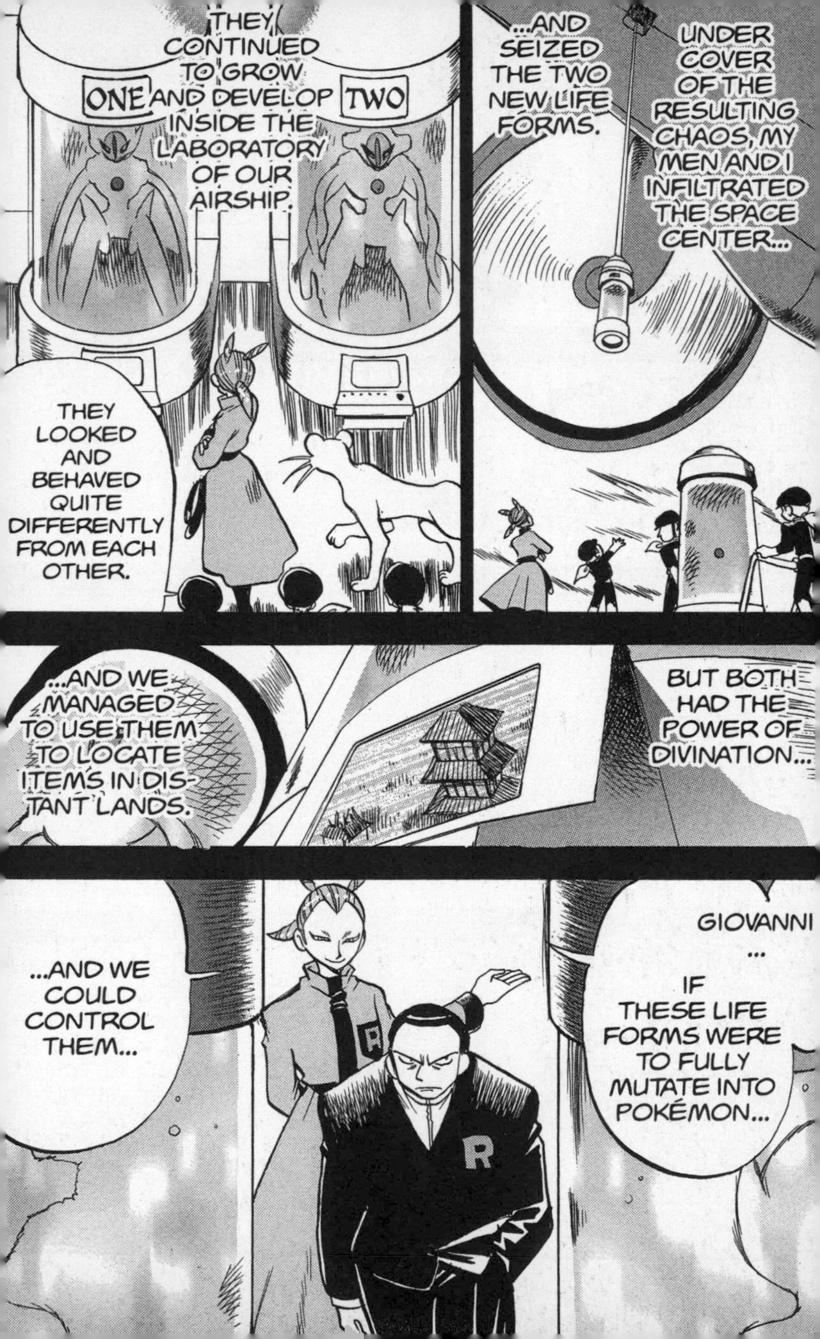
UNDER COVER OF THE RESULTING CHAOS, MY MEN AND I INFILTRATED THE SPACE CENTER...
...AND SEIZED THE TWO NEW LIFE FORMS.
THEY CONTINUED TO GROW AND DEVELOP INSIDE THE LABORATORY OF OUR AIRSHIP.
TWO
ONE
THEY LOOKED AND BEHAVED QUITE DIFFERENTLY FROM EACH OTHER.
BUT BOTH HAD THE POWER OF DIVINATION...
...AND WE MANAGED TO USE THEM TO LOCATE ITEMS IN DISTANT LANDS.
GIOVANNI ... IF THESE LIFE FORMS WERE TO FULLY MUTATE INTO POKÉMON...
...AND WE COULD CONTROL THEM...

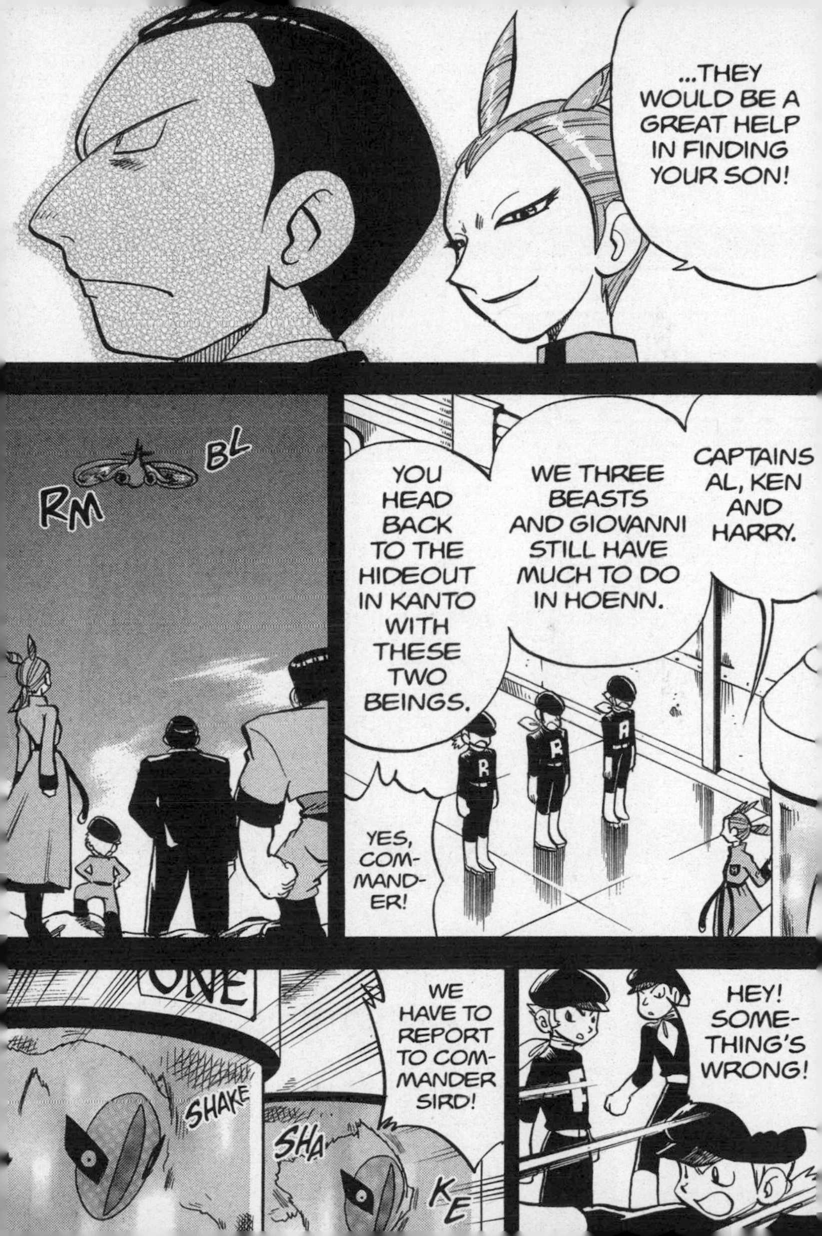
...THEY WOULD BE A GREAT HELP IN FINDING YOUR SON!
CAPTAINS AL, KEN AND HARRY.
WE THREE BEASTS AND GIOVANNI STILL HAVE MUCH TO DO IN HOENN.
YOU HEAD BACK TO THE HIDEOUT IN KANTO WITH THESE TWO BEINGS.
YES, COM-MAND-ER!
RM
BL
HEY! SOME-THING'S WRONG!
ONE
WE HAVE TO REPORT TO COM-MANDER SIRD!
SHAKE
SHAKE

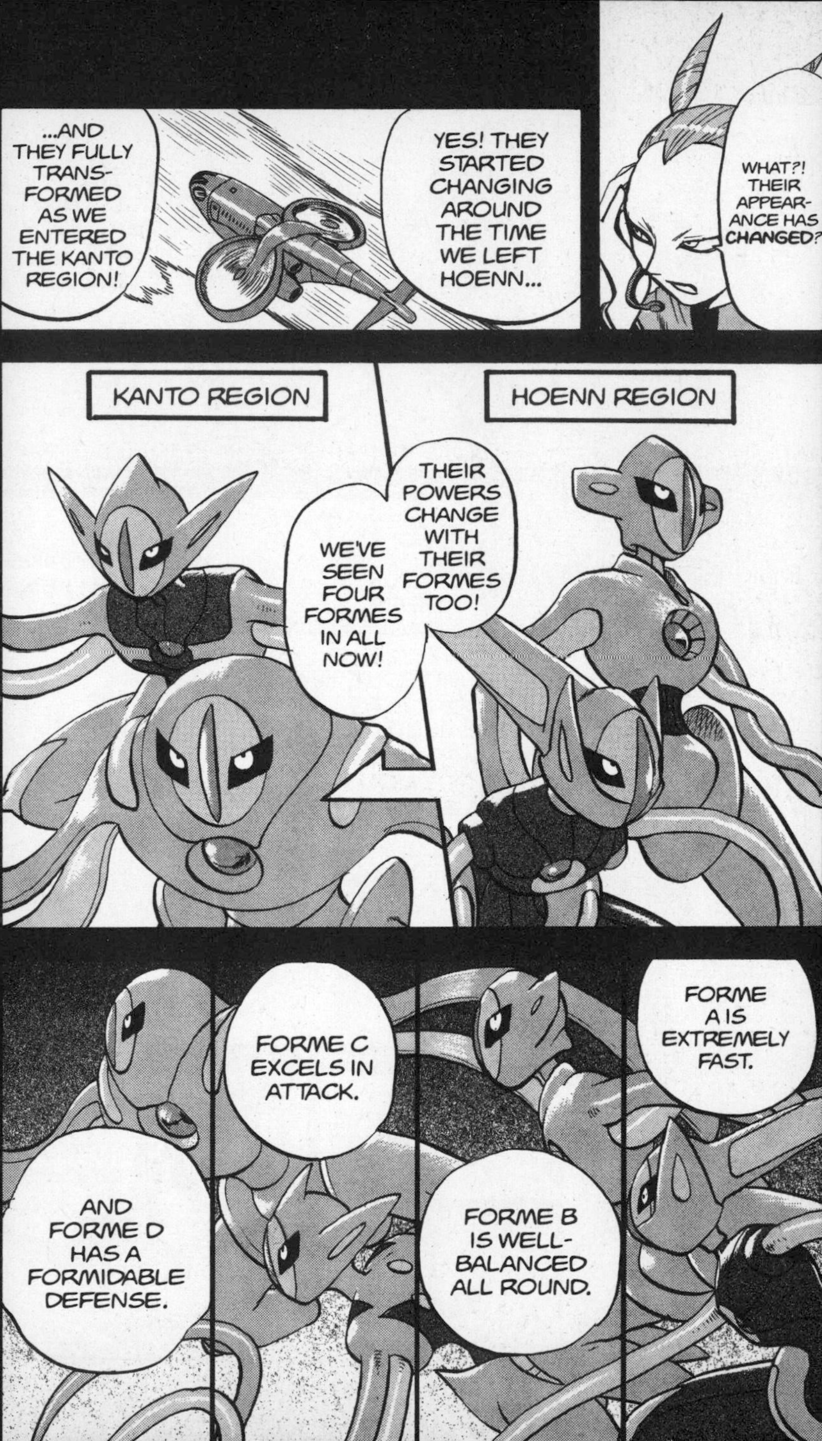
WHAT?! THEIR APPEARANCE HAS CHANGED?
YES! THEY STARTED CHANGING AROUND THE TIME WE LEFT HOENN...
...AND THEY FULLY TRANSFORMED AS WE ENTERED THE KANTO REGION!
HOENN REGION
KANTO REGION
THEIR POWERS CHANGE WITH THEIR FORMES TOO!
WE'VE SEEN FOUR FORMES IN ALL NOW!
FORME A IS EXTREMELY FAST.
FORME B IS WELL-BALANCED ALL ROUND.
FORME C EXCELS IN ATTACK.
AND FORME D HAS A FORMIDABLE DEFENSE.

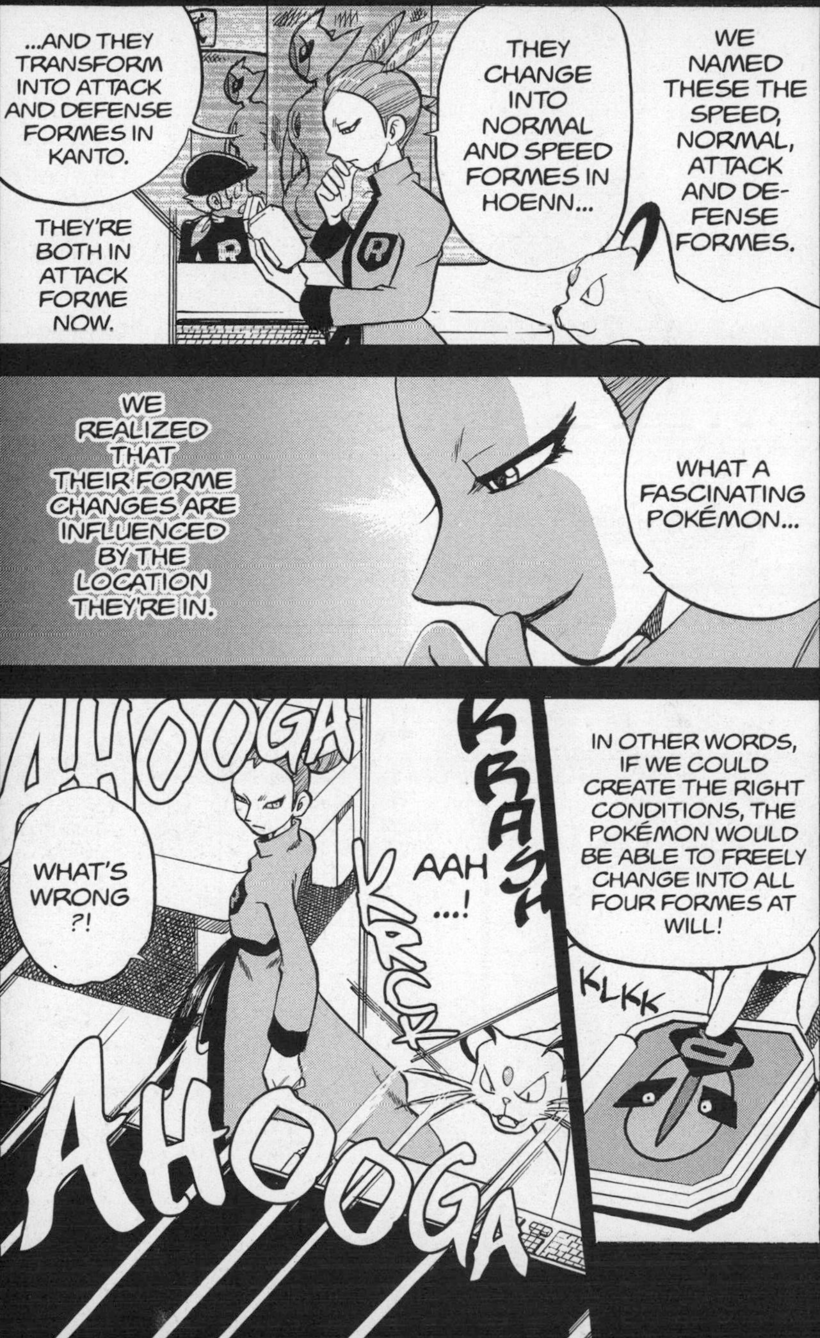
WE NAMED THESE THE SPEED, NORMAL, ATTACK AND DEFENSE FORMES.
THEY CHANGE INTO NORMAL AND SPEED FORMES IN HOENN...
...AND THEY TRANSFORM INTO ATTACK AND DEFENSE FORMES IN KANTO.
THEY'RE BOTH IN ATTACK FORME NOW.
WHAT A FASCINATING POKÉMON...
WE REALIZED THAT THEIR FORME CHANGES ARE INFLUENCED BY THE LOCATION THEY'RE IN.
IN OTHER WORDS, IF WE COULD CREATE THE RIGHT CONDITIONS, THE POKÉMON WOULD BE ABLE TO FREELY CHANGE INTO ALL FOUR FORMES AT WILL!
KLKK
KRASH
AAH ...!
AHOOGA
WHAT'S WRONG ?!
KRCK
AHOOGA

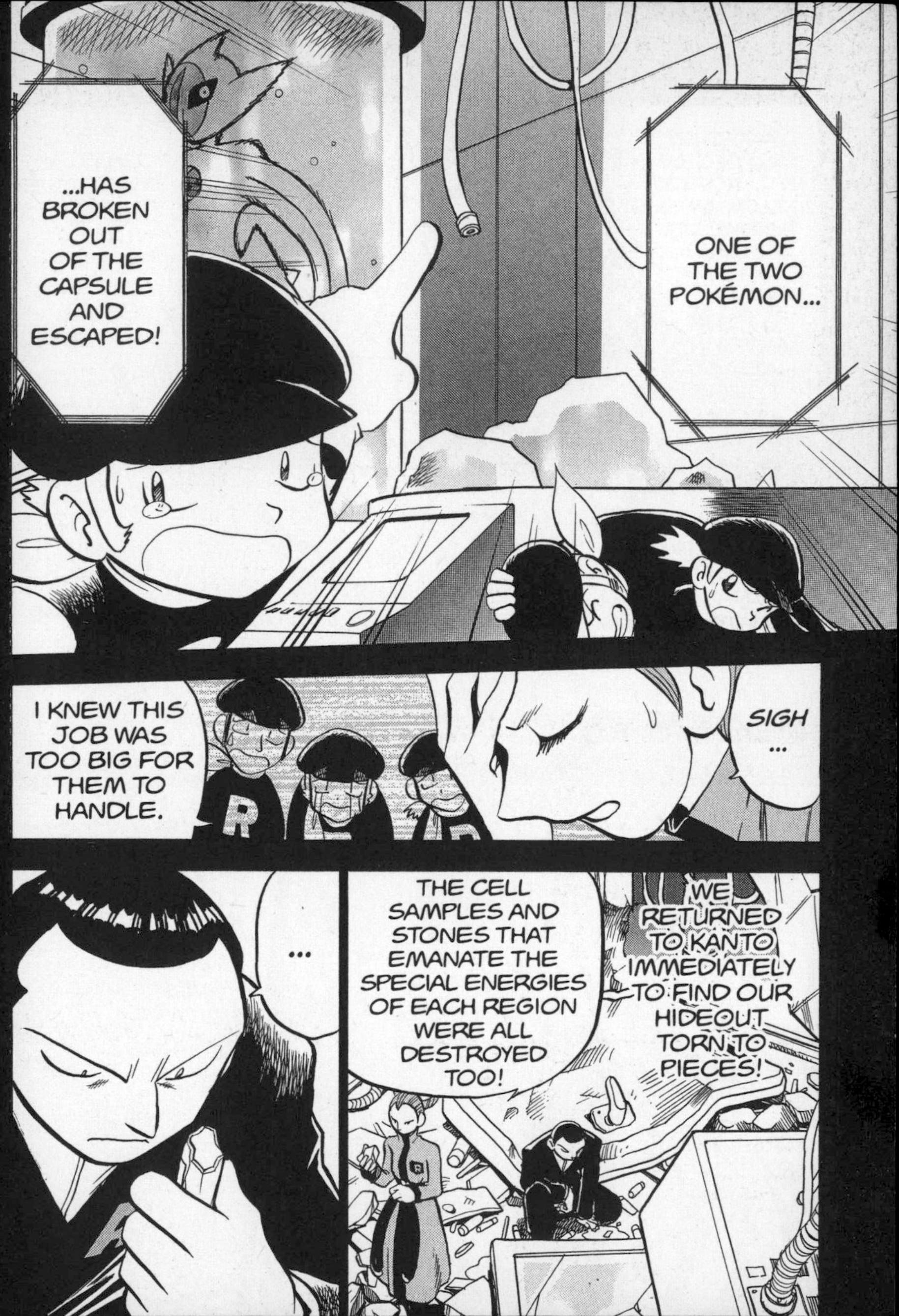
ONE OF THE TWO POKÉMON...
...HAS BROKEN OUT OF THE CAPSULE AND ESCAPED!
SIGH ...
I KNEW THIS JOB WAS TOO BIG FOR THEM TO HANDLE.
WE RETURNED TO KANTO IMMEDIATELY TO FIND OUR HIDEOUT TORN TO PIECES!
THE CELL SAMPLES AND STONES THAT EMANATE THE SPECIAL ENERGIES OF EACH REGION WERE ALL DESTROYED TOO!
...

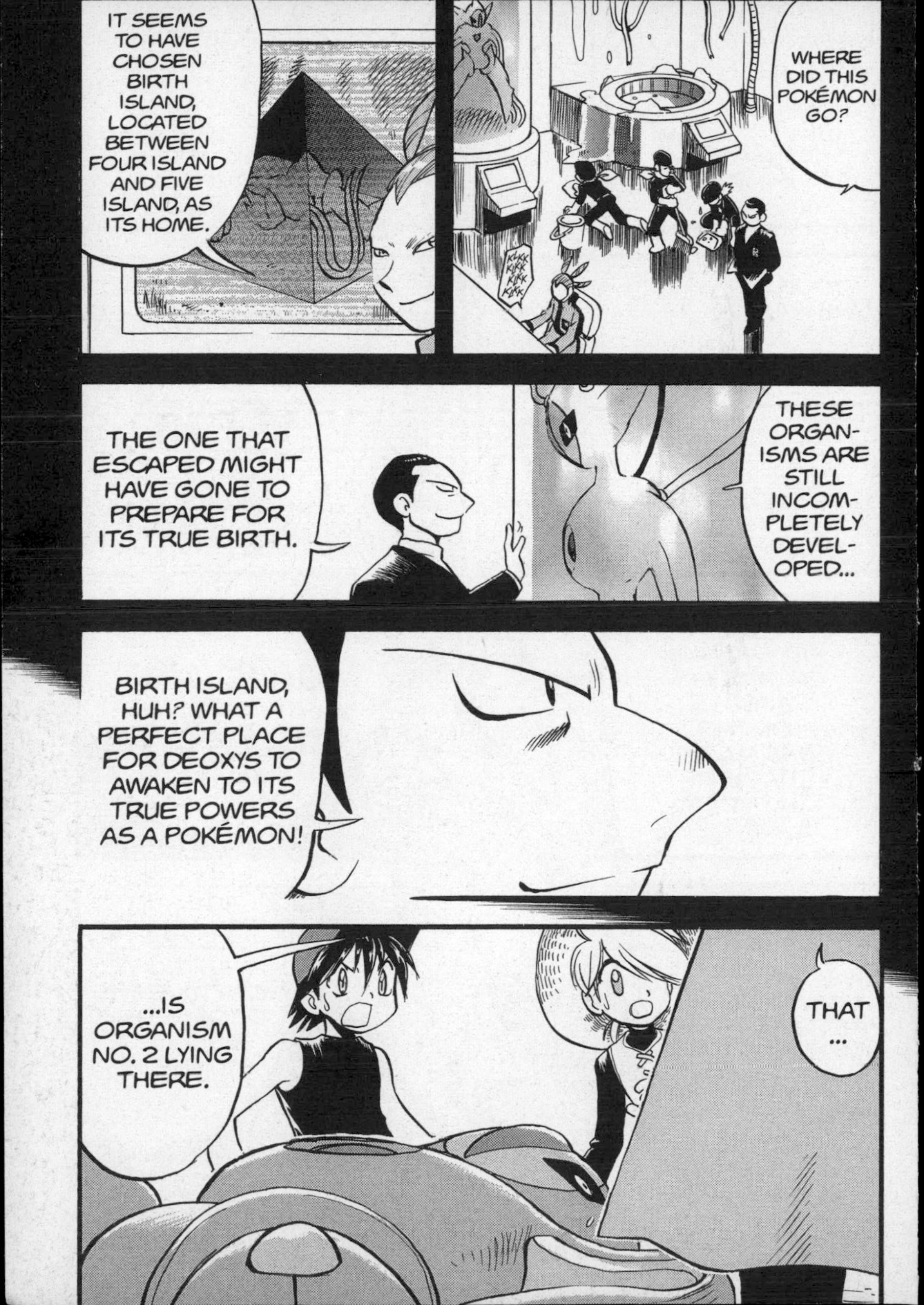
WHERE DID THIS POKÉMON GO?
IT SEEMS TO HAVE CHOSEN BIRTH ISLAND, LOCATED BETWEEN FOUR ISLAND AND FIVE ISLAND, AS ITS HOME.
THESE ORGAN-ISMS ARE STILL INCOM-PLETELY DEVEL-OPED...
THE ONE THAT ESCAPED MIGHT HAVE GONE TO PREPARE FOR ITS TRUE BIRTH.
BIRTH ISLAND, HUH? WHAT A PERFECT PLACE FOR DEOXYS TO AWAKEN TO ITS TRUE POWERS AS A POKÉMON!
THAT ...
...IS ORGANISM NO. 2 LYING THERE.

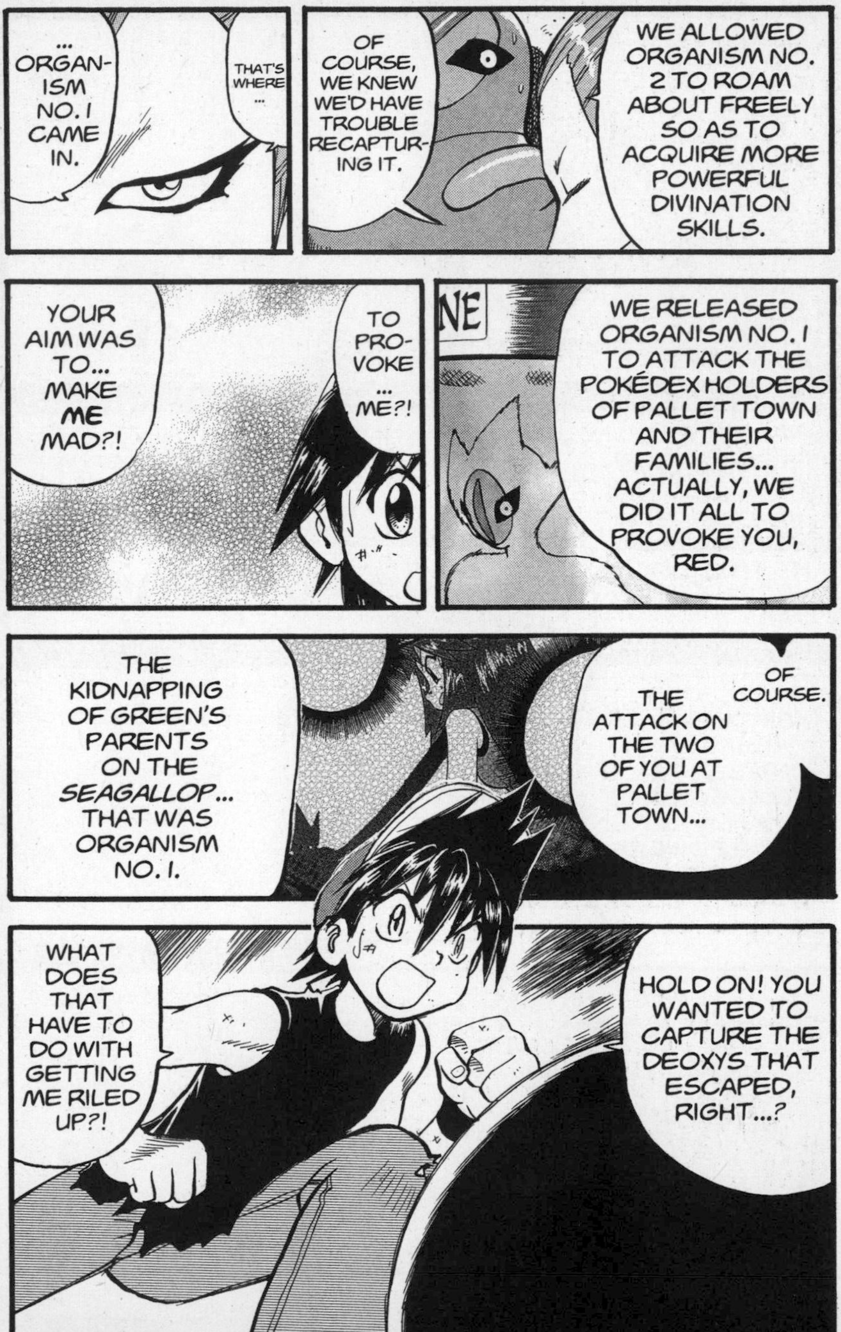
WE ALLOWED ORGANISM NO. 2 TO ROAM ABOUT FREELY SO AS TO ACQUIRE MORE POWERFUL DIVINATION SKILLS.
OF COURSE, WE KNEW WE'D HAVE TROUBLE RECAPTURING IT.
THAT'S WHERE ...
... ORGANISM NO. 1 CAME IN.
NE
WE RELEASED ORGANISM NO. 1 TO ATTACK THE POKÉDEX HOLDERS OF PALLET TOWN AND THEIR FAMILIES... ACTUALLY, WE DID IT ALL TO PROVOKE YOU, RED.
TO PROVOKE ... ME?!
YOUR AIM WAS TO... MAKE ME MAD?!
OF COURSE.
THE ATTACK ON THE TWO OF YOU AT PALLET TOWN...
THE KIDNAPPING OF GREEN'S PARENTS ON THE *SEAGALLOP*... THAT WAS ORGANISM NO. 1.
HOLD ON! YOU WANTED TO CAPTURE THE DEOXYS THAT ESCAPED, RIGHT...?
WHAT DOES THAT HAVE TO DO WITH GETTING ME RILED UP?!

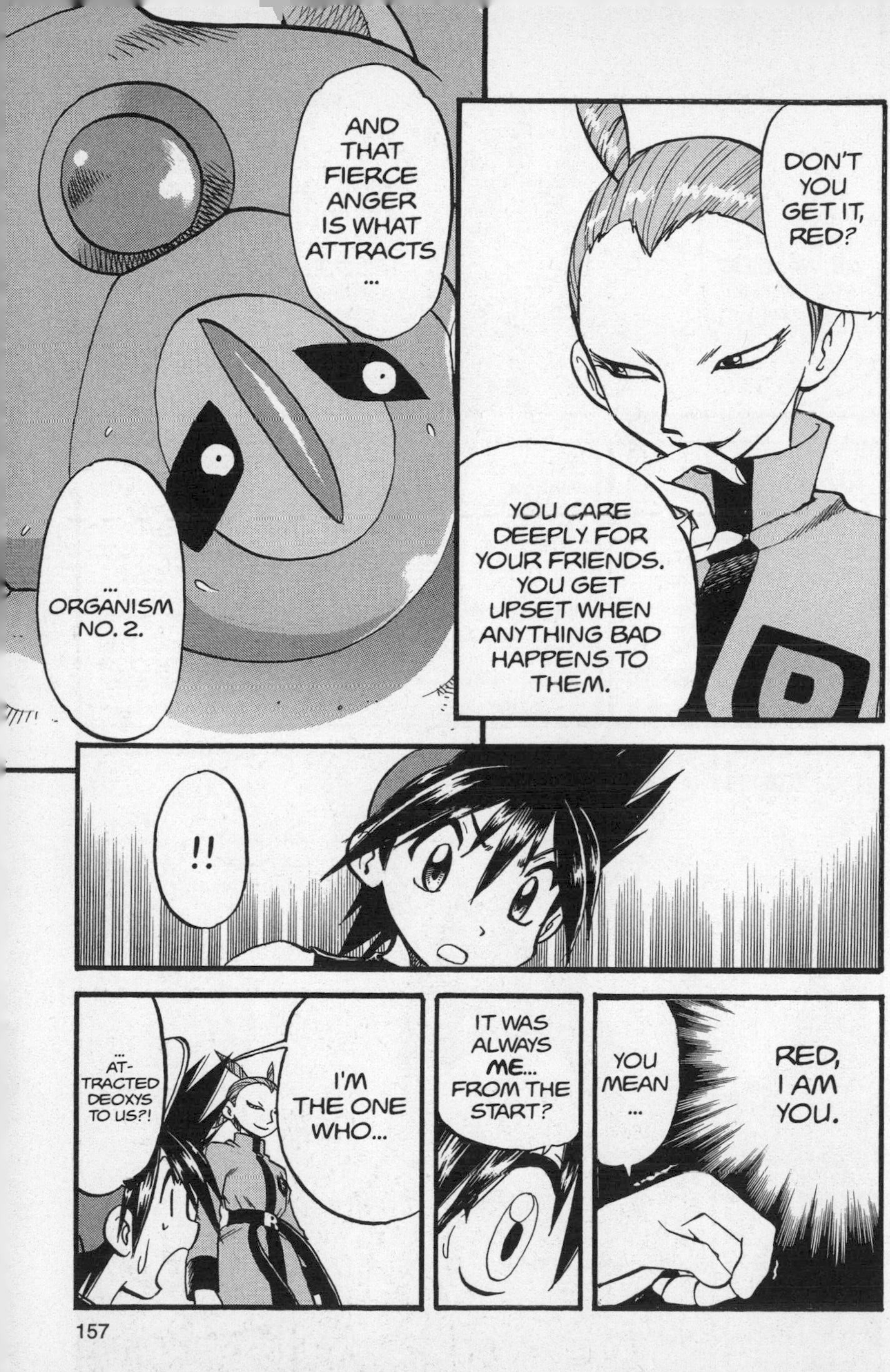
DON'T YOU GET IT, RED?
YOU CARE DEEPLY FOR YOUR FRIENDS. YOU GET UPSET WHEN ANYTHING BAD HAPPENS TO THEM.
AND THAT FIERCE ANGER IS WHAT ATTRACTS ...
... ORGANISM NO. 2.
!!
RED, I AM YOU.
YOU MEAN ...
IT WAS ALWAYS ME... FROM THE START?
I'M THE ONE WHO...
... AT-TRACTED DEOXYS TO US?!

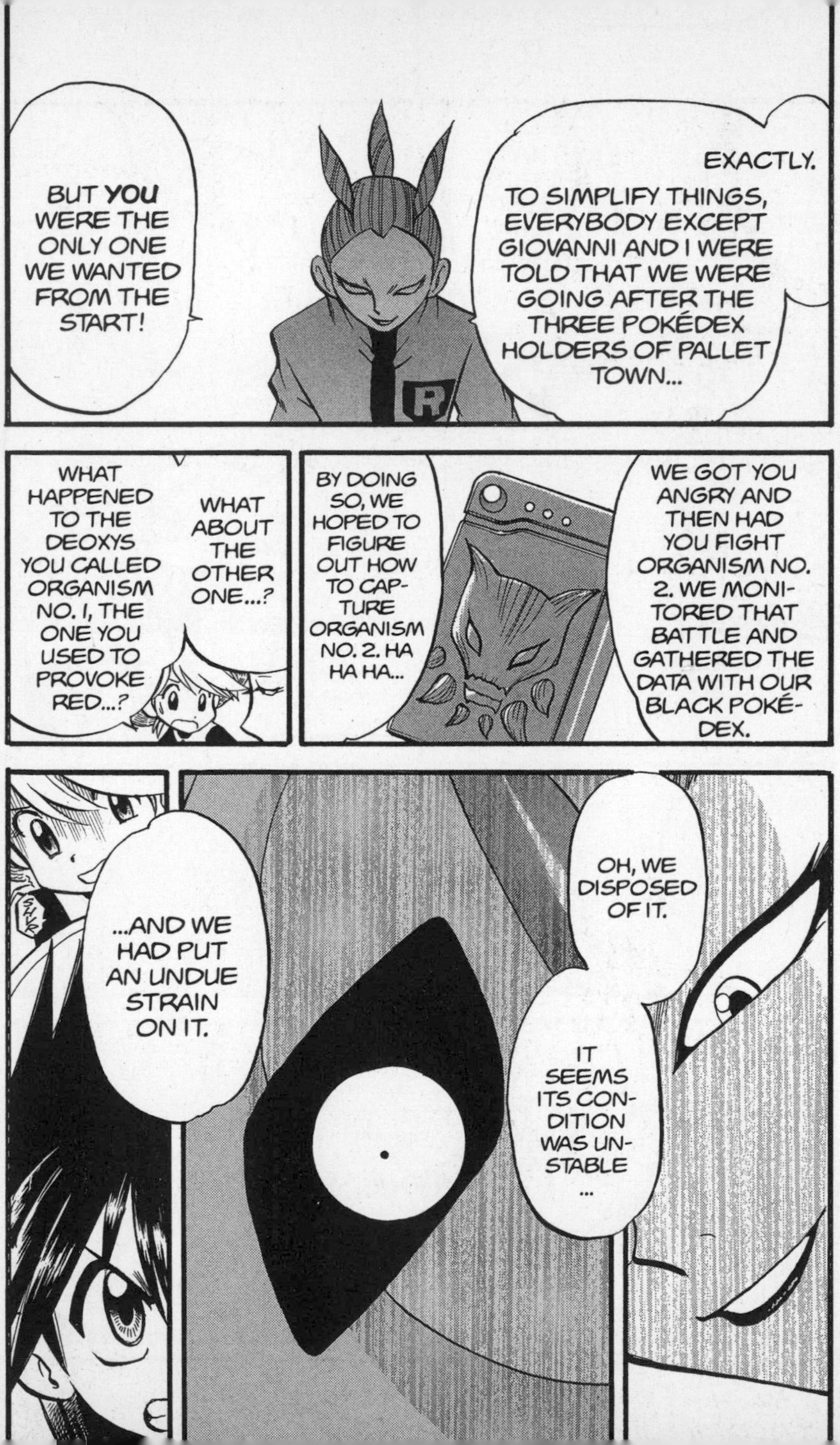
EXACTLY.
TO SIMPLIFY THINGS, EVERYBODY EXCEPT GIOVANNI AND I WERE TOLD THAT WE WERE GOING AFTER THE THREE POKÉDEX HOLDERS OF PALLET TOWN...
BUT **YOU** WERE THE ONLY ONE WE WANTED FROM THE START!
WE GOT YOU ANGRY AND THEN HAD YOU FIGHT ORGANISM NO. 2. WE MONITORED THAT BATTLE AND GATHERED THE DATA WITH OUR BLACK POKÉDEX.
BY DOING SO, WE HOPED TO FIGURE OUT HOW TO CAPTURE ORGANISM NO. 2. HA HA HA...
WHAT ABOUT THE OTHER ONE...?
WHAT HAPPENED TO THE DEOXYS YOU CALLED ORGANISM NO. 1, THE ONE YOU USED TO PROVOKE RED...?
OH, WE DISPOSED OF IT.
IT SEEMS ITS CONDITION WAS UNSTABLE...
...AND WE HAD PUT AN UNDUE STRAIN ON IT.

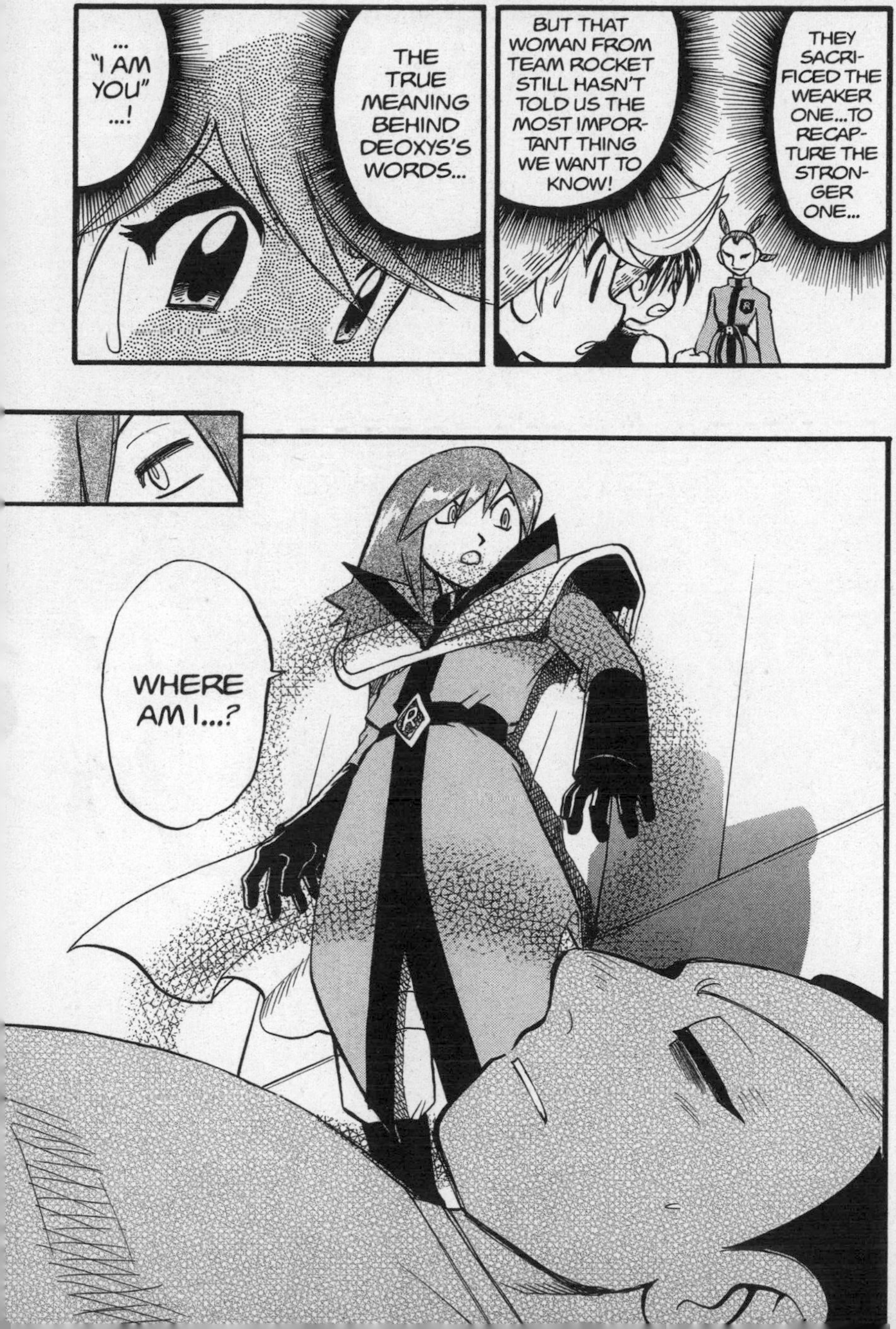
THEY SACRI-FICED THE WEAKER ONE...TO RECAP-TURE THE STRON-GER ONE...
BUT THAT WOMAN FROM TEAM ROCKET STILL HASN'T TOLD US THE MOST IMPOR-TANT THING WE WANT TO KNOW!
THE TRUE MEANING BEHIND DEOXYS'S WORDS...
... "I AM YOU" ...!
WHERE AM I...?

•Adventure 297•
Mewtwo Comes Through

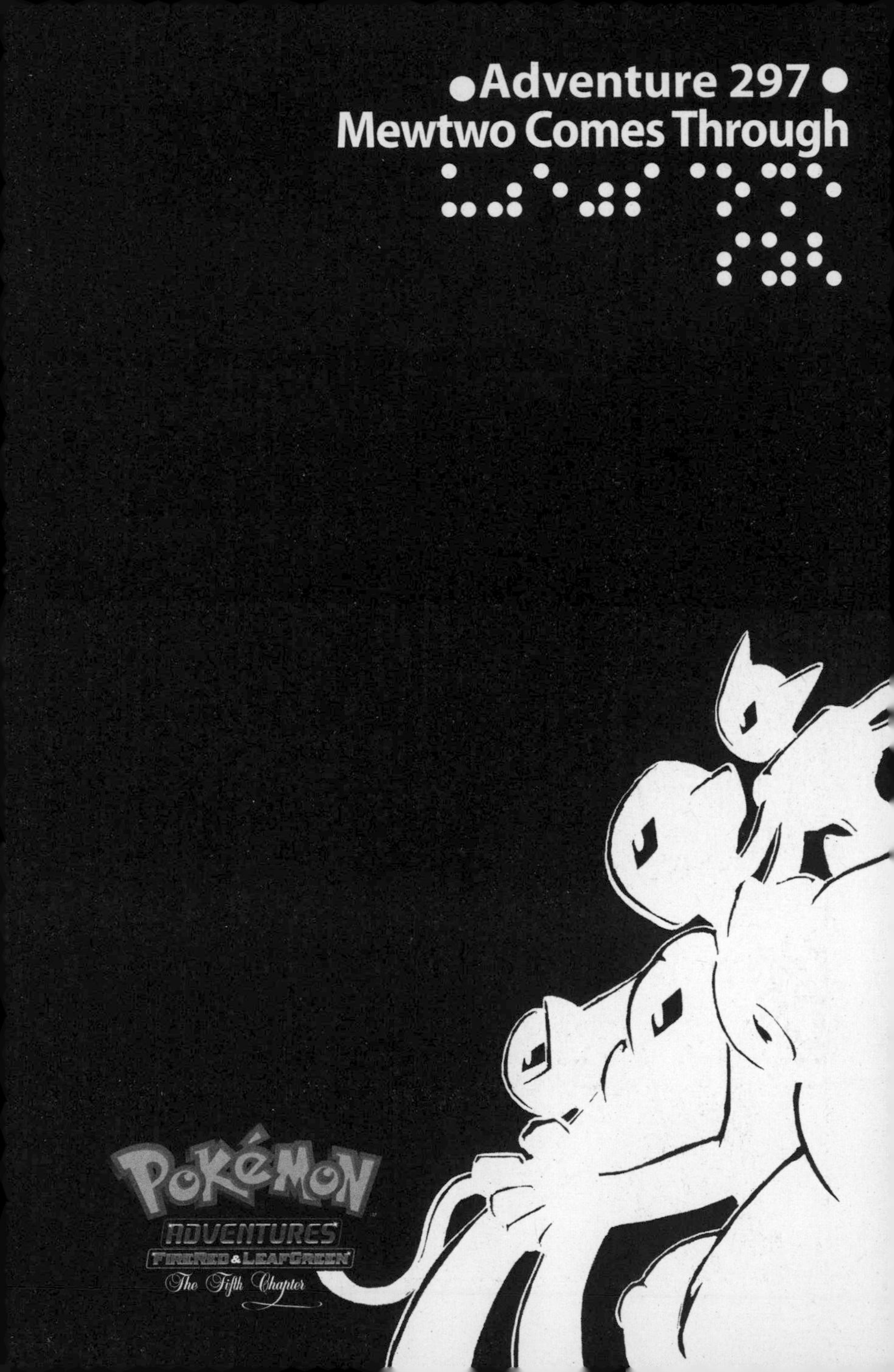

Pokémon Adventures
FireRed & LeafGreen
The Fifth Chapter

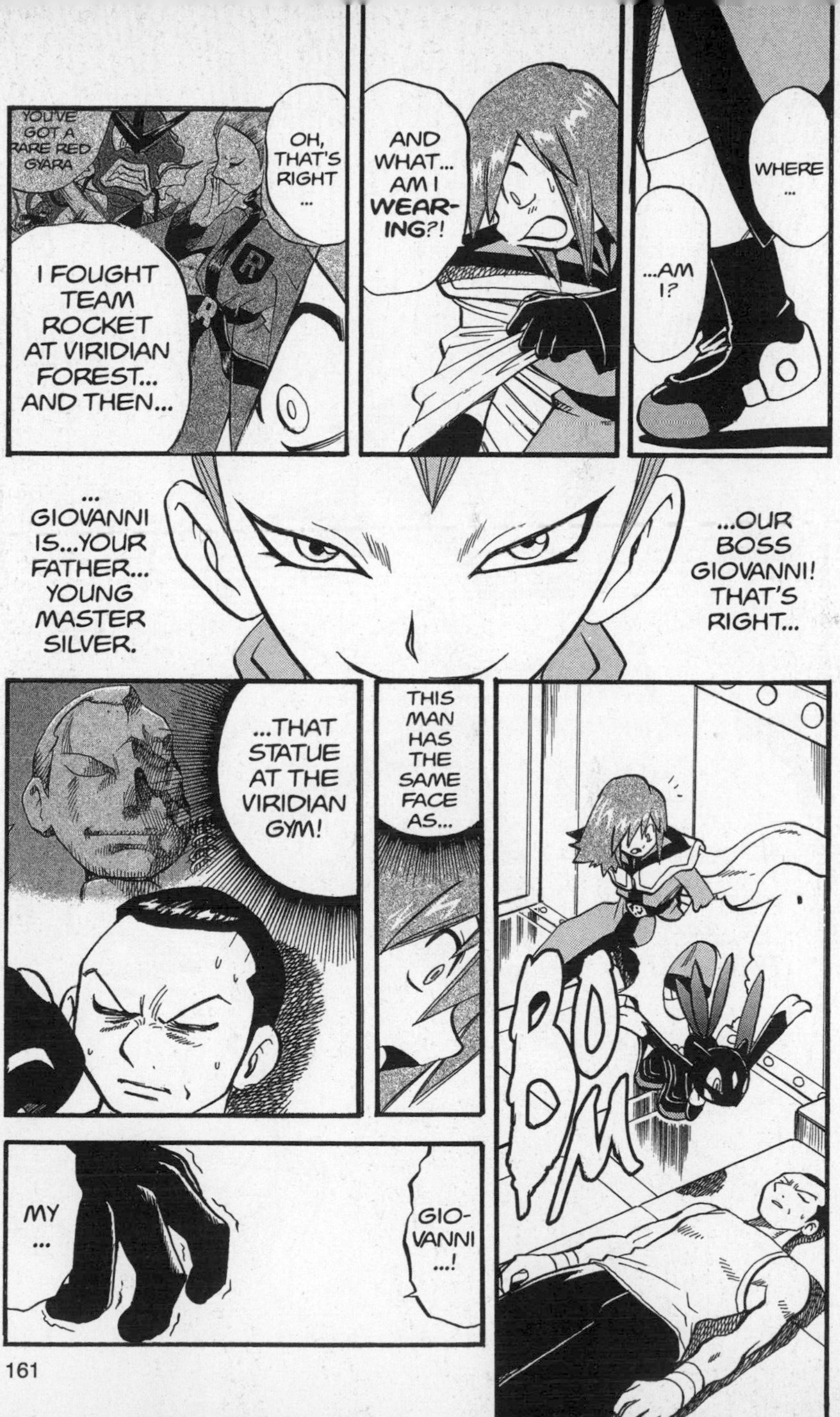
WHERE ...
...AM I?
AND WHAT... AM I WEARING?!
OH, THAT'S RIGHT ...
YOU'VE GOT A RARE RED GYARA
I FOUGHT TEAM ROCKET AT VIRIDIAN FOREST... AND THEN...
...OUR BOSS GIOVANNI! THAT'S RIGHT...
... GIOVANNI IS...YOUR FATHER... YOUNG MASTER SILVER.
BOOM
THIS MAN HAS THE SAME FACE AS...
...THAT STATUE AT THE VIRIDIAN GYM!
GIO-VANNI ...!
MY ...

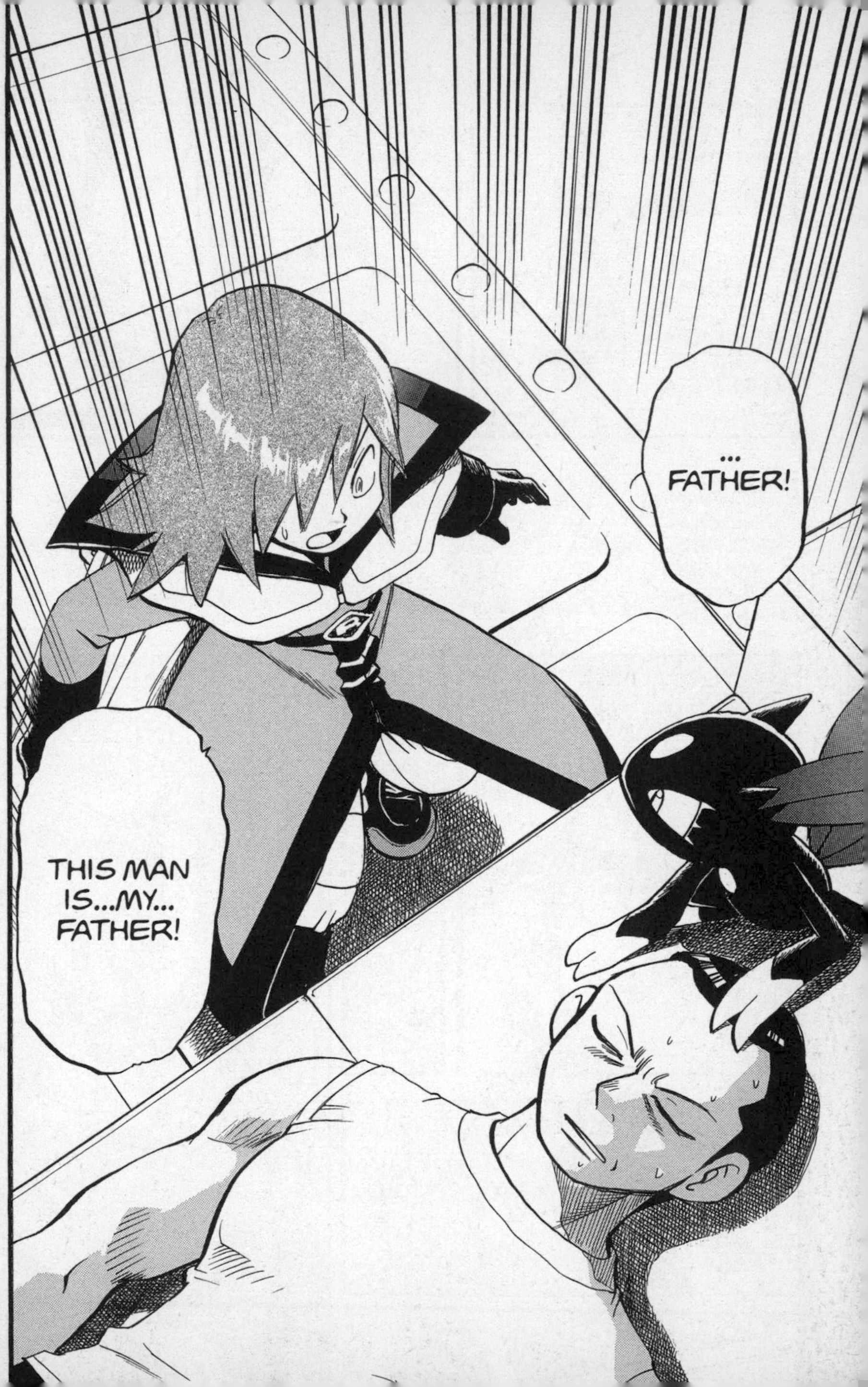

... FATHER!
THIS MAN IS...MY... FATHER!

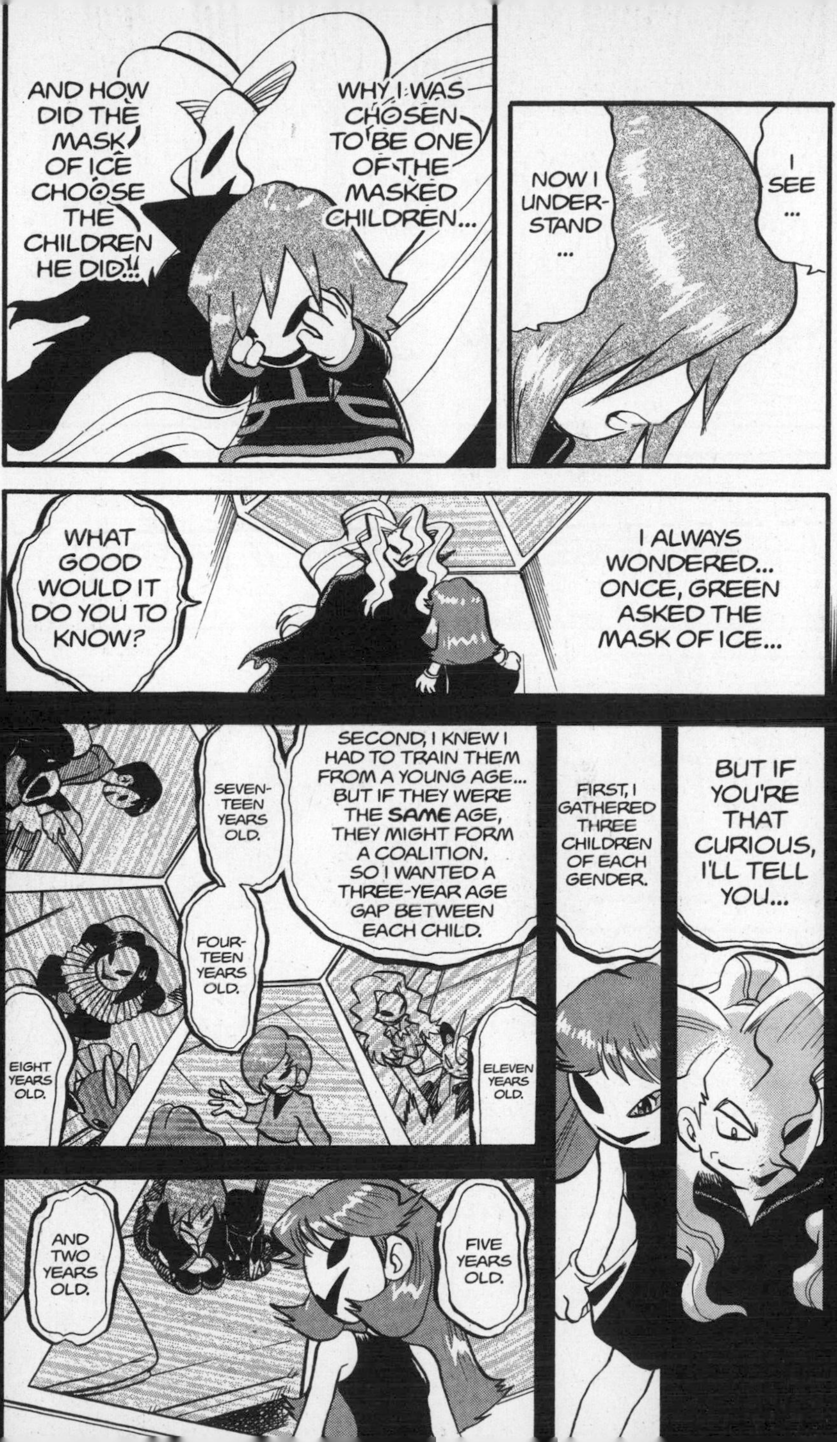
I SEE ...
NOW I UNDERSTAND ...
WHY I WAS CHOSEN TO BE ONE OF THE MASKED CHILDREN...
AND HOW DID THE MASK OF ICE CHOOSE THE CHILDREN HE DID!!
I ALWAYS WONDERED... ONCE, GREEN ASKED THE MASK OF ICE...
WHAT GOOD WOULD IT DO YOU TO KNOW?
BUT IF YOU'RE THAT CURIOUS, I'LL TELL YOU...
FIRST, I GATHERED THREE CHILDREN OF EACH GENDER.
SECOND, I KNEW I HAD TO TRAIN THEM FROM A YOUNG AGE... BUT IF THEY WERE THE SAME AGE, THEY MIGHT FORM A COALITION. SO I WANTED A THREE-YEAR AGE GAP BETWEEN EACH CHILD.
SEVENTEEN YEARS OLD.
FOURTEEN YEARS OLD.
ELEVEN YEARS OLD.
EIGHT YEARS OLD.
FIVE YEARS OLD.
AND TWO YEARS OLD.

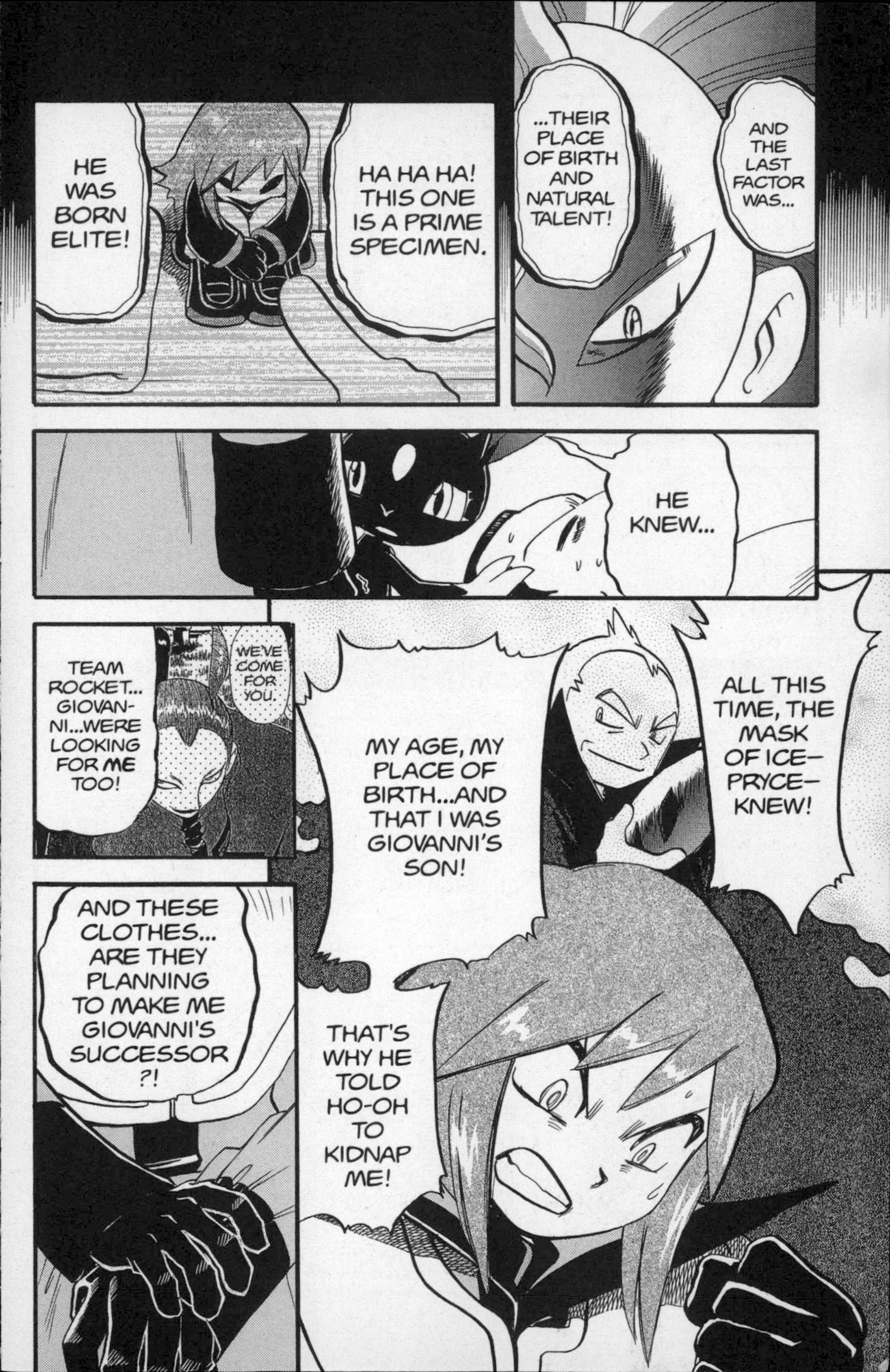
AND THE LAST FACTOR WAS...
...THEIR PLACE OF BIRTH AND NATURAL TALENT!
HA HA HA! THIS ONE IS A PRIME SPECIMEN.
HE WAS BORN ELITE!
HE KNEW...
ALL THIS TIME, THE MASK OF ICE—PRYCE—KNEW!
MY AGE, MY PLACE OF BIRTH...AND THAT I WAS GIOVANNI'S SON!
THAT'S WHY HE TOLD HO-OH TO KIDNAP ME!
WE'VE COME FOR YOU.
TEAM ROCKET... GIOVANNI...WERE LOOKING FOR ME TOO!
AND THESE CLOTHES... ARE THEY PLANNING TO MAKE ME GIOVANNI'S SUCCESSOR?!

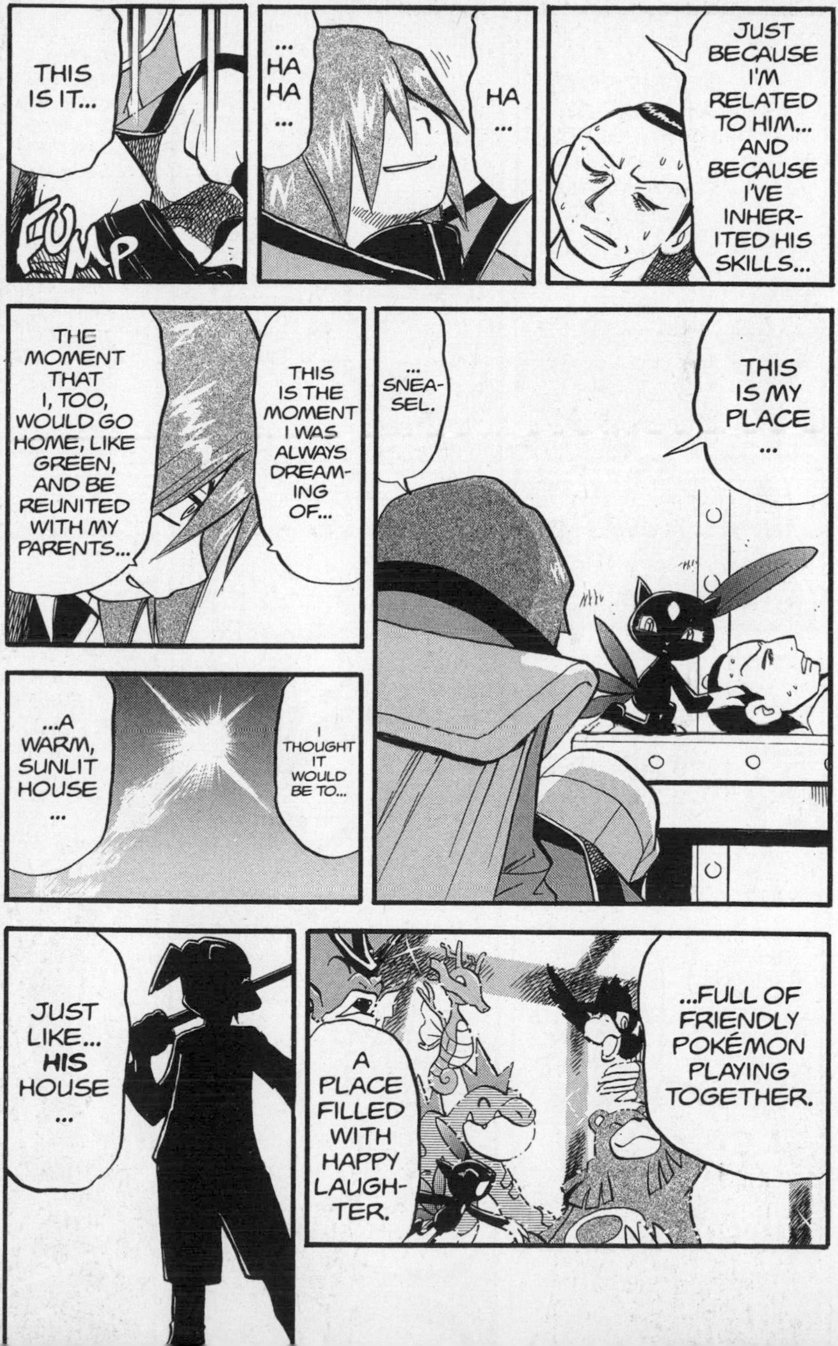
JUST BECAUSE I'M RELATED TO HIM... AND BECAUSE I'VE INHER-ITED HIS SKILLS...
HA ...
... HA HA ...
THIS IS IT...
FUMP
THIS IS MY PLACE ...
... SNEA-SEL.
THIS IS THE MOMENT I WAS ALWAYS DREAM-ING OF...
THE MOMENT THAT I, TOO, WOULD GO HOME, LIKE GREEN, AND BE REUNITED WITH MY PARENTS...
I THOUGHT IT WOULD BE TO...
...A WARM, SUNLIT HOUSE ...
...FULL OF FRIENDLY POKÉMON PLAYING TOGETHER.
A PLACE FILLED WITH HAPPY LAUGH-TER.
JUST LIKE... **HIS** HOUSE ...

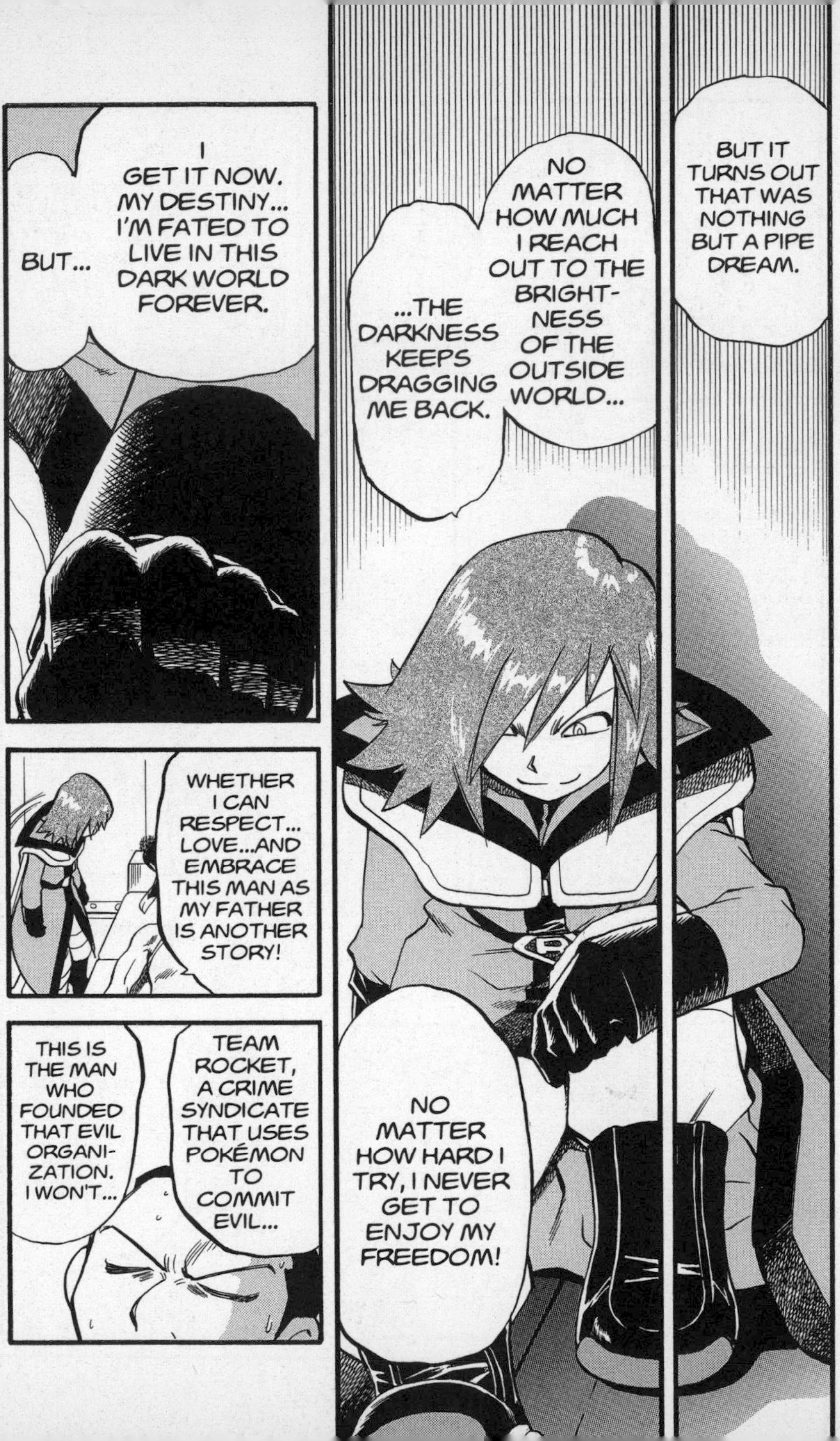
BUT...
I GET IT NOW. MY DESTINY... I'M FATED TO LIVE IN THIS DARK WORLD FOREVER.
WHETHER I CAN RESPECT... LOVE...AND EMBRACE THIS MAN AS MY FATHER IS ANOTHER STORY!
THIS IS THE MAN WHO FOUNDED THAT EVIL ORGANI-ZATION. I WON'T...
TEAM ROCKET, A CRIME SYNDICATE THAT USES POKÉMON TO COMMIT EVIL...
...THE DARKNESS KEEPS DRAGGING ME BACK.
NO MATTER HOW MUCH I REACH OUT TO THE BRIGHT-NESS OF THE OUTSIDE WORLD...
NO MATTER HOW HARD I TRY, I NEVER GET TO ENJOY MY FREEDOM!
BUT IT TURNS OUT THAT WAS NOTHING BUT A PIPE DREAM.

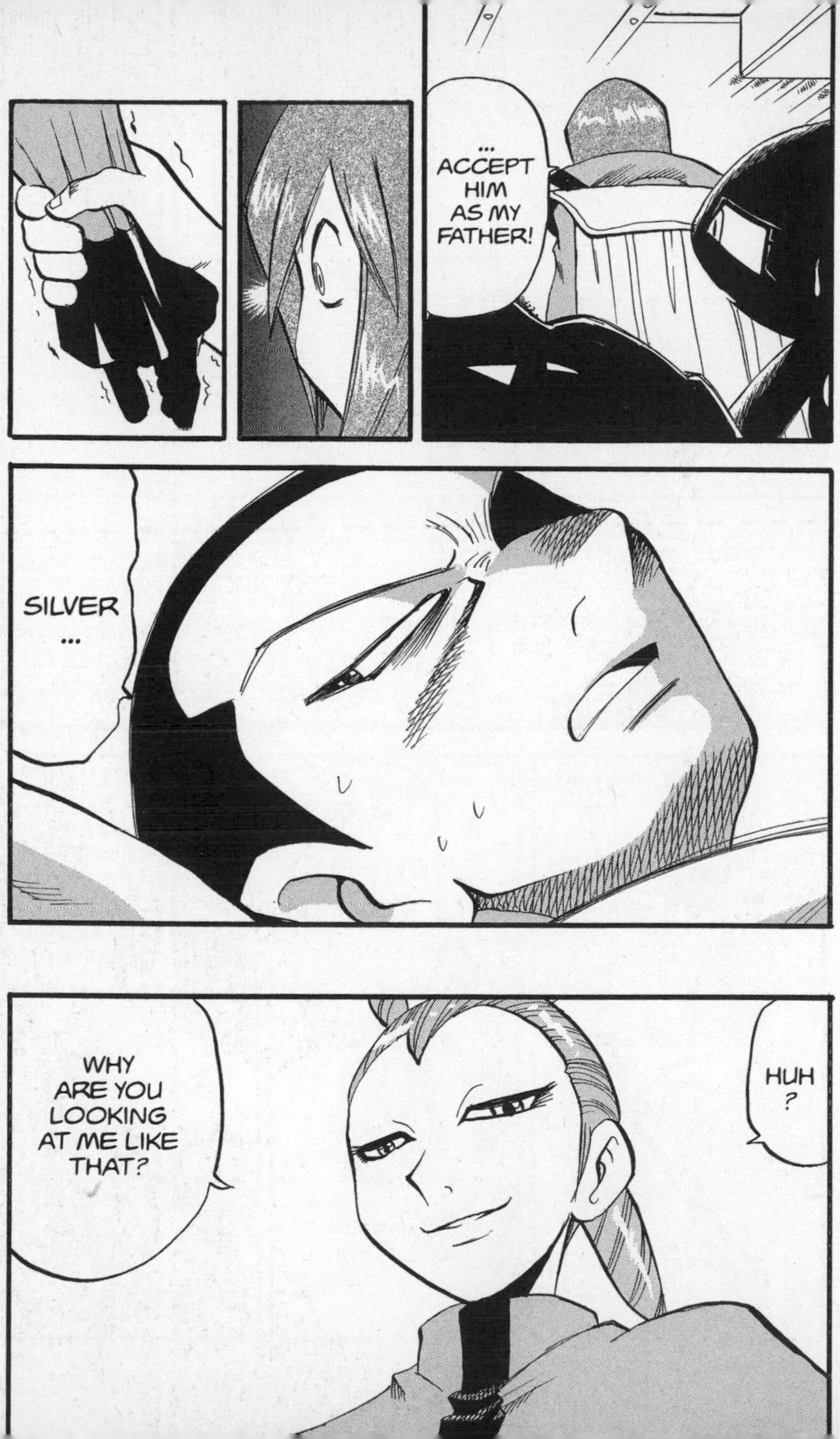
... ACCEPT HIM AS MY FATHER!
SILVER ...
HUH ?
WHY ARE YOU LOOKING AT ME LIKE THAT?

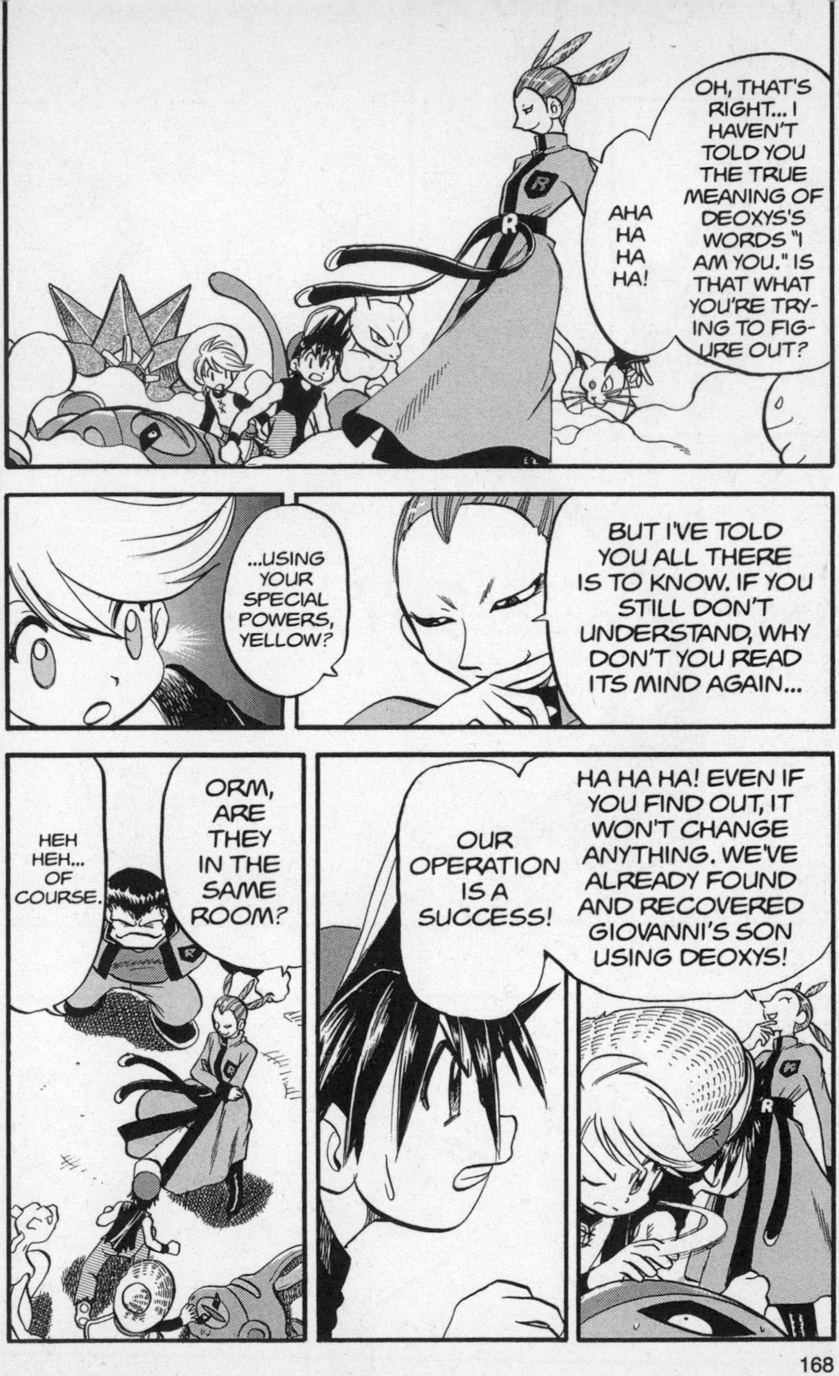

OH, THAT'S RIGHT... I HAVEN'T TOLD YOU THE TRUE MEANING OF DEOXYS'S WORDS "I AM YOU." IS THAT WHAT YOU'RE TRYING TO FIGURE OUT?
AHA HA HA HA!
BUT I'VE TOLD YOU ALL THERE IS TO KNOW. IF YOU STILL DON'T UNDERSTAND, WHY DON'T YOU READ ITS MIND AGAIN...
...USING YOUR SPECIAL POWERS, YELLOW?
HA HA HA! EVEN IF YOU FIND OUT, IT WON'T CHANGE ANYTHING. WE'VE ALREADY FOUND AND RECOVERED GIOVANNI'S SON USING DEOXYS!
OUR OPERATION IS A SUCCESS!
ORM, ARE THEY IN THE SAME ROOM?
HEH HEH... OF COURSE.

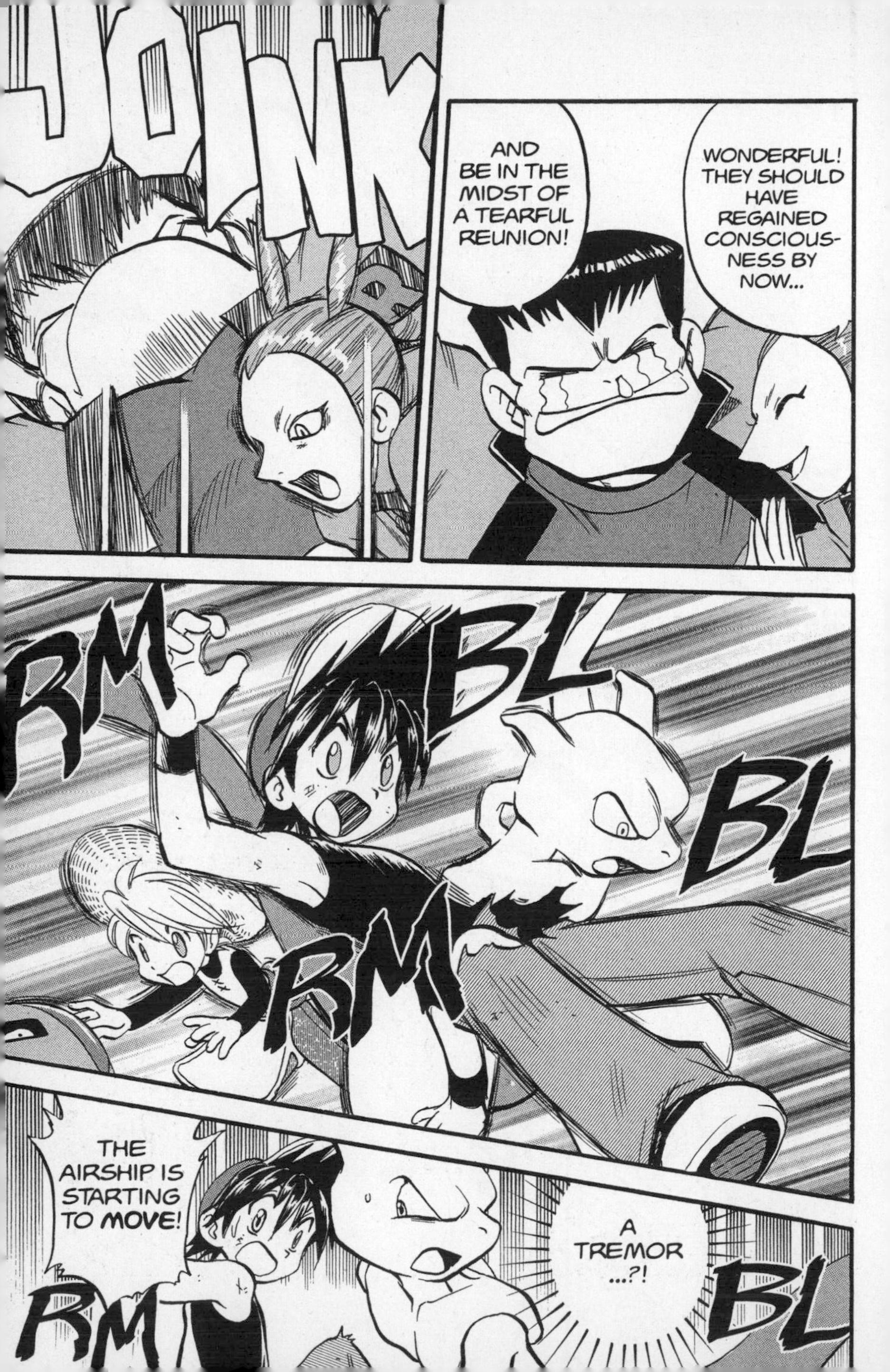
WONDERFUL! THEY SHOULD HAVE REGAINED CONSCIOUSNESS BY NOW...
AND BE IN THE MIDST OF A TEARFUL REUNION!
JOINK
BL
BL
RM
RM
A TREMOR ...?!
THE AIRSHIP IS STARTING TO MOVE!
BL
RM

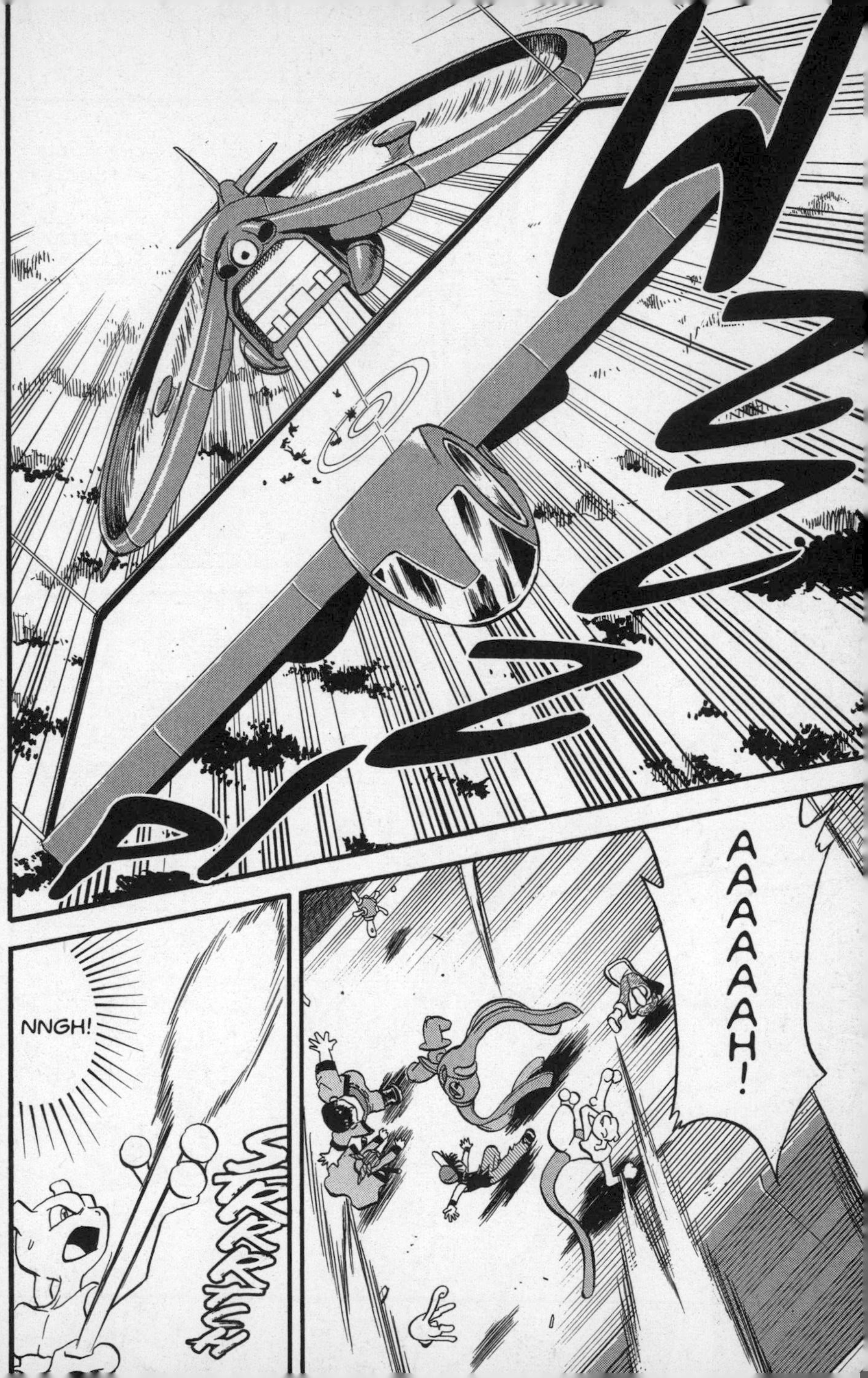
AAAAAAAH!
NNGH!

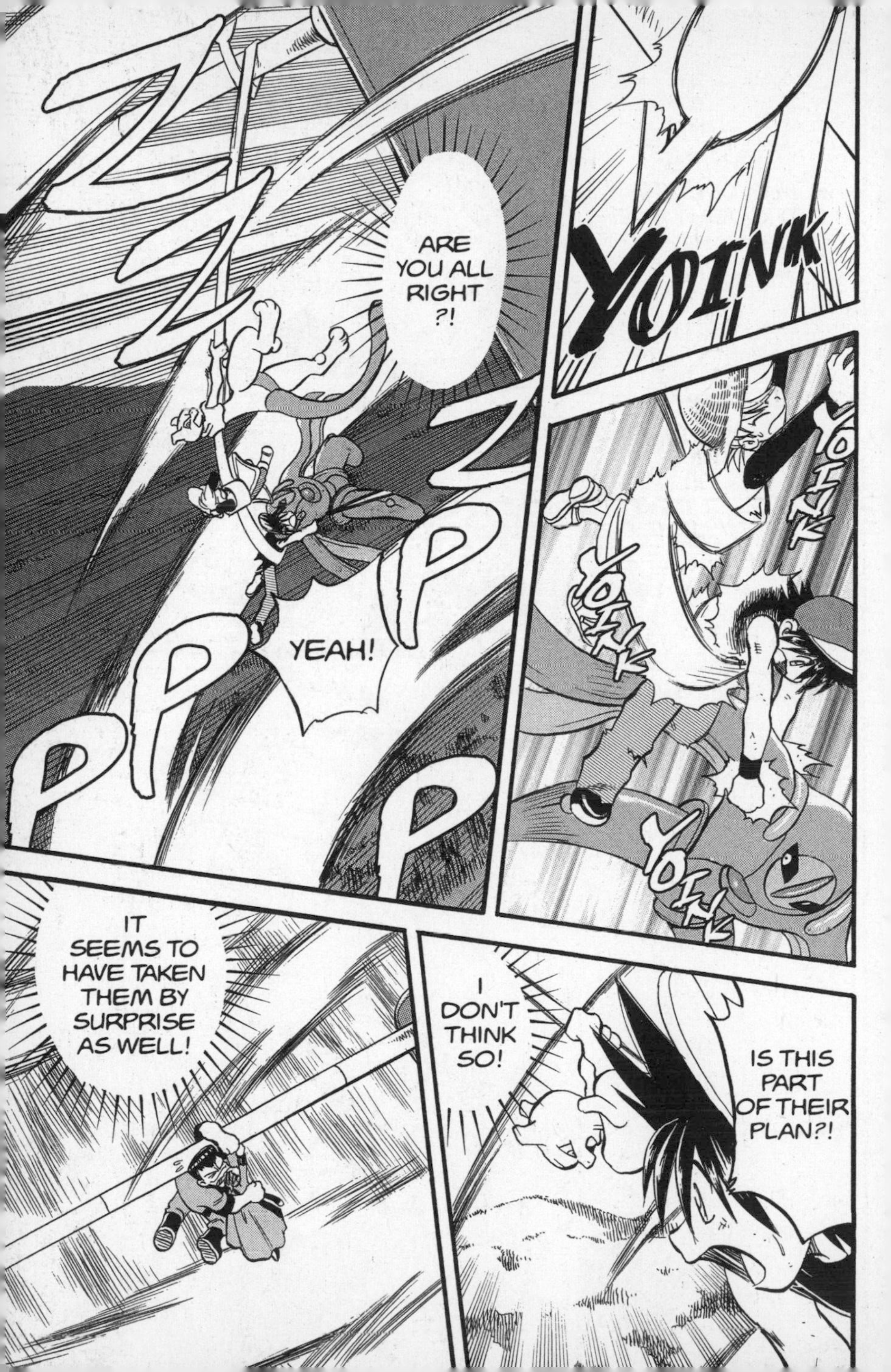
YOINK
YOINK
YOINK
YOINK
ARE YOU ALL RIGHT?!
YEAH!
IS THIS PART OF THEIR PLAN?!
I DON'T THINK SO!
IT SEEMS TO HAVE TAKEN THEM BY SURPRISE AS WELL!

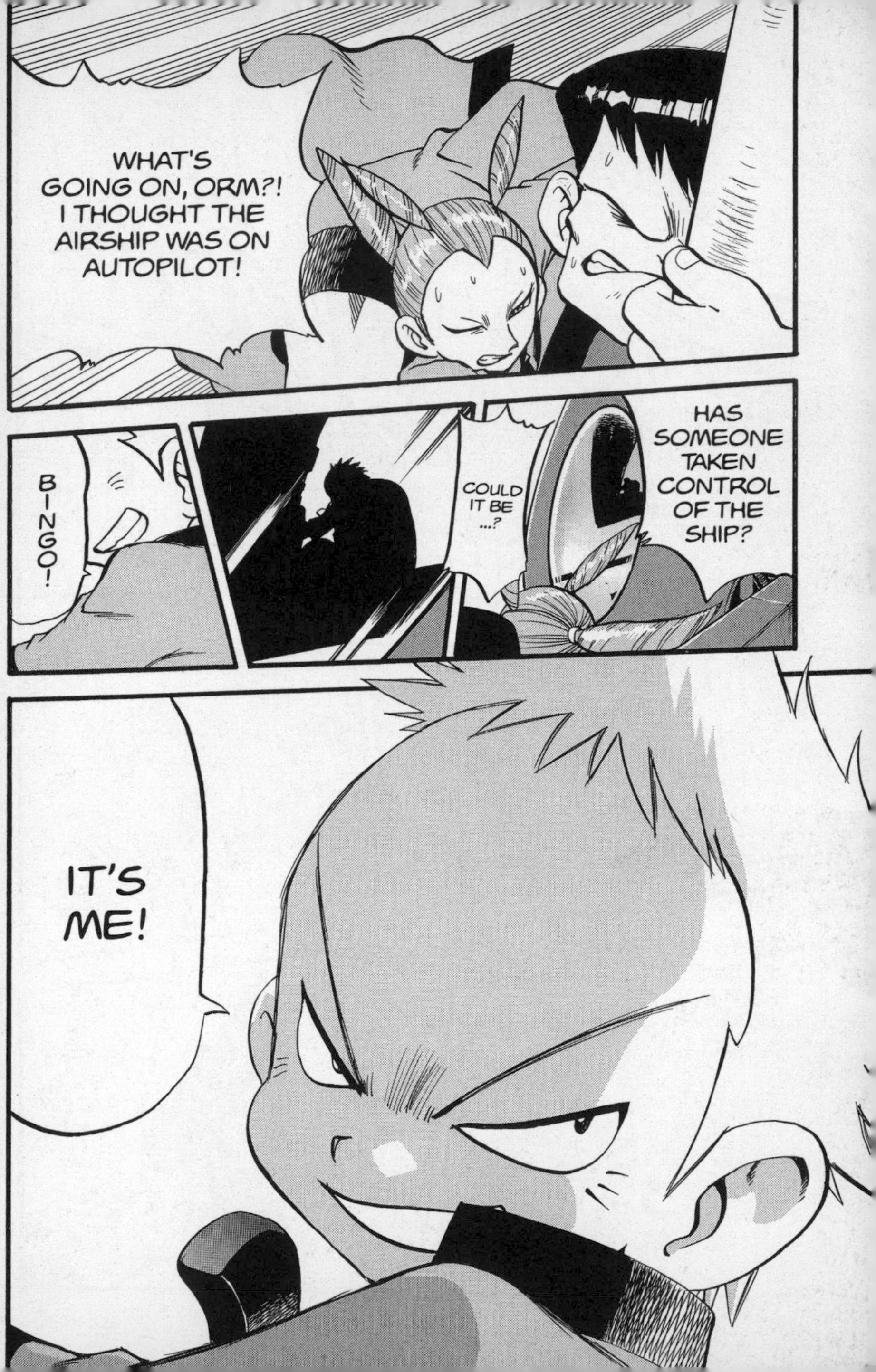

WHAT'S GOING ON, ORM?! I THOUGHT THE AIRSHIP WAS ON AUTOPILOT!
HAS SOMEONE TAKEN CONTROL OF THE SHIP?
COULD IT BE ...?
BINGO!
IT'S ME!

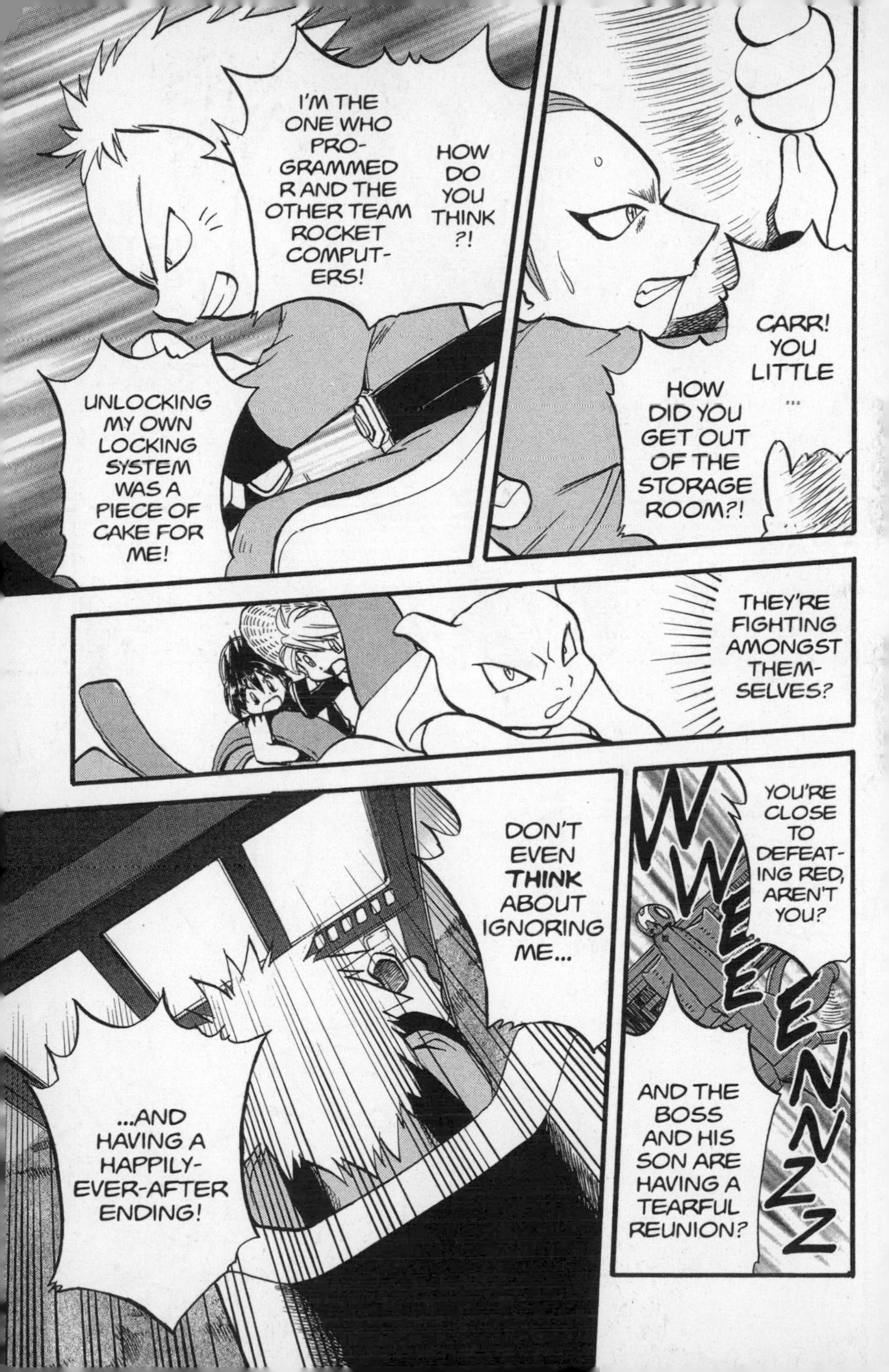
CARR! YOU LITTLE ...
HOW DID YOU GET OUT OF THE STORAGE ROOM?!
HOW DO YOU THINK ?!
I'M THE ONE WHO PRO-GRAMMED R AND THE OTHER TEAM ROCKET COMPUT-ERS!
UNLOCKING MY OWN LOCKING SYSTEM WAS A PIECE OF CAKE FOR ME!
THEY'RE FIGHTING AMONGST THEM-SELVES?
YOU'RE CLOSE TO DEFEAT-ING RED, AREN'T YOU?
WWEEENNZZ
AND THE BOSS AND HIS SON ARE HAVING A TEARFUL REUNION?
DON'T EVEN **THINK** ABOUT IGNORING ME...
...AND HAVING A HAPPILY-EVER-AFTER ENDING!

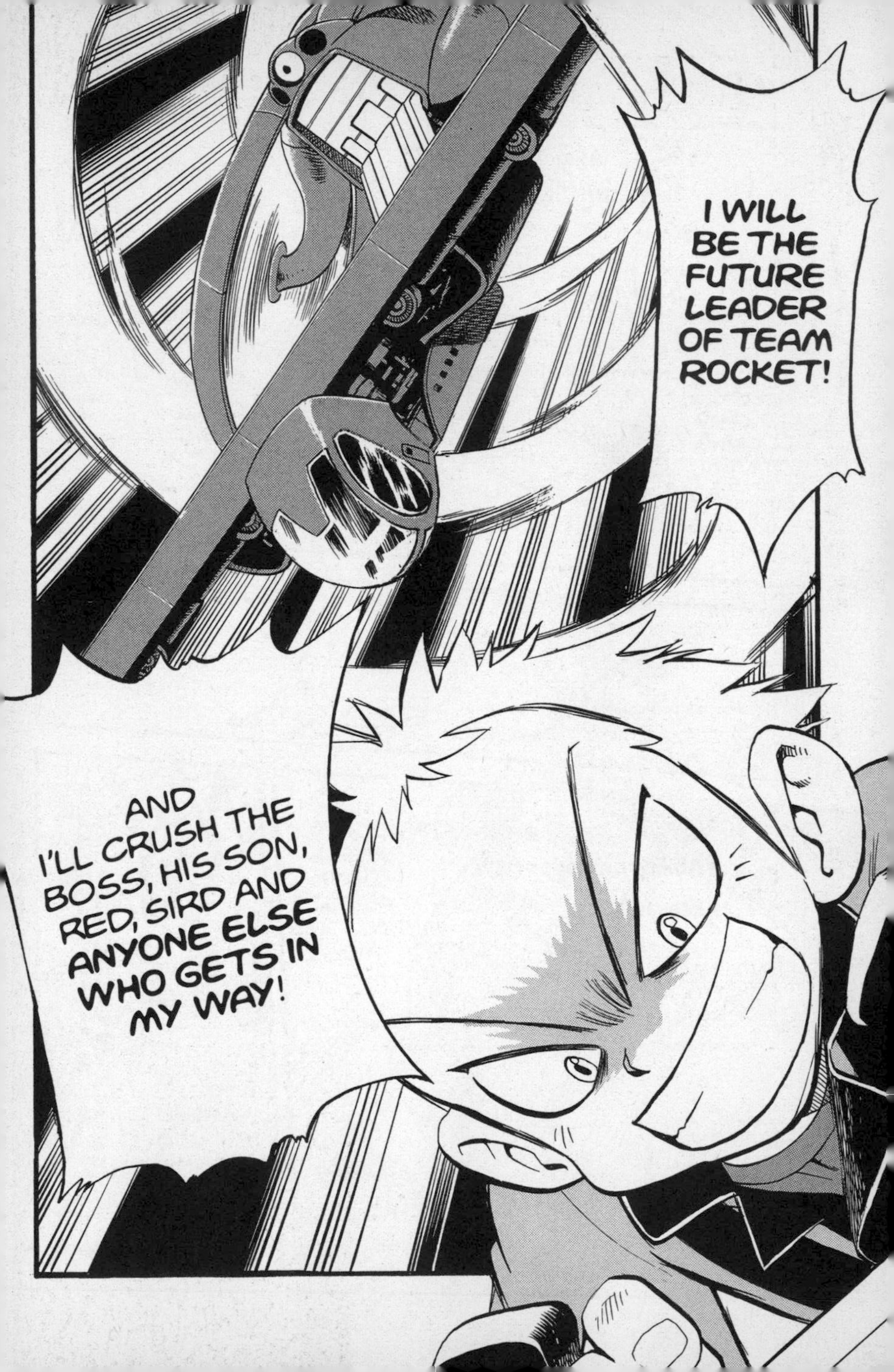
I WILL BE THE FUTURE LEADER OF TEAM ROCKET!
AND I'LL CRUSH THE BOSS, HIS SON, RED, SIRD AND ANYONE ELSE WHO GETS IN MY WAY!

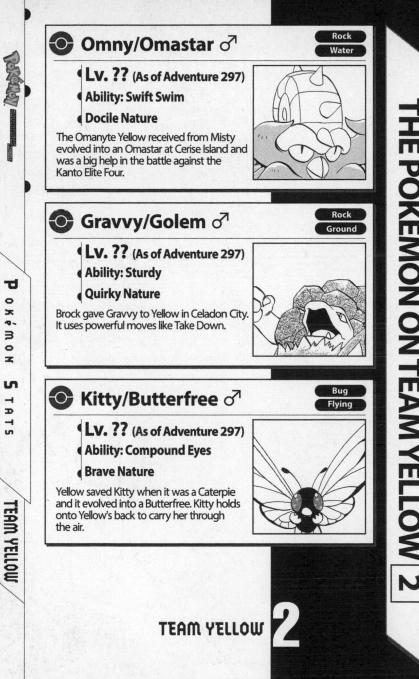

THE POKÉMON ON TEAM YELLOW 2

POKéMON STATS

TEAM YELLOW

Omny/Omastar ♂

Rock
Water

- **Lv. ??** (As of Adventure 297)
- **Ability: Swift Swim**
- **Docile Nature**

The Omanyte Yellow received from Misty evolved into an Omastar at Cerise Island and was a big help in the battle against the Kanto Elite Four.

Gravvy/Golem ♂

Rock
Ground

- **Lv. ??** (As of Adventure 297)
- **Ability: Sturdy**
- **Quirky Nature**

Brock gave Gravvy to Yellow in Celadon City. It uses powerful moves like Take Down.

Kitty/Butterfree ♂

Bug
Flying

- **Lv. ??** (As of Adventure 297)
- **Ability: Compound Eyes**
- **Brave Nature**

Yellow saved Kitty when it was a Caterpie and it evolved into a Butterfree. Kitty holds onto Yellow's back to carry her through the air.

TEAM YELLOW 2

● Adventure 298 ●
Start the Countdown, Starmie

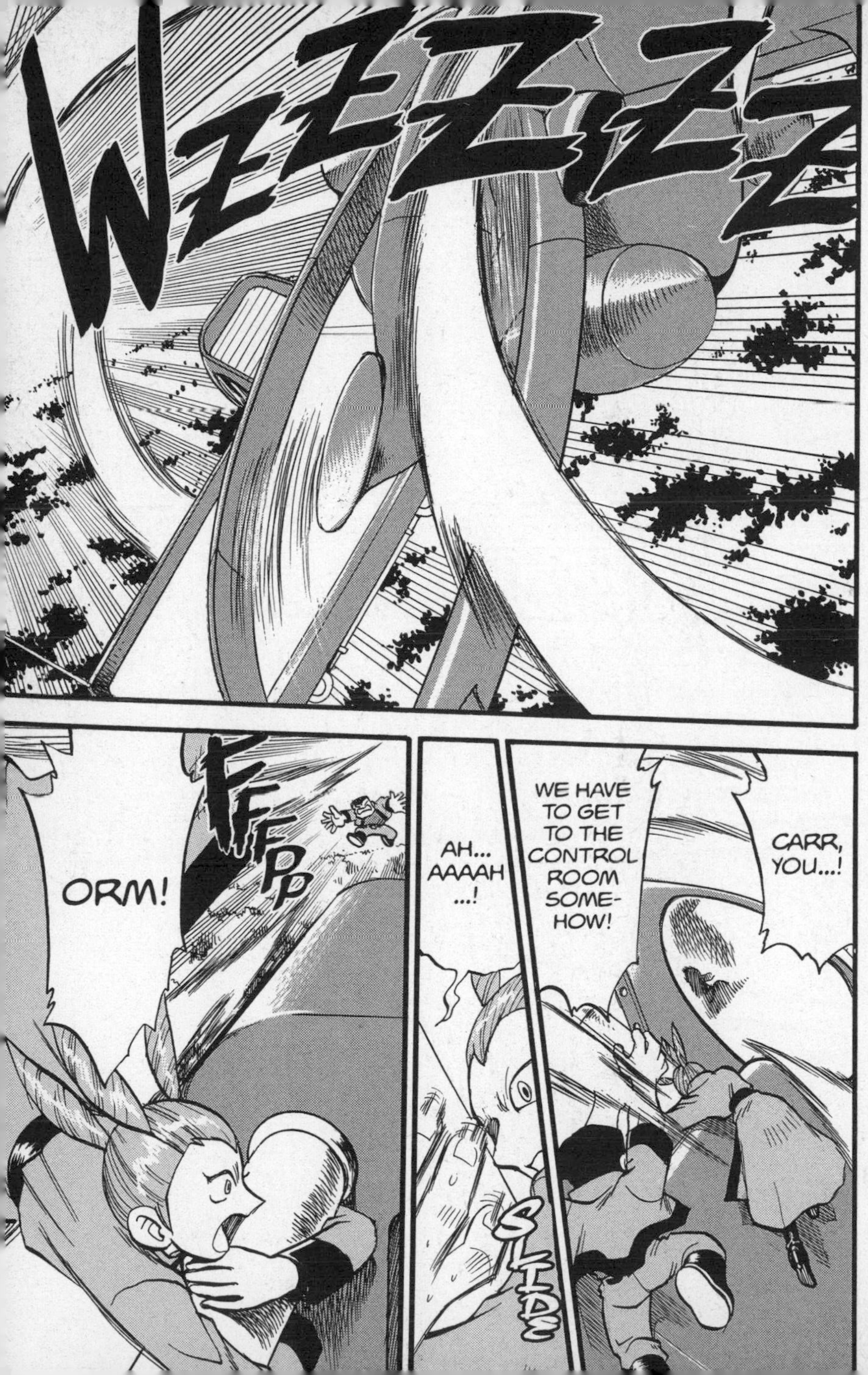

WZZZZZZ
CARR, YOU...!
WE HAVE TO GET TO THE CONTROL ROOM SOME-HOW!
AH... AAAAH ...!
SLIDE
FFFPP
ORM!

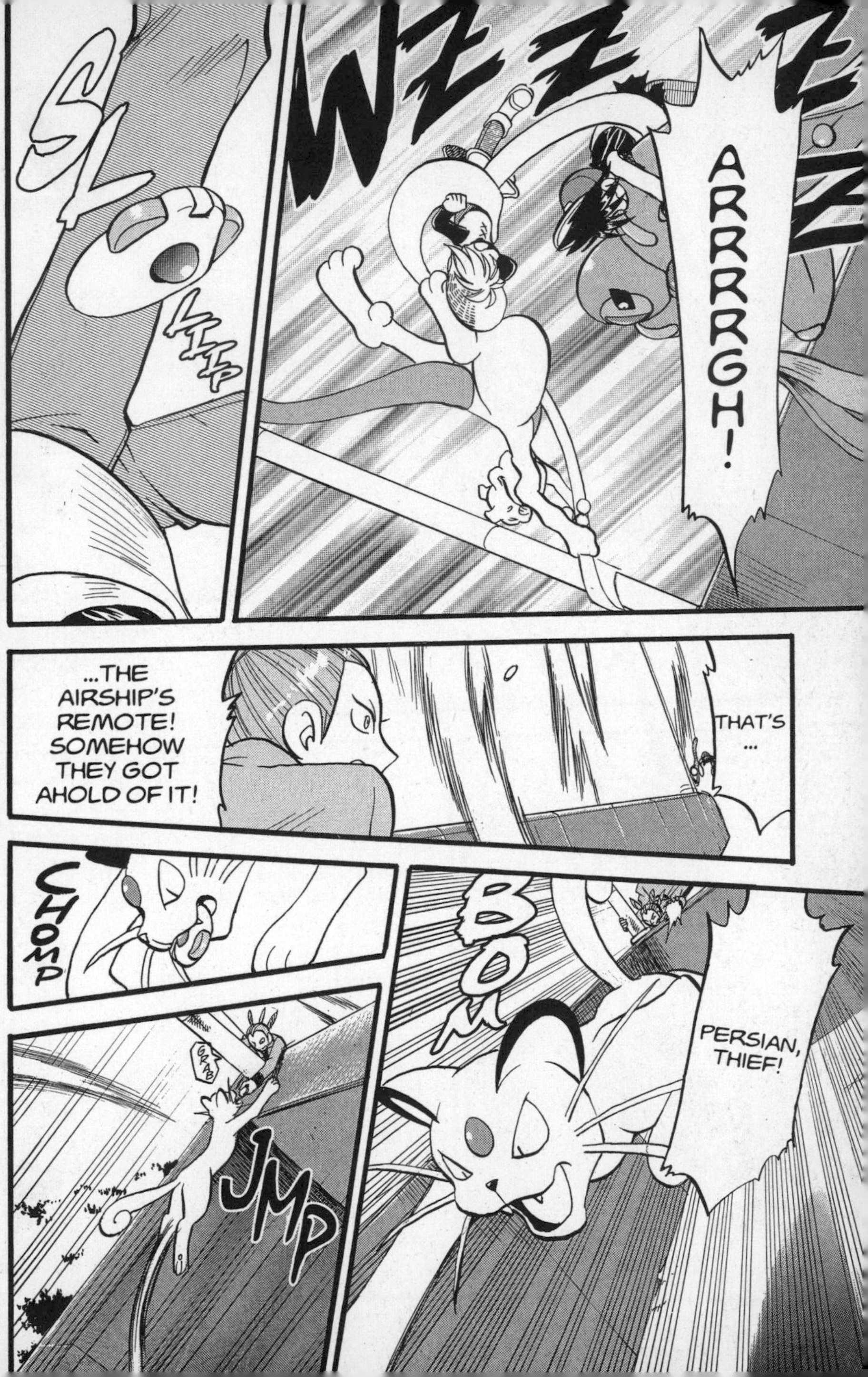
ARRRRGH!
THAT'S ...
...THE AIRSHIP'S REMOTE! SOMEHOW THEY GOT AHOLD OF IT!
BOOM
PERSIAN, THIEF!
CHOMP
GRAB
JMP

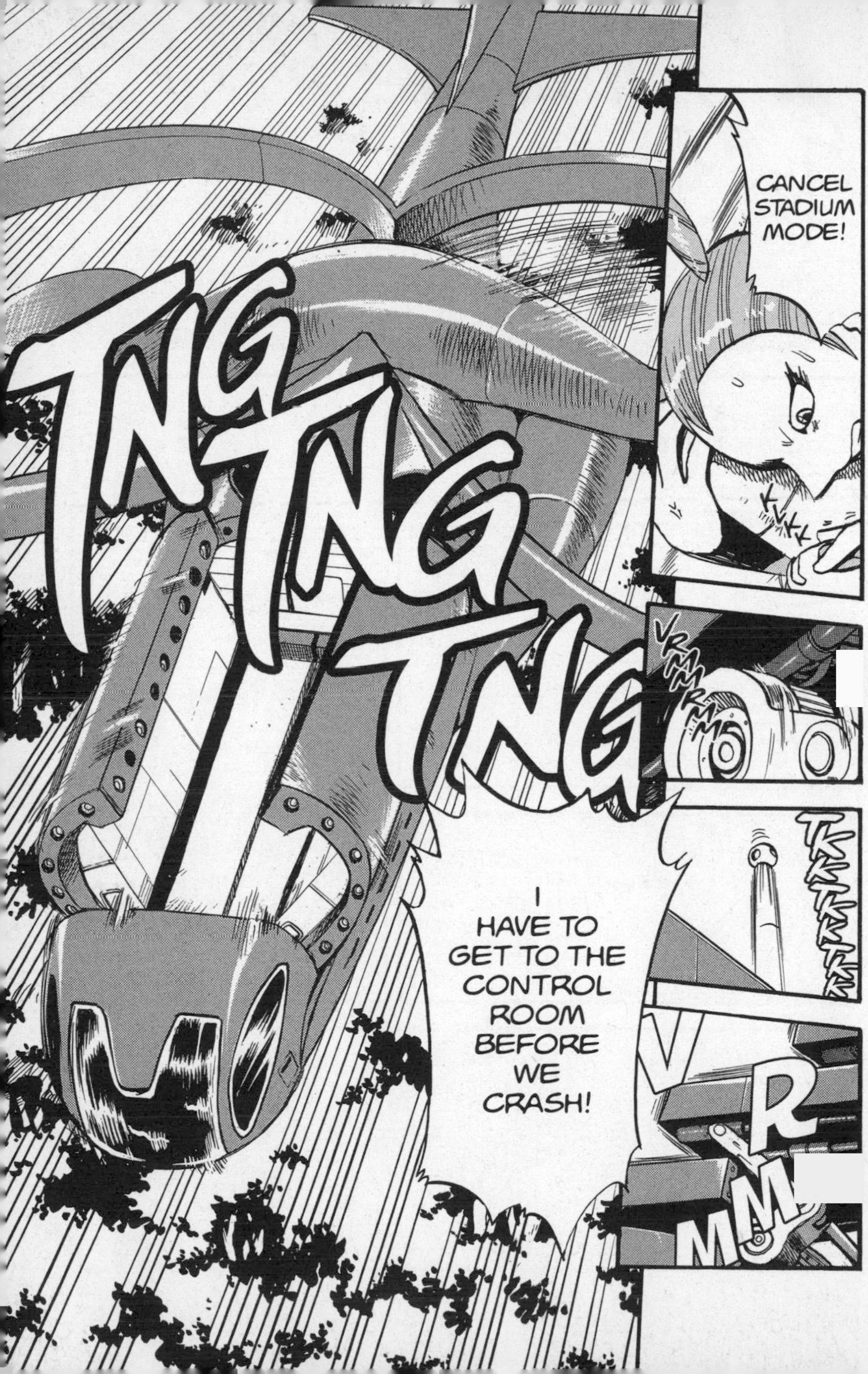
CANCEL STADIUM MODE!
TNG TNG TNG
I HAVE TO GET TO THE CONTROL ROOM BEFORE WE CRASH!

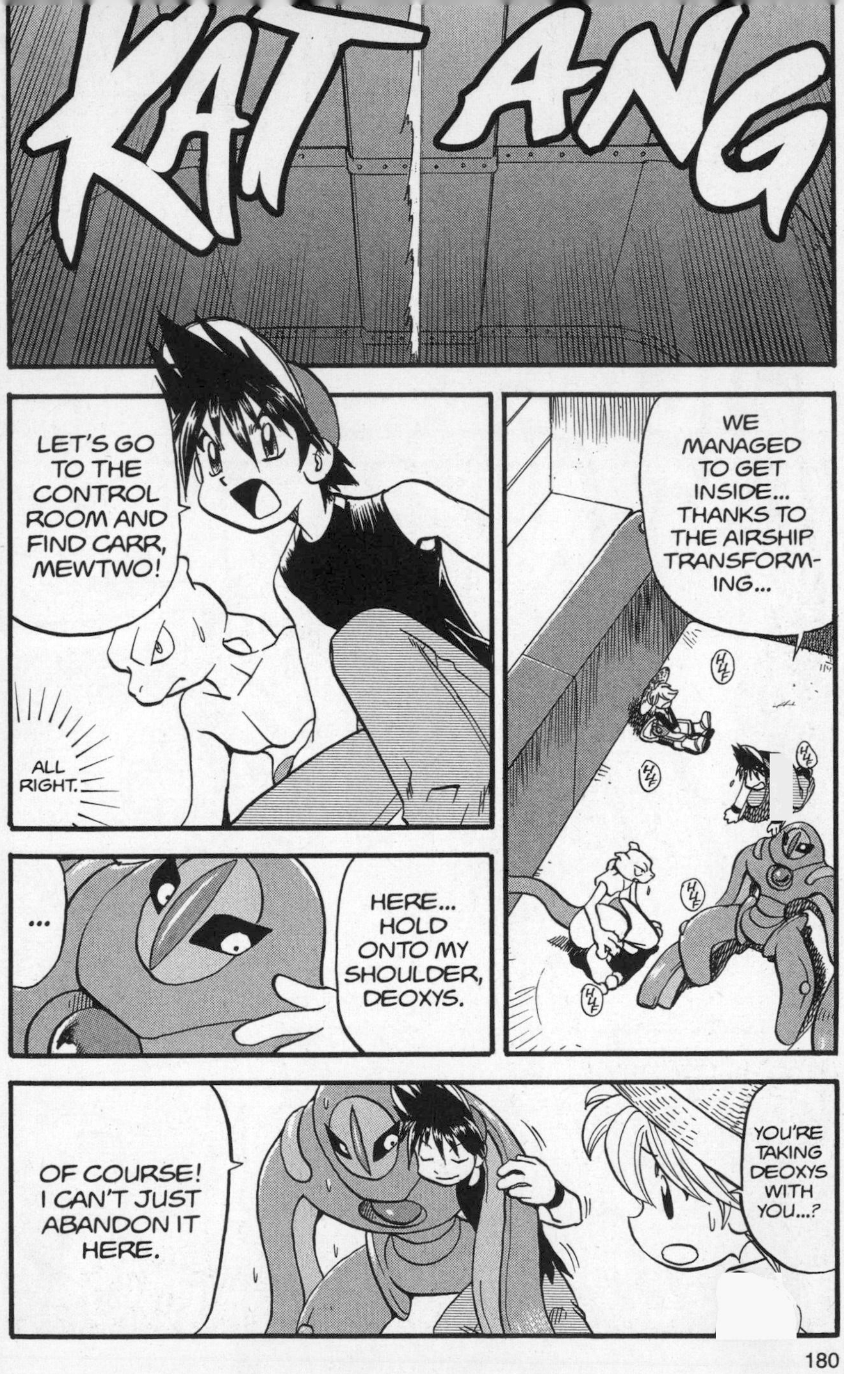
KATANG
WE MANAGED TO GET INSIDE... THANKS TO THE AIRSHIP TRANSFORMING...
LET'S GO TO THE CONTROL ROOM AND FIND CARR, MEWTWO!
ALL RIGHT.
HERE... HOLD ONTO MY SHOULDER, DEOXYS.
...
YOU'RE TAKING DEOXYS WITH YOU...?
OF COURSE! I CAN'T JUST ABANDON IT HERE.

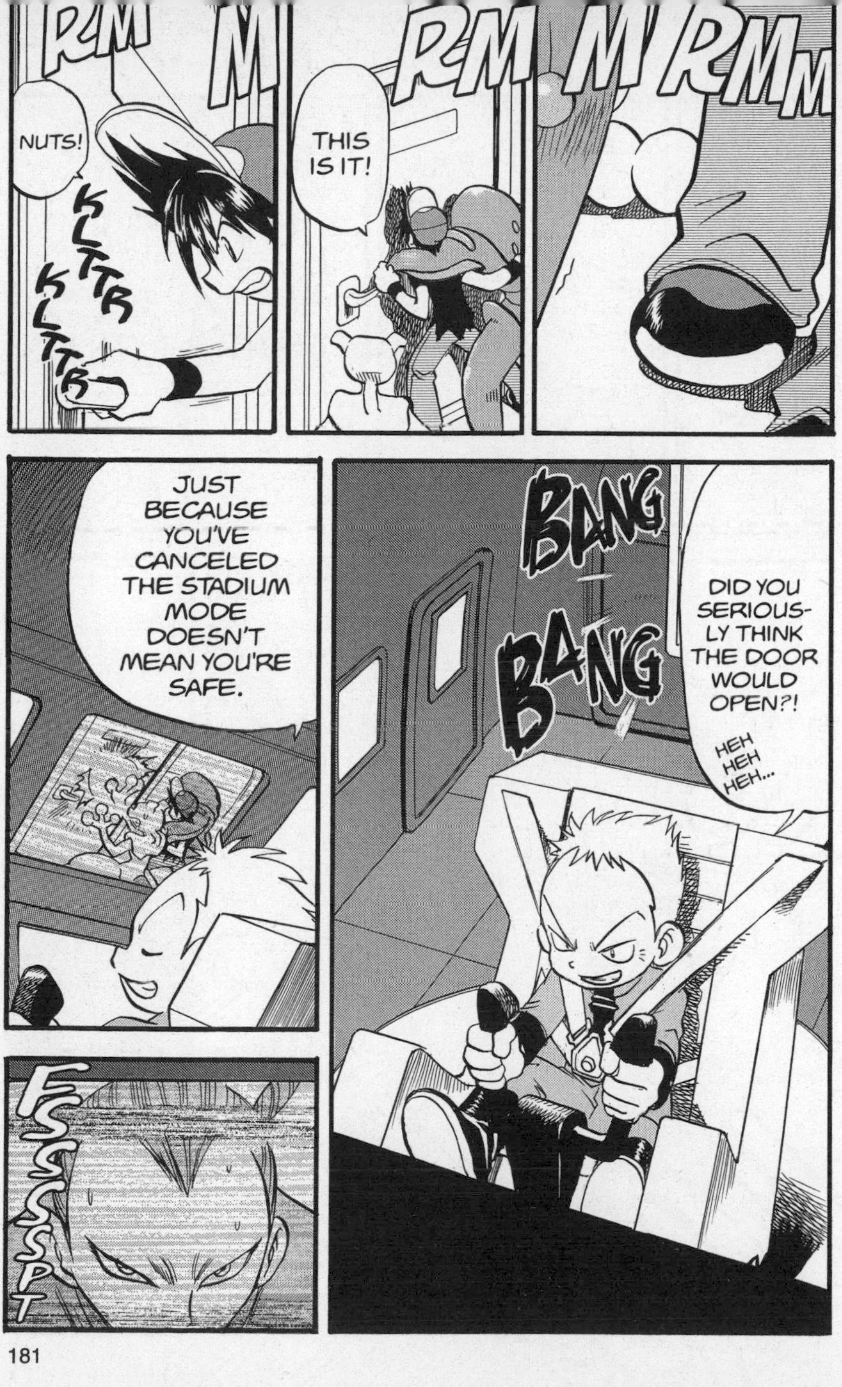
M RMM
RM
THIS IS IT!
RM M
NUTS!
KLTTR KLTTR
BANG BANG
DID YOU SERIOUS-LY THINK THE DOOR WOULD OPEN?!
HEH HEH HEH...
JUST BECAUSE YOU'VE CANCELED THE STADIUM MODE DOESN'T MEAN YOU'RE SAFE.
FSSSSPT

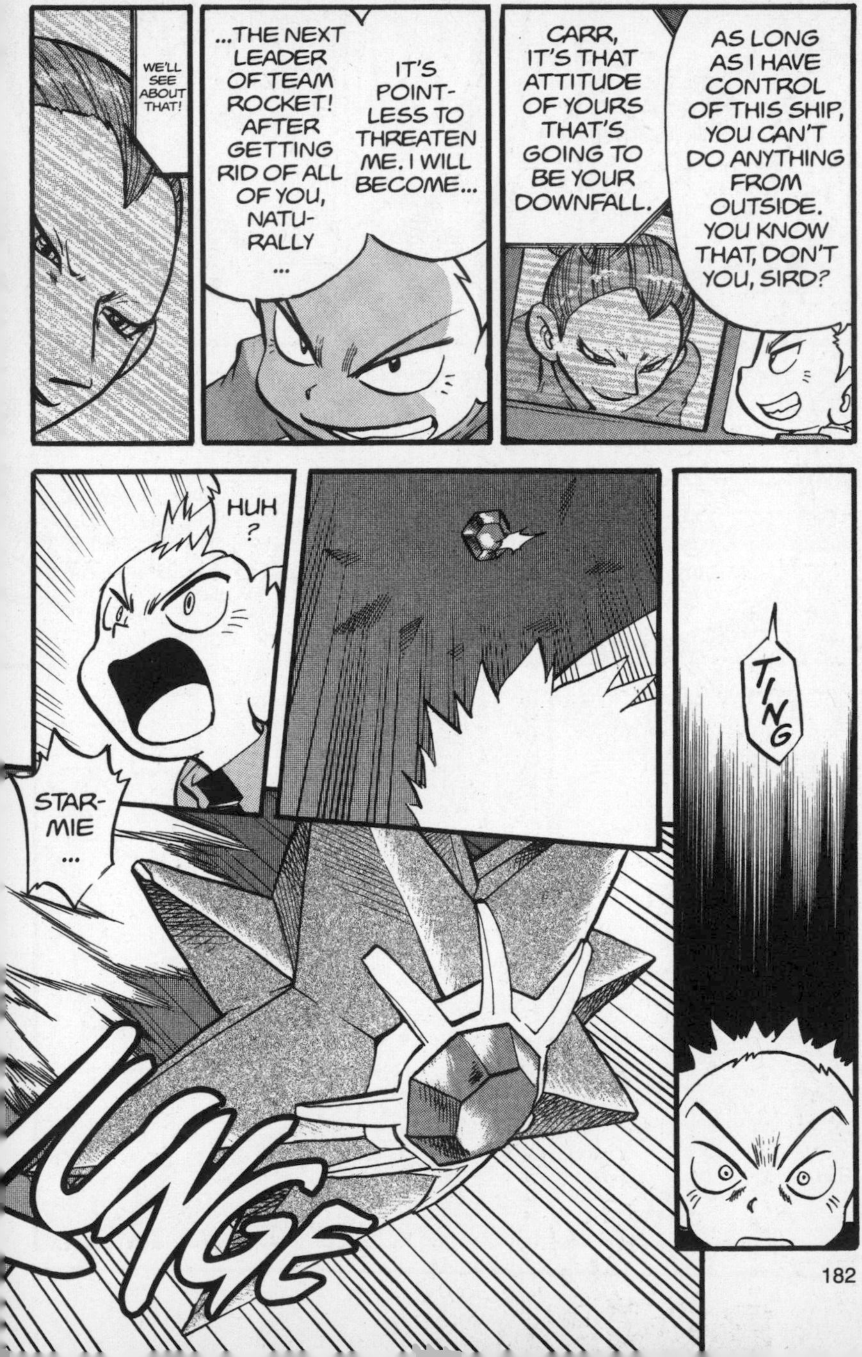
AS LONG AS I HAVE CONTROL OF THIS SHIP, YOU CAN'T DO ANYTHING FROM OUTSIDE. YOU KNOW THAT, DON'T YOU, SIRD?
CARR, IT'S THAT ATTITUDE OF YOURS THAT'S GOING TO BE YOUR DOWNFALL.
IT'S POINT-LESS TO THREATEN ME. I WILL BECOME...
...THE NEXT LEADER OF TEAM ROCKET! AFTER GETTING RID OF ALL OF YOU, NATU-RALLY...
WE'LL SEE ABOUT THAT!
TING
HUH?
STAR-MIE...
UNGE

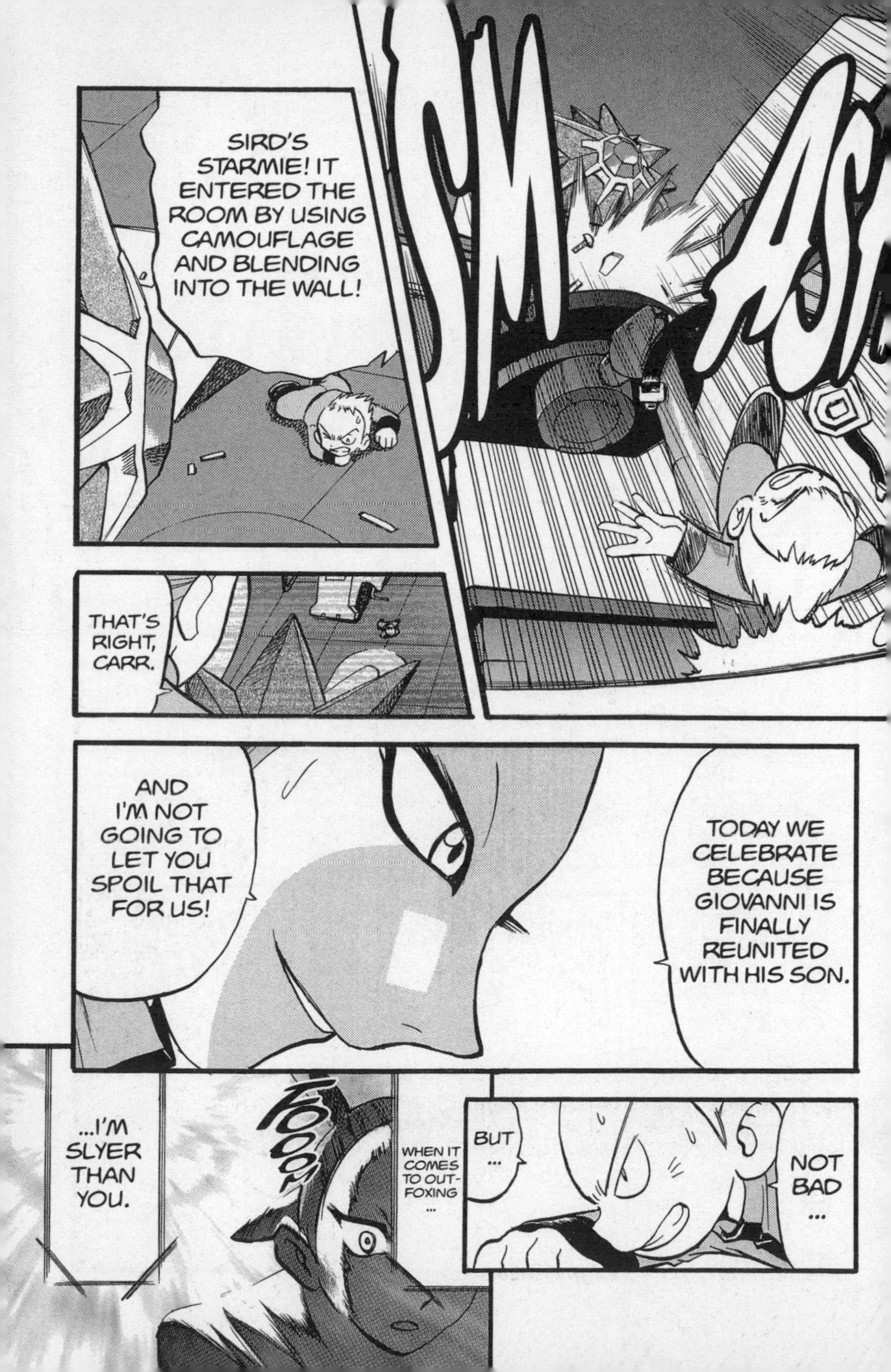
SMAS
SIRD'S STARMIE! IT ENTERED THE ROOM BY USING CAMOUFLAGE AND BLENDING INTO THE WALL!
THAT'S RIGHT, CARR.
TODAY WE CELEBRATE BECAUSE GIOVANNI IS FINALLY REUNITED WITH HIS SON.
AND I'M NOT GOING TO LET YOU SPOIL THAT FOR US!
NOT BAD ...
BUT ...
WHEN IT COMES TO OUT-FOXING ...
...I'M SLYER THAN YOU.

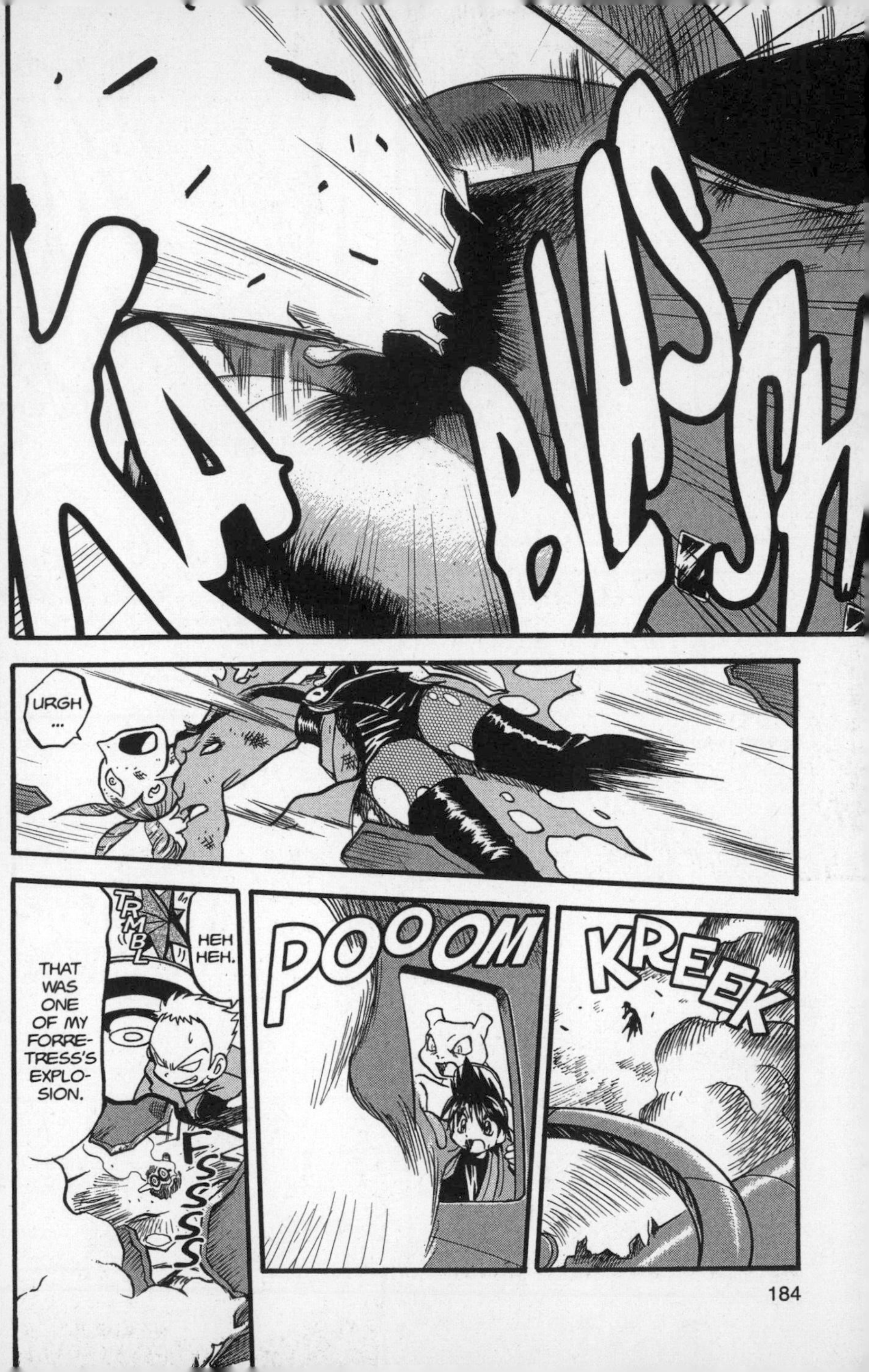
KABLASH
URGH ...
KREEK
POOOM
TRMBL
HEH HEH.
THAT WAS ONE OF MY FORRETRESS'S EXPLOSION.
FSSSSS

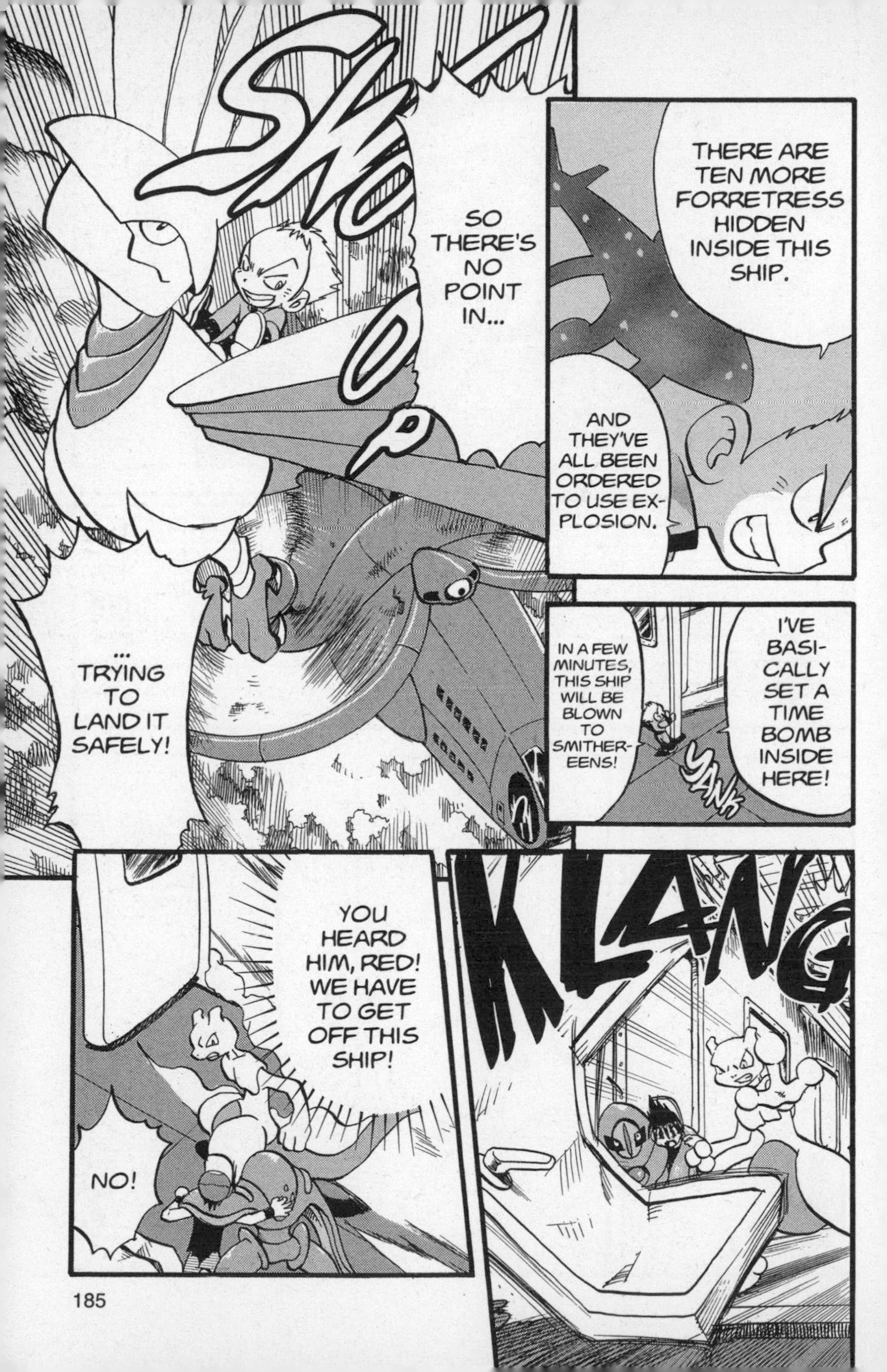
THERE ARE TEN MORE FORRETRESS HIDDEN INSIDE THIS SHIP.
AND THEY'VE ALL BEEN ORDERED TO USE EX-PLOSION.
I'VE BASI-CALLY SET A TIME BOMB INSIDE HERE!
IN A FEW MINUTES, THIS SHIP WILL BE BLOWN TO SMITHER-EENS!
YANK
SHOOP
SO THERE'S NO POINT IN...
... TRYING TO LAND IT SAFELY!
KLANG
YOU HEARD HIM, RED! WE HAVE TO GET OFF THIS SHIP!
NO!

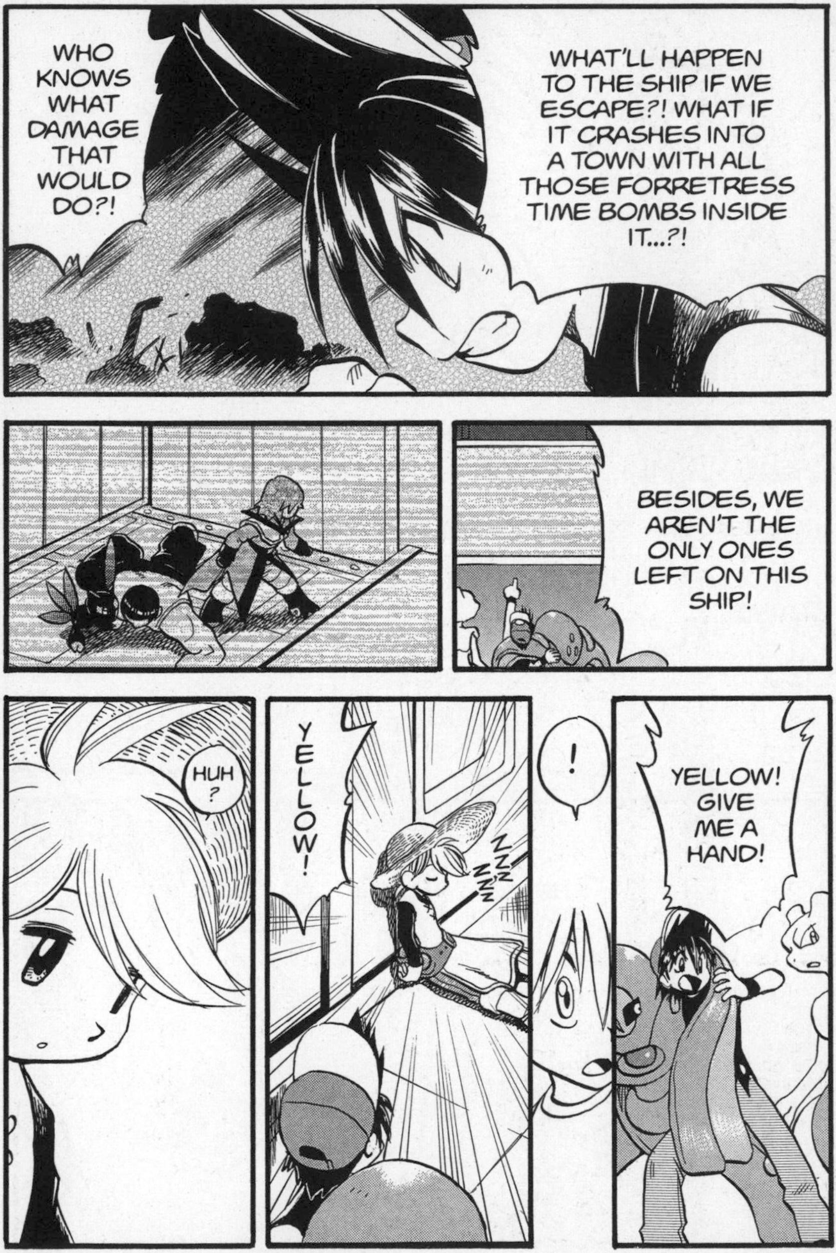
WHAT'LL HAPPEN TO THE SHIP IF WE ESCAPE?! WHAT IF IT CRASHES INTO A TOWN WITH ALL THOSE FORRETRESS TIME BOMBS INSIDE IT...?!
WHO KNOWS WHAT DAMAGE THAT WOULD DO?!
BESIDES, WE AREN'T THE ONLY ONES LEFT ON THIS SHIP!
YELLOW! GIVE ME A HAND!
!
YELLOW!
ZZZ
HUH?

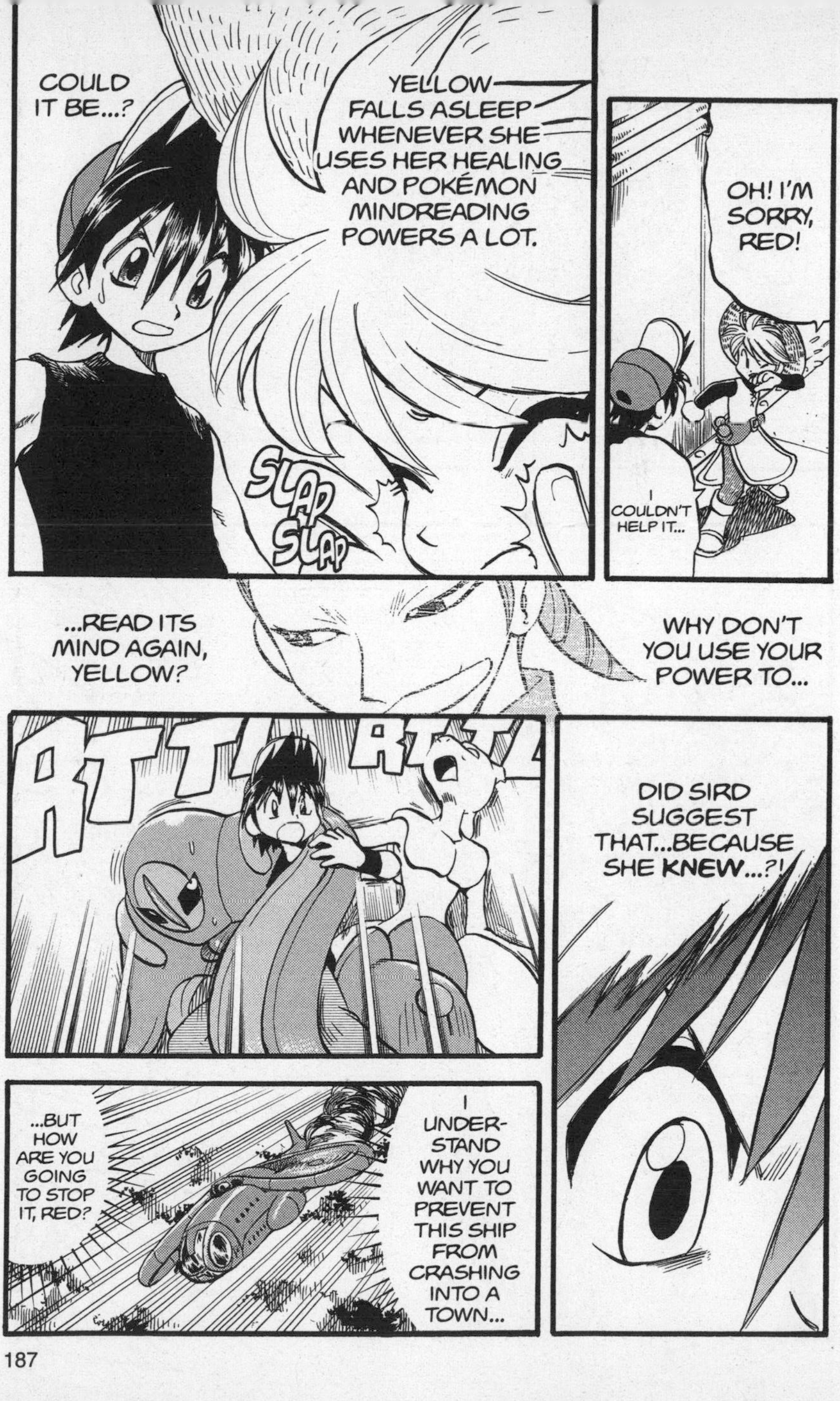
OH! I'M SORRY, RED!
I COULDN'T HELP IT...
YELLOW FALLS ASLEEP WHENEVER SHE USES HER HEALING AND POKÉMON MINDREADING POWERS A LOT.
COULD IT BE...?
SLAP SLAP
WHY DON'T YOU USE YOUR POWER TO...
...READ ITS MIND AGAIN, YELLOW?
DID SIRD SUGGEST THAT...BECAUSE SHE **KNEW**...?!
I UNDER-STAND WHY YOU WANT TO PREVENT THIS SHIP FROM CRASHING INTO A TOWN...
...BUT HOW ARE YOU GOING TO STOP IT, RED?

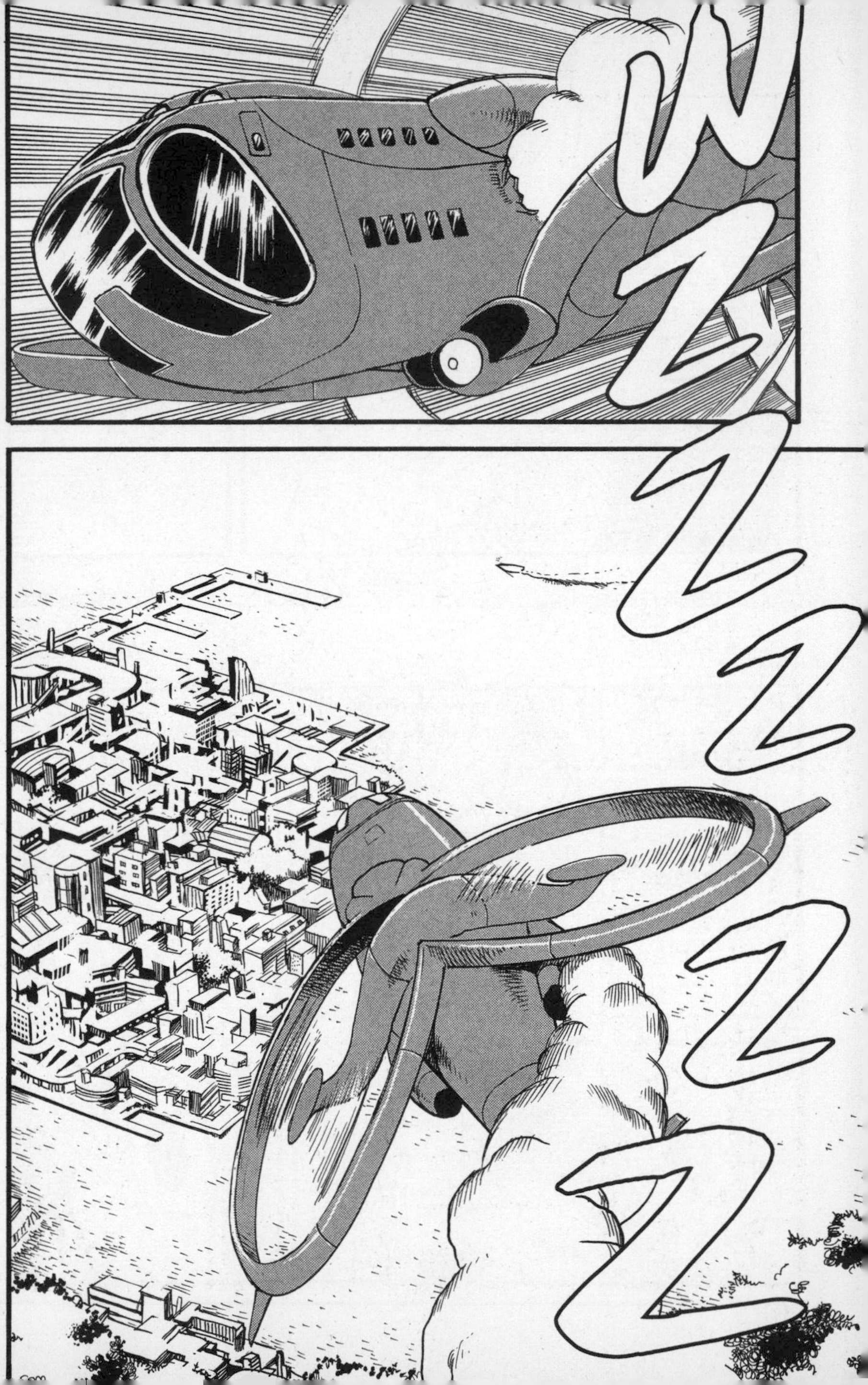

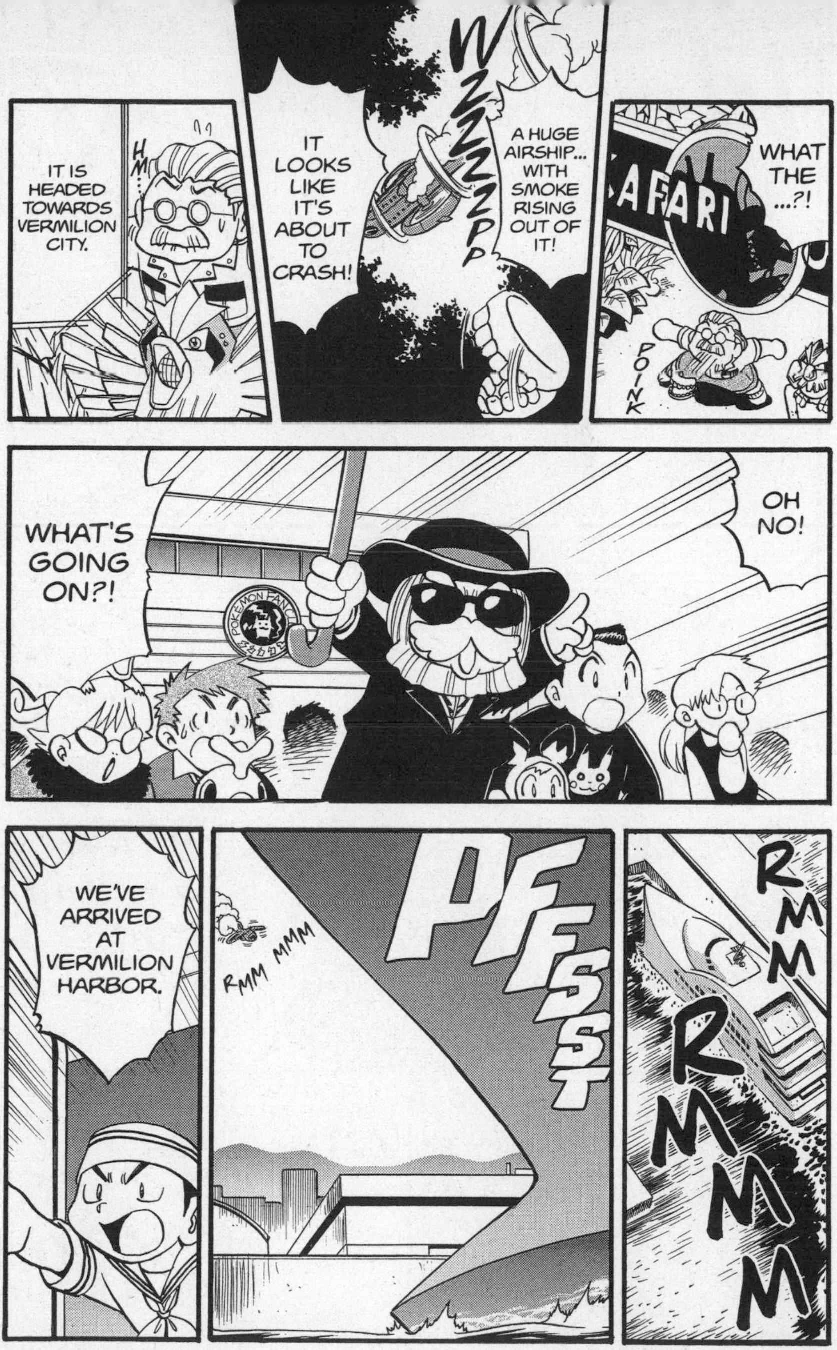
WHAT THE ...?!
POINK
A HUGE AIRSHIP... WITH SMOKE RISING OUT OF IT!
WZZZZZPP
IT LOOKS LIKE IT'S ABOUT TO CRASH!
HM...
IT IS HEADED TOWARDS VERMILION CITY.
OH NO!
WHAT'S GOING ON?!
RMM
RMMMMM
PFFSST
RMM MMM
WE'VE ARRIVED AT VERMILION HARBOR.

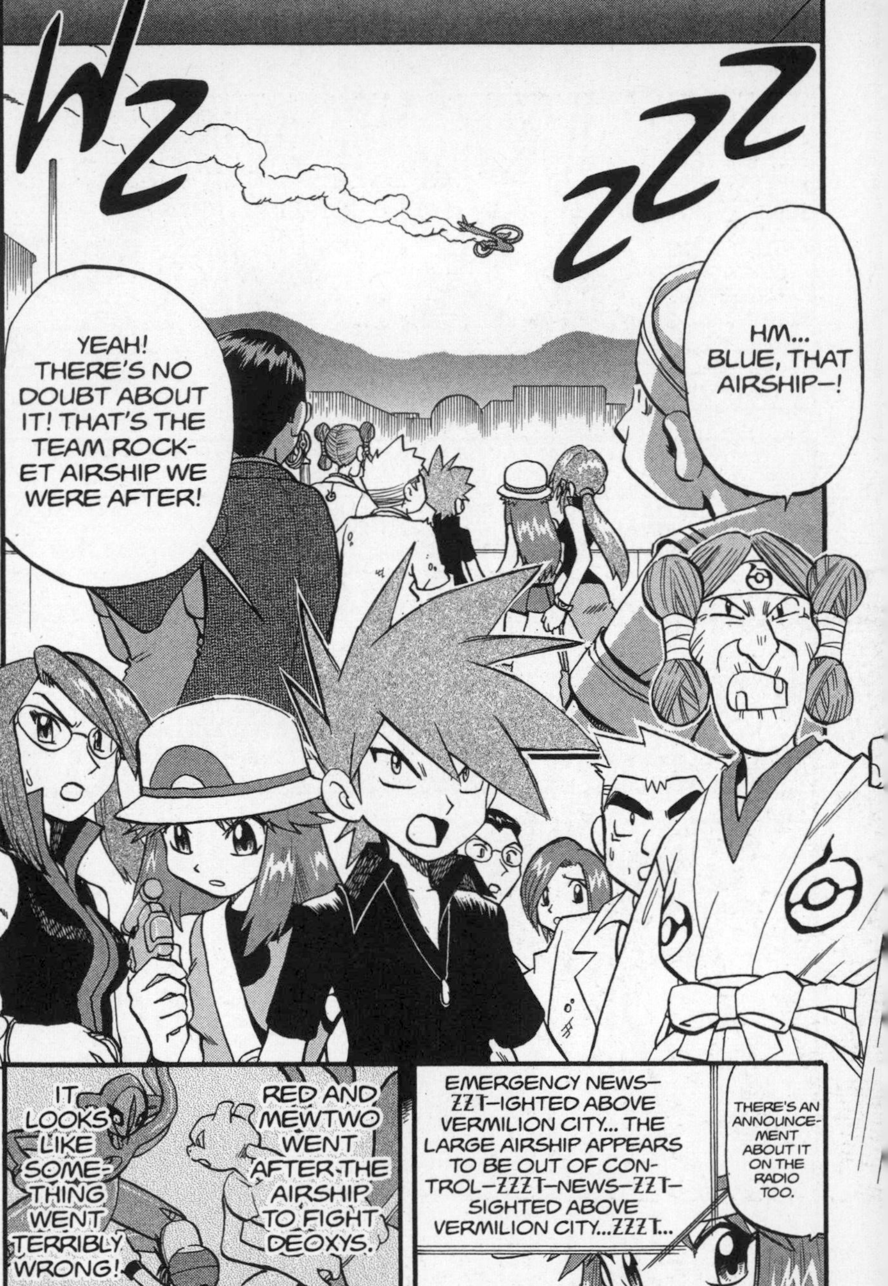
WZZZZZ
HM... BLUE, THAT AIRSHIP—!
YEAH! THERE'S NO DOUBT ABOUT IT! THAT'S THE TEAM ROCKET AIRSHIP WE WERE AFTER!
THERE'S AN ANNOUNCEMENT ABOUT IT ON THE RADIO TOO.
EMERGENCY NEWS—ZZZT—IGHTED ABOVE VERMILION CITY... THE LARGE AIRSHIP APPEARS TO BE OUT OF CONTROL—ZZZT—NEWS—ZZT—SIGHTED ABOVE VERMILION CITY...ZZZT...
RED AND MEWTWO WENT AFTER THE AIRSHIP TO FIGHT DEOXYS.
IT LOOKS LIKE SOMETHING WENT TERRIBLY WRONG!

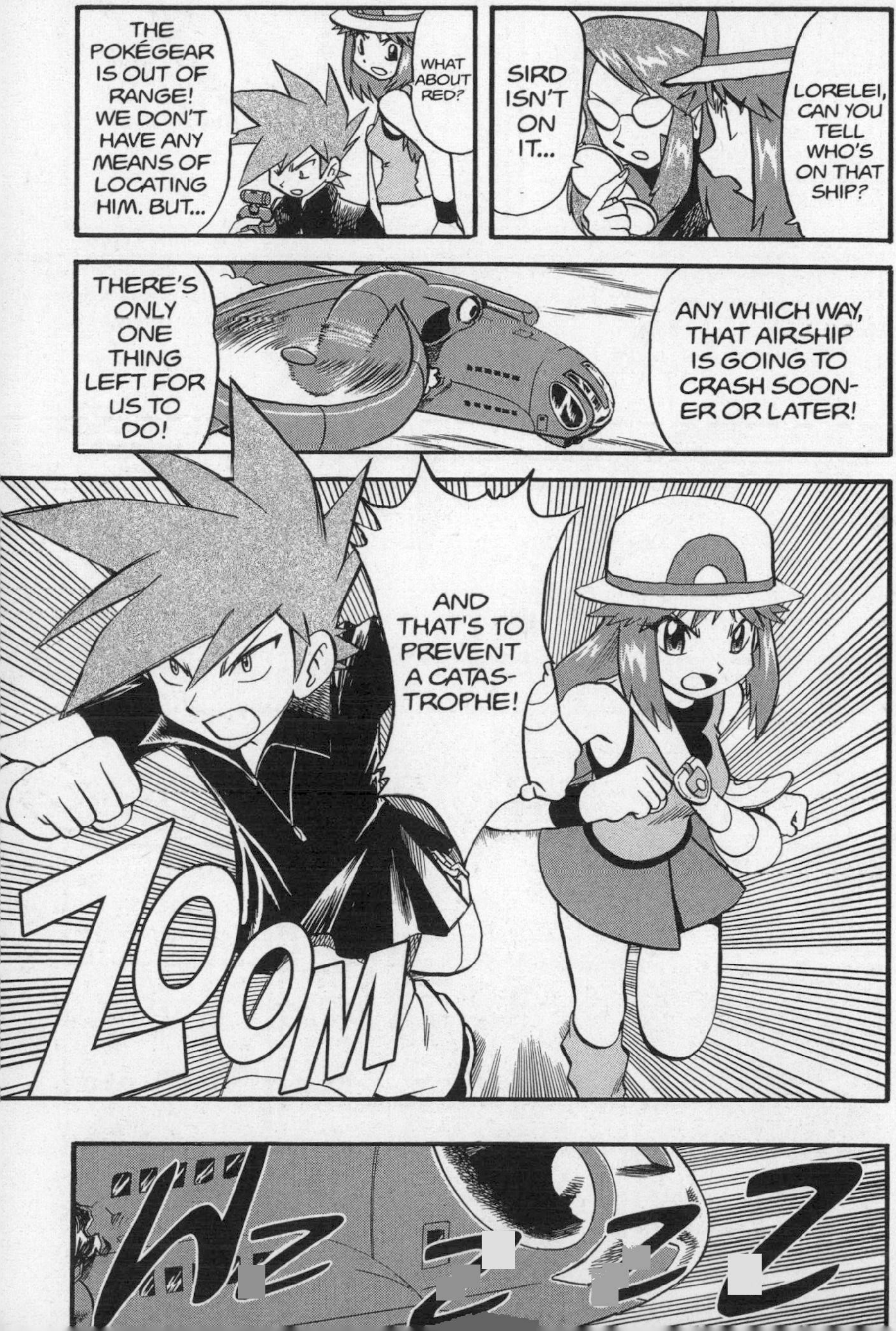
LORELEI, CAN YOU TELL WHO'S ON THAT SHIP?
SIRD ISN'T ON IT...
WHAT ABOUT RED?
THE POKÉGEAR IS OUT OF RANGE! WE DON'T HAVE ANY MEANS OF LOCATING HIM. BUT...
ANY WHICH WAY, THAT AIRSHIP IS GOING TO CRASH SOONER OR LATER!
THERE'S ONLY ONE THING LEFT FOR US TO DO!
AND THAT'S TO PREVENT A CATASTROPHE!
ZOOM

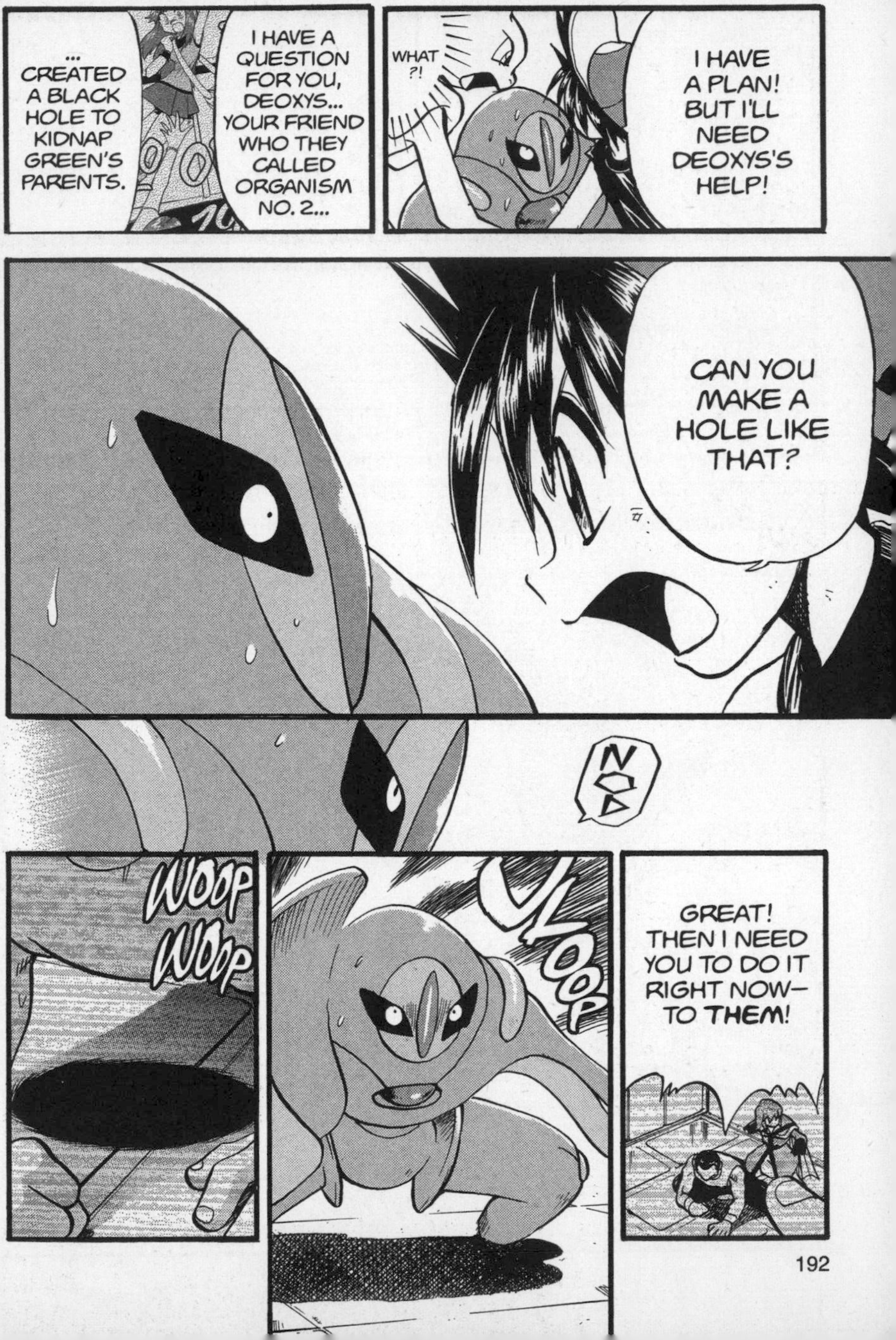
I HAVE A PLAN! BUT I'LL NEED DEOXYS'S HELP!
WHAT ?!
I HAVE A QUESTION FOR YOU, DEOXYS... YOUR FRIEND WHO THEY CALLED ORGANISM NO. 2...
...CREATED A BLACK HOLE TO KIDNAP GREEN'S PARENTS.
CAN YOU MAKE A HOLE LIKE THAT?
NOD
GREAT! THEN I NEED YOU TO DO IT RIGHT NOW— TO THEM!
VOOOP
WOOP WOOP

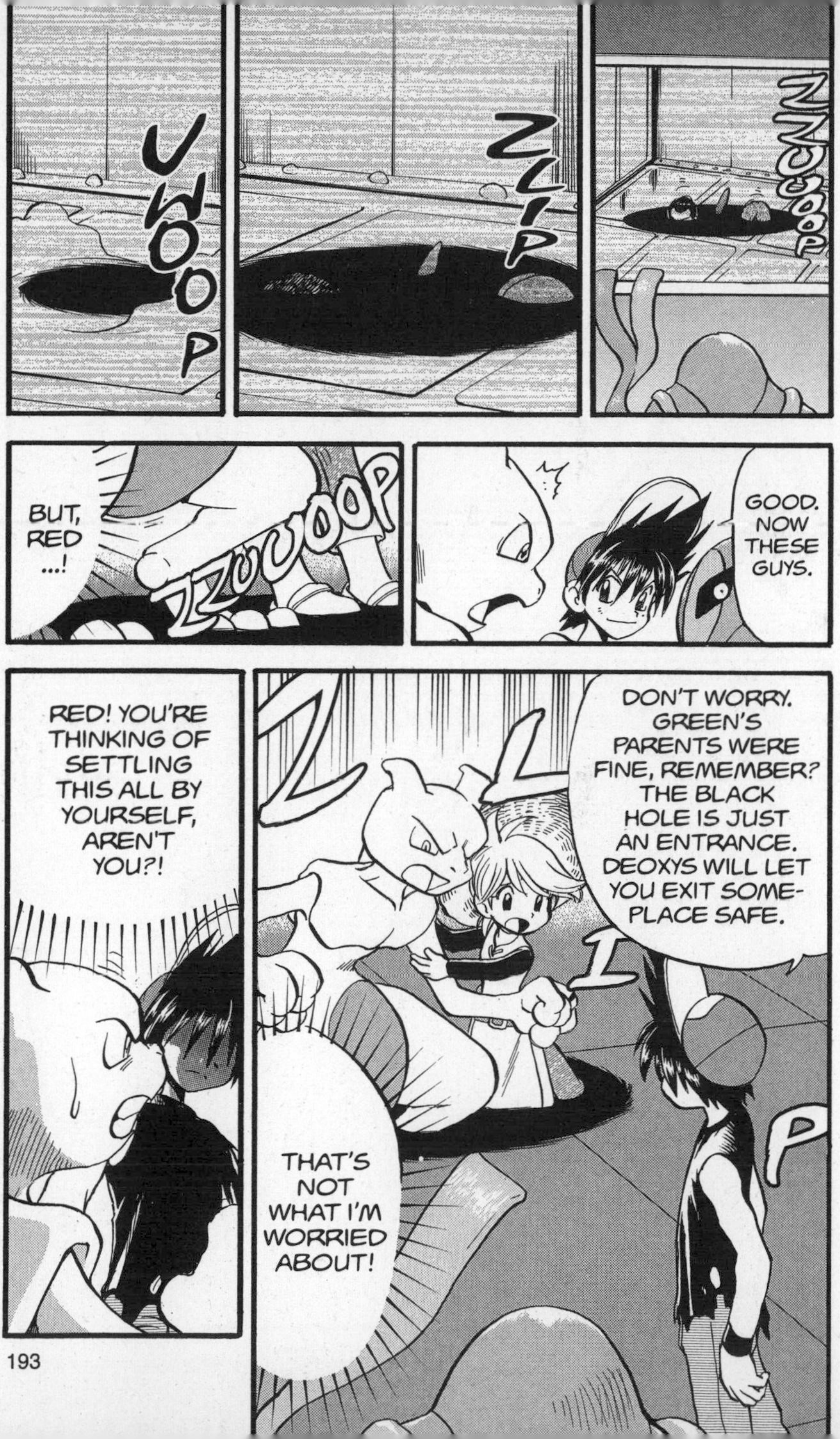
ZZUOOOP
ZLIP
UWOOP
GOOD. NOW THESE GUYS.
ZZUOOP
BUT, RED ...!
ZLIP
DON'T WORRY. GREEN'S PARENTS WERE FINE, REMEMBER? THE BLACK HOLE IS JUST AN ENTRANCE. DEOXYS WILL LET YOU EXIT SOME-PLACE SAFE.
THAT'S NOT WHAT I'M WORRIED ABOUT!
RED! YOU'RE THINKING OF SETTLING THIS ALL BY YOURSELF, AREN'T YOU?!

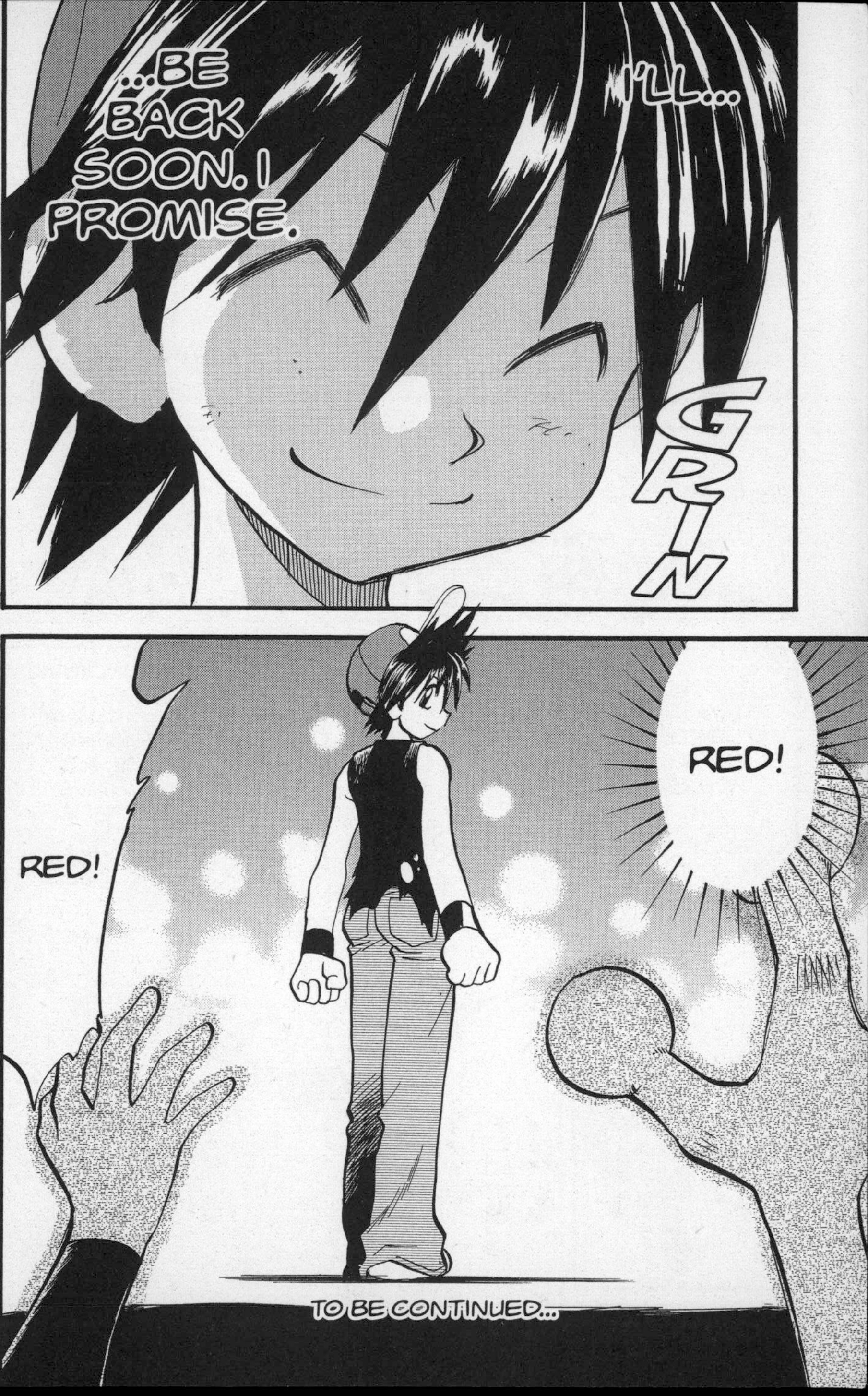
I'LL...
...BE BACK SOON. I PROMISE.
GRIN
RED!
RED!
TO BE CONTINUED...

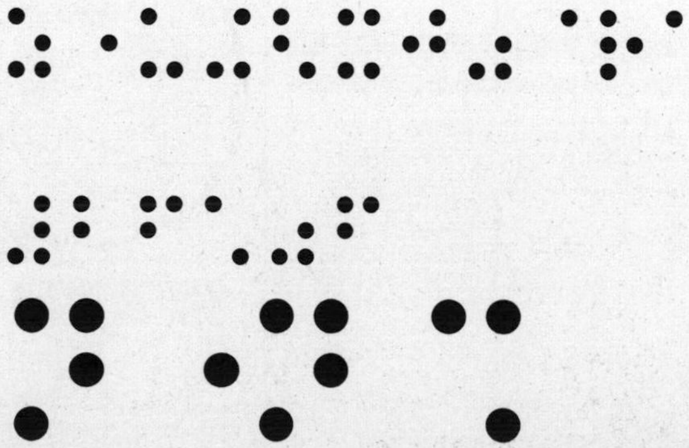

DEOXYS

SPECIAL FEATURE: DNA POKÉMON.

DEOXYS IS A POKÉMON WITH SEVERAL MYSTERIOUS POWERS. THIS IS THE DATA GATHERED ON DEOXYS IN THE MIDST OF THE PRECEDING FIERCE BATTLE, REVEALING THE FORMIDABLE POWER OF THE ENERGIES OF THE UNIVERSE.

THE SECRET BEHIND ITS ORIGIN FINALLY REVEALED!

DEOXYS'S ROOTS LIE IN A SPACE VIRUS. IT CAME DOWN TO EARTH ON A METEOR.

1 ORIGIN

A ROCKET LAUNCHED FROM THE MOSSDEEP SPACE CENTER CAME ACROSS A VIRUS IN OUTER SPACE AND BEGAN TO CONDUCT EXPERIMENTS ON IT. DURING THE EXPERIMENTS, THE VIRUS WAS EXPOSED TO A LASER BEAM, WHICH CAUSED IT TO MUTATE. THE VIRUS HAS NOW TURNED INTO A NEW ORGANISM...

THIS NEW ORGANISM TRAVELED TO OUR HEROES' WORLD BY CLINGING ONTO THE GRAND METEOR. BOTH WERE RECOVERED BY THE MOSSDEEP SPACE CENTER AND KEPT THERE.

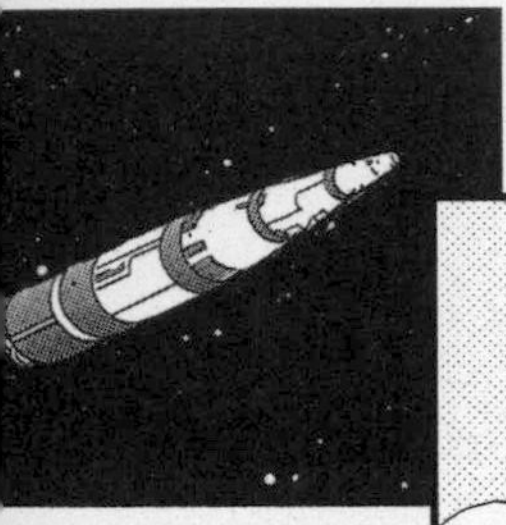

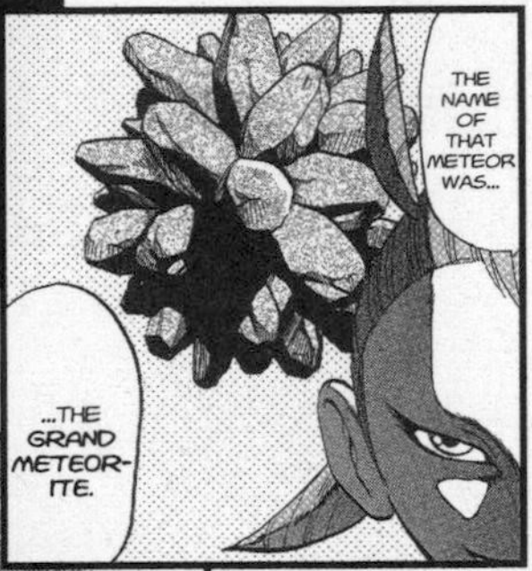
THE NAME OF THAT METEOR WAS...
...THE GRAND METEOR-ITE.

THE ROCKET THAT SCOVERED THE VIRUS AND POSED IT TO THE LASER.

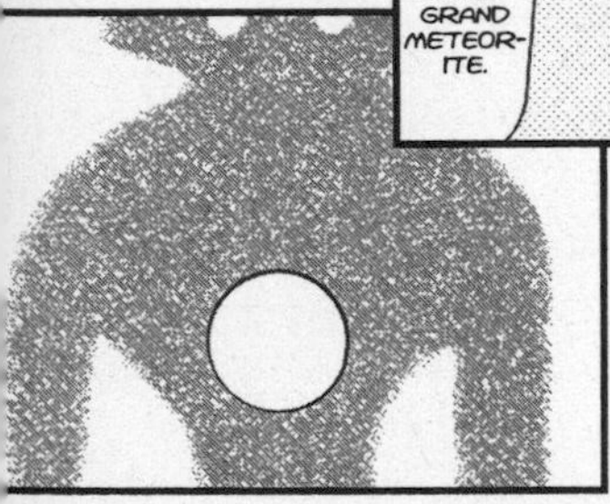

◀▲PROFESSOR COZMO GOT AHOLD OF THE GRAND METEOR. MEANWHILE, THE VIRUS BEGAN TO GROW LIMBS AROUND ITS CORE.

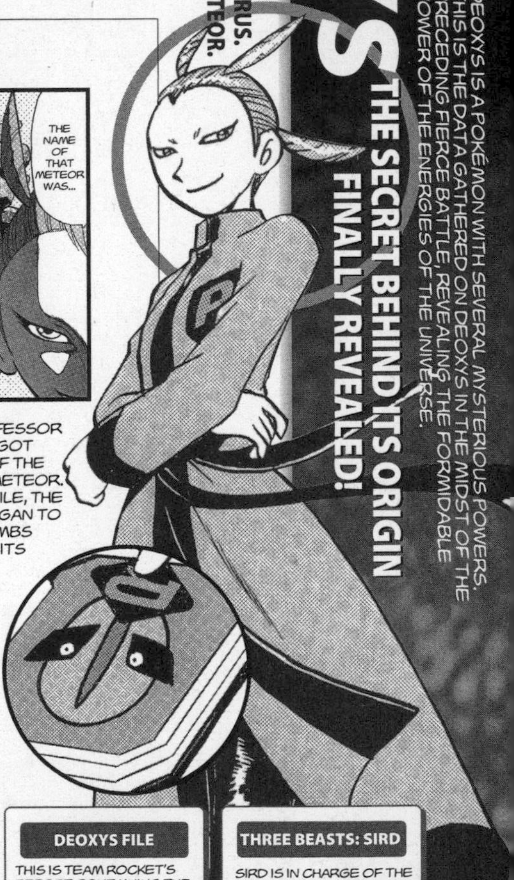

● TWO NEW ORGANISMS ARE SPAWNED.

THE TWO ORGANISMS ARE TILL INCOMPLETELY FORMED ND ARE NOW HOUSED INSIDE EAM ROCKET'S AIRSHIP.

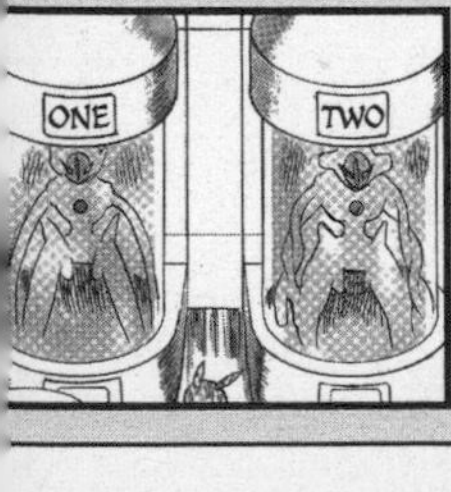
ONE
TWO

THESE TWO ORGANISMS WERE HOUSED AT THE SPACE CENTER. THEY WERE STOLEN BY TEAM ROCKET AND NAMED ORGANISM NO. 1 AND ORGANISM NO. 2. NO. 2 ESCAPED.

DEOXYS FILE

THIS IS TEAM ROCKET'S REPORT CONTAINING THE FULL DETAILS OF THEIR "OPERATION-D," A STUDY OF DEOXYS.

THREE BEASTS: SIRD

SIRD IS IN CHARGE OF THE RESEARCH ON DEOXYS. SHE HAS DIVULGED SOME OF ITS SECRETS.

2 FORMES

IT HAS BEEN REVEALED THAT DEOXYS IS ABLE TO ALTER ITS SHAPE INTO SEVERAL DIFFERENT FORMES. ITS POWERS CHANGE SIGNIFICANTLY DEPENDING ON ITS FORME.

3 CHANGE

WE'VE ALSO DISCOVERED THAT THE CHANGE IN FORME IS TRIGGERED BY THE ORGANISM'S LOCATION. THAT'S WHY DEOXYS BEGAN TO TRANSFORM DURING ITS JOURNEY.

4 RECAPTURE

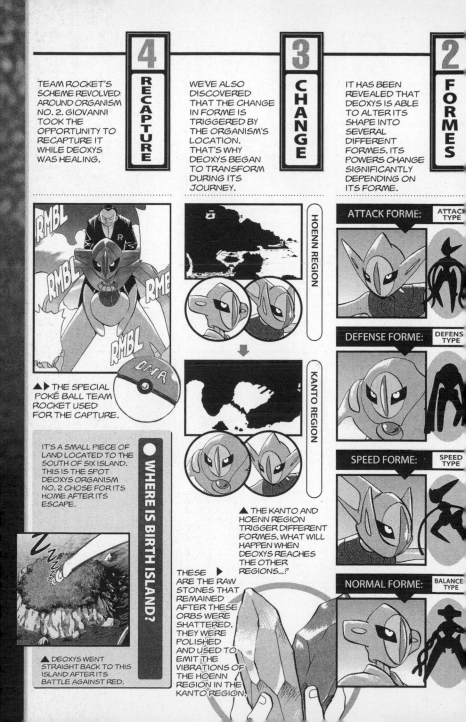

TEAM ROCKET'S SCHEME REVOLVED AROUND ORGANISM NO. 2. GIOVANNI TOOK THE OPPORTUNITY TO RECAPTURE IT WHILE DEOXYS WAS HEALING.

ATTACK FORME: ATTACK TYPE

DEFENSE FORME: DEFENSE TYPE

SPEED FORME: SPEED TYPE

NORMAL FORME: BALANCE TYPE

HOENN REGION

KANTO REGION

▲ THE KANTO AND HOENN REGION TRIGGER DIFFERENT FORMES. WHAT WILL HAPPEN WHEN DEOXYS REACHES THE OTHER REGIONS...?

THESE ▶ ARE THE RAW STONES THAT REMAINED AFTER THESE ORBS WERE SHATTERED. THEY WERE POLISHED AND USED TO EMIT THE VIBRATIONS OF THE HOENN REGION IN THE KANTO REGION.

RMBL
RMBL
RMBL
RMBL

▲▶ THE SPECIAL POKÉ BALL TEAM ROCKET USED FOR THE CAPTURE.

● WHERE IS BIRTH ISLAND?

IT'S A SMALL PIECE OF LAND LOCATED TO THE SOUTH OF SIX ISLAND. THIS IS THE SPOT DEOXYS ORGANISM NO. 2 CHOSE FOR ITS HOME AFTER ITS ESCAPE.

▲ DEOXYS WENT STRAIGHT BACK TO THIS ISLAND AFTER ITS BATTLE AGAINST RED.

5 CAPABILITIES

AS A DNA POKÉMON FROM OUTER SPACE, DEOXYS HAS MANY UNIQUE AND POWERFUL CAPABILITIES.

DIVINATION

DEOXYS CAN FIND THE OWNER OF AN OBJECT BY SIMPLY TOUCHING IT.

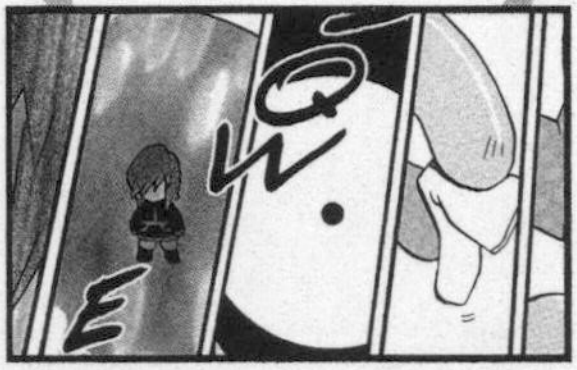

▲ DEOXYS QUICKLY DISCOVERED SILVER'S WHEREABOUTS.

FIST

DEOXYS USES ITS FIST AND TENTACLES IN ITS NORMAL FORME, AN ALL-AROUND FORME THAT CAN HANDLE ANY TYPE OF BATTLE.

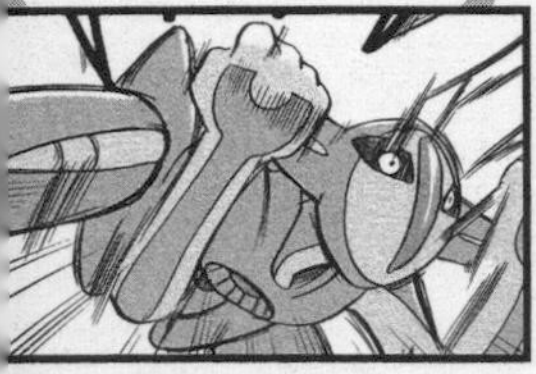

IT USES ITS FISTS FOR OSE COMBAT.

MOST POWERFUL MOVE: PSYCHO BOOST

A POWERFUL MOVE WHICH ONLY DEOXYS CAN USE. RED'S TEAM WAS DEFEATED WITH JUST THIS MOVE!

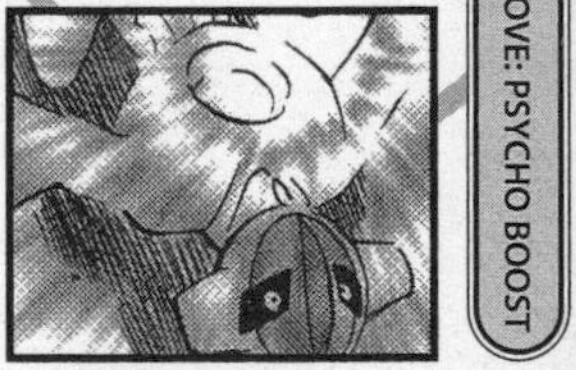

▲ AN AWESOME MOVE. POWER: 140.

BLACK HOLE

DEOXYS CAN CREATE A BLACK HOLE THAT CONNECTS TO A MYSTERIOUS VOID TO CAPTURE ITS OPPONENT. THE BLACK HOLE CAN APPEAR ANYWHERE.

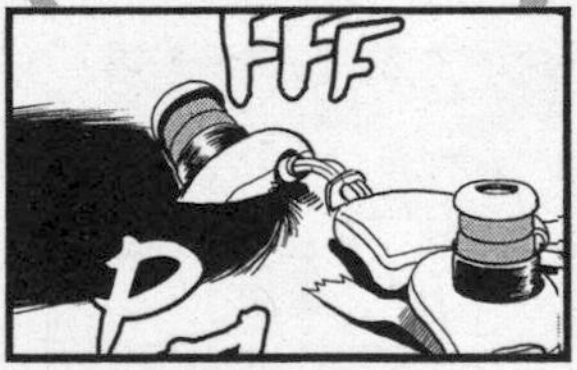
FFF

▲ IT WAS ABSORBED INTO THE DARKNESS.

DUPLICATES

DEOXYS CAN CREATE IMEROUS DUPLICATES AND CONTROL THEM FROM A DISTANCE. EACH ONE ISN'T VERY TRONG BY ITSELF, BUT HEY CAN OVERWHELM THEIR OPPONENT BY FORCE OF NUMBERS.

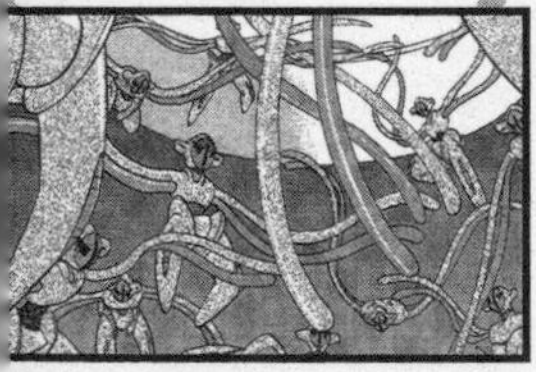

'NNUMERABLE DUPLICATES AND IN OUR HEROES' WAY.

DELTA SHIELD

THIS TRIANGULAR SHIELD INCREASES DEOXYS'S POWER AND PROTECTS IT FROM ATTACKS. IT CAN BE USED WHILE MOVING. DEOXYS OFTEN RAISES THIS SHIELD TO PROVIDE AN OPPORTUNITY TO RESTORE ITS STRENGTH.

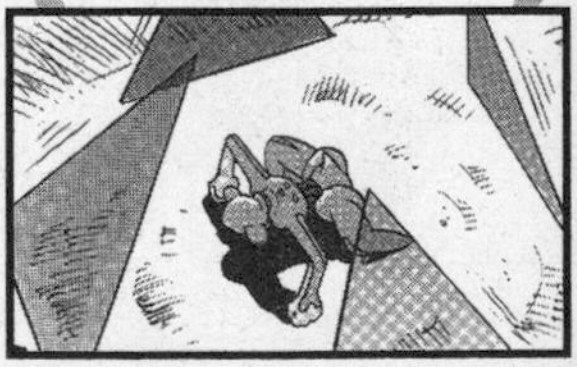

▲ AKA "THE MOVING SHIELD"

DECEPTION

DEOXYS CREATES AN AURORA IN FRONT OF ITS BODY TO DISGUISE ITS ACTUAL FORME. A HIGHLY ADVANCED TACTIC WHICH IS ESPECIALLY USEFUL WHEN BATTLING TRAINERS WHO ARE GOOD AT STRATEGIZING AGAINST DIFFERENT POKÉMON TYPES.

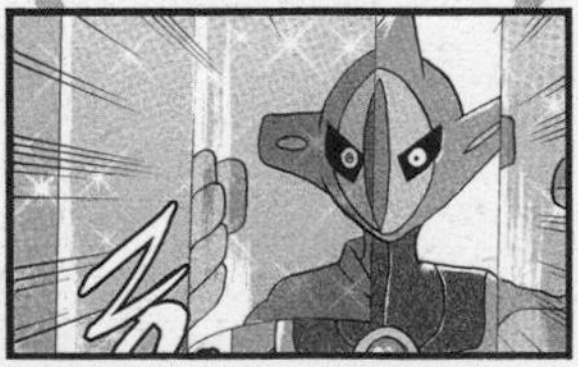

▲ THIS IS ACTUALLY ATTACK FORME, NOT NORMAL FORME.

WHAT WILL BECOME OF DEOXYS...?

DEOXYS HAS BEEN DEFEATED AND HAS LOST ITS ABILITY TO CHANGE INTO FOUR DIFFERENT FORMES. NEVERTHELESS, MANY VILLAINS WISH TO HARNESS ITS UNIQUE POWERS. DEOXYS APPEARS TO BE IN GREAT DANGER!

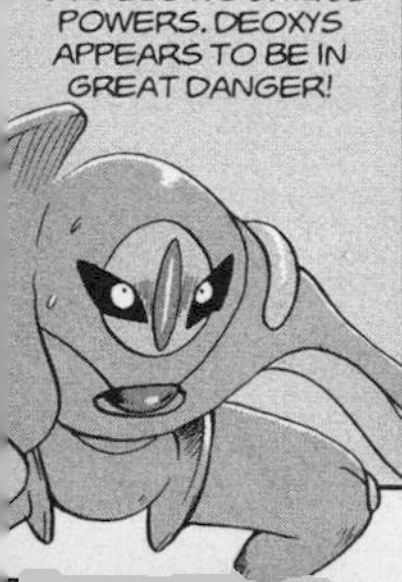

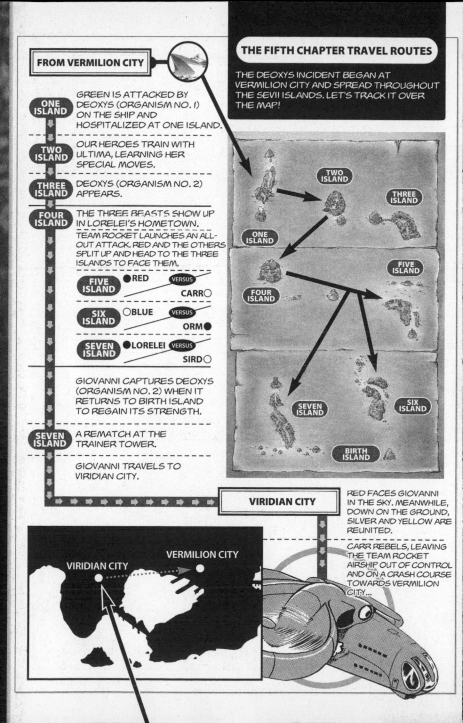

THE FIFTH CHAPTER TRAVEL ROUTES

THE DEOXYS INCIDENT BEGAN AT VERMILION CITY AND SPREAD THROUGHOUT THE SEVII ISLANDS. LET'S TRACK IT OVER THE MAP!

FROM VERMILION CITY

ONE ISLAND — GREEN IS ATTACKED BY DEOXYS (ORGANISM NO. 1) ON THE SHIP AND HOSPITALIZED AT ONE ISLAND.

TWO ISLAND — OUR HEROES TRAIN WITH ULTIMA, LEARNING HER SPECIAL MOVES.

THREE ISLAND — DEOXYS (ORGANISM NO. 2) APPEARS.

FOUR ISLAND — THE THREE BEASTS SHOW UP IN LORELEI'S HOMETOWN. TEAM ROCKET LAUNCHES AN ALL-OUT ATTACK. RED AND THE OTHERS SPLIT UP AND HEAD TO THE THREE ISLANDS TO FACE THEM.

FIVE ISLAND — ●RED VERSUS CARR○

SIX ISLAND — ○BLUE VERSUS ORM●

SEVEN ISLAND — ●LORELEI VERSUS SIRD○

GIOVANNI CAPTURES DEOXYS (ORGANISM NO. 2) WHEN IT RETURNS TO BIRTH ISLAND TO REGAIN ITS STRENGTH.

SEVEN ISLAND — A REMATCH AT THE TRAINER TOWER.

GIOVANNI TRAVELS TO VIRIDIAN CITY.

VIRIDIAN CITY

RED FACES GIOVANNI IN THE SKY. MEANWHILE, DOWN ON THE GROUND, SILVER AND YELLOW ARE REUNITED.

CARR REBELS, LEAVING THE TEAM ROCKET AIRSHIP OUT OF CONTROL AND ON A CRASH COURSE TOWARDS VERMILION CITY...

TWO ISLAND

THREE ISLAND

ONE ISLAND

FIVE ISLAND

FOUR ISLAND

SEVEN ISLAND

SIX ISLAND

BIRTH ISLAND

VERMILION CITY

VIRIDIAN CITY

●Adventure 299●
Distant Relation Deoxys

POKéMON ADVENTURES FIRERED & LEAFGREEN The Fifth Chapter

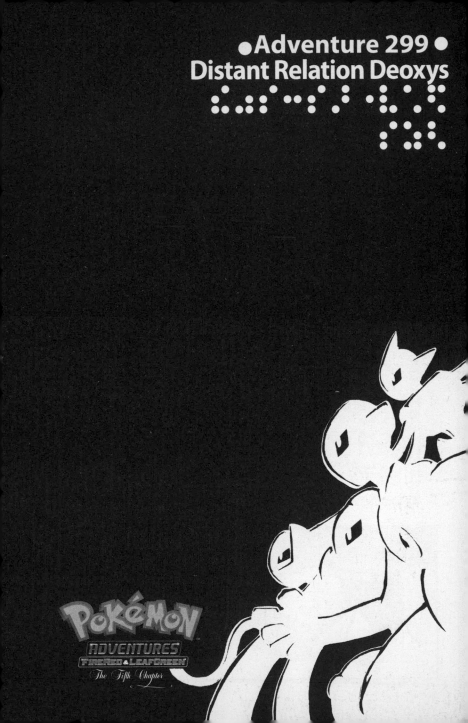

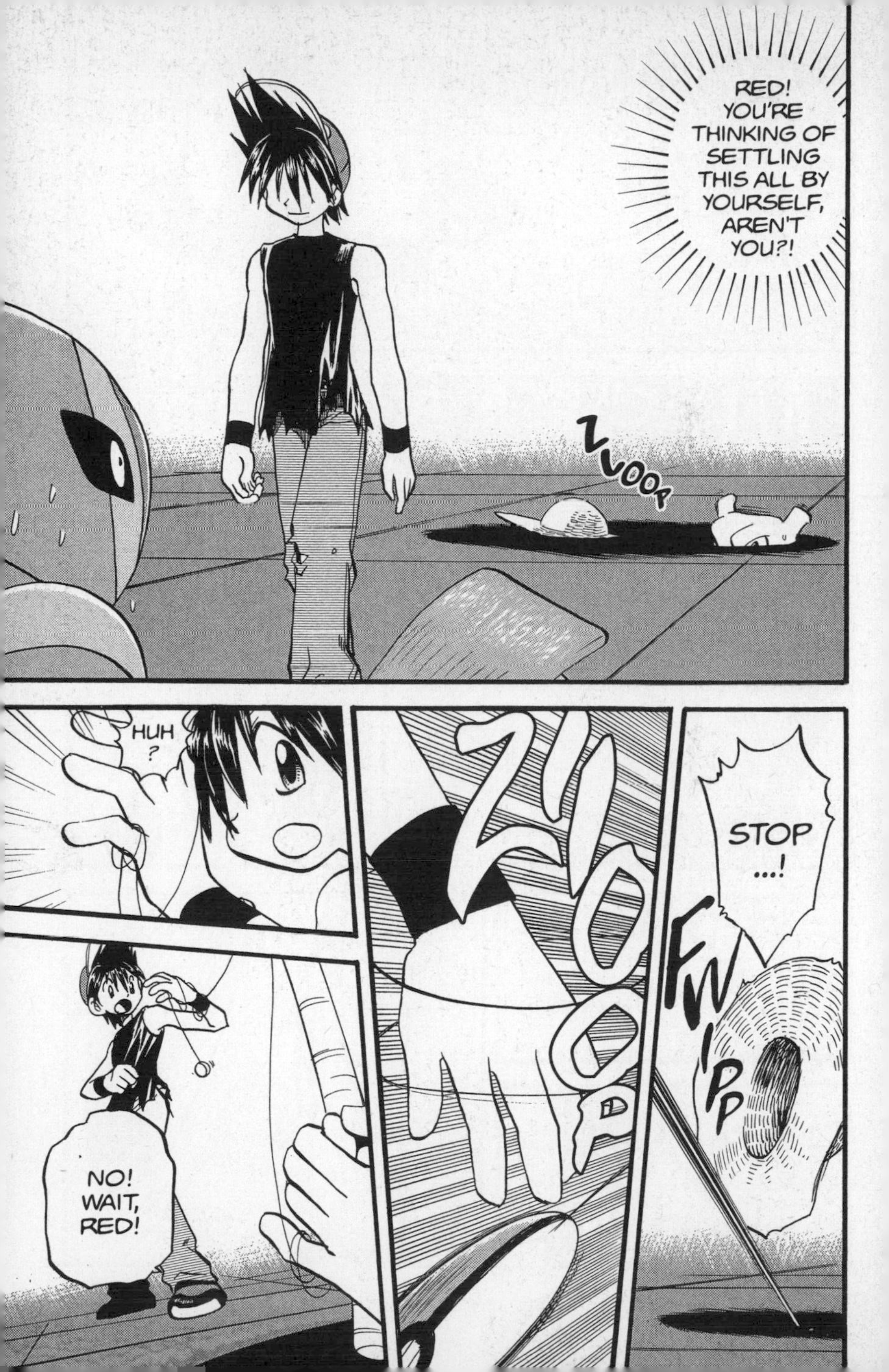
RED! YOU'RE THINKING OF SETTLING THIS ALL BY YOURSELF, AREN'T YOU?!
ZVOOP
STOP ...!
FWIPP
ZVOOP
HUH ?
NO! WAIT, RED!

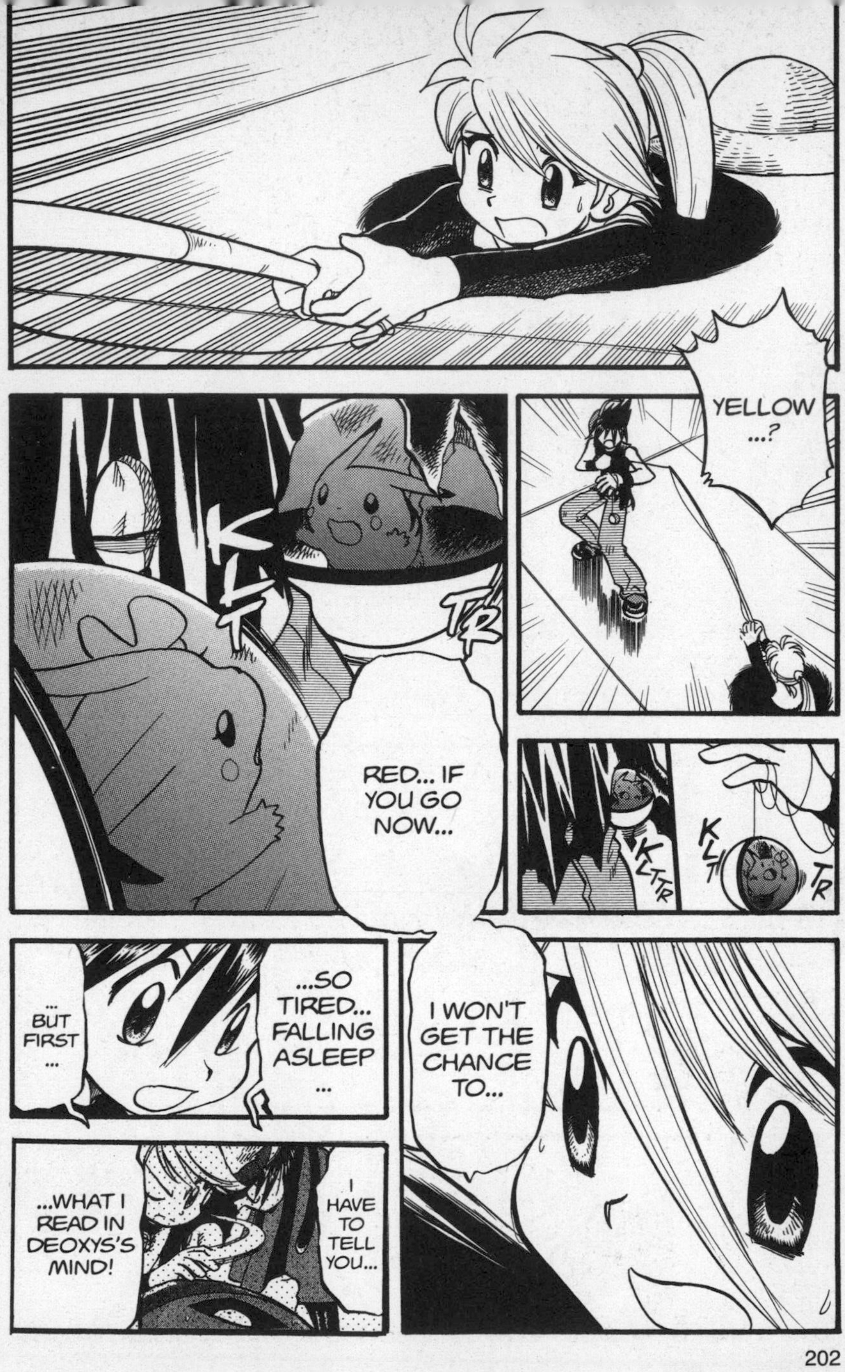
YELLOW ...?
KLT
TR
KLTTR
KLT
TR
RED... IF YOU GO NOW...
I WON'T GET THE CHANCE TO...
...SO TIRED... FALLING ASLEEP ...
... BUT FIRST ...
I HAVE TO TELL YOU...
...WHAT I READ IN DEOXYS'S MIND!

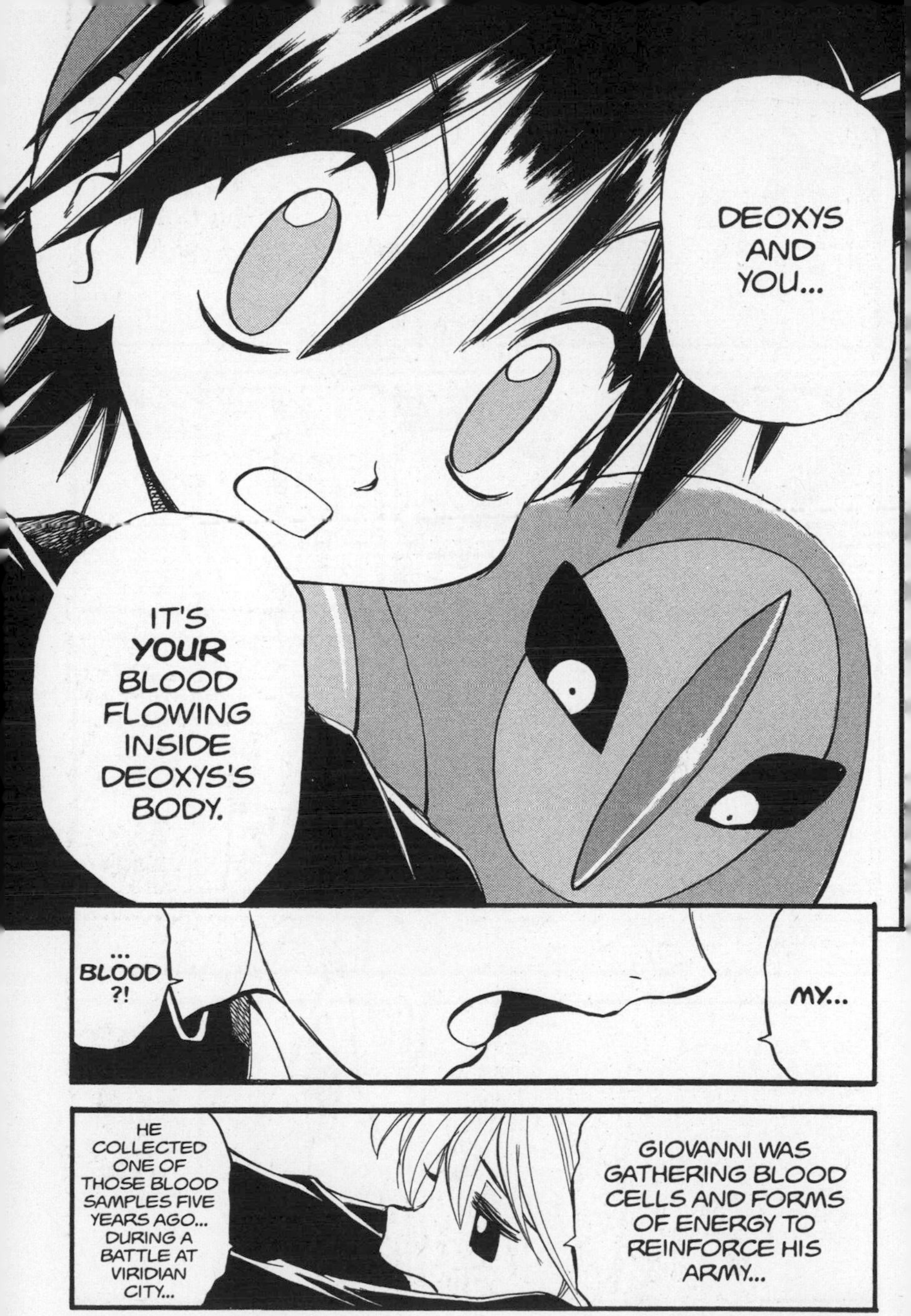
DEOXYS AND YOU...
IT'S **YOUR** BLOOD FLOWING INSIDE DEOXYS'S BODY.
MY...
...BLOOD?!
GIOVANNI WAS GATHERING BLOOD CELLS AND FORMS OF ENERGY TO REINFORCE HIS ARMY...
HE COLLECTED ONE OF THOSE BLOOD SAMPLES FIVE YEARS AGO... DURING A BATTLE AT VIRIDIAN CITY...

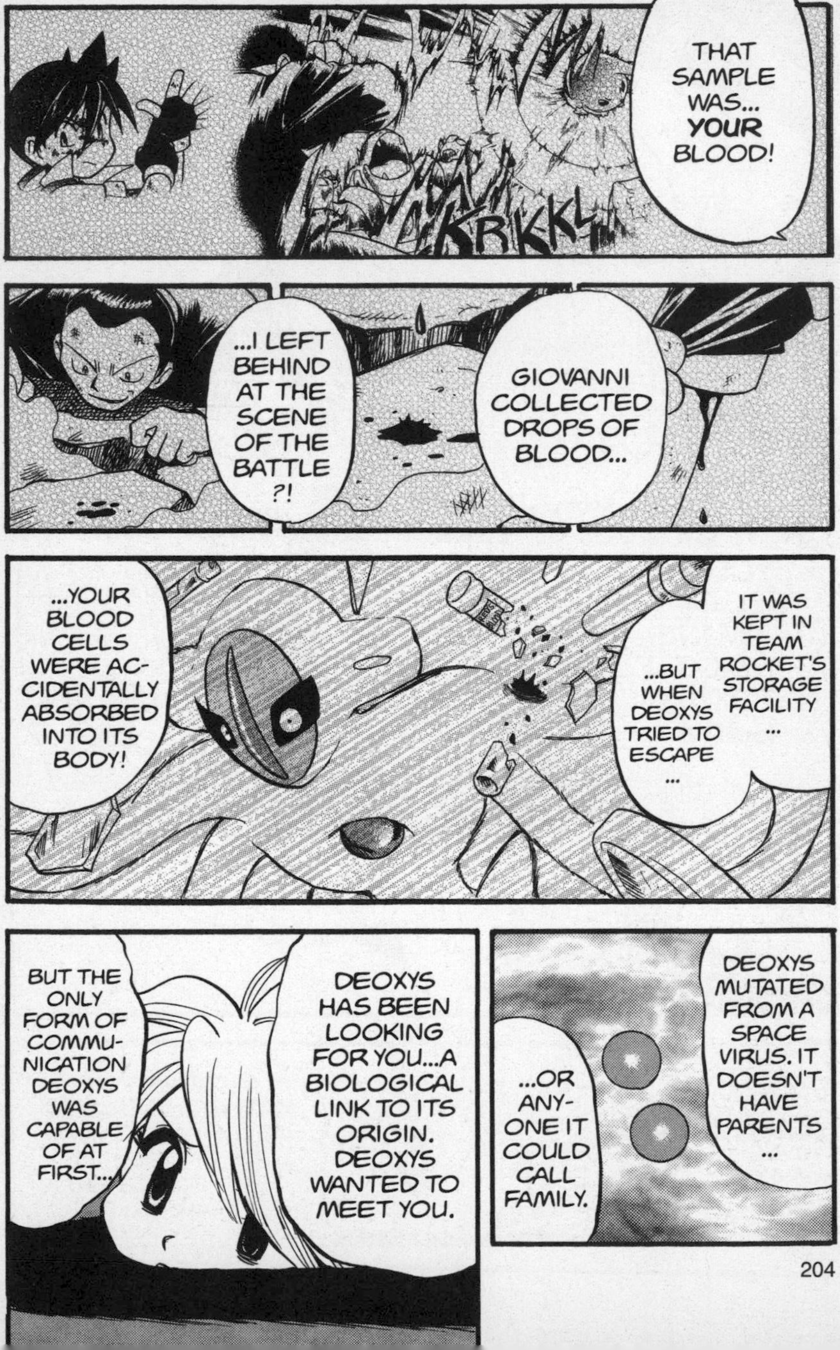
THAT SAMPLE WAS... **YOUR** BLOOD!
KRKKL
GIOVANNI COLLECTED DROPS OF BLOOD...
...I LEFT BEHIND AT THE SCENE OF THE BATTLE ?!
IT WAS KEPT IN TEAM ROCKET'S STORAGE FACILITY ...
...BUT WHEN DEOXYS TRIED TO ESCAPE ...
...YOUR BLOOD CELLS WERE ACCIDENTALLY ABSORBED INTO ITS BODY!
DEOXYS MUTATED FROM A SPACE VIRUS. IT DOESN'T HAVE PARENTS ...
...OR ANYONE IT COULD CALL FAMILY.
DEOXYS HAS BEEN LOOKING FOR YOU...A BIOLOGICAL LINK TO ITS ORIGIN. DEOXYS WANTED TO MEET YOU.
BUT THE ONLY FORM OF COMMUNICATION DEOXYS WAS CAPABLE OF AT FIRST...

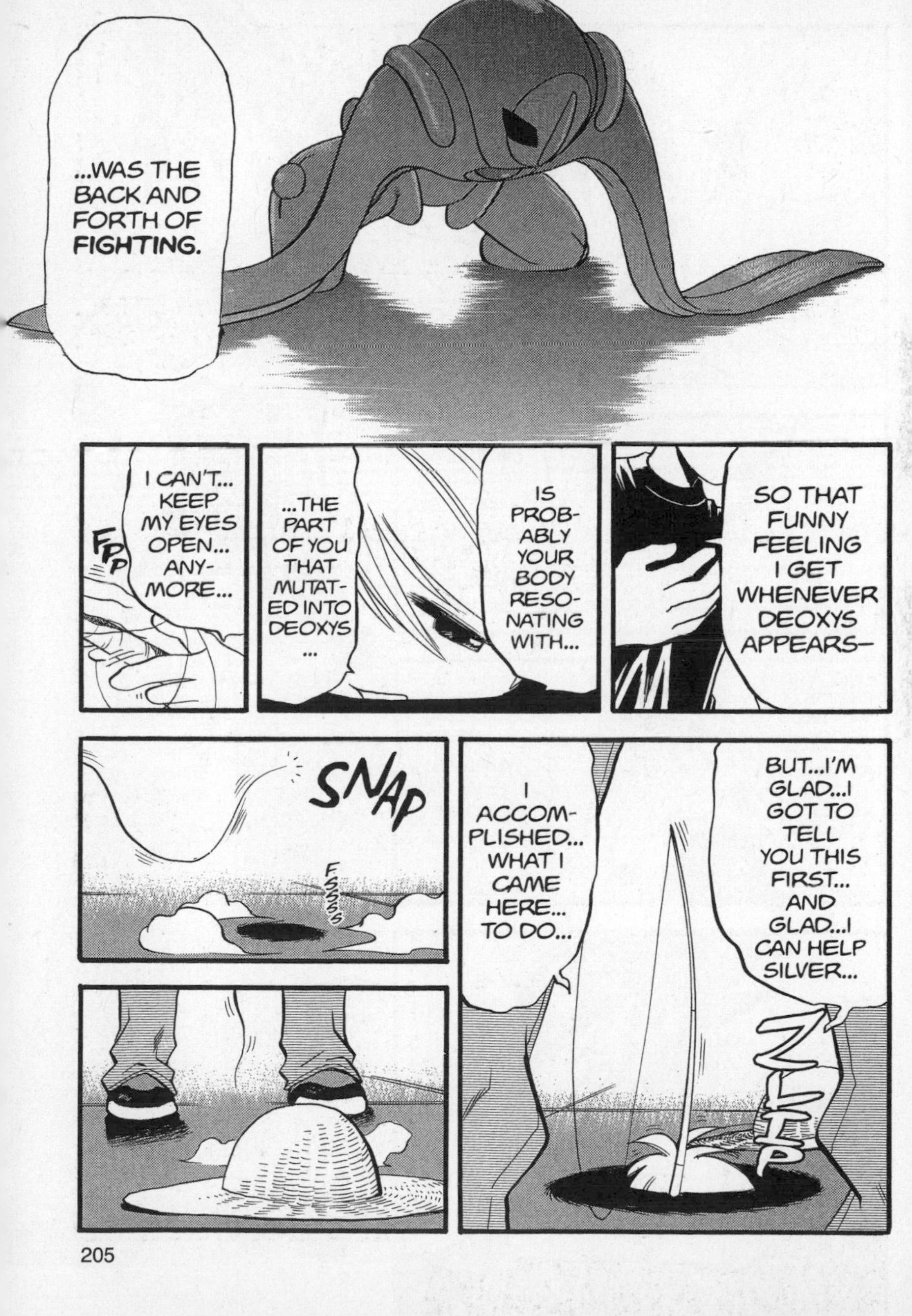
...WAS THE BACK AND FORTH OF FIGHTING.
SO THAT FUNNY FEELING I GET WHENEVER DEOXYS APPEARS—
IS PROB-ABLY YOUR BODY RESO-NATING WITH...
...THE PART OF YOU THAT MUTAT-ED INTO DEOXYS ...
I CAN'T... KEEP MY EYES OPEN... ANY-MORE...
FPP
BUT...I'M GLAD...I GOT TO TELL YOU THIS FIRST... AND GLAD...I CAN HELP SILVER...
I ACCOM-PLISHED... WHAT I CAME HERE... TO DO...
ZZLIP
SNAP
FSSSS

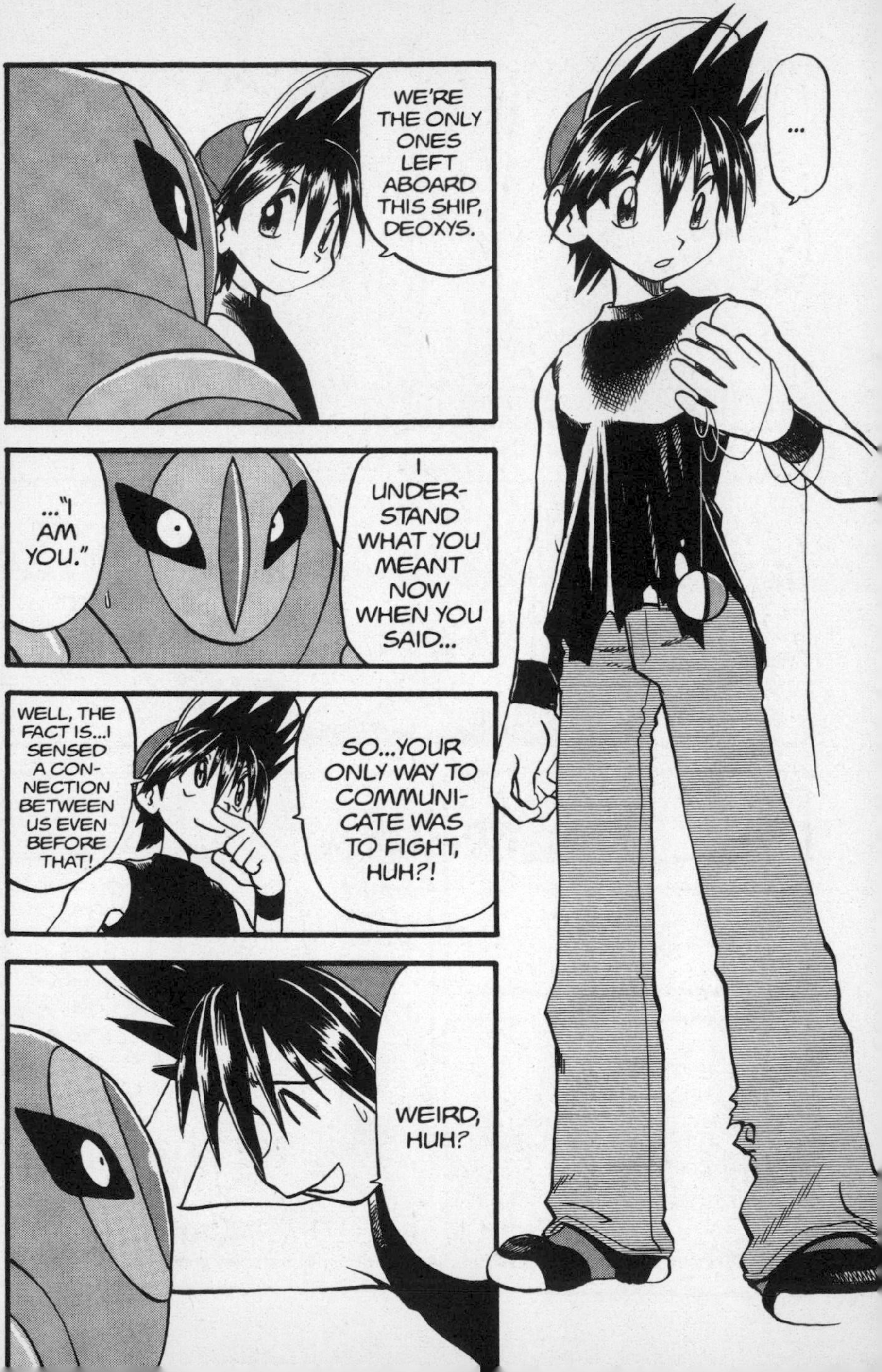
...
WE'RE THE ONLY ONES LEFT ABOARD THIS SHIP, DEOXYS.
I UNDER-STAND WHAT YOU MEANT NOW WHEN YOU SAID...
..."I AM YOU."
SO...YOUR ONLY WAY TO COMMUNI-CATE WAS TO FIGHT, HUH?!
WELL, THE FACT IS...I SENSED A CON-NECTION BETWEEN US EVEN BEFORE THAT!
WEIRD, HUH?

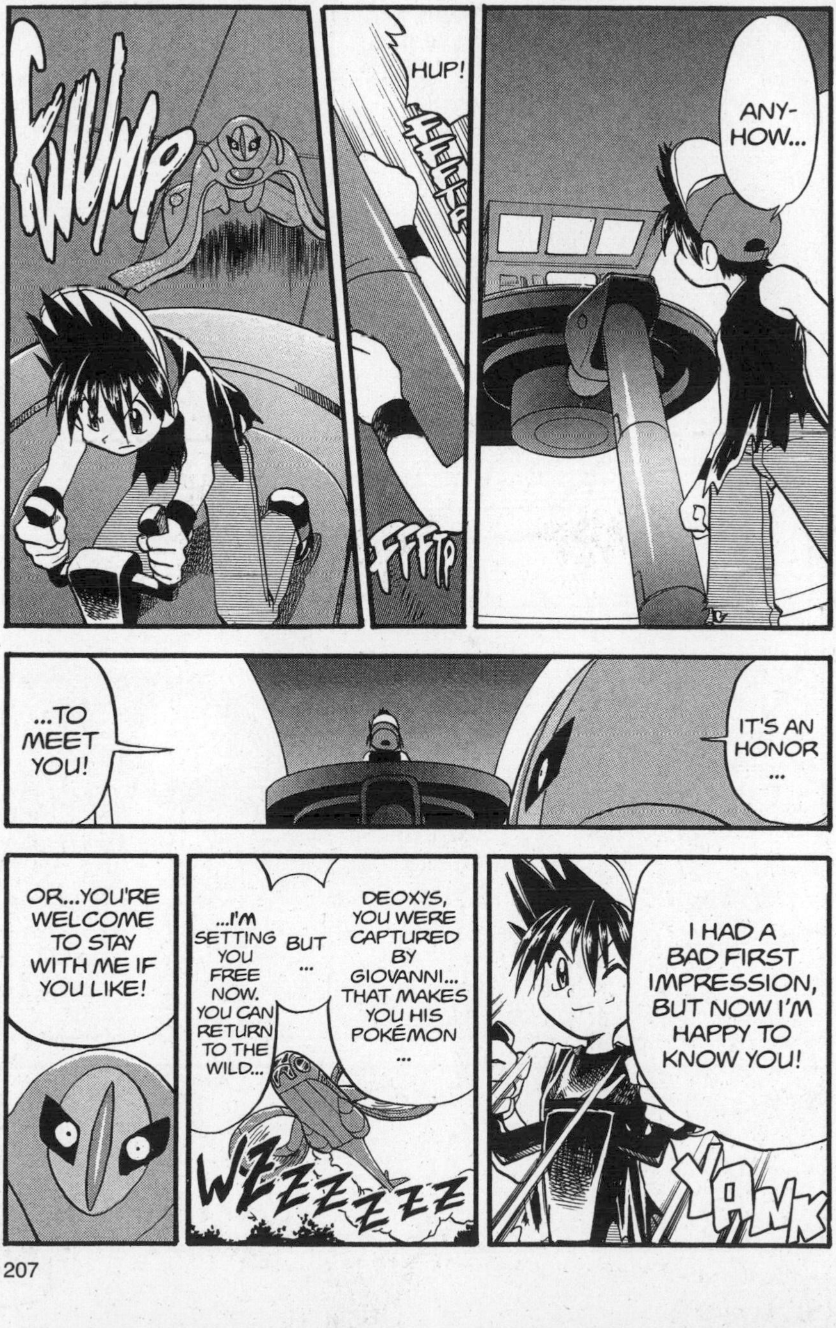
ANY-HOW...
HUP!
FFFTP
FWUMP
IT'S AN HONOR ...
...TO MEET YOU!
I HAD A BAD FIRST IMPRESSION, BUT NOW I'M HAPPY TO KNOW YOU!
YANK
DEOXYS, YOU WERE CAPTURED BY GIOVANNI... THAT MAKES YOU HIS POKÉMON ...
BUT ...
...I'M SETTING YOU FREE NOW. YOU CAN RETURN TO THE WILD...
WZZZZZZZ
OR...YOU'RE WELCOME TO STAY WITH ME IF YOU LIKE!

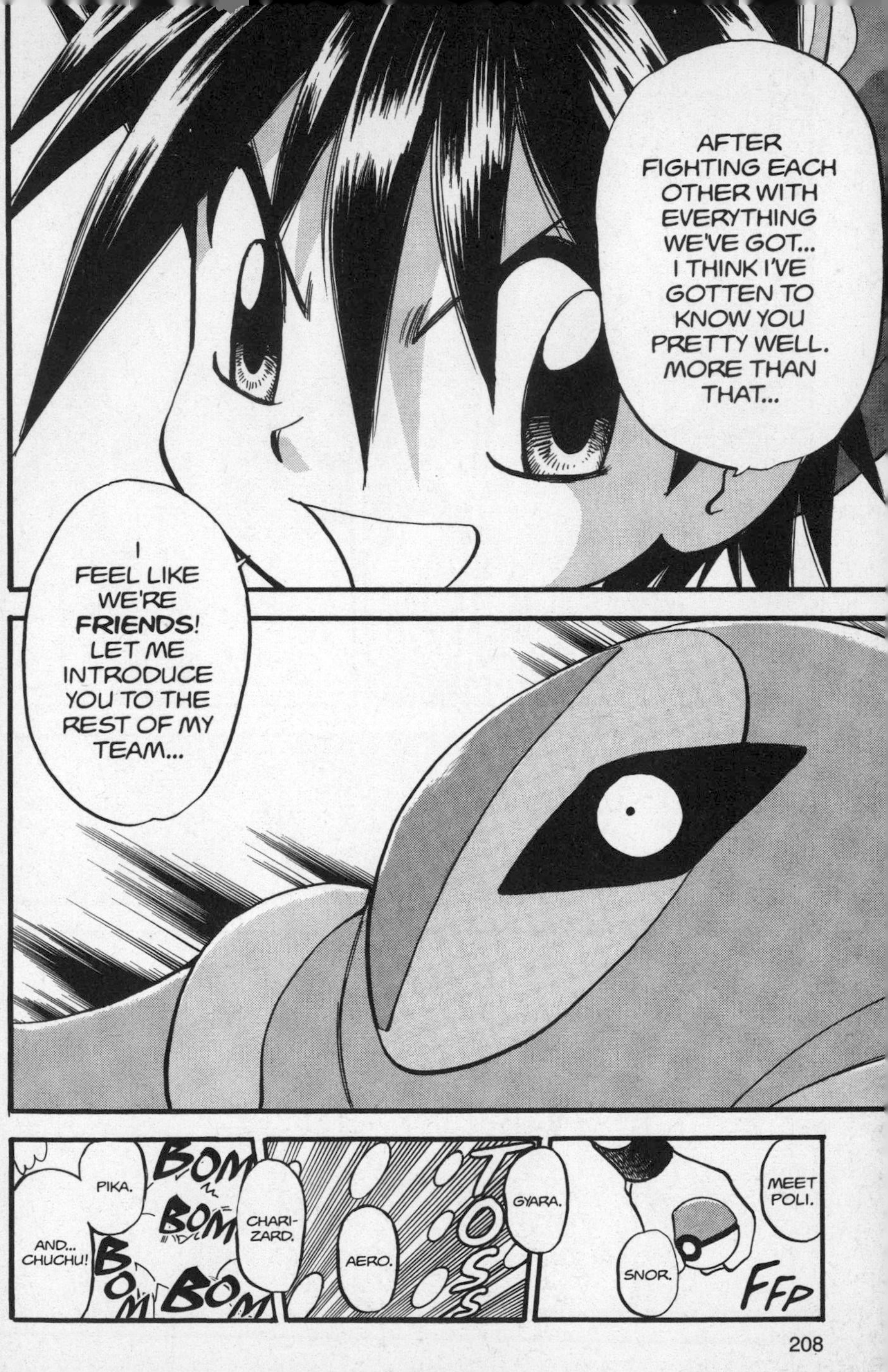
AFTER FIGHTING EACH OTHER WITH EVERYTHING WE'VE GOT... I THINK I'VE GOTTEN TO KNOW YOU PRETTY WELL. MORE THAN THAT...
I FEEL LIKE WE'RE **FRIENDS**! LET ME INTRODUCE YOU TO THE REST OF MY TEAM...
MEET POLI.
SNOR.
FFP
GYARA.
TOSS
CHARI-ZARD.
AERO.
BOM
BOM
PIKA.
BOM
BOM
BOM
AND... CHUCHU!

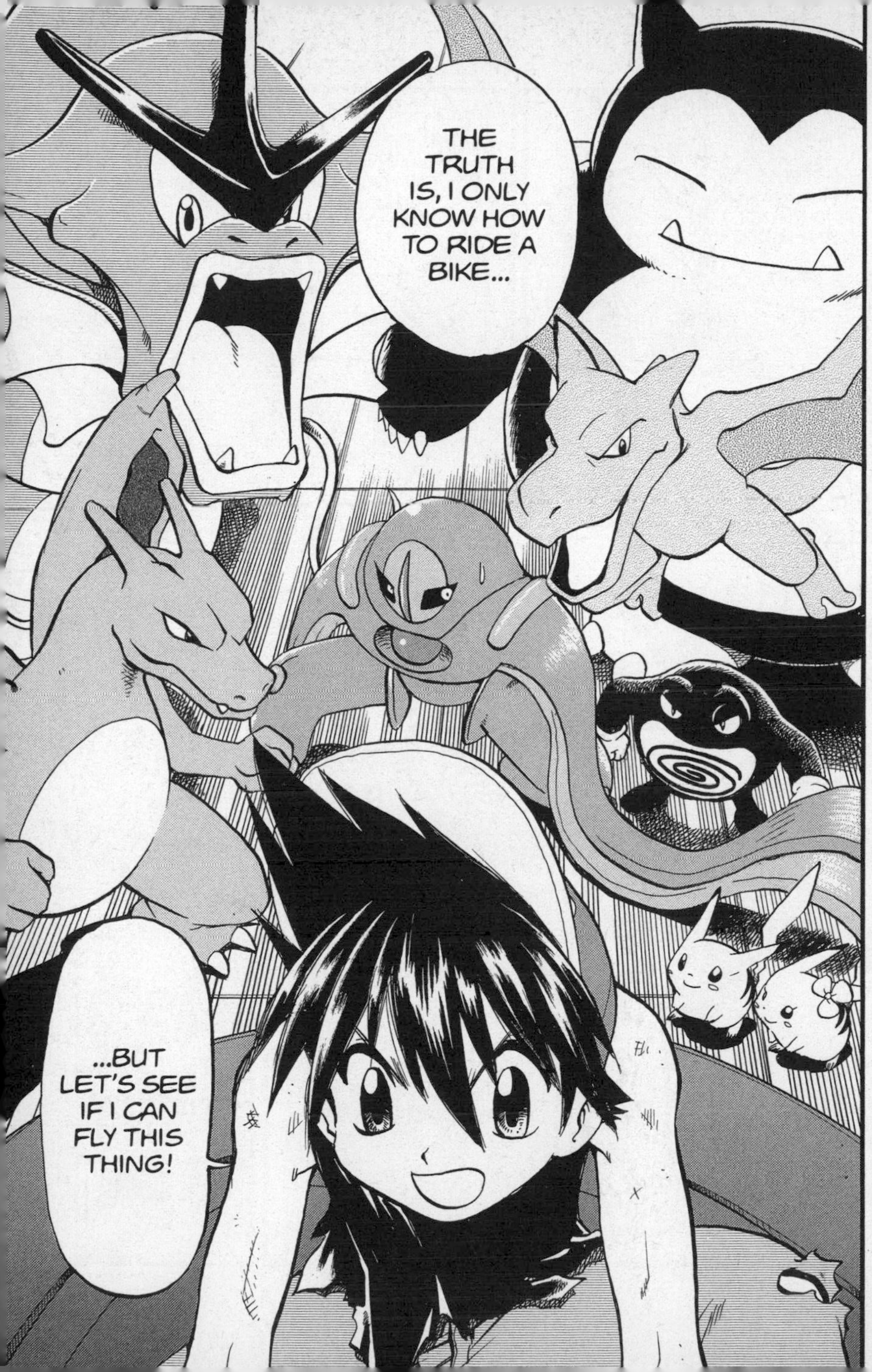
THE TRUTH IS, I ONLY KNOW HOW TO RIDE A BIKE...
...BUT LET'S SEE IF I CAN FLY THIS THING!

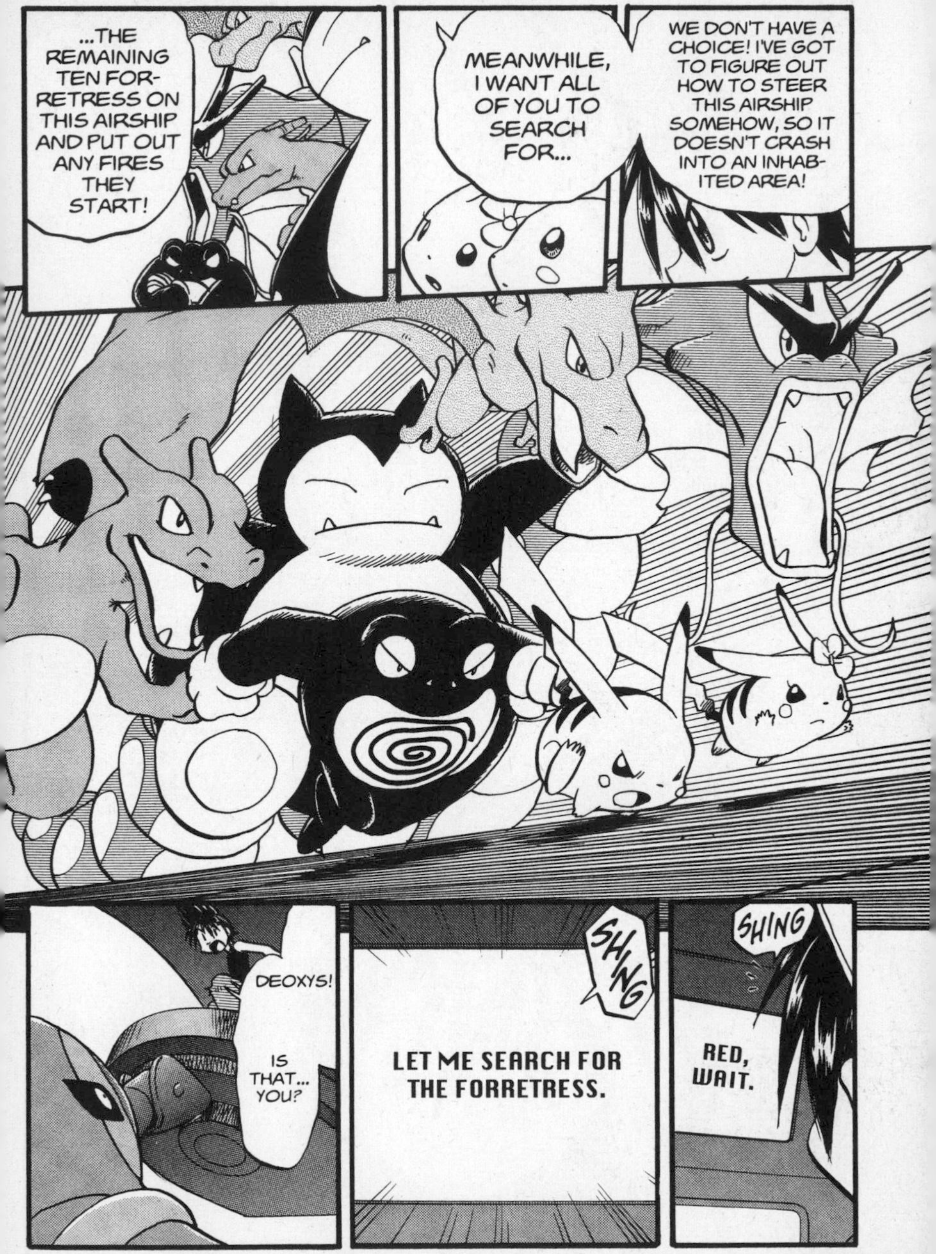
WE DON'T HAVE A CHOICE! I'VE GOT TO FIGURE OUT HOW TO STEER THIS AIRSHIP SOMEHOW, SO IT DOESN'T CRASH INTO AN INHABITED AREA!
MEANWHILE, I WANT ALL OF YOU TO SEARCH FOR...
...THE REMAINING TEN FORRETRESS ON THIS AIRSHIP AND PUT OUT ANY FIRES THEY START!
SHING
RED, WAIT.
SHING
LET ME SEARCH FOR THE FORRETRESS.
DEOXYS!
IS THAT... YOU?

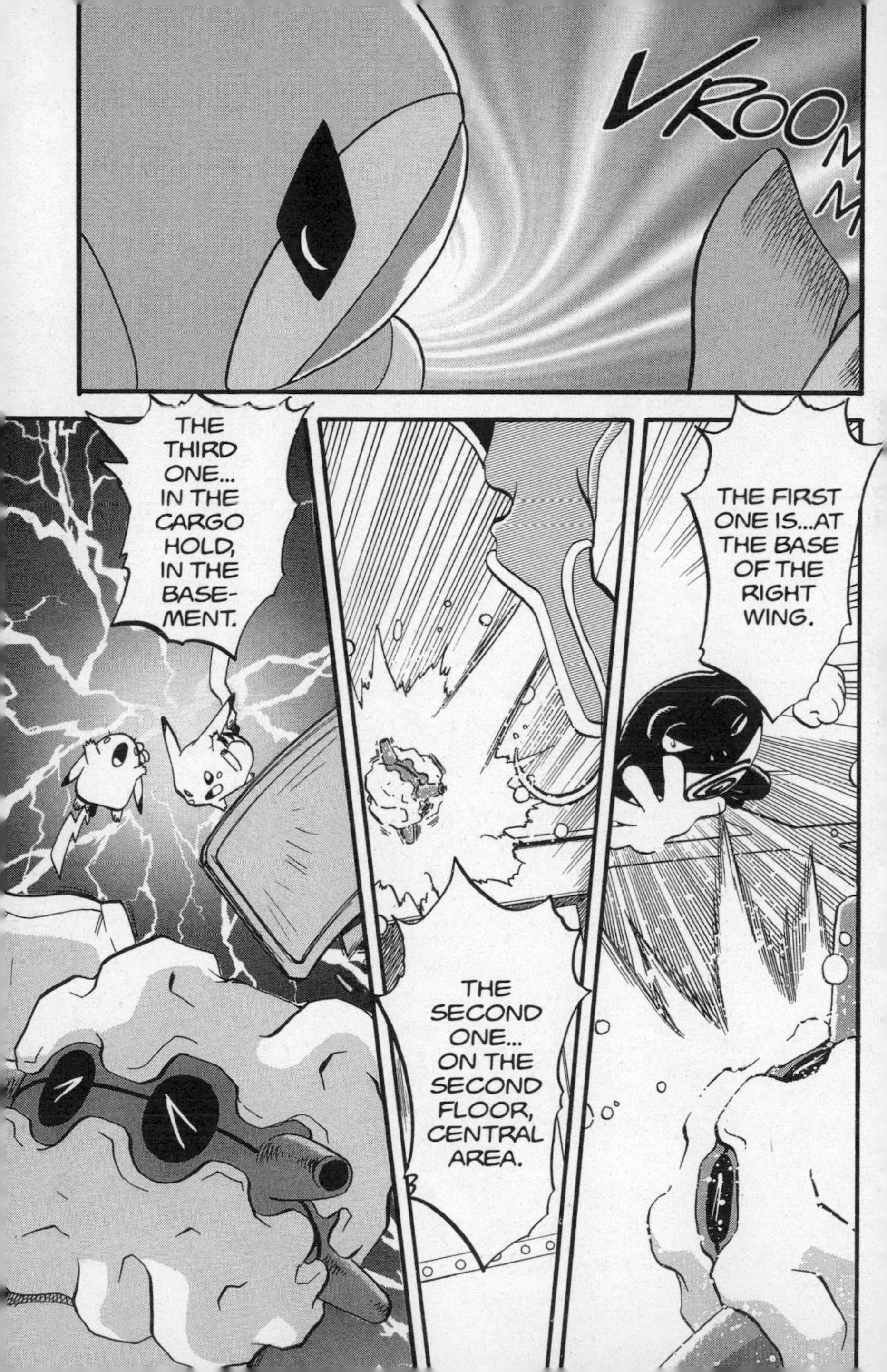
VROOMMM
THE FIRST ONE IS...AT THE BASE OF THE RIGHT WING.
THE SECOND ONE... ON THE SECOND FLOOR, CENTRAL AREA.
THE THIRD ONE... IN THE CARGO HOLD, IN THE BASE-MENT.

•Adventure 300•
Right on Time, Rhydon

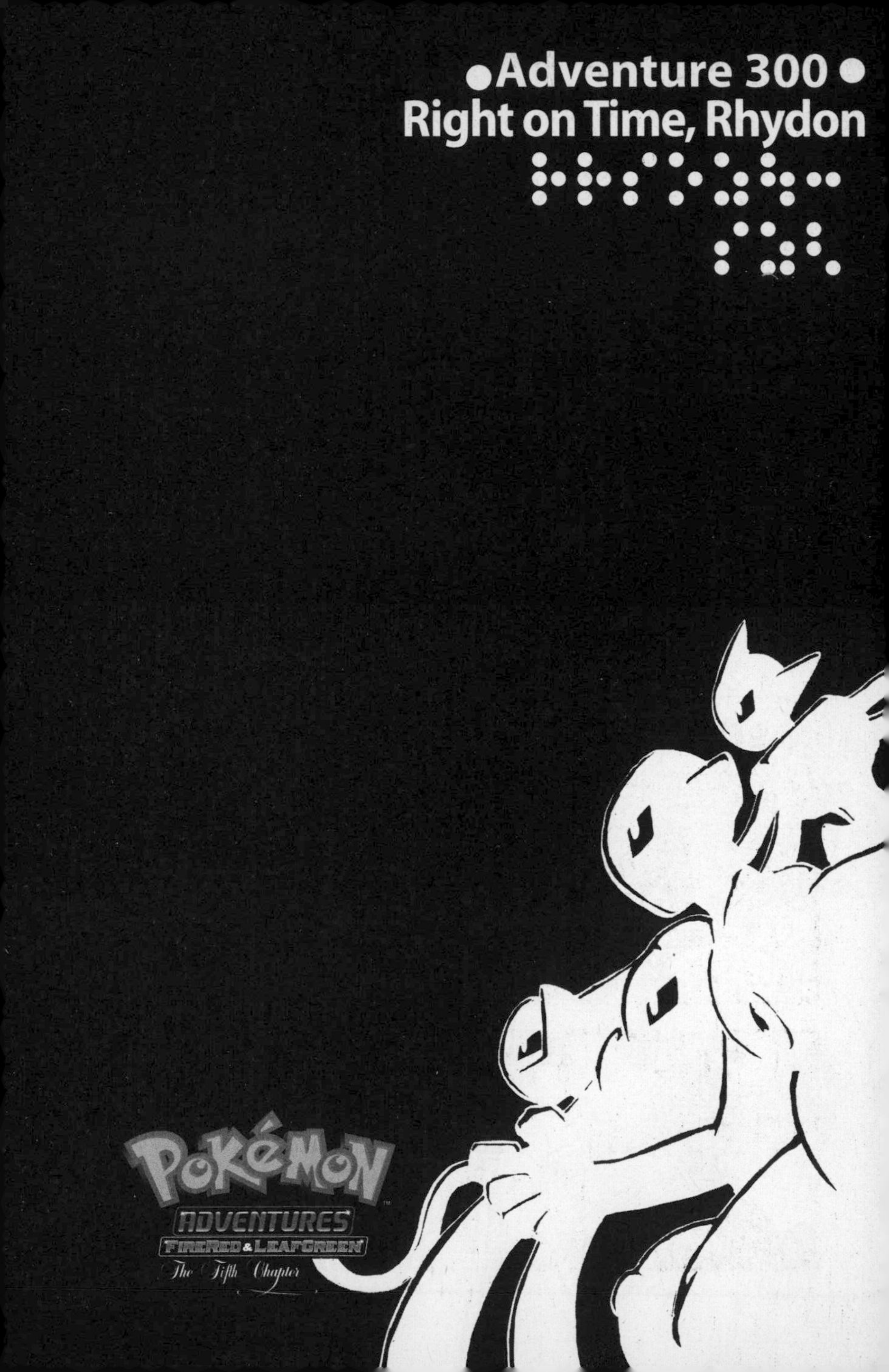

Pokémon Adventures
FireRed & LeafGreen
The Fifth Chapter

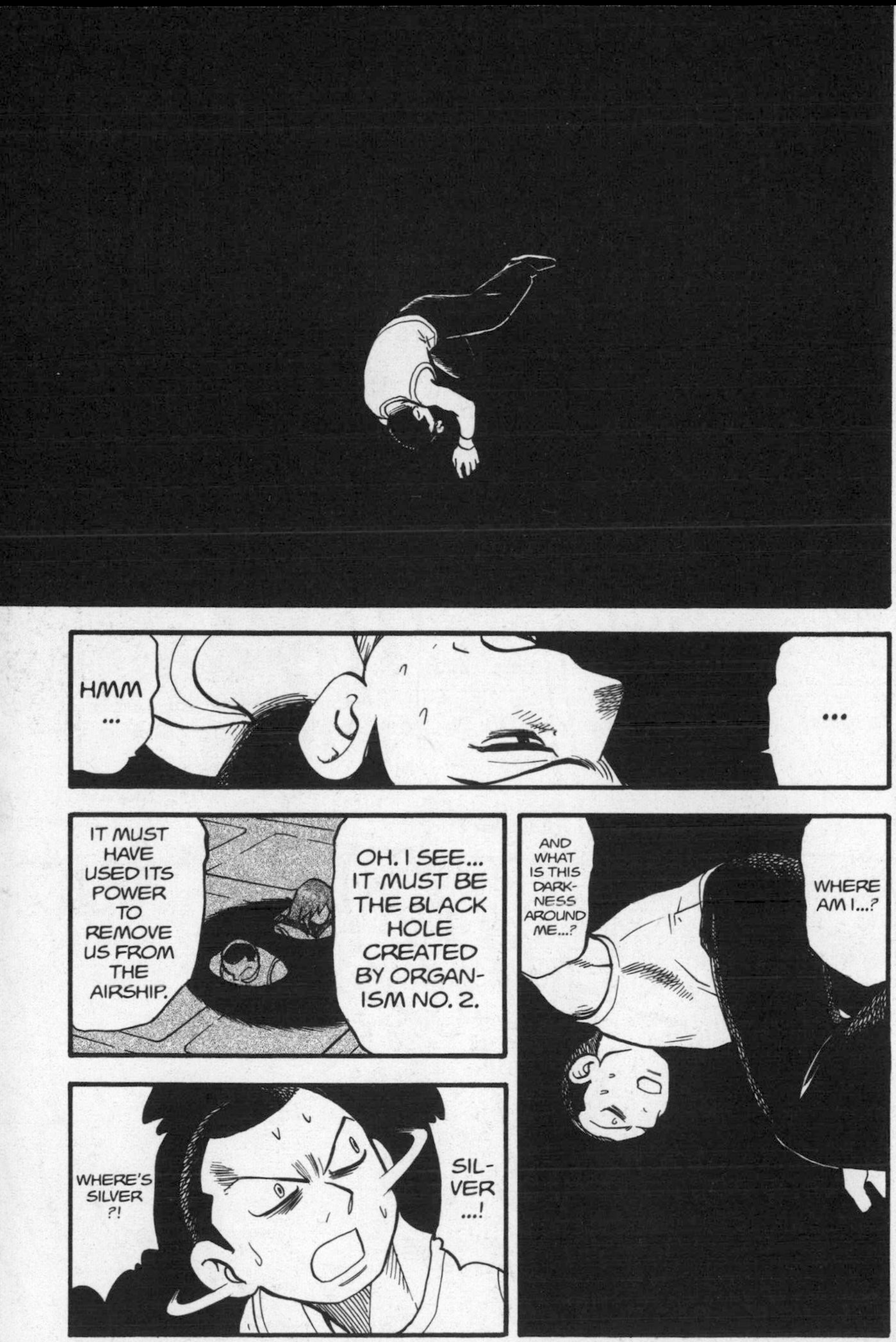
...
HMM...
WHERE AM I...?
AND WHAT IS THIS DARKNESS AROUND ME...?
OH. I SEE... IT MUST BE THE BLACK HOLE CREATED BY ORGANISM NO. 2.
IT MUST HAVE USED ITS POWER TO REMOVE US FROM THE AIRSHIP.
SILVER...!
WHERE'S SILVER?!

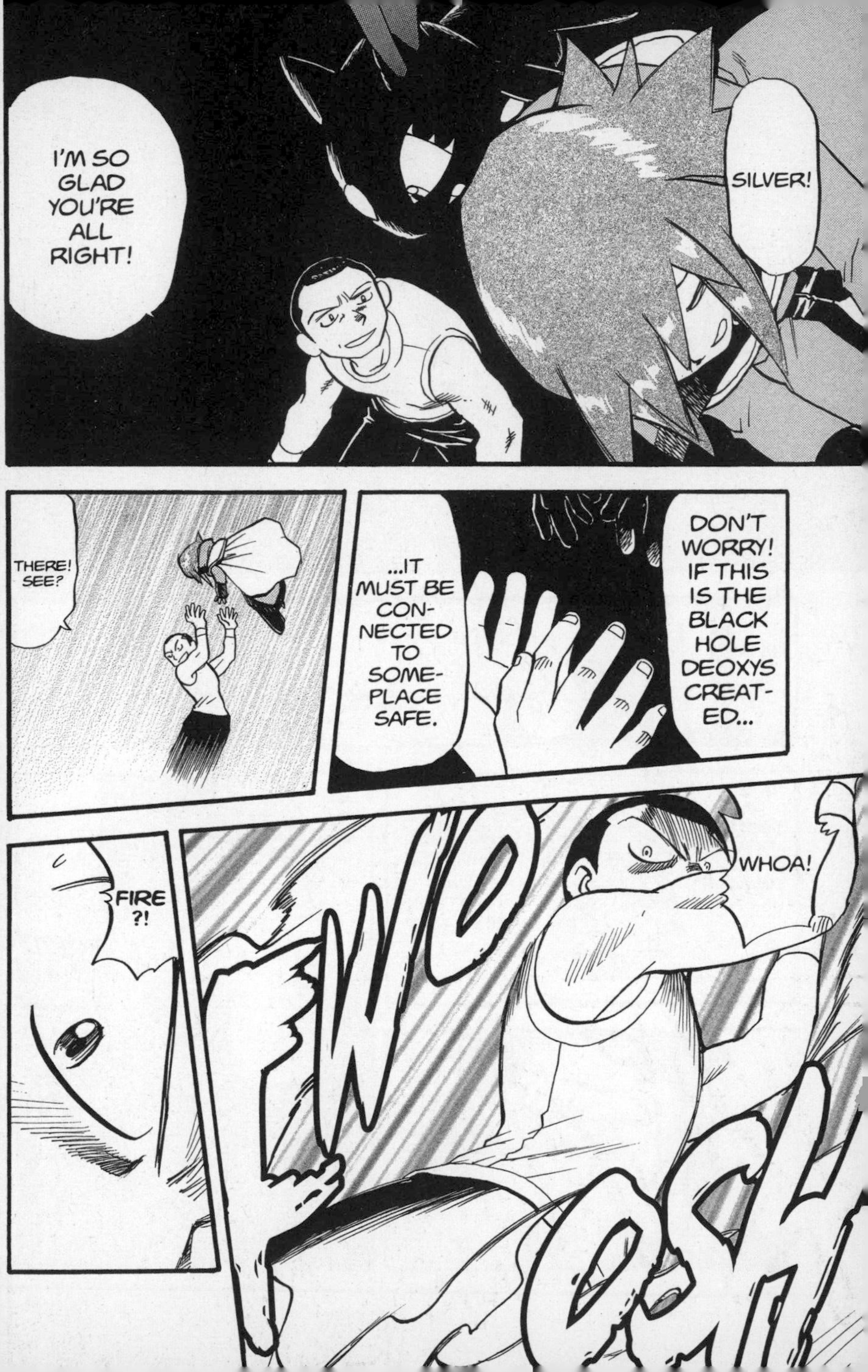
SILVER!
I'M SO GLAD YOU'RE ALL RIGHT!
DON'T WORRY! IF THIS IS THE BLACK HOLE DEOXYS CREATED...
...IT MUST BE CONNECTED TO SOMEPLACE SAFE.
THERE! SEE?
WHOA!
WOOSH
FIRE?!

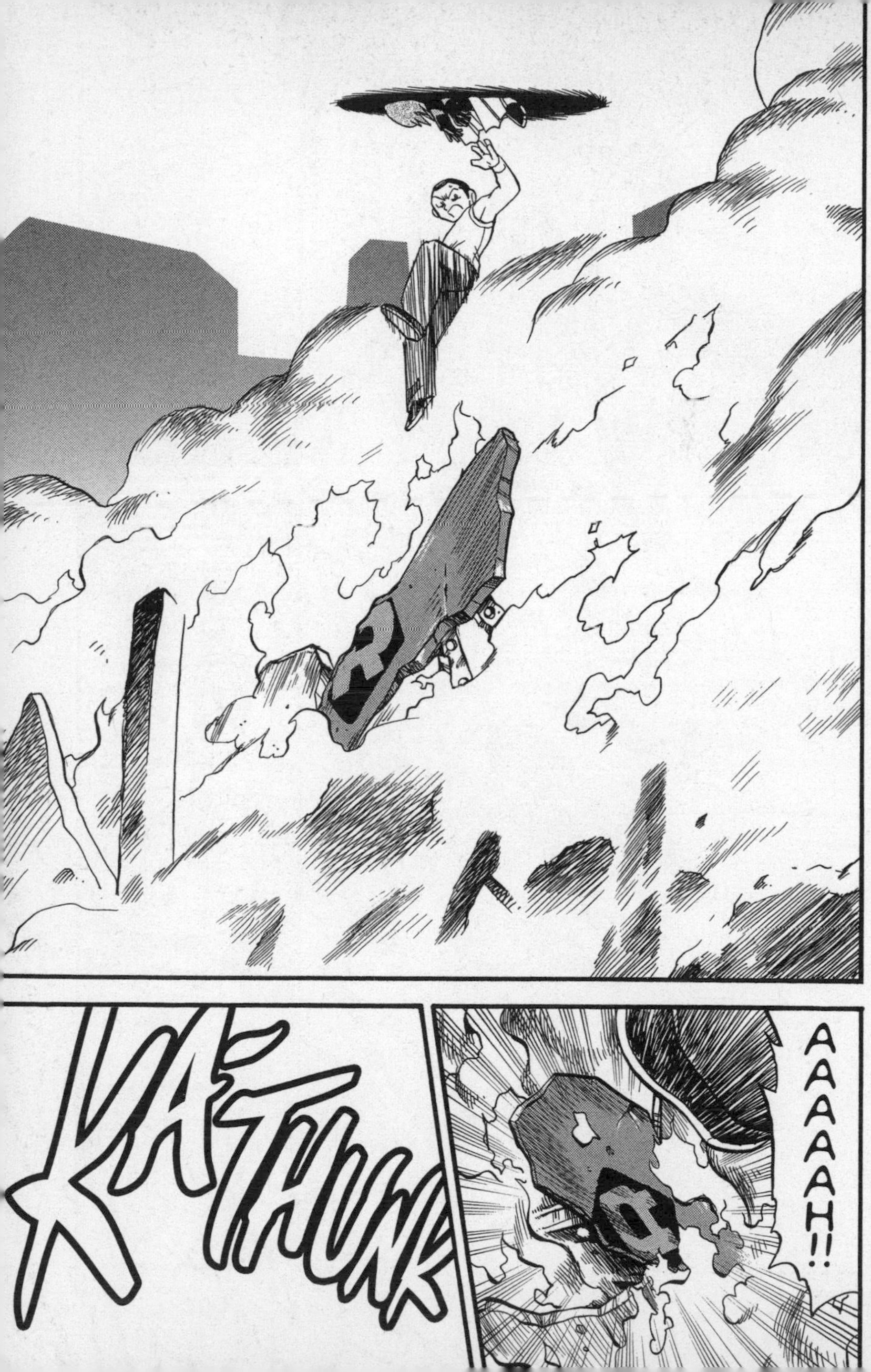

AAAAAH!!
KATHUNK

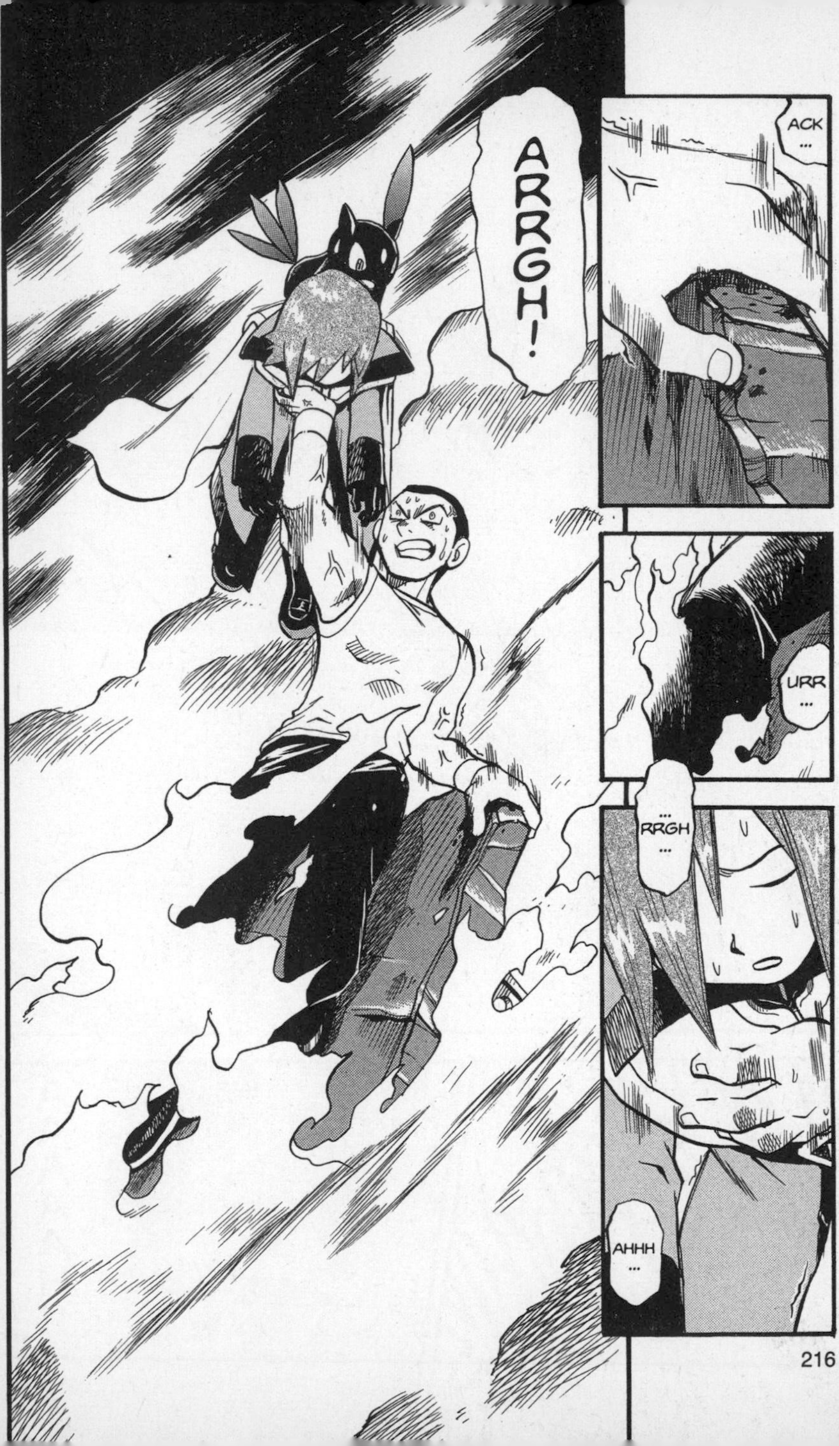
ACK ...
URR ...
... RRGH ...
AHHH ...
ARRGH!

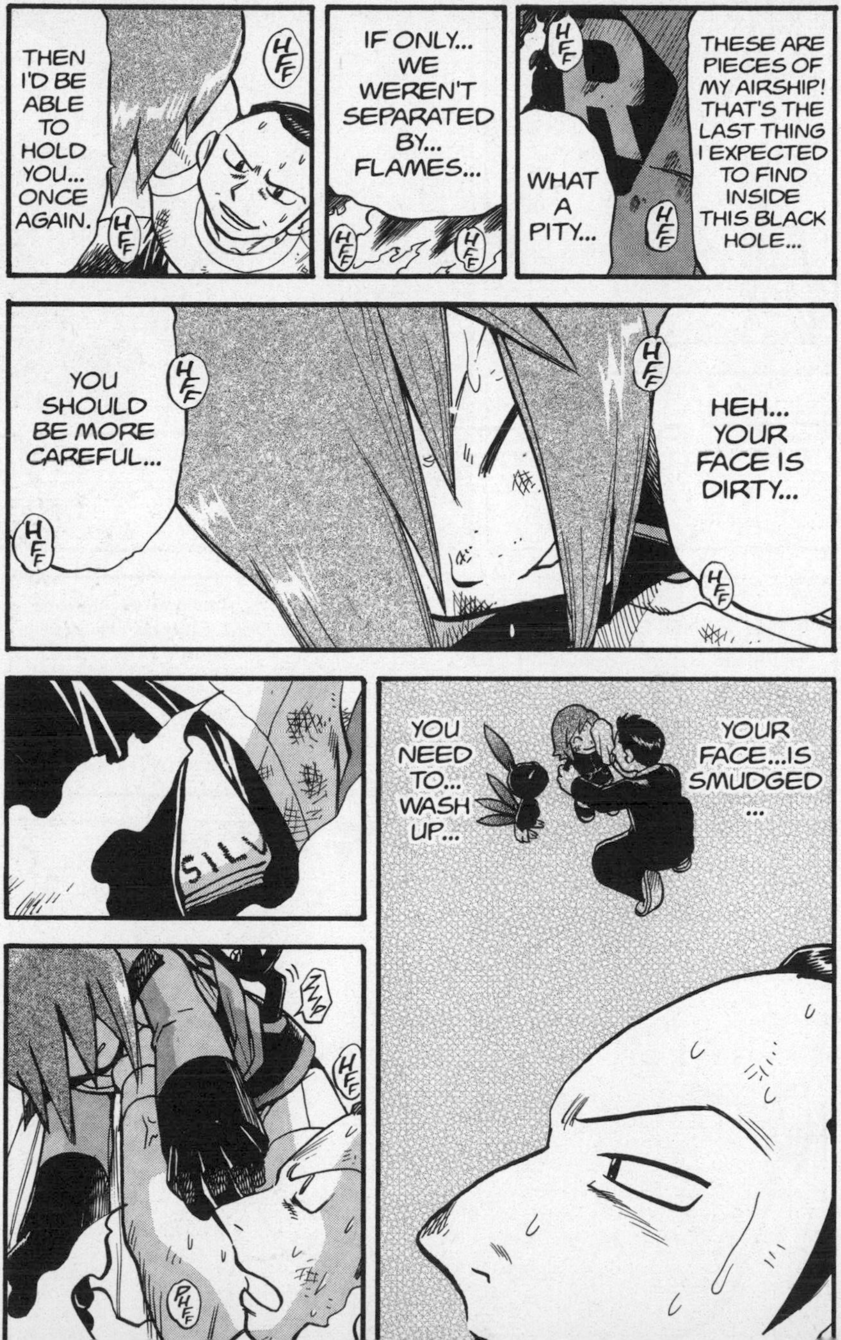
THESE ARE PIECES OF MY AIRSHIP! THAT'S THE LAST THING I EXPECTED TO FIND INSIDE THIS BLACK HOLE...
HFF
WHAT A PITY...
HFF
IF ONLY... WE WEREN'T SEPARATED BY... FLAMES...
HFF
HFF
HFF
THEN I'D BE ABLE TO HOLD YOU... ONCE AGAIN.
HFF
HFF
HEH... YOUR FACE IS DIRTY...
HFF
HFF
YOU SHOULD BE MORE CAREFUL...
HFF
YOUR FACE...IS SMUDGED ...
YOU NEED TO... WASH UP...
SILV
ZMP
HFF
PHFF

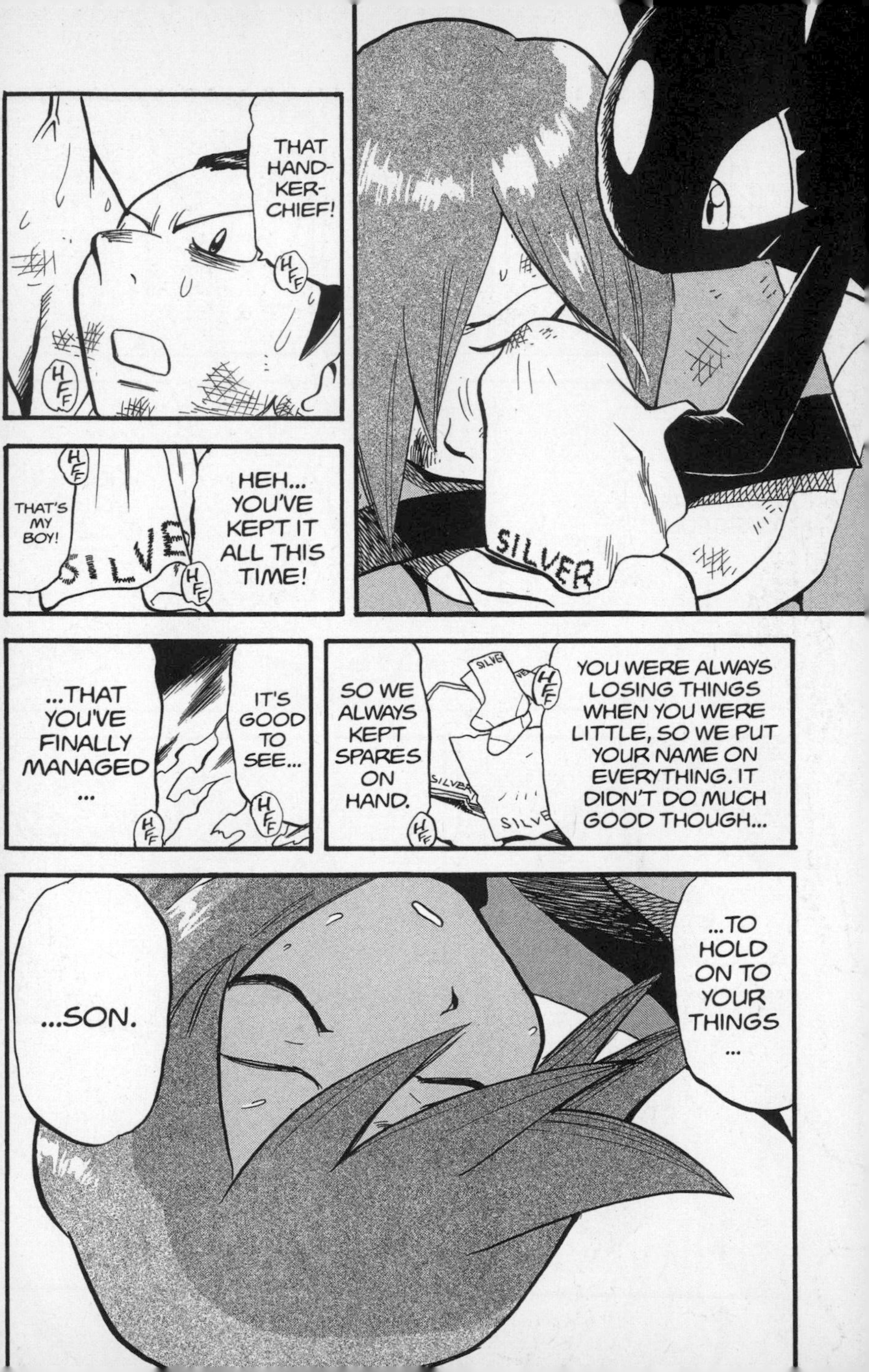
SILVER
THAT HANDKERCHIEF!
HFF
HFF
HEH... YOU'VE KEPT IT ALL THIS TIME!
HFF
THAT'S MY BOY!
HFF
YOU WERE ALWAYS LOSING THINGS WHEN YOU WERE LITTLE, SO WE PUT YOUR NAME ON EVERYTHING. IT DIDN'T DO MUCH GOOD THOUGH...
HFF
SO WE ALWAYS KEPT SPARES ON HAND.
HFF
IT'S GOOD TO SEE...
HFF
...THAT YOU'VE FINALLY MANAGED ...
HFF
...TO HOLD ON TO YOUR THINGS ...
...SON.

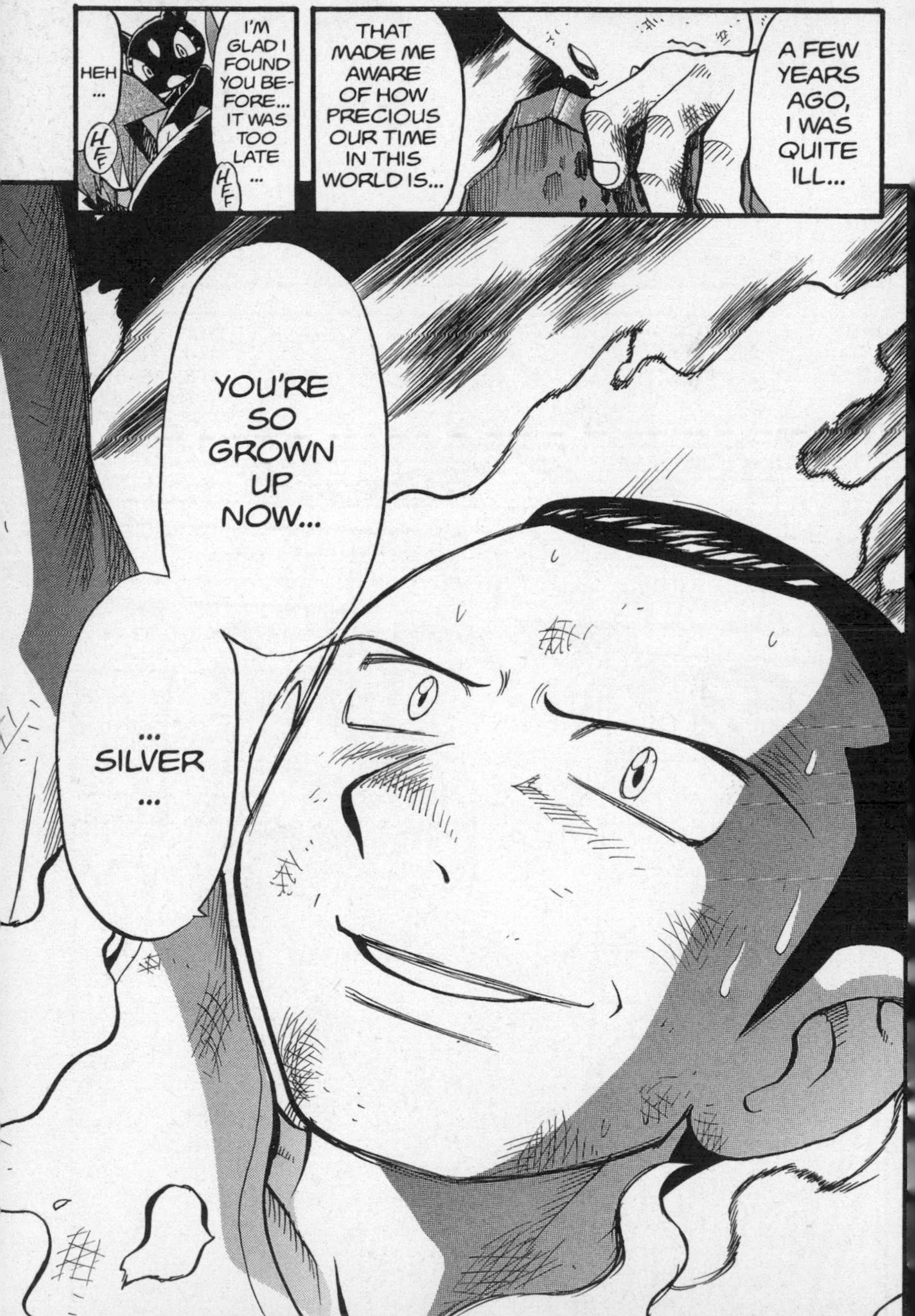
A FEW YEARS AGO, I WAS QUITE ILL...
THAT MADE ME AWARE OF HOW PRECIOUS OUR TIME IN THIS WORLD IS...
I'M GLAD I FOUND YOU BE-FORE... IT WAS TOO LATE ...
HEF
HEH ...
HEF
YOU'RE SO GROWN UP NOW...
... SILVER ...

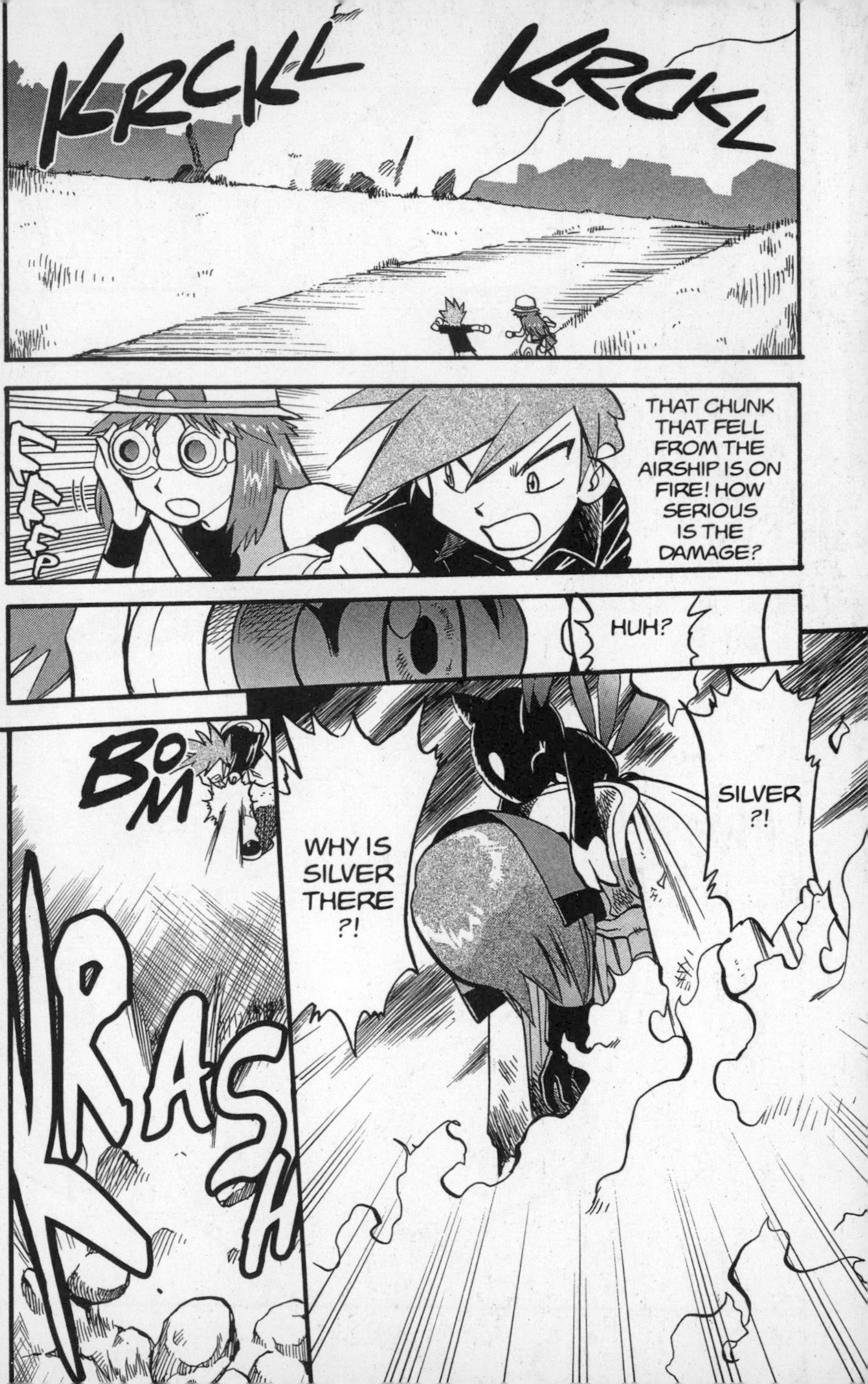
KRCKL
KRCKL
THAT CHUNK THAT FELL FROM THE AIRSHIP IS ON FIRE! HOW SERIOUS IS THE DAMAGE?
HUH?
SILVER ?!
WHY IS SILVER THERE ?!
BOM
KRASH

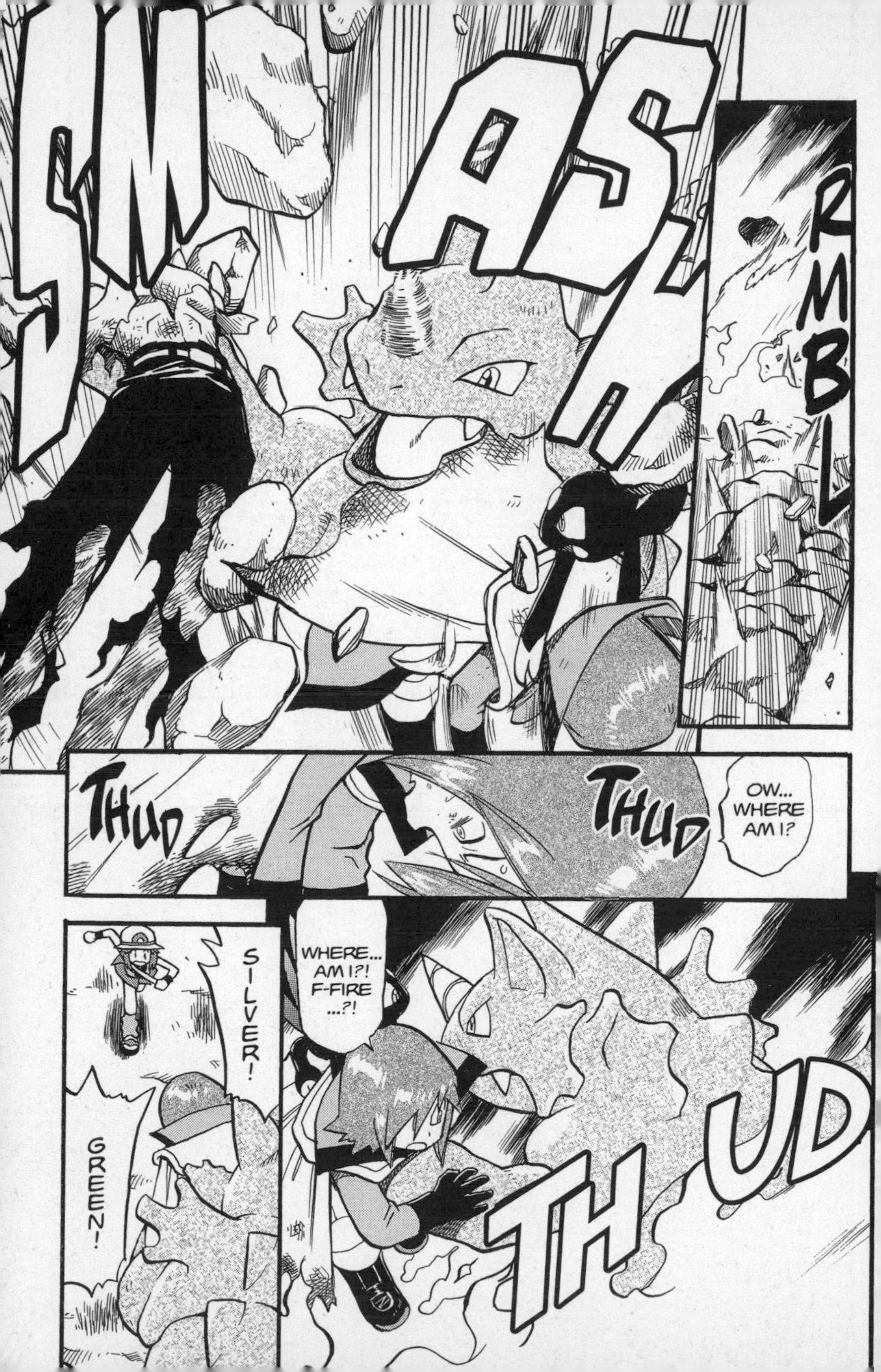
RMBL
SMASH
OW... WHERE AM I?
THUD
THUD
WHERE... AM I?! F-FIRE ...?!
THUD
SILVER!
GREEN!

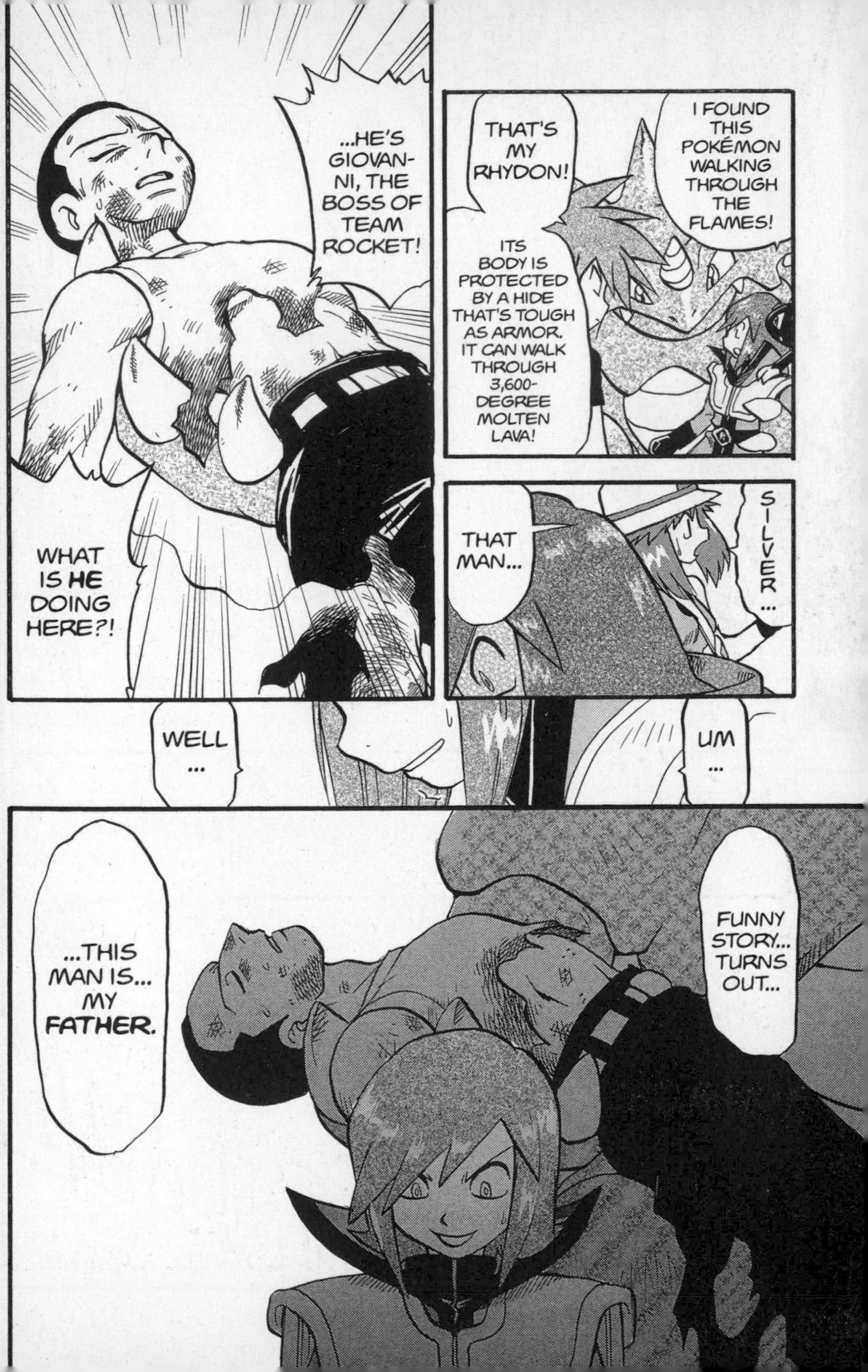
I FOUND THIS POKÉMON WALKING THROUGH THE FLAMES!
THAT'S MY RHYDON!
ITS BODY IS PROTECTED BY A HIDE THAT'S TOUGH AS ARMOR. IT CAN WALK THROUGH 3,600-DEGREE MOLTEN LAVA!
SILVER ...
THAT MAN...
...HE'S GIOVANNI, THE BOSS OF TEAM ROCKET!
WHAT IS **HE** DOING HERE?!
UM ...
WELL ...
FUNNY STORY... TURNS OUT...
...THIS MAN IS... MY **FATHER**.

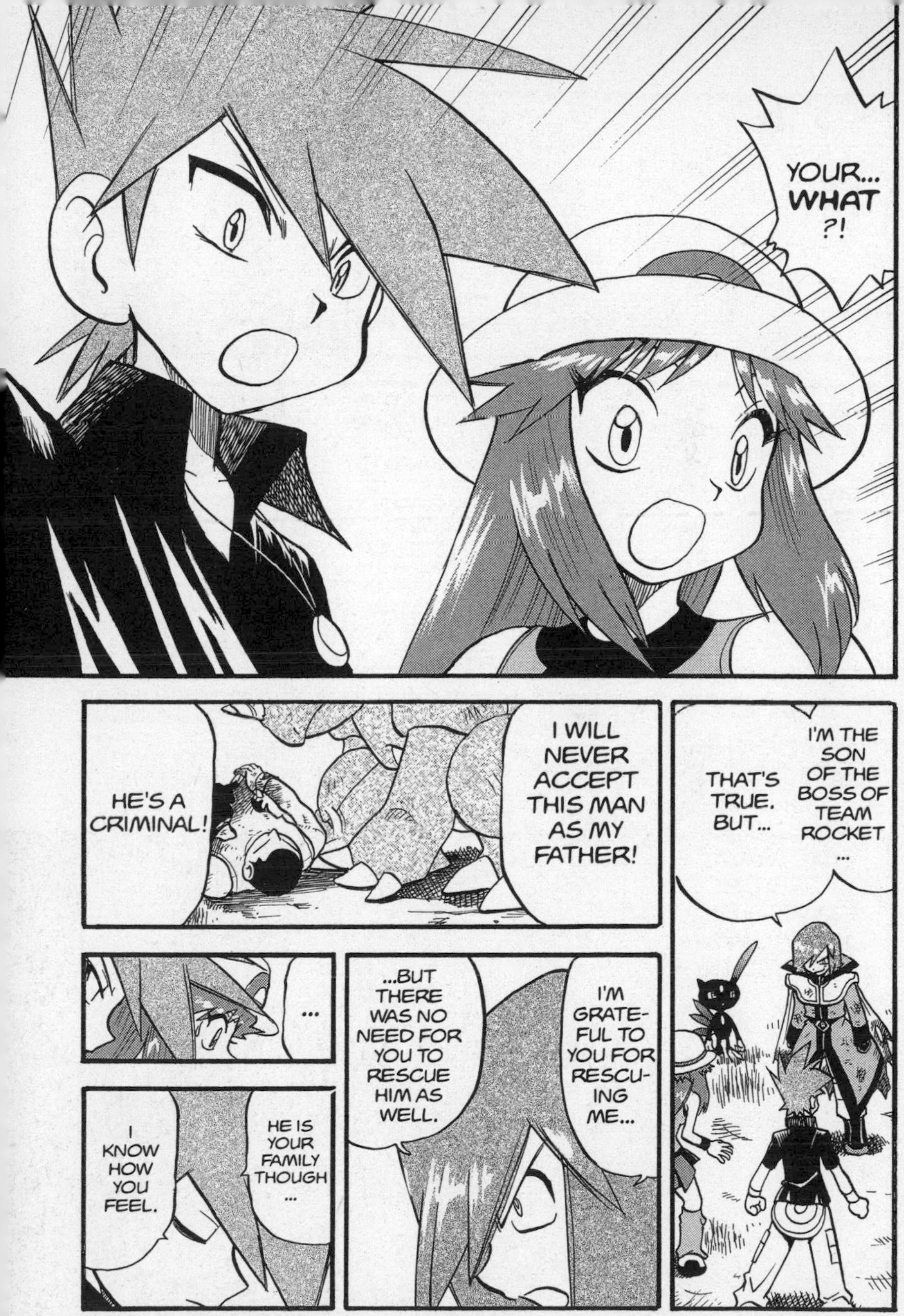

YOUR... WHAT ?!
I'M THE SON OF THE BOSS OF TEAM ROCKET ...
THAT'S TRUE. BUT...
I WILL NEVER ACCEPT THIS MAN AS MY FATHER!
HE'S A CRIMINAL!
I'M GRATE-FUL TO YOU FOR RESCU-ING ME...
...BUT THERE WAS NO NEED FOR YOU TO RESCUE HIM AS WELL.
...
HE IS YOUR FAMILY THOUGH ...
I KNOW HOW YOU FEEL.

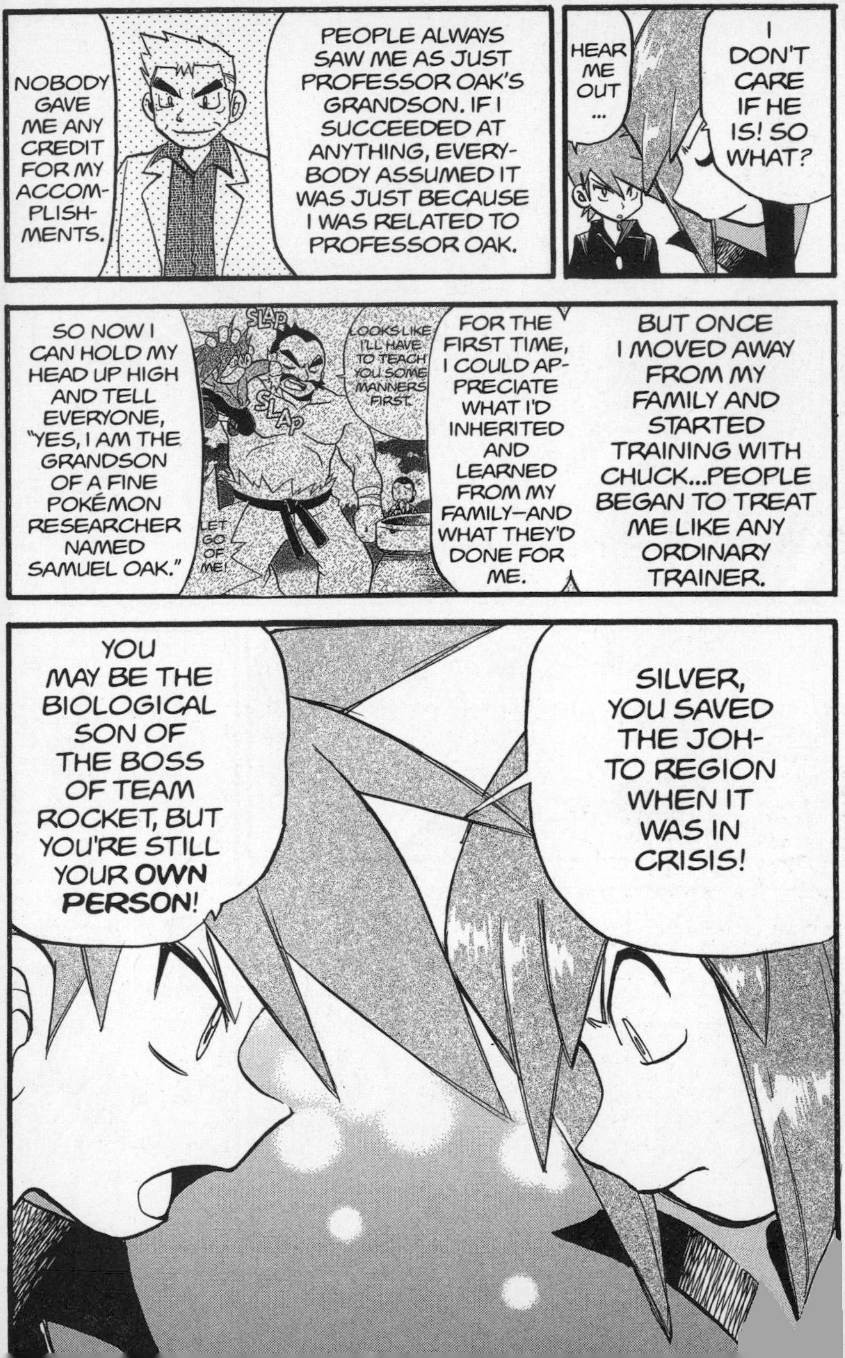
I DON'T CARE IF HE IS! SO WHAT?
HEAR ME OUT ...
PEOPLE ALWAYS SAW ME AS JUST PROFESSOR OAK'S GRANDSON. IF I SUCCEEDED AT ANYTHING, EVERYBODY ASSUMED IT WAS JUST BECAUSE I WAS RELATED TO PROFESSOR OAK.
NOBODY GAVE ME ANY CREDIT FOR MY ACCOMPLISHMENTS.
BUT ONCE I MOVED AWAY FROM MY FAMILY AND STARTED TRAINING WITH CHUCK...PEOPLE BEGAN TO TREAT ME LIKE ANY ORDINARY TRAINER.
FOR THE FIRST TIME, I COULD APPRECIATE WHAT I'D INHERITED AND LEARNED FROM MY FAMILY—AND WHAT THEY'D DONE FOR ME.
LOOKS LIKE I'LL HAVE TO TEACH YOU SOME MANNERS FIRST.
SLAP
SLAP
LET GO OF ME!
SO NOW I CAN HOLD MY HEAD UP HIGH AND TELL EVERYONE, "YES, I AM THE GRANDSON OF A FINE POKÉMON RESEARCHER NAMED SAMUEL OAK."
SILVER, YOU SAVED THE JOHTO REGION WHEN IT WAS IN CRISIS!
YOU MAY BE THE BIOLOGICAL SON OF THE BOSS OF TEAM ROCKET, BUT YOU'RE STILL YOUR **OWN PERSON**!

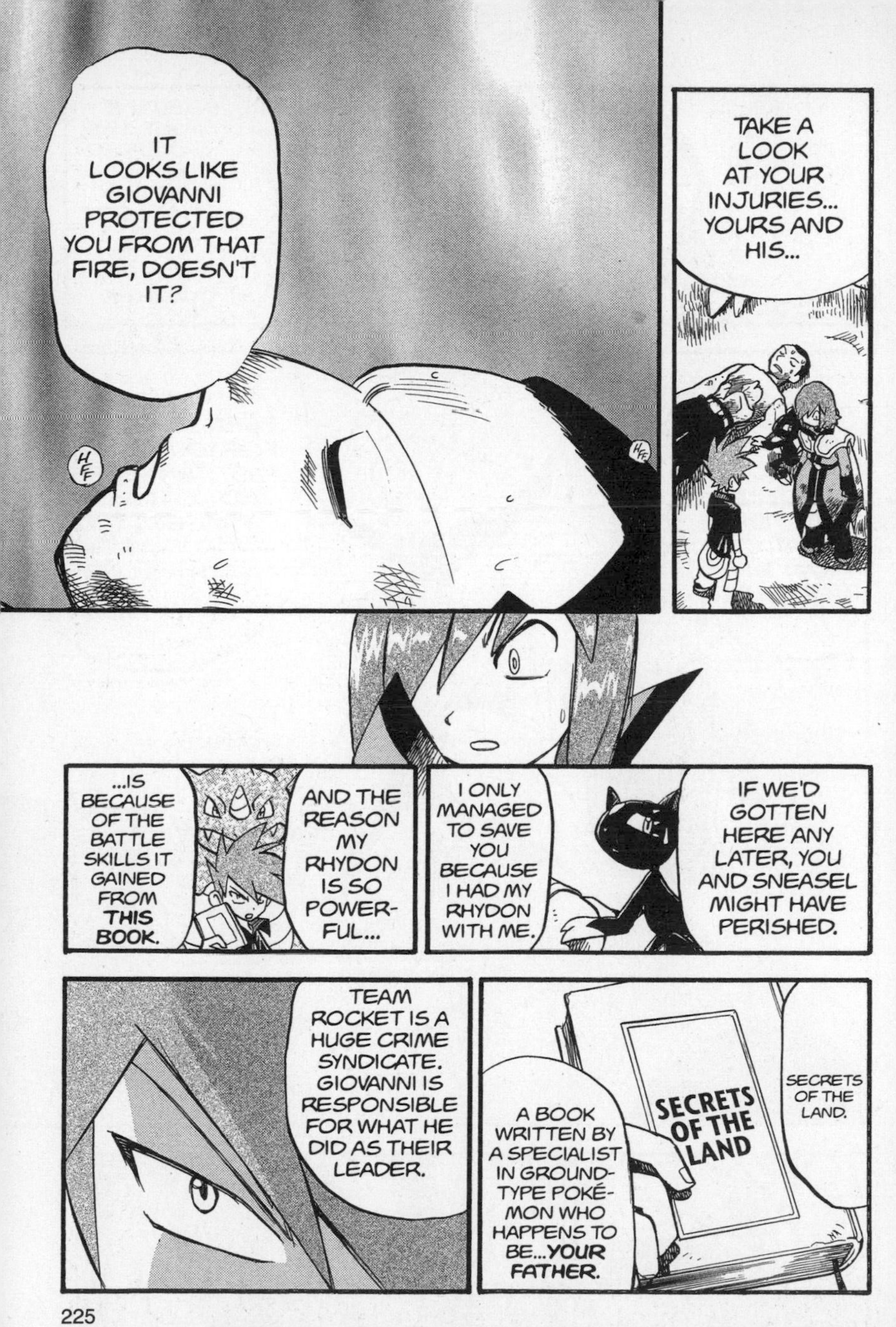
TAKE A LOOK AT YOUR INJURIES... YOURS AND HIS...
IT LOOKS LIKE GIOVANNI PROTECTED YOU FROM THAT FIRE, DOESN'T IT?
HFF
HFF
IF WE'D GOTTEN HERE ANY LATER, YOU AND SNEASEL MIGHT HAVE PERISHED.
I ONLY MANAGED TO SAVE YOU BECAUSE I HAD MY RHYDON WITH ME.
AND THE REASON MY RHYDON IS SO POWERFUL...
...IS BECAUSE OF THE BATTLE SKILLS IT GAINED FROM **THIS** BOOK.
SECRETS OF THE LAND.
SECRETS OF THE LAND
A BOOK WRITTEN BY A SPECIALIST IN GROUND-TYPE POKÉMON WHO HAPPENS TO BE...**YOUR FATHER**.
TEAM ROCKET IS A HUGE CRIME SYNDICATE. GIOVANNI IS RESPONSIBLE FOR WHAT HE DID AS THEIR LEADER.

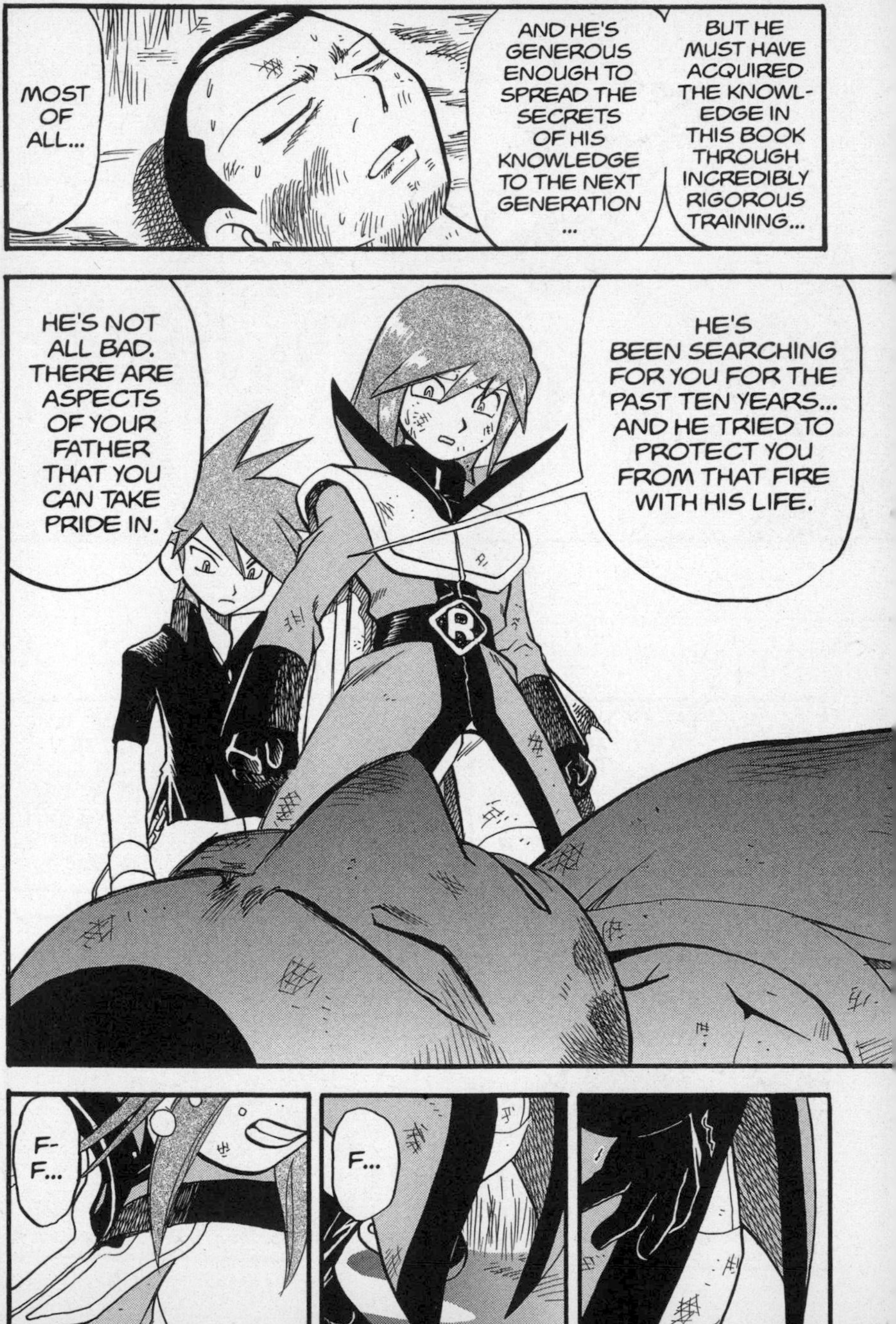
BUT HE MUST HAVE ACQUIRED THE KNOWL-EDGE IN THIS BOOK THROUGH INCREDIBLY RIGOROUS TRAINING...
AND HE'S GENEROUS ENOUGH TO SPREAD THE SECRETS OF HIS KNOWLEDGE TO THE NEXT GENERATION ...
MOST OF ALL...
HE'S BEEN SEARCHING FOR YOU FOR THE PAST TEN YEARS... AND HE TRIED TO PROTECT YOU FROM THAT FIRE WITH HIS LIFE.
HE'S NOT ALL BAD. THERE ARE ASPECTS OF YOUR FATHER THAT YOU CAN TAKE PRIDE IN.
F...
F- F...

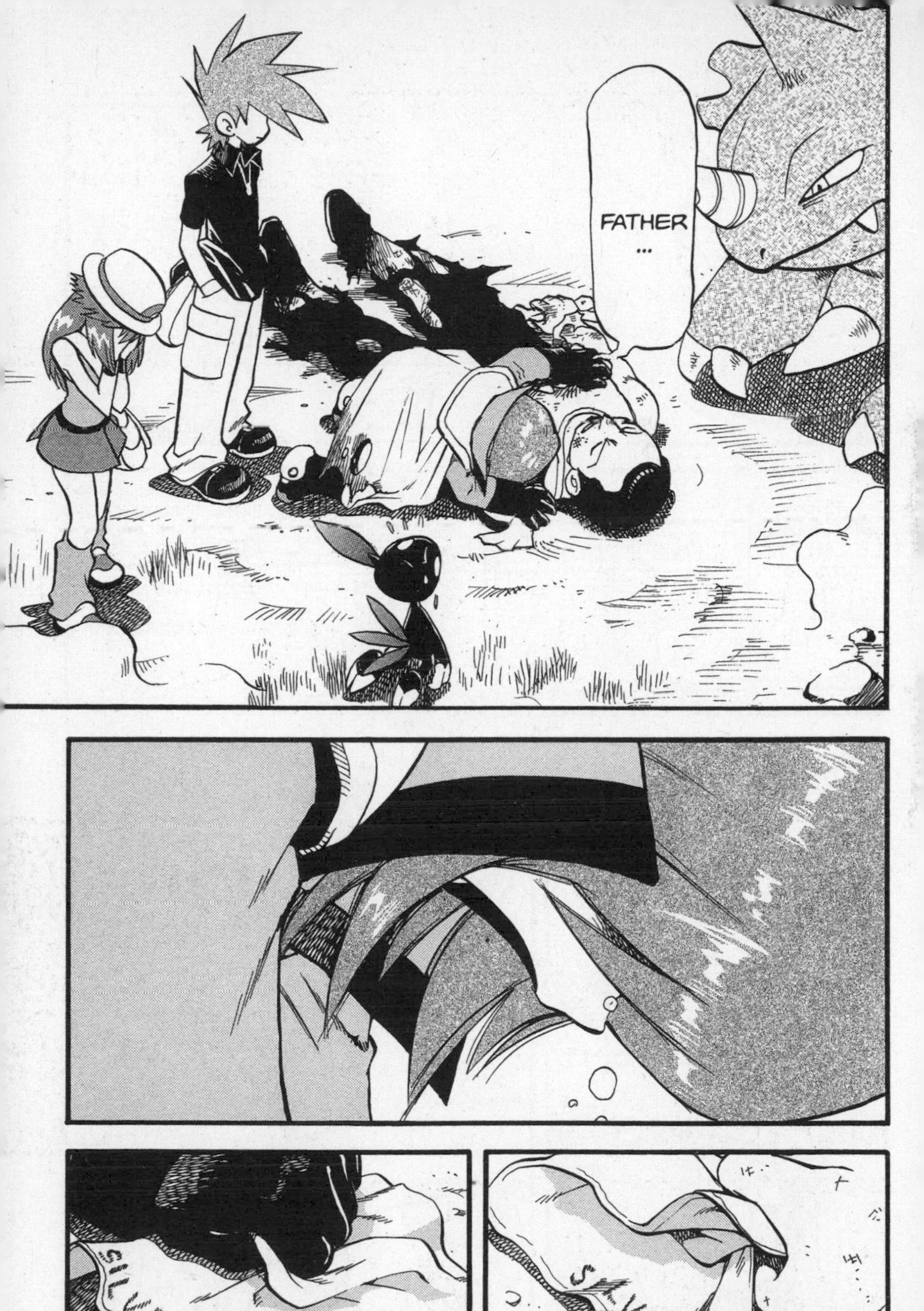
FATHER
...

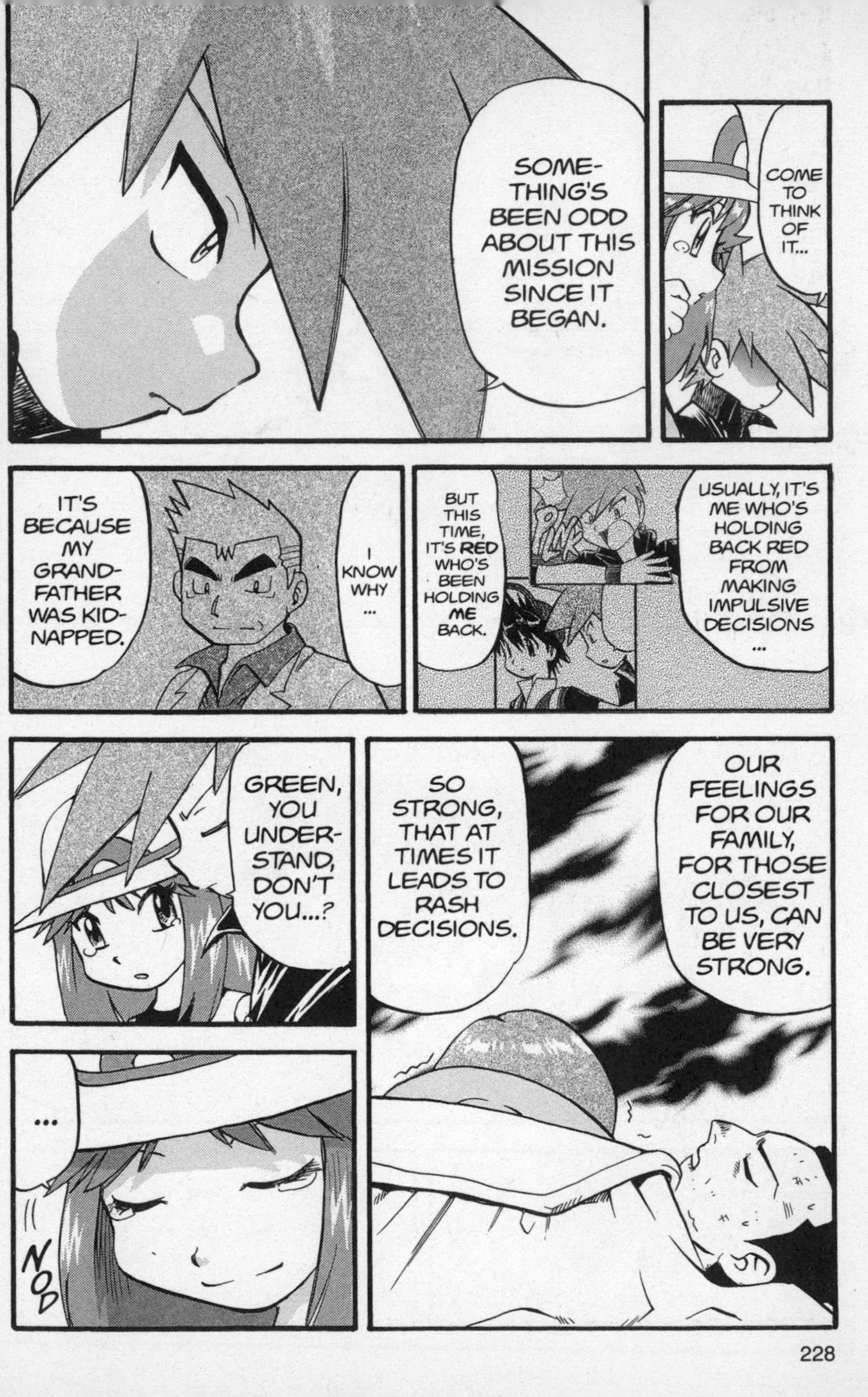
COME TO THINK OF IT...
SOME-THING'S BEEN ODD ABOUT THIS MISSION SINCE IT BEGAN.
USUALLY, IT'S ME WHO'S HOLDING BACK RED FROM MAKING IMPULSIVE DECISIONS ...
BUT THIS TIME, IT'S RED WHO'S BEEN HOLDING ME BACK.
I KNOW WHY ...
IT'S BECAUSE MY GRAND-FATHER WAS KID-NAPPED.
OUR FEELINGS FOR OUR FAMILY, FOR THOSE CLOSEST TO US, CAN BE VERY STRONG.
SO STRONG, THAT AT TIMES IT LEADS TO RASH DECISIONS.
GREEN, YOU UNDER-STAND, DON'T YOU...?
...
NOD

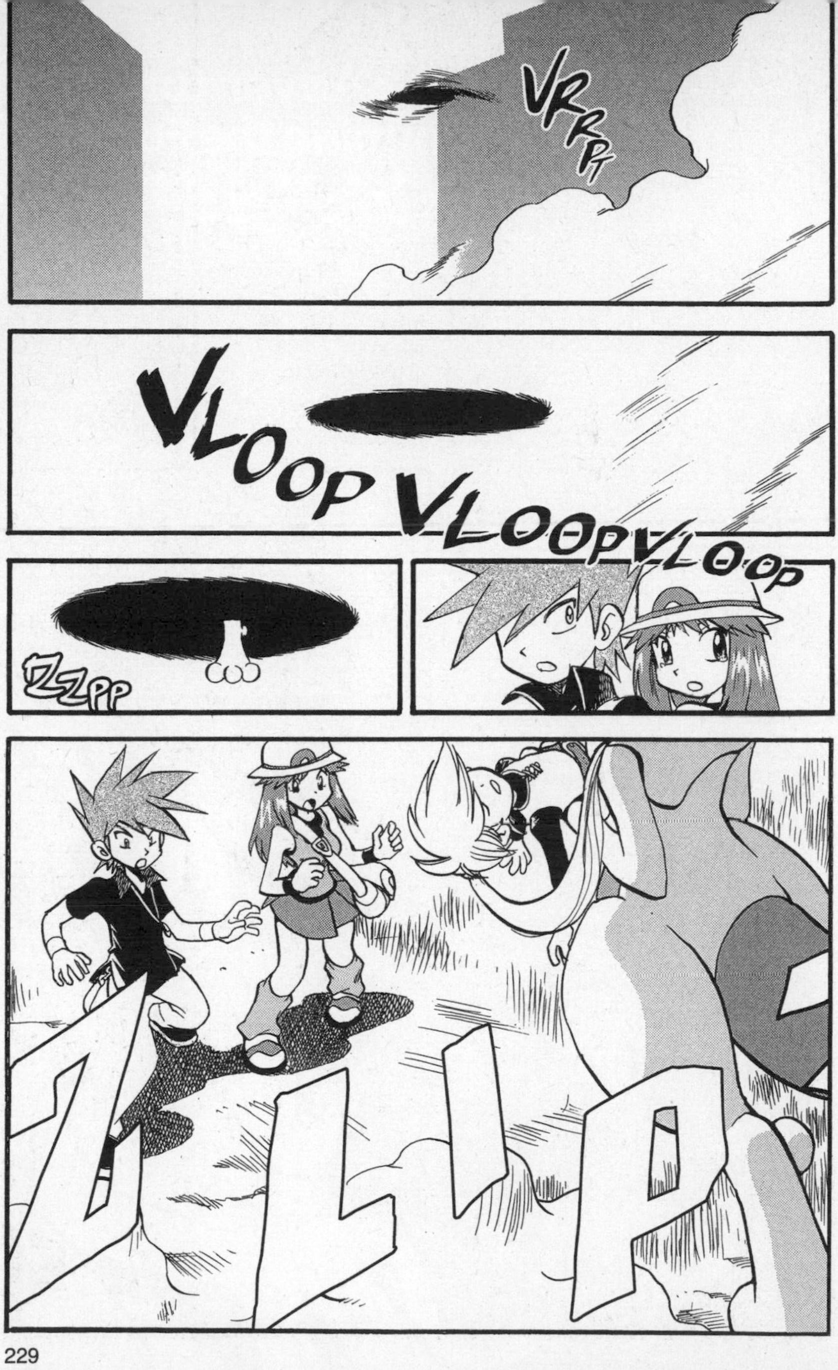
VRRPT
VLOOP
VLOOP
VLOOP
ZZZPP
ZLIP

●Adventure 301●
Storming the Forretress

Pokémon Adventures
FireRed & LeafGreen
The Fifth Chapter

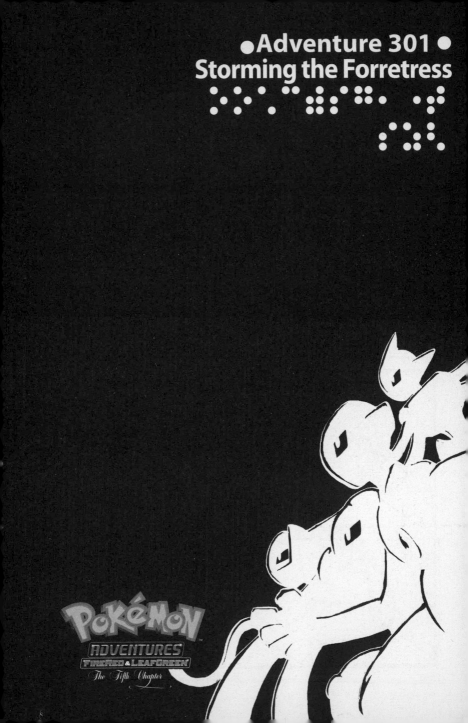

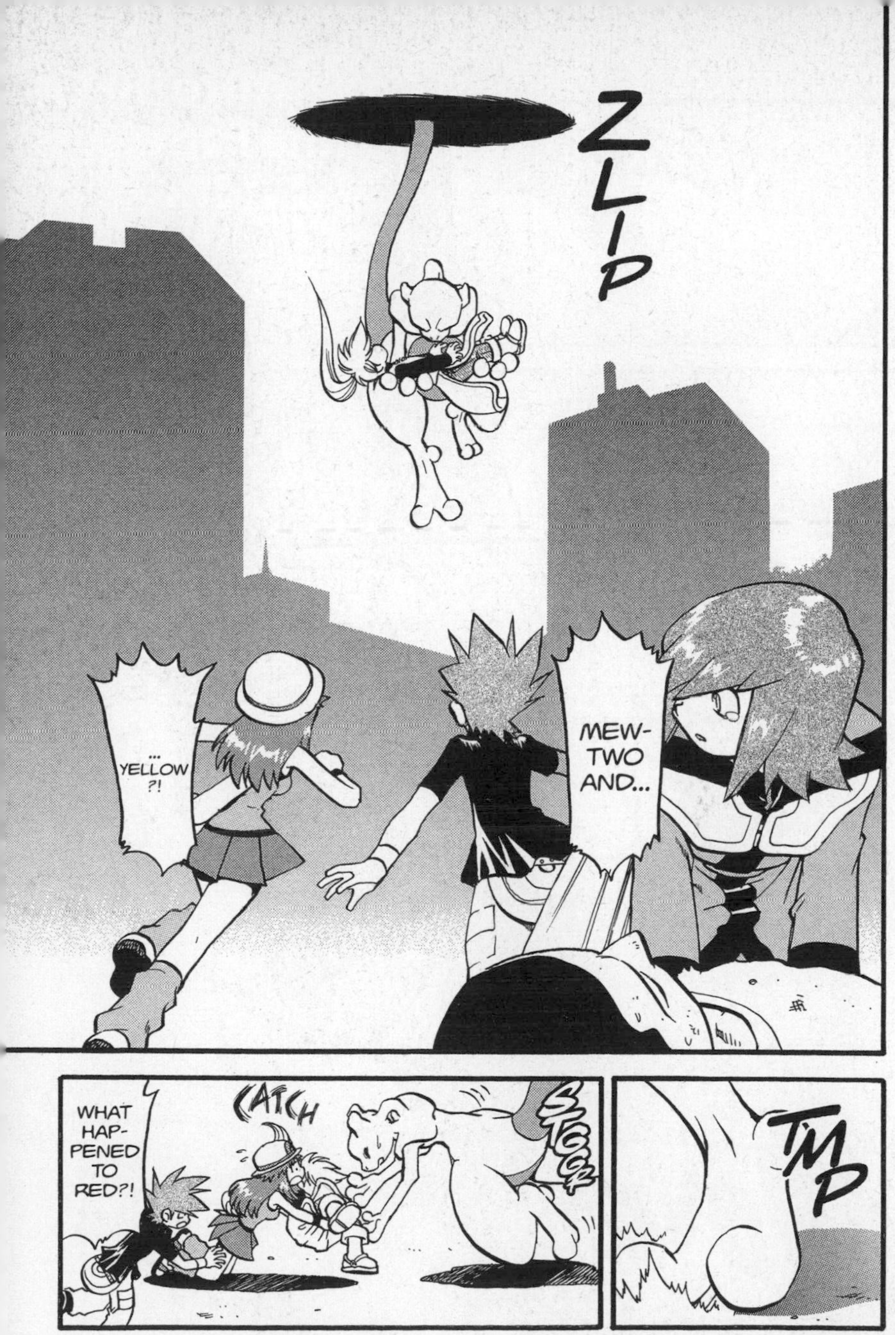
ZLIP
MEW-TWO AND...
...YELLOW?!
TMP
CATCH
WHAT HAP-PENED TO RED?!

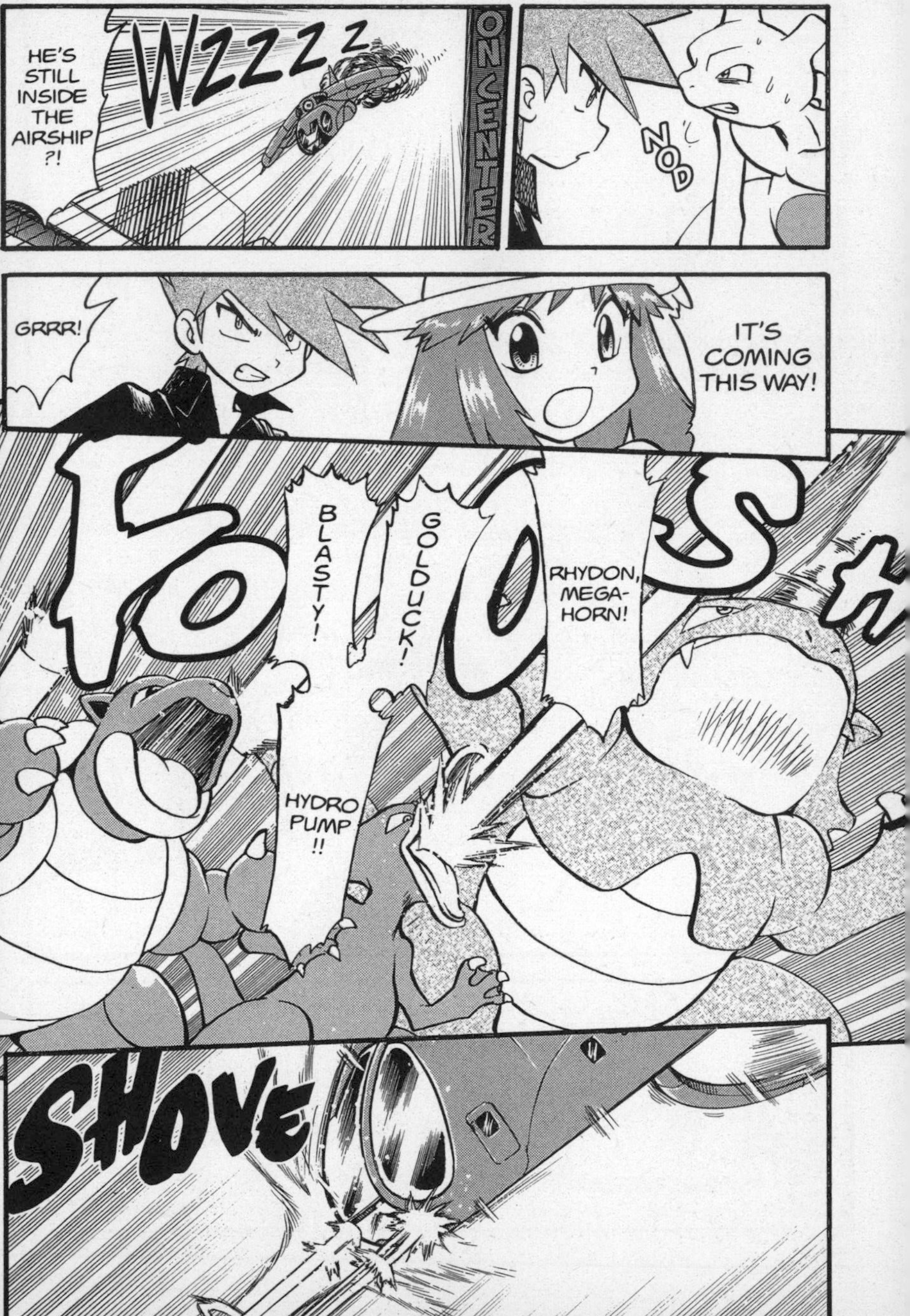
NOD
ON CENTER
WZZZZZ
HE'S STILL INSIDE THE AIRSHIP ?!
IT'S COMING THIS WAY!
GRRR!
RHYDON, MEGA-HORN!
GOLDUCK!
BLASTY!
HYDRO PUMP !!
SHOVE

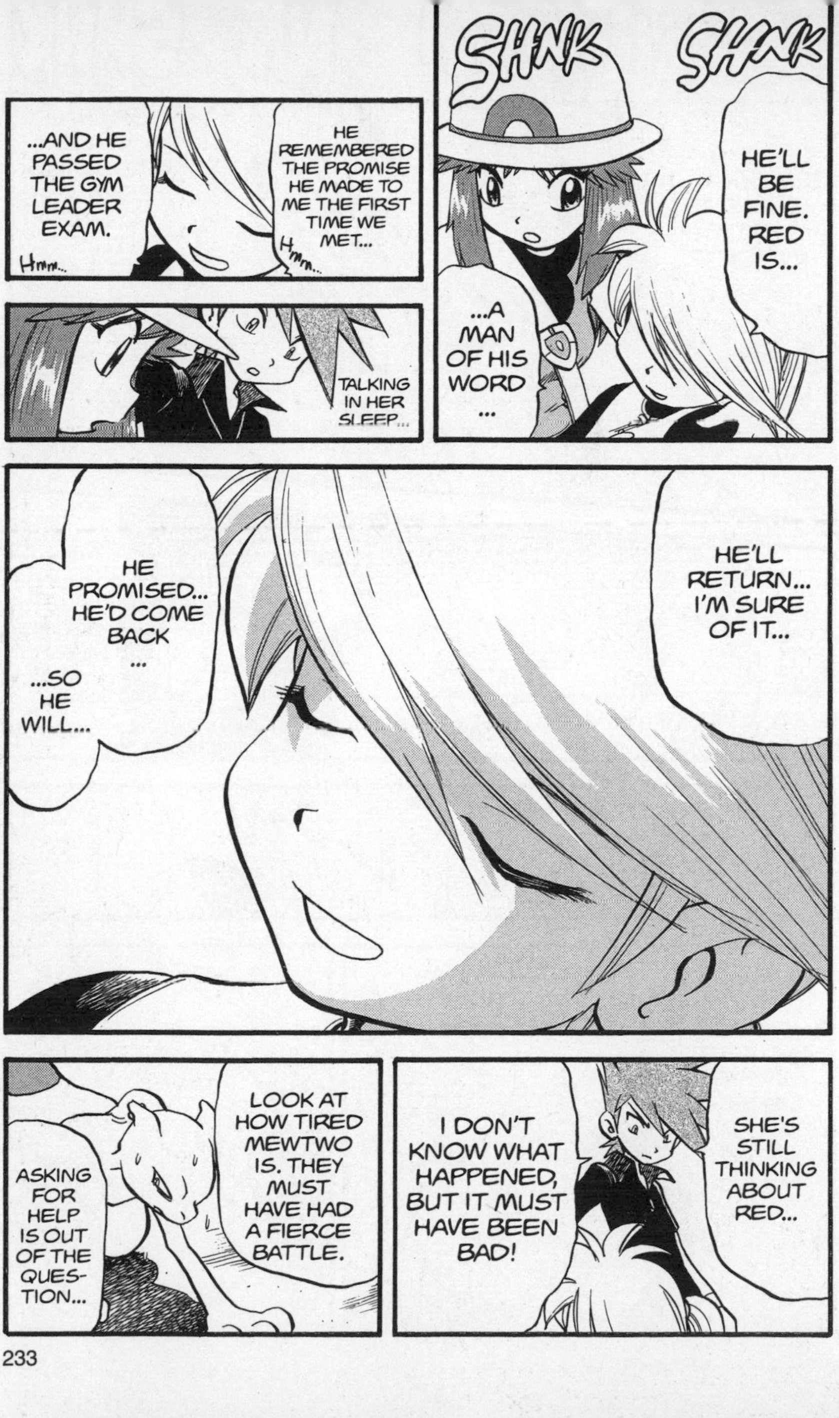
SHNK SHNK
HE'LL BE FINE. RED IS...
...A MAN OF HIS WORD ...
HE REMEMBERED THE PROMISE HE MADE TO ME THE FIRST TIME WE MET...
Hmm...
...AND HE PASSED THE GYM LEADER EXAM.
Hmm...
TALKING IN HER SLEEP...
HE'LL RETURN... I'M SURE OF IT...
HE PROMISED... HE'D COME BACK ...
...SO HE WILL...
SHE'S STILL THINKING ABOUT RED...
I DON'T KNOW WHAT HAPPENED, BUT IT MUST HAVE BEEN BAD!
LOOK AT HOW TIRED MEWTWO IS. THEY MUST HAVE HAD A FIERCE BATTLE.
ASKING FOR HELP IS OUT OF THE QUES-TION...

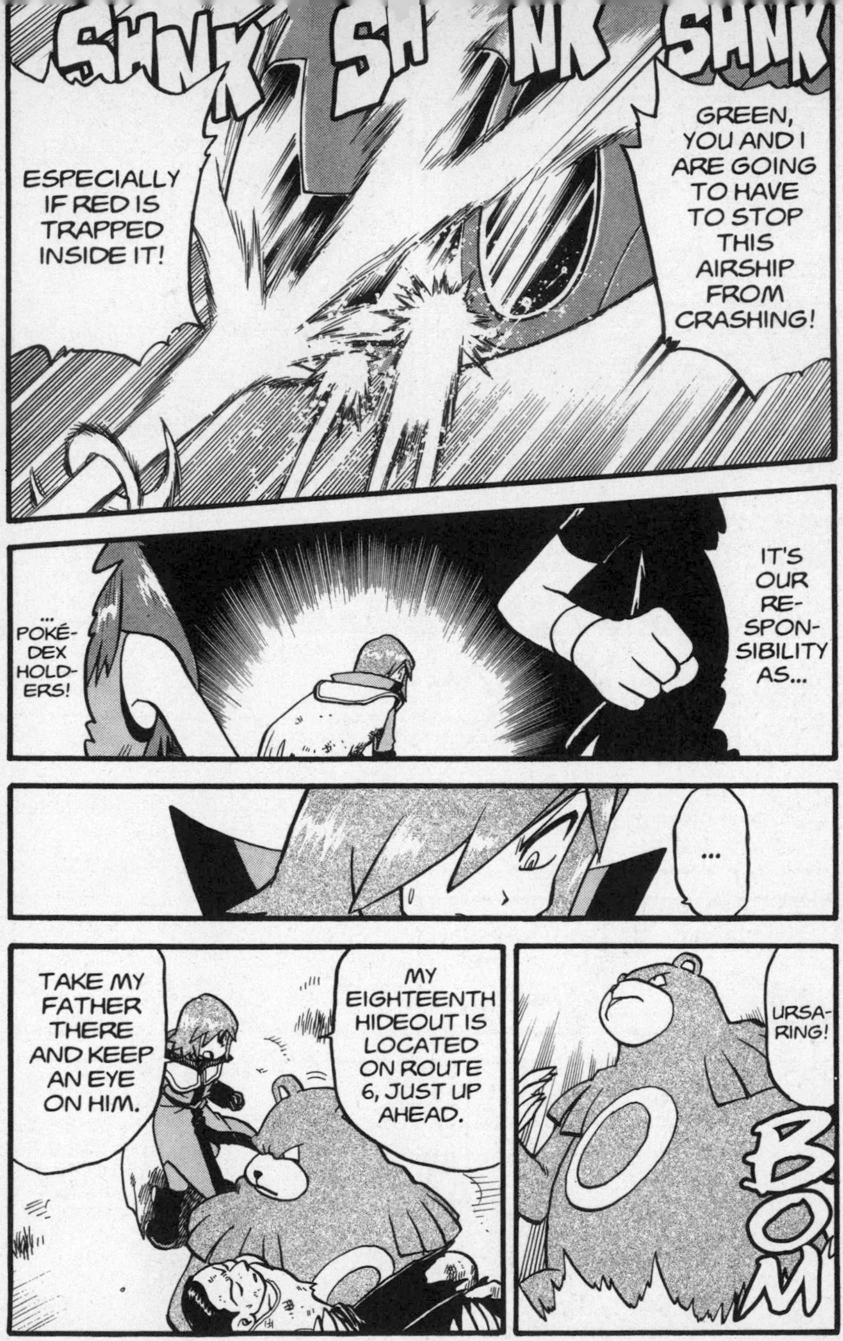
SHNK
SH
NK
SHNK
GREEN, YOU AND I ARE GOING TO HAVE TO STOP THIS AIRSHIP FROM CRASHING!
ESPECIALLY IF RED IS TRAPPED INSIDE IT!
IT'S OUR RE-SPON-SIBILITY AS...
... POKÉ-DEX HOLD-ERS!
...
URSA-RING!
BOOM
MY EIGHTEENTH HIDEOUT IS LOCATED ON ROUTE 6, JUST UP AHEAD.
TAKE MY FATHER THERE AND KEEP AN EYE ON HIM.

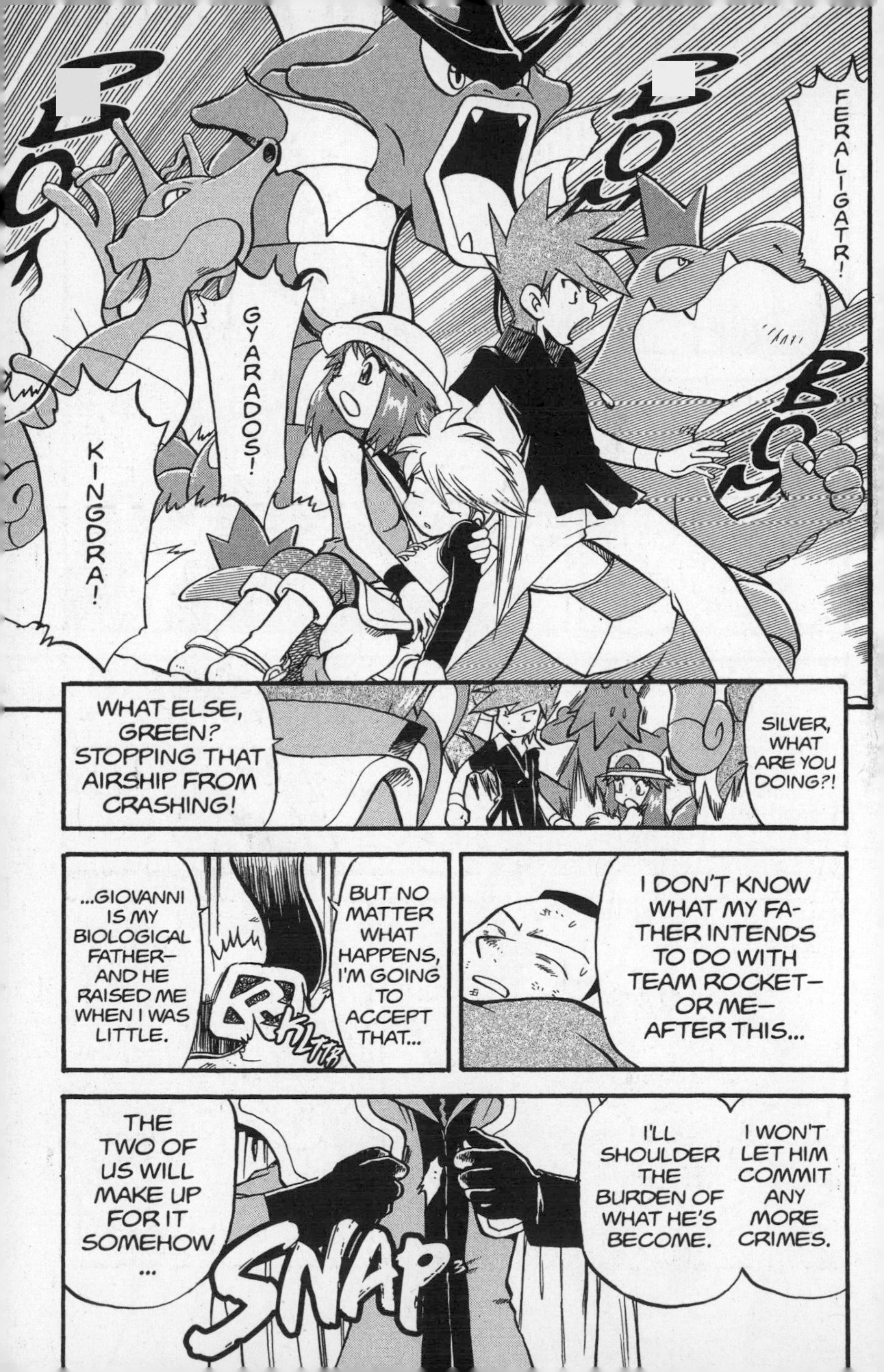
FERALIGATR!
BOOM
GYARADOS!
KINGDRA!
SILVER, WHAT ARE YOU DOING?!
WHAT ELSE, GREEN? STOPPING THAT AIRSHIP FROM CRASHING!
I DON'T KNOW WHAT MY FATHER INTENDS TO DO WITH TEAM ROCKET— OR ME— AFTER THIS...
BUT NO MATTER WHAT HAPPENS, I'M GOING TO ACCEPT THAT...
...GIOVANNI IS MY BIOLOGICAL FATHER— AND HE RAISED ME WHEN I WAS LITTLE.
I WON'T LET HIM COMMIT ANY MORE CRIMES.
I'LL SHOULDER THE BURDEN OF WHAT HE'S BECOME.
THE TWO OF US WILL MAKE UP FOR IT SOMEHOW ...
SNAP

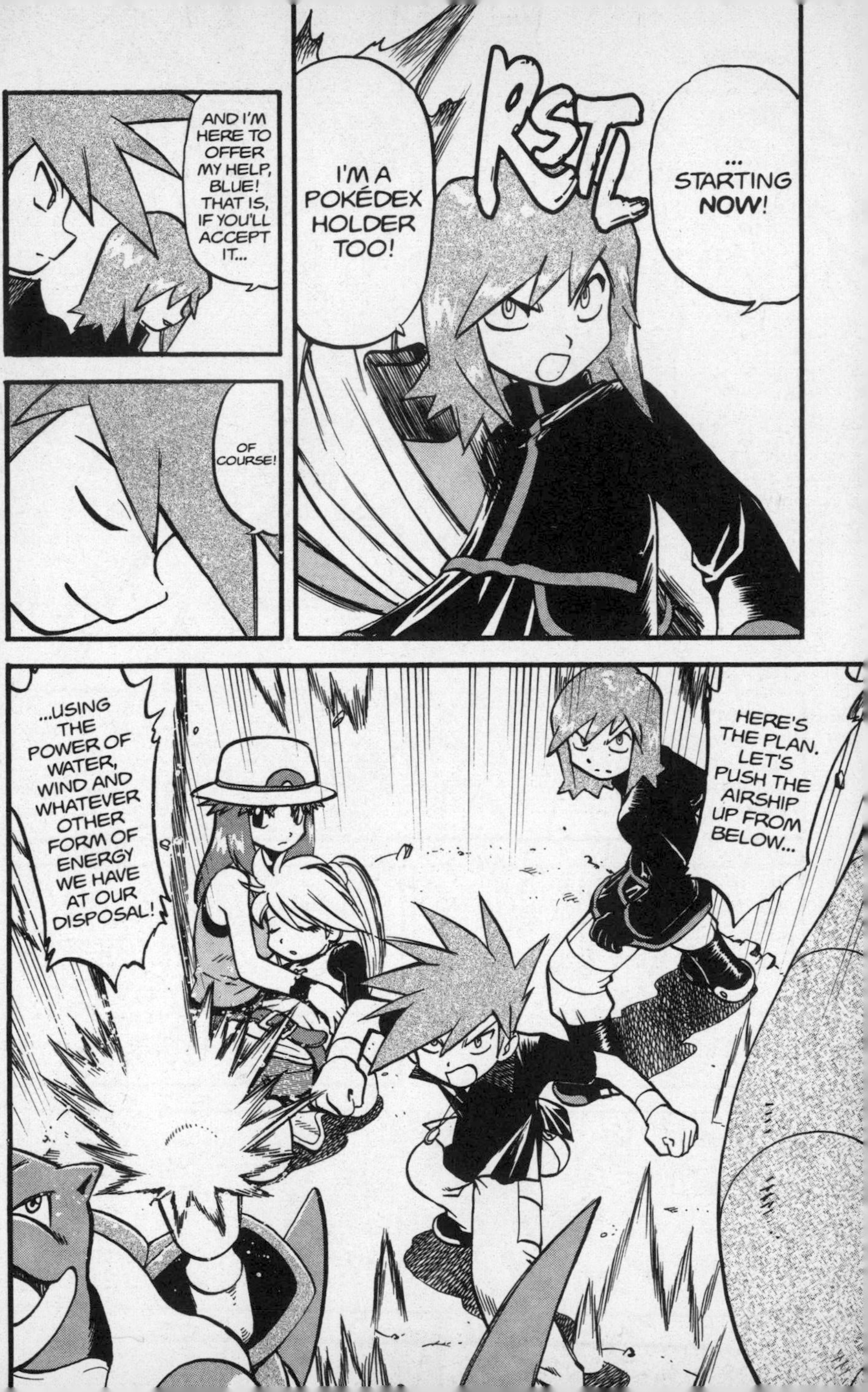
... STARTING NOW!
RSTL
I'M A POKÉDEX HOLDER TOO!
AND I'M HERE TO OFFER MY HELP, BLUE! THAT IS, IF YOU'LL ACCEPT IT...
OF COURSE!
HERE'S THE PLAN. LET'S PUSH THE AIRSHIP UP FROM BELOW...
...USING THE POWER OF WATER, WIND AND WHATEVER OTHER FORM OF ENERGY WE HAVE AT OUR DISPOSAL!

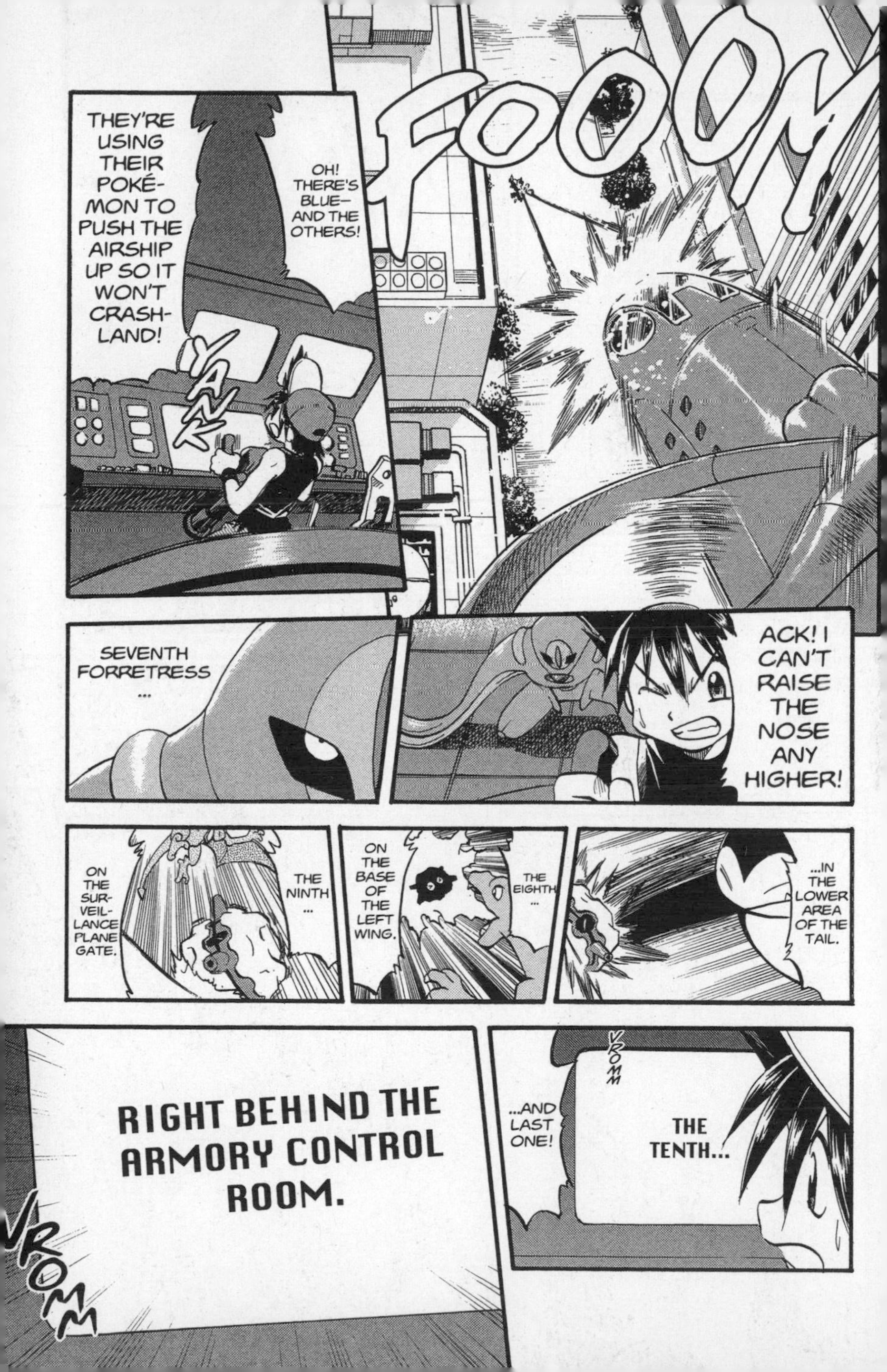
FOOOM
OH! THERE'S BLUE— AND THE OTHERS!
THEY'RE USING THEIR POKÉMON TO PUSH THE AIRSHIP UP SO IT WON'T CRASH-LAND!
YANK
ACK! I CAN'T RAISE THE NOSE ANY HIGHER!
SEVENTH FORRETRESS ...
...IN THE LOWER AREA OF THE TAIL.
THE EIGHTH ...
ON THE BASE OF THE LEFT WING.
THE NINTH ...
ON THE SUR-VEIL-LANCE PLANE GATE.
VROMM
THE TENTH...
...AND LAST ONE!
RIGHT BEHIND THE ARMORY CONTROL ROOM.
VROMM

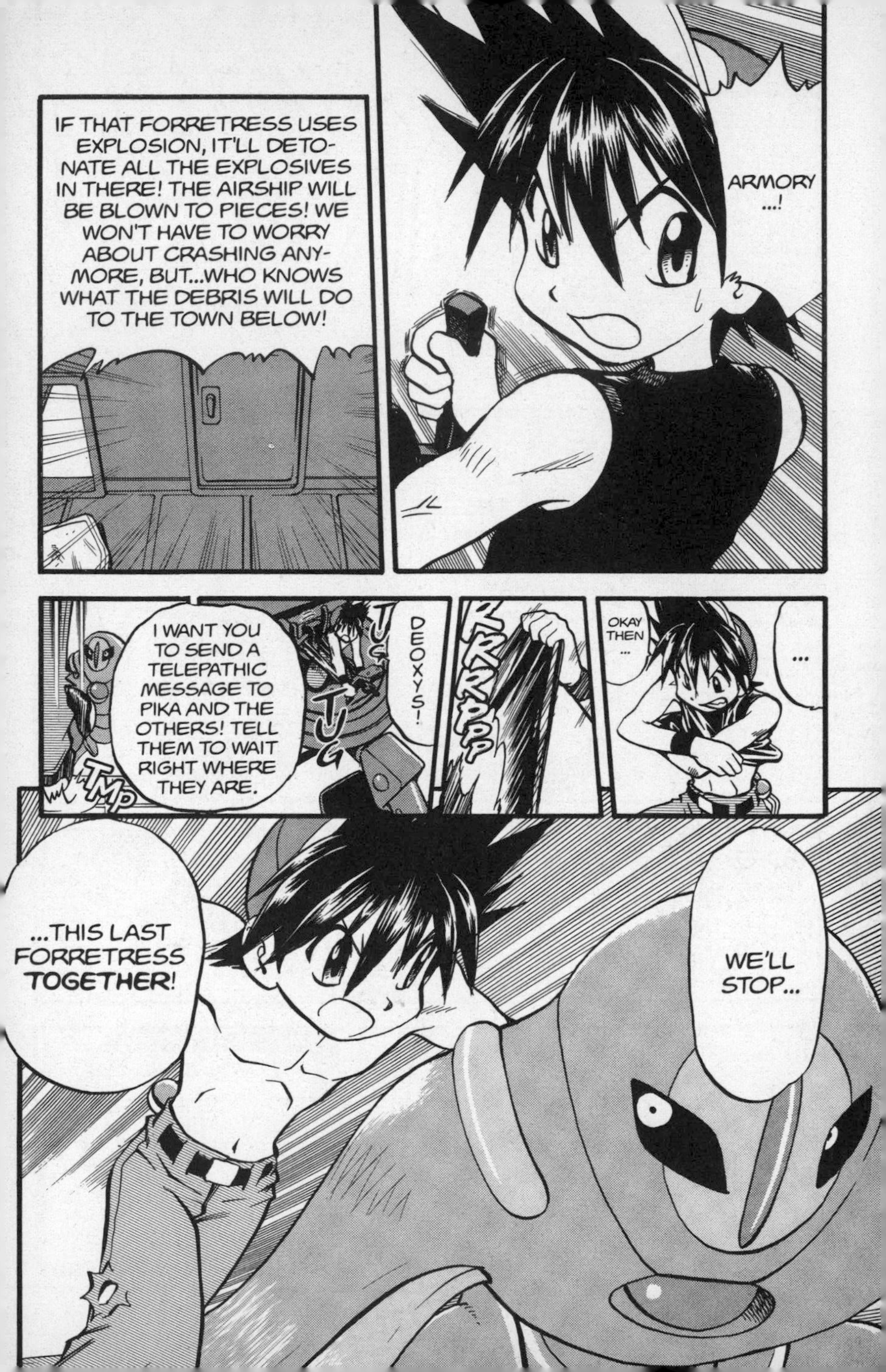
ARMORY ...!
IF THAT FORRETRESS USES EXPLOSION, IT'LL DETONATE ALL THE EXPLOSIVES IN THERE! THE AIRSHIP WILL BE BLOWN TO PIECES! WE WON'T HAVE TO WORRY ABOUT CRASHING ANYMORE, BUT...WHO KNOWS WHAT THE DEBRIS WILL DO TO THE TOWN BELOW!
...
OKAY THEN ...
KRRRPPP
DEOXYS!
TUG
TUG
I WANT YOU TO SEND A TELEPATHIC MESSAGE TO PIKA AND THE OTHERS! TELL THEM TO WAIT RIGHT WHERE THEY ARE.
TMP
WE'LL STOP...
...THIS LAST FORRETRESS **TOGETHER**!

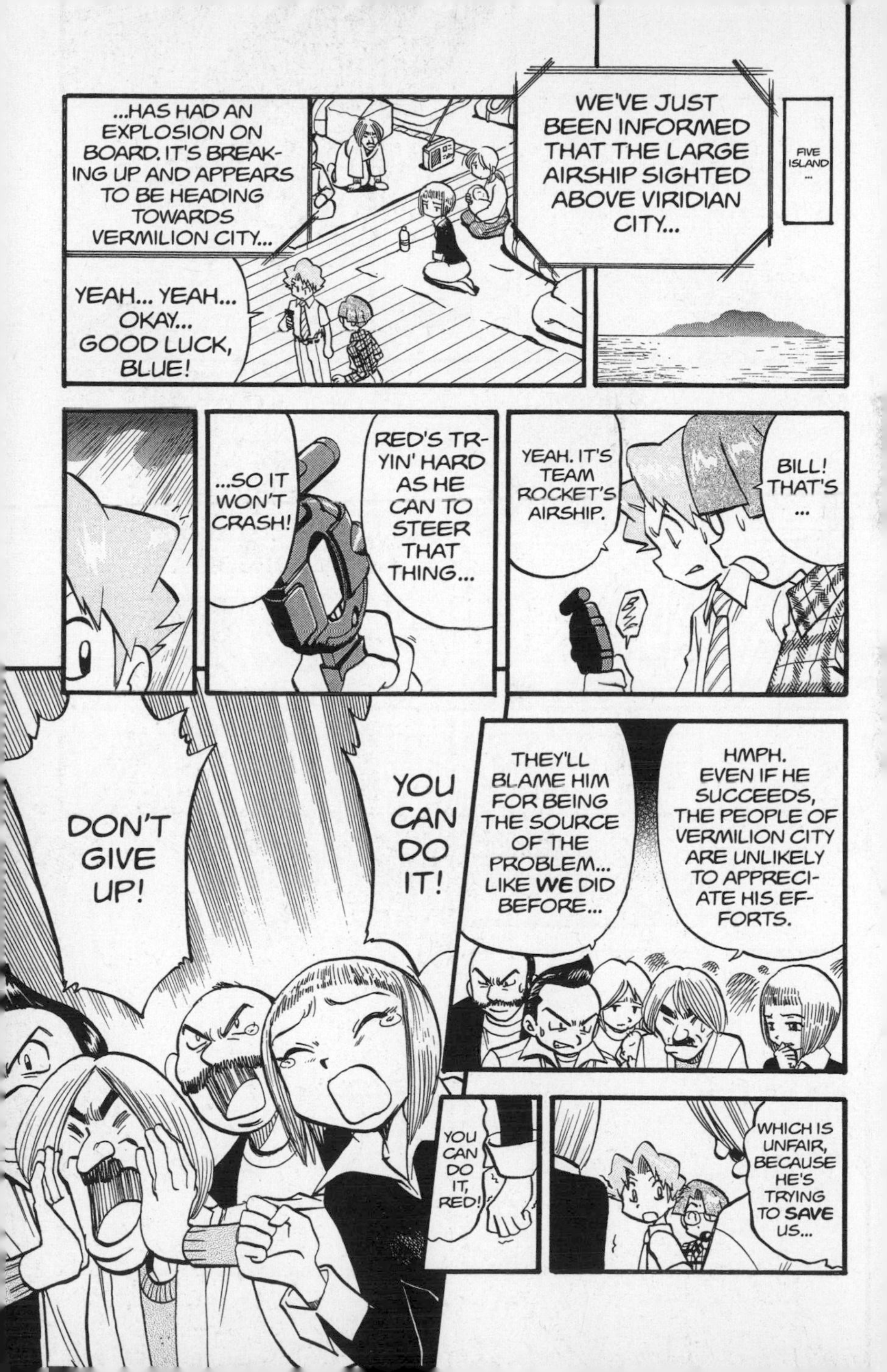

FIVE ISLAND...
WE'VE JUST BEEN INFORMED THAT THE LARGE AIRSHIP SIGHTED ABOVE VIRIDIAN CITY...
...HAS HAD AN EXPLOSION ON BOARD. IT'S BREAKING UP AND APPEARS TO BE HEADING TOWARDS VERMILION CITY...
YEAH... YEAH... OKAY... GOOD LUCK, BLUE!
BILL! THAT'S ...
YEAH. IT'S TEAM ROCKET'S AIRSHIP.
RED'S TRYIN' HARD AS HE CAN TO STEER THAT THING...
...SO IT WON'T CRASH!
HMPH. EVEN IF HE SUCCEEDS, THE PEOPLE OF VERMILION CITY ARE UNLIKELY TO APPRECIATE HIS EFFORTS.
THEY'LL BLAME HIM FOR BEING THE SOURCE OF THE PROBLEM... LIKE **WE** DID BEFORE...
WHICH IS UNFAIR, BECAUSE HE'S TRYING TO **SAVE** US...
YOU CAN DO IT!
DON'T GIVE UP!
YOU CAN DO IT, RED!

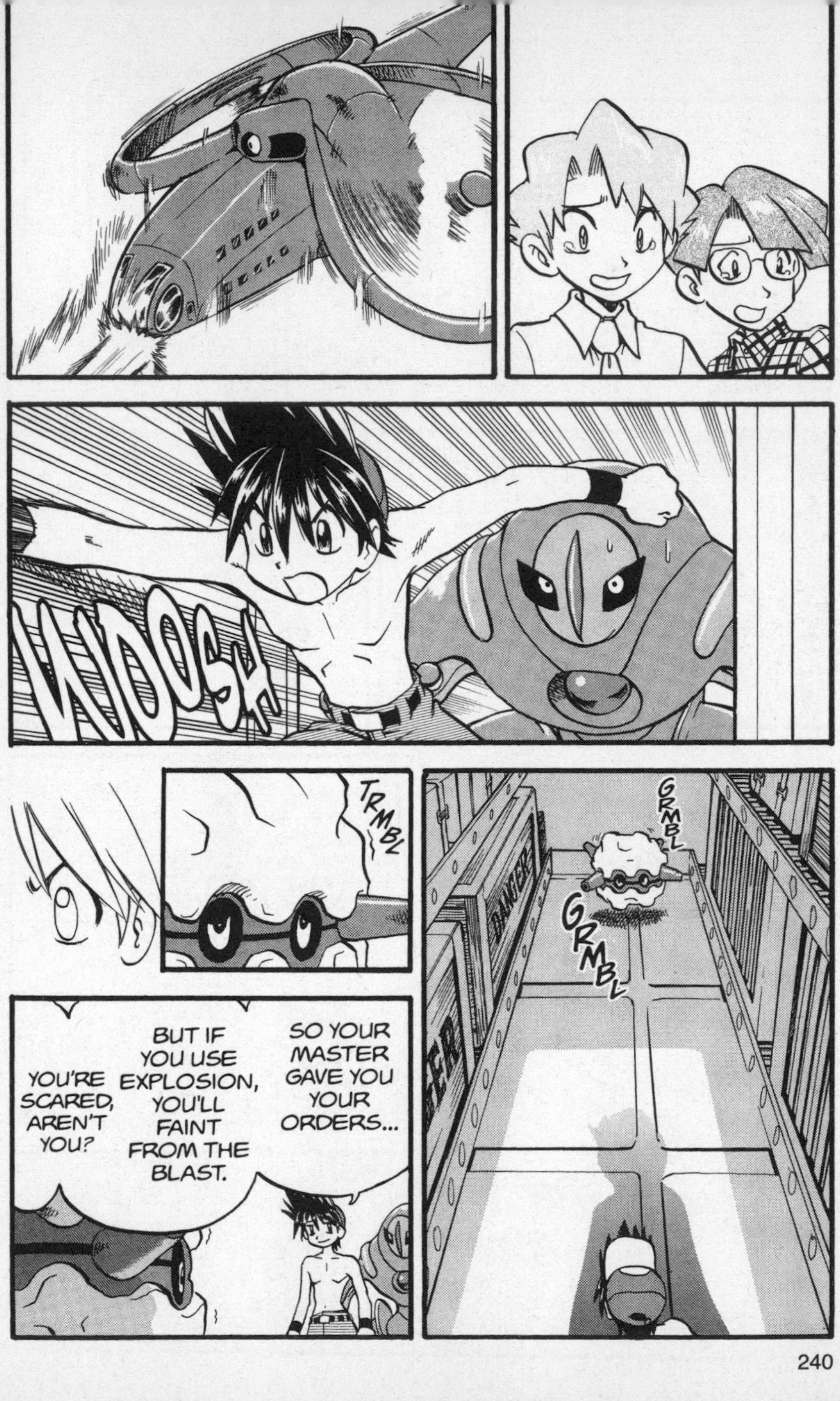
WOOSH
GRMBL
GRMBL
TRMBL
SO YOUR MASTER GAVE YOU YOUR ORDERS...
BUT IF YOU USE EXPLOSION, YOU'LL FAINT FROM THE BLAST.
YOU'RE SCARED, AREN'T YOU?

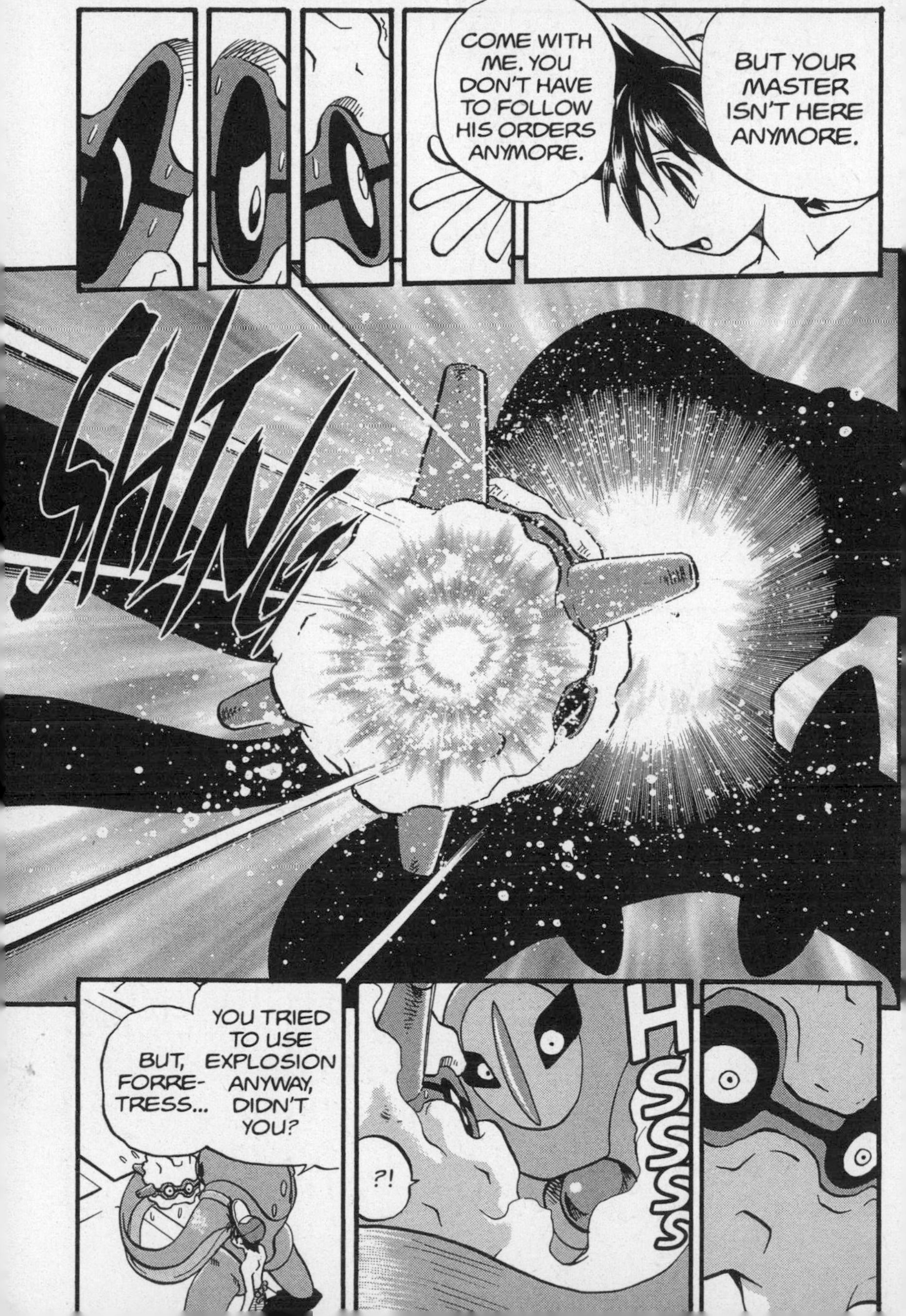
BUT YOUR MASTER ISN'T HERE ANYMORE.
COME WITH ME. YOU DON'T HAVE TO FOLLOW HIS ORDERS ANYMORE.
SHING
HSSSS
?!
BUT, FORRE-TRESS... YOU TRIED TO USE EXPLOSION ANYWAY, DIDN'T YOU?

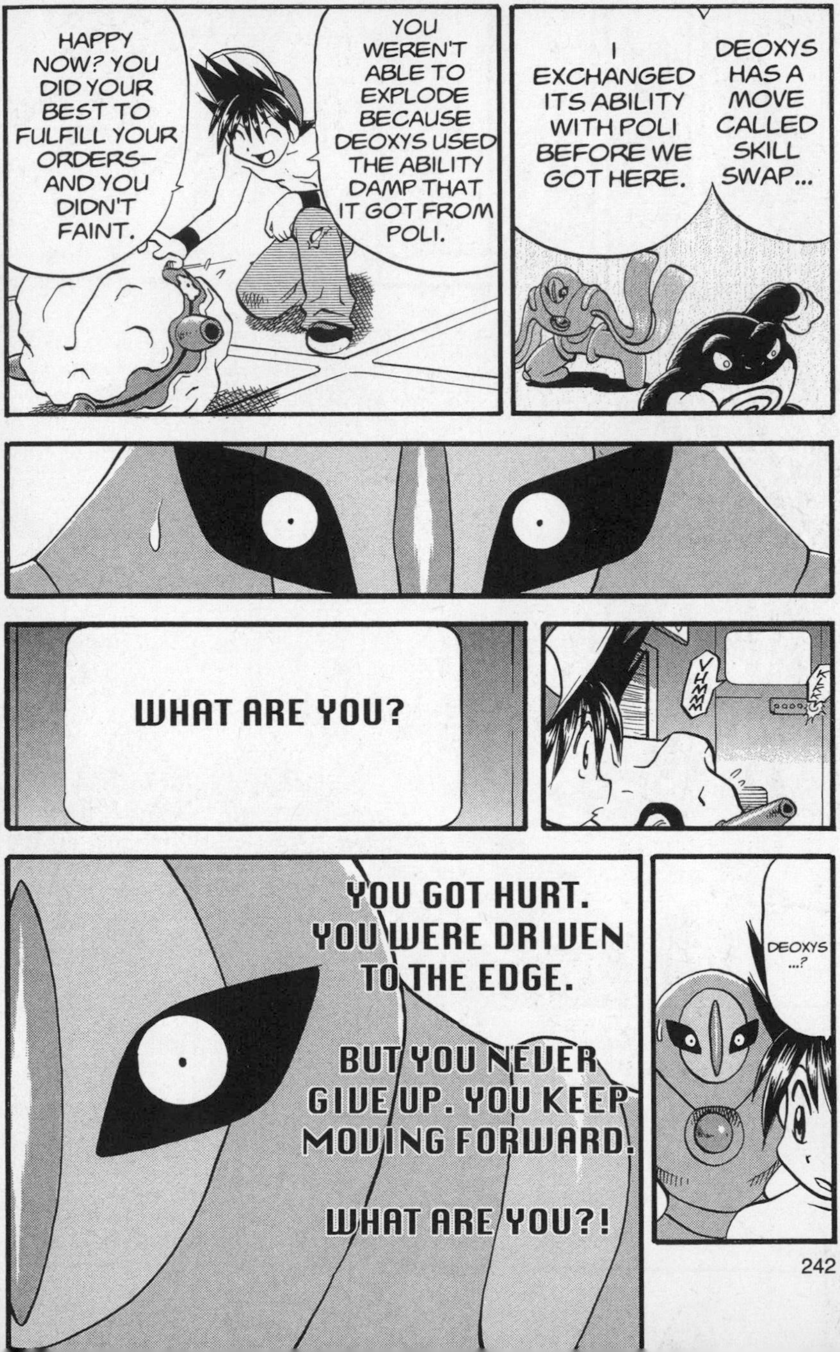
DEOXYS HAS A MOVE CALLED SKILL SWAP...
I EXCHANGED ITS ABILITY WITH POLI BEFORE WE GOT HERE.
YOU WEREN'T ABLE TO EXPLODE BECAUSE DEOXYS USED THE ABILITY DAMP THAT IT GOT FROM POLI.
HAPPY NOW? YOU DID YOUR BEST TO FULFILL YOUR ORDERS— AND YOU DIDN'T FAINT.
VHMMM
WHAT ARE YOU?
DEOXYS ...?
YOU GOT HURT. YOU WERE DRIVEN TO THE EDGE.
BUT YOU NEVER GIVE UP. YOU KEEP MOVING FORWARD.
WHAT ARE YOU?!

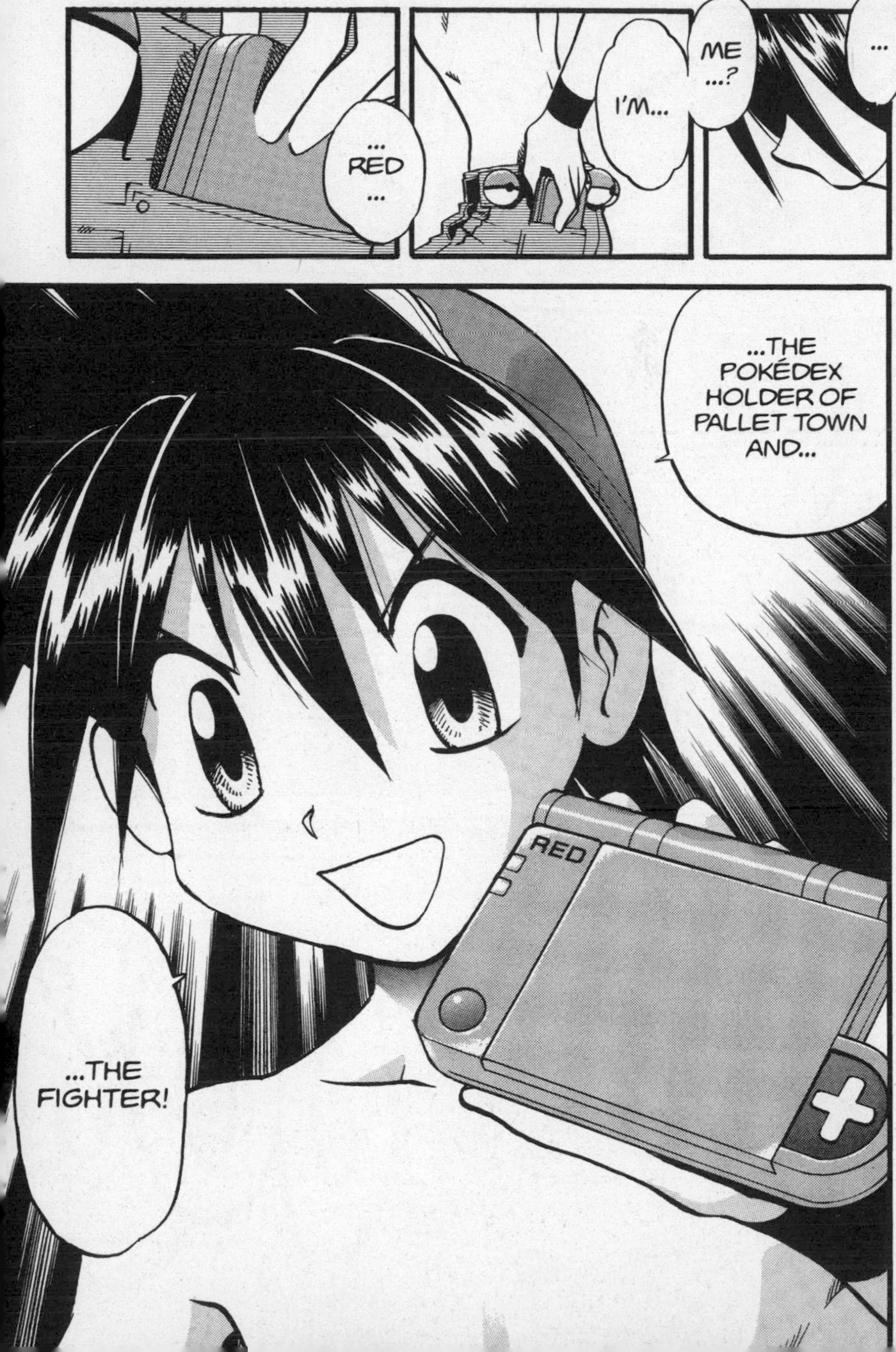
...
ME ...?
I'M...
... RED ...
...THE POKÉDEX HOLDER OF PALLET TOWN AND...
RED
...THE FIGHTER!

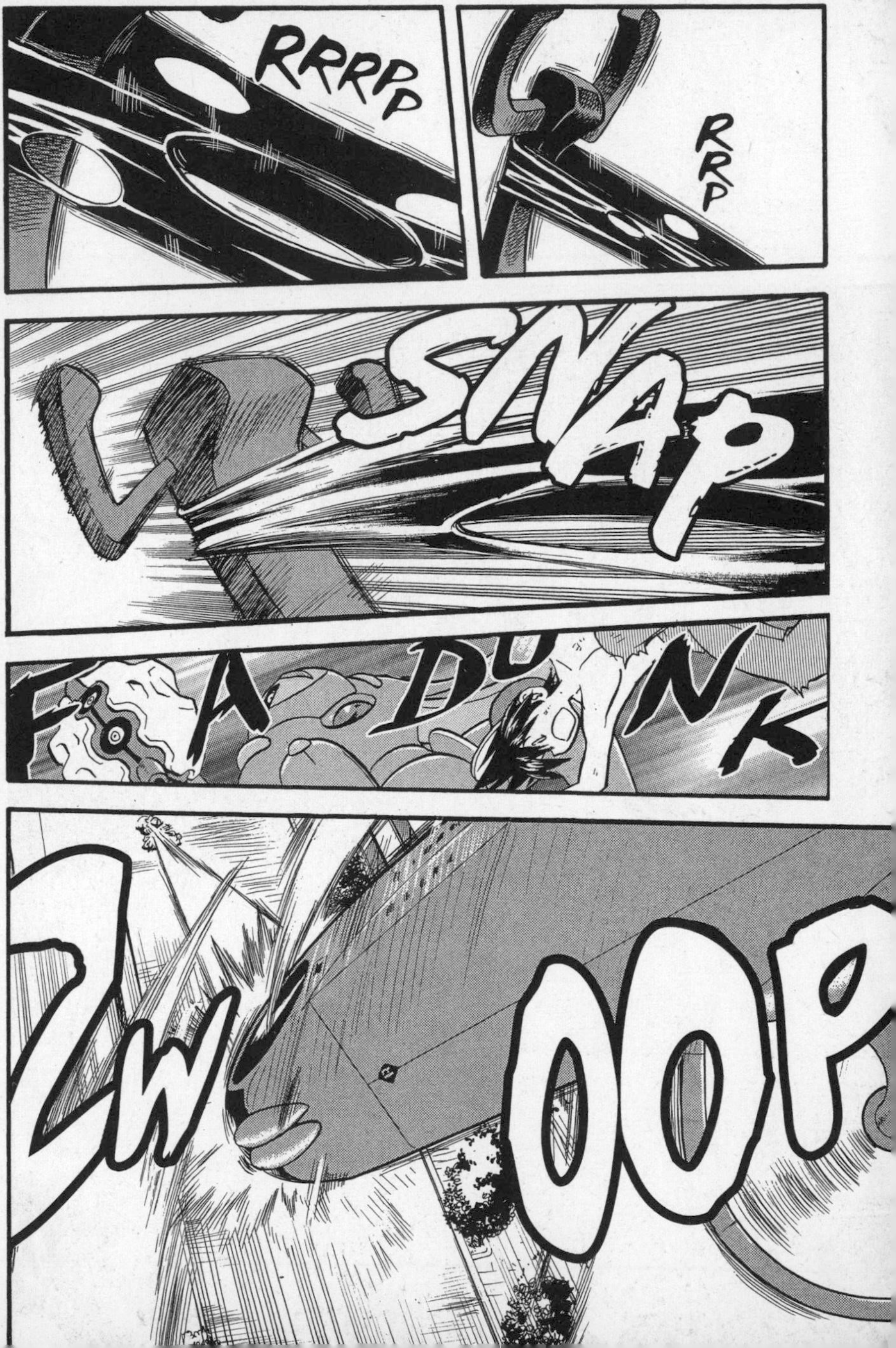
RRP
RRRPP
SNAP
FADUNK
ZWOOP

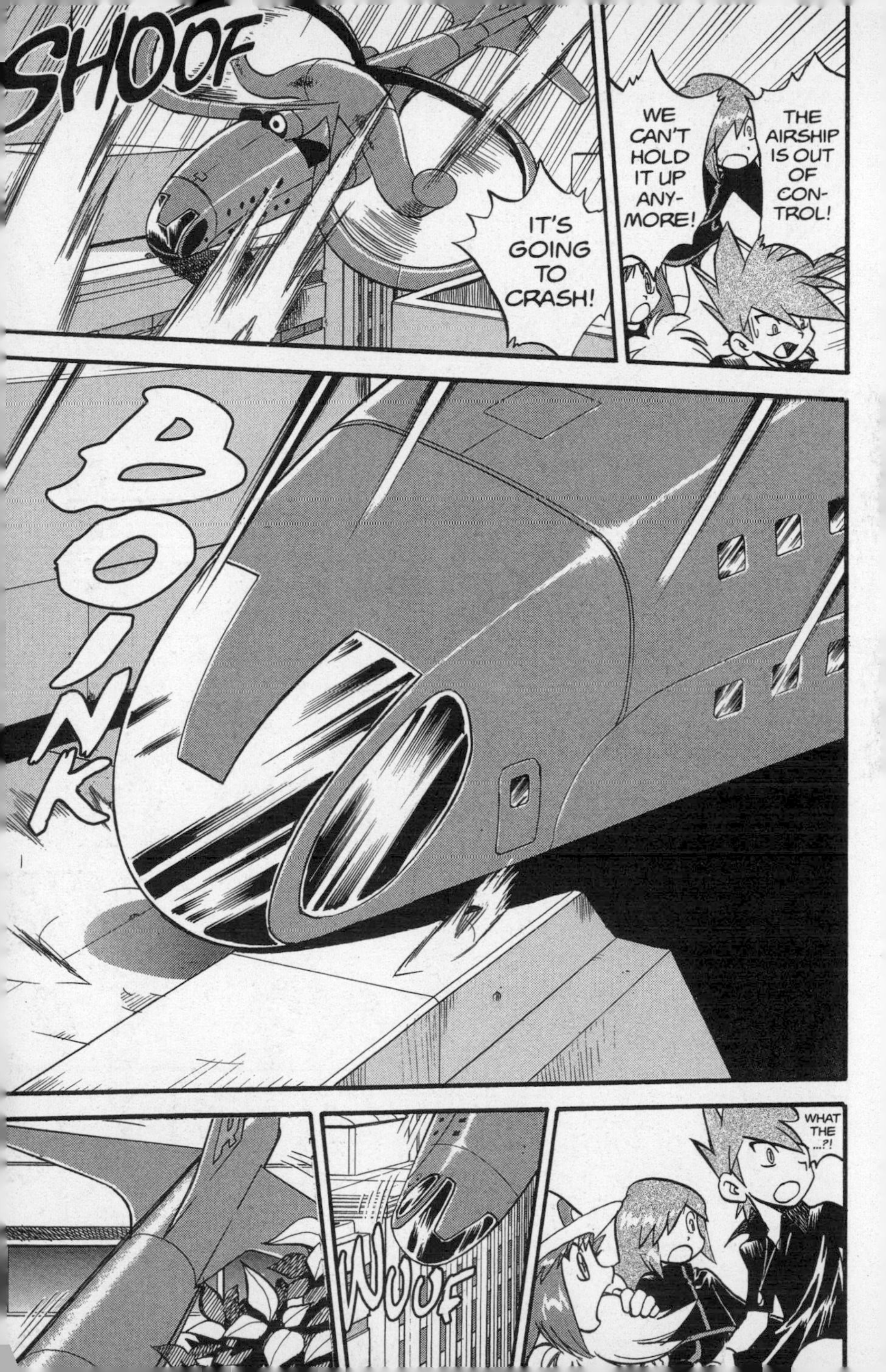

THE AIRSHIP IS OUT OF CONTROL!
WE CAN'T HOLD IT UP ANYMORE!
IT'S GOING TO CRASH!
SHOOF
BOINK
WHAT THE ...?!
WUUF

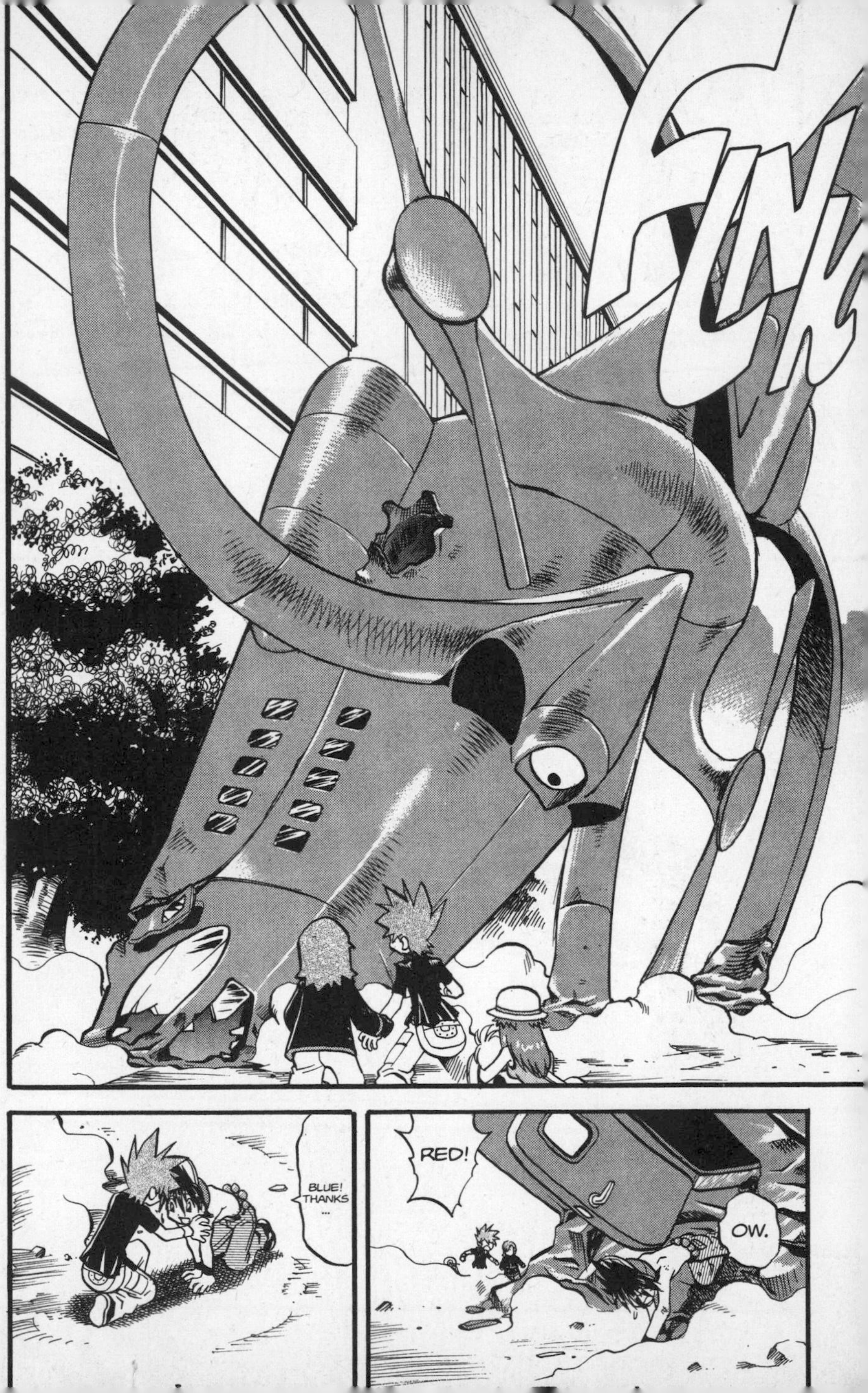
RED!
OW.
BLUE! THANKS ...

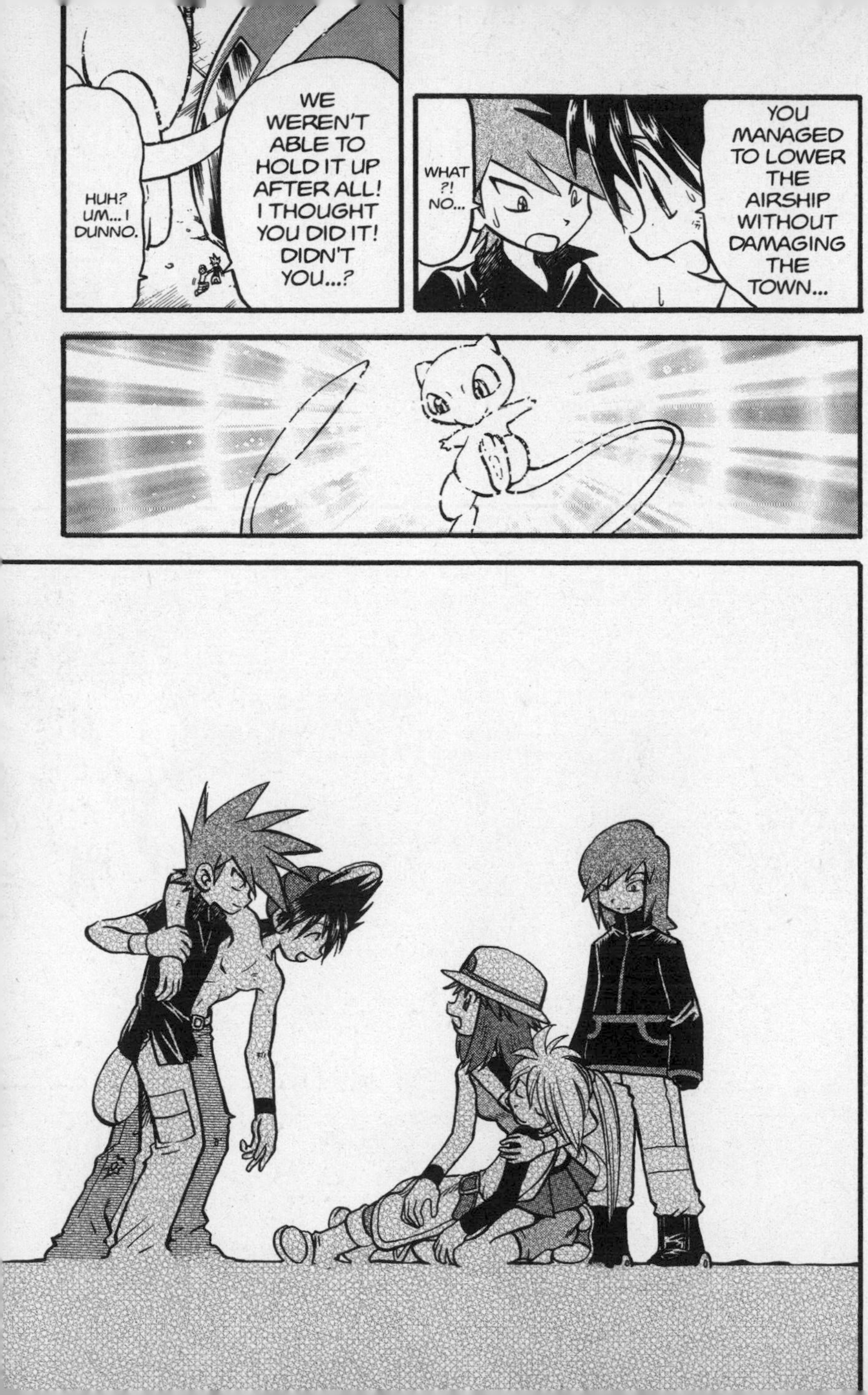
YOU MANAGED TO LOWER THE AIRSHIP WITHOUT DAMAGING THE TOWN...
WHAT?! NO...
WE WEREN'T ABLE TO HOLD IT UP AFTER ALL! I THOUGHT YOU DID IT! DIDN'T YOU...?
HUH? UM... I DUNNO.

●Adventure 302●
Phew for Mew

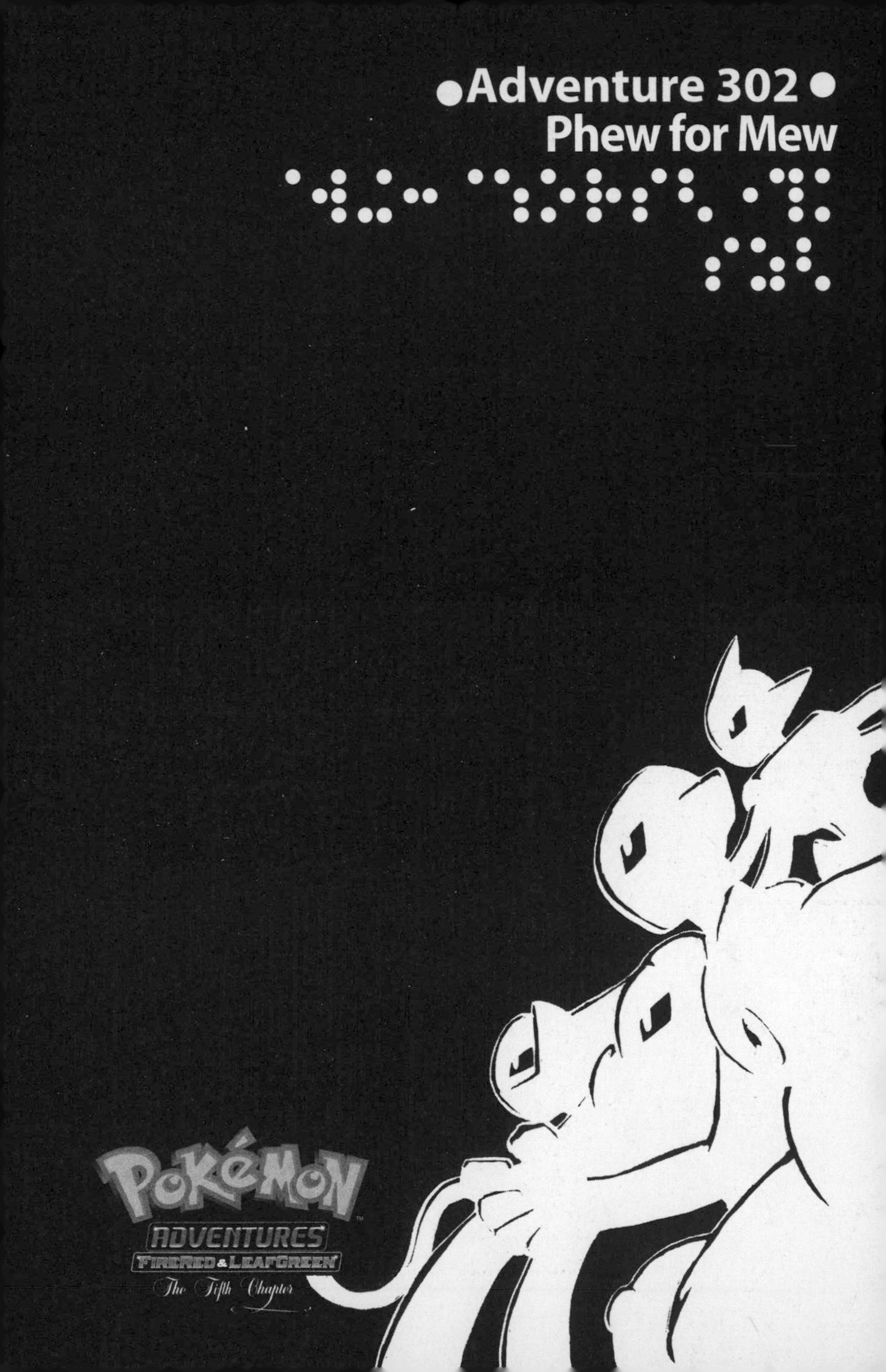

Pokémon
ADVENTURES
FireRed & LeafGreen
The Fifth Chapter

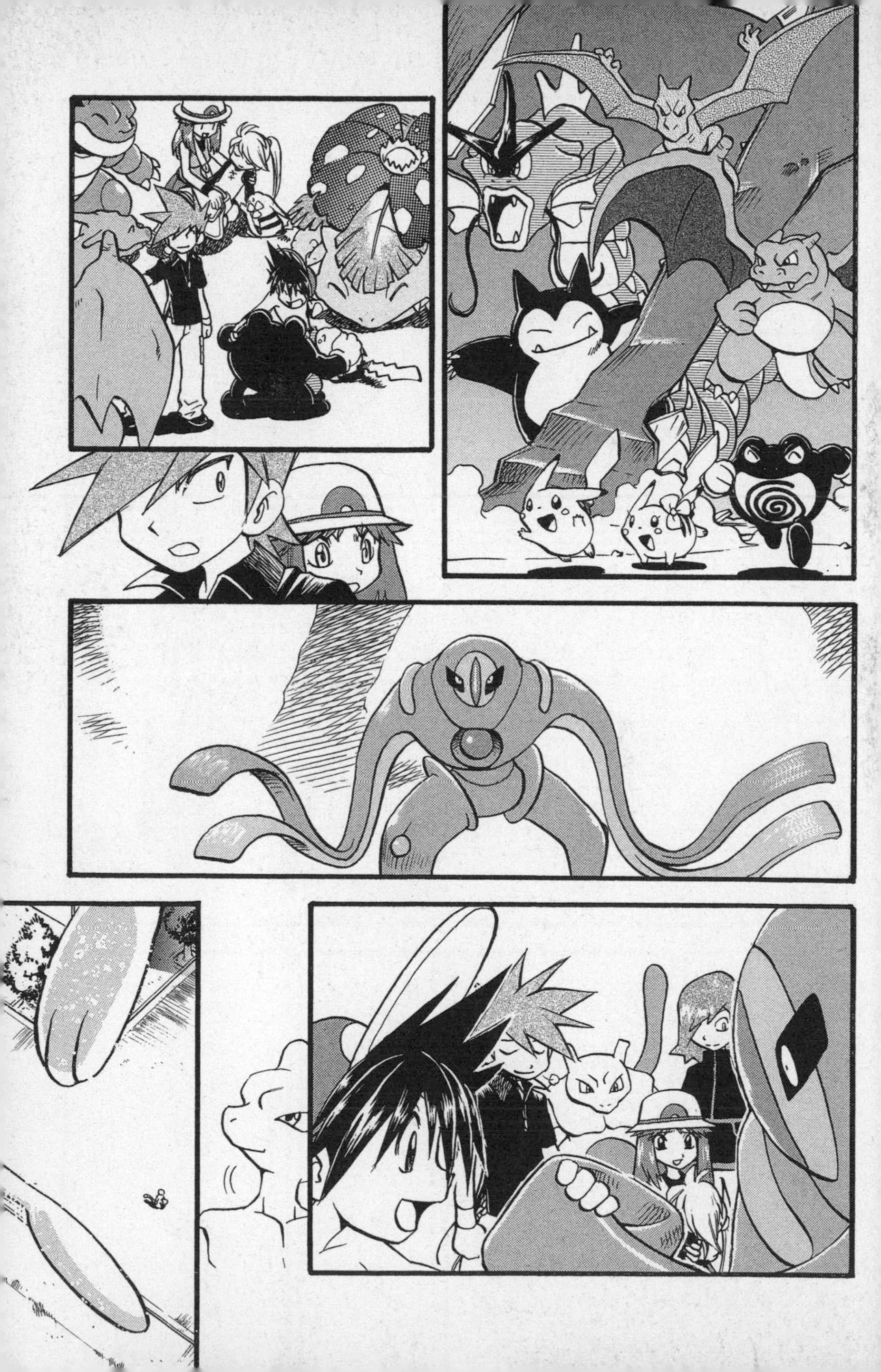

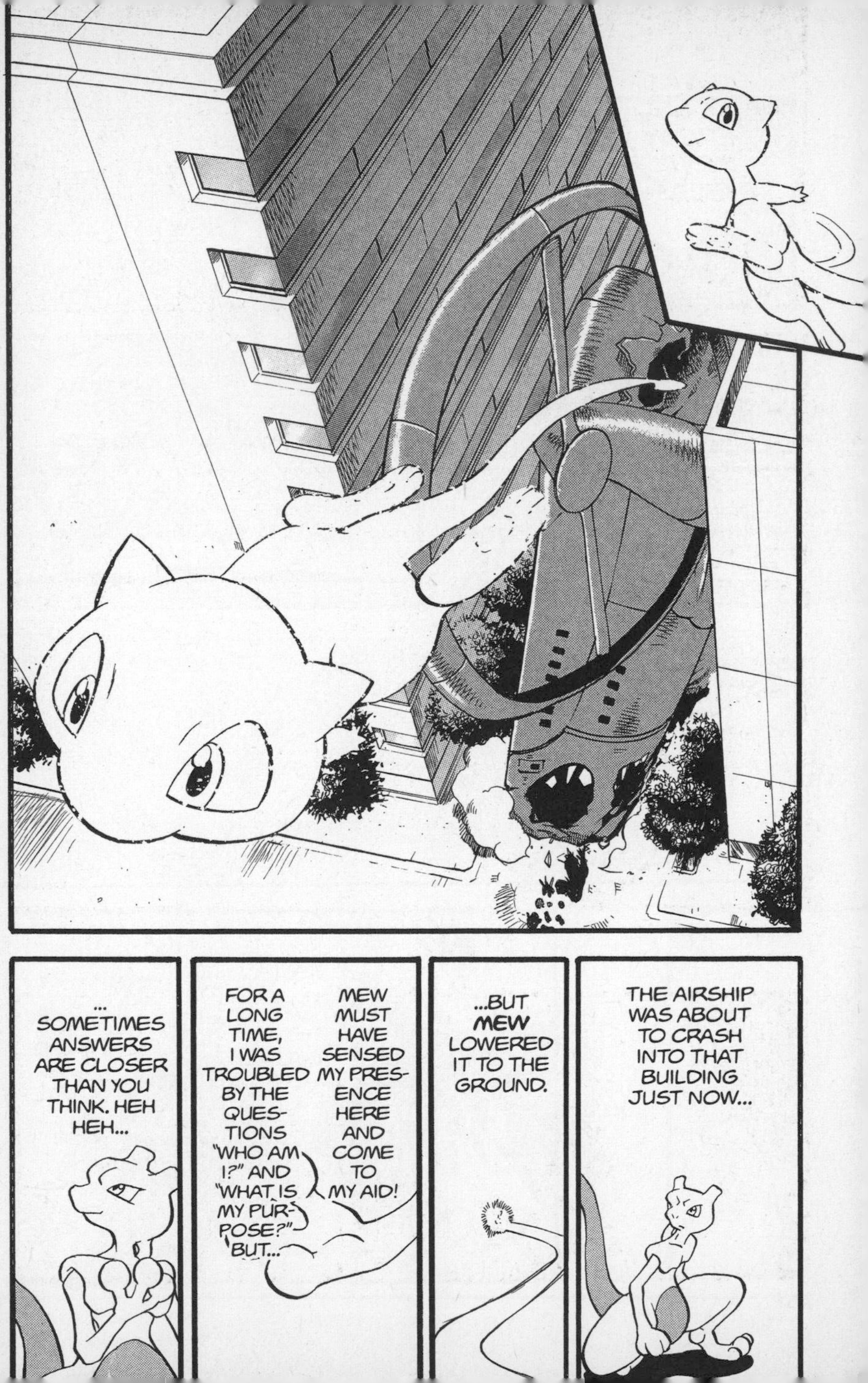
THE AIRSHIP WAS ABOUT TO CRASH INTO THAT BUILDING JUST NOW...
...BUT MEW LOWERED IT TO THE GROUND.
MEW MUST HAVE SENSED MY PRESENCE HERE AND COME TO MY AID!
FOR A LONG TIME, I WAS TROUBLED BY THE QUESTIONS "WHO AM I?" AND "WHAT IS MY PURPOSE?" BUT...
... SOMETIMES ANSWERS ARE CLOSER THAN YOU THINK. HEH HEH...

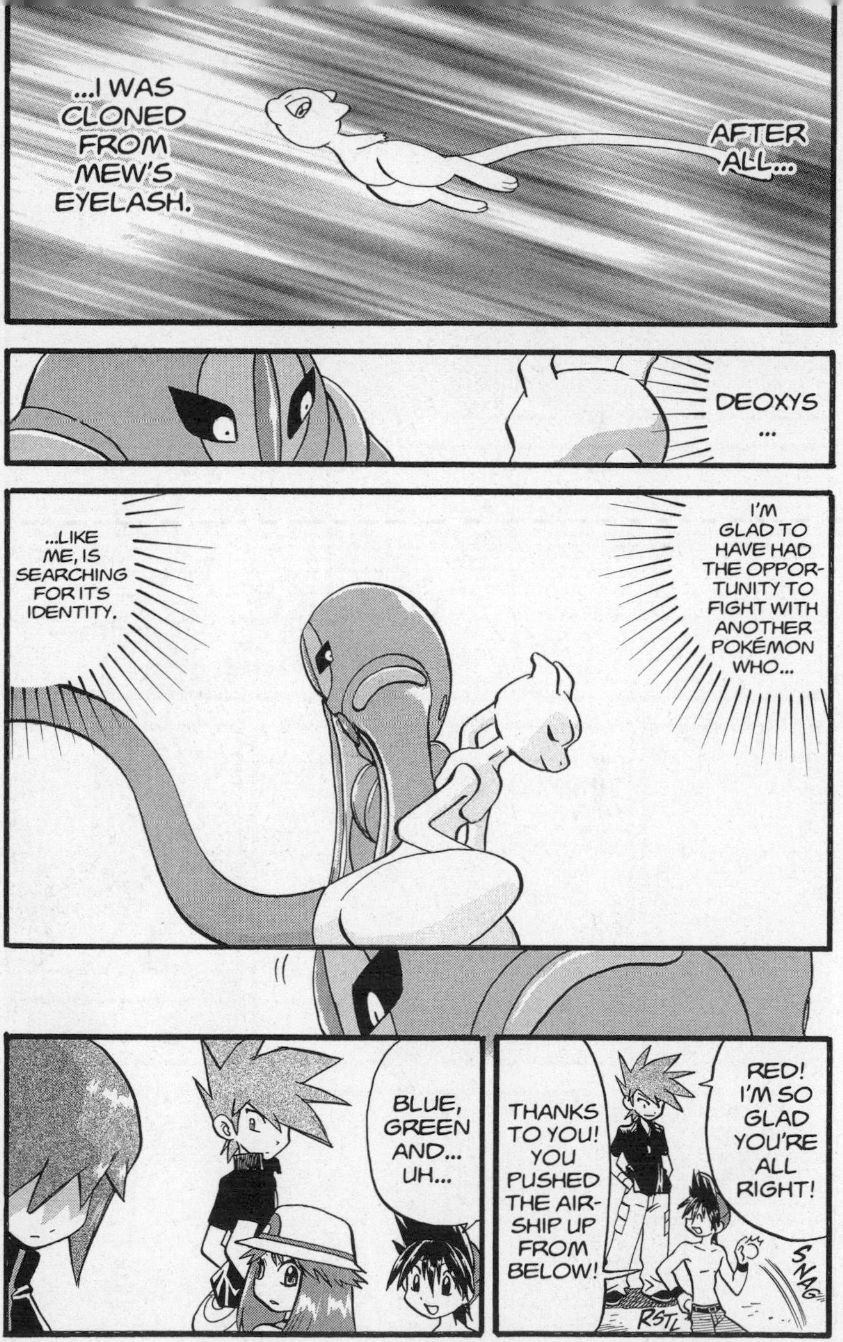
AFTER ALL...
...I WAS CLONED FROM MEW'S EYELASH.
DEOXYS ...
I'M GLAD TO HAVE HAD THE OPPOR-TUNITY TO FIGHT WITH ANOTHER POKÉMON WHO...
...LIKE ME, IS SEARCHING FOR ITS IDENTITY.
RED! I'M SO GLAD YOU'RE ALL RIGHT!
THANKS TO YOU! YOU PUSHED THE AIR-SHIP UP FROM BELOW!
SNAG
RSTL
BLUE, GREEN AND... UH...

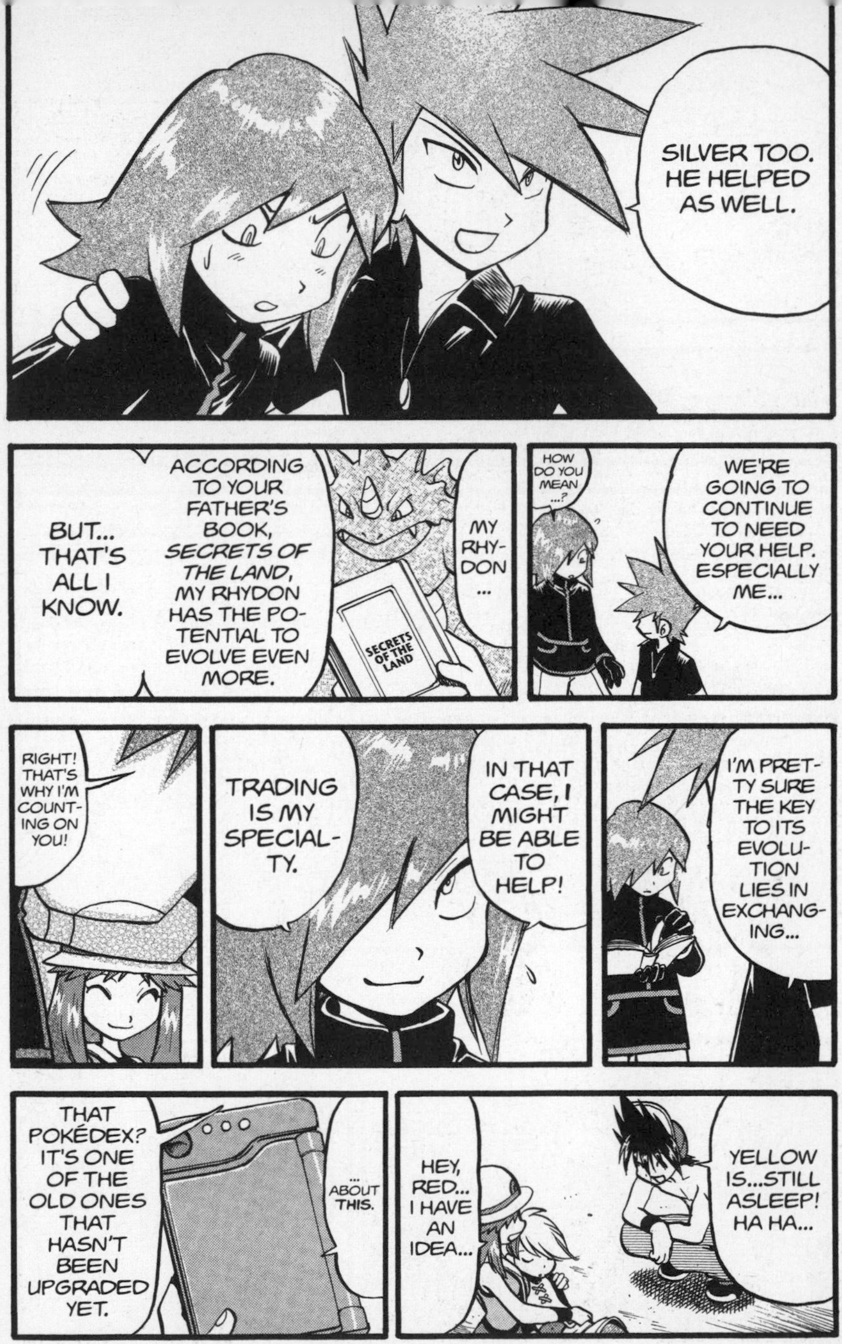
SILVER TOO. HE HELPED AS WELL.
WE'RE GOING TO CONTINUE TO NEED YOUR HELP. ESPECIALLY ME...
HOW DO YOU MEAN ...?
MY RHYDON ...
ACCORDING TO YOUR FATHER'S BOOK, *SECRETS OF THE LAND*, MY RHYDON HAS THE POTENTIAL TO EVOLVE EVEN MORE.
SECRETS OF THE LAND
BUT... THAT'S ALL I KNOW.
I'M PRETTY SURE THE KEY TO ITS EVOLUTION LIES IN EXCHANGING...
IN THAT CASE, I MIGHT BE ABLE TO HELP!
TRADING IS MY SPECIALTY.
RIGHT! THAT'S WHY I'M COUNTING ON YOU!
YELLOW IS...STILL ASLEEP! HA HA...
HEY, RED... I HAVE AN IDEA...
... ABOUT **THIS.**
THAT POKÉDEX? IT'S ONE OF THE OLD ONES THAT HASN'T BEEN UPGRADED YET.

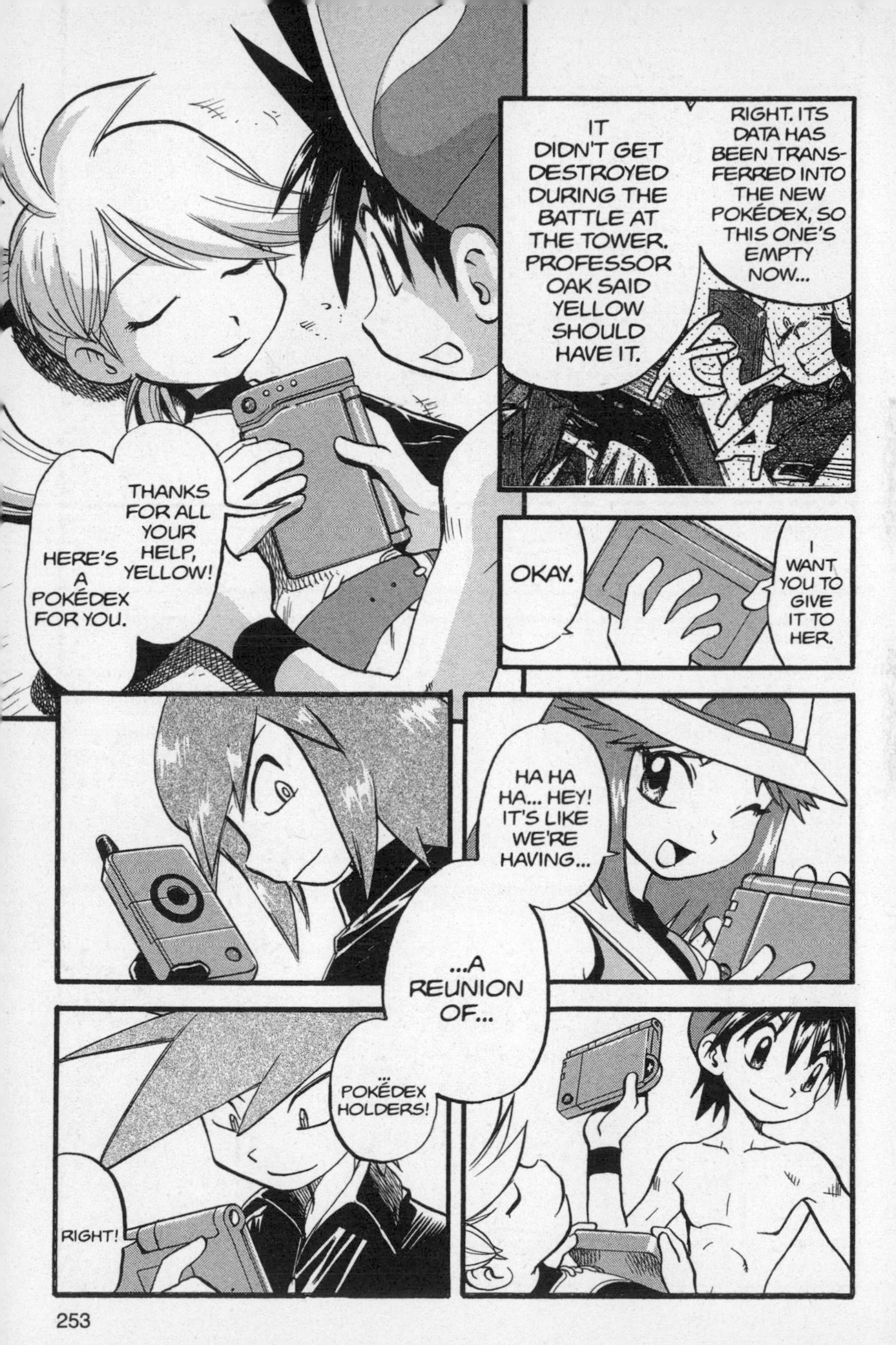
RIGHT. ITS DATA HAS BEEN TRANS-FERRED INTO THE NEW POKÉDEX, SO THIS ONE'S EMPTY NOW...
IT DIDN'T GET DESTROYED DURING THE BATTLE AT THE TOWER. PROFESSOR OAK SAID YELLOW SHOULD HAVE IT.
I WANT YOU TO GIVE IT TO HER.
OKAY.
THANKS FOR ALL YOUR HELP, YELLOW!
HERE'S A POKÉDEX FOR YOU.
HA HA HA... HEY! IT'S LIKE WE'RE HAVING...
...A REUNION OF...
...POKÉDEX HOLDERS!
RIGHT!

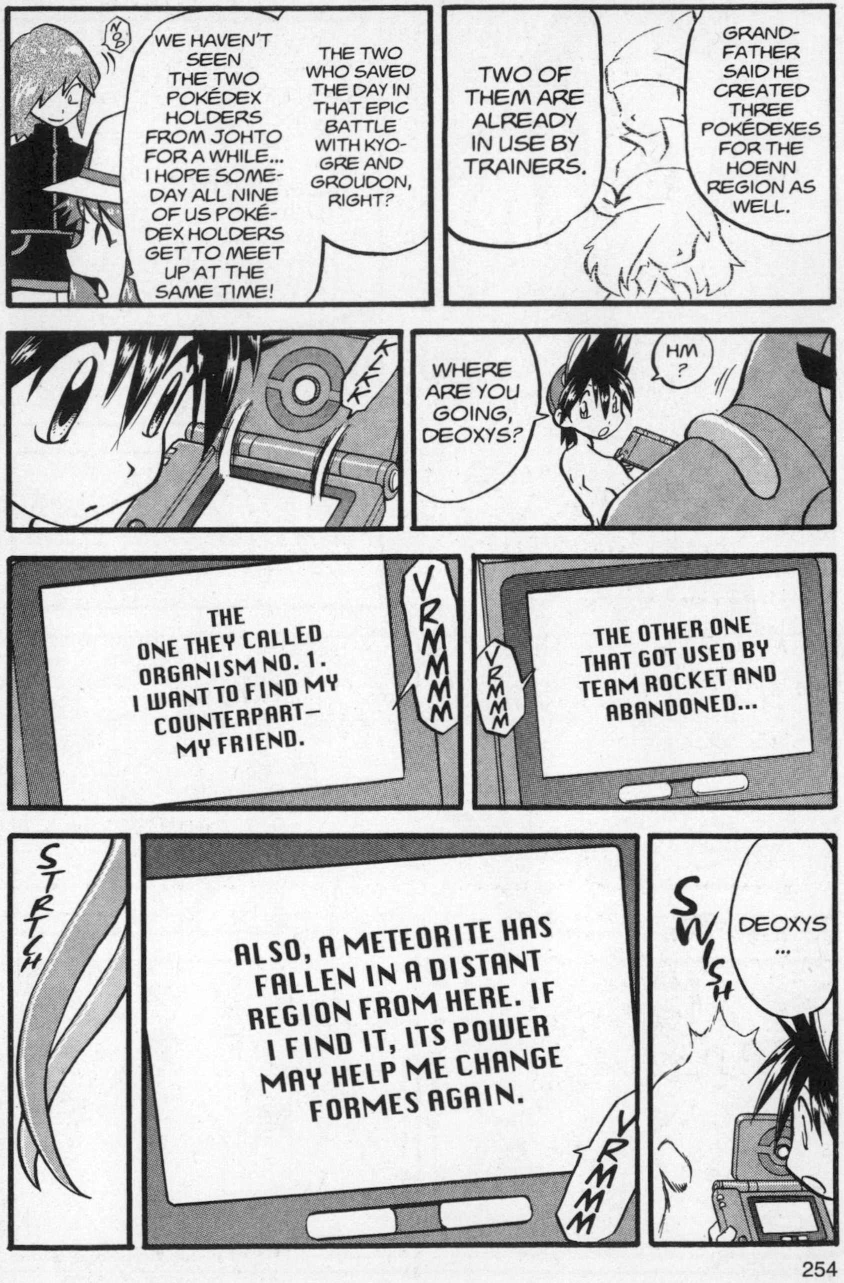
GRAND-FATHER SAID HE CREATED THREE POKÉDEXES FOR THE HOENN REGION AS WELL.
TWO OF THEM ARE ALREADY IN USE BY TRAINERS.
NOD
THE TWO WHO SAVED THE DAY IN THAT EPIC BATTLE WITH KYO-GRE AND GROUDON, RIGHT?
WE HAVEN'T SEEN THE TWO POKÉDEX HOLDERS FROM JOHTO FOR A WHILE... I HOPE SOME-DAY ALL NINE OF US POKÉ-DEX HOLDERS GET TO MEET UP AT THE SAME TIME!
HM?
WHERE ARE YOU GOING, DEOXYS?
KLKK
VRMMM
THE OTHER ONE THAT GOT USED BY TEAM ROCKET AND ABANDONED...
VRMMMM
THE ONE THEY CALLED ORGANISM NO. 1. I WANT TO FIND MY COUNTERPART—MY FRIEND.
DEOXYS...
SWISH
VRMMM
ALSO, A METEORITE HAS FALLEN IN A DISTANT REGION FROM HERE. IF I FIND IT, ITS POWER MAY HELP ME CHANGE FORMES AGAIN.
STRTCH

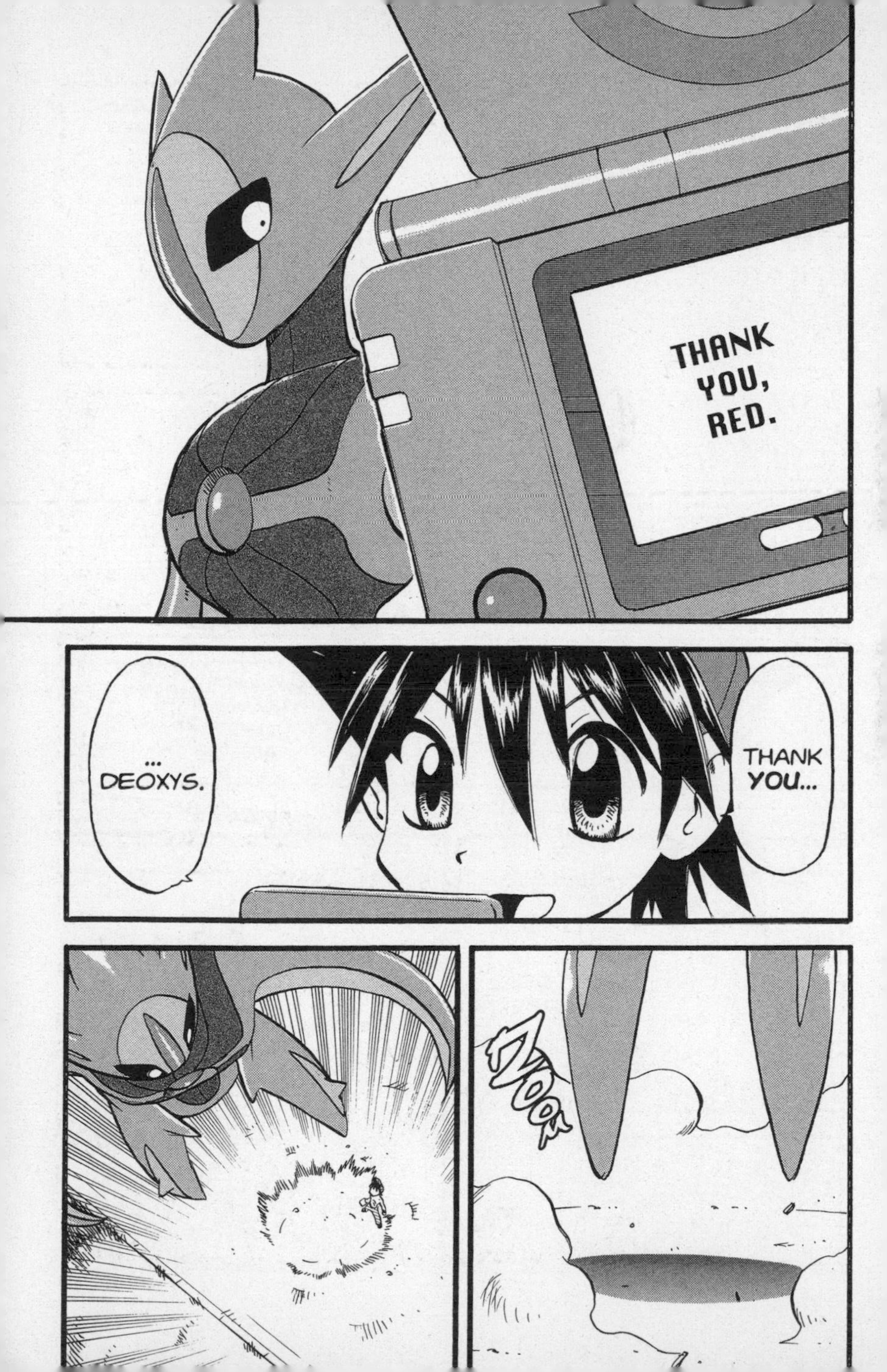
THANK YOU, RED.
THANK YOU...
...DEOXYS.
ZVOOF

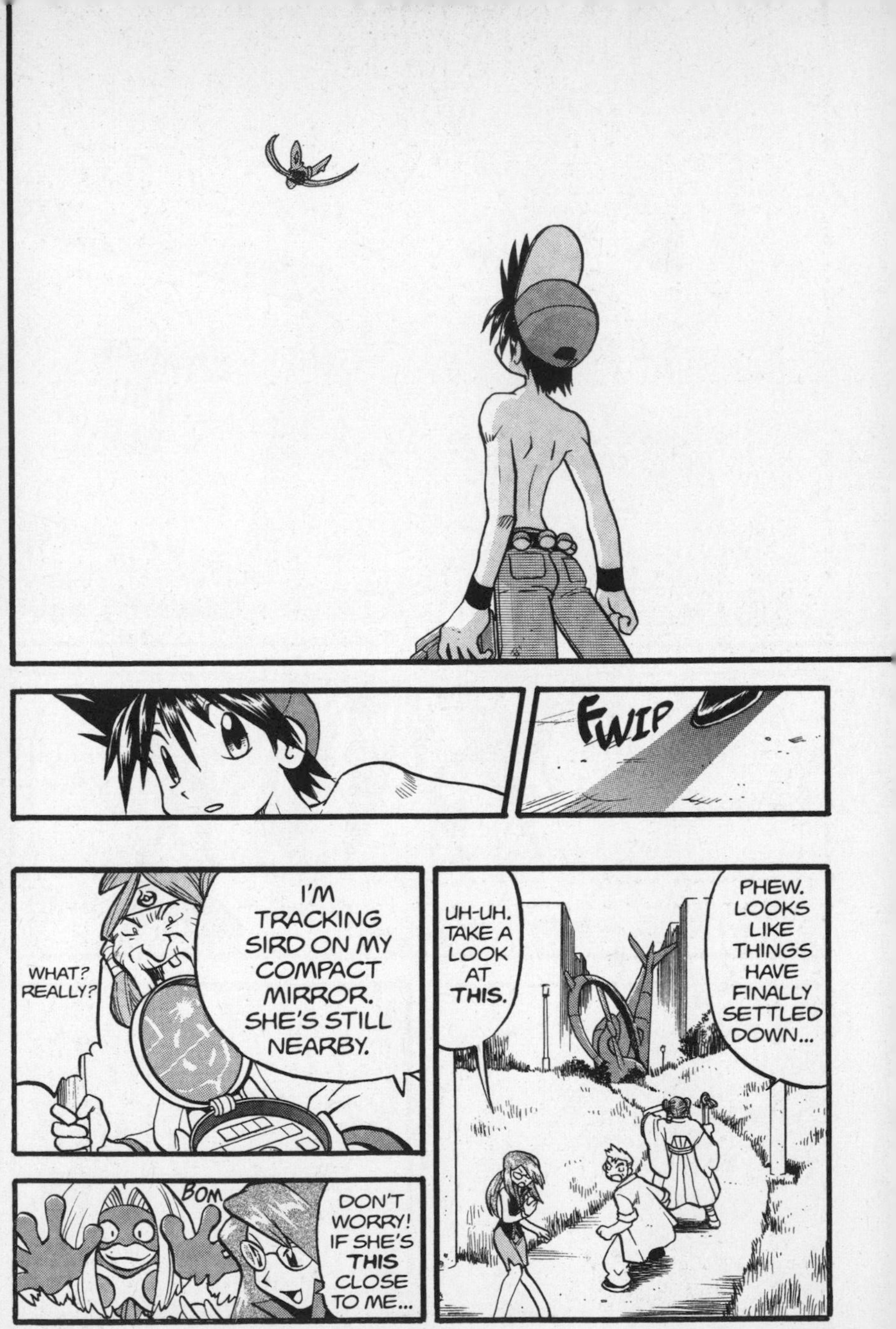
FWIP
PHEW. LOOKS LIKE THINGS HAVE FINALLY SETTLED DOWN...
UH-UH. TAKE A LOOK AT THIS.
I'M TRACKING SIRD ON MY COMPACT MIRROR. SHE'S STILL NEARBY.
WHAT? REALLY?
BOM
DON'T WORRY! IF SHE'S THIS CLOSE TO ME...

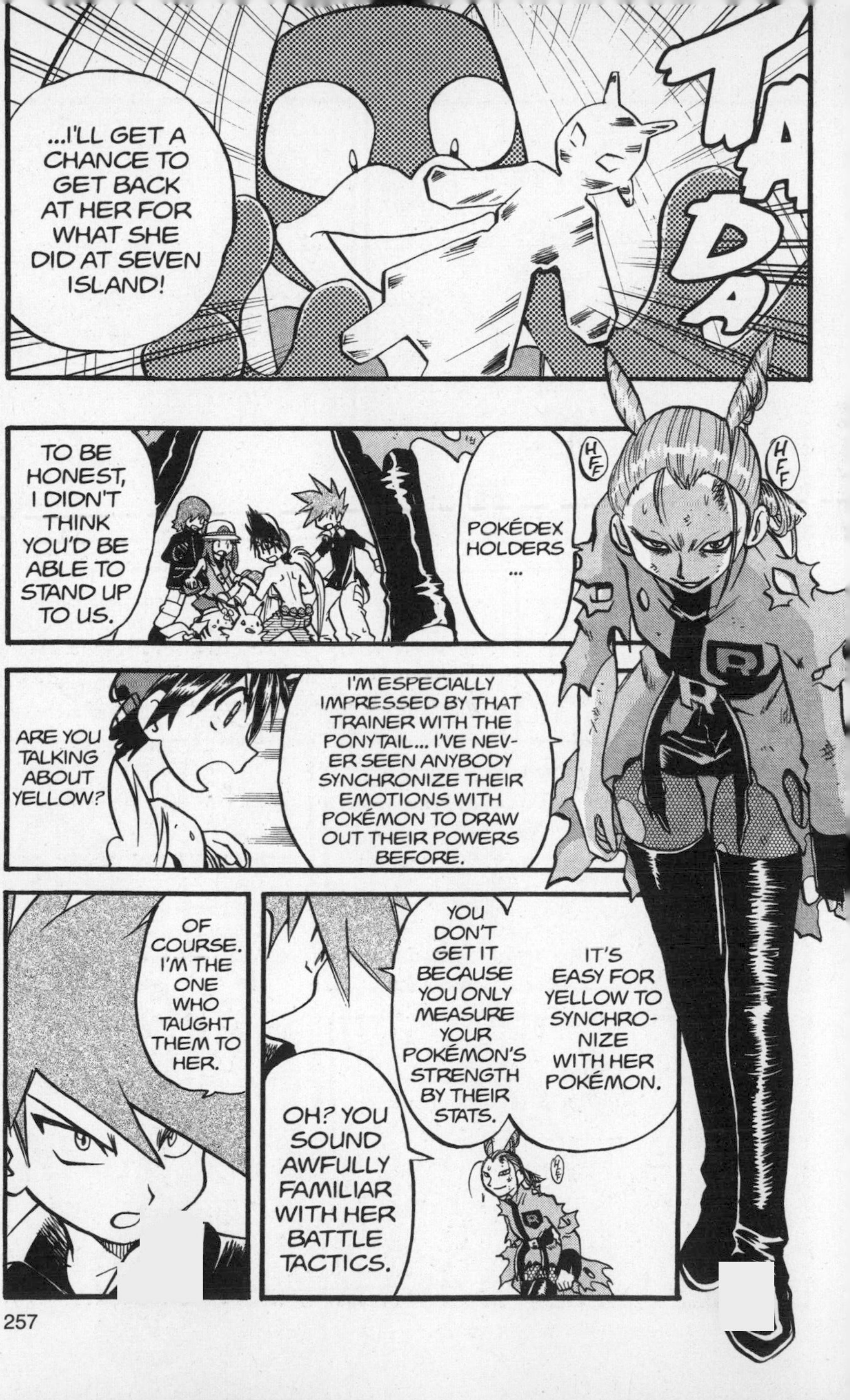
TA DA
...I'LL GET A CHANCE TO GET BACK AT HER FOR WHAT SHE DID AT SEVEN ISLAND!
HFF
HFF
POKÉDEX HOLDERS ...
TO BE HONEST, I DIDN'T THINK YOU'D BE ABLE TO STAND UP TO US.
I'M ESPECIALLY IMPRESSED BY THAT TRAINER WITH THE PONYTAIL... I'VE NEVER SEEN ANYBODY SYNCHRONIZE THEIR EMOTIONS WITH POKÉMON TO DRAW OUT THEIR POWERS BEFORE.
ARE YOU TALKING ABOUT YELLOW?
IT'S EASY FOR YELLOW TO SYNCHRONIZE WITH HER POKÉMON.
YOU DON'T GET IT BECAUSE YOU ONLY MEASURE YOUR POKÉMON'S STRENGTH BY THEIR STATS.
OH? YOU SOUND AWFULLY FAMILIAR WITH HER BATTLE TACTICS.
HFF
OF COURSE. I'M THE ONE WHO TAUGHT THEM TO HER.

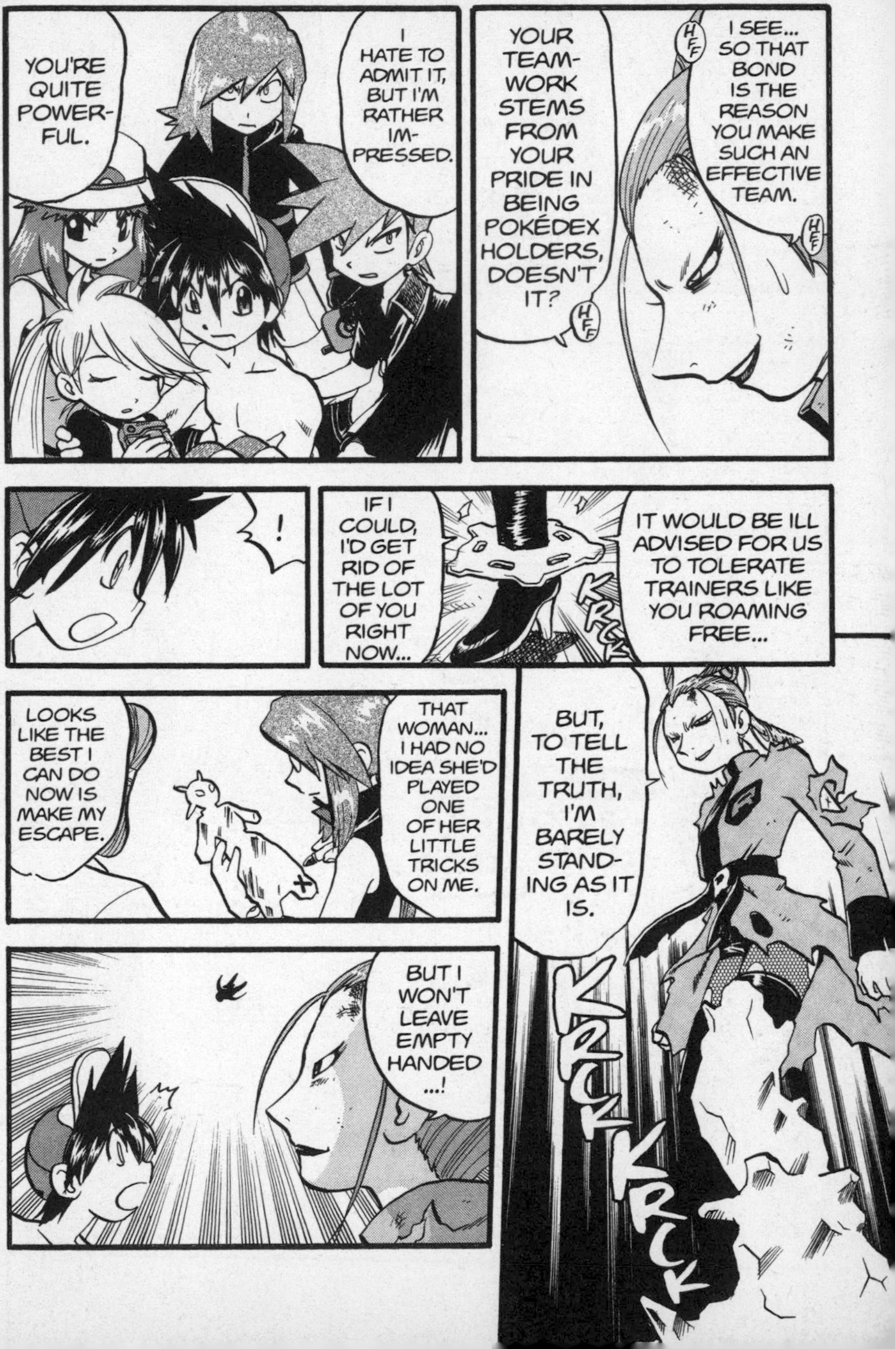

HFF
I SEE... SO THAT BOND IS THE REASON YOU MAKE SUCH AN EFFECTIVE TEAM.
HFF
YOUR TEAM-WORK STEMS FROM YOUR PRIDE IN BEING POKÉDEX HOLDERS, DOESN'T IT?
HFF
I HATE TO ADMIT IT, BUT I'M RATHER IM-PRESSED.
YOU'RE QUITE POWER-FUL.
IT WOULD BE ILL ADVISED FOR US TO TOLERATE TRAINERS LIKE YOU ROAMING FREE...
KRCK
IF I COULD, I'D GET RID OF THE LOT OF YOU RIGHT NOW...
!
BUT, TO TELL THE TRUTH, I'M BARELY STAND-ING AS IT IS.
KRCK
KRCK
THAT WOMAN... I HAD NO IDEA SHE'D PLAYED ONE OF HER LITTLE TRICKS ON ME.
LOOKS LIKE THE BEST I CAN DO NOW IS MAKE MY ESCAPE.
BUT I WON'T LEAVE EMPTY HANDED ...!

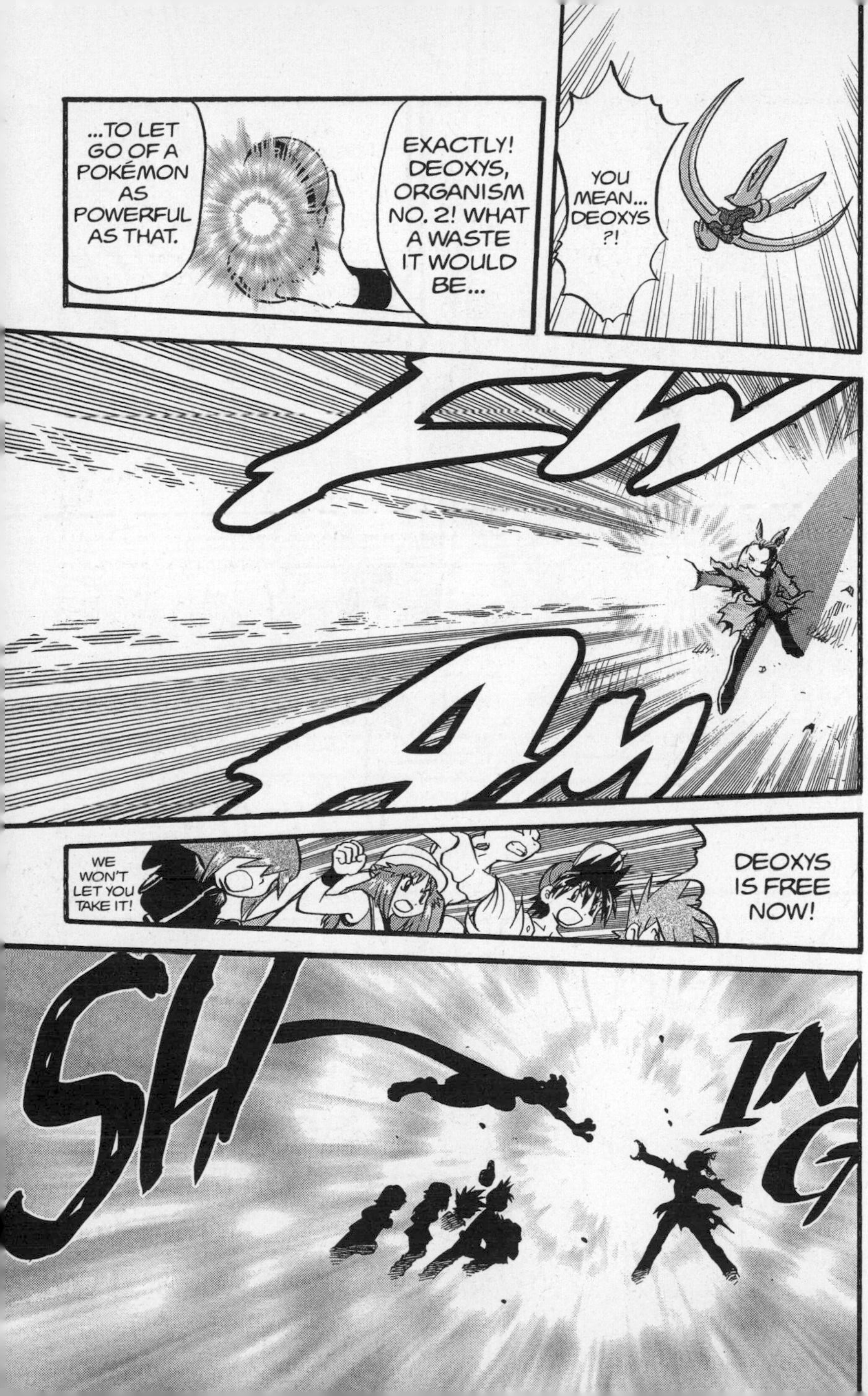
YOU MEAN... DEOXYS ?!
EXACTLY! DEOXYS, ORGANISM NO. 2! WHAT A WASTE IT WOULD BE...
...TO LET GO OF A POKÉMON AS POWERFUL AS THAT.
DEOXYS IS FREE NOW!
WE WON'T LET YOU TAKE IT!

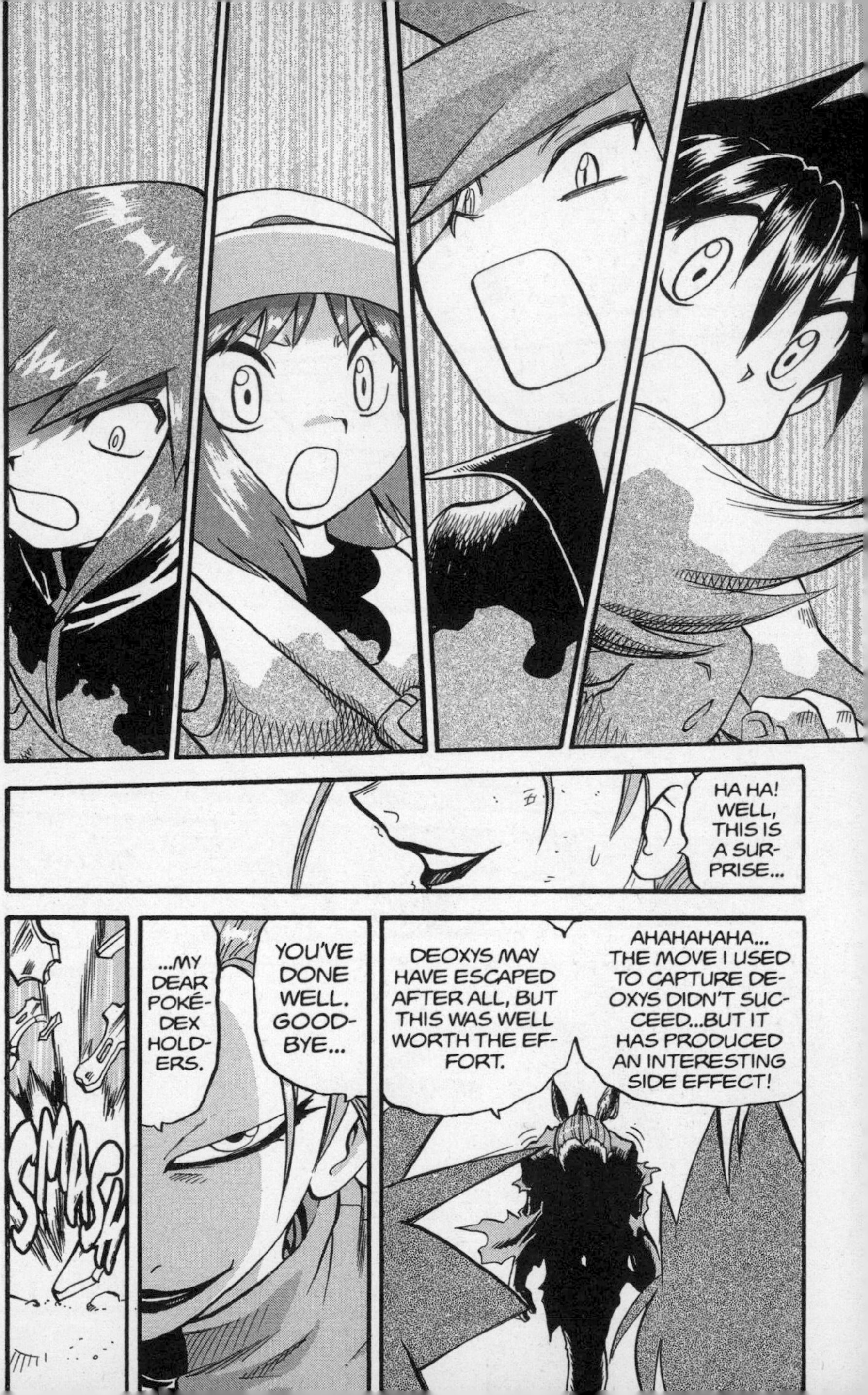
HA HA! WELL, THIS IS A SUR-PRISE...
AHAHAHAHA... THE MOVE I USED TO CAPTURE DE-OXYS DIDN'T SUC-CEED...BUT IT HAS PRODUCED AN INTERESTING SIDE EFFECT!
DEOXYS MAY HAVE ESCAPED AFTER ALL, BUT THIS WAS WELL WORTH THE EF-FORT.
YOU'VE DONE WELL. GOOD-BYE...
...MY DEAR POKÉ-DEX HOLD-ERS.

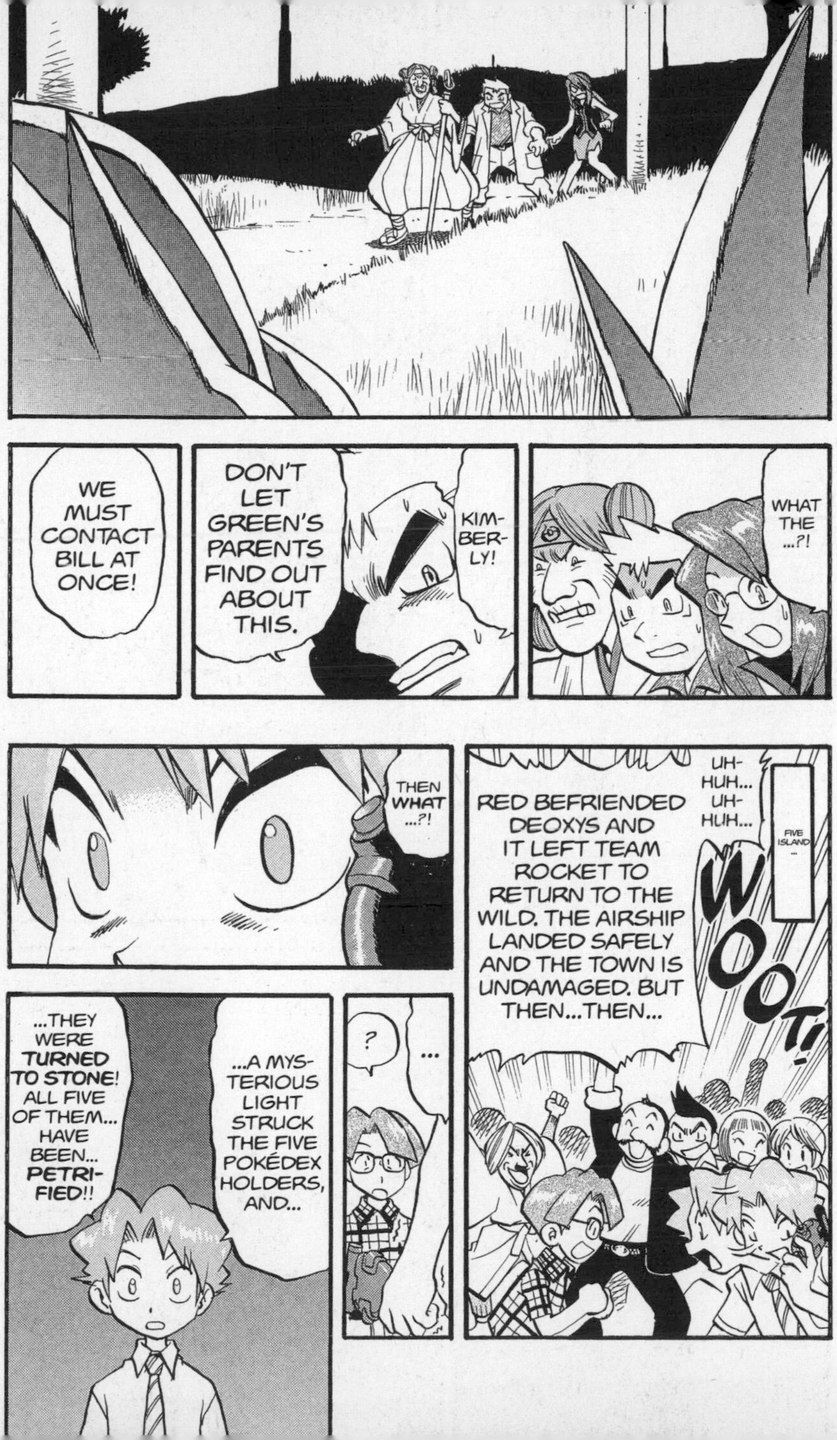

WHAT THE ...?!
KIM-BER-LY!
DON'T LET GREEN'S PARENTS FIND OUT ABOUT THIS.
WE MUST CONTACT BILL AT ONCE!
FIVE ISLAND...
UH-HUH... UH-HUH...
RED BEFRIENDED DEOXYS AND IT LEFT TEAM ROCKET TO RETURN TO THE WILD. THE AIRSHIP LANDED SAFELY AND THE TOWN IS UNDAMAGED. BUT THEN...THEN...
WOOT!
THEN **WHAT** ...?!
...
?
...A MYSTERIOUS LIGHT STRUCK THE FIVE POKÉDEX HOLDERS, AND...
...THEY WERE **TURNED TO STONE!** ALL FIVE OF THEM... HAVE BEEN... **PETRIFIED!!**

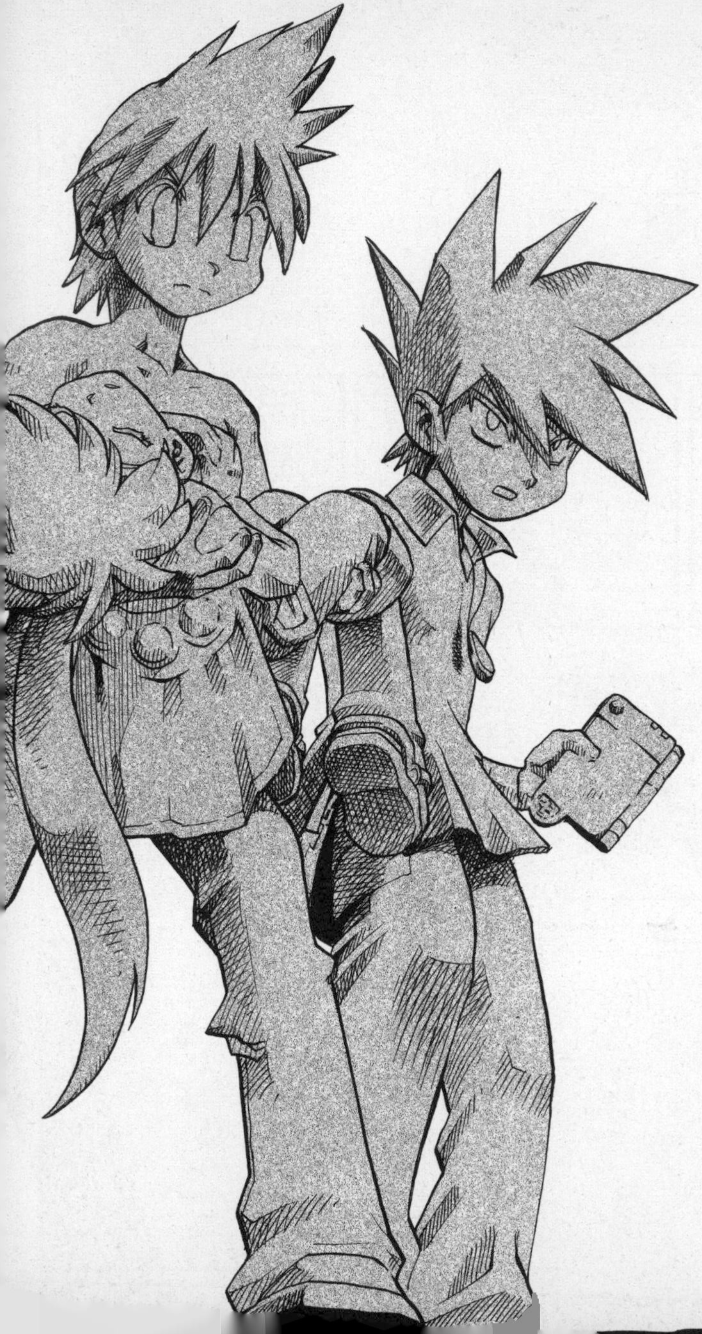

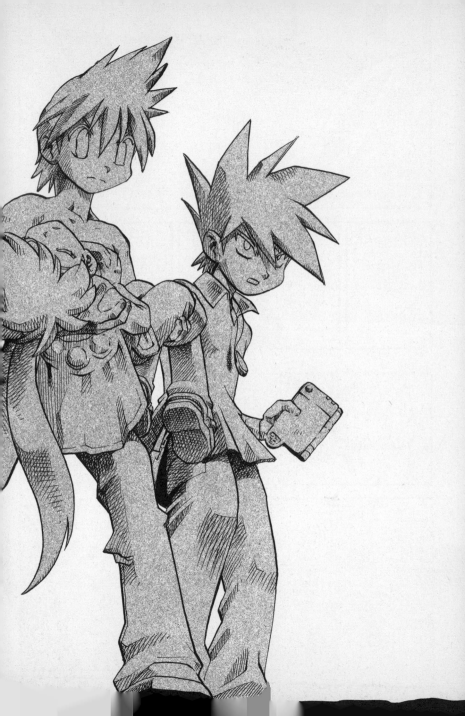

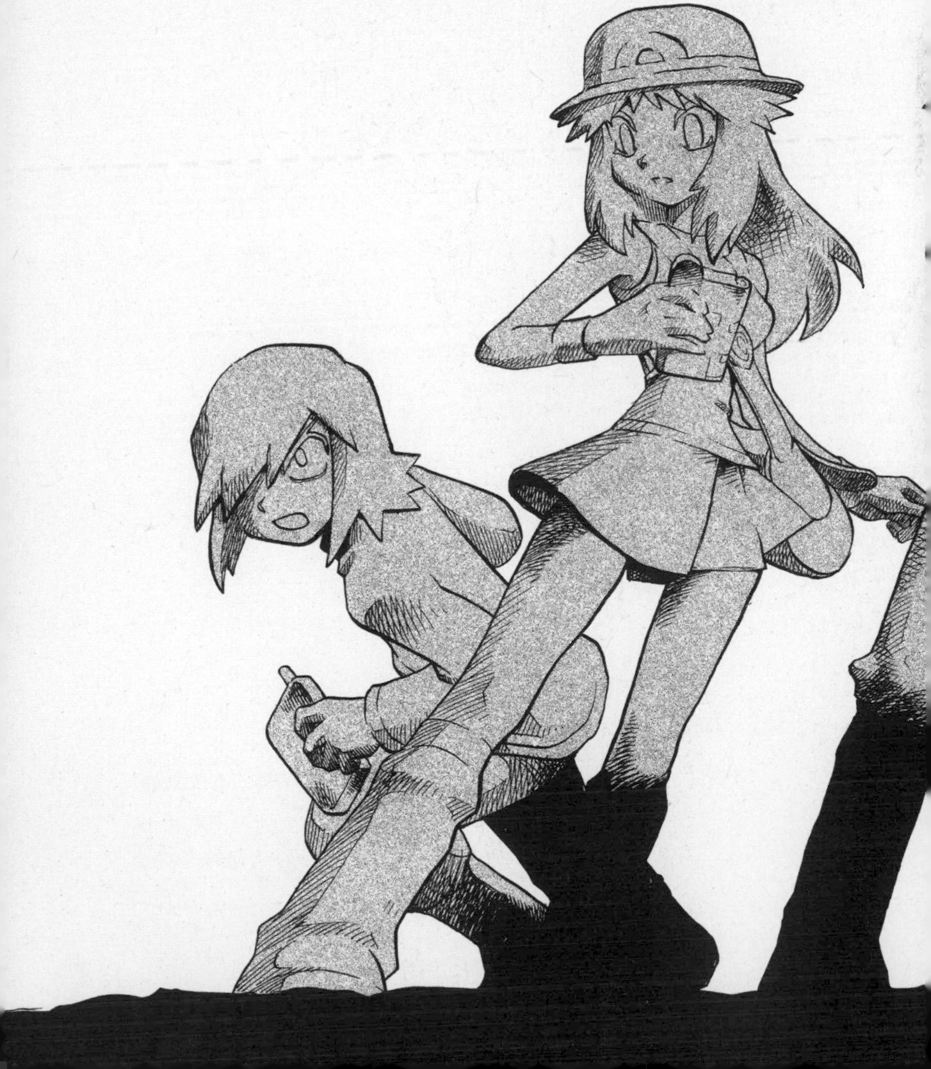

Fin The Fifth Chapter

FireRed & LeafGreen

Pokémon Adventures FireRed & LeafGreen 5

The Fifth Chapter

SECRET JAPANESE-BRAILLE SUBTITLES DECODED!

Volume 23

Defeat and Frustration continues in volume 24

23

The Fifth Chapter

Subtitles List

The Fifth Chapter
Subtitles List

Volume 24

Chapter 280: Red the Underdog
Chapter 281: Secret of the Forme Change
Chapter 282: The Qualifications of a Pokédex Holder
Chapter 283: The Reason to Fight
Chapter 284: Mewtwo Joins In
Chapter 285: A Tower with a Mind of Its Own
Chapter 286: Attack of the Duplicates
Chapter 287: Hometown Viridian City

The Final Battle continues in volume 25

24

Volume 25

Chapter 288: Destroy the Restrainer
Chapter 289: Viridian City in Mind
Chapter 290: The Mid-Air Battle Arena
Chapter 291: Final Battle
Chapter 292: Your Father Is Giovanni!
Chapter 293: Aurora Illusion
Chapter 294: End of the Illusion
Chapter 295: Last Shot
Chapter 296: Deoxys and Its Roots
Chapter 297: Carr's Revolt
Chapter 298: Escape from the Black Hole
Chapter 299: Instinct Calls
Chapter 300: The Soul of a Father
Chapter 301: Red the Fighter
Chapter 302: The Bonds of the Pokédex Holder

25

Message from
Hidenori Kusaka

Deoxys is the main character of the Fifth Chapter. I still remember the surprise I felt the first time I saw it. It has such a unique design that I kept asking myself, "What kind of Pokémon is that?!" I later learned about its Attack and Defense Formes and that it originated in outer space—which made it all the more intriguing! The FireRed & LeafGreen story arc has been running for 38 months, but even after all that time, I feel like Deoxys hasn't run out of surprises for us yet!

Message from
Satoshi Yamamoto

The fifth chapter is finally reaching its climax. The dots are starting to connect... The characters and Pokémon are intertwined by the strings of fate! Vol. 25 will have one of the most dramatic stories in the Pokémon Adventures series. I hope you enjoy it!

New Adventures Coming Soon...

Meet an odd new Pokémon Trainer named Emerald who claims to like Pokémon Battles—but not Pokémon! How can that be? And with that attitude, how will he fare on the Pokémon Battle Frontier when he challenges powerful Factory Head Noland and impatient Pike Queen Lucy?

And what Legendary Pokémon and evil organization will become Emerald's even greater challenge...?

PERFECT SQUARE
POKÉMON™
ADVENTURES
EMERALD
26
VOLUME TWENTY-SIX
Story by Hidenori Kusaka
Art by Satoshi Yamamoto

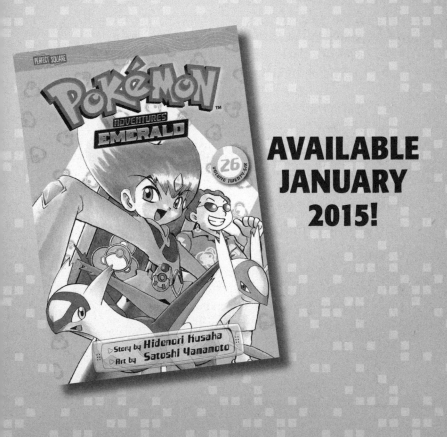

AVAILABLE JANUARY 2015!

POKÉMON™
BLACK & WHITE

STORY & ART BY SANTA HARUKAZE

YOUR FAVORITE POKÉMON FROM THE UNOVA REGION LIKE YOU'VE NEVER SEEN THEM BEFORE!

REALLY? YOU THINK WE CAN'T CRACK THOSE QUIZZES ?
IT'S IMPOSSIBLE!
UNSOLVABLE QUIZZES?!
SCRAGGY THE GENIUS WILL FIGURE OUT THE ANSWERS!
tup tup tup tup

POKÉMON
BLACK & WHITE
POCKET COMICS
STORY & ART BY SANTA HARUKAZE

Available now!

A pocket-sized book brick jam-packed with four-panel comic strips featuring all the Pokémon Black and White characters, Pokémon vital statistics, trivia, puzzles, and fun quizzes!

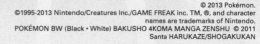

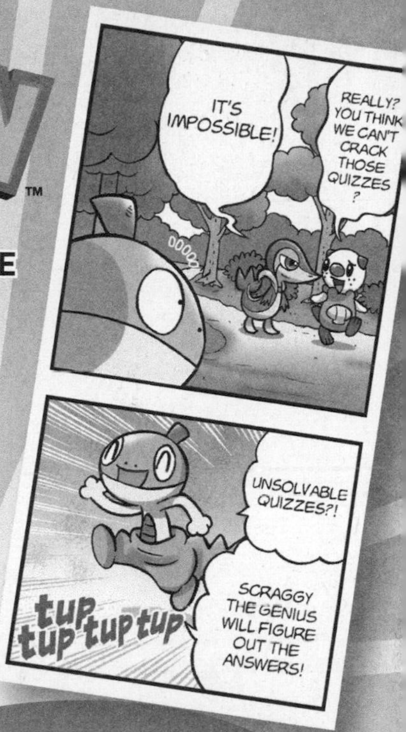

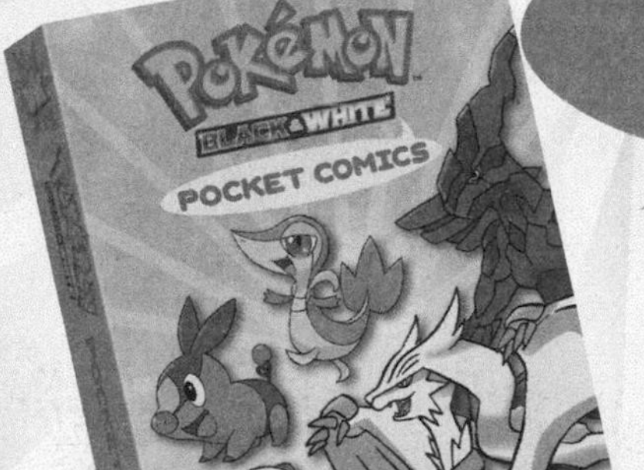

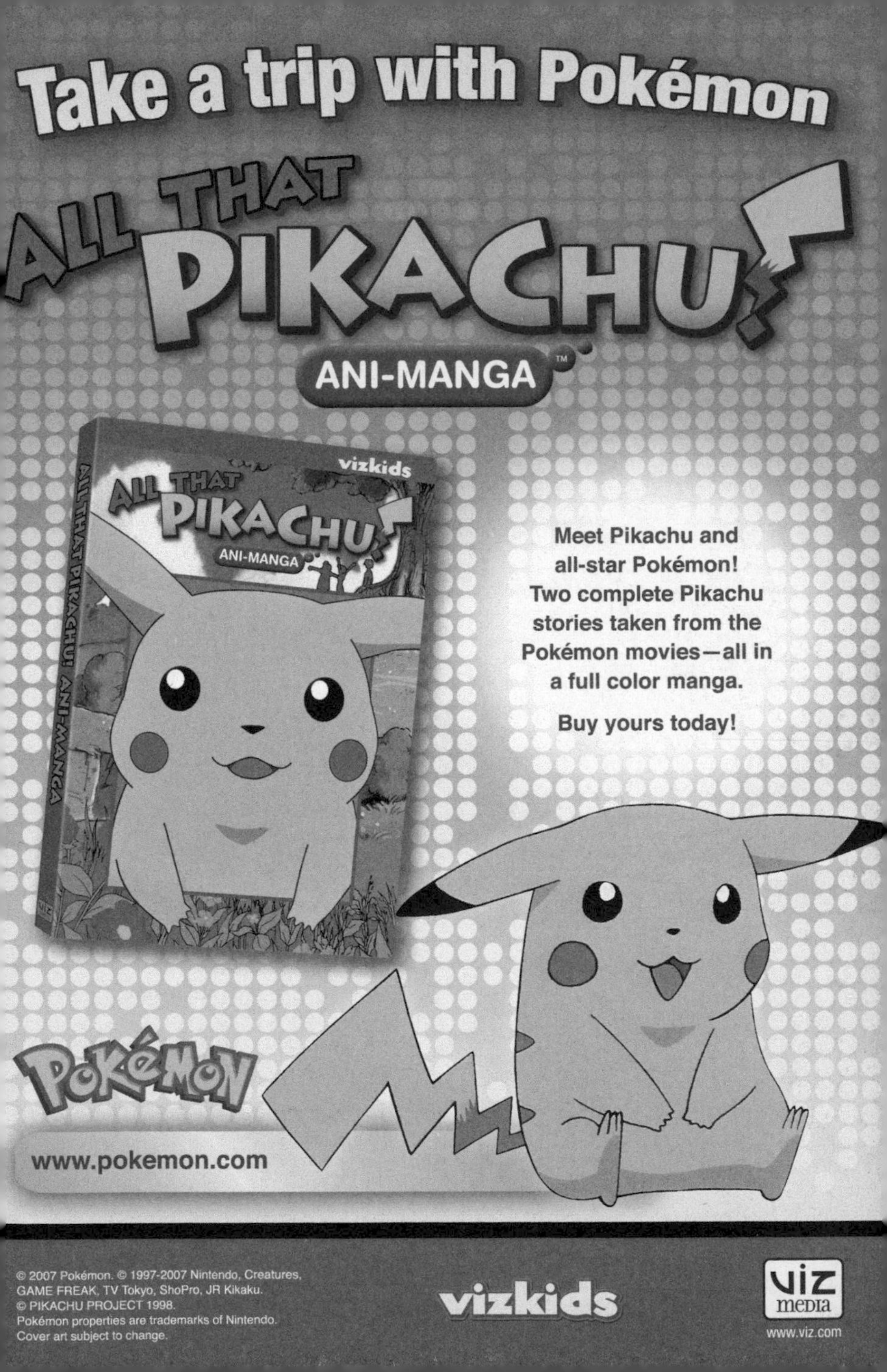
Take a trip with Pokémon
ALL THAT PIKACHU!
ANI-MANGA™
vizkids
ALL THAT PIKACHU!
ANI-MANGA
ALL THAT PIKACHU! ANI-MANGA
Meet Pikachu and all-star Pokémon! Two complete Pikachu stories taken from the Pokémon movies—all in a full color manga.
Buy yours today!
POKÉMON
www.pokemon.com
© 2007 Pokémon. © 1997-2007 Nintendo, Creatures, GAME FREAK, TV Tokyo, ShoPro, JR Kikaku.
© PIKACHU PROJECT 1998.
Pokémon properties are trademarks of Nintendo.
Cover art subject to change.
vizkids
VIZ media
www.viz.com

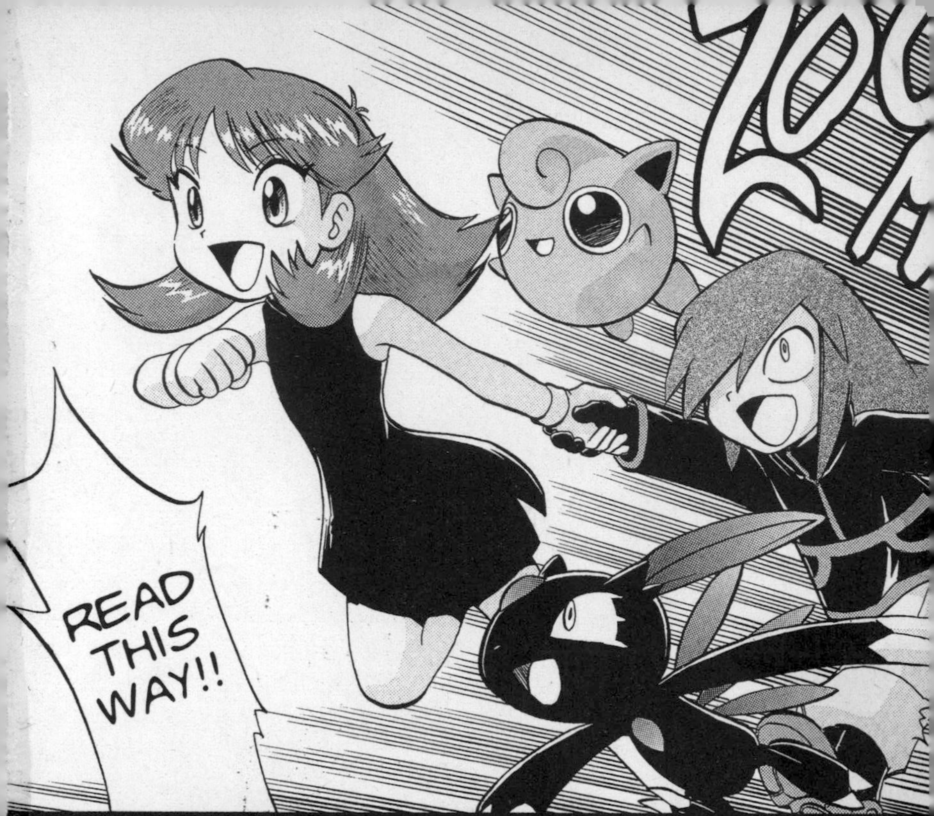
READ THIS WAY!!

THIS IS THE END OF THIS GRAPHIC NOVEL!

To properly enjoy this VIZ Media graphic novel, please turn it around and begin reading from right to left.

This book has been printed in the original Japanese format in order to preserve the orientation of the original artwork.

Have fun with it!

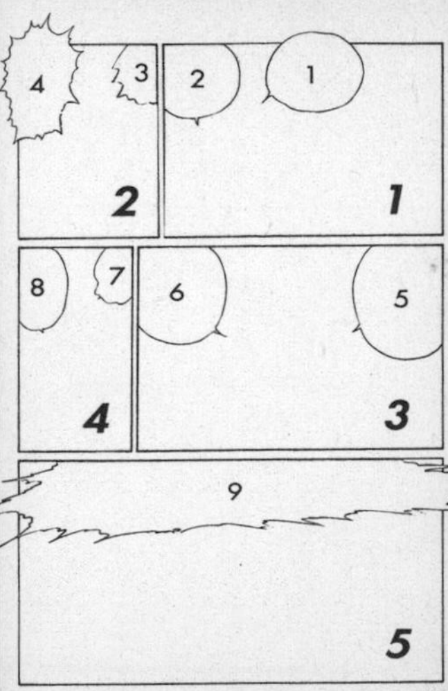

FOLLOW THE ACTION THIS WAY.